W9-CQW-027

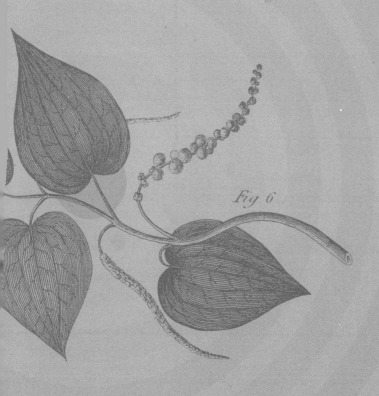

Fig 6

THE CUSANUS GAME

The
CUSANUS
GAME

WOLFGANG JESCHKE

Translated by
ROSS BENJAMIN

A Tom Doherty Associates Book
New York

This is a work of fiction. All of the characters, organizations, and events portrayed in this novel are either products of the author's imagination or are used fictitiously.

THE CUSANUS GAME

Copyright © 2005 by Wolfgang Jeschke

English translation copyright © 2013 by Ross Benjamin

Originally published as *Das Cusanus-Spiel* by Droemer Verlag, an imprint of Droemersche Verlagsanstalt Th. Knaur Nachf. GmbH & Co. KG, in Munich, Germany.

All rights reserved.

A Tor Book
Published by Tom Doherty Associates, LLC
175 Fifth Avenue
New York, NY 10010

www.tor-forge.com

Tor® is a registered trademark of Tom Doherty Associates, LLC.

The Library of Congress Cataloging-in-Publication Data is available upon request.

ISBN 978-0-7653-1908-1 (hardcover)
ISBN 978-1-4299-8871-1 (e-book)

Tor books may be purchased for educational, business, or promotional use. For information on bulk purchases, please contact Macmillan Corporate and Premium Sales Department at 1-800-221-7945 extension 5442 or write specialmarkets@macmillan.com.

First Edition: October 2013

Printed in the United States of America

0 9 8 7 6 5 4 3 2 1

For Julian and Rosi

Contents

BOOK THREE

BOOK FOUR

BOOK FIVE

Time is an unfolding of God.

—Nicolaus Cusanus

What is fascinating about the principle of the kaleidoscope is that it suffices to shift but a tiny fragment of reality into another position in order to create new, unexpectedly variegated fantasy worlds, which delight the eye and the mind.

—Jeremias Wolf

The world is everything that is the case and also everything that can be the case.

—Anton Zeilinger

THE CUSANUS GAME

PROLOGUE

Emilio was woken by the wopp-wopp of the weak repellers. Perhaps animals had stumbled into the border surveillance. When he heard the hum and rumble of heavy repellers and the howl of the vortex launchers, he stood up and stepped outside the tent. The moon shone in the west.

Suddenly he heard a cry in the camp, then loud, vehement words. Bakhtir came marching toward him, beside himself with anger; with kicks and punches he drove two young men in front of him. They seemed dazed and did not even try to evade the head driver's blows. Ghamal and Pietro; they were in shock. Emilio grabbed an armful of branches and threw them into the embers to kindle a fire. Both of the boys had bloody noses and bruises on their faces and arms—marks of the repellers.

"At least they got such a scare that they turned around," Bakhtir exclaimed with a voice as if his throat were constricted, "but Ibrahim and Hakim . . ."

He broke off and tried in vain to suppress a sob.

"Your son?" asked Emilio.

Bakhtir nodded silently. Emilio grasped him by the shoulder. "You go into your tent!" he shouted at the two young men, who cowered before him and held their heads in pain. "We'll speak about this tomorrow."

They struggled to their feet and staggered away.

"That crazy Ibrahim!" cried Bakhtir; it sounded like a wail. "He persuaded Hakim and the two others to come with him. I should have put that fellow in chains."

Furiously, he kicked a stone into the fire.

"Try to calm down, Bakhtir," said Emilio. "We will find out what happened."

"Do you think there's still hope?"

The caravan leader shrugged silently and looked down at the ground.

"Hakim!" Bakhtir cried out into the plain. There the fog had spread like a milky lake out of which the treetops rose. "Hakim!"

No answer. The lights had gone out. The howling of the wolves and the rumbling of the repellers had fallen silent. The newly kindled fire blazed, illuminating the faces of the men. Bakhtir wept.

AN HOUR AND a half after sunrise, the airship appeared. When it was floating over the campsite, the whine of the jets died away and it descended. Shortly before landing, they once again briefly hissed, and the supple, light gray plastic body of the zeppelin, which was covered with a glistening film on its back and flanks, broke open at the bottom like a soft pod and released containers that arranged themselves into two rows.

The drivers began emptying the containers. They were filled with packaged loads, cocooned in silvery plastic threads. These were now exchanged for the goods brought by the caravan. Emilio checked the electronic identification of the packages with his device. On the LED appeared numbers, quantities of items and descriptions of goods, as well as names and addresses of the respective recipients.

The men were about to heave the loads onto the animals' backs and tie them down when the figure of a man in a Euro-blue protective suit appeared in the opening at the front of the zeppelin. His polarized helmet visor revealed no face. He raised his hand and exclaimed, "Hello, Emilio!" He then added gravely, "Please come with me."

Bakhtir spoke up hoarsely. "My son," he said, "was one of the boys who . . ."

There was a brief, heavy silence. Then the man in the protective suit said, "You may come too."

He climbed the aluminum ladder into the cockpit. Emilio and Bakhtir followed. Behind them servos hoisted the containers into the cargo area and fastened them in their foam troughs. Emilio could not believe his eyes; the cockpit was far more spacious than the external dimensions suggested.

"My boy," Bakhtir said in a near-whisper. "Is he . . ."

"I'm sorry," said the man in the protective suit. "Unfortunately nothing remains of either of them. They ran straight into a laser fan."

"My son," Bakhtir sobbed. As if of its own volition, his hand pulled his revolver from his belt and pointed it at the pilot in the protective suit.

"Stop this nonsense, man!" cried the pilot. "From where you're standing, you could damage a lot of outrageously expensive electronics and trigger the self-defense, if you shoot. So put that thing away!"

Emilio reached out toward the revolver, but it was too late. Bakhtir had fired two shots at the man's chest. The double wreath of Euro-stars remained intact, but an alarm siren began to bleat, and somewhere the hiss of escaping gas could be heard.

"Hold the man back, Emilio!" shouted the pilot, slapping with his glove at the large panel of switches on the left shoulder of his protective suit. "He seriously believes that I'm here in the flesh. And now get out of here as fast as you can, damn it! From here I have no control over the aircraft's self-defense."

The next instant the man in the protective suit was gone. The room had been reduced to a third of its length and was filling up with whitish smoke from the floor. Where the two shots had hit the wall there was crackling, and the alarm siren would not stop bleating. The smoke thickened. Bakhtir coughed and doubled up, causing even more gas to stream into his lungs.

"Out! Out! Out!" shouted Emilio.

He grasped Bakhtir by the shoulders, drove him to the hatch, pushed him out and jumped after him. With a snap the hatch of the cockpit sealed shut behind him. They crawled out from under the airship—not a second too soon, for the engines were firing already and the aircraft took off. Emilio and Bakhtir threw sand at each other to stifle the flames licking at their djellabas; then they squatted down, vomited, and coughed their guts out.

"This was a needless tragedy, caravan leader," said the voice of the man in the protective suit from the device on Emilio's belt. "You must impress upon your people that we are not running an adventure playground here. This is a border that nothing and no one can penetrate. It is the border between past and future."

Emilio spat to get rid of the acrid, burning taste in his mouth.

"And on which side lies the future?" he asked.

André laughed.

"Here the clocks go faster, and have done so for more than five hundred years. Look at your calendar, Emilio. It shows the year 1425. Here we live in the middle of the twenty-first century."

"Then we still have a lot of time," replied the caravan leader.

The man on the other side of the border didn't answer. And Emilio saw that the light had gone out. The connection had been broken.

Book
ONE

I

The Horse on Via Garibaldi

I once thought that truth could be found better in darkness. But of great power is the truth in which possibility itself shines brightly. Indeed, it shouts in the streets . . . With great certainty it shows itself everywhere easy to find.

NICOLAUS CUSANUS

From behind the barrier of stacked-up sandbags, a man appeared.
"Halt!" he cried. "Halt, signorina! You can't drive across here!"
He had a rifle under his arm and, despite the heat, a blue knitted wool cap on his head. I was about to turn left onto the Ponte Sisto, but the engine stalled. The indicator light blinked red. I gave the battery a kick, but the thing was totally dead. The man came running across the street with a sideways gait, leaning his right shoulder somewhat forward—probably because of his weapon—and limping a bit. Breathing heavily, he grabbed the handlebars of my Lectric and held on to them.

"Let go right now!" I shouted, kicking at his knee, but he dodged and tightened his grip.

"Listen, signorina! I'm really trying to help you. You can't cross here. See for yourself."

Only now did I notice that there was a tank on the other side of the river, at the turn onto Piazza Trilussa, and two more armored vehicles had driven up, one close behind the other, on Lungotevere della Farnesina. Soldiers in light blue EuroForce combat uniforms stood there, heavily armed and with technical equipment on their backs.

I stepped down, pulled my crash helmet off my head, shook my hair out, and looked back. The street lay deserted before me.

"But I live over there," I said, "on Via Garibaldi."

The man shook his head, pulled a crushed pack of Nazionali from his shirt pocket, fished one out and stuck it between his lips, dug out an ancient Camel Zippo lighter, flicked it open, and lit the cigarette. Greedily he sucked in the smoke. He's definitely pretty sick, I thought in passing. His cheeks were pale and sunken and covered with gray stubble. Greasy gray curls hung out under the edge of his wool cap, which bore the Juventus emblem in front. He raised his face, bared his yellow teeth, and let the smoke stream out between them.

"Riders on horseback," he said, coughing into his arm held in front of his mouth. "Riders on horseback," he repeated in a tone as if he were speaking of something particularly abhorrent. With the rifle he pointed across to the opposite bank. "Three or four. Armed. Moros, in the middle of the city—in broad daylight. It would be time to blow up the bridge."

"And you think that would stop them?" I asked. "The river is gone."

He shook his head. "Here no one's getting across. We'll make sure of that," he asserted, pointing with his thumb over his shoulder.

I saw rifle barrels jutting over the barrier of sand-filled gray and black plastic bags and from the second- and third-floor windows. The display windows of the sporting goods store on the ground floor were blockaded with cabinets and overturned tables. "Around the clock," he assured me.

Along the left bank, similar makeshift barricades of sandbags and car tires had been piled up to shoulder height on the sidewalk in front of the houses. The only way to reach the entrances to the houses was sideways through a sort of labyrinthine passage.

To fill all the sandbags was no problem, for in the months of dryness the hot south wind had deposited pale drift sand from the Sahara all over the city on the outside steps and in the entrances to the houses. Now it nestled against the foot of soot-covered walls—several feet high in many places.

The man with the wool cap suddenly raised his head as if he were picking up a scent. From Saint Peter's Square, where a unit of the EuroForce light air cavalry was stationed, I heard the sound of approaching helicopters. From there they patrolled the city and flew missions to secure the southern belt highway and give the convoys covering fire. That was during the day—at night no one dared to use the southern Grande Raccordo Anulare between Via Aurelia and Via Appia, when car tires burned in the lanes and sniper fire was to be expected. Sometimes the stink of burnt rubber reached as far as Trastevere.

The whipping sound grew louder; two shadows in gray and brown camouflage paint emerged one after the other from the haze in low-altitude flight and took shape over the Ponte Mazzini. The funnel-shaped double barrels of the ShriekGuns projected downward from their bellies like the stingers of monstrous insects. The rotors spun deafeningly and raised dust from the bone-dry riverbed, which clouded the air even more and filled it with the stink of old death.

The helicopters suddenly rose high and leaned into a sharp right turn. I saw only briefly the white helmets with the flipped-down data visors shimmering between the reflections on the plastic bubbles of the cockpits; then the machines had disappeared behind the pines on the Gianicolo hill. After that the sonar weapons screamed for several minutes.

The man flicked his cigarette butt into the gutter and nodded to me.

"Now you can cross, signorina," he said, eyeing appreciatively my laced suede vest, as if he were permitting himself only now to cast a glance at something other than the supposed front line. Sweat trickled down between my breasts and ran over my belly. I wiped my forehead with my hand.

"You should look for another apartment," he said. "Trastevere has been given up since the police station on Via Garibaldi was closed. You're not safe over there anymore. You should get that straight, signorina. The west side of the city has been in the hands of the Moros for a long time. There have been lootings in the Vatican. Despite the EuroForce guards." He spat. "Since Papa Coward absconded to Salzburg, not a damn soul cares what happens here."

"There can't be much left there," I said. "Most of it was brought to Vienna and Budapest a long time ago."

"You should see what the Americans and Japanese are making off with."

"On behalf of UNESCO."

"Don't make me laugh," he said, pulling his wool cap off his head and wiping his face with it.

I shrugged and tried to start the engine, but the battery indicator light blinked red. I had already noticed on Via dei Cerchi, shortly before Piazza Bocca, that it was almost dead. It hadn't charged the previous night: power outage—lately there was one every other day.

"Do you live alone?" the man inquired. "Here in the house there are still apartments. Safe apartments. I'm the super here. Ask for Dino, if you're interested."

"Thanks, signore!" I called over my shoulder, hanging the helmet on the handlebars and pushing my Lectric between the concrete-encased posts onto the Ponte Sisto. "I'll get back to you on that."

"You're welcome to move in with me, my dear!" he shouted, and laughed bleatingly.

"I'll think about it."

THE SOLDIERS ON Piazza Trilussa waved me through. With their light blue ceramic armor and helmets, their flipped-down VR-visors, laser-aiming devices, whip antennas, and heavy hand weapons, they looked like upright crustaceans.

As I turned onto Via Garibaldi, I saw that it had been closed off halfway up with coils of razor wire. An officer raised a hand and stopped me. He was around thirty, of medium height; with his closely trimmed full beard and his brown curls under the light blue beret, he was really good-looking. From the walkie-talkie in the breast pocket of his camouflage bulletproof vest, a voice chattered excitedly.

"Where do you want to go, signorina?" he asked. Judging by the dialect, he was from the north, like most of them. Bologna, perhaps, or Modena.

"I live up there—to the right, across from the convent of Santa Maria dei Sette Dolori."

"Then you should pack your suitcases. You're better off moving across the river. Here there are more and more guys who will make short work of a young girl like you."

"There are guys like that on the other side too."

He laughed sarcastically. "You're probably right. But this here is no longer a secure zone. You enter at your own risk—that you should know."

He pulled a lever and a gap opened in the coil of wire. I pushed my Lectric between the dangerous-looking, chest-high loops, which were covered with razor-sharp blades a handbreadth apart. The barrier closed behind me.

At that moment three explosions could be heard in close succession up on the Gianicolo, then a fourth, and once again the infernal howl of the ShriekGuns broke out. I stood still. Sweat poured down my ribs. It wasn't only the heat, which had been weighing down on the city for months like a smothering dusty pillow—it was pure fear. I felt my intestines twist into a knot and my knees threaten to give out under me.

"Get out of here, signorina! Off the street!" the officer shouted behind me.

I couldn't make out any immediate danger. A helicopter with whirring rotors kept appearing over the pines, and its engine noise, which sounded like the rattle of shots being fired, was accompanied by the shrill screaming and subsonic hum of its sonar guns, which shook my bones and threatened to shatter my skull; then it disappeared again. The hill seemed to be enveloped in smoke, as if the dry trees on its summit had caught fire.

"Go, signorina, go!"

I turned around. God, what did the guy want?! The voice in his breast pocket was squawking excitedly. He was waving his arms.

"Take cover!"

I leaned my Lectric against a trellis with flower troughs in which pale pink rhododendrons had perished in cracked hard soil, and sought shelter in the entrance to a former restaurant, the door of which was boarded up.

Suddenly I heard the clatter of hooves and looked up with surprise. From the Porta San Pancrazio, a riderless horse came bursting down the hill at full gallop, a heavy farm horse; a dun—with rolling eyes, waving mane, and extended tail—dashed past me and toward the barricade as if out of its mind from the noise, was about to leap over it, hesitated at the last moment, frightened by the soldiers standing on both sides of the road, slipped, spraying sparks, on the cobblestones that formed an island there in the soft asphalt, could no longer slow itself down, and plunged with flailing forelegs directly into the coils of wire.

How it screamed! I hadn't known that horses were capable of such sounds. It was a constant shrill wailing as if from a person in extreme torment.

The soldiers, who wanted to rush to the rescue, recoiled in fright from the kicking hooves. In its panic the animal got itself ever more hopelessly tangled in the wire barrier. The razor-sharp blades dug ever deeper into its flesh; blood streamed onto the pavement. The officer shouted an order and drew his pistol. Crouching, he approached the animal and shot a laser beam into its wide-open mouth. A whitish red fountain erupted between its ears and stained the fur on its back with dark spots. The animal went silent and seemed to shake its head incredulously; then its jaw sank between its twitching forelegs onto the barbed wire. Suddenly there was a smell of singed hair and burnt flesh. The horse's eyes looked like peeled hardboiled eggs.

I had to turn away, and sat down in a daze on one of the two plastic chairs, which, once white but now yellowed and gray from the dust and the corrosive air, decayed among the dried-out flower troughs.

ROYAL PUB was written in gold letters on a moss-green sign with peeling paint. Renata and Marco had sometimes come here when they had visited me. And CarlAntonio, the mutant, the "boy with his clever backpack," as the students good-naturedly called him. For others, the Siamese twins were the "Monster of Cattenom." While Antonio sat there turned away and stared dully at the street, Carl, his "backpack," had chatted with us. CarlAntonio were the most lovable thing the dark heart of Europe had left us.

The Royal Pub had closed the previous autumn and never reopened.

I stood up and avoided looking at the dead horse. Via Garibaldi was still deserted. A dozen people stared out the windows. Once it would have been hundreds; onlookers would have swarmed around the cadaver like flies, so that the soldiers would have had trouble keeping them away. Where had all those people gone? The fact that there were barely any illuminated windows in the evening was not only due to people's fear of snipers—they had meanwhile moved away. Trastevere was almost as empty as it had been a thousand years before, when only a few fishermen and herdsmen lived on the bank of the Tiber.

I CARRIED MY Lectric up the steps to the front door. In the hallway, the usual mess: broken-open, twisted metal mailboxes, some stuffed full to bursting with leaflets and district newspapers. The floor was littered with a layer of electronic confetti, DotChips and VidDiscs and dirty envelopes torn open in search of cash.

No word from Mother. Is Grandmother still alive? Why does Mother still not have an ICom, so that you could call her? Why doesn't she send an e-mail to the institute, as I've implored her again and again?—the only reliable way in times like these. But she prefers to live in the previous century. Keeps an eye out for the mailman. You'd need a time machine to stay in contact with her. Was she always this way? Probably Father already found her old-fashioned. I don't know. He was always up with everything that was currently in fashion. That was his job. Oh, Father.

I plugged the Lectric into the charger in the hallway, locked it up with the chain, and stuck a 100-Euro-Chip into the slot. The eye of the battery glowed reassuringly green; so there was power.

"Is that you, Signorina Ligrina?"

"It's me, Stavros."

He emerged from the shadows and leaned his Uzi in the corner. A bear of a man, barefoot, wearing only Bermuda shorts, blue and white in the colors of his homeland, with HELLAS printed on one leg, PATRIA on the other. He dried his bull neck and close-cropped hair with a gray towel.

"Couldn't it be cleaned up a little bit here?" I asked him.

He looked around as if he were seeing the mess in the hallway for the first time, let his glass eye wander over it as if he first had to scan the image of the disorder in order to perceive it at all. He rubbed his laser-ravaged chest, on which bushy islands of gray and black hair grew between pools of smooth, melted-looking pale pink—his painful memento of the lost naval battle of Icaria.

"What for?" he mumbled with a dragging voice. "No one lives here any-more."

"Am I no one?"

"*Scusi*, signorina." His intact blue-black eye smiled.

He put his arm around me and gave me a fatherly pat on the shoulder. He smelled terribly of garlic and sweat. Sometimes, when he was a bit drunk, his tongue prosthesis took on a life of its own; it crept out of the corner of his mouth like a curious, flesh-colored amphibian, replete with thousands of glittering nanosensors, and explored his stubble-covered cheek and his chin. In Turkish captivity they had cut out his tongue. "*Imaste dio . . .*" blared the portable radio back in his chamber. I liked him, felt safe when he was in the house.

THE WATER WAS brown and smelled stagnant. As I stepped out of the bathroom, I heard the rumbling engine noise of a heavy machine down on the street. I peered through the curtain. They were trying to lift the horse cadaver out of the barrier with the help of a mobile crane, but the bowels were so tangled in the loops of the razor wire that they could not be separated. The intestines had to be cut loose. Excrement and bodily fluids poured out onto the pavement. My stomach clenched into a small, hard ball, into a fist thrusting upward. I ran back into the bathroom, pushed my damp hair out of my face and held it together with my fist behind my neck, while I vomited into the toilet bowl. "*Anigho to stoma*," Mikis Theodorakis sang with a loud voice, Stavros's patriotic friend.

My God, did the Greeks have only one composer in four thousand years? We could easily have given them two or three dozen.

TOWARD MORNING TRASTEVERE was burning, down on Piazza Bernardino da Feltre. It took almost an hour for the fire department to arrive, because the roadblocks that fearful residents had erected to protect themselves had to be removed.

*   *   *

WHEN I CAME from the university in the afternoon, Via dei Fori Imperiali was closed, as was Cavour and Piazza del Colosseo. Not by the police, nor by the military—there were no uniforms in sight far and wide—but by supporters of the Praetorians. The convoy was heading toward Piazza Venezia: trucks full of electronic and holooptic equipment, flanked by drivers in black leather on Harleys without mufflers. Bald, colorfully tattooed heads, thick necks, fat faces, painted with chalk and black stripes straight across the eyes. Bodyguards. On a rolling platform was a bizarre cage resembling a litter, from which ribbons in the national colors fluttered under colored awnings. In it a young, dark-skinned woman was chained up, a delicate girl with smooth black hair styled in Egyptian fashion into a helmet. She was naked and wore a silver ring pierced through her nose. She shook her head and raised her chin proudly. Jerkily, she tried to stand up, but a movement of the vehicle threw her back into the pillows.

The Praetorians were preparing one of their holoshows. All morning loud snatches of music could be heard from Piazza Venezia. Wagner, I assumed—undoubtedly a copy of the "artistically controversial" productions of *The Ring* by Sigurd Wagner and Lutz-Loki von Stein, in which boars had supposedly been castrated on the open stage.

I had to take a detour, heading south on Amba Aradam and Terme di Caracalla, and finally came out at Via Aventino. It was early afternoon. The sky was shrouded in dusty smog, in which a hazily shining sun had nested for weeks. It seemed to have moved closer and swollen to three times its size. I got off, leaned my Lectric on the railing of the Ponte Palatina, and looked down into the dried-out riverbed. In the embankment walls yawned the mouths of forgotten ducts, from which stinking secretions dripped, congealing into puddles of organic pitch—millennia-old veins in the body of the city, which eluded the cartography of the sewer maps. Even the deepest points of the riverbed had been baked into a cracked morass. The dogs and cats that ventured under the arches of the Ponte San Fabricio at Isola Tiberina and the Ponto Rotto in search of water scarcely had a chance against the rats or fell victim to the ravens that kept an eye on their territory from the dried-out plane trees along the Pierleoni promenade. The pits and hollows between the rocks encrusted with bird droppings were littered with skulls and skeletal remains of small mammals—mostly pets abandoned by their owners when they moved away.

Silence surrounded me. Not a sound could be heard, in the middle of the city. There was not a single vehicle on the riverside roads. They had disappeared without a trace, the beautiful cars with the enchanting names: the Alfa Romeos and Lamborghinis, the Jaguars and Mercedes-Benzes, the Porsches and Fiat Luxes, the Chevrolets and Bugattis. Once they had roared down these roads, but now their names sounded more like those of long-extinct noble houses. The sources had run dry from which they drew their power. There was gasoline only for public service vehicles and for the military—or for groups like the Praetorians, who had good connections with military officers.

Not a breeze stirred. The plane trees along the riverside lane had shed their withered leaves. It seemed to me as if they were holding their breath. Suddenly I heard a soft whimper behind me. I turned around and saw a killer dog.

"Help me!" he croaked. His lifeline on the top of his head was almost closed. Only a sliver as wide as a finger shimmered murky red, and his short, dark brown fur had already become discolored; jaw and ears showed the typical ghostly blue-white of approaching death. From his jowls dripped mauve saliva. His sticky fur smelled of wet excrement, and his rattling breath stank of inner putrefaction. The rejection of the implanted larynx had begun.

"Help me," he whined. He had clamped his tail between his hind legs.

"I can't help you. Go to your master," I replied gruffly.

He raised his head and barked hoarsely. Was it a weak cough? A sad laugh?

He could hardly stand up for hunger and exhaustion. His tongue hung out of his mouth. His bloodshot eyes stared at me pitifully. I turned away. These genetically modified animals got to me. No doubt he had killed people. That was what they were made for. Laboratory products. Intelligent killers. He was a dog, but he bore a little bit of human being within him, which they had implanted in him. When these animals became useless, they were gassed or given a lethal injection. But they were cunning, and some got away in time. That didn't help them, however, for they had a built-in clock that indicated their expiration date. Death began from within.

I rummaged in the basket on the handlebars and found a bar of chocolate that had gotten soft. I put it on the ground in front of him, to avoid coming into contact with his saliva, for you couldn't know what viruses had been custom-made for them in order to control their lifespan. He sniffed at the bar and slid his almost transparent tongue over it, then devoured it greedily.

"Thanks," he panted; a thin thread of blood ran out of the corner of his mouth. It was clear: Soon the ravens would come.

Suddenly deafening crashes of thunder could be heard in the east over the city center, and an eruption of colored laser light rose into the sky; it flickered through the haze as if the sun had now finally reached the earth and had begun to interact with the atmosphere. Cascades of fire flooded downward and rose up again like faculae from a corona. And above them rang out the shrill cries and the laughter of the Valkyries, who, wrapped in fluttering robes of blazing colors and shadows, stormed through the sky on their steeds in a wild gallop. *Hiaha! Hiaha! Hoyotoho! Hoyotoho! Hiaha!* The haze over the riverbed turned into a circling, screaming inferno of white and gray as hundreds of gulls suddenly descended. And in no time the ravens were there too—dozens of them, flying up out of the plane trees with flapping wings to defend their territory in a concerted action. And as quickly as it had come, the apparition of birds was gone again. A few white feathers fluttered downward.

The sky over the city had turned steel blue. Copper-colored lasers flashed through the haze; between gray-black graphite crags the glaring orange river of lava moved slowly eastward. Solar matter. Erupting prominences, blazing filaments.

Moss-gray domes bulged, bathed in liquid silver, under which shadowy riders in bronzed armor gathered. Mighty steeds with a shoulder height of twenty yards. Snorting that reverberated loudly from the facades of the houses, as if you were standing among the animals, the creak of leather, the clang of weapons. Heavy helmets, adorned with cow horns or buzzard wings—closed visors. A signal was given, and the hunt went on. The infernally loud music soared, sank, soared again. *Hoyotoho! Hoyotoho! Hiaha! Hiaha!*

I hated those fascists, but you had to grant them one thing: They knew how to stage their spectacles. By selecting specific, particularly grandiose opera scenes and revamping them to the point of perversion, they created the backdrop for their excessive experience of life. Their production was, as always, impressive and technically perfect, but in its mythical pomposity inhuman and sometimes disgusting.

I remembered an evening the previous autumn when I had ended up at a performance of *Aida* with Bernd, my boyfriend, which the notorious Condottiere Sergio had personally staged. He had transformed the north side of Piazza Navona into a city gate of Thebes—the great stone faces of the monumental statues severe and dignified, still unscathed by the Coptic and Islamic iconoclasts and the sandstorms from the Libyan Desert. As ever-thicker clouds of fog drew closer from the Nile and the daylight faded, the colossal statues stood out more and more clearly; between them, to the electronically reproduced sound of fanfares, the triumphal procession surged in, Radames at the head, followed by his officers in absurd gaudy uniforms, behind them slaves hauling the rich spoils—gold and ivory.

On the gallery, dressed entirely in gold and under a canopy of peacock feathers, amid priests and dignitaries: *il re*—with crook and flail as insignia of power and crowned with the sun disk between the horns of Hathor, surrounded by his royal guard of bird-headed Osiris warriors with metallically shimmering neck feathers and steel-blue beaks. At his side Seth in a scarlet robe, god of violence and rape. *"Trema, vil schiava."*

The face of the ruler appeared in close-up, was optically blown up to the size of a four-story house. *"Salvator della patria,"* he bellowed, as windows opened in his eye sockets as on a screen—as if rectangular holes had been punched in them. Blackness behind them, then suddenly dark skin, slave skin, so extremely enlarged that you saw every pore, every little hair, every bead of sweat, and then—like lightning—a lash of a whip whizzing downward through the air. Breaks in the skin, beads of blood appeared. The next stroke whizzed downward. The beads spattered. *"Nulla a te negato sarà in tal,"* cried the amputated-seeming mouth of the king, *"lo giuro per la corona mia, pei sacri Numi."* The sound of his voice, amplified a thousand times, thundered down to the Ponte Parione and could undoubtedly be heard as far as Tiburtino and Salario, while the echo boomed back from Capitolino and Aventino.

As the naked temple dancers offered the king and the priests the treasures of the vanquished, an expanding projection was suddenly superimposed over the image: Il Condottiere himself, shoving his erect member into the mouth of a black slave girl. It was a live recording. The spectators held their breath; only a few, disgusted by the performance, turned away. Some could not conceal their excitement, rummaged with their hands in their pants pockets. A number of the girls with white-painted faces screamed with rapture and groped at their leather outfits as the triumphal march progressed.

"Bite his dick off!" I shouted. No, I didn't shout it. I knuckled under like

everyone else—accepted it, that disgusting provocation, that travesty of fellatio, that outrageous humiliation of a woman. *"Tu prostata nella polvere."* I
accepted it out of fear of the genetically modified Rottweilers, growling and
tugging impatiently at their chains, because they could smell the excitement of the spectators. But they were held back by the grinning bodyguards, who kept a watchful eye on the audience and closely monitored
whether resistance stirred anywhere. "Death, death," the animals panted
hoarsely, and their life-seams on their heads shone fresh.

"Come on, Bernd," I said. "Let's go."

He didn't hear me.

"Come on," I implored.

Yes, it was loud, but he was staring with fascination as the Condottiere
climaxed and raised both arms triumphantly. And as he stuffed his member back into the black leather uniform, the girl vomited onto the stage.
Gray-yellow slime ran down her chin. The triumphal march seemed never-
ending.

Those pigs! But it was typical for them: They fired up their audience
with special laser effects and with deafening sound, went to the limit—and
then a step beyond it, to test the spectators, to see whether resistance
stirred. If that happened, they struck—hard and mercilessly—unleashing
their cruel dogs and igniting naked terror.

I felt tears running down my cheeks, turned around and hurried away.
Bernd didn't even notice.

That evening the ICom on my lapel chirped.

"Yes, Luigi?"

"A call for you, Domenica."

"Who is it?"

"Keller, Bernd."

"No!"

A minute later it chirped again.

"Yes?"

"A call for you, Domenica."

"Who is it?"

"Keller, Bernd. Shall I accept?"

"No!"

Again it chirped.

"We're *incommunicado*, Luigi!" I commanded.

"If you say so, Domenica."

The chirping stopped.

"I never want to see him again!" I shouted at my reflection. "Gets turned on when a vile fascist pig humiliates a woman on the open stage by using her like . . . like a urinal!"

That evening I sensed what a stranger he had become to me. Or had he always been a stranger to me, and I had merely never noticed?

AT THAT TIME, the Praetorians were already the true rulers of the city. Where they appeared there was never a uniform in sight, neither police nor military nor EuroForce. They ruled the road, roared with their heavy motorcycles down Via Appia Nova or Corso d'Italia and wantonly swept the rest of the traffic aside. No one intervened; no one dared to oppose them. Even EuroForce shied away from taking them on. According to rumors, the officers made deals with them: fuel, weapons, lasers, high-tech electronics in exchange for dirty operations against supposed Moros in the Mezzogiorno, on the Gaeta-Termoli line, which had no more chance of being held than the earlier Salerno-Brindisi line had. Or on the coast, when a few dozen Africans, Greeks, Albanians, Croatians, or Montenegrins had once again tried to enter the country illegally at night with Mafia speedboats. And many an officer had nothing against mounting one of the chained-up, long-legged beauties from Senegal or the Christian-Ethiopian mandated territory of the former Sudan, whom you could shoot in the head if—in an officers' club mood—you felt like it, without anyone asking questions.

What sort of obscenity had they come up with this time to give people a thrill? Would they disembowel a person? Stick some illegal immigrant from the Balkans or Africa whom their dogs had only caught but not killed into a suit of armor and fry him with microwaves, then peel him out of the shell like a boiled lobster? I shuddered.

The laughter of the Valkyries had ceased; the fire in the sky had gone out.

I spat over the railing into the dried-out riverbed and turned around. The dog was gone.

I pushed my Lectric across the bridge. Then I started the engine and drove home, taking Anguillara and Sanzio. One-way streets. I was going the wrong way. But who still bothered about things like that?

*　*　*

THAT NIGHT I dreamed about a dog. It lay in the dried-out riverbed. Its sand-colored fur was filthy. A raven had dug its talons into its head and was pulling at its dark jowls.

"Help me," said the raven.

The dog looked at me out of empty eye sockets and smiled.

II

CarlAntonio

> If we begin to consider how many thousands of individual events were necessary to bring about our situation here and now, and how many thousands of individual events that did not occur could have prevented it, then the most certain thing we know, namely our situation here and now, takes on an extraordinary degree of improbability.
>
> ALEXANDER DEMANDT

The students of my generation prided themselves on being particularly sexually permissive and not getting into committed relationships—at most for a brief time. We followed our inclinations, moved in for a spell with this guy, for a spell with that girl, until another interesting relationship came along—but I had really fallen a bit in love with Bernd. He was a handsome fellow with his long, dark blond hair, which hung down to his shoulders; a lean, sinewy body, which was entrancing to touch; his light skin, which looked like bronze after a few days of sun and which I never got tired of stroking and caressing with my fingertips.

He looked like his sister Birgit, who was four years older than he was, just as tall and lean and athletic.

Yes, Birgit . . .

"You're sleeping with her," I accused him in a voice embittered by jealousy. "You're always going 'home' to her! You're always murmuring with her via Com! Are you enslaved to her, or what?! Your own sister?"

He stared at me in confusion—anxious like a cornered animal.

"At least admit it already! I don't care! Do you hear? I don't give a damn!"

I cared. I definitely cared.

"Are you crazy?" he shouted at me angrily. "You don't understand anything!"

No, I didn't understand anything. What did I know at the time about fixations? About the hardships of a small boy who had lost his father and mother? Who clung to his older sister, because she was his only refuge in an incomprehensible, hostile world? I knew only that Birgit was an extraordinarily beautiful woman. Every man desired her, but none could boast of having "won" her. The news would have spread like wildfire. And then there was the almost painful resemblance to Bernd . . .

No, I didn't understand anything.

They came from Wiesbaden and were on vacation with their parents on the Adriatic when the disaster happened. Vacationers from the worst-hit areas had been "advised" against returning until "things were under control." But cities like Wiesbaden, Worms, or Mainz would never be "under control" again, at least not in this century. How were 180 kilograms of plutonium-238 to be brought "under control," which, vaporized, had spread over thousands of square miles and had a half-life of 87 years? It could have been even worse, some scientists had the nerve to declare, for plutonium-239 takes 24,000 years before only half of it has decayed into uranium. But even in fractions of one millionth of a gram, both are highly radiotoxic and carcinogenic when inhaled. To say nothing of the radioactive strontium and caesium isotopes, which had also been released in the explosion and had been borne eastward by the wind, deep into Bohemian and Polish regions.

The people who were on vacation in Italy when it occurred had been housed in camps near Rimini and Livorno and left in the dark about the true magnitude of the catastrophe. Thus many of them had tried to return home on their own, intending to see for themselves what was going on and save at least a few valuables and important family property—papers, photos, bankbooks and other documents. Thus Bernd and Birgit's father too had set off one day. When he didn't return and no news arrived, their mother left the two children behind with friends and headed north in search of him. She was never heard from again. The military made short work of and no distinction between looters and former residents who illegally infiltrated restricted areas. Most of them were soon so contaminated by radiation that they were not even allowed to return to the "free" areas anymore. They were interned, received meager medical care, and wasted away. The death books of Osnabrück, Magdeburg, Bayreuth, and Würzburg listed far from everyone who lay in the mass graves of the "border towns" of Kassel, Heidelberg, Bad Neustadt, Schweinfurt, and Jena. For many, identification was impossible, and they had to be buried quickly.

At the time, Bernd was two years old and Birgit six. A rich German chose a dozen children whose parents were missing. Bernd and Birgit, who were very beautiful children, were among them; they grew up in a country house near Siena and received an education with the most up-to-date curricula.

Then something must have happened to Birgit to make her so aloof toward men, but neither of them ever said a word about it. Birgit ran away with her brother from the house of their "benefactor"—she must have been eleven or twelve at the time. They struggled along, lived for a few years in a commune of the "Acqua è Vita" movement, which destroyed lawn sprinklers on golf courses and cricket fields and cut through hoses at night. With the increasing water shortage, a few splinter groups of the AèV then grew more and more violent, and when the first millionaire families were found drowned in the swimming pools of their secure grounds, the antiterror units cracked down hard. They stormed the communes of the movement and liquidated them. Bernd and Birgit got lucky. They were not shot dead like many of the members, but landed in prison—for only a few weeks, as the state already had enough mouths to feed.

Finally they came to Rome, took their entrance exam at the university, and were accepted into the Facoltà di Scienza. Both chose biology with a focus on botanical ecotechnology.

That's where we met.

"Do you have an older sister?" she asked me.

"Not that I know of," I replied. "I don't have any siblings."

"Strange," said Birgit, clasping my chin and moving it back and forth. "She wore her hair somewhat shorter, but the same face shape"—she ran her thumb over my cheek and chin—"exactly the same."

"Hey! What's the deal?" Indignantly, I shook off her hand. I didn't like to be touched so intimately—and especially not by her.

"Leave her alone, Birgit," said Bernd. "You heard her say she doesn't have a sister."

She whipped around to him. Her tightly woven braid lashed her shoulder, and her beautifully curved mouth sneered, but she said nothing. With a broad, expressive mouth like that, with its nimble lips and corners, some people can say everything without uttering a word. And the mouth said: "I won't do anything to her, your little pet," while her big blue-gray eyes looked him over with amusement.

Arrogant bitch!

Her long earrings made of red glass balls strung on thin silver chains, arranged according to size and hanging almost down to her shoulders, swung as she turned to me again. She raised her eyebrows at a steeper angle. "It was just a question. It's strange, isn't it? Ask the backpack. He was there."

She gestured with a nod to CarlAntonio, turned away, and left with those graceful, lithe movements characteristic of runners or high jumpers to devote her attention to other guests at her party.

Birgit was probably six feet tall, everything about her was large, but that didn't detract from her femininity in the slightest. Her figure was perfectly proportioned. Bernd and she could have been twins, but she was not only older than he was, she was also more mature. She had had her experiences early, had had no choice.

Men, as attracted as they were to her, feared her; they were afraid she might make disparaging remarks, for her sarcasm was scathing.

When she wore her hair loose, it framed her face in soft, dark blond waves. Then she seemed to be a different woman: more accessible, more sensual, more vulnerable. Perhaps she braided it tightly back from her face so that it accentuated her broad cheekbones, lent her a severe, unapproachable appearance. It was as if she had erected ramparts from which she looked down at us. Then the color of her eyes seemed changed too; a cool green mingled with the blue-gray of her gaze. Eyes like the sea northwest of St. Kilda, as Marcello claimed—Viking eyes.

"How do you actually know what the sea looks like near St. Kilda?" Renata had asked Marcello, who was passionately in love with Birgit at the time and had let himself be carried away to the point of making this rapturous comparison. He wrinkled his forehead with annoyance and looked at Renata appraisingly. But she had asked in all seriousness, with innocently raised eyebrows.

"None of you have ever read a Viking novel, or what?" He flashed his eyes at us angrily. Everyone was looking at him mockingly, which riled him even more. "No clue about *Red Orm* or *Eric Brighteyes*. About anything!"

"Ah, *that's* where you got it from," said Renata, nodding with understanding.

"You're all terrible philistines!" he shouted, throwing his hands up and shaking his black curls uncomprehendingly.

I too admired Birgit, even though she didn't like me. Perhaps I even loved her a little, but the sight of her hurt me in a strange way. And I was jealous, because I sensed from the beginning that Bernd would never be able to part from her.

For a long time, I didn't want to believe it.

"You really don't have a sister?" Carl asked, reaching back and tapping Antonio on the shoulder so that he stayed put. "What a shame."

"Now you're starting with that too!"

He scrutinized me with his lively dark brown eyes, clasped his narrow, triangular chin—which rested on his sternum—with thumb and forefinger, as if he could thereby wrench it out of its bony entrenchment, and pursed his lips thoughtfully. Antonio, patient as a mule, munched a sandwich. Mayonnaise and bits of egg were stuck to his chin.

"Really a shame," said Carl. "We would have liked to meet her. She really had an incredible resemblance to you. Perhaps not quite as pretty as you"—he eyed me appraisingly—"but just as stylishly dressed."

"Stop it, you old charmer."

He grinned. "Well, a bit older, in her early thirties or so, I'd guess. Let me tell you what happened. We were sitting in Emanuele on Santa Maria Maggiore. You know the place, of course. Birgit, Marcello, and us. Having coffee. We thought it was you when we saw 'you' from afar, and—strangely—we all had the feeling that she knew us, was almost about to greet us but then changed her mind at the last moment. Oho, we thought, so our Domenica is picking up rich uncles." He laughed.

"There was an older man there, you see, in his late fifties or so. No longer quite so fresh, but a stylish fellow: dove-gray pants, dark blue jacket, straw hat, sunglasses. Made an impression, you couldn't deny it. Now she's embarrassed, we thought at first, she doesn't want to introduce him to us. Got dressed up and put on makeup to look older. But then we saw that it couldn't be you after all. The woman really was older than you. And her hair was shorter than yours, cut about medium length."

He shook his head. "It must have been her older sister, we told ourselves. She has been keeping her from us."

Antonio, who had silently consumed his sandwich, wanted to move on, but Carl reached back and poked him hard so that he stayed put.

"I just wanted to tell you, Domenica."

"I don't know anything about a sister, although . . . who knows? My father supposedly got around. He didn't miss any chances—so my mother claims anyway."

Carl grinned and shook his head appreciatively. "Is your mother actually still alive?" he asked.

"I hope so. Haven't heard anything from her for months. And I can't reach her, because she doesn't carry an ICom."

"Is that possible? It's compulsory."

I shrugged. "In Genoa they're apparently not too particular about it. You know, she's one of those people who are still living in the last millennium. Really. She keeps an eye out for mailmen. She wants nothing to do with e-mail. She doesn't understand anything about it, she says. You know, my mother writes me letters and probably sticks them in a mailbox that no one has emptied for years."

"It's not unheard-of," said Carl. "But there are still mailmen. Like us, for example. Antonio!" He snapped his fingers. Antonio, who had in the meantime gotten hold of some nuts or potato chips, stopped chewing and turned his head so I could see his coarse, bulbous-nosed profile. "Wipe your mouth and give Domenica her envelope."

With a strained frown, Antonio rummaged in his shabby brown shoulder bag, which he wore strapped over the misshapen poncho that served both of them as a shared article of clothing, and passed half a dozen identical envelopes over his shoulder. Carl took them impatiently from his hand and handed me one of them with a sigh. It bore the Vatican insignia.

Personal was written on it.

"Thanks," I said.

"They arrived today at the institute. A whole bundle. Direct from the Holy Father in Salzburg."

He nodded.

"Well, at least from the Holy See. For everyone who applied last year to that Rinascita Project."

The contents of the envelope felt like a VidChip.

"Good luck," said Carl, drained his glass with a forceful jerk of his torso, ran the back of his hand over his lips, and handed the glass over his shoulder for Antonio to put down.

I knew that Carl drank vast quantities of red wine. He literally had to drink for two, while Antonio seemed to be more responsible for the nourishment of their shared body.

"We have to move on. Still have a few letters to deliver," he said with a smile, slapping Antonio on his bald head. Antonio pushed off, and Carl strained to peer forward over his shoulder past the thick, protruding ears in order to direct him.

Antonio and his "backpack" Carl. After the disaster, there had been countless cases of mutations, but the pair of twins was definitely the most gruesome of all the monsters—while also the most likable. Many deformed children—people spoke vaguely of "tens of thousands"—who were born after the catastrophe of 2028 had quietly been registered as "stillbirths." Premature birth had been induced and the fetuses removed to save the lives of the mothers. CarlAntonio's deformation, however, was unique, so grotesque and so scientifically interesting that it was preferable to sacrifice the life of the mother to save the object of medical interest for study. In any case, the doctors at the Brothers of Mercy Hospital of the University of Regensburg regarded this as the right decision, and because it was a good Catholic university, the monster was even baptized: The Siamese twins received the names Karl and Anton. Their mother came from Offenbach, which, like Frankfurt, was directly at the edge of the death corridor; she had lived in one of the large refugee camps of the southern Upper Palatinate.

The deformation was indeed grotesque. Both brothers had a fully developed head and upper body, but merged under the shoulder blades and were conjoined at the spine from the sacrum to the coccyx. While Antonio had a fully formed body—exceptionally formed, some women claimed—Carl's chest was narrow and bulged steeply. His head sat neckless on the torso; the lower jaw was fused with the sternum, which lent his posture a servile and simultaneously rebellious quality and his voice a strained, asthmatic timbre. His small pelvis stuck out at a right angle over Antonio's backside and formed a baggy hollow of skin that was closed by the rudimentary little legs and oversized feet, which were reminiscent of the flippers of seals, when he bent them in an embryo-like fashion. Behind it the surgeons had created an artificial passage where Carl's only half-formed digestive tract now ran into that of Antonio. Only in that way could the twin survive. On the other hand, despite state-of-the-art medical technology, the "backpack" could not simply be removed from Antonio, because the nerve pathways of both bodies intersected in the lower area—which resulted in strange physical as well as psychic reactions.

On top of that, they needed each other in yet another way. What would the melancholy, clumsy, somewhat retarded Antonio have done without his "backpack" full of intelligence, wit, spirit, and imagination? What would

Carl be without Antonio, who sustained him with his healthy appetite and his robust body, which he battened on and lived off like an exotic epiphyte?

There were women who were sexually attracted to the monstrous physique, but it required some skillfulness—and Carl's help getting the shared body to the necessary blood alcohol level—to bring Antonio out of his apathy, stimulate him, and arouse his dull libido. While Antonio ultimately toiled away silently and unflaggingly, so the stories went, Carl on his back screamed like an excited chimpanzee; he threw his head back and forth so violently that the saliva sprayed from his lips, and writhed as if he wanted to break free from his twin. And when Antonio, grunting, finally climaxed, Carl's lower body had turned into a swollen mass that looked like the butt of a baboon, and a shape the length of a finger, purple and thin, jutted from his loins.

CarlAntonio lived above all off being a monster; some dottori at the Policlinico on Piazza Sassari lived off it as well—and probably better. On the side, the two brothers ran errands for the botanical institute of the university.

CarlAntonio. Back then they were still alive. They had just turned twenty, if I remember correctly. But shortly thereafter, it happened. The Hobbits ambushed them, those racists in their gray loden jackets and lederhosen and pointy felt hats on which they stuck feathers of dead birds, those self-proclaimed guardians of the genetic inheritance and preservers of the purity of the Aryan race.

Carl was still alive when they were found—for he had his own heart and his own lungs. They had used a knife. Hobbits always use knives, hunting knives or butcher knives, which they grandiosely call "swords." They had slit open Antonio's belly and had not forgotten to mutilate him; they had blinded him and hacked his face to pieces, as they always do, because they cannot tolerate a subhuman—a nonhuman—having a human face.

Carl made a detailed statement, but the police wouldn't do anything, we were all sure about that. You could tell by the officers' faces; they were no different from the Hobbits, sympathizers from the bottom of their hearts—their uniforms couldn't fool us. Carl had not seen much, had only felt the terrible pain. His voice was weak and toneless. It was as if his brother's mind had escaped into him at the moment of horror, seeking refuge in his head, with all its dullness and lethargy. And gradually, death too came creeping over and nested in his breast and grew into a suffocating, dark weight. But it took hours before it crushed him. The end came with a desperate rearing up, as if he still wanted to break free of his brother's cooling body after all, and with rattling breath, he flailed around.

Just when we all believed that the worst was over, he asked for a mirror so that he could see his twin's face one more time. The ward doctor fulfilled his request. He had two mirrors brought over and positioned in such a way that his wish was granted. Carl wept when he saw the maimed face of his brother. Fifteen minutes later he too was dead.

I UNFOLDED MY battered flexomon, smoothed it out and pressed it to the wall, then inserted the TV modem into my ICom until it clicked into place. Luigi's input tongue darted out, I put the papal chip on it, and Luigi swallowed it like a frog swallowing a fly. The golden keys on a blue background appeared on the flexomon.

"You are Domenica Ligrina," said a pleasant male voice. "Allow me to introduce myself. I am Bertolino Falcotti from the Istituto Pontificale della Rinascita della Creazione di Dio, San Francesco. Please wait a moment."

The signal on the monitor switched into IA-mode.

"Would you like visual contact?"

"Yes, please," I replied. "One moment."

I pinned the camera to the middle of the flexomon. A red dot appeared on the upper edge of the monitor, immediately followed by another. The papal emblem disappeared, and I was looking into a study, saw a desk with piles of books and periodicals, between them a thick, burning candle.

"I'm glad that you are still interested in working together, Signorina Ligrina."

The man sitting behind the desk nodded amiably to me. He was dressed casually, wore a black button-down shirt, the sleeves rolled up above the elbows. In his early forties, by my estimation, though the slightly graying hair on the sides made him appear older. His glasses flashed. Dimples formed in his cheeks when he smiled. That lent him a certain charm. He could have been an assistant at the university. In any case, he did not look like the clergymen I'd dealt with previously. Behind him, on the whitewashed wall, I spotted an icon, its gold shining out of the gloom.

"First, if you permit me, I would like to ask you a few personal questions." He was quiet and well spoken. "Beforehand, I must alert you to the fact that this conversation is being recorded. Do you agree nonetheless to answer questions about yourself?"

I shrugged. "To whom will the recording be made accessible, Signore Falcotti?"

"Only the committee that decides on your application."

"And who are they?"

"Unfortunately, I cannot answer that question."

"You are not permitted to answer it."

He raised his hands in a conciliatory fashion. "For me there's no difference."

"All right, I agree."

He nodded and brushed back his short-cropped hair with his fingertips; fleetingly he touched a slight unevenness at his left temple. An implant? He had a thin, well-proportioned, almost boyishly handsome face. The glasses gave him an aloof quality, and perhaps he wore them for that very reason.

"I don't need to tell you that, at the end of our conversation, both interactive data carriers are ROM. That gives them the character of a document that is not accessible to unauthorized individuals without your express approval."

"With the exception of the committee."

"You have already agreed to that."

"That's correct."

"But enough with the formalities." He opened a file. A window popped up on my flexomon, and the image of my father appeared. The picture must have been taken years before his death. A dark blue shirt, a white single-breasted jacket. His eyes flashed boldly from under the brim of his panama hat.

"Authorized material from the registration authorities," explained Falcotti. I suddenly realized that I was smiling at the photo on the monitor, and I immediately pulled myself together.

"Your father's name is Giacomo?"

"No—his name was Jacopo! He is no longer alive."

Falcotti looked up and scrutinized me. Had there been too much intensity in my voice? Or grief? Why should I have concealed it? Even if it was more than ten years earlier. I had loved him from the time I was a small child. And later I could not be angry with him when I heard that he had had frequent affairs. He was often on the go and as a textile sales representative constantly came into contact with beautiful women—models, owners of boutiques. On the contrary, I had been proud of him. He was . . . a man of the world. Good-looking, always elegantly dressed. He had to be. And he always made jokes that Mother either didn't get or didn't want to get, because she was much too sober and humorless to appreciate our silliness. I was always delighted when he winked at me conspiratorially from under the brim of his panama hat, and I would double up with laughter. I enjoyed when he took me out, to the holos, to eat ice cream or visit a museum. Then I felt like one of his "hussies," as Mother called them with a venomous look and a shrill voice, although I had no idea what she meant by that. Women liked him, and he liked them. I could not grasp why Mama wept so often.

"He died in an accident?"

"He died in the attack on the Naples–Rome express near Mondragone in September 2039, which took so many lives."

"I remember. It was terrible."

All the travelers from the Mezzogiorno who resided south of the Gaeta-Termoli line and had no special permission to travel north had been refused tickets and reservations in Naples and had been forcibly prevented from getting to the platforms where the trains to Rome departed. The city was seething with unrest, and the Stazione Centrale resembled a besieged fortress. Special police units cracked down hard on the demonstrators and hermetically sealed off the train station. The Neapolitans were outraged at being equated with the Moros. Under strict security measures, the Naples–Rome express finally rolled out of the station. Half an hour later, shortly after Falciano-Mondragone, an explosive charge was detonated in the first car of the fully occupied high-speed train as it entered a tunnel. It was never possible to determine how many people died in the inferno, for despite all the security there had been many passengers on board who had no reservation. The official statements put the number of dead at 412, but according to estimates, more than 500 people must have lost their lives in the attack. No corpses were found, only a compressed mass of steel, aluminum, charred plastic, and protein that had agglomerated into a hard plug in the tunnel tube. It took weeks of work to gouge it out. That same year the terror bombings began against authorities and politicians in Rome, but the regime remained firm. It stuck to a plan envisaging a sort of tiered system of dams against immigration from the south to the north to stem the tide of people from the Mezzogiorno. Meanwhile the rivers of refugees had long flowed past it along the coasts.

"What was your father's occupation?"

"He was a sales representative for textiles. In the end, mainly for holo-textiles produced by a Korean company, which were really in fashion in those days."

Falcotti smiled to himself. So he was familiar with those garish, lewd, glitter miniskirts with the sewed-in chips, which came out in the early thirties and were an absolute hit: shameless HoloClips, which could be activated with a skilled twitch of the hip, which conjured away the material for seconds and were programmed with all manner of intimate scenes, from the harmless groping of a soft-core porno about fellatio to hard-core penetration—and that in bright metallic and vivid colors.

Mother made sure that Father never took them out of his sample cases at home, because she loathed that "disgusting stuff" from the depths of her soul. "We live off it," Father had replied, shrugging. "It's not simple today, believe me."

"Your mother is still alive?" asked Falcotti.

An image of my mother appeared. A pretty woman, who had probably been really sexy in her youth before grief and disappointment had consumed her charm. A pale face that had become a bit doughy with time. The pallor was accentuated by her curly black hair, which she wore pinned up in the back in an old-fashioned way and from which one or two corkscrew curls always hung down on the side. Oh yes, her slightly receding chin, the constantly mournful pursed lips, the sad, always somewhat reproachful look, the tiny bite of bitterness in the left corner of her mouth, which had deepened with the years . . . Would I look like that one day, I wondered involuntarily. The resemblance was unmistakable, but I had my father's eyes—and his chin too!

Falcotti observed me. I wrinkled my forehead and sighed. "Yes. She moved to Genoa a few years ago, to live with her mother when my grandfather died."

Grandfather! How distant were the times when I got to spend my vacation with him? He had been such a lovable man, who had kept his sense of humor despite everything. Back then he seemed ancient to me, although he was not yet sixty, and he walked laboriously on crutches. A few thugs from the Mafia had mauled him when he still had his café on Piazza Caricamento near the Palazzo San Giorgio on the harbor. He had refused to pay them protection money, because he already had a contract with the Moros. The Mafiosi were going all out at the time—the south was increasingly slipping away from them, and so they were attempting to gain the upper hand in the north by force. A hopeless undertaking, at least in Genoa, for the city had been firmly under the control of the Africans for more than sixty years.

The Moros were generous: They compensated him for the injuries and paid for the operations. I did not grasp at the time what getting shot in the knees meant. My grandfather never uttered a word about the pain inflicted on him by this barbaric injury and he would not have tolerated any pity, but he enjoyed my affection. I loved him—most of all his big fleshy ears, which I touched with a mixture of shyness and admiration when he let me. And I loved going grocery shopping with him. I sat on his lap and we whirred in the wheelchair down the road and across the big parking lot to the supermarket.

With that memory, my nose filled with the scent of freshly brewed coffee that emanated from his clothes because he sat behind the counter all day operating the espresso machine, removing the steaming metal filter, knocking it out on the edge of an old coffee-soaked wooden drawer, and filling it carefully with freshly ground coffee.

With the compensation from the Moros he had been able to buy a small terrace café overlooking the city, along with the house attached to it. It was on a quiet street, which had lost its significance due to the construction of the highway. My mother moved there after Father's death, because it had become too dangerous in Frascati for a single mother with an adolescent daughter. Actually, that gave her a pretext to help her mother with the household chores and Grandfather in the café, for they could no longer manage on their own.

The summers became more overpowering with each year. Day after day you saw the hopeless deployment of fire-extinguishing planes, of fire brigades and volunteers. Burning forests on Sardinia, Corsica, and Corfu. Seas of flames on the Peloponnese and the Balkans, ash-clouded sky and people fleeing. Helicopters with food and drinking water in areas surrounded by fires.

The hills above Genoa were magnificent. Most mornings, a breeze wafted up from the sea and alleviated the heat, while it took your breath away in the city below. In the late afternoon, the wind from the hills stirred, filling the evening with the fragrance of herbs and cool pine needles. We all had our hands full. Most of the time, the terrace was already full of guests at ten in the morning—excursionists from the cities on the coast— and after sunset all those craving a breath of air and a cool drink. Business was good.

When the last guests had left and the weather permitted it, I pushed Grandfather out onto the terrace in his wheelchair and he showed me the stars.

"You have to come visit us sometime over Christmas vacation, Domenica, then we could look into the galaxy. The Sagittarius Arm is visible then, brimming with stars. Now, in summer, only a few neighbors can be seen, which belong to the Orion Arm like us: Vega, Deneb, Antares, Altair, Arcturus, and Spica, and the brightest over there in the Perseus Arm. Beyond that begins the great void," he told me enthusiastically.

He knew all the strange-sounding names of the stars, which the Arabs had given them: Sirah, Algorab, Algenib, Shedir, Albireo, Achernar, Alamak, Sadalmelik, Merak, Alcyone, Dubhe, Zubeneschamali, Zubenelgenubi, Zubenelakrab, Ras Alhague, Aldebaran, Alderamin, Hadar, Enif, Furud, Sulafat, Sadalsuud—names as smooth and sparkling as polished gemstones.

"Those people lived under a close sky," Grandfather explained. "They needed only to look up when they camped at night in the desert."

And I pictured a caravan camp on a moonless night. The snorting of the camels somewhere in the darkness, the last tea, heavily sweetened and with a few sprigs of fresh mint in the glass, had long since been finished, the embers of the fire had been consumed, the sand was cool, the sky had spread out its treasures.

Yes, I owed the sky to Grandfather. He had made it accessible to me, and my interest in it had never died. On starry nights I could sit outside for hours and go on journeys with my eyes, tens of thousands of light-years away through the depths of the universe, which remain closed to most, because no one handed them the key to this treasure chest.

Vacation in Genoa. All that was now fifteen years in the past. Grandfather was long dead. What might it look like there today?

"Are you in contact with her?" asked Falcotti.

"Sorry?"

"With your mother?"

"I haven't heard from her for about three months. I've called her from time to time, when I could get through, but . . . well, we never had too much to say to each other."

She spoke on the telephone only rarely. "I'll write to you," she said. — "What are you going to write to me? In Rome there hasn't been regular postal delivery for a long time." — "What nonsense. Letters are still delivered everywhere." — "Mother, believe me, not here." — "I'll write to you," she said, and hung up.

Sometimes I thought she was no longer in her right mind. Perhaps it was all a bit too much for her. She could no longer keep up.

"Do you love her?"

"She always made it really hard for me. When you ask me so directly—I like her, but love . . . hm, actually no."

He made a note on his computer.

"You have siblings?"

"No."

"Any other relatives? Uncles, aunts?"

"No."

"Your paternal grandparents?"

"Dead."

"Friends with whom you are particularly close?"

"Friends, yes. Fellow students. But no committed relationships."

I didn't mention Bernd. At that point we had slept together just three or four times. I had no idea how our relationship would develop.

Falcotti nodded. "You seem to be someone who manages well alone. That's important."

"Why?"

"Our project involves missions that must sometimes be performed by individuals operating completely on their own. Possibly without outside help."

"Fieldwork?"

"Yes, something like that."

That was unusual.

"But fieldwork is usually conducted by teams," I asserted.

Falcotti placed his fingertips together. "Unfortunately, that will not be possible in this case."

"Will this work be abroad? I mean, outside Italy?"

"Yes. Mainly. But I ask you to understand, Signorina Ligrina, that I cannot disclose any details to you before it has been decided whether you will be among the final candidates."

"Sounds mysterious, Signore Falcotti."

He shrugged meaningfully.

"Will this potentially be a permanent job?"

"It will potentially be a permanent job."

Should I get my hopes up? It would be premature—the disappointment would then be all the more intense.

"That will be all for today, Signorina Ligrina. Thank you for answering my questions so openly. I appreciate your cooperation, especially as I am prohibited from giving you further information about the nature of our project. Should the preselection committee choose you, we will arrange a personal interview. In the meantime we would like to ask you to submit to a thorough medical examination at the polyclinic on Piazza Sassari. Ask for Professor Pietro Dalmatini and make an appointment. The examination is, of course, free of charge. The expenses will be paid by the institute."

I WAS NOT granted the privilege of meeting Professor Dalmatini personally. I had to content myself with a young assistant doctor named Dolfredi, who had a thin, overhanging mustache and had eyes only for his equipment. An old nurse, who lavished her motherliness on me, patted me incessantly. I had to lie down naked in a body-shaped tub lined with white plastic. The doctor then gave me an injection in the back of my hand. The last thing I knew I was sliding through a gleaming chrome portal into the maw of a machine; then I was suddenly knocked out. When I came to after two hours of unconsciousness, I was lying safely and cozily in a recovery room on a rolling bed. My clothes were next to me on a chair. Someone had taken care to cover me with a quilted blanket. Doctor Dolfredi? I flung the blanket off me and got dressed.

He actually knocked before he came in.

"Yes?" I asked gruffly.

Doctor Dolfredi looked at me with surprise, then gazed questioningly at the computer screen on his wrist.

"Oh, this will take a few hours," he said, holding up a chip. "They want to know a lot about you."

"Who?"

He examined thoroughly the label on the plastic-wrapped chip. "Istituto Pontificale della Rinascita della Creazione di Dio, San Francesco," he read aloud. "The Pope himself!"

His mustache rose as he smiled, revealing a thick mouth with soft, pink, saliva-moistened lips, which I could never stand on men. He bared his buckteeth, between which the mashed remains of a tramezzino were stuck.

"If he even knows about this Istituto," he added.

I glowered at him. His revolting smile disappeared.

* * *

AFTER THAT I heard nothing for several months. It was impossible to avoid the impression that the whole Rinascita Project had been abandoned.

To my knowledge, the initiative for it had originally come from John XXIV, who had displayed a strong commitment to environmental issues. His successor Paul VII certainly did not have much interest in the Creazione di Dio when he wore the tiara that he had bought back from an impoverished sheik in exile with donation funds. Instead, he set to work developing Castel Gandolfo into an impregnable fortress, had deep underground galleries driven into the mountain walls surrounding the lake, in which he planned to store the treasures of the Vatican Museums in order to protect them from the dangers of the new mass migration and preserve them for posterity. His building zeal was too great for his weak heart.

Finally, Paul VIII did not attach particularly great importance to the Creatio or the art treasures; he was much more concerned with his personal security. Soon after assuming office, he moved his residence to Mantua, only to relocate shortly thereafter to Salzburg. As a Hungarian, he probably felt more at home there. In Austria jubilation burst out; South Tyrol, Friuli, and Slovenia had been annexed to the state territory, and now the Holy Father was residing in Salzburg. For the Romans, however, the Pope was from that point on as dead as his predecessors, and some Italian cardinals demanded his deposition. The little people called him Papa Coniglio, Papa Coward.

Perhaps he had decided to abandon the Rinascita Project. And Falcotti was entrusted with other tasks.

I spoke to fellow students who had applied too. No one had heard anything more about it, and all inquiries regarding a Vatican institute of that name came to nothing. Nothing could be found on the Net either. It seemed no longer to exist, had disappeared without a trace—and with it Bertolino Falcotti.

"A papal miracle," Birgit commented mockingly.

I no longer had high hopes, but somehow I could not entirely believe that Signore Falcotti had taken leave of us in this impolite way. Had something happened to him? Was he traveling?

III

Ghost Towns

For nothing is found in time except the now.

NICOLAUS CUSANUS

How many of the residents of Rome had remained? A hundred thousand? Five hundred thousand, as the Capitol claimed? Or was it only fifty thousand? The fact was that the water and power supply had broken down in the southern districts. The green tank trucks of the AMNU drove with armed escort to Borgata, Ostiense, and Garbatella, and the fire department roared down Cristoforo Colombo but usually turned around without having achieved anything, because it was shot at. Over Cecchignola and Torrenova there were often black columns of smoke, and the smell of burning car tires frequently reached the city center.

Life went on, at least in the center, but the quartieri at the periphery had become more villagelike. People moved closer together, clustered around public fountains, small markets, parishes, formed supply and security associations. In between were ghost towns.

And no one knew exactly how many people still lived behind the high walls and wrought-iron gates of the countless tiny monasteries, where they safeguarded their relics, documents, and folios.

The unthinkable had very gradually become thinkable: The Caput Mundi, the center of the world, might one day have to be given up. An outrageous idea for many. And this time the armed hordes were coming from the south. They said it was the Moros, the blacks, the Africans, but it was people from the Mezzogiorno, whose vineyards had been scorched and whose livestock had perished of thirst in the blazing heat as the breath of the desert wafted toward their fields.

* * *

WHEN THE HOT wind blew up Via di San Grigorio and the Colosseo stood out like a somber fortress against the cinnamon-colored sky, in which the sun no longer had a definite place, breathing in the lecture halls and laboratories became a torment. Around eight in the morning, the thermometer was already at one hundred degrees. We took our Wallet PCs and Notepads and tramped through the sand between the dried-out palms in front of the Facoltà di Ingegneria on Via Eudossiana. The "Scuola di Ingegneria Aerospaziale"—what lofty plans we once had! We stopped in the shade of the wall behind the dust-covered car wrecks, on the roofs of which feral cats slept, and sought refuge on the cool marble slabs of San Pietro in Vincoli. While outside the hot breath of the future could be felt, heralding the arrival of Africa, inside wafted the cool air of the past.

There, Nico, I encountered you for the first time, where under the pale grave slab, bordered with a band of black and pink marble, your bones lie:

NICOLAVS D'CVSA CARD.

A coat of arms on the wall, which shows a fat red crayfish served on a spade-shaped tray sitting on a netlike placemat made of red strings and tassels, Cryfftz, Krebs, crayfish, an *Astacus astacus*, which has long since disappeared from the rivers of Central Europe—and with absolute certainty from the Moselle. Above it, on the broad, colored bas-relief by Andrea Bregno, you kneel, on the left, with folded hands, at the feet of St. Peter—the broad-brimmed traveling hat, as big as a wagon wheel, leaning against your body. Opposite you an angel with golden wings and glad tidings. This was my favorite spot: The grave of Cardinal Nicolaus Cusanus—as he was named after his birthplace of Kues.

AFTER MOVING OUT of the Città Universitaria on Piazzale San Lorenzo, our institute was at first situated in the small box of a house at the foot of the tower of the Borgia dynasty on the northwest corner of Piazza di San Pietro in Vincoli, where the members of the Facoltà di Impianti Nucleari previously had their laboratories. Here Ettore Majorana had done his research, the brilliant nuclear physicist who disappeared mysteriously and whose fate was never cleared up.

We had moved into the monastery on the west side of the piazza, which had offered Lebanese Christians refuge during the Muslim fundamentalist persecutions in Beirut. They had returned home after the Peace of Rabat, and the Technical University had acquired the building. With the large dormitories, the spacious corridors and staircases, it seemed more like a hospital from the century before last. From the high ceilings decorated with stucco hung Oriental lamps made of openwork brass, which served the purpose of illumination less than they did that of archiving decades of dead insects.

In the basement corridors stood dozens of high beds made of brass tubing, which—according to the ingenious system of a custodian—had been stacked crosswise up to the ceiling in order to save space. Countless mattresses quietly moldered away. Two or three of the beds were always ready for use, because ever since the Parco di Traiano, once a popular "getaway" for students, had turned into a wasteland in which not a blade of grass grew, they went off to the basement when they wanted to be undisturbed. Or they crept into the church of San Pietro, where those who had been raised strictly Catholic got an extra kick by doing it at the feet of the horned Moses, who, the tablets of the law clamped under his arm and indignant at so much sinfulness, looked away with darkened brow.

I lay on my back on the cool marble slab. Bernd sat next to me and typed on his Palmtop, while I lost myself in my thoughts. This Nico—had he been like Bernd when he was young? I imagined him tall and lean; narrow face, straight, aristocratic nose. But he had actually been the son of a river boatman, a successful merchant named Krebs—spelled Cryfftz in his native dialect—which means crayfish. He had retained the name, had borne the crayfish on his coat of arms. He had always been proud of his simple origins. Ultimately, he was named curial cardinal and vicar general of Rome by Pope Pius II; thus he held the second-highest ecclesiastical office as the Pope's representative.

What moved such men to join the clergy, to place themselves in the service of the Church and the Holy See? To renounce having a wife and children? Certainly, in his day, it had been the only way for a gifted young man to study, attain education, and rise in the hierarchy of society. Or had it been his religiosity, the decision to do something for God's Creation, for the Church, which, responsible for His kingdom on Earth, at that time was in a desolate state, in danger of failing to fulfill God's mission? I decided to delve deeper into the life and work of that impressive man.

If I were to encounter him here and now . . .

I closed my eyes and ran my hand along Bernd's lean, tanned thigh, on which silky blond hair sprouted.

"Hey!" said Bernd, moving away from me as I slid my fingers into his shorts.

"Take me," I said.

He looked at me with a mixture of horror and disgust.

"Are you crazy?"

"We wouldn't be the only ones . . ." I replied, gesturing with a nod to Rita, who was sitting on Eduardo's lap with her eyes closed and gyrating her thin hips.

Bernd stared into the semidarkness of the nave and took a while to grasp what was happening in the opposite aisle under the side altar with the painting of St. Augustine by Guercino. He jumped up.

"All of you must be nuts! Here in the church!" he snarled, gathering up his things and running to the entrance.

"They're going to elect you pope!" I shouted after him, frustrated and disappointed—and angry with myself.

Rita turned her head toward me, without pausing for even a moment in her sensual rhythm. I sank back on the cool, smooth stone and breathed deeply. Soon the *Astacus astacus* would drive its claws into my sinful flesh as a punishment.

I looked to the left—and saw that the winged Grim Reaper on the wall, adorning the tomb of Cinzio Aldobrandini, was staring at me with blazing eyes, the bony fingers of his right hand wrapped in a strangling grasp around an hourglass. I jumped with fright. It must have been the lighting in the church that made the eye sockets blaze bright white. He looked terrifying.

Rita and Eduardo strode toward the exit, Rita smiling abstractedly, Eduardo rubbing morosely with the ball of his thumb at a semen stain on his jeans.

SUMMER SOLSTICE. As they did every year, the Hobbits organized big parades. Tents, campfires, songs. Hobbits appeared only in "packs." Never alone. Alone they were cowardly. United they were cruel and dangerous. They "cleansed" the city, hunted for "Moros." And the Praetorians supported them in this. The police remained invisible. EuroForce stayed out of it.

For several nights already, the dull drumming and singing of the "pack" on the Gianicolo could be heard. The fires blazed, silent vigils were held. For the remains of the West? Hobbits in droves with pointy gray felt hats, earth-colored loden jackets or cloaks, with knives in the wide leather belts on their lederhosen: hunting knives, army knives, and double-edged daggers, to crusade against the Moros, to hunt, mutilate, and kill them.

During the day, the race of dwarves was nowhere to be seen. Did they crouch in their musty caves, in the root system of crude Nordic mythology, in their cartoon world with electronic icons of the forever bygone and forever resurgent? Their underground realm was the vast labyrinth of the Vatican bus station inside the Gianicolo, a dark, deserted network of concrete caverns in which abandoned bus wrecks from the states of Eastern Europe rusted away. In them they had discovered ancient, blood-soaked, half-decayed flags, relics of long-forgotten battles, which pilgrims from Poland and the Baltic states had brought with them to have them blessed by the Pope but which had remained unblessed after the death of John Paul II. With them they covered their "fallen heroes," and on them they swore loyalty and obedience to their leaders.

On the night of June 22, the hunt was on. When darkness fell, the shooting began, and it lasted through the whole night. Constant shouting and the frenetic barking of dogs could be heard, and a wild drumming that was recorded by synthesizers and amplified so intensely that the windows rattled and you could almost feel it in your skin.

Between the backyard of the house in which I lived and the summit of the hill there had once been a botanical garden, which had belonged to our institute, but at some point all the trees had been cut down. They had been sick from exhaust gases, it was claimed, but Stavros had shaken his head and said that the motive had been to have an open field of fire from the police station, so that no one could sneak up within throwing range. In any case, the trees were gone—and, in the meantime, so was the police station.

Bernd had stayed at my place. We had made love in the darkness. No one turned on the light at night, for fear of drawing fire—even if only from hobby snipers in the neighborhood. Sometimes flashes of light blazed over the roofs and lit up the facades of the houses, and glaring reflections crisscrossed the ceiling with stroboscopic patterns.

At midnight we opened a bottle of sparkling wine. It was somewhat warm, because the power had been out all day. The alcohol, the flashes of light, and the incessant drumming turned us on. Only toward morning did I fall asleep in exhaustion.

The howling of ambulances woke me. It seemed never-ending—half a dozen. They must have been parked nearby. The rhythmic blinking of their red lights swept across the ceiling. The drumming had gone silent. The shooting had ceased. Bernd was asleep. I stood up and opened the curtain a crack. It was a vision of horror. I had never seen anything like it. The victims of the night's combat were being brought down from the hill. It must have been a real battle, a war.

On Via Garibaldi seven white and red ambulances from the Policlinico of the Città Universitaria over on Via Tiburtina were parked in a row. Doctors and helpers bustled about. In the courtyard of the convent, medical teams attended to the injured. The nuns—only eight or nine still lived on the vast premises—had opened the wrought-iron gate. The small front courtyard, which usually served as a parking lot for guests and visitors, had turned into a makeshift field hospital. A priest strode from one stretcher to the next, before they were lifted up and pushed into the vehicles.

On the street the dead had been lined up along the convent wall below the entrance. The line kept getting longer. Some of them had no more faces, others were charred down to their hips; blackened ribs poked through the ruptured skin of the torsos. Their hands had been bound behind their backs with wire, a gasoline-filled car tire hung around their necks and ignited. "Kentucky" was what this ghastly method of execution was named— after the American fried chicken. Stavros had explained that to me; I had not wanted to believe it. He was down below, walking along the line of corpses and scrutinizing every single one with an expert eye.

Suddenly I sensed that Bernd had come up behind me. He thrust his hands under my T-shirt and kneaded my breasts as he pushed his stiff member between my legs and began to pant excitedly. I broke free of him and shouted with disgust, louder than intended, "Let me go! You're no better than those fascists!" With a violent movement I wiped the tears from my face. "That turns you on, huh?"

He stared at me with astonishment, and his erection dwindled. "Hold on a second! What's the matter with you?"

"How can you be thinking . . . about *fucking* at the sight of those corpses?"

He brushed his long blond hair from his face and looked morosely out the window.

"Most of those people are looters and murderers. Moros. They've been making the city unsafe for weeks."

"Most of those people are simple country boys from the Mezzogiorno who have been driven from their land by the drought. They were desperate and hungry," I replied.

"Then they should report to one of the aid organizations. They'll get ration cards and a place in one of the refugee camps."

"That's coming from you, of all people? You should really know better! The population of Europe declines by two million each year. What happens to all those people?"

"Most of them die of cancer."

"And thousands die every month on the coast. Supposedly attacked and killed by feral dogs. Meanwhile the Praetorians are directing the movements of those semi-intelligent killer beasts by computer."

Bernd shrugged. "They keep the illegal immigrants at bay, don't get their hands dirty, and save on food for the animals too."

"Ugh!"

Bernd spread his arms. "That's just how it is. How can we change it?"

"What kind of country has this become? I'm ashamed. People are murdered in cold blood. Like them down there. Look at them! No one even thought of protecting them. Or did you hear a EuroForce helicopter last night?"

"They were probably otherwise engaged."

"I'm sure of it. One crow doesn't peck another's eyes out. They're all in cahoots. And these poor people were left to the Hobbits and the Praetorians with their killer dogs. It's fun, a hunt like that! They wore down their victims with vibrasound and deceived them with battlefield holos so that they sought cover where there was no cover, and then they picked them off like rabbits. That's how it goes!" I sobbed.

Bernd looked at me helplessly.

"You're right. That's how it goes," he said faintly.

A woman in the convent courtyard had sunk to her knees, raising her fists in an accusatory fashion and exclaiming curses. One of the nuns put her arm around her and tried to comfort her. One after another the ambulances started and drove away with howling sirens. Others arrived.

"There's no way you can go on living here, Domenica. You can move in with me. Birgit definitely won't have anything against it."

"Oh, thank you for the generous invitation. Did you ask her permission, then?"

The thought of his arrogant sister, who never spoke anything but German with him, only intensified my helpless anger. At times like this, I could imagine them doing it with each other, he and that beautiful woman who aroused the desire of all men but didn't let any of them near her.

"I'd rather not chance her slamming the door in my face. I'll find something."

He shrugged and got dressed. "I'll help you move."

"Not necessary. I'll manage."

All morning ambulances came and took away the injured amid howling sirens. There must have been more than a hundred. Then—much more quietly—the dead. There had been forty-six, Stavros told me later. Mainly Italians from the south, maybe a dozen Albanians and Africans.

IT WASN'T HARD to find an apartment. Luigi took care of it for me. He asked me what I wanted and plunged into the Net. Five minutes later he gave me half a dozen addresses. I chose one and he finalized the contract with the landlord's ICom.

The apartment was only ten minutes away from the institute on Via Merulana, right behind the Terme di Traiano. The landlord, one Signore Paolini, was happy to rent for four hundred euros a three-room apartment for which he would have gotten five times that amount ten years earlier. He had put up his wife and his two small daughters with relatives in Bergamo— for safety reasons, as he confided in me—and amused himself with an Austrian woman, who seemed to be a relentlessly cheerful spirit, with up-swept blond ringlets, always smiling, trilling, and giggling—and dressed in hideously patterned baby-pink pantsuits. But she still didn't manage to dispel the deep sadness that dwelled in Signore Paolini's dark eyes and in the corners of his drooping mustache.

"Rome is dying," I said to him the next morning when I paid the rent.

Signore Paolini counted the money; the cigarette in the corner of his mouth gave off smoke into his eyes, and he squinted. He looked at me and nodded, but his mind was elsewhere. His bony figure only half filled his shabby coffee-colored bathrobe.

"*Gern hab ich die Frau'n geküßt . . .*" a jaunty tenor belted out in German from the squalid speaker of a portable radio on a small table with a crocheted tablecloth next to the kitchen door.

"Who is dying?" asked his girlfriend from the kitchen.

My landlord dismissed her question with a weak movement of his hand and let out a rattling cough.

"Who is dying?" she wanted to know.

He gave me a sad look, blew the smoke out his nostrils, and stubbed out the cigarette in an overfilled ashtray. His fingers were yellow with nicotine.

"I am," he grumbled, "if you keep pestering me with your questions."
His girlfriend stuck her head out the kitchen door.
"Hello," I said.
She waved to me with freshly painted nails.
"You grouch," she said to Signore Paolini. "Light me a cigarette."

IV

Imaste Dio

Clocks had two functions, in my view. The first was to tell people what time it is, and the second to impress on me that time is a mystery, an unrestrained, boundless phenomenon that eludes understanding and that we, for lack of better options, have given a semblance of order. Time is the system that must ensure that everything does not happen at once.

CEES NOOTEBOOM

I called a taxi and went to Via Garibaldi to get the rest of my belongings. The driver could not be persuaded to wait for me and drove off as soon as I got out. With surprise I noticed that the trash in the hallway was gone. The overstuffed mailboxes had been emptied; the floor was not only swept, but even mopped.

"Stavros! Did you do this? You've earned a bottle of ouzo."

No answer. I went to the back and cast a glance into his small cubbyhole, which served as his living space and bedroom. Stavros wasn't there. He must have gone shopping or was having a drink somewhere.

I went upstairs and packed the rest of my things in two big travel bags—clothing, shoes, and linens in one; computer, books, DVDs, CDs, and chips in the other. For my kitchenware I had gotten a moving box; on top was the big porcelain vase I had been lugging around with me for many years. It was glazed midnight blue, with magnificent white herons strutting around, sheltered by bamboo branches—a memento of my father. He had brought it back from a trip at some point; perhaps a Korean business associate had given it to him. In any case, I cherished it. In autumn I always filled it with long dry grass, in early spring with broom flowers, to entice the season's arrival ahead of time.

When I had carried everything down, Stavros still wasn't there. Should

I leave him a message? No, I wanted to say good-bye to him in person, thank him, and present him with a bottle of ouzo that Vasilios, a Greek student, had obtained for me through connections.

The street was deserted under the hot, hazy sky. Someone had washed the blood, the ashes, and the soot of the corpses from the pavement. The water had long evaporated. Somewhere a woman was weeping. The gate to the convent was open. It was usually closed, so I went through with curiosity. It was Sister Anna, tears running down her face. Two priests stood with her, talking to her reassuringly with serious expressions. A dark car was parked in the courtyard.

They had not yet noticed me. I backed away and turned to leave.

"Signorina Ligrina!" Anna called after me. "There you are."

I stopped, turned around, and approached her. "Yes, Sister?"

"Look what has happened," she sobbed. "It's terrible."

She took me by the arm and led me through the entrance into the corridor of the convent. The blue-gray and white marble-tiled floor was littered with shards. The whole glass facade facing the convent garden was shattered; the wall opposite it was riddled with bullet holes. In the reception area to the left of the entrance, next to the wooden telephone booth, I saw a large, blackish, sticky stain, on which flies had gathered.

"This is where they shot Signore Vulgaris."

"Stavros?" I gasped.

My chest constricted. I looked around in horror. There were shards everywhere. Someone had spray-painted the outline of his head and upper body in bright orange on the wall, on the tiles the outline of his legs and his weapon. Here he had died, not three yards from the convent's Com system. "How on earth did this happen? Who was it?" I asked in dismay.

"We don't know. We were attacked this morning. What godless barbarians! They killed Sister Oeconomica in her office and took all the money. Sister Carlotta and little Magdalena they shot down in the kitchen. They were brought to the clinic."

A cherrywood-and-glass case in which the Christ Child had stood—the life-size figure of a blond boy of about ten with a halo and a sash over his arm raised in blessing—had been reduced to rubble. Tatters of satin hung on the worm-eaten laths of the smashed rear wall. Pieces of the gilded aureole lay scattered over the floor; the statue had been mutilated beyond recognition. The white sash, embroidered with golden letters spelling IO SONO L'AMORE, lay over a severed hand.

"They killed the Savior," the Sister sobbed. "He died for me."

I saw that she was trembling all over. It wasn't fear; it was a fit of religious ecstasy. She kneeled down on the shards and crossed herself.

"He bears my wounds," she declared shrilly, spreading her arms. "He is a miracle!"

My chest felt tight. I sensed all sympathy dying away in me, for I could not share such feelings.

"Sister, I . . . It was too much for you. Come on," I said.

I helped her to her feet and supported her. She staggered alongside me. We walked down the corridor. Glass crunched under my shoes. Soberly, I took a closer look at the destruction. Another pool of blood with the outline of a human figure in bright orange. Farther back, outside the door to the mother superior's office, a third.

The looters must have possessed incredible firepower. The walls displayed hundreds of bullet holes. I cast a glance into one of the alcove-like small rooms. A large glass case, which had contained a blue, white, and gold-painted Madonna with child and a dusty little bouquet of dried flowers, was also destroyed. The Christ Child was gone. The Madonna's head was missing. Worm-eaten wooden splinters jutted out of her chest and neck. Next to that a gutted ancient television set; a pious amateur craftsman had replaced the screen with a glass window, behind which a depiction of the Annunciation could be seen. It was unscathed.

We returned to the entrance hall. High up on the wall hung a double portrait: two ovals of Jesus and his mother in the style of the sentimentalized Sacred Heart devotion surrounded by a gilded frame. Christ pulled open his red robe and exposed his pierced heart.

Stavros did not exhibit his wounds. The ravaged battlefield of the Aegean War, which he bore on his chest, had been plowed anew.

"What a world!" Anna sobbed. "What a time! Oh, Holy Mother of God, help us!"

In the convent garden, a fountain burbled. Birds chirped. The clematis nodded in the light breeze, which wafted through the shot-up windows. The rosebushes so fondly tended by the sisters were in full bloom and exuded their fragrance. How many afternoons had I spent on this island of quiet in the middle of the city, sitting at one of the stone tables and reading?

Destroyed. The convent would be closed.

It had been four men. Stavros must have noticed the attack and rushed to the rescue. He had cornered and shot dead three of them. The fourth must have hidden in the convent garden, lying in wait for him as he tried to fight his way to the telephone to call for help. How often had I told him that he should pin an ICom to his collar? He would have been able to order an automatic distress call and stay under cover. As it was, the fourth had picked him off through the window and had escaped.

It had not been Moros, but most certainly specialists from the Balkans, who stole sacred art in Rome at the behest of galleries and private collectors in the Far East and overseas, especially Mass utensils, altarpieces, statues, and incunabula. What they had expected to gain from the attack on this impoverished, small convent, which had sheltered and fed pilgrims to Rome for two hundred years, was a mystery. Cheap altar utensils made of zinc, statues made of wood and plaster, painted with loving care, but without any aesthetic value.

"Rome is dying," I said hoarsely to the two priests standing in the parking lot in the convent courtyard and waiting for Anna. They looked at me uncomprehendingly and somewhat reprovingly. Then they told Anna to pack up her personal things. She would be housed temporarily in a different building, until it was decided what would happen.

Anna and I pressed our cheeks together to say good-bye. Finally I too could cry.

I WENT THROUGH the whole house, ringing the doorbell at every apartment. No one opened the door. A few apartments were unlocked; they were empty. Rats had moved in; they had gnawed away at boxes and plastic bags to build their nests. Everywhere I was confronted by the acrid smell of their excretions. On the stained carpet were dried-up droppings. In the bathrooms cockroaches rustled. I opened the window in the stairwell. The rear courtyard was covered with dozens of shiny black plastic garbage bags, which bore the AMNU sign of the city administration and would probably never be picked up. Many of the bags had been gnawed at; their contents had decomposed and putrefied. Between them crawled rats. It stank horribly. Fat flies buzzed around like stray bullets and crashed against the windowpane. I held my breath and hurriedly closed the window, but the whole house had long since inhaled the effluvium. It seemed to have crept into the walls and to adhere to the wallpaper like a sticky exhalation. It revolted me.

I went downstairs to Stavros's apartment and pocketed the CDs with the patriotic songs of his favorite composer. It was important to me to honor his memory in that way.

When I stepped onto the street, three teenagers were about to shoot at my vase with an AeroBlaster; they had gotten the vase from the hallway of the house and placed it on the front steps.

"What's this all about?" I shouted at them.

"Do you want to buy it, signora?" the leader asked with a grin, a kid, maybe fourteen years old.

His incisors looked like spade blades in the upper jaw of his thin, pimply face. His left fist was tattooed with a blue scorpion. He raised it at me, as if he wanted to transfix me with that gesture.

"It belongs to me," I snapped at him.

The boys laughed.

"Five hundred euros," the leader demanded impassively, pumping his weapon.

I restrained my anger and decided to play along.

"All right," I said. "I'll give you fifty euros. You go buy yourselves some ice cream and leave my vase alone. Okay?"

"Five hundred."

"Fifty."

The vase burst into pieces. Bamboo branches plummeted from the midnight blue sky and buried the strutting herons. I cried out with anger and pain, rushed over, and grabbed the neck of the vase, which had remained intact.

"A thousand," said the boy, pumping his weapon again and pointing it at me. Suddenly I was afraid. Now he's going to shoot, I thought. The tiny hard plastic shuriken, propelled by air pressure, were not able to penetrate deep into the skin, but they caused painful bruises even through clothing. And if they hit you in the eye . . .

With a howl I hurled the neck of the vase into his face—with the absolute certainty that I would at that same moment feel the sharp plastic granules tearing the skin off my cheeks. Nothing happened. I opened my eyes. The boy was licking the blood from the corner of his mouth, where the broken piece had hit him. He had lowered his weapon. The other two fellows had backed away a few paces. Silence.

"You'll make a brave Hobbit!" I exclaimed scornfully.

He grinned at me and raised his fist with the scorpion.

"I'm a Praetorian," he declared, too proud to wipe the blood off his chin, then turned around and walked away. His sidekicks followed him. Bodyguards. Führer pose. Oh, God! Always the same dumb male games.

Crying, I sat over the shards of my vase on the steps leading up to an empty house.

"Call me a taxi," I said to Luigi through my sobs.

"Please repeat," he replied.

He could not identify my weepy voice. I cleared my throat and tried to speak normally.

"Call me a taxi, Luigi!"

"Yes, Domenica."

Only the third taxi driver was willing to come to Trastevere.

That evening I got drunk off Stavros's ouzo and played Stavros's CDs at full blast. The songs of Theodorakis. Why hadn't we Italians produced such a composer in five hundred years?

"Rome is dying!" I shouted drunkenly out the window.

It was after midnight. No one heard me. No one answered. A bell tolled somewhere, dull and muffled, as if from the ocean floor, from a sunken ship. In the south the haze was illuminated by deep red flashes. Heat lightning? Or was it muzzle flash? Had the bombardment of Rome begun? Was the storming of the city at hand?

V

Witch-Burning

Why do we remember the past but not the future?

STEPHEN HAWKING

Cardinal Nicolaus Cusanus counted the leather containers that were attached to the packsaddles of the beasts of burden. In Brussels he had managed to acquire state-of-the-art astronomical instruments and in Leuven several scholarly manuscripts, which he had had carefully packed for the journey. He reassured himself that everything was still there.

The morning dawned.

"Get up!" the captain of the city guard shouted.

Three darkly dressed figures, who had been cowering next to the landing, rose. Their clothing was dirty; their sidelocks curled from under their hats and hung down to their chests. The three men had been bound together with thin chains, the older one between the two younger ones. They wore wretched footgear; the toes of one of the men peeked out from his shoe. Two officers of the city guard drove them from behind with their pikes. The three prisoners eyed the weapons silently and impassively. They shivered in the morning cold.

"They've known for more than twenty years that they are not permitted to stay in the city at night," the captain declared to no one in particular, as if he had to excuse his official act, "but they try again and again." When no one paid attention to him, he barked: "Move! Or do I have to make you?"

"You don't have the say around here!" exclaimed the ferryman. "This ferry is from Deutz. We ferrymen are not subject to the city council of Cologne, but to the archbishop. Bear that in mind. Remove the chains from those men!"

At that moment, a rat crawled out from between the planks, an enormous animal of an unusual color—more grayish white with reddish spots than grayish brown. Sniffing, it scurried along the edge of the dock. One of the officers jabbed at it with his pike—playfully, more to scare it away than to impale it. Like lightning, the rat had jumped on the weapon, had climbed the shaft in no time, and stood a handbreadth from the officer's face. The rat then made a noise that sounded to the cardinal, from where he was standing, almost as if it had spoken, hissing a warning. But that was nonsense, of course.

The man recoiled in fright and threw the spear away from him. "The devil!" he cried, pale with horror, took a stumbling step back, and fell on his behind. "The devil!" The pike clattered to the ground, and the rat disappeared between the planks over the water.

The cardinal turned with surprise to the man, who sat on the ground and gawked around, his eyes wide with terror. "The devil?" the cardinal asked with curiosity, scrutinizing the man.

"Apologies, Your Eminence," said the captain, signaling to the officer with a brusque hand gesture to pull himself together and get up from his undignified position. He then got to work unlocking and removing the prisoners' chains. He threw them grumpily over his shoulder. Then he turned away and spat in the river.

Nicolaus scrutinized the prisoners, who seemed not to have even noticed the incident with the rat. They made an apathetic impression as the officers drove them onto the ferry with their pikes. He had endorsed the expulsion of the Jews from the city, but the measure had not brought about the hoped-for solution. The conflict between the council and the archdiocese continued to smolder, and Hussite-influenced preachers constantly rekindled the acrimonious atmosphere between the denominations and religious currents. For many, Rome's word carried no more weight. No one seemed to want to obey. The world was in a state of dissolution.

The cardinal nodded to his groom to lead the horses onto the ferry. Their hooves clip-clopped on the planks, and the man tethered the four animals to the railing side by side. They were uneasy and eyed anxiously the foaming dark water of the river. The ferryman shouted a command, and the ungainly, heavy vessel cast off. With their long oars the oarsmen pushed it off from the rocking, wooden dock. It started to turn. The river was already swollen, even though it was only mid-March. In the Black Forest and in the Vosges, the thaw had probably already begun.

"Row!" the ferryman shouted at his oarsmen. "Or do you want to dock in Düsseldorf instead of in Deutz? Row!"

The cardinal turned to his young companion, who wore a blue beret on his thick, shoulder-length hair, on which he had boldly stuck three quills as a sign of his occupation.

"Well?" asked Nicolaus, resuming the conversation that had been broken off for a while. "What else happened?"

"If I may, Your Eminence, since when does much happen in Cologne?" asked Geistleben, taking his knapsack off his shoulders and dropping it next to him on the floor. "A handful of little Roman monks arrived who fled from Constantinople, because the Turk is approaching the gates. They moan and ramble on about the end of the world and scrounge and beg for benefices. Oh yes, and on Candlemas a little witch was burned on the Old Market square. But you have surely heard about that."

"Not a word," Nicolaus replied, shaking his head with displeasure. "Is it spreading here too, that awful folly of torturing women and putting them to death?"

"Yes, certainly. It is getting worse everywhere. People are afraid of the spawn of the Antichrist, who gnaw at the limbs of the Church and eat their way deeper and deeper into its heart."

"What sort of talk is that, Geistleben? It is not the Antichrist who gnaws, it is greed that gnaws, it is vanity that gnaws, it is lust that gnaws in the flesh of our brothers and sisters."

"Well, indeed, that is your affair, noble lord. You undoubtedly understand more about it . . ."

"Quite true."

"But the East will fall, Your Eminence. Half the Empire—"

"What else was to be expected? I saw it with my own eyes, Geistleben. Catacombs full of writings, accumulated for centuries, with the knowledge of millennia from all over the world. But no one reads it; no one can even sort through it! Schemers and empty-headed scholars swarm over it like rats. Everyone gnaws at everyone else. Often at their own flesh. No wonder, then, the enemies are lurking. That's how it is everywhere. Here in our lands too. It was often painful, what I saw on my journey to Flanders and the Netherlands. It fills me with bitterness and rancor. As for the archbishop, however—we spoke daily during the concilium, but he did not mention a word about having held a witch trial."

"Well, Your Eminence, he seemed to have been not at all certain at first. Once before he had been at odds with the Pope, old von Moers. After almost forty years in office—simply excommunicated."

"That was Pope Eugene. He held it against him that he had voted against him at the Council of Basel."

"But that was a deep shock for him in his old age."

"Pope Nicholas reinstated him. He won't want for anything."

"Certainly not."

"When I stayed here on Christmas and New Year's Day, I heard rumors of a woman who had been found with a strange collection of herbs. Was she the one?"

"Yes, she was."

"And the trial? Why the harsh sentence?"

"As for the trial, my lord, things got away from him. There was again conflict with the city council over jurisdiction. Tempers flared. He sought advice and support from the highest authority. A commission was to come from Rome, to investigate the case, whether devil's work was actually involved . . ."

"Why wasn't the woman forced to renounce all vengeance and banished from the city, as usual? Why did she have to be put to death?"

"There were inflammatory speeches. A young priest was very active, a zealot from Swabia, Bartholomäus von Dillingen is his name—he is a preacher at St. Maria im Kapitol. People call him 'Witch Bart.' If I may, Your Eminence, an evil snooper. He watched her every step for weeks. After his sermons, an angry crowd always proceeded to the Old Market square and demanded that she be made short work of. She was ultimately turned over to the episcopal judge, for the archbishop insisted on the main jurisdiction, as the law would have it. A serf who encountered her in the summer on the Moselle testified that, without touching him, she used devilish powers to cast him to the ground with such force that he was black and blue all over his body and felt pains in his chest for weeks. He heard laughter that sounded like the bleating of a goat and could smell the definite stink of sulfur. A citizen with whom she lodged testified that she told her that one could fly from Cologne to Rome in an hour. And under torture she spoke heedlessly. She confessed to having flown through the air herself. It was the herbs, though, that determined the outcome."

"How so?"

"Over the whole summer she had gathered a collection of seeds— kernels from grain and fruit, blossoms from all sorts of flowers and plants. For medicinal purposes, she claimed. These seeds were sorted neatly into little canvas pouches and labeled and inscribed with Latin words. But these words were incomprehensible. A sort of secret system of classification, Your Eminence, which . . . well, so it seemed to me, was strangely coherent, but of which no one had ever heard, as the professors of medicine brought in from the university confirmed. This system pointed to heretical, arcane knowledge and could not possibly be of godly origin . . ."

"Of devilish origin, then . . ."

"The commission of professors came to that conclusion. The young woman could not be saved. One thing followed another. Everything happened very quickly. And the citizens were content when the sentence was issued and carried out immediately. And the archbishop washed his hands in innocence as Pontius Pilate had done formerly."

"So they truly did make short work of her."

"Well, she actually brought it on herself. She lied through her teeth. Went so far as to claim that the Holy Father himself sent her to collect little seeds and flowers."

"The Holy Father?"

"Yes, in order to save Creation, she asserted."

The cardinal shook his head. "She was surely confused. An unfortunate creature. The woman should not have been treated that way. Such a thing is shameful."

"Verily, I look at it the same way. Especially as she had more education than could be ascribed to the devil, or—if I may—to the archbishop, for that matter."

"How so? Was she a nun? From what order?"

"I don't think so. It's odd . . . no one who had sworn a vow of humility would have spoken like that. And her Latin, oh my . . ."

"A noblewoman then?"

"Not a chance!"

"A simple woman? You are making me curious."

"You will be even more surprised, Your Eminence, when I tell you that she wrote you letters. It emerges from them that she seemed to be quite well acquainted with you."

"What do you mean, she was acquainted with me? Was she from here? From Koblenz? From the Moselle?"

"No, certainly not. No one really knows where she was from. Some claim that she came from Amsterdam, others that she was from Sweden, was the assistant of a court physician there. Her appearance, her speech pointed more to a Roman, perhaps Florence, Siena . . . who knows? But definitely not from the countryside. By no means. She was educated. Knew things even I had never heard of. At times, I thought she had . . ."

"Yes?"

". . . come from another world."

"You mean, from distant lands?"

"Very distant lands, Your Eminence. Of which we still know nothing."

"A sibyl perhaps, from the Orient?"

The scholar shook his head hesitantly. "Those prophetesses speak obscurely. She spoke more with the light of certainty. It seemed to me—how should I put it—as if the darkness were in our heads more than in her words, if you understand what I mean, Your Eminence."

The cardinal lowered his gaze thoughtfully. "From where might she have known me? Did she ever cross paths with me? Did she speak with me? In Rome perhaps? But I don't remember ever having met a woman of that sort . . ."

"It does not seem so. I don't think she knew you by sight. It is more— how should I put it—as if she were acquainted with your writings and with you as a very famous man."

"You're speaking in riddles, Geistleben. How could she have been acquainted with my writings? And me, a very famous man? That I am not, God knows. She must indeed have been confused."

"It would not have been a surprise. She had, after all, spent months in the dungeon. The icy cold had afflicted her. She was sick and desperate. Without friends or acquaintances. In the end, death must have seemed to her like a salvation."

"What barbarity, to burn a woman alive! I would not have thought old von Moers capable of it. Sat meek as a lamb by my side during the synod. As if butter wouldn't melt in his mouth. Lo and behold, old Dietrich! Perhaps that is why he did not even mention a word about . . . Did she confide in you personally?"

"No. I caught only fleeting glimpses of her now and then, when she was brought to an interrogation. I read the transcripts."

"You were permitted to see them?"

"Well . . . as a scribe in the chancery of the archbishop I could not help taking notice of them. I worked for him for almost a year. I write quickly and largely flawlessly, you should know. But now boredom drives me onward."

"The letters to me . . . ?"

"Are in the records. They will—I assume—eventually be delivered to you, because the case has been concluded. But so that you would not have to wait too long, I took the liberty of copying for you one or two letters that came into my view, Your Eminence."

"So you copied documents that are under lock and key and—I presume—classified . . . ?"

"Well, apparently not so classified. Far more than that, they are incomprehensible, mysterious—but extremely remarkable."

"You are carrying the copies with you?"

"Yes, indeed. I fetched them from the hiding place as the synod members set off and your departure too was approaching. I hastened after you to be on the ferry with which you are crossing."

"And intend to sell the copies to me now, I assume, after you have sufficiently piqued my curiosity."

"Stop it, Your Eminence! You have a reputation as an experienced merchant, especially when it comes to rare items."

"Copies of obscure letters from an alleged little witch, who, in a state of confusion, claimed to know me. Indeed, Geistleben, a rare item. I have to grant you that."

"I foresaw it: There would be no chance of haggling with you, Your Eminence. I will give them to you as a gift. You are known throughout the land as a generous man. Your magnanimity is proverbial."

"Now, now! Do not mock. I know what people say about me."

"Nothing could be further from my mind! You will certainly repay a poor little scribe and traveling scholar, noble lord."

"How about it, Geistleben? I saw you working diligently during the synod. I can always use a scribe who is quick with the quill and has a sharp mind. Good at copying writings of all sorts and tongues."

"Many thanks, Your Eminence, for your confidence and your magnanimous offer, but I am drawn away. I would like to finally move on. First Strasbourg, then Paris, to study there the Lullian art of which I have heard."

"You mean that Majorcan's art of creating knowledge by means of a little mechanism—click, clack—without exerting the mind and calculating—from one to two to three—the wisdom of God's Creation?"

"If I may, Your Eminence, it might, I think, be the true future of all philosophizing: counting, measuring, weighing, calculating. Not the errors, superior attitudes, and disputes over authorities of the past and present.

Computing! The little witch writes it at one point: You will one day be credited with having advanced this very thing."

"Me? That is as bold as it is incredible, Geistleben. True, I have—it was a long time ago, I think it was in the year '26, when I was still Giordano Orsini's secretary—examined the work of Raymundus Lullus. While rummaging around here in Cologne, I found it among many other writings. The cardinal pointed out to me that there was an extensive, almost entirely unexplored library here. He had a nose for such things."

"I too discovered it here. It intrigued me."

"I made excerpts back then, but I never found time to devote myself seriously to that *Ars Magna,* as its creator so vainly called it. Only I have reservations about ceding the practice of philosophy to the mechanics and clockmakers. Although . . . Well, indeed, at the Camaldolese monastery Val di Castro, after a dispute with Toscanelli, I wrote down a few thoughts on weighing, which . . . I will delve deeper into it, when time permits . . . But no, how would that woman . . ."

"Does anyone know what the future will bring, Your Eminence? Besides God, perhaps the devil . . . and a little witch now and then?"

"Moor the vessel!" the ferryman shouted to the oarsmen.

On the riverside two young men had hastened over and caught the lines that were thrown to them. Horses were harnessed, a dozen or more, to tow the heavy vessel upstream to the upper dock, for the leeway was surely three thousand feet. The breath of the animals steamed in the cool morning air. Up on the bank Jewish children stood in the wet grass. Wrapped in rags—barefoot. They followed the horses at a proper distance, for the towing men swung their whips widely. A pale sun rose between cloud banks and turned animals and people into gold-enveloped silhouettes.

"I hope to be in Rome again by summer, Geistleben," said the cardinal. "If your wanderlust should lead you there, you would be a welcome guest."

"You are too kind, Your Eminence. I am honored by your offer."

"You would then have to tell me about the Lullian art, if it has been taught to you in Paris."

"It will be my pleasure, Your Eminence."

The groom led the animals by the reins up the dock, held the stirrup, and helped the Cusan mount. The cardinal held up the tied-up scroll with the letters.

"Thank you!" he called to the scholar, who had shouldered his knapsack. "God bless you."

"Farewell, Your Eminence."

"We set off," the cardinal commanded, taking the reins. "I want to be in Heisterbach with the Cistercians for sext and in Andernach for vespers. The day is short, and I hate journeying in the dark."

The groom nodded, leaped into the saddle, and fastened together the reins of the pack animals. Then they rode off, leaving behind the voices of the children ringing out in the cool morning air.

A couple of geese flew low over the reeds along the river. The heavy, rhythmic beat of their wings sounded like the lusty moans of two lovers. The groom turned his face away and grinned.

VI

In Vincoli

This game, I say, signifies the movement of our soul from its kingdom to the kingdom of life, in which there is rest and eternal happiness. In its center presides Jesus Christ, our king and the giver of life. Since he was similar to us, he moved the sphere of his person so that it came to rest in the middle of life, leaving us an example so that we would do as he had done and our sphere would follow his, although it is impossible for another sphere to reach its resting place in the same center of life where the sphere of Christ rests. For there is within the circle an infinity of places and abodes.

NICOLAUS CUSANUS

The lecture had been canceled. I had an hour and strolled across the piazza in front of San Pietro in Vincoli. For the first time I realized that the old church looked more like a market hall with several of its gates closed on nonshopping days. Only with difficulty could the portal be made out in the shadow of the portico. I walked around the northern side of the church; from behind the building looked even more odd: an architectural jumble of alterations and additions, so that you could scarcely make out the apse. An old, rounded brick wall rose to half the height of the main building and was crowned with a pitched roof. A murky, makeshift window was installed in it. It could just as well have been a stair tower or the silo of an old storehouse. Over many centuries, the whole complex seemed to have surrounded itself with armor like a mutant crustacean. Into the grooves and hollows of this armor had grown metal rain gutters and water conduits, plastic drainpipes as well as a chaotic network of power lines, lightning conductors, and antenna wires—like forgotten drains and sensors on a corpse after a failed surgery. Dead vines hung down like rotten bandaging.

I went back and turned the corner onto Via Eudossiana, where a mobile kiosk offered ice cream and drinks to students and tourists in the summer. On that day too it stood in its spot, but business was bad. Most of the departments of the university next door had been dissolved. The tourists didn't come. Only rarely did a small group of Chinese or Japanese visitors stray there to admire the horned Moses.

That was where I had met Bernd the previous year.

"May I treat you to some ice cream?" he had asked me. I had smiled at him, for he seemed terribly shy. He was in his early twenties and good-looking with his long blond hair. It had clearly been difficult for him to speak to me. As I scrutinized him, he actually turned red.

"Well, if you're treating me to something, then I'd prefer a soda," I said.

We had walked for an hour in the Terme di Traiano. It already looked bad there at the time. The grass had dried up into a yellow-brown mat; the bushes were bare. Only the trees still found some water in the depths, but had shed most of their leaves in order to reduce the evaporation surface area. Even the pines had scattered an unusually thick carpet of needles. Green lizards scurried across the path; their bizarrely serrated body markings could have been designed by a Japanese lacquer artist.

That had been a year earlier. Now the park was beset by wandering dunes, and it was dangerous to enter it after nightfall because the Praetorians trained their packs of semi-intelligent, genetically modified dogs there.

Bernd studied ecotechnology and took his courses in botany at our institute. He brought the Rinascita Project to my attention, and many of us botanists hoped to get a job there. We saw it as a unique opportunity, for what need would there be for botanists if the plants died?

THE CONVENT OF the Piccole Sorelle dei Poveri behind high walls on the southern side of Piazza San Pietro we called the "aviary," because it was occupied by little white birds. The order was founded in France, and still most of the Little Sisters were French. Strangely, they were all dainty and small, as if they had been bred especially for this convent, and they always appeared in small twittering groups. You never saw one of them alone. In the morning they flocked to their tasks in the city. Probably most of them worked as language teachers. In the late afternoon they returned and disappeared into the aviary behind the high walls. In the evening the gate to the convent was closed tight and secured with a thick chain.

As I drove to the institute on June 30—the last day of the semester—all of Rome seemed to have begun to decompose. A sickeningly sweet corpse smell rose from the sewers, as if a seismic shift had opened ancient, previously undiscovered catacombs, and from the gaping mouths of the cellar windows wafted the stink of mold and rot. The air felt tallowy—smelled rancid, as if it had taken on a greasy, sweaty state. The sky dimmed leadenly.

I drove across the piazza past the aviary to the parking lot, secured my Lectric, and was about to walk to the institute when Gina approached me and said, "We're all in the church." She cast an uneasy glance at the sky. I followed her, and together we entered the church. I was about to sit down in "my" spot bordered by pink marble, the cool grave slab of Nicolaus Cusanus, when I felt wetness. The marble tiles and slabs were covered with a shimmering sheen, and with my fingertips I touched a damp film.

A trough of the Icelandic Low, deviating far south, extended over France into the western Mediterranean. Its cold air tongue pushed its way under the oppressive, dust-laden pall of smog that had accumulated over a year and a half of drought and lifted it up a few yards. That was enough.

A peal of thunder rolled over the city, louder than any decibels the Praetorians had ever produced. We hurried outside. In the meantime, it had gotten as dark as if a solar eclipse were taking place. The air seemed to have congealed; a gray ground fog formed, creeping out of the sewers. Lightning flashed, lit up the whole sky like the inside of a gas-discharge lamp, and another peal of thunder rolled over the city. And then the beast that had lain over the city and smothered it for more than a year began to vomit. First came surreally large black and yellow globs that smacked into the sand and onto the pavement like bird droppings. In no time the ground was sprinkled and then covered with that sticky substance. Then the heavens began to roar like a cataract, and a few seconds later water came pouring down as if it formed a solid mass. And suddenly the ground was littered with a million foamy bubbles like gray-brown toad spawn, which the next moment were riddled by the impact of a stream of crystal clear bullets; they burst in white explosions and excavated one fleeting crater after another. Lightning incessantly lit up the darkness, and the peals of thunder merged into a deafening crescendo unlike anything I had ever witnessed before. We watched a group of the Piccole Sorelle who appeared at the cavernous descent of Via San Francesco di Paola. With hitched-up habits the nuns approached the gate of the aviary like a flock of white bantam chickens. They kept slipping on the slick layer that covered the pavement, and had trouble fighting their way through the masses of water, which flooded the piazza from one minute to the next and created an enormous lake in the southwest corner. In the past, the water could have drained unimpeded through a small alleyway onto Via degli Annibaldi toward the Colosseo, but around the turn of the century some shortsighted building department official had issued a permit for the alley to be walled off, forcing the floods to seek a different outlet; they found it very quickly in the tunnel of Via San Francesco di Paola, which swallowed them like a thirsty throat, until it was clogged by sand.

The thunderstorm moved on, but the heavy rain persisted. The monotonous pelting sound put me in a dreamy mood, and I had the sensation that the piazza was ascending like a spacious elevator toward the heavens.

It rained all evening and half the night. The sirens of emergency vehicles and fire trucks could be heard again and again. Most of the students spent the night in the bed basement of the institute. The custodian grumpily gave his permission and reprovingly eyed the wine bottles that we had gotten at the supermarket. I offered him one of them. He scrutinized me severely, ran his hand with a sigh through his gray fringe of hair, then smiled, grabbed the bottle, and stashed it in the pocket of his gray work coat.

The first daylight transported us into another world. It was lined with blue. The sun had its place again; the air was as cool as silk and flushed the lungs with invigorating freshness. This must be how salmon feel, I said to myself, when they have gone beyond the fetid waters at the mouth and are approaching the source. The palms in front of the institute glistened and gleamed under a clear, bright sky; the facades of the houses, still gnawed at by sulfuric acne and darkened by smog the day before, appeared as if they had been freshly whitewashed. The tower of the Borgia dynasty looked imposing and almost restored. The sand drifts on the steps and along the walls were gone; the piazza, on the other hand, looked like an oasis in the desert, or rather like a field of sand with a massive shallow puddle. And Via San Francesco di Paola no longer existed. Gone was the street sign on which generations of students had immortalized themselves with their initials; gone was the blind white eye in the aureole under the ancient lamp, which stared vacantly at those who descended Via San Francesco—actually not a road but a cavernous passage with steps—to Via Cavour; gone, too, was the old lamp. It had been ground away by the sand masses sliding through. The passage itself had turned into a compactly sand-filled tunnel.

Since an excavator could not be used, the sand had to be dug out and vacuumed up by the fire department.

We students helped out, and fourteen large truckfuls of sand were removed from the hole—plus one of the nice little white sisters. She had apparently not managed to climb the rest of the steps against the power of the cascading water and had been buried and smothered by the sand masses borne along by it. She seemed tiny laid out on the stretcher, and her little legs, which stuck out of the dirty white habit, looked like those of a small bird. Poor *sorella*, I thought, as the helpers carried her across the piazza to the convent, how fragile they actually are.

So it was a sad day, even though the light broke through for the first time in many months and gave back colors to the world. And above us the swifts grazed with their blade-wings the fresh blue with which the sky was lined.

The evening filled the horizon with molten orange, in which steel gray rafts of scabby cinders drifted; behind that a vast lagoon of turquoise and cobalt opened up, above which a soft lime green floated like a breath— dreamy coasts over the horizon, drawn on our retinas by stray photons, deceptive ethereal forms, engulfed by darkness within minutes.

That night we saw the stars again for the first time in a long while. But the next day the temperature already rose above one hundred degrees again. The relentlessly hot air of Africa breathed down our necks, and the desert returned to besiege the city anew.

As IF THE peristalsis of a long-dead body had suddenly been reactivated by a vigorous enema, the river had returned. It was indescribable, all that it carried along with it. At the Ponte Rotto, a barrier had formed, consisting of household items, mattresses, plastic bags, shopping carts, bicycles, branches, boards, and the decomposed cadavers of animals and birds, which had heaped up into a ten-foot-tall cliff obstructing the water. The vast quantities of sand had formed new islands rutted with deep drainage channels. Half the Sahara must have been in the streets of Rome. The sand, fine as dust, had within minutes clogged all the sewers. Soon a disgusting sludge rose up in tens of thousands of basements and low-lying dwellings, and what had amassed there then began to stink. A miasma spread, compared with which the effluvia of the Pontine Marshes could have passed for the atmosphere of a climate therapy resort. It was only a matter of time before yellow

fever, malaria, and cases of dysentery would appear, for the muck had undoubtedly sloshed into many wells.

The decayed tooth stump of the Castle of St. Angelo, which had displayed its concentrated ugliness for a few days, was enveloped by a sickly
haze, and passed very gradually into a sort of virtual state, which allowed it
to slide into a parallel universe. The Rome of our reality went on dying, but
somehow the boundaries between the dimensions became blurred.

THE TEMPORARY RESURRECTION seemed to have had an impact on the
Vatican peristalsis as well, for the vanished Istituto Pontificale della Rinascita della Creazione di Dio, San Francesco reappeared as if from a parallel
world.

My ICom chirped.

"Yes, Luigi?"

"A call, Domenica."

"Who is it?"

"Falcotti, Bertolino."

"That can't be!"

"Would you like to accept?"

"Yes."

"Have lightning and thunder brought you back to life, Signore Falcotti?"
I asked point-blank.

He laughed. "Are you still interested in the prospect I held out to you in
our previous conversation?"

"I've completed my degree, thank God. Botany was the last department
that still held proper exams here this spring."

"I know. Most of the others have long since headed north."

"So I urgently need a job. After this semester, my scholarship expires. I
can't afford to be choosy."

"Well, it . . . it is not a job in that sense. As I already mentioned last time
we spoke, it is a . . . longer-term commitment."

"Even better. Abroad?"

"Within Europe, yes."

"No problem, Signore Falcotti."

"Excellent. I will be at the university the day after tomorrow. Would you
have time for a conversation in person?"

"I have all the time in the world."

"How enviable."

We made an appointment.

I HAD NEVER before been on the top floor of the university. In the hallway stood discarded furniture: ancient desks, which still had glass inkwells set into a narrow board over the lid; the folding seats were as tiny and cramped as if they had once served first-graders or Lilliputians. Next to the desks was a row of ugly chairs made of steel tubing with worn and slit-open white plastic upholstery, from which the yellow stuffing poured like old fat.

Had I strayed into a wing that was no longer used? No, the room number Signore Falcotti had given me checked out. I knocked—no response. I pushed down the handle; the door was unlocked. Afternoon light streamed through half-open blinds into the large room. On the whitewashed wall behind the desk shone the gold from a gloomy icon. It was the room I had seen over the Vid connection during our first conversation. On the desk burned a thick yellow wax candle, emitting a cozy scent of honey. From hidden speakers came soft choral singing, which had a strangely light, dancing quality. On the large surface of the desk I saw an open laptop, surrounded by piles of books and periodicals. On top lay a fish paperweight, an astonishingly lifelike reproduction of a gilthead bream. It raised its head grimly and rested on its ventral fins.

"Hello!" I called, but no one seemed to be there. I was about to leave when I heard a voice behind me in the hallway. Signore Falcotti was smaller and slighter than the image on the monitor had led me to suspect. The small rectangular reading glasses had slipped down almost to the tip of his nose. He wore baggy black jeans and an open-necked white shirt with the sleeves rolled up halfway under a shabby light brown leather vest.

With both hands he clasped my outstretched hand, as if we were old friends. He had a natural warmth, without any posture of exaggerated priestly attention, to which I had always been averse.

"Please take a seat, Signorina Ligrina," he said, gesturing to a leather armchair in front of the desk.

"Thank you."

I sat down and involuntarily crossed my legs, before I realized that that was not exactly appropriate for the present occasion, that my demeanor left something to be desired, which could have negatively influenced the decision. How could I have been so thoughtless as to put on a knee-length skirt for an interview with a clergyman? Too late. And a demure tug at the hem of the skirt would only have drawn even more attention to it. I hoped that he did not misunderstand the exposure of my knees, but rather interpreted it as a sign of my easygoing nature.

Signore Falcotti seemed not even to have registered it; his eyes were fixed on his laptop monitor. He was probably about to access my data. I noticed that I was inwardly tense. The fragrance of honey from the candle made my head a bit fuzzy, and I wondered in passing whether he had already had the close-cropped beard when we spoke over VidCom. No, I had a good memory for things like that; he must have grown it in the interim, and it suited him really well.

"Is the music bothering you?" he suddenly asked, looking at me.

"No, I find it interesting. For all its seriousness, somehow cheerful."

He nodded. "Perotin. Twelfth century."

He lifted the paperweight from the open periodical and closed it.

"The gilthead bream looks very real," I said.

He gazed at the object in his hand. "You might find it hard to believe, but it *is* real."

"Cast in synthetic resin?"

"No. It somehow turned into synthetic resin itself. It went through some sort of mysterious transubstantiation. A friend brought it back from Venice for me."

"It's amazing what can be accomplished these days."

He nodded and brought his fingers together into a gable. "So you are still interested in the work?"

"We new graduates don't have a wide range of options. My scholarship has expired."

"I mean genuine interest in serving God's Creation."

"If I look at our world that way . . . yes, Signore Falcotti."

He nodded. My gaze fastened on his left temple. As I had suspected, he did indeed wear an implant, which showed under the skin. It was a slender cross, about an inch and a half long. His glasses flashed in a streak of sunlight that fell through the blinds, and I could not make out his eyes. Falcotti seemed to mean it entirely in earnest: God's Creation . . . Well, he believed in that. But I wondered whether I believed in it, and involuntarily shrugged.

"To be honest, I hadn't expected to hear anything more about this project. It has been almost two years since I applied."

"My apologies," he said, pursing his lips uncomfortably. "There were some ... uh ... shifts in objectives as a result of the ... uh ... change in the office of the Holy Father."

I could imagine that. Under Paul VII everything that John XXIV had initiated in the environmental domain had undoubtedly been quashed. But I would not have expected that Paul VIII would have been interested in efforts of that sort. He was appreciative of art, a lover of music, but a revival of God's Creation following St. Francis, as John had propagated—that I could not see him embracing. Perhaps he loved flowers, but the gardens of Hellbrunn were surely sufficient for that. There must have been more behind it.

"But we also had serious technical problems."

"Money?"

"Money is always a problem, but in our case the problems had more to do with physics and logistics. Let's leave that aside, though. I wanted to finally meet you in person and ask you a few more questions," said Falcotti.

"Does that mean that I am among the final candidates for a job?"

He placed both hands on the desk and said with a decisive nod, "Yes."

"Why didn't you tell me that right away, Signore?" I asked with a somewhat shrill voice.

Pleasure took my breath away. I would have liked best to jump up and clasp his hand gratefully. I had stood up halfway, but he directed me with a gentle gesture to take a seat again, and typed something into his laptop.

"The final decision has not yet been made, Signorina Ligrina," he said. He folded his hands and went on somewhat more formally, "Was there a concrete reason for your interest in nature that moved you to study botany?"

"Yes," I said hesitantly. "As strange as it sounds, it was a painting in the Vatican Museums, which made a deep impression on me as a child. I remember it so clearly because I was there with my father. The week before he died."

MY FATHER HAD driven with me to Rome at seven o'clock in the morning in order to beat the masses of visitors, and we were the first to be admitted. I had really been looking forward to this trip. I was always delighted when Father did something with me—he so rarely had time. But after we had roamed three dozen halls, I was—my God, I was only twelve—pretty bored of the numerous paintings and statues assailing me, the countless Madonnas, the angels, the grim-looking apostles, the martyred figures of the Holy One, and finally the varnished dark globes and old maps. Then I suddenly saw the painting. It hung not far from the exit in a small room and surpassed all the others in its colorfulness and beauty. It was called *Adam and Eve in the Earthly Paradise*. An artist named Peter Wenzel had painted it. His portrait hung on the rear wall of the room. An older man with milk-white hair down to his collar, a pale complexion, wearing a white ruffled shirt and a black dress coat. He scrutinizes the viewer with a cool, searching, and yet slightly anxious, aloof gaze from dark brown eyes. In his strangely misshapen right hand he holds a bouquet of paintbrushes.

The *Paradise* was at first glance my favorite painting. I always wanted to get a replica of it, but during my studies that didn't come to pass. And when I was one day in the Vatican again years later, I could no longer find it. It had been taken down and brought to safety along with most of the other paintings.

I was fascinated by the painting. The longer I looked at it, the more details I noticed. My father was already getting impatient, tapping his thigh with the tightly rolled-up *Corriere*.

"How can anyone invent something so beautiful?" I asked.

"*Invent?*" replied my father, raising his eyebrows with astonishment. "That's not *invented*, Domenica. Such animals and plants exist. Or they used to, anyway."

"Where?"

"What do I know," he said, shrugging. "You have to ask Grandfather. He knows more about these things than I do and has a lot of books about them."

"CAN YOU STILL remember details of the painting?" asked Falcotti.

"Oh, that was over ten years ago!"

"Just give it a try."

"All right. I would say it is over six feet tall and maybe ten feet wide. It depicts an idyllic river landscape. I remember a large shady tree in the foreground on the left."

"Can you see this tree in your mind's eye?"

"Hm . . . yes, actually," I said hesitantly.

I saw every detail in my mind's eye. Summoning visual impressions from my memory came easily to me.

"It's a grape tree; large blue grapes are growing on it. They're ripe."

"A grape *tree*? I thought that grapes grow on vines."

"Yes, but only because the plant is cut back each year. If it were permitted to develop naturally, then the *Vitis vinifera* would grow into a tree like the one in the painting: sixty feet tall and with a trunk at least five feet thick."

"I didn't know that. What else do you remember?"

"Under the *Vitis vinifera* stands a camel. Two cows are lying to its right. Behind them is a tiger; in front of them, a lion and a lioness stride by, but the cows are not the least bit unsettled. In the center, the view opens onto a winding river, on the banks of which palms and willows grow. A deer and a zebra can be seen. In the foreground on the right stands another large tree—an apple tree, as is fitting in Paradise. If I remember correctly . . . hm, I would say, a *Malus sylvestris* or *domestica*. Eve has just picked an apple and is handing it to Adam, who is sitting on the ground. A boa constrictor hangs from a branch; on another a chimpanzee is gesticulating excitedly. There are colorful birds everywhere, parrots, macaws. They are perched on the branches or flying through the air. Toward the front on the right stands a white horse, seen from behind, and . . . yes, a rooster. I remember a rooster. And a huge elephant in the background on the right, raising its trunk . . . But tell me, is this important, Signore Falcotti?"

He looked up, for he had been absorbed in his monitor. Had he called up the image to test my powers of recollection? The cross in his temple seemed to be pulsating.

"How do you mean?" he asked.

"Is it important for my work that I remember a painting I saw more than ten years ago?"

He stroked his beard thoughtfully.

"A good visual memory is extremely important for the planned work," he explained hesitantly. "It can sometimes save your life."

The argument could not be dismissed.

"In the wild?" I asked.

"In the wild, yes. But it is really a gift from God to possess a good visual memory, or even an eidetic memory. I envy anyone who has been endowed with that. Where the brain stores these vast quantities of data is a mystery. How do you do that?"

I could not help laughing. "I don't know."

I TOLD HIM nothing about the strange experience that we, Father and I, had had when we were standing before the painting. Perhaps that was why the image had stuck in my mind so clearly. I was still contemplating the details when a woman entered the room behind us. She let out a stifled cry, prompting me to turn around. She had covered her mouth with her hand and was staring with astonishment at the painting, then at me, and then at

Father. She was pretty, wore her dark hair medium-length and had a faint resemblance to my mother, but was younger. She seemed distressed for some reason. Her dark eyes were wide with terror. Her intense gaze frightened me so much that my stomach tightened.

"You . . ." she said, raising her hand with a jerky movement to her forehead. I suddenly had a throbbing headache, and a piercing voice screamed in my skull: *No! No! No!*

"Is something wrong, young woman?" my father asked her. "Do you need help?"

"I've made a terrible mistake," she whispered. "Please forgive me."

She was white as a sheet as she backed away unsteadily, groping for something to hold on to.

No! No! No! The word rang out repeatedly in my head, which felt like it was about to burst. I raised my fists to my temples and began to sob. Father looked at me in confusion, took me in his arms, and held me tight.

"Are you okay, *cara*?" he asked me worriedly, leading me to a bench. "Sit down for a moment."

"I'm leaving," the woman asserted, shaking her head vigorously, as if she were trying to drive away bad thoughts. "I'm leaving . . ."

But she did not seem to be capable of that. Weakness threatened to overwhelm her; she struggled to stay on her feet, staggering against the wall. A guard rushed over from the next room and supported her, offered her a chair, and was about to call for medical help via his walkie-talkie, but she declined.

I doubled up with pain. My bowels felt like they were filled with cold stones. I shook my head, didn't know what to do. Through the open door I saw the guard leading the woman to a bench in the next room, on which she sat down.

"Calm down, my child," my father said again and again, stroking my hair. "It's the heat, right? The poor air quality here. All the people. Come on, let's go to the cafeteria. It's right across from the exit. Come on, Domenica."

We left. Only slowly did the pressure in my chest abate. The voice in my head faded away gradually, and the cramp in my belly subsided. Father was so lovingly worried about me. I sensed his warm affection—I loved him.

A week later he was dead.

I PLACED MY hands in my lap. Falcotti looked at me motionlessly. Both of us were silent. Finally he nodded and cleared his throat.

"Were there other reasons for your interest in nature at such an early age?"

"Yes, but that's a long story."

"Tell it to me, Signorina Ligrina. We have all the time in the world, as you so nicely phrased it. And I enjoy listening to you."

"Don't take this the wrong way, but you sound like a psychologist."

"Oh, I *am* a psychologist," he explained with a smile, raising his eyebrows as if my unawareness had surprised him. "I work as a recruiting office, so to speak. It's among my duties to find the right people for our missions and get to know them. My employers are quite strict. They set high standards."

I grinned at him, and he smiled back.

"Tell me," he urged me.

"Well, all right. As a child I got to spend summer break every year with my mother's parents in Genoa. They had a small café for excursionists overlooking the city. Occasionally they rented a room to extended-stay guests. One of those guests—it might have been the following year, in the summer of 2040—was an American woman. She was conducting some sort of botanical field research . . ."

SARAH! SHE IMPRESSED me beyond measure, aroused my childlike enthusiasm. She showed me that the plants directly in front of our noses, in our immediate vicinity, all around us, form a fascinating world, in which most people stumble around blindly. She made clear to me—though at the time I often did not yet understand what she meant—that all this surrounding us—plants, animals of all sorts—is vital for us human beings, because we cannot even exist without it.

That had already been demonstrated to us in the Mezzogiorno several years earlier. Nonetheless, no one quite grasped it—no one wanted to grasp it. They blamed the government, which was too weak, lacked the necessary military toughness, and let the UN order it around. On television we saw olive trees and grapevines in flames, houses and vehicles too, sometimes people. The Moros were to blame, was the general opinion. Then came repeated shootings, hunts for foreigners, and massacres of refugees from the south and from the Balkans. But why would the immigrants lay waste to the land that was their only chance of survival? It was the withdrawing troops who, in accordance with the scorched-earth policy, were setting fire to the houses to eliminate hiding places and create an open field of fire. The forests were as dry as tinder; the crops in the fields were pitifully low and withered. A spark sufficed to turn whole tracts of land into blazing infernos. And when the wind blew from the southeast, dense clouds of smoke darkened the sky over the Gulf of Genoa; the sun shone like a sickly, reddened eye. And then ash fell like a soundless gray rain, onto the terrace, onto the table-cloths, onto our skin. The ashes of trees, the ashes of houses, and—yes, sometimes probably even the ashes of people.

The people in the south believed that they were losing their land to the Moros, while they were actually losing it to the sun. Africa itself was approaching—as unstoppably as its continental plate, which had been pushing against southern Europe for millions of years, slowly, with a speed akin to that of fingernails growing, but unrelentingly.

Sarah was the type of American whose enthusiasm for her scientific work knew no bounds. She *lived* for her job; everything else was without meaning. She worked on one of those "Gaia" or "Noah's Ark" projects, of which there were dozens at the time, with the mission of quickly collecting as much of the worldwide diversity of genetic material as could still be saved for the future in the face of accelerating species extinction.

Sarah—she seemed to always have on the same black, much-too-large T-shirt with white sweat stains down to the waist and armholes so wide that you could see her breasts: tiny forms that nonetheless hung limply from her ribs. She always had a sunburned red nose, from which the skin peeled, because she was outdoors from morning to night. And her frizzy hair—she just had hair, no hairstyle, as is common among female American students—she tied back thoughtlessly into a bushy ponytail. But she was no longer a student; she had made a name for herself with a paper on new arid Mediterranean ecologies. Sometimes scholars from some environmental institute in Rome or Bologna would show up at our door, men in dark suits and ties, who appeared somewhat confused when she introduced herself to them.

When I saw her for the first time, she was sitting in her faded, ripped jeans and dirt-encrusted running shoes, stirring her cappuccino and laughing cheerfully behind her small round wire-rimmed glasses. "Domenica! What a beautiful name," she said with her piercing, high voice. "But child, believe me, no one in the States would consider naming their daughter 'Sunday.'"

The smell of her T-shirt mingled with that of the fresh coffee. She usually sat on the terrace early in the morning. The foldable satellite dish sat on the cement wall; the unrolled solar cell film glittered in the sun, and the laser eye stared southward into the geostationary orbit. She scratched around in her hair with the data stylus of her electronic notebook and dictated in whiny English her report to the Artificial Intelligence of her institute in San Diego, of which I did not understand a word.

When she was not off on one of her excursions, Sarah usually stayed with us. She had asked Grandfather's permission to use his library when the Internet failed her, but most of what she found in the reference books she declared point-blank to be "bullshit."

During the two months in which Sarah was with us, a strange relationship developed between her and me. I watched her store her finds and samples—mostly plant parts, seeds, leaves, or flowers—in plastic bags she tore from a compact roll, write the place of discovery, date, and species with her stylus in her notebook, which then spat out tiny self-adhesive labels, and weld the bags with a thermocouple on the edge of her device. With what primitive methods I later had to perform the same work!

Sometimes Sarah brought me with her on her excursions. When she took on a new area, she would remove her glasses and clean them, wipe the sweat from her brow with her forearm, and stand there silently for ten or fifteen minutes intently scrutinizing the surroundings. She seemed to circle and mark this and that in her mind.

"You first have to figure out the presumed geologic substrate you have in front of you, child," she explained to me. "You can do that by means of indicators: trees, bushes, things like that. Then the conditions of the terrain: Where is there flowing water and where is it headed? Where is it retained? Then you know where what you're looking for is at home. Searching costs far too much time and usually leads to nothing. You have to approach it and say: If it grows here, then only here and nowhere else. Only in that way can you acquire a feel for the local ecosystem."

And she showed me examples: friendship among plants, coexistence and interdependence, aversion and intolerance.

On one of those excursions, as Sarah was working on the slope of a small hidden cove, I discovered the dead white whale. Through the branches of the dying trees I suddenly saw it drifting close to the shore. I climbed down to the narrow pebble beach and stared at the cadaver with fascination. The whale was perhaps thirty or forty feet long and must have been dead for a long time already, for the smell of putrefaction filled the air. The whole cove was enveloped by a sweet miasma. But that didn't bother me. I thought of

Captain Ahab and his raging against the notorious albino, the veteran of the seas with half a dozen twisted harpoons in its neck, as I had seen it in the old film with Gregory Peck. But the cadaver looked more peaceful. The animal was one of the few marine mammals that had survived the murderous whaling in the previous century and the death of plankton in the southern seas and the Arctic in this one. And now it had perished miserably here.

Why had the lonely wanderer come to the Gulf of Genoa to die? Had it been fascinated by the black undersea glaciers that had poured out of the burning *Haven* over the shoulder of the Ligurian Sea eighty years earlier? There on the sea floor stretched a dead landscape, which absorbed every ray of light falling into the depths. The hardened pitch gave the water a strange taste, which almost all living things avoided. Had my white whale penetrated into this dark, lifeless world in order to explore it? Had it, the pale creature, sought death in this darkness?

"It stinks!" Sarah exclaimed with a shrill voice, holding her sunburned nose.

"A white whale," I said wistfully.

"A *physalus*," she explained, "a fin whale. The white that you see there is not the skin, but the blubber. The skin has been eaten away by birds and marine animals. Now they are feeding on the layer of fat."

Did she notice my disappointment?

"Supposedly there used to be whole herds of fin whales here. Spotted and bottlenose dolphins too. The Gulf of Genoa used to be famous for its wealth of shrimp and fish. The seagrass meadows of Cinque Terre and Portofino were unique spawning grounds. All sorts of sponges and algae, even corals. Popular grazing areas for marine mammals. That's all over," she said with a shrug.

"Too late for an ark," I said.

"Definitely too late for this creature," Sarah replied, nodding at the bobbing cadaver. "That's why we should save what can still be saved. When climate change occurs as quickly as it has this time, the plants have no time to migrate. They are overrun. If things go on like this, in a hundred years it will look like the Sahel here. Take my word for it, child."

In autumn Sarah left us to continue her research in Slovenia. She had planted a seed in me. And it had fallen on fertile ground.

I TOLD FALCOTTI nothing about the white whale, of course—my shame in having mistaken a half-decayed cadaver for Moby Dick was reason enough for that. It simply did not fit into the background of an aspiring biologist.

"One last question, Signorina Ligrina. Suppose I had the power to stop and turn back time: What situation would you wish to be sent back to so that you could undo a decision or set things on a different course?"

I looked at him with surprise. I wasn't sure what he meant. Was it a psychological test?

"A strange question," I said.

Falcotti shrugged. "Say whatever springs to your mind," he urged.

"All right. I would wish to be at the Napoli Centrale train station on September 16, 2039, at 4 P.M. Then I would stop my father from getting on the ill-fated train to Rome. I mean, no. I would, of course, try to warn the authorities about the planned attack . . ."

I faltered. He smiled and nodded at me encouragingly.

". . . if something like time travel were ever possible. But how would something like that be possible?"

"Yes, of course." Falcotti nodded and made a note. "And if I had the power to transport you to any century, which would you choose?"

The conversation was growing more and more puzzling, but I decided to play along.

"The fifteenth century," I said.

"An interesting time. The century of Leonardo and Michelangelo, of Botticelli and Bosch, of Alberti and Ariosto, of Savonarola and Machiavelli . . ."

"And of Nicolaus Cusanus."

He looked up with surprise and nodded. "An extremely interesting man. He was a confidant of the Holy Father Pius II, cardinal, and papal legate. Have you studied his work?"

I shook my head. "He's our neighbor here, so to speak. He's buried around the corner."

"In San Pietro in Vincoli, yes. That was his church. He was from Germany."

"I know. From Kues, a small town on the Moselle. Not far from Cattenom. Kues is in the middle of the death zone."

"I never realized that. Of course," he replied, nodding.

"His heart is buried there, in accordance with his wishes, for he really loved his home."

"He died in Todi, as far as I know. In Umbria."

"I thought he died here in Rome."

"No, he died of an epidemic, like his friend, Pope Pius II, and many others who had gathered there for a crusade to wrest Constantinople from the Turks. The undertaking had to be aborted. That was 1464, if I remember correctly. He was only sixty-three years old," said Falcotti.

"It is said that he spent almost all his income to buy up the best vineyards in the area around Kues in order to secure his goal in life: to establish a foundation for needy old people. It still existed, incidentally, when the disaster happened. It had lasted for almost six centuries."

"I see you have studied him after all, Signorina Ligrina."

"Not in earnest. I just watched the DVD that's sold to tourists in San Pietro. I've taken a look at his philosophical writings, but I can't find my way into the thinking of that time. It strikes me as so . . . labyrinthine, as if you were constantly going around in circles and getting nowhere. But from what I've heard about him in history of science courses I've always had the impression that he was far ahead of his time."

"Did you say, 'in circles'?" Falcotti gestured with a nod to a low table at the other end of the room. "Are you familiar with that?"

The surface of the table, a square roughly five feet long by five feet wide, was bordered by a low raised edge and consisted of a pale, polished wooden board with a sort of target made of dark wood inlaid in it.

Falcotti stood up. "Come with me," he said.

On closer examination, I saw that the wooden board displayed concentric circles. The areas enclosed by the circles were marked with the numerals 1 to 9 from outside to inside; the circle in the center bore no number. On the edge lay wooden balls, as big as oranges. Falcotti grabbed one of them, drew back his arm, and threw it with a slight swing almost parallel to the outer circle onto the target. It described a bizarrely crooked path inward and stopped on the eight.

"Give it a try."

He handed me the ball, which he had fished out of the spiral with a small wooden rake. It was not a uniformly round ball, I immediately noticed, but rather it had a hollow on one side, as if a smaller ball had been gouged out of the larger ball, shifting the center of gravity from the middle far into the concave part of the object. That explained the erratic path it described.

"What is this?" I asked. "A refined form of bocce or boules?"

"It's the game of spheres, the *ludo globi*, which Nicolaus Cusanus invented shortly before his death. Whoever manages with his throws to come

closest to the center is the winner. Any attempt to reach the center by aiming directly at it inevitably fails. But with time you can attain a certain skill
for getting close to the target in a circuitous way. Try it!"

I threw the "ball" much too forcefully onto the target. It wobbled wide
of the mark and ended up on the opposite side on the one.

"Try again!"

This time the object rolled close to the center, but again came to rest on
the one.

"Don't give up," Falcotti said with a smile. "That is—among other
things—the point."

This time the ball landed more softly, parallel to the lines of the circles,
with the convex side facing the edge, and the *globus* did indeed roll on a
strongly curved path toward the center, until it came to a standstill on the
eight.

"That's really good," said Falcotti. "You're learning fast."

"And *what* am I learning?"

"There are various interpretations of this game. Cusanus himself attrib-
uted several qualities to it. One of the most important is that it entertains the
players, puts them in a cheerful mood, and teaches them to sustain defeats
lightheartedly and good-humoredly. For it's a fact that the movement of the
globus is fundamentally unpredictable. Even if the starting conditions were
exactly the same, every throw is different. With that Cusanus is trying to tell
us that no two events are ever entirely alike and so exact prognoses are never
possible. The deeper level is of a symbolic nature: In the center of the field,
in the tenth, innermost circle, which bears no number, is Christ. To follow
him directly is fundamentally impossible; for that we people are too flawed—
that is, each of us has his dent. On our life's path we inevitably go astray, even
if we aim steadfastly to reach our goal, to reach God. But if we strive toward
it with patience, we can nonetheless come quite close to our goal."

He drew back his arm and brought the *globus* onto a course that proceeded wide of the mark over the two and three with an increasing curve,
finally ending up on the nine.

"I see that you'll do it one day, Signore Falcotti."

Smiling, he shrugged and looked at me over the rim of his glasses.

"No prognoses, Signorina Ligrina! Who knows, maybe you're about to
overtake me."

VII

A Chicken for Cusanus

All these various visible forms are enclosed in the world. And yet if it were possible for someone to be situated outside the world, the world would be invisible to him.

NICOLAUS CUSANUS

Oh my! I beg your pardon, Your Eminence. We were not expecting you. We thought you were still staying in Cologne. Oh God, I was planning to go to the market tomorrow morning to buy some things to which you are partial, as I know from the past. Oh, Your Eminence. What am I doing standing here before you? Please . . ."

"But Katrin! Are you seriously going to sink to your knees before me? Stand up and let me embrace you. And don't call me 'Your Eminence'! What did you always call me when I was still dean at St. Florin?"

"I wouldn't dare."

"Nico, you called me, and you were like a mother to me. Let us stick with that, Katrin."

"But you have become such an exalted man. You come right after the Holy Father, says Helwicus."

"Well, isn't it so?" the dean broke in. "It is said that Pope Nicholas is your friend and values your advice."

"Indeed, we see eye to eye in many respects."

"What am I doing here?" the old housekeeper lamented, spreading her arms. "Completely unprepared. I can offer a chicken, roasted in butter and rosemary, but cold. The bread is fresh."

"I'm not hungry. We did not set off from Andernach until after lunch today. In the morning I had to dictate an urgent letter to the chapter of St. John's in Osnabrück. But I'm thirsty. I could certainly do with a glass of wine."

"Wine from home?"

"Yes. Do you have some from my father's vineyards?"

"Indeed, we do. Every year your brother Johannes sends us a tun down the Moselle. It is the best wine far and wide."

"Then bring me a flagon of that, Katrin, so that I may at least taste a mouthful of home."

"You mean, you're not going to ride up to Kues?" asked the dean.

"I would be delighted to, but I don't have the time, Helwicus. I'm expected in Frankfurt. And next month I shall be in Brixen once again. I would have liked to ride up to Kues to check on things and see how far the plans for the foundation have come to fruition, but I have trustworthy people under my brother's supervision who are advancing my cause and managing it well."

"I heard the same."

"Did you also hear about the execution in Cologne on Candlemas? Of the young woman who was deemed guilty of witchcraft and was burned at the stake?"

"Yes, I heard about that. Tilman von Linz was present at the proceedings as an adviser to Dietrich. There was again a great deal of conflict between the city council and the archbishop, as usual, this time in the matter of jurisdiction. And the people were completely beside themselves, wanted to finally see a witch burn with their own eyes."

"This woman wrote me letters."

"Did I hear you correctly? She wrote *you* letters?"

"Yes, look! Now I will finally take some time to read them," said the cardinal, tossing the tied-up scroll onto the large table. "They are copies. One of the archbishop's scribes gave them to me. Geistleben is his name. He and I crossed to Deutz on the same ferry."

The cardinal took a penknife and cut the strings, filled the goblet that had been set down before him with wine, and drank from it in small, sampling sips.

"The wine is good," he said, nodding appreciatively; then he began to read.

Later Katrin brought him a candle. And when it had burned down, she lit a second one for him and placed additional candles nearby.

And Nicolaus Cusanus read and read.

"YOU HAVE NOT even touched the chicken, my lord. I knew that it was not to your taste."

"No, Katrin," the cardinal said, lost in thought. "That is, yes." He turned away. "East of Cattenom the land is black, deep into Bohemian and Polish regions," he murmured, "as can be seen from orbit."

"I will bring you warm milk."

"Is Helwicus up yet?"

"Yes. Shall I summon him?"

"Please do."

"Do you know where Cattenom is, Helwicus?" he asked the dean.

"Oh, I believe there is a hamlet by that name up at the top of the Moselle, in Lotharingia, not far from Metz. I'm not certain, but Adrien, the fisherman who brings us his catch every Thursday evening, comes from that area. I will ask him."

"In Lotharingia?" the cardinal repeated reflectively. "East of Cattenom the land is black . . ."

"I don't understand."

The cardinal stuck a fingernail under the hardened wax of the burned-down candle and detached it from the table.

"Mysterious, all this," he murmured.

"What the little witch wrote to you?"

"That was no witch who was executed there. It was a strange woman. Mad, perhaps, but knowledgeable and acutely perceptive. She foresaw a future we cannot even imagine."

The cardinal looked exhausted after staying awake all night. He turned to the window and rubbed his chin. Day had come, but dense mist veiled the river, so that the opposite bank could not be seen.

"'East of Cattenom the land is black,' she writes, 'deep into Bohemian and Polish regions, as can be seen from orbit.' — What does she mean by 'orbit'? The circle of the Earth? A circle above the Earth? It would have to be a bird that could soar as high as the sphere of the moon in order to see that far. An angel . . . ?"

At a loss, the cardinal shook his head. "The black blade that had pierced the heart of the continent." The plague? A conflagration? A festering wound of the earth itself?

The Cusan looked out over the meadows around the mouth of the Moselle. They stretched almost down to Andernach, a vast wetland from which myriad mosquitoes swarmed up in the summer. A nuisance for man and beast, as he recalled. What a carefree time that had been, when he had still performed his duty as a dean here at St. Florin!

Mist rose like smoke from extinguished fires. An army camp of ghosts, which had moved on through time. The cardinal hunched his shoulders as if a chill had seized him.

"Todi," he murmured.

"I beg your pardon?" the dean asked in confusion.

"She writes: 'Beware of Todi.' What is supposed to await me there? What did she mean by that?"

He turned away from the window and looked with tired eyes at Helwicus. "It should not have been doctors and judges questioning her, but scholars. It ought to have been determined where she came from and with whom she had studied. She must have come from a part of the world of which we know nothing, but whose wise men certainly seem to have knowledge of us. The case of this woman should have been decided in Rome. Now it is too late."

He tossed the copies onto the table and rubbed his eyes. In his youth, impressed by the words of famous authorities and frightened by accounts of the evil influences of the *superstitio*, he too had demanded the extermination of witches and wizards. With unease he remembered his sermon *Ibant magi*, which he had delivered on Epiphany of the year 1431. Now, twenty years later, he thought differently about those things. He had conquered his fear of the devil, countered it with the clarity of his thinking, which had sprung from his faith. The darkness no longer scared him.

"I will try to sleep for a few hours," he sighed, and blew out the candle.

VIII

Light-Clipper

Imagination is a straightforward form of virtual reality. What may not be so obvious is that our "direct" experience of the world through our senses is virtual reality too. For our external experience is never direct; nor do we even experience the signals in our nerves directly—we would not know what to make of the streams of electrical crackles that they carry. What we experience directly is a virtual-reality rendering, conveniently generated for us by our unconscious minds from sensory data plus complex inborn and acquired theories (i.e., programs) about how to interpet them . . . Every last scrap of our external experience is of virtual reality. And every last scrap of our knowledge—including our knowledge of the non-physical worlds of logic, mathematics and philosophy, and of imagination, fiction, art and fantasy—is encoded in the form of programs for the rendering of those worlds on our brain's own virtual-reality generator.

DAVID DEUTSCH

H e's a strange guy, that Falcotti," Birgit said indignantly, when we met a few days later at a party at Marcello's and started talking about the job interviews. "He wanted to play the Grand Inquisitor, don't you think? He's a snoop! He wanted to know more about my private relationships than about my professional qualifications. I told him it was none of his business. He just grinned stupidly and took notes. What's that all about?"

Bernd looked uneasy, as he always did when his sister got worked up. And she was practically seething as she continued to tell us about her conversation with Falcotti.

" 'Okay,' I said to him, 'I'm really interested in the job, but first I would like to know what it involves. You're constantly beating around the bush, and I'm supposed to tell you all sorts of things about my private life. I'm not

telling you anything until you tell *me* what you actually want from us, what
the deal is with this Rinascita, how much it pays per month, and where we
are being sent. Because if what it boils down to is that I'm going to be wearing a protective suit and collecting mutated mold fungi between Mainz
and Frankfurt until I'm hopelessly poisoned by radiation, then we can forget it,' I told him. 'I've been there already, and that was enough for me, that
I can assure you.' — 'Where did you get an idea like that?' he asked me,
wide-eyed. — 'Because *that's* the sort of thing volunteers are always being
sought for. I've seen people who were sent in there for only a few days. Afterward they looked like hell had spat them out. I'll never forget that.' —
'I'm sure you're right,' he replied, 'but our work does not consist of . . .' — 'I'm
listening,' I said to him. 'We would never send you into a radioactively
contaminated area,' he declared, looking at me in that angelically pious
way I absolutely can't stand. 'But if you have reservations . . .' — 'Yes, I
have reservations,' I replied. 'What's with all this secrecy? I'd like a
straight answer from you.' He shrugged. 'I'm sorry,' he said, 'I cannot provide you with more information at this stage in the interview process.' —
'Then I'm sorry too,' I said to him, and with that our conversation was
over. I suppose that meant I was off the list. So much for Rinascita della
Creazione. Screw it!"

She drained her glass in one gulp and slammed it down on the table so
hard that Bernd and I jumped.

"Have you really been in a contaminated area before?" I asked Birgit.

"Yes."

"Secretly?"

She turned down the corners of her mouth in her characteristic fashion.
A bitter smile. "Of course. How else—on one of the organized sightseeing
tours to the death zone?" she replied brusquely.

Birgit shrugged heavily. I noticed that she had tears in her eyes. I'd
never seen her like that before.

"You have absolutely no idea how messed up the environment is there.
The land is worse than dead. It's condemned never to bear normal life
again. Chaos has truly consumed it. I'd always thought those reports were
a bunch of fantasy crap: the shadow world threatening us, spreading, eating
its way from the edges into our reality. But damn it, it's really true! It's as if
you weren't even on Earth anymore! The plants don't know anymore what
they're supposed to look like; they've forgotten what color they're supposed
to be. The shape of their flowers, the time of their ripening—everything is

out of control! It's genetic chaos. Have you ever seen black clematis? Or black larkspur? Red tree fungi, the size of satellite dishes? And with some of the plant monsters growing there, you'd have to do a genetic analysis to figure out what they evolved from."

She covered her mouth with her hand, as if she wanted to stop herself from talking. No one said anything. We'd never seen an outburst like that from her before.

Marcello finally broke the uncomfortable silence.

"What were you doing there?" he asked. "I mean . . . you were risking your life. Why . . . ?"

She turned away. Her braid brushed her shoulder. "I was searching for our parents."

"And were you able to find out anything?"

She shook her head, wiped tears from the corner of her eye. All of us looked silently past one another.

What an awful party, I thought. For heaven's sake!

"So I won't get the job," she blurted out. "The hell with it."

"I've declined too," said Bernd.

I looked at him, taken aback.

"You were offered a job, and you just blew it off? For God's sake, we all know how hard it is to get anything these days. We can't afford to be choosy, damn it!"

He avoided my eyes.

"I'll find something else," he said dismissively. "And so will Birgit."

Bernd seemed relieved that he had withdrawn his application. I suddenly felt really cold inside. I had secretly always hoped that we could somehow work together. He had simply thrown in the towel. Didn't he want to stay in contact with me? The more I thought about it, the more I realized that it didn't have to do with me personally, but rather that his shyness and reserve, which I so liked about him, were nothing but an expression of his indecisiveness. He had never had to make a decision, and he would never make a decision. Birgit would always do that for him.

"The two of you are acting as if the offer had come from the Mafia. It's from the Vatican, for crying out loud!" I exclaimed. "Who says they're planning to send us to Germany?"

Everyone looked at me.

"Because that's where Creation is really dead. If they take the Rinascita thing seriously, then they have to start there," Birgit replied vehemently.

"And as for the Vatican: Do you have any idea how many people it has exploited for its purposes? People of good faith?"

"Stop it, you two!" cried Bernd.

"What's that supposed to mean?" I said heatedly. "There are lots of places on this earth where Creation desperately needs a rebirth. Besides, I don't think that the Vatican feels called to fix the damage the French have done."

"How do you know?" Birgit asked derisively.

"As far as I know, they intend to clean up there themselves."

"Well, then they're going to be busy for the next three hundred thousand years."

"Everyone is pitching in. It's a task for the whole world," Marcello interjected in a conciliatory tone. "Everyone has the right to decide for themselves whether they take part or not. And if I were to be sent there, I would go."

"Good boy," Birgit blurted out. "But have a few of your stem cells frozen beforehand."

"I just don't think that we're going to be sent there," I insisted, but suddenly I was no longer so sure.

"Me neither," said Renata. "What could we do there as botanists?"

"Life counts," Bernd broke in. "Damage assessment."

"Nonsense," Renata snapped at him. "It's too late there for all that."

"If I were you, I would definitely take a really close look at the small print," Birgit advised us. "From the beginning, I've had a feeling that there's something shady about this. What's with all the secretiveness?"

"Have you guys noticed that this Falcotti wears a small cross as an implant on his temple?" asked Marcello.

"You can't miss it," said Birgit.

"Direct contact to the man upstairs," Bernd sneered.

"Listen," I said to him. "That's his business. We shouldn't make fun of it."

Birgit looked at me and smiled coldly. "And why not?" she asked.

"I've often seen Jesuits with those," Renata broke in. "They used to wear them on their collars."

"Could be a BCI," said Marcello.

"A what?" I asked.

"A Brain-Computer Interface," he explained. "An implant that gives you direct access to the networks."

I shrugged and looked inquiringly at Renata. She nodded. "A window into cyberspace."

"Well, so what?" said Birgit. "Computer-assisted smartass."

"Were you guys asked too what time you'd want to be sent to if that were possible?" Marcello asked, steering the conversation in another direction.

Birgit waved the question aside. "That was clearly part of some psychological test. Do you know what I answered? A week before the Cattenom disaster, with a well-armed strike force, I said. To neutralize the idiots there on time."

Bernd nodded. His eyes shone.

Oh, Bernd, I thought.

"I can't imagine any task that would be assigned to such a motley group," said Marcello.

"What do you mean?" I asked.

"They made Ernesto an offer too."

"Which Ernesto?"

"Ernesto Caputi. He studied physics."

"He'll get a Geiger counter hung around his neck," Birgit declared, laughing a bit too loudly. "That's obvious."

She was sad—and a little drunk.

"And Marco too."

"Which Marco?"

"Marco Brescia. I think you know him, Domenica."

"Yes, I remember."

"As for him, I'm sure that he can't tell a columbine from a carrot," Birgit said. "He's a medievalist."

I was fed up with all the chatter and went out into the kitchen. Renata was slicing bread with a large kitchen knife. As she did so, I saw for the first time that she was missing part of the pinky and ring finger on her left hand. She noticed that I was staring at the mutilation.

"You should be more careful with the knife," I hastened to say casually, nodding at her hand.

She raised it and held it in front of my eyes. "Bang," she said.

I looked at her questioningly.

"Have you ever seen lattice towers flying?" she asked. "Like falling angels. With outspread wings and hurling thunderbolts."

"You were with Alto Adige? Did you blow up power lines too?"

She nodded and gazed at her mutilated fingers. "I got lucky," she said. "I sacrificed only two inches. The Austrians never caught me. Otherwise it would have certainly turned out worse."

She raised the bread knife to her throat. The bright specks in her dark brown eyes flashed like fragments of amber. Her cheeks had turned red. I had never seen her so cheerful.

"You're glad that you have a job prospect."

Renata nodded. A happy smile lit up her round, almost peasantlike face. Her muted charm revealed itself only at second glance. She had beautifully curved eyebrows and a small, heart-shaped mouth she never put makeup on; her small, even teeth dug involuntarily into her lip when she thought hard. Her curly hair she wore combed back simply, looped in a loose knot and held with a sort of clasp—a smooth, bulbous piece of pinewood that looked like a small, half-opened fist, in which her hair was fastened with a long pointed pin. On the rounded "back of the hand," the object was sky blue with alpine flowers painted on it by a naive artist of her homeland. Obviously a very old piece.

Renata came from the region of Bolzano. After the "referendum" and the "annexation" of South Tyrol, she had joined the freedom movement Alto Adige and had fled from the Austrian security service to Venice. There she had struggled along with various jobs and fulfilled her university entrance requirements.

As a child Renata had already learned to conceal herself from the eyes of the occupiers and to move without attracting attention. I remember how surprised I was when I touched her for the first time. Renata had often sat in front of me at lectures. One day it struck me how shabbily she was dressed. Her clothing was clean, but threadbare and patched in several places; clearly she could not buy anything new. That was an unfamiliar experience for me, for I had never had to give clothing a second thought. Father had had connections with textile companies and fashion studios; mother's closets overflowed with outfits, dresses, skirts, pants, blouses, and sweaters that she had not worn even once, because they were too fashionable for her, and she, as she put it, did not want to walk around like "one of those hussies" with whom he dealt—strictly professionally, as he insisted. In my school and university years, I had helped myself to this supply without a thought and had rarely had to buy anything. The next time I went home, I packed a large plastic bag full of clothes that might fit Renata and brought them back for her. She scrutinized me, but said nothing.

"If you want to have this stuff," I said, "I really don't need it."

She did not even glance into the bag, just stared at me silently.

"I've been wanting to give it away for a long time," I said with a shrug; I almost felt as if I had to apologize for the gift.

Finally, with a rapid hand motion I had noticed her make a few times before, she brushed her upper lip and the tip of her nose, as if she had a sniffle. Then she reached for the bag, put her arms around me, and whispered, "Thanks." It sounded as if she was moved, but it might have only been the throaty sound of her native dialect. I took her in my arms, probably more overwhelmed than she was by my own generosity and kindheartedness—and as I did so, I realized with astonishment how dainty and delicate-boned she felt. She must have weighed less than 110 pounds and was as lithe as a cat.

My Renata. How much easier it would have been if we had been able to stay together.

OF THE ROUGHLY thirty applicants, five were left: Renata Gessner and Marcello Tortorelli, both botanists, who had taken the exam with me; Ernesto Caputi, who studied theoretical physics and had specialized in boundary layer quantum phenomena; Marco Brescia, who had gotten his degree in European history of the late Middle Ages; and me. The rest had not qualified or had backed out like Birgit and Bernd when the rumor surfaced that the Istituto della Rinascita was planning to send the recruits into the death zone to take stock of the devastation.

"A CALL, DOMENICA."

"Who?"

"Keller, Bernd."

"Accept. — Yes, Bernd?"

He hemmed and hawed. "You shouldn't sign the contract, Domenica."

"What's that supposed to mean? Do you want me to pass up this opportunity? You know well how difficult it is for us to find a job. So leave me alone, all right? I accept your decision, even though I'm disappointed about it. I'd always imagined that we could set off together and . . . But okay. You made your decision. If you even made it. Was it your own decision?"

"Domenica . . . That's not so important . . ."

"Yes, it is, damn it! It's very important!" I blurted out. "You've hidden behind her back again. As always. I bet you're calling me secretly."

"Don't get so worked up. I just want to give you some advice."

"And what's your advice? Not to sign the contract. For what reason? Give me a reason!"

He was silent. Then he said, "I can't. It has to be of your own free will. You have to decline or take the job of your own free will."

Gradually I was getting angry.

"What is this nonsense, Bernd?"

"I just . . . They're doing something with you. Something bad. Something monstrous. I saw today what they . . ." His voice was trembling. He broke off.

"What did you see?" I asked, disconcerted.

I had never known him to act like this. He was distressed.

"I can't tell you."

"Listen, Bernd. We've known each other for such a long time. What's going on?"

"Please, let it be, Domenica. Please . . . for your sake . . ."

"Now talk already!"

"I can't tell you, Domenica. Believe me, I can't."

"And *why* can't you?"

"It . . . it would destroy the world."

"Say that again."

"It would destroy the world. Our world."

I took a few deep breaths. "Are you crazy?"

"No."

The silence drew itself out.

"Okay, Bernd. Thank you for your advice."

"But it really has to be your absolute free will, whatever you do."

"I understand."

I had not understood a word.

"WHO ACTUALLY STARTED this urban legend that we would be sending you into radioactively contaminated areas?" Falcotti asked us during the final meeting.

"I don't know," I answered evasively.

"I heard it from Birgit Keller," said Marcello, "our fellow botany student. She had applied too."

Falcotti nodded.

"Well, the opposite is the case," he said emphatically. "We will be sending you individually into areas of Europe that are still absolutely unpolluted and scarcely touched—at least as far as fieldwork is concerned. The physicists and historians will be needed at the base from which we operate in order to support the people outside and ensure their return. Therefore you will have to complete quite different trainings. Those will be conducted in Venice, because here in Rome we don't possess the necessary technical equipment. Your later place of operation will be Amsterdam. As strange as it may sound, the center of the Istituto Pontificale della Rinascita della Creazione di Dio is under construction there. It's an ecumenical project and serves exclusively scientific, technical purposes. It's about the salvation of God's Creation, the salvation of the future, yes"—he spread his arms in an all-embracing gesture—"about the preservation of this our universe."

"Oho," Renata said sarcastically. "Then let's get cracking. To my knowledge, we have only the one."

Falcotti looked at her thoughtfully and nodded. "You're quite right, Signorina Gessner. We do."

"A CALL, DOMENICA."

"Who?"

"Ligrina, Maria."

"Accept!—Mother! Finally!"

Right at the outset I once again made the mistake of asking her how she was doing. It just slipped out of me, and that same moment I knew I shouldn't have done it, for as usual she began to complain. It was all too much for her, the house and the café, and Grandmother was no help to her; on the contrary, more and more she had to take care of the old woman as well.

"Mother, I have a job!" I interrupted her lament. "A steady job for at least two years! I'm going to Venice and then to Amsterdam."

"Why would you do that, child? How can anyone in these uncertain times hit on the idea of going abroad? Now, when everything is topsy-turvy, ever since the EU was dissolved and the Moros and other foreigners have been threatening us from all sides."

"Mother, I have to advance in my career. Finding a job today as a botanist is hard."

"Come to Genoa. Here there are enough trees and plants to study. Here you'll be in good hands." In my mind I saw myself cleaning the house, sweeping the terrace, wiping the tables, and serving guests late into the night, who always talk the same stupid nonsense and expect you to be unable to contain yourself with laughter at their dumb jokes.

"Mother, I have to finally earn my own money . . ."

"I know that sort of talk. You're your father's daughter all right. He always had some excuse to slip away. He never showed consideration for me. I might have guessed that you'd abandon me too."—Were those tears in her voice?—"I'm always left standing alone . . ."

Yes, she really was crying. Oh God!

"You can always reach me under this code, Mother, wherever I am. Where are you calling from? Do you finally have an ICom?"

Of course, she must have had one, or else my device could not have identified her.

"The call was disconnected by the other party, Domenica. Would you like me to reestablish the—"

"No, thank you, Luigi. I've had enough for today."

IT WAS STILL dark when we rode out to the Leonardo da Vinci Airport. We had only hand luggage with us; the rest of our things had been sent ahead by freight, for even though none of us had a lot, it amounted to a small relocation. Falcotti had advised us that it was better to move out of our apartments. Signore Paolini, my landlord, had acknowledged the news with a silent shrug and had given me one of his saddest looks.

Each of us was dozing in a seat on the small bus, which had pulled up whisperingly in front of the institute at three in the morning. We had celebrated our departure there with far too much red wine. Neither Bernd nor Birgit had shown up. I had not expected that, but you made the good-bye much easier for me that way, Bernd.

The fuel cell worked soundlessly; only the noise of the tires could be heard as we rolled through the silent, empty streets. The traffic lights were turned off or destroyed; many probably had been for years. There was rarely an illuminated window. Only on Via della Magliana were there a few streetlights burning at irregular intervals. On the side of the highway to Fiumicino, wrecked vehicles gutted by fire came into view again and again; our headlights yanked them out of the darkness and then let them sink back into it. Drones came flitting through the sky like bats, briefly hovered over us and checked the identification of the vehicle and our ICom chips, only to dart away on their nightly hunt.

A wide perimeter around the airport was closed off and secured with double razor wire as well as a high-voltage fence. Every hundred yards there was a tank. We had to pass through three security checkpoints. At each one a uniformed man stuck his head in, stared at his Palmtop, and matched our IComs with the chips of the accompanying documents our driver handed over to him. At the third one Marcello jumped up and rushed to the door.

"Stay here! Do not get off the bus!" the security officer barked.

Marcello ignored the command, pushed past him, went plunging off the bus—and was looking into the barrel of a submachine gun pointed at his head.

"Don't move!"

Another uniformed man rushed over and cocked his weapon. They tried to drive Marcello back onto the bus, but he suddenly doubled up and vomited. The security officers jumped back so that their uniforms would not be soiled, seized him from the right and left by his upper arms, and dragged him to the roadside, where he puked the contents of his stomach into the dead gray grass. The vomit, in the aggressive ice-blue xenon light that suddenly stabbed down at a slant in front of us from the sky, looked like blood. I shuddered. Out of nowhere a military drone appeared over the bus and circled the vehicle. The two rotors of the aircraft whirred almost soundlessly, which intensified the sense of menace, while with its jerky dragonfly-like movements it kept its double-barreled weapon constantly aimed at us.

"Hey! Hey! Hey!" cried our driver, throwing up his arms and dropping them onto the steering wheel.

They pushed Marcello onto the bus. One of the security officers waved his submachine gun.

"Drive on!" he shouted.

The door closed with a sigh. Marcello flopped down into his seat. His face was ashen and covered with sweat. He was struggling for breath. Renata grabbed him by the shoulders from behind.

"You are *never* to do that!" she cried, hitting his shoulders with her fists. "*Never! Never! Never!*"

Marcello turned his head crossly and tried to fend her off.

"What did you want me to do, puke all over the bus?"

"That doesn't matter. You can easily die that way, you hear? Those guys are scared. They're nervous. It happens very fast, believe me! In a situation like that you have to stay completely calm. And whatever you do, just don't move."

"Oh, leave me in peace," he murmured.

He was again overcome by nausea. He averted his head and pressed his hand to his mouth.

"Let him be," I said to Renata, putting my arm around her soothingly. She was trembling all over. I had never seen her so worked up.

"In situations like that I've seen many a friend—" She broke off.

"Calm down, Renata. Nothing happened."

The bus drove on slowly. We passed a burned-up delivery truck that was in the left lane. The metal was annealed and looked eerily pale; the back tire was still smoking. The downdraft from the rotors of a hovering drone blew the black curls across the asphalt. The strobelike glare of its searchlight ran across our faces in order to consign them to some electronic catacombs.

THE AIRPORT SCREENING dragged on endlessly. In the meantime, dawn was already breaking. Our travel documents were double- and triple-checked. Here and there protests among the waiting passengers grew loud. They had no effect. I was reminded of the television reports on the situation in Naples when the Gaeta-Termoli line was established. That was how far north the African continent had pressed in twelve years. We Romans had suddenly become Moros.

I looked out at the new launch system through the large shatterproof windowpane. Soon the sun would rise. A light-clipper crouched, darkly glistening, on a stratolifter at the end of the ramp of the linear accelerator, as if the darkness of the night with its glitter of stars had been compressed into an elegant sculpture. The broad, sweeping wings of the flying wing aircraft were encrusted with a sprayed-on film of solar cells, which completely absorbed the light. The panoramic windows on the edges of the wings were brightly illuminated and looked like closely arrayed faceted eyes, which stared alertly into the brightening sky. Slowly it began to move, gliding with increasing speed on the monorail of the magnetic levitation train, which rose in a gentle curve. It accelerated the machine to three hundred miles per hour, and then it ignited with a blue flash the double engines of the remote-controlled hydrogen booster at the tail of the stratolifter, which bore the aircraft upward. With its gleaming flame the lifter burned such a steep vapor trail into the morning sky that it looked as if the ramp of the magnetic train continued into the high atmosphere in the form of a thick white braid that the wind billowed rapidly northward. At a height of 115,000 feet, the lifter would uncouple and return. The plane, with the sun on its dark shoulders, would then race against the day to New Caracas, Sydney, or Tokyo, or as far as the dikes of Singapore.

In the meantime, the second plane with its fully fueled lifter had been hoisted onto the catapult, and a third and fourth were preparing for takeoff. The light-clippers had to scale the sky at daybreak; those with the greatest distance to cover went first.

We had to wait until the first lifter came back. It descended, clusters of landing gear extending downward, touched down, and released half a dozen wildly dancing braking parachutes. Finally we could take off.

We flew on a twin-engine turboprop with Fiat hydrogen engines. The plane was designed for eighty passengers and filled to capacity. It purred almost soundlessly, heading northward at two hundred miles per hour. From that height it could be made out clearly that the forest damage in the Abruzzo region had progressed further than the last satellite photos I had seen at the institute had suggested.

Ernesto was asleep in the seat next to me. I wondered once again what a quantum physicist could contribute to Rinascita della Creazione di Dio. "That's quite simple to answer," he had said to me when I had asked him about it. "Creation consists of quanta. Perhaps our job will be just to bring them back into their divinely ordained order." So he didn't know either.

We were already over the Po Delta when Ernesto finally awoke. The water glistening in the morning light and the floating farms on it looked like shimmering natural silk with dark rectangles printed on it.

"What sort of technical equipment is there in Venice that is unavailable in Rome?"

He looked at me sleepily and shrugged. "Since the beginning of this century, Venice has been the world capital of virtual reality. That's where cutting-edge research is conducted: optics, holography, simulation. And for ten years the Japanese have had a high-tech base there: the NNTR is restoring the city literally from the ground up."

"NNTR?"

"Nippon NanoTech Research. They're using various nanotechnologies to turn the rotten wooden foundation in the subsoil into a load-bearing and resistant substance. So far with moderate success and some unexpected side effects. In the Middle Ages whole forests were rammed into the mud of the lagoon that once stretched between Pula and the Peloponnese. Maybe they need you botanists to determine the wood species that were used back then so that they can program their tiny machines properly."

"Botany deals only very marginally with wood, Ernesto," I replied. "Wood is a *product* of nature, a cadaver of a once-living thing, so to speak. Interesting at most for age determination in connection with paleobotanical questions."

He yawned. You could at least feign a little bit of interest, you arrogant egghead, I thought.

"And Toshiaki Ishida and his team are there too. Number one in RT."

"What's that?"

"Ray tracing. Surfaces are covered with microscopic optic elements that simulate computer-operated structures. That achieves an effect similar to what chameleons or octopuses do with their skin cells."

"What's the point of that?"

He shrugged and went on: "Or random objects are computer-generated in a holographic rendering. They construct virtual realities that you can't distinguish from reality. That began in the 1980s with film. Lucasfilm was the first. The entertainment industry put a lot of money into these studies in order to make the animations more and more realistic. Then the U.S. Army further advanced research in this area—just think of the battlefield holos used to deceive enemy reconnaissance. Suddenly there was money in abundance. But the Japanese are foremost today in this field of optics. Do you remember the movie *Final Fantasy,* by Hironobu Sakaguchi? It came out around the turn of the century."

"No, I'm not familiar with it."

"A purely computer-animated production of incredibly lifelike detail. You think you're looking at real people. Every single hair, every impurity of skin. Absolutely perfect! Ishida was his disciple. That movie is second to none. I see a connection there, incidentally, to the Netherlands, where similar studies are being conducted at the CIA."

"The CIA?" I asked in confusion.

"Not the Americans, for heaven's sake. The Casimir Institute in Amsterdam. It's known as the center for quantum gravity and multidimensional boundary layer studies."

"Then maybe we're going to plant the world with holographic flowers and reforest it with virtual trees," I commented jokingly.

Ernesto didn't laugh. From the perspective of quantum physics, such a world was perhaps completely indistinguishable from the real one. Patterns in photon drifts, mobile atoms, molecular concentrations and interactions, the pull of nuclear forces and gravity. Reality originates in the brain, projections on the inner screen with vague correspondences in the real world, that much was clear to me; they are distorted reproductions, at most parallelisms. Like the pins in the cylinder of a music box in relation to the melody? Where had I read that? Nonetheless, they were astonishing references. Analog efficiency optimization: Here the evolution of consciousness had had to overcome the highest threshold; selection had raged mercilessly. Only those who bore the best image of their environment in their minds were capable of surviving. The interface had been developed to perfection, so that consciousness had the impression of sitting directly behind the eyes like a pilot in the cockpit, looking directly out into reality. A fallacy as a trick of survival, for this supposedly real world exists only in the head. The actual real world is entirely different, something absolutely foreign. — Or maybe not?

I remembered the lectures on the physiology of perception. The blue of the sky: There are no blue photons. Nothing about light is blue. There's no blue coloration of the retina—no trace of blue in the signal that shoots into the brain through the optic nerve. The blue of the sky is solely in the mind of the beholder, is the impact of an electromagnetic vibration of a particular wavelength transformed into a color sensation, the result of a collision of subatomic particles—a correspondence in different reality media. Still, perhaps there were more correspondences between the inner and outer reality media than the neuroscientists and cognitive scientists thought. We're not so far apart, after all, my dear Ernesto, I said to myself, we biologists and you quantum physicists.

Ernesto had mentioned the chameleon. That animal had mastered the art of turning the inner reality into the outer one, reverse-translating it, so to speak, and it served as a symbol for that mental step. It provided the crosscheck, so to speak: outer—inner—outer. And still more remarkable was the octopus, which produced within seconds a whole spectrum of external features, as if it possessed the magical powers of a shape-shifter. Nature is full of camouflage, Richard Fortey had noted half a century earlier, but human beings are the only living creatures on Earth who find pleasure in deceiving themselves. They are bent on developing that art to absolute perfection.

But to what end? Is that a sensible step in evolution or a step into the abyss?

Questions upon questions . . .

IX

The Border

A land is never poorer than when it seems to overflow with riches.

LAO TZU

The caravan leader looked at the device on his belt and pointed out the direction to the men, mustached fellows with turbans or scarves wrapped around their heads. They laid their dusty carpets in the grass and unrolled them toward the southeast. After the men had said their prayer, they stood up and bowed one last time toward the dark half of the sky. The evening air was damp and cool. The path of the sun was still low in the sky, but it was already perceptibly ascending from its winter camp, each day a finger's breadth; for the time being, however, it was still too weak to burn away the fog that lay over the Po Plain in winter. But the dust and ash in the high atmosphere augured magnificent sunsets.

The previous night the caravan had camped at a mountain oasis below Monte Scarabello; it had been a cold night. Now they had reached the edge of the plain, where the Baganza Valley opens up toward the north. Near Marzolara, within sight of the border, they set up camp. They had arrived at their destination. The drivers had relieved the camels of their loads and led them to the riverbed to drink, where water came out of the ground between flat boulders. Now the animals were grazing on the grass-covered western slope, at the foot of which the men had lit a fire.

"Over there begins, as some claim, the promised land," said the caravan leader, pointing northward with his chin into the hazy plain. After twenty days of steppe, bare mountains, and stretches of desert, the green of the vegetation was pleasing to the eye.

"But it's not our land," he went on, "and we have no place there."

He paced up and down before the men, who now sat by the fire and had placed kettles on the stones to brew tea. The evening light poured coral-red through the cloud banks over the western horizon and died away only very gradually.

"Some refuse to believe it," he went on. "There are always men among those I lead here who consider themselves clever enough to surmount the border and enter this supposed paradise. They cherish the belief that they could find asylum there."

The caravan leader eyed the young men.

"Be advised: No one has ever succeeded in that. The border cannot be surmounted. And it is deadly."

He spat into the fire and ran his finger under the edge of the turban over his forehead, in order to loosen it.

"Some claim that on the other side of the border is a land in which milk and honey flow. That's nonsense. True, the people there don't suffer from hunger, indeed, they are immeasurably rich in comparison to us, but they don't share with us, because they know that not enough would remain for them of that to which they lay claim. So they defend their wealth tooth and nail. They live in fear, for they regard their land as an island in chaos. And they are afraid that this island could go under; beset by storm surges, it could be swept away. That's why they have surrounded themselves with a wall of weapons, which extends from the icy Norwegian Sea across Eastern Europe to here and from here westward to the great sea, which follows the Biscay dam, the Wales-Ireland dam, and then the curve of the North Sea and from there stretches back up to the Norwegian Sea. This island Europe is a world unto itself, which has nothing to do with the world we know."

In the growing darkness the animals could be heard picking greedily at the lush grass. They had drunk their fill and belched rumblingly.

"Behind that wall live more old people than in the whole rest of the world combined. And for many of those old people, time doesn't pass anymore. They have decided that time has to stand still, and they believe they can stop the flow of time. They possess many technical capabilities that we do not even understand. Sometimes, however, we reap some of those benefits. That's the basis of our business. For we have things to offer in exchange that they with all their technology are unable to produce."

The caravan leader pointed to the loads. "Spices," he said. "Coffee, cocoa, tobacco. Those are the things that they need from us. And that's why we're here." He rose. "For that we receive from them solar technology, radio technology, medical equipment, medicine, vaccines."

A few of the men laughed halfheartedly, exposing gaps between their teeth.

"But what they don't give us are weapons," he said, nodding emphatically. "And in weapons technology they are unsurpassed. That's why this border is impregnable and deadly. Those many old people who don't want to die and perhaps cannot die spend their wealth to have ever more perfect weapons developed. For they are haunted by the fear that something might change, after all. That something from outside might infiltrate. That time might start flowing again and disaster would take its course."

With his coarse boot he kicked a smoldering branch back into the fire and made an all-embracing gesture with his hand toward the north and the west.

"Even though you see no one anywhere, you can be sure that we are under constant observation. Not one of our steps escapes them, not one movement. You can trust no dragonfly, no fly, for it could be an MAV, a mini-drone."

Some of the men laughed uneasily.

"Don't laugh!" snapped Bakhtir, the head of the drivers, who was stuffing his waterpipe. "Emilio is right. Not even your crab lice can be trusted."

Hakim, his son, who crouched beside him and filled the glass container of the pipe with fresh water, giggled. His father gave him a kick. "I said not to laugh."

"You have no idea," the caravan leader went on, "what battlefield holos are, and I won't even try to explain it to you. Only this: If you see a house, there is not necessarily a house far and wide, but you can be sure that very nearby a deadly trap lies in wait, a meat grinder that will snap at you with steel teeth or a bone breaker that will crush you to a pulp."

Bakhtir nodded in agreement as he lit his pipe.

"The same goes for trees and bushes," declared Emilio, handing his tin cup to a driver, who filled it with tea from a large sooty pot. "There's not necessarily a tree or bush growing far and wide, but you can be sure that very nearby a laser is pointed at you, which will burn you to ashes. So be warned!"

When the brass sky had lost its last glow and night had fallen, a colored cluster of lights could be seen rising in the northwest and striving toward the zenith. A beam of light stabbed down to Earth, to which the shape seemed fastened like a dragon to a tight leash. When it had reached the zenith, the leash tore and faded, and the cluster of lights drifted away across the sky toward the southeast, until it disappeared in the Earth's shadow. It was a solar satellite of the ESA, which had unloaded its yield at one of the European tracking stations. Sixteen such energy farms were operated by the ESA at that time in medium Earth orbit in order to satisfy the insatiable voracity of the old continent for electric power—which was needed for the operation of its electronic heart, its complicated network of internal organs, and its deadly periphery.

The drivers, who had watched the spectacle with a mixture of curiosity and awe, now wrapped themselves in their djellabas against the emerging cold. They sat by the fire and smoked. The caravan leader stood up, walked a few steps into the darkness, and sat down on a stone. He took a small device, which was secured with a chain, out of the breast pocket of his jacket and activated it by pushing a button on the side. At a distance of a couple miles, a tiny but incredibly bright blue light shone. Additional light signals in red and yellow flashed here and there on the plain. The LED display of the device brightened. He pushed on it with his thumb. A bright white dot appeared far in the north, rose rapidly into the sky, suddenly stood still and burned for a few seconds in a glaring light, then went out.

"Hello, Emilio," said a voice from the device. "You've returned. Welcome to the border. How are you doing?"

"I'm doing well, André. I have sixty-seven heavily laden animals with me. I was able to procure almost everything that was requested. But you've long since known that."

André laughed. "We'll load your freight in the morning. The exchange will take place at the usual time, two hours after sunrise. Agreed?"

"Agreed."

They had set out from Reggio di Calabria along the old Via Francigena, the medieval road of the Franks, later highway A12—by way of Civitavecchia, Tarquinia, Grosseto, Livorno, Pisa, Viareggio, Massa, and Carrara, because on the coastal plain watering places could still be found and the terrain was more surveyable. Near Aulla they had turned northward, heading up the Magra Valley into the mountains, past Pontrémoli and Berceto, then through the Passo della Cisa and following the course of the Baganza to Marzolara, where the valley opened into the Po Plain and shortly before Parma the old road was blocked by the border. The journey had taken them twenty-two days.

"This time we again chose the safe route through the coastal plain."

"I know. We had you under satellite surveillance the whole time, of course. If we had detected signs of an ambush, support would have been on its way immediately. Along the southern border, we have supersonic drones in the air all the time; they could be in Rome in ten minutes, in Naples in fifteen, and in Reggio in twenty."

"I know, André, but on my side of the world time flows more slowly. So much speed would only unnecessarily frighten my men. Besides, I need watering places and campsites; I have to secure the favor and the goodwill of the local rulers. We journey under the protection of the Emir of Perugia. He is a powerful man, and he is feared for his punitive expeditions."

"He offers his protection at a high price."

"In return his soldiers are reliable. He recruits his troops from among the Muslim Bosniaks. That way he can take it for granted that they will not make common cause with the Serbs and Croats or the Albanian warlords lurking in the Abruzzo region."

"I understand, Emilio. You know that better than I. You know your world. All right, see you tomorrow."

"Good night, André."

"Good night."

Emilio turned off the device.

"He's back," Bakhtir, who had come up beside him, said softly, pointing with a nod to the hill in the southeast.

Emilio raised the binoculars to his eyes. In the dwindling light, he could make out the figure standing motionless on the summit and observing them.

"For whom might he be spying?" asked Bakhtir.

"No idea," replied Emilio. "He has his mascot with him again too. What sort of animal might that be?"

"Looks like a rat," said Bakhtir.

Emilio shook his head doubtingly. "It's too big for that."

He lowered the binoculars. When he looked up again, the figure was gone.

THAT NIGHT EMILIO was woken by the *wopp-wopp* of the weak repellers. Perhaps animals had stumbled into the border surveillance. When he heard the hum and rumble of heavy repellers and the howl of the vortex launchers, he stood up and stepped outside the tent. The moon shone in the west.

Suddenly he heard a cry in the camp, then loud, vehement words. Bakhtir came marching toward him, beside himself with anger; with kicks and punches he drove two young men in front of him. They seemed dazed and did not even try to evade the head driver's blows. Ghamal and Pietro; they were in shock. Emilio grabbed an armful of branches and threw them into the embers to kindle a fire. Both of the boys had bloody noses and bruises on their faces and arms—marks of the repellers.

"At least they got such a scare that they turned around," Bakhtir exclaimed with a voice as if his throat were constricted, "but Ibrahim and Hakim . . ."

He broke off and tried in vain to suppress a sob.

"Your son?" asked Emilio.

Bakhtir nodded silently. Emilio grasped him by the shoulder. "You go into your tent!" he shouted at the two young men, who cowered before him and held their heads in pain. "We'll speak about this tomorrow."

They struggled to their feet and staggered away.

"That crazy Ibrahim!" cried Bakhtir; it sounded like a wail. "He persuaded Hakim and the two others to come with him. I should have put that fellow in chains."

Furiously, he kicked a stone into the fire.

"Try to calm down, Bakhtir," said Emilio. "We will find out what happened."

"Do you think there's still hope?"

The caravan leader shrugged silently and looked down at the ground.

"Hakim!" Bakhtir cried out into the plain. There the fog had spread like a milky lake out of which the treetops rose. "Hakim!"

No answer. The lights had gone out. The howling of the wolves and the rumbling of the repellers had fallen silent. The newly kindled fire blazed, illuminating the faces of the men. Bakhtir wept.

AN HOUR AND a half after sunrise, the airship appeared. When it was floating over the campsite, the whine of the jets died away and it descended. Shortly before landing, they once again briefly hissed, and the supple, light gray plastic body of the zeppelin, which was covered with a glistening film on its back and flanks, broke open at the bottom like a soft pod and released containers that arranged themselves into two rows.

The drivers began emptying the containers. They were filled with packaged loads, cocooned in silvery plastic threads. These were now exchanged for the goods brought by the caravan. Emilio checked the electronic identification of the packages with his device. On the LED appeared numbers, quantities of items and descriptions of goods, as well as names and addresses of the respective recipients.

The men were about to heave the loads onto the animals' backs and tie them down when the figure of a man in a Euro-blue protective suit appeared in the opening at the front of the zeppelin. His polarized helmet visor revealed no face. He raised his hand and exclaimed, "Hello, Emilio!" He pointed to Bakhtir. "Are you the father of the one boy?"

"Yes," Bakhtir said hoarsely.

A spark of hope flickered in his eyes.

"Both of you please come with me."

He climbed the aluminum ladder into the cockpit. Emilio and Bakhtir followed. Behind them servos hoisted the containers into the cargo area and fastened them in their foam troughs. Emilio could not believe his eyes; the cockpit was far more spacious than the external dimensions suggested. Along the longitudinal wall of the room was a wheeled stretcher. On it lay Hakim.

"Baba!" he cried with a pitiful voice.

"My boy," said Bakhtir, who was about to rush over to him, but Emilio seized him by the shoulders and held him back.

He saw that the boy had a broken spine. His body was motionless from the chest down. Only his head and arms were moving; on his elbows he tried to crawl off the stretcher, but wide elastic bands bound his paralyzed body to it.

"Baba!" he whimpered.

Bakhtir looked at him with growing horror.

"Of the other one," said the man in the protective suit, "unfortunately nothing remains. He ran straight into a laser fan. As for him"—he gestured with a head movement to Hakim—"a heavy repeller broke all his bones. The spine too."

"My son," Bakhtir said tenderly, pulling his revolver from his belt and holding it to Hakim's head.

The boy stared at him in horror; his whimpering grew louder.

"Stop this nonsense, man!" cried the pilot in the protective suit. "From where you're standing, you could damage a lot of outrageously expensive electronics and trigger the self-defense, if you shoot. So put that thing away!"

Bakhtir saw with horror that he had pushed the barrel of his weapon halfway into the boy's head. Aghast, he drew it back, pointed it at the pilot, and fired two shots at the man's chest. The double wreath of Euro-stars remained intact, but an alarm siren began to bleat, and somewhere the hiss of escaping gas could be heard.

"Hold the man back, Emilio!" shouted the pilot, slapping with his glove at the large panel of switches on the left shoulder of his protective suit. "He seriously believes that we're here in the flesh. And now get out of here as fast as you can, damn it! From here I have no control over the aircraft's self-defense."

"Baba!" Hakim cried pitifully, desperately thrashing his head back and forth and staring through them as if they had suddenly become invisible.

The next instant the wheeled stretcher was gone, as well as the man in the protective suit. The room had been reduced to a third of its length and was filling up with whitish smoke from the floor. Where the two shots had hit the wall there was crackling, and the alarm siren would not stop bleating. The smoke thickened. Bakhtir coughed and doubled up, causing even more gas to stream into his lungs.

"Out! Out! Out!" shouted Emilio.

He grasped Bakhtir by the shoulders, drove him to the hatch, pushed him out, and jumped after him. With a snap the hatch of the cockpit sealed shut behind him. They crawled out from under the airship—not a second too soon, for the engines were firing already and the aircraft took off. Emilio and Bakhtir threw sand at each other to stifle the flames licking at their djellabas; then they squatted down, vomited, and coughed their guts out.

"We have brought the boy to the clinic in Mantua. He will stay there until he has healed. Then you can take him with you the next time you come," said the voice of the man in the protective suit from the device on Emilio's belt. "And one more thing, caravan leader: Impress upon your people that we are not running an adventure playground here. This is a border that nothing and no one can penetrate. It is the border between past and future."

Emilio spat to get rid of the acrid, burning taste in his mouth.

"And on which side lies the future?" he asked.

André laughed. "Here the clocks go faster, and have done so for more than five hundred years. Look at your calendar, Emilio. It shows the year 1425. Here we live in the middle of the twenty-first century."

"Then we still have a lot of time," replied the caravan leader.

The man on the other side of the border didn't answer. And Emilio saw that the light had gone out. The connection had been broken.

Book
TWO

The Toad in Castello

And from this, the conclusion that the universe is finite and the world is unique no more follows than that therefore monkeys are born tailless, that owls see at night without glasses, that bats make wool. in addition, it is never possible to make the inference: the universe is infinite, there are infinite worlds.

GIORDANO BRUNO

I jumped up from an oppressive dream that dissolved within seconds into confusion and slipped away from me. Ashes, I thought. Ashes. I must have said it aloud, for Ernesto was looking at me strangely. His ICom, which he wore as an eyebrow piercing, glowed in the backlight like a fresh drop of blood on his temple.

The plane was already in its final descent, gliding in over Mestre and following the northern shore of the lagoon. Venice, to our right—a mass of shelter-seeking tiled roofs packed around the silver question mark of the Canal Grande—was surrounded by a staggered ring of sausage-shaped rubber rafts, over which there was fog. Far east was the Lido Dam, which shielded the lagoon from the Adriatic like a long, thin arm.

"My God, how ugly," I said, pointing down to the floating off-white objects.

Ernesto leaned forward and looked out. "But necessary," he declared. "A cryobarrier."

"So that the muck from Mestre doesn't slosh into the city?"

"No, more likely so that the tiny nanomachines can't get out and scatter all over the world. Damn tricky task they're carrying out here for the first time on a grand scale. But it seems to be working. Part of the foundation has apparently already been restored."

We touched down close to the water. AEROPORTO MARCO POLO was written on the white facade of the airy new airport terminal.

A stocky, cheerfully grinning Japanese man awaited us at the exit, holding up a sign with our names. He introduced himself as Kazuichi Inoue.

"The subway to the arsenal still isn't running," he said apologetically. "We'll have to take a detour."

We took the airport bus along the northern shore of the lagoon and across the Ponte della Libertà to the Ospedale Santa Chiara, where a motorboat picked us up. It buzzed down the Canal Grande, turned left at Santa Geremia into the Canale di Cannaregio, and went through the ghetto, past small old houses, in which for many centuries there had been Jewish shops, kosher butchers, and secondhand dealers. Now antique shops, Internet cafés, and tiny restaurants had been established there. Then the motorboat went out into the lagoon. A fresh northeast wind blew toward us; it was cool, though the sun was shining. The air smelled damp and salty from the churned-up water. Gulls dipped and soared, squawking. We continued along the Sacca della Misericordia and the Fondamenta Nuove and past a light blue box at the end of a floating dock, which rolled in the waves. OSPEDALE was written in black letters on a yellow background over the windows. A bit farther on, we turned into the Rio di Santa Giustina, a canal at the other end of which a massive gloomy brick castle loomed over the houses. Its huge semicircular arched windows overlooked the city like the seemingly sleepy eyes of a monstrous lurking toad, which had wedged itself in between the old houses of Castello.

"What is that?" I asked. "A church?"

The sight of the building was oppressive.

"That's the dog run," Renata explained, wrinkling her nose. "San Lorenzo. The Dominican monastery. The headquarters of the dogs of God. The Inquisition in this city once reigned here."

"Were heretics burned here too?"

"No. The Signoria would not have tolerated the Inquisition usurping so much power. But they had their spies and lackeys here too. Scholars definitely did well to avoid the mainland. But even here in the city they weren't safe. Giordano Bruno was imprisoned for almost a year in San Lorenzo. A local merchant had lured him into a trap and betrayed him to the Dominicans. Later he was handed over to the Vatican."

"I never understood that. He was a scholar known throughout Europe—"

"—for his antiauthoritarian attitude and his unconventional views," Renata interrupted me with a shrug. "But what was he to a Venetian merchant? That's the question, Domenica. An apostate Dominican, and rebellious to boot, because he brazenly defied his order; a little monk who had the nerve to call Jesus an Oriental magician and who rambled on about inhabited worlds beyond the moon with which under the present circumstances it was undoubtedly impossible to carry on any dealings in the foreseeable future. Why should someone incur trouble with the Pope for such a dubious fellow? Away with him! Off to Rome! Let them do with him in the Vatican what they please. And that they did."

Renata was right. I had lived long enough near Piazza Campo de' Fiori, where the horror of the stake-burnings remains palpable to this day, where, according to the calculations of a statistician, the ground had been so saturated with the ashes of the victims burned at the stake that the air still contained molecules of them. The idea of breathing in remains of Giordano Bruno, who had been burned at the stake there, had always sent shivers down my spine, and whenever I crossed the piazza I had held my breath until I got dizzy.

"A ghastly hovel," I said.

"And the building was thoroughly renovated only at the beginning of the century."

"Why wasn't it torn down?"

"Nothing is ever torn down here, Domenica. Everything here is protected as a cultural heritage site."

The boat was moored in front of a building with a marble facade in a strange mixture of classical and baroque architecture, as only the nineteenth century in its immoderate historicism could have brought forth; over mighty portals flanked by Ionic columns were the words:

ISTITUTO TECNICO PAOLO SARPI

On the right side, next to the tunnel-like passage of Calle San Francesco, it was flanked by a strange building with a Renaissance facade that included three marble sarcophagi at a lofty height—perhaps the final resting places of highly renowned engineers and inventors. The idiosyncratic architectural solution made an impression less sublime than it was ridiculous, for it seemed like a bizarre, vertically constructed bathhouse, in the stone tubs of which sweaty technicians could have their backs scrubbed. It was the former church of Santa Giustina, in which a museum for the history of technology had been established, as I later learned.

Through the portal flanked by columns made of polished dark wood we entered another world. Only the old marble floor had been left untouched; everything else was glass and brightness by means of refined indirect lighting. Palms and papyrus plants in troughs exuded freshness. There was a slight whiff of frangipani in the air. Was it a shady garden? Was a scent synthesizer fooling my nose with vibrations? Somewhere water burbled. To the right next to the entrance blazed a bougainvillea. I surreptitiously ran the back of my hand over the flower petals. It was real.

Right at the entrance, a sculpture stood between palms. It portrayed a kneeling old bald-headed man wearing a toga. His mouth was open in a painful cry; he had wrapped his arms comfortingly around the shoulders of a younger man, who lay half-upright before him on the ground, a hand covering his face in agony. Apparently he had been blinded.

On the wall behind the sculpture hung an oval painting. It was the portrait of a middle-aged man in monastic dress, with clear, knowingly gazing eyes under thin, widely curved eyebrows. His mouth was framed by a dark beard, his nose jutted out, his forehead was broadly domed under short-cropped brown hair.

FRA PAOLO SARPI was inscribed on the small brass plaque under the painting.

"The teacher of Galilei," declared Ernesto, who had stopped next to me. "He was luckier than Bruno. As a native-born Venetian, he enjoyed the protection of the city, but the fundamentalists got him nonetheless and mutilated his face so badly with knives that he could never show himself again in public."

I thought of CarlAntonio.

"He was our most significant scientist in the sixteenth century. He became famous as a historian, for"—he shrugged with a sigh—"in Venice scientists have never counted for much."

"That has changed with Professor Ishida, I've heard."

Ernesto cast me a surprised glance, then laughed. "You can say that again."

We waited.

PROFESSOR TOSHIAKI ISHIDA insisted on greeting us in person, our escort informed us. With a billowing, open lab coat he finally strode hastily through the glass door, which soundlessly slid aside, a short, slight man around fifty years old, with his VR glasses casually pushed up on his forehead, as if he wished to demonstrate that even an extremely important experiment could not prevent him from welcoming us.

"My young friends!" he exclaimed in perfect Italian, spreading his arms. "Welcome to this beautiful city! Welcome to our institute. I hope you had a pleasant journey."

Then he repeated the gesture of greeting silently in Japanese; he placed his fingertips together and bowed several times.

He had short gray hair and almost white side-whiskers that stuck out a handbreadth from the periphery of his face like a grotesque ridden-up ruffled collar. His alert black eyes flashed triumphantly.

"Oh, God," whispered Marcello. "Looks like a macaque."

"Then be careful around him," Renata said with a chuckle. "Macaques are agile—and they bite."

I had trouble suppressing the urge to burst out laughing.

"Shh!" Kazuichi hissed.

"Indeed. He's his own logo," Ernesto murmured.

I noticed that his skin was greased with a cream or oil that, depending on the angle of the light, caused iridescent color patterns to appear on it .

"I know that in Europe people usually greet each other with a handshake," declared Ishida, raising both hands, which suddenly scintillated in all colors of the rainbow. "As a rule, we here in the institute refrain from that. Not out of impoliteness"—he raised his chin, the ruffled collar stuck out even more—"nor for hygienic or other medical reasons, but rather solely for technical reasons. You will all understand that in due time. Incidentally, you are staying very close to here. It's the red house to the right up on the Rio, No. 2821 N, about a hundred and fifty yards from here. Mr. Kazuichi Inoue, one of my assistants—you know him already, of course— will attend to you. He will show you your apartments shortly. Your luggage is already there. We'll do everything we can so that you feel comfortable here with us. But first familiarize yourselves with the city, to the extent that you are not already familiar with it." And raising a shimmering finger, Professor Ishida added: "Get a pathfinder tattoo. Here in Venice it can easily come to pass that you end up in a blind alley or even in a canal."

Renata sniffed disdainfully.

Professor Ishida's raised palms flashed, and he bowed in parting. "Thank you."

The glass door snapped aside and closed behind him. A billowing white silhouette faded away on the other side. The professor hurried back to his experiment.

Suddenly I noticed that I was dead tired.

"How did you Japanese people learn to speak such fabulous Italian?" Marco asked our escort, as we walked along the Fondamenta Santa Giustina to our housing.

"Ha," Kazuichi replied, grinning. "Piped in."

"Piped in?"

He jerkily lowered his thick head. I would have to get used to his manner of nodding.

"SimStim," explained Kazuichi. "Simulated stimulation. Deliberately induced imaginings. Ideally via Brain-Computer Interface."

He tapped his temple, and I noticed that he wore, half covered by his bristly black hair, an implant the size of a euro-cent piece under his skin. I was horrified; I had long since decided never to have one of those brain pacemakers implanted in me. How could you know where your own memories ended and the Net began?

"If you don't want to wear your own BCI," he said, as if he could read my mind with that thing, "you have to undergo an indirect SimStim treatment. That's an elaborate procedure, which lasts until the data packets have been individually fed to you. A few electrodes are stuck to your forehead and you are slid into a tube. After a few days you begin to think in the desired language and talk away: Uzbek, Visigothic, Middle High German, Aramaic, Martian—whatever your heart desires."

"That's impossible," I blurted out with astonishment.

"It has been possible for a long time," he said, nodding to me. "In the meantime, you can also have yourself programmed with sense impressions of animals, of dolphins or wild cats or birds. That's only more complicated and not entirely risk-free. Have you never heard of the 'Flight of the Condor,' by Luciero Montalban? The mental symphonies of Fautin and Norrevang?"

He shook his head with a laugh when he saw that we were staring at him blankly.

"Where are you from, people?" he asked.

"I thought those are VR spectacles," Marco interjected suspiciously. Perhaps he believed our tutor was pulling our leg.

"The VR provides only the scenery," explained Kazuichi. "The smell, the taste, the physical sensations, the actual kick—that comes from the inducer. Via BCI or conventional SimStim."

"Are you experimenting with that here?"

Again that exaggerated nod.

"I thought you worked with holography."

"It's all related," replied Kazuichi, scratching his temple where the cent showed under the skin. "Reality models. That includes photon manipulation too—spatial, temporal . . ."

"Light?" Marco asked, frowning and stroking his thin, shaved head. It was not his field—nor mine. Ernesto, walking on the other side of the Japanese man, smiled indulgently at so much ignorance. Suddenly I had the impression that Kazuichi was listening inwardly. Was he heeding the voice of his master? Or the whispering of the Net?

"You mean optics?" he asked Marco distractedly. "Yes, optics too, of course. We work on real reality," he explained. "That will be clear to you in due time."

I had stopped and looked to the right. Directly behind the old building of the institute was a huge building complex, which in its bareness and featurelessness resembled an airplane hangar or a military technical facility. It extended eastward to the church of San Francesco and northward almost to the water of the lagoon.

"Oh," said our Japanese guide, eyeing the white block. "Someone has been fiddling with a switch again." He shook his head with amusement.

I didn't understand the remark, but I was too tired to ask what he meant.

OUR APARTMENTS WERE on the southwest and northwest sides of the four-story house. The corners of the building had been constructed as balconies overlooking the northwest lagoon with San Michele as well as the city to the south. The view did not much interest me, however. I decided to leave my suitcases unopened, and I lay down for an hour.

When I visited Renata later in her apartment on the fourth floor, she was standing with a glass of orange juice at the balcony railing. Ernesto was sitting in an armchair in the living room.

"Shall I bring you a glass of juice too?" he asked me.

"Yes, please. Where are Marcello and Marco?"

"I think they're lying down," he replied.

I stood next to Renata. She was looking across to the distant mountains rising from the gray-green haze of the plain, their pale summits showing faintly against the clear, light blue afternoon sky.

"Homesick?" I asked.

She frowned and wrinkled her snub nose. After a moment's hesitation she shook her head wordlessly, but I noticed the pain behind her determination not to let herself be overwhelmed by emotions. I quickly changed the subject.

"Is that snow?" I asked, gesturing with a nod to the mountain range. "I've never seen snow. In reality, I mean."

"Lime," said Renata.

"Limestone?"

"The corals and shells of the Tethys Sea—compacted and lifted into the sky. It was once the coast of North Africa. That's where I come from," she said with a smile. "That always fascinated me as a child. To have been born on the northern coast of Africa."

"A Moro in disguise," said Ernesto. "I've suspected you for a long time."

"Hey!" I cried in shock as my eyes wandered toward the southeast. "That's impossible!"

The bare, windowless block of the institute had disappeared. Instead the architecture of the old Istituto Tecnico Paolo Sarpi in its boring regularity of black-stained cornices and tall double-gabled windows extended eastward as far as the slender brick tower of the Campanile di San Francesco. Ernesto came out onto the loggia.

"Look at that," I said. "I swear that an hour ago there was a smooth white block here at least two hundred yards long."

"Are you sure?"

"Absolutely."

He ran his hand through his short brown hair, which was already thinning quite a bit on top, and nodded at me. "Ray tracing," he explained. "It's an optical trick."

"How do they do that?"

"It's not even that new. Sasha Migdal, a Russian quantum physicist, already patented it last century, in the nineties. He called it 'Metaflash' or 'Metastream,' a computerized reproduction of three-dimensional surfaces. It was a trixel technology."

"Holographic?" asked Renata.

"Yes, something like that, merely more refined. Television works with pixels—two-dimensionally. Here, three coordinates of a picture element are stored. These days, people are working with additional dimensions. Subtle information about surface texture."

"Those are just games," I broke in.

Ernesto nodded, but he had not even been listening. "The military technicians call it WaveCam—wave camouflage. Or Overlay, because it is superimposed on real or projected surfaces. Visible light is modulated by invisible light. In that way, you can make a coarse surface appear smooth as a mirror or make an even surface appear structured. You can cover it with fur, present it as overgrown with plants, or adapt it entirely to the surroundings."

"Now hold on," I said. "The chameleon has been doing that for more than fifty million years."

"Some octopuses too," added Renata. "Have you ever seen how they do that? It's incredible! One glance at the background, and the surface of their body turns a split second later into its photographic image."

"Nanos machinulis," said Ernesto; it sounded almost reverent.

"What does that have to do with nanos?" she asked with a frown.

"The surface of the building has been sprayed with smartdust. The particles assume the function of monitors. They group themselves into picture elements. With a computer you can thereby simulate any structure and alter it constantly. Do you see the shadows of the cornices and intrados? They follow exactly the position of the sun."

"Might the professor have sprayed himself with something like that?" I asked. "He looked as if he had applied some sort of cream."

"That looked gross," said Renata, wrinkling her nose. "And then that straw star of a beard. A strange fellow."

"That iridescent coating on his skin?" Ernesto reflected. "Maybe so. Perhaps they use that to simulate tactile and haptic impressions." He became really excited. "Of course! Why didn't I think of that before? The sense of touch is the most difficult to simulate. Ishida is trying to do that with smartdust. Directly on the skin. Probably the substance contains graphite and reacts to electromagnetic fields. That's brilliant!"

We work on real reality, Kazuichi had declared. *That will be clear to you in due time.*

"But what, for heaven's sake, does that have to do with botany?"

"Well, they're obviously trying to re-create reality as closely as possible. Of course that includes trees, bushes, grass . . ." he speculated, but it didn't sound very convincing.

"Photos or videos would be sufficient for that," I replied.

"Think of extinct plants. Suppose they want to simulate a primeval jungle, with giant ferns, giant horsetails, and other plants. For that you have to know exactly what those plants once looked like."

"Ernesto, no one knows what those plants once *really* looked like. What we see in textbooks are reconstructions that have been made on the basis of fossils and in comparison with current species that are regarded as their descendants or relatives."

"That may be true. But perhaps that's enough. Perhaps the simulation doesn't have to be so exact. Perhaps an approximation is enough."

"Hm."

"That reminds me of those countless old *Jurassic Park* movies," Renata interjected.

"Why not?" replied Ernesto. "But instead of a movie, a SimStim total artwork, in which you can *smell* the cadavers of those beasts and *taste* their blood."

"Well," I said, "if you like that sort of thing . . ."

"You wouldn't believe how many people are completely crazy about such sense impressions."

"The site where the institute now stands supposedly used to be a huge empty area on which two ancient rusty gas holders stood," said Renata. "The old people here told me that. I worked nearby for a few months."

"In the Ospedale?" I asked her.

She shook her head. "In the Ospedaletto of the Chiesa di Santa Maria dei Derelitti. That's an old people's home on Calle Barbaria delle Tole. It must have been abandoned in the meantime. Back then they had already stopped taking in old people. I always liked visiting that church over there."

She gestured to the narrow campanile beyond the institute building. "That's San Francesco della Vigna. There used to be a vineyard there. Sometimes the monastery garden is open. It's absolutely silent there. You really believe you are in a garden in which time came to a standstill centuries ago," she said dreamily, running her hand across her forehead. "Until the tolling of the campanile bell brings you back into the present."

She smiled at me and added: "By the way, when the death knell sounds from San Francesco at midnight on Shrove Tuesday, the Carnevale di Venezia is carried to its grave."

"Oh," said Ernesto, but we could tell by looking at him that this information did not mean much to him.

At the time, I had no idea how many hours I would spend in that monastery garden—with an anxious heart and desperate hope.

II

Scarabeo

We have to learn to look at space and time differently, as participants in a relational world rather than the stage in an absolute world.

LEE SMOLIN

So this was the glorious Venice—somewhat old and rotten and putrid seen from up close, I said to myself, but thanks to the Consorzio Venezia Nuova, the Association of International Private Committees for the Safeguarding of Venice, UNESCO, and Japanese high tech, on the road to recovery.

Here too time folded back on itself, the past was intertwined with the present as in Rome and in other ancient Italian cities. But at first glance this city struck me as absolutely un-Italian, foreign, Oriental. Certainly, it had for centuries been an—often ungrateful—bastard of the Eastern Roman Empire.

But that first impression deceived. It was not at all characterized by that sublime Byzantine laziness, that sleepy indifference and dreamy idleness, but rather by rapacity and ingenuity. You needed only to observe the Canal Grande on a normal weekday, the busy back and forth of the suppliers, deliverers, and collectors, to feel the engine of restlessness, bustle, and acquisitiveness. Behind the magnificent facades of the palazzi—then as now—profits had always been made without reservation. That was and is the pride of this city, the core of its history.

Because of its geographic location, Venice had never used land vehicles. The nerve of modernity leads only to the periphery at Santa Lucia. There it was severed. In the city itself, as had been the case for centuries, only the patter and shuffle of human feet could be heard. That produces the nostalgic illusion of timelessness, to which the contemporary individual, stressed by noise, only too easily succumbs. And the inhabitants of this island had made a business out of that too.

So this was the much-extolled robber bride of the eastern seas, done up extravagantly, though by no means tastelessly, and, as she aged, increasingly dependent on the attentions of her admirers.

WE WERE GIVEN ample time to settle in. Kazuichi attended to us. Two days after our arrival he provided us with our work equipment.

"This is the Scarabeo," he explained, handing us a Wristtop, a flat transparent device with a strap and a metallic-coated surface. "It's compatible with any ICom. That means you can ask a question via your ICom, and it will get you the answer from the Web or wherever. The Scarabeo is the best server technology currently available; it is equipped with the most up-to-date semantic and ontological search programs and will get you all the data you need. If vocal does not suffice, then there's a Vid here—" He tapped on the tiny screen. "If the size does not suffice, then you stick this here somewhere—" He unfolded a piece of film, slapped it against the wall, and smoothed it out. "On demand, there's animation. The slicing has three presentation levels: infotainment, high, and top—also with VR optics or as a holo, as needed. The Scarabeo has access to all public Nets; also available are all films, operas, operettas, musicals, and the whole tralala down to folklore. Okay? Shunts for institute networks or other exclusive or arcane infopools with special permission are built in, of course. Got it?"

I nodded hesitantly.

"I work with a BCI," said Kazuichi, tapping his temple. "That's not everyone's thing, I know. But I have gotten so used to it that I could no longer live without the thing. I'd feel as if I were in a dark cell—sensory deprivation. I need the Web around me, like a spider. If I don't have constant access to all data—without any time lag—then I get sick."

Renata looked at me. I shrugged.

"I've already worked with something similar," said Ernesto, turning the Scarabeo between his fingers. "We called them Minatori. Browsers for the library computers. With them you descend into the mines of knowledge."

"How poetic," Kazuichi said without a trace of irony. "The Scarabeo is the next generation; it has about ten thousand times the capacity. It got its name because it combs through the dung that human civilization has heaped up in ten millennia of written culture—from clay tablets to infoflashes. It scrapes together what you need and rolls it into bite-sized—"

"Hey! Yuck!" exclaimed Renata.

"Well—into *manageable* portions, okay?" Kazuichi said with a grin. "As is proper for a dung beetle. You should always carry it with you. At work, I mean. Or privately too . . ."

Did I want to know everything at all times? Did I ever want to live on a data garbage dump? Oh God, no. The ICom was already a burden for me sometimes. But I could order it to leave me alone and hold all calls. To be unreachable—at least for a brief time, before you're reminded by the Net to plug in again. It was unfortunately only a privilege of the rich and powerful not to be constantly available.

MY SCARABEO SURPRISED me with a detailed training program for the next weeks: specialization in the ecology and flora of Central Europe. At the same time, language courses were on the agenda. Dutch at the top. We were to receive our special training in Amsterdam and would possibly be assigned fieldwork there too—far outside the death zone. Bernd's fears had remained unfounded.

On my wrist bloomed corncockle and spreading wallflower. "*Agrostemma githago . . .*" Luigi prompted from the Scarabeo's store of knowledge. "*Erysimum repandum.*" They were so present that I thought I could smell their wild earthy scent. The pinnate brushes of the small pasque flower (*Pulsatilla pratensis*) took shape, and the swollen lips of the lady's slipper (*Cypripedium calceolus*). The good king Henry (*Chenopodium bonus-henricus*) extended its tight umbel toward me. The cabbage thistle (*Cirsium oleraceum*) demonstrated prickly defiance. The hairy willowherb (*Epilobium hirsutum*) grew forth in its starred purple. The timid little red tips of the bog asphodel (*Narthecium ossifragum*), the refined chador of the hoary plantain (*Plantago media*), the ringing white bells of the sidebells wintergreen (*Orthilia secunda*), and the whispering little helmet of the Manchurian monkshood (*Aconitum variegatum*), the blue eyes of the common chicory (*Cichorium intybus*) gazed at me and the golden ones of the liverwort . . .

"*Hepatica nobilis . . .*"

"Thanks, Luigi," I said. "That's enough work for today. We'll review it again later."

Most of those beautiful fragile creatures had long since departed reality. Some had already gone extinct in the twentieth century; many had been claimed by the terror of the twenty-first. So many dead—wiped out, lost forever. The Scarabeo conjured them up from old plant books, from specialized botanical literature and encyclopedias, re-creating them before my eyes in precisely detailed holographs, plucking them for me in Walahfrid Strabo's *Hortulus* and with Besler's help in the gardens of Johann Conrad Freiherr von Gemmingen, once prince bishop of Eichstätt.

Did Sarah now work with something like this too? Probably she didn't need it, because she always knew best. What had become of her? Probably she had long since returned to her country, held a professorship or headed an institute. I decided to have my device search for her website, but could not remember her last name.

DR. MONDOLONI WAS a friendly, considerate, and quiet man in his midthirties. He was a head taller than I, slender, and almost bald. What remained of his hair had been cut to a millimeter in length. His thick, dark eyebrows looked like caterpillars over two gently gazing dark brown eyes.

"He's gay," said Marco, who had a lot to do with him, because his brain was being stuffed with medieval dialects by the bushel in the form of intensive treatments.

I shrugged.

"For God's sake, nowadays you can do something about that," Marco blurted out.

"Why should he?" I replied. "I like him the way he is."

Dr. Mondoloni's language laboratory was in the basement of the old building up on the Fondamenta. Through the window children's shouting and the chugging of the boats on the Rio Santa Giustina could be heard. He could have scanned my ICom without saying anything to me, but that would have seemed impolite to him, judging from my impression of him. He sat down opposite me on a chair, smiled at me encouragingly, took a notepad and pen, questioned me, and took notes.

"Have you ever worked with dream screens before, Signorina Domenica?" he asked with a soft voice.

"No. I didn't even know that such a thing existed."

He raised his thick black eyebrows and nodded. "They're daydreams of a sort, based, like many interface technologies these days, on simulated stimulation of sense impressions, known as SimStim—that is, on induced memories of experiences that you yourself have not had. But don't worry, I won't tamper irresponsibly with your memory. It's my job to impart language skills to you. After a few sessions, you'll have the sensation that buried childhood memories have become accessible again. And these memories are linked with linguistic memories. You will feel as if you had grown up as a small child in another linguistic environment, as if you had learned that language naturally but since forgotten it. And suddenly the memory resurfaces."

I had to stretch out on a narrow chaise lounge, and Dr. Mondoloni fastened electrodes to my forehead and temples. The touch of his fingers was as delicate and gentle as if I were being grazed by down. I looked anxiously up at the dome of his head. As many as a hundred living and dead languages were filed away in there, Marco had asserted. The thick black caterpillars of his eyebrows crawled toward each other, rose, sank, wriggled, recoiled from each other, and approached each other once again as in a bizarre mating ritual—reduced to a strictly arranged synchronized ballet. He noticed my gaze and smiled.

"I wish you a pleasant shopping expedition in Amsterdam, Signorina Domenica."

"What do you mean?" I asked, and then . . .

I STOOD ON the Noordermarkt square, a shopping basket on my arm, as Mother always gave it to me to take along. The clock on the church tower across the square struck twice—so it was half past eleven. I was running late. I walked past the poultry and cheese stalls alongside the Prinsengracht to the north end of the square, where the vegetable and fruit sellers offered their wares. The stalls were already half empty. With fascination I stopped in front of the flower stalls. That concentrated luminosity of the asters: yellow, orange, red, and brown—waning joyfulness of summer. A last summoning of warmth and already an autumnal scent of heaviness and moisture, of ripeness.

I knew that the woman whose stall was in front of the church always had the largest selection of apples. She pulled her strong red hands out from under her green apron and turned to me.

"*Kan ik u helpen?*" she asked.

"*Ik wil appels kopen. Welke zijn goed?*"

"*Ik heb nieuwe Elstars.*"

"*Geeft u mij maar een kilo.*"

The market woman gathered the apples into a bag and weighed them. I put the bag in the basket and paid.

"*U spreekt mijn taal absoluut perfekt. Waar heeft u dat geleerd?*" she asked me. So it was apparent that I wasn't from around here.

"*Datzelfde zou ik u kunnen vragen,*" I replied, and was suddenly no longer certain whether we had previously been communicating in Dutch or Italian.

A parrot squawked: *"Kan ik u helpen?"*

Next to the fruit stall a showman had pitched a tent. In front of it was a barrel organ to which the parrot was chained. A boy in overalls, who was barefoot despite the already autumnal coolness, carried a box of apples through the entrance to the tent, from which at that moment the showman emerged. He had on clown makeup and wore a coarse black-and-white-checkered shirt, a multicolored vest, and baggy pants made of black velvet with wide suspenders made of the same material.

The showman went to the barrel organ and began to turn the crank. A folksy melody rang out. *"Kan ik u helpen?"* squawked the parrot, scurrying aside on its perch. The man looked strangely familiar to me and I approached him with curiosity. He half-averted his face, but I saw clearly, standing out at the temple under the chalk-white makeup, the small slender cross he wore under his skin.

"Signore Falcotti!" I blurted out. "How is that possible?"

He continued to turn the crank as he looked at me with his black-rimmed eyes. His large, bright, red-painted mouth stretched into a smile.

"You recognized me right away?" he asked.

"Yes."

The boy carried another box of apples into the tent. His legs were tanned, his feet dirty. He picked out an apple, tossed it back and forth between his hands three or four times, winked conspiratorially at me, and bit into it.

I knew at that moment that everything around me was not reality. Rather, I felt as if I were acting in a play, standing on a stage or a movie set, but there was no script or screenplay. It was all so absurd. The barrel organ had gone silent.

"Let's go inside," said Falcotti, holding up the flap at the entrance to let me in. In the middle of the tent was a wooden table on which the boy had set six or seven boxes of apples.

I was reminded of my early childhood: Behind my parents' house stretched a large garden with several apple trees. One of them stood close to the house, and its branches jutted over the railing of the balcony on the second floor. When the trees were in bloom, thousands of bees swarmed around them, and the blossoms were full of those buzzing insects. When I was two or three years old, I had at an unattended moment gone out on the balcony through the door from my parents' bedroom, had unsuspectingly grabbed at the blossoms, and had promptly been stung by a bee. The jolt at the sudden, unexpected pain was elemental—like a powerful electric shock. Horrified, I ran into the room, got tangled in the curtains at the door, and fell down. My father was standing in front of the mirror. With a glance he grasped the situation, rushed over to me, picked me up, and pressed me to his chest. I couldn't speak, couldn't even scream. "It will get better soon, my child," he said close to my ear. "It will get better soon."

It didn't get better soon. An ambulance brought me to the hospital, because I went into anaphylactic shock. I almost could have died, my father later told me. As a child I didn't understand what death meant, but the horror that pierced me to the core like a sharp wedge and incapacitated me so that I couldn't even scream was lodged deep in my soul. I had felt creaturely fear for the first time. That's what death must be like, suddenly pouncing on you, I often said to myself later. And from that point on, my throat always constricted when I saw bees or wasps near me.

Falcotti eyed me, waiting.

"You look funny," I lied.

"Do you think so?"

His hair was stiffened with gel and stuck out in spikes. The colorful patchwork vest was shabby and the greasy high collar of the shirt was torn under the ear. He shrugged apologetically. "As a psychologist one is sometimes forced to take on strange roles. In your case, however, I was happy to do so," he said, pulling with two fingers on his painted lower lip.

"What do you mean?"

Falcotti gazed silently at his reddened fingertips. His dark eyes looked out through the white makeup as through the eyeholes of a mask. That was when I noticed that he had shaved off his beard. He took a small, curved knife, grabbed one of the apples, and sliced it. Suddenly his hand and his forearm were covered with bees, crawling all around on his skin.

"Watch out!" I cried in horror.

Falcotti looked at his hand. The insects did not seem to bother him in the least.

"They won't do anything to me," he assured me.

"Were those creatures inside the apple?" I asked in amazement.

"No, in the blossom," he replied.

"Well, yes, but . . ."

"I know: You're thinking that was a long time ago. The time in between—that seems mysterious to you. But there's an explanation. I will give it to you, but I have to ask you to keep absolutely silent about it."

A bee crawled across his cheek. He brushed it away. Suddenly the bees had been disturbed by something and began to swarm. Their threatening buzzing filled the tent. I turned on my heel, ran out, and crashed into the barrel organ. It began to play . . .

Then the world disintegrated, morphed into a polished metallic tube, in which shadows of four-dimensional figures moved.

"*Kan ik u helpen?*" squawked the parrot, but it had already dissolved, as had the chain, the barrel organ, the whole Noordermarkt square.

GRADUALLY I CAME to and had a throbbing headache. I heard voices, people laughing and chatting, but so softly that I couldn't understand a word. A church clock struck at the edge of audibility.

I ran my hands across my forehead to massage my aching temples—and reached into a spider's web of electrodes, which withdrew from the touch like almost-insubstantial undersea creatures. The voices vanished. I seemed to have somehow triggered an alarm, for Dr. Mondoloni's face appeared at the entrance to the tube.

"Everything all right?" he asked, sliding back the tubular equipment.

"I can't say," I murmured. "A bit of a headache."

"That's normal," he explained, spraying an ethereal substance on his fingertips and beginning to massage my forehead and temples with circular movements, as his caterpillar eyebrows resumed their mating ritual. I couldn't watch them, and closed my eyes. Within seconds the pain dissipated, but I was enjoying the touch of his fingers.

"That was strange," I said.

"Strange?"

"Yes, a grotesque situation."

Dr. Mondoloni stopped and stood up. I got up too and fixed my hair.

"Can we do another session tomorrow? It's better if we start off—"

"If you promise not to unleash bees on me again, Doctor."

"Bees?" he asked, visibly perplexed.

He held the chip he had ejected from the console up to the light, as if he could spot an insect embedded in it as in amber.

"Don't tell me you didn't know that."

"No, I really don't know it," Mondoloni emphasized, clearing his throat self-consciously. "That isn't directly related to the language lesson, Signorina Domenica. It's a sort of vaccination for your training—custom-made by the boss himself. I don't know the formula. I know only that it serves your protection."

"You had promised not to tamper with my brain."

"There can be no question of that," he said, looking at me ingenuously with his gentle, sad eyes. "We have merely mobilized your own defenses. Your memories, which you acquired naturally at some point and which were slumbering in you, were invoked and intensified."

"Hm. You can say that again." I looked at him thoughtfully. "A sort of blocking?"

"More of a conditioning. It is unfortunately necessary."

"Does everyone receive it?"

"Of course. It's required if you work here at the institute."

I put on my anorak. He hastened to help me into it.

"Well, then, see you tomorrow. Without bees, Doctor. I'll take you at your word. Because I hate those creatures."

"I might have guessed as much," replied Dr. Mondoloni, smiling sadly.

"THEN THE IDIOT knocks over the bottle of gasoline. It immediately ignited, of course. In the blink of an eye everything was in flames, and pounds of explosives were lying around on the table. 'Get out of here!' I shouted. 'Get out!' But he just gawked at me in terror, with a totally blank stare. I grabbed him by the shoulder, pushed him out of the tent, and flung myself to the ground. At that moment there was a bang. The tent was torn to pieces. Burning shreds flew across the whole square and landed on the market stalls all around and on the cobblestones . . . Phew!"

Renata gazed at her mutilated hand as if she had to check whether she had suffered new injuries.

"Really shrewd, that old fox," she said.

"Ishida? You can bet your life on it," I agreed.

Renata nodded. "Deep-seated fears. For you, it's bees; for me, fire, explosions. That rascal brainwashed us."

"Mondoloni spoke of necessary conditioning."

"That's just another way of saying it. But what were we being conditioned for?"

"I'm sure we'll find out soon."

III

The Executioner at the Ponte del Paradiso

As the visible is in truth, it is not seen by you; the same is true of hearing and the other senses . . . Therefore, he is irrational who thinks that he knows something in truth but is ignorant of truth.

NICOLAUS CUSANUS

From my balcony I had a magnificent view toward the northwest. In the foreground was the Isola di San Michele, which had run aground forever in the shallow water of the lagoon. Beyond it, in the distance, rose the pale summits of the Carnic Alps; they floated above the haze of the plain like a fleet in full sail.

The walk from the institute, through narrow streets and across small squares, to Campo Santi Giovanni e Paolo, on which the massive brick church and the Ospedale stood, took seven or eight minutes; from there it was another twelve to fifteen minutes to San Marco.

Marcello and Kazuichi had come along. We trotted up and down steps, across little bridges, left, right—Kazuichi leading the way with almost somnambulistic certainty.

"Piped in?" I asked him. "The city map, I mean."

He stopped and raised his pinky. It looked greasy, as if he had dipped it in oil. Kazuichi turned his body to the right—the finger splayed toward the left. He turned his body to the left—the finger maintained its direction and crept under the ring finger.

"Does it function as a compass?" I asked.

Kazuichi shook his head with a laugh. "No, it's my pilot. My pathfinder. It knows its way around any city if I retrieve the data from a satellite."

He gestured vaguely up at the southern sky.

"Nanotechnology?"

"Yes, vibrotactile induction," he confirmed.

"May I touch it?"

Kazuichi's finger did not feel greasy at all. More like it was glazed—and hot, as if intense activities were under way in the coating on the skin.

"Smartdust?" asked Renata.

Kazuichi nodded.

Marcello inspected the finger warily. His freshly washed black ringlets shone. He shook his head. "Well, I'll be."

"That's nothing," said Kazuichi. "You'll become familiar with all sorts of things here. You'll be extremely well equipped when you head off on your excursions."

"And where will we be heading?" I tried to fish for information.

"I don't know," he said. "You'll be told in Amsterdam. All botanical activities proceed from there. Here in Venice there's nothing on that scale. Our work here is, as it were, only on a local scale."

"And from Amsterdam—we will be heading all over the world?"

"Yes, that too. But beforehand you have to learn to move in the terrain that we create for you. That's our job."

I thought of Sarah. She had been able to survey the terrain like no one else—the natural terrain.

"Holographic terrain?"

"Yes, yes." He nodded emphatically. "We work on real reality, universal reality. And you have to be able to move with absolute certainty in it, so that we don't lose you. With absolute certainty."

"Like your finger here in the city."

"Ha! In any city," he replied with a chuckle.

Marcello stared, pale and somewhat disgusted, at the iridescent finger, which seemed to be leading a mysterious life of its own.

RENATA HAD WARNED me. "San Marco will overpower you," she had said. "You have to contemplate the details. Wherever you look, you see beauty, perfect craftsmanship, everything lovingly fashioned and imaginatively composed."

We strolled through the Merceria Orologio and suddenly it was before us.

It stunned me with its ornate magnificence, as can be mustered only by vast riches. An overflowing treasure chest, brimming with the spoils of countless plunders, a done-up pirate bride showered with jewelry, in whose décolletage four horses had been stuck for fun.

I stopped and caught my breath. The presence of that basilica was overwhelming.

Renata, who had stopped as well, nodded to me with a smile.

"I warned you," she said.

Kazuichi had led the way and was heading toward a café called Chioggia on the piazzale opposite the Palazzo Ducale, where two Japanese men and three Western Europeans sat, engaged in conversation. A tall redhaired man—probably in his mid to late thirties—seemed to be leading the discussion.

Kazuichi approached the table and was about to introduce us, when the redhead turned around, stood up, rushed over to me, and embraced me as if we were old friends.

"Hello, Domenica. How are you doing?"

I stiffened.

"Hey. Hold on," I said somewhat crossly, because I could never stand such intimacies. "Do we even know each other?"

"Oh," he said self-consciously with an unmistakably Dutch accent, rubbing the red stubble on his chin. "Things can change."

Oh, so you're that type, I thought. No, my dear, we've never met. I would remember that. I almost would have fallen for it, it had sounded so genuine.

He held out his large, slender hand to me. For a moment, I hesitated, and then I grasped it.

"Apparently, you already know my name. What's yours?"

"This is Frans van Hooft," said Kazuichi.

"Just Frans," he said, grinning at me.

He was still acting as if we were old friends.

"Frans works at our institute too," Kazuichi went on. "When he finds time for it."

He then introduced the others at the table. The other two Europeans were Dutch as well, one of them from the Christiaan Huygens Institute in The Hague, the other from the "CIA" Ernesto had mentioned. The two Japanese men at the table seemed to be from the local NNTR.

"Sometimes I'm . . . uh . . . a bit rash," Frans said apologetically, pushing over another table and some chairs so that we could sit down with the others.

"We've never met, right?" I asked, making sure.

"Who knows?" he said. "It's often strange. Maybe it comes with the times."

"The times?"

He shook his head. "Forgive me, Domenica. Just joking. Okay?"

"We can remain on a first-name basis, I have nothing against that," I said. "All of us here are, if I've understood that correctly. But permit me a question: Is that always your way?"

"Always," he assured me.

"But that doesn't suit you. Honestly."

"I thought nothing of it. You know, Holland is small. Everyone knows everyone there," he said, obviously straining for a plausible explanation.

I eyed him as he turned his attention to the others at the table. Frans was really good-looking. He was more than a head taller than I, perhaps six-two. He stooped somewhat, as is often the case with people who already stand out as children due to their above-average height. He was lean, almost bony, with gray-green eyes and medium-length reddish blond hair. His handshake had felt good—warm and strong, somehow confidence-inspiring. I didn't find him unpleasant—on the contrary—but something was off about him. His greeting had been genuine and spontaneous. Still . . . I was completely certain that I'd never seen him before, and yet he seemed somehow familiar to me. How was that possible? I was overcome with a feeling of uncertainty. Damn it, I said to myself, the guy actually succeeded in making me think about him.

"What would you like to drink?" he asked us when the waiter appeared. "It's on the city."

"Why is that?" I asked Kazuichi.

"When Frans is not traveling for us, he works for the city. Our institute is helping Venice rise to new glory. Restauro e Risanamento Conservativo," he declared loftily. "International funds are allocated for it. Venice has been broke for centuries. But life is good here."

I ordered a Campari soda with ice. On the table were half a dozen plastic bags with handwritten labels. *Larix*, I read, and *Quercus ilex*. In the bags were wood chips and small pieces of tree bark. One of the other two Japanese men at the table—polite, but rather taciturn—gathered them up and slipped them into his briefcase when he noticed my interest. He pretended to be quickly making room because the waiter was coming with our drinks. Then both of them gulped down their cups of coffee, stood up, nodded good-bye, and left. Kazuichi called something after them in Japanese.

"Do those two also work at the institute?" I asked.

Kazuichi shook his head. "No, they're also part of the NNTR, but deal with applied nanotechnology and work on the foundations."

"The most important thing," Frans was saying to his countrymen, "is to memorize well the relevant details—the most distinctive ones. Do you see the crenellations up there on the roof edge of the Palazzo Ducale?" he asked, pointing over his shoulder with his thumb. "How many are there?"

"Thirty-six," said one of the Dutch men, whom he had introduced as Kees.

"Yes, thirty-six," said the other—his name was Laurens—who had also looked up and counted silently.

"Wrong!" Frans said triumphantly. "Anyone want to bet?"

The two men gave each other bemused looks.

"You both made two mistakes. You counted the crenellations on the left side up to the gable—eighteen—and then simply extrapolated and doubled that. But you should have counted all the crenellations. For there are thirty-seven and not thirty-six. There's one more on the right side."

Everyone looked up and counted, including me. Indeed, he was right. On the left, between the dainty turret and the gable over the lion with its paw on an open book and a man kneeling before it: eighteen; to the right of it, nineteen.

"Why two mistakes?" Kees asked, frowning.

Frans turned to him and replied: "True mastery in architecture lies not in symmetry but in slight deviations from it. Some claim that that is what distinguishes human measure from that of mathematics and physics. But that's not true. Symmetry breaking is among the constitutive fundamental conditions of the universe. Without it our cosmos would not even exist; a nanosecond after its emergence, it would have dispersed into energy and sunk back into the quantum ocean."

"How come?" Marcello murmured with surprise.

"That's true," I said.

Frans looked at me with a smile and nodded.

"Not until the late twentieth century did physicists figure that out," he said. "Artists, however, seem to have always known it. On the buildings of famous architects you will always find such subtle asymmetrical displays of individuality. You just have to look closely." He leaned back. "I have no trouble with that. God—or my parents' genes—endowed me with a photographic memory. That's why I'm employed as a sort of traveling camera. And that will also be the job for which you will be trained," he added, turning his attention to everyone. "You always have to memorize precisely your immediate surroundings. Your life can depend on it."

Renata looked at me and shook her head questioningly.

"Falcotti said the same exact thing to me," I said, turning to her. "It seems to be a requirement for our job. Orientation in the terrain, he said."

Kazuichi suddenly chuckled. Did he find that funny? Frans had a serious look on his face. If this fellow, I thought, with his trained eye and his photographic memory, really believed he had met me before, then . . . Nonsense, it had only been a charming come-on after all. A joke.

"Are you familiar with Venice?" he asked me.

"No, I've never been here before. Disgraceful, right?"

"These days nothing is as easy as it was thirty years ago. Freedom of movement is obsolete in Europe. In the past—yes, that was wonderful."

"You're talking as if you had experienced it."

He nodded.

Above San Giorgio appeared the magnificent *Archduke Leopold* with its three horizontal bands of red, white, and red, flying over the lagoon on its way from Dubrovnik or Trieste to Madrid or Lisbon. The black double-eagle peered down threateningly. From the nose and the two passenger gondolas hung long, narrow pennants, which billowed in the wind. The turbines whined at full power.

"Venice is a beautiful city," Frans said with a sigh.

"And it's going to be even more beautiful, I've heard," I interjected.

He raised his shoulders and his hands as if he were fending off a compliment aimed at him personally. "We're all doing our best."

He tilted his head and smiled at me. "Might I help you explore the city? It would be my pleasure, Domenica."

I gave him a carefully measured smile and replied: "That's an offer I can't resist."

"Then we'll get started in the next few days, as soon as Professor Ishida allows us time for it."

"Frans knows the city like no other," Kazuichi asserted. "He was involved from the beginning as . . . uh . . . adviser on historical matters . . ."

He broke off when Frans cleared his throat, and gave a suddenly somewhat forced smile.

"Did you study art history?" I asked.

Frans cast a help-seeking glance at Laurens and Kees. "Actually not so much," he replied. "More . . . hm . . . technical history. History of architecture . . . along those lines."

"Frans specialized in wood," explained Kees, the young man from the

CIA. "Underneath us are millions upon millions of tree trunks. Wood from an area of more than a thousand miles—from the Venetian Alps, Slovenia, Istria, Croatia, Dalmatia, Albania, down the whole coast as far as Greece. Even from the Taurus Mountains and Lebanon. A restoration of the foundations can be successful only if we know exactly what wood was used in the construction of a palazzo or a house, so that the nanos can be programmed accordingly."

"Hey, that interests me," I interjected. "I'm a botanist. How do you determine that? The trunks have been stuck in the mud for centuries."

"More like silt and sand. Caranto they call it here."

"Fine. But they must be in stages of increasing decay. They must be petrified or reduced to rotten, salt-infused tissue."

Frans ran his hand uneasily across his forehead and puffed out his cheeks. "Samples are . . . uh . . . brought to the surface and analyzed."

"Like the samples your colleagues took with them?"

Frans nodded.

"Are you pulling our legs, or what?" I snapped. "That was fresh wood. Larch and holly oak."

Frans shrugged, but did not give a reply.

"No, no," Laurens, the other young Dutch man, reassured me. "Those are samples of the same wood that was used back then. The molecular structure is being investigated, the genome decoded. Then the Japanese construct their smart little nanos, which they set loose on the foundations to restore them cell by cell."

"I see," said Marcello.

Kazuichi raised his pathfinder finger and gazed at it. Frans stared at the table.

"All this will be explained to you in detail," he said. "But we don't want to preempt Professor Ishida. You have to understand that."

"I HAVE A feeling they're keeping something important from us. That makes me really edgy. I keep coming across strange incongruities. And they're feeding us hints, evasive answers, and lies."

Renata pushed the last of her linguine with mussels in lemon sauce back and forth and wound it around her fork. "They have instructions not to preempt their guru. Frans said so clearly. Professor Ishida insists on introducing us personally to the scope of our duties, cocky as he is. He'll make a show out of it, you'll see."

"My God, we signed a contract! Why won't anyone finally come clean with us?"

Renata shrugged. "I have a feeling we're still being tested. And as long as they're already paying our salary, I can wait and see what happens."

"Still . . ."

I looked up at the sky. It was already dark, even though it was still early evening. In the distance rumbled thunder; wind stirred. Somewhere a loose shutter clattered. A sheet, torn from a high clothesline between the windows, sailed over Campo San Lio like a harpooned ray and got caught, flapping, between wires.

"We'd better pay," I suggested. "Why don't they debit it from our IComs, like they do everywhere else?"

Renata laughed. "Not in the Olandese Volante, Domenica. They take only cash, just like a hundred years ago. And they still write the bill by hand. It's part of their image. But they also make the pasta by hand, just like a hundred years ago."

"That I have nothing against."

The other patrons had already departed or sought refuge inside the restaurant. Two waiters rescued the place settings and the utensils from the three short rows of tables that had been set up between the entrance and the pozzo on the small square. FREEDOM FOR FRIULI AND ALTO ADIGE, someone had sprayed with inelegant handwriting in ugly sulfur yellow on the gray sandstone of the pozzo. I beckoned to the waiter, placed the money on the tablecloth, and weighted down the bills with a plate.

"Do you think we'll get home dry?"

"If not, we'll have another espresso on Campo Formosa or at the Colleoni and wait until the storm has blown over."

We didn't make it. As we turned the corner onto Salizada San Lio, the storm broke.

"I know a shortcut!" Renata cried over the patter of the rain, and started to run. I followed her back around the corner and along Calle del Paradiso. Above me shutters were being hurriedly closed and latched. In front of me were steps; Renata had already climbed them and was hurrying down the other side. I lost sight of her. Above me, slanted to the left, spanning the street, I saw a slender filigree stone triangle. I hastened up the steps, blinded by the rain. It was a bridge. Under it the black water of a canal.

Suddenly I saw a face—only for the split second of a glaring lightning flash, followed immediately by a brief crash of thunder and darkness—the unearthly bearded face of an executioner under a turban looking at me indifferently. The executioner raised the ax . . .

I don't know whether I cried out in terror. I staggered with weak knees down the steps, did not dare to look up again, stumbled to the right along the Fondamenta and then to the left down a narrow street leading out onto Campo Santa Maria Formosa.

The square was deserted. Renata was nowhere to be seen. The raindrops made bubbles in the puddles. The Café da Egidio, which had been our destination, was unlit. Suddenly I was overcome by fear that I had veered off course and ended up in a strange world. I looked around. There was no one in sight on the vast square. I suddenly felt as if I were the last human being on the planet. Everyone else had abandoned it. The rain pounded on the tin roof of the kiosk and the porch overhang of the house to my right.

"Where are you?" shouted Renata. She appeared under the awning of the Al Burchiello.

She had covered her head with a plastic bag like a three-cornered hat and was waving. I rushed over to her, full of mortal fear.

"What happened?"

I slipped in a puddle. She caught me. Water ran down her face. I buried mine in her shoulder and sobbed, clinging to her as if she were the last handhold in an unknown universe.

"What's the matter, Domenica?"

"I met my executioner," I gasped.

"Your executioner?" she asked uncomprehendingly.

Renata held me steady with her small, strong hands and pushed me away from her until she could look into my face.

"He raised the ax."

"You're all mixed up, girl. Let's get a grappa."

The sharp taste did me good. Gradually I composed myself and stopped trembling. I closed my eyes and took a deep breath.

"That must have been the head over the gate at the Ponte del Paradiso. But it looks more dumb than threatening," Renata said with a laugh. "And how could it raise an ax? It's just a head."

"He raised the ax," I insisted.

IV

Letters from a Witch

The crux of evolutionist historicism: this past is not among the forebears of our present.

JEREMIAS WOLF

The cardinal counted the leather containers that were attached to the packsaddles of the beasts of burden. In Brussels he had managed to acquire state-of-the-art astronomical instruments and in Leuven several scholarly manuscripts, which he had had carefully packed for the journey. He reassured himself that everything was still there.

The morning dawned.

"Get up!" the captain of the city guard shouted.

Three darkly dressed figures, who had been cowering next to the landing, rose. Their clothing was dirty; their sidelocks curled from under their hats and hung down to their chests. The three men had been bound together with thin chains, the older one between the two younger ones. They wore wretched footgear; the toes of one of the men peeked out from his shoe. Two officers of the city guard drove them from behind with their pikes. The three prisoners eyed the weapons silently and impassively. They shivered in the morning cold.

"They've known for more than twenty years that they are not permitted to stay in the city at night," the captain declared to no one in particular, as if he had to excuse his official act, "but they try again and again." When no one paid attention to him, he barked: "Move! Or do I have to make you?"

"You don't have the say around here!" exclaimed the ferryman. "This ferry is from Deutz. We ferrymen are not subject to the city council of Cologne, but to the archbishop. Bear that in mind. Remove the chains from those men!"

At that moment, a rat crawled out from between the planks, an enormous animal of an unusual color—more grayish white with reddish spots than grayish brown. Sniffing, it scurried along the edge of the dock. One of the officers jabbed at it with his pike—playfully, more to scare it away than to impale it. Like lightning, the rat had jumped on the weapon, had climbed the shaft in no time, and stood a handbreadth from the officer's face. The rat then made a noise that sounded to the cardinal, from where he was standing, almost as if it had spoken, hissing a warning. But that was nonsense, of course.

The man recoiled in fright and threw the spear away from him. "The devil!" he cried, pale with horror, took a stumbling step back, and fell on his behind. "The devil!" The pike clattered to the ground, and the rat disappeared between the planks over the water.

The cardinal turned with surprise to the man, who sat on the ground and gawked around, his eyes wide with terror. "The devil?" the cardinal asked with curiosity, scrutinizing the man.

"Apologies, Your Eminence," said the captain, signaling to the officer with a brusque hand gesture to pull himself together and get up from his undignified position. He then got to work unlocking and removing the prisoners' chains. He threw them grumpily over his shoulder. Then he turned away and spat in the river.

Nicolaus scrutinized the prisoners, who seemed not to have even noticed the incident with the rat. They made an apathetic impression as the officers drove them onto the ferry with their pikes. He had endorsed the expulsion of the Jews from the city, but the measure had not brought about the hoped-for solution. The conflict between the council and the archdiocese continued to smolder, and Hussite-influenced preachers constantly rekindled the acrimonious atmosphere between the denominations and religious currents. For many, Rome's word carried no more weight. No one seemed to want to obey. The world was in a state of dissolution.

The cardinal nodded to his groom to lead the horses onto the ferry. Their hooves clip-clopped on the planks, and the man tethered the four animals to the railing side by side. They were uneasy and eyed anxiously the foaming dark water of the river. The ferryman shouted a command, and the ungainly, heavy vessel cast off. With their long oars the oarsmen pushed it off from the rocking, wooden dock. It started to turn. The river was already swollen, even though it was only mid-March. In the Black Forest and in the Vosges, the thaw had probably already begun.

"Row!" the ferryman shouted at his oarsmen. "Or do you want to dock in Düsseldorf instead of in Deutz? Row!"

The cardinal turned to his young companion, who wore a blue beret on his thick, shoulder-length hair, on which he had boldly stuck three quills as a sign of his occupation.

"Well?" asked Nicolaus, resuming the conversation that had been broken off for a while. "What else happened?"

"If I may, Your Eminence, since when does much happen in Cologne?" asked Geistleben, taking his knapsack off his shoulders and dropping it next to him on the floor. "A handful of little Roman monks arrived who fled from Constantinople, because the Turk is approaching the gates. They moan and ramble on about the end of the world and scrounge and beg for benefices. Oh yes, and a little witch is about to be put on trial. But you have surely heard about that."

"Not a word," Nicolaus replied, shaking his head with displeasure. "Is it spreading here too, that awful folly of torturing women and putting them to death?"

"Yes, certainly. It is getting worse everywhere. People are afraid of the spawn of the Antichrist, who gnaw at the limbs of the Church and eat their way deeper and deeper into its heart."

"What sort of talk is that, Geistleben? It is not the Antichrist who gnaws, it is greed that gnaws, it is vanity that gnaws, it is lust that gnaws in the flesh of our brothers and sisters."

"Well, indeed, that is your affair, noble lord. You undoubtedly understand more about it . . ."

"Quite true."

"But the East will fall, Your Eminence. Half the Empire—"

"What else was to be expected? I saw it with my own eyes, Geistleben. Catacombs full of writings, accumulated for centuries, with the knowledge of millennia from all over the world. But no one reads it; no one can even sort through it! Schemers and empty-headed scholars swarm over it like rats. Everyone gnaws at everyone else. Often at their own flesh. No wonder, then, the enemies are lurking. That's how it is everywhere. Here in our lands too. It was often painful, what I saw on my journey to Flanders and the Netherlands. It fills me with bitterness and rancor. As for the archbishop, however—we spoke daily during the concilium, but he did not mention a word about planning to hold a witch trial."

"Well, Your Eminence, he seems to be not at all so certain. He doesn't want to make any mistakes. Once before he has been at odds with the Pope, old von Moers. After almost forty years in office—simply excommunicated."

"That was Pope Eugene. He held it against him that he had voted against him at the Council of Basel."

"But that was a deep shock for him in his old age."

"Pope Nicholas reinstated him. He won't want for anything."

"Certainly not."

"When I stayed here on Christmas and New Year's Day, I heard rumors of a woman who had been found with a strange collection of herbs. Is she the one?"

"Yes, she is."

"And she is to be put on trial?"

"The archbishop has sought advice and support from the highest authority. A commission is to come from Rome, to investigate the case, whether devil's work is actually involved . . ."

"Why wasn't the woman forced to renounce all vengeance and banished from the city, as usual?"

"There were inflammatory speeches. A young priest was very active, a zealot from Swabia, Bartholomäus von Dillingen is his name—he is a preacher at St. Maria im Kapitol. People call him 'Witch Bart.' If I may, Your Eminence, an evil snooper. He watched her every step for weeks. After his sermons, an angry crowd always proceeds to the Old Market square and demands that she be made short work of. She was ultimately turned over to the episcopal judge, for the archbishop is insisting on the main jurisdiction, as the law would have it. He had her interrogated. She was found guilty, but he isn't doing anything. He's biding his time."

"What were the results of the interrogations?"

"A serf who encountered her in the summer on the Moselle testified that, without touching him, she used devilish powers to cast him to the ground with such force that he was black and blue all over his body and felt pains in his chest for weeks. He heard laughter that sounded like the bleating of a goat and could smell the definite stink of sulfur. A citizen with whom she lodged testified that she told her that one could fly from Cologne to Rome in an hour. And under torture she spoke heedlessly. She confessed to having flown through the air herself. It was the herbs, though, that determined the outcome."

"How so?"

"Over the whole summer she had gathered a collection of seeds— kernels from grain and fruit, blossoms from all sorts of flowers and plants. For medicinal purposes, she claimed. These seeds were sorted neatly into little canvas pouches and labeled and inscribed with Latin words. But these words were incomprehensible. A sort of secret system of classification, Your Eminence, which . . . well, so it seemed to me, is strangely coherent, but of which no one has ever heard, as the professors of medicine brought in from the university confirmed. This system points to heretical, arcane knowledge and cannot possibly be of godly origin . . ."

"Of devilish origin, then . . ."

"The commission of professors came to that conclusion. The young woman lied through her teeth. Went so far as to claim that the Holy Father himself sent her to collect little seeds and flowers."

"The Holy Father?"

"Yes, in order to save Creation, she asserted."

The cardinal shook his head. "She is surely confused. An unfortunate creature. The woman should not be treated this way. Such a thing is shameful."

"Verily, I look at it the same way. Especially as she has more education than can be ascribed to the devil, or—if I may—to the archbishop, for that matter."

"How so? Is she a nun? From what order?"

"I don't think so. It's odd . . . no one who has sworn a vow of humility would speak like that. And her Latin, oh my . . ."

"A noblewoman then?"

"Not a chance!"

"A simple woman? You are making me curious."

"You will be even more surprised, Your Eminence, when I tell you that she wrote you letters. It emerges from them that she seems to be quite well acquainted with you."

"What do you mean, she is acquainted with me? Is she from here? From Koblenz? From the Moselle?"

"No, certainly not. No one really knows where she is from. Some claim that she comes from Amsterdam, others that she is from Sweden, was the assistant of a court physician there. Her appearance, her speech point more to a Roman, perhaps Florence, Siena . . . who knows? But definitely not from the countryside. By no means. She is educated. Knows things even I have never heard of. At times, I think she came . . ."

"Yes?"

". . . from another world."

"You mean, from distant lands?"

"Very distant lands, Your Eminence. Of which we still know nothing."

"A sibyl perhaps, from the Orient?"

The scholar shook his head hesitantly. "Those prophetesses speak obscurely. She speaks more with the light of certainty. It seemed to me—how should I put it—as if the darkness were in our heads more than in her words, if you understand what I mean, Your Eminence."

The cardinal lowered his gaze thoughtfully. "From where might she know me? Has she ever crossed paths with me? Has she spoken with me? In Rome perhaps? But I don't remember ever having met a woman of that sort . . ."

"It does not seem so. I don't think she knows you by sight. It is more— how should I put it—as if she were acquainted with your writings and with you as a very famous man."

"You're speaking in riddles, Geistleben. How could she be acquainted with my writings? And me, a very famous man? That I am not, God knows. She must be confused."

"It would indeed be no surprise. She has, after all, spent months in the dungeon. The icy cold has afflicted her. She is sick and desperate. Without friends or acquaintances."

"Did she confide in you personally?"

"No. I caught only fleeting glimpses of her now and then, when she was brought to an interrogation. I read the transcripts."

"You were permitted to see them?"

"Well . . . as a scribe in the chancery of the archbishop I could not help taking notice of them. I worked for him for almost a year. I write quickly and largely flawlessly, you should know. But now boredom drives me onward."

"The letters to me . . . ?"

"Are in the records for the commission from Rome. They will—I assume—eventually be delivered to you, as soon as the case is concluded. But so that you would not have to wait too long, I've taken the liberty of copying for you one or two letters that came into my view, Your Eminence."

"So you copied documents that are under lock and key and—I presume—classified . . . ?"

"Well, apparently not so classified. Far more than that, they are incomprehensible, mysterious—but extremely remarkable."

"You are carrying the copies with you?"

"Yes, indeed. I fetched them from the hiding place as the synod members set off and your departure too was approaching. I hastened after you to be on the ferry with which you are crossing."

"And intend to sell the copies to me now, I assume, after you have sufficiently piqued my curiosity."

"Stop it, Your Eminence! You have a reputation as an experienced merchant, especially when it comes to rare items."

"Copies of obscure letters from an alleged little witch, who, in a state of confusion, claimed to know me. Indeed, Geistleben, a rare item. I have to grant you that."

"I foresaw it: There would be no chance of haggling with you, Your Eminence. I will give them to you as a gift. You are known throughout the land as a generous man. Your magnanimity is proverbial."

"Now, now! Do not mock. I know what people say about me."

"Nothing could be further from my mind! You will certainly repay a poor little scribe and traveling scholar, noble lord."

"How about it, Geistleben? I saw you working diligently during the synod. I can always use a scribe who is quick with the quill and has a sharp mind. Good at copying writings of all sorts and tongues."

"Many thanks, Your Eminence, for your confidence and your magnanimous offer, but I am drawn away. I would like to finally move on. First Strasbourg, then Paris, to study there the Lullian art of which I have heard."

"You mean that Majorcan's art of creating knowledge by means of a little mechanism—click, clack—without exerting the mind and calculating—from one to two to three—the wisdom of God's Creation?"

"If I may, Your Eminence, it might, I think, be the true future of all philosophizing: counting, measuring, weighing, calculating. Not the errors, superior attitudes, and disputes over authorities of the past and present. Computing! The little witch writes it at one point: You will one day be credited with having advanced this very thing."

"Me? That is as bold as it is incredible, Geistleben. True, I have—it was a long time ago, I think it was in the year '26, when I was still Giordano Orsini's secretary—examined the work of Raymundus Lullus. While rummaging around here in Cologne, I found it among many other writings. The cardinal pointed out to me that there was an extensive, almost entirely unexplored library here. He had a nose for such things."

"I too discovered it here. It intrigued me."

"I made excerpts back then, but I never found time to devote myself seriously to that *Ars Magna*, as its creator so vainly called it. Only I have reservations about ceding the practice of philosophy to the mechanics and clockmakers. Although . . . Well, indeed, at the Camaldolese monastery Val di Castro, after a dispute with Toscanelli, I wrote down a few thoughts on weighing, which . . . I will delve deeper into it, when time permits . . . But no, how would that woman . . ."

"Does anyone know what the future will bring, Your Eminence? Besides God, perhaps the devil . . . and a little witch now and then?"

"Moor the vessel!" the ferryman shouted to the oarsmen.

On the riverside two young men had hastened over and caught the lines that were thrown to them. Horses were harnessed, a dozen or more, to tow the heavy vessel upstream to the upper dock, for the leeway was surely three thousand feet. The breath of the animals steamed in the cool morning air. Up on the bank Jewish children stood in the wet grass. Wrapped in rags—barefoot. They followed the horses at a proper distance, for the towing men swung their whips widely. A pale sun rose between cloud banks and turned animals and people into gold-enveloped silhouettes.

"I hope to be in Rome again by summer, Geistleben," said the cardinal. "If your wanderlust should lead you there, you would be a welcome guest."

"You are too kind, Your Eminence. I am honored by your offer."

"You would then have to tell me about the Lullian art, if it has been taught to you in Paris."

"It will be my pleasure, Your Eminence."

The groom led the animals by the reins up the dock, held the stirrup, and helped the Cusan mount. The cardinal held up the tied-up scroll with the letters.

"Thank you!" he called to the scholar, who had shouldered his knapsack. "God bless you."

"Farewell, Your Eminence."

"We set off," the cardinal commanded, taking the reins. "I want to be in Heisterbach with the Cistercians for sext and in Andernach for vespers. The day is short, and I hate journeying in the dark."

The groom nodded, leaped into the saddle, and fastened together the reins of the pack animals. Then they rode off, leaving behind the voices of the children ringing out in the cool morning air.

A couple of geese flew low over the reeds along the river. The heavy, rhythmic beat of their wings sounded like the lusty moans of two lovers. The groom turned his face away and grinned.

"OH MY! I beg your pardon, Your Eminence. We were not expecting you. We thought you were still staying in Cologne. Oh God, I was planning to go to the market tomorrow morning to buy some things to which you are partial, as I know from the past. Oh, Your Eminence. What am I doing standing here before you? Please . . ."

"But Katrin! Are you seriously going to sink to your knees before me? Stand up and let me embrace you. And don't call me 'Your Eminence'! What did you always call me when I was still dean at St. Florin?"

"I wouldn't dare."

"Nico, you called me, and you were like a mother to me. Let us stick with that, Katrin."

"But you have become such an exalted man. You come right after the Holy Father, says Helwicus."

"Well, isn't it so?" the dean broke in. "It is said that Pope Nicholas is your friend and values your advice."

"Indeed, we see eye to eye in many respects."

"What am I doing here?" the old housekeeper lamented, spreading her arms. "Completely unprepared. I can offer a chicken, roasted in butter and rosemary, but cold. The bread is fresh."

"I'm not hungry. We did not set off from Andernach until after lunch today. In the morning I had to dictate an urgent letter to the chapter of St. John's in Osnabrück. But I'm thirsty. I could certainly do with a glass of wine."

"Wine from home?"

"Yes. Do you have some from my father's vineyards?"

"Indeed, we do. Every year your brother Johannes sends us a tun down the Moselle. It is the best wine far and wide."

"Then bring me a flagon of that, Katrin, so that I may at least taste a mouthful of home."

"You mean, you're not going to ride up to Kues?" asked the dean.

"I would be delighted to, but I don't have the time, Helwicus. I'm expected in Frankfurt. And next month I shall be in Brixen once again. I would have liked to ride up to Kues to check on things and see how far the plans for the foundation have come to fruition, but I have trustworthy people under my brother's supervision who are advancing my cause and managing it well."

"I heard the same."

"Did you also hear about the witch they plan to bring to trial in Cologne?"

"Yes, but only vaguely. There are many rumors going around in Cologne. I think it will turn out the same way as in the year '46 with that sorceress. The city council had her banished. A lenient sentence for the woman."

"This time, perhaps not, the way things stand."

"Maybe so. I heard a conflict broke out between the archbishop and the council. Tilman told me about it; he is on hand as an adviser to him. Now they are waiting for a commission from Rome to attend to the case."

"This woman wrote me letters."

"Did I hear you correctly? She wrote *you* letters?"

"Yes, look! Now I will finally take some time to read them," said the cardinal, tossing the tied-up scroll onto the large table. "They are copies. One of the archbishop's scribes gave them to me. Geistleben is his name. He and I crossed to Deutz on the same ferry."

The cardinal took a penknife and cut the strings, filled the goblet that had been set down before him with wine, and drank from it in small, sampling sips.

"The wine is good," he said, nodding appreciatively; then he began to read.

Later Katrin brought him a candle. And when it had burned down, she lit a second one for him and placed additional candles nearby.

And Nicolaus Cusanus read and read.

"YOU HAVE NOT even touched the chicken, my lord. I knew that it was not to your taste."

"No, Katrin," the cardinal said, lost in thought. "That is, yes." He turned away. "East of Cattenom the land is black, deep into Bohemian and Polish regions," he murmured, "as can be seen from orbit."

"I will bring you warm milk."

"Is Helwicus up yet?"

"Yes. Shall I summon him?"

"Please do."

"Do you know where Cattenom is, Helwicus?" he asked the dean.

"Oh, I believe there is a hamlet by that name up at the top of the Moselle, in Lotharingia, not far from Metz. I'm not certain, but Adrien, the fisherman who brings us his catch every Thursday evening, comes from that area. I will ask him."

"In Lotharingia?" the cardinal repeated reflectively. "East of Cattenom the land is black . . ."

"I don't understand."

The cardinal stuck a fingernail under the hardened wax of the burned-down candle and detached it from the table.

"Mysterious, all this," he murmured.

"What the little witch has written to you?"

"This is no witch. It is a strange woman. Mad, perhaps, but knowledgeable and acutely perceptive. She foresees a future we cannot even imagine."

The cardinal looked exhausted after staying awake all night. He turned to the window and rubbed his chin. Day had come, but dense mist veiled the river, so that the opposite bank could not be seen.

"'East of Cattenom the land is black,' she writes, 'deep into Bohemian and Polish regions, as can be seen from orbit.' — What does she mean by 'orbit'? The circle of the Earth? A circle above the Earth? It would have to be a bird that could soar as high as the sphere of the moon in order to see that far. An angel . . . ?"

At a loss, the cardinal shook his head. "The black blade that had pierced the heart of the continent." The plague? A conflagration? A festering wound of the earth itself?

The Cusan looked out over the meadows around the mouth of the Moselle. They stretched almost down to Andernach, a vast wetland from which myriad mosquitoes swarmed up in the summer. A nuisance for man and beast, as he recalled. What a carefree time that had been, when he had still performed his duty as a dean here at St. Florin!

Mist rose like smoke from extinguished fires. An army camp of ghosts, which had moved on through time. The cardinal hunched his shoulders as if a chill had seized him.

"Todi," he murmured.

"I beg your pardon?" the dean asked in confusion.

"She writes: 'Beware of Todi.' What is supposed to await me there? What does she mean by that?"

He turned around decisively.

"Frankfurt will have to wait. I will send a messenger to say that I will be coming three or four days later. Today I will ride back to Cologne. I have to speak with this woman. It should not be judges questioning her, but scholars. It ought to be determined where she comes from and with whom she has studied. She must come from a part of the world of which we know nothing, but whose wise men certainly have knowledge of us. This case is too important to be left to the council of the Cologne citizenry or Dietrich von Moers. I have to talk to the archbishop, have to urge him not to do anything overhasty. This case must be decided in Rome."

"Very well, Your Eminence," said the dean.

"Katrin, summon the archbishop's groom for me, who rode with me yesterday. He is to saddle the horses and accompany me back to Cologne."

V

Nanos Machinulis

The living world is dying; the natural economy is crumbling beneath our busy feet. We have been too self-absorbed to foresee the long-term consequences of our actions, and we will suffer a terrible loss unless we shake off our delusions and move quickly to a solution. Science and technology led us into this bottleneck. Now science and technology must help us find our way through and out.

EDWARD O. WILSON

There are still a lot of tourists here," I said.

"But not half as many as there used to be. Only about twenty percent of the applications are granted," Frans replied.

"Why don't they close off Venice entirely, as long as it's a construction site?"

"What would the people who still reside here live off?" He spread his arms. "There are only fifty thousand of them anyhow. It used to be four times as many. It would mean decline. The social structure would break down. The city must live on."

"But it's sick."

"All the more reason we have to make sure it lives on. Certainly, it could be turned into a museum, but that wouldn't be Venice anymore, but rather a sort of Disneyland that is opened in the morning and in which the lights are turned out in the evening."

We walked to the Rialto and took the vaporetto. The sun was shining, but it was low in the southwest, and the air on the water was damp and cold. Some of the palazzi along the Canal Grande looked as if they had been hoisted off their foundations, those had been replaced with new ones, and the buildings had then been put back on them. The stone steps and piers looked new; the grime and the slippery growth of algae had disappeared.

Those that had not yet undergone nanotechnological renewal now looked all the worse.

At San Stae we got off and walked along the salizzada, bearing right where the street opened onto a jumble of little bridges crisscrossing a system of branching canals. Frans suddenly stopped and looked around. Then he walked down to the water and scrutinized the walls just above the surface. On the damp brick facade of the house on the small square someone had sprayed graffiti: a green buglike or crustacean monster with a snake head, from whose mouth a forked tongue darted out between sharp, bloody fangs. The eyes glowed malevolently in bright red. Above it were the words NO NANOS! and below it ITALIA NOSTRA. I climbed down to Frans, who was crouching on a step just over the water.

"Do you see that?" he asked.

"What's that?" I asked, disgusted. "Looks like pus."

He raised a finger. "Those are several billion dead nanos."

"Several *billion?*"

I looked around in the indistinct glow of twilight and saw that all along the waterline between the stones of the houses' foundations poured slime the yellow of broom flowers, as if the old walls were suppurating.

He activated his ICom. "I'm here on Campo San Boldo. Someone released something here. Yes, it looks to me like quite a lot. It could spread during the flooding tonight through the western canals. I think you should send a few rush-troopers here right away."

"Rush . . . ?"

"R.U.S.H. That's the NNTR's rapid response team," he explained, turning to me. "The name comes from their rucksack helicopters." Frans bent over, scratched with his fingernail at the sticky secretion, and sniffed it. He screwed up his face.

"Chloroacetamide," he said. "The usual. Probably forty, fifty liters."

He looked up at the facade.

"Parrocchia San Giacomo da l'Orio. Yes, you can land here. The square is big enough. Pozzo in the center. No problem. Over."

He wiped his finger with a tissue.

"Those idiots use this to kill off the nanos that are supposed to stabilize the wood of the pylons," he explained. "It takes a great deal of effort to develop those tiny biotechnicians. Each one is a specialist in a very particular species of wood. It responds to very specific genetic structures. They give it the signal that activates its programming. And that tells it what it has to do."

"The genes of holly oaks and larches?"

"Theoretically, yes. But there are deviations, depending on where the wood comes from, where it grew. In addition, at times of intense construction activity those wood species were very expensive. So many master builders secretly mixed other types of wood with them. That's what makes the reconstruction so difficult."

"How do you know all this?" I asked him.

"I've been with the organization for six years."

"But you're not a nanotechnician."

"No. Nor a lignologist. Unfortunately. More a sort of traveler."

"Dealing in wood?"

"Something like that."

"I thought you were an architectural historian. So you claimed, at least."

"The two are not mutually exclusive, are they?"

"You're making fun of me."

"No, Domenica. I . . ."

"Listen, Frans. We really don't have to deceive each other. I don't know what this is about. I've signed a contract as a botanist to participate in an environmental project. Okay? But for more than a month we, my fellow students and I, have been confronted with nothing but strange secretiveness. That's frustrating. We're kept in the dark, put off, fed half-truths, presumably even lied to at times . . ."

"No, Domenica. To make it clear between us once and for all: There are no half-truths here and definitely no lies. Has it ever crossed your mind that all this might be part of your training?"

"A test of our patience?"

"Something like that. In any case, the selection process is not yet complete. The reason for the strict secrecy is that there's a great deal of extremely sensitive data in connection with the Rinascita Project, which is not intended for public consumption. It must under no circumstances reach the media or be made public, because it would change our world from the ground up."

That sounded somehow familiar to me. I remembered the strange call from Bernd in Rome. Had some sort of conspiracy of silence been established? But something like that could not be sustained. In the long run, it was impossible. Unless . . . I suddenly had the sensation that I could no longer think clearly.

"That all sounds pretty dramatic. Don't you think?" I said.

"It *is* dramatic, Domenica, and could be really dangerous in its ramifications. Besides, it's not my job to brief you on your mission. Professor Ishida reserves that for himself alone. But he will do so only after your conditioning is complete."

"You mean our brainwashing?"

"God, no! I said 'conditioning.' It's in all our interest that as few people as possible know about our missions. It's a responsibility that sometimes demands everything from us."

"Diving and scraping wood samples from the foundations of the buildings?"

Frans looked at me uncomprehendingly, then laughed out loud and put his arm around me. Why did that touch seem so familiar to me?

Suddenly I heard a soft whirring above us and saw four figures in yellow protective suits approaching from the east with gleaming rotors strapped to their backs. Two unmanned aircraft with equipment followed. They landed between the houses.

"Let's get something to eat," said Frans.

We had strolled down narrow streets and stepped out onto the large Campo San Giacomo. We crossed the square, heading toward a trattoria: Capitan Uncino. The sign displayed a musketeer who had with a lunge speared three fish on his sword; his raised left arm was adorned with a golden hook, which had replaced the severed hand.

The establishment was almost empty. It seemed to have seen better days, but it looked cozy. In the back, next to the entrance to the kitchen, was a man-sized grandfather clock with a semicircular top and a face made of wrought brass. The hands pointed to a quarter to six.

The owner, a round, almost bald man, emerged from the kitchen and raised his fleshy paw in greeting. He wore a shirt with wide armholes and had tied an ugly gray plastic apron around his belly, on which blood and the remains of fish innards were stuck.

"Hello, Frans!" he exclaimed. "Where did you find this pretty little angel?"

"She only recently came down from the sky, and is named Domenica."

"Hello, Domenica. Good evening."

The owner returned to the kitchen, warbling to himself. A young woman served us. She had black-painted lips and short hair dyed carrot-red, which looked like the plastic fur of a cuddly toy. Her black jeans stretched across her ample behind.

When we had eaten our pasta, the owner came to our table and greeted us with a handshake. His plump face shone; on his pale forehead below his receding hairline beads of sweat stood close together like bloated transparent leeches.

"I assume you will have the fish I recommend to you as always," he said to Frans, giving him a friendly pat on the shoulder. "Today I have something very special for you."

He went into the kitchen and came back with a greasy plastic bag. He had put on a pair of kitchen gloves. Carefully he pulled out a fish about a foot long and placed it in front of Frans on a napkin.

"Look at this beautiful lucerna," he said. "Would you rather have it grilled or steamed?"

The fish was still alive, but its movements were somehow limited. It didn't wriggle, as one expects from freshly caught fish, but writhed sluggishly, as if in slow motion. The young woman who was about to set our table let out a soft cry, dropped the little basket of bread and utensils on the table, and strode hurriedly to the entrance on her platform shoes.

"Stay here!" the owner shouted brusquely.

She stopped, but remained at the door.

The fish's dorsal fin was erect and looked like a serrated blade. It emitted a soft groan that sounded almost like a grumble. I extended a finger.

"Don't touch!" Frans said hastily.

He himself seemed to have no inhibition, pulled a small knife with a curved blade from his pocket, flipped it open, and positioned the fish in front of him. The gills opened and closed in a slowed-down rhythm. The mouth worked hard; the eyes were clouded by a gray-white haze. Frans stuck the blade in under the gills. The body tissue visibly resisted his efforts, even though the knife seemed to be very sharp. At first blood still came out, but at the belly the flesh seemed to have the consistency of hard rubber and farther back of synthetic resin, which a knife could no longer handle. Frans's fingers and the blade were covered with a glittering film, which was reminiscent of gold leaf particles.

Smiling to himself, the owner had followed his efforts. "Well," he said. "Isn't it a fine specimen?"

Some of the patrons who had since arrived had approached our table and were watching. Their faces reflected a mixture of repugnance and curiosity.

"You're making a real mess here with that nano stuff for your restauratio," said the owner.

An old man with a white mustache nodded grimly.

Frans rubbed together the tips of his thumb and forefinger, with which he had held the fish in place, as if he were checking whether his skin was already forming a hardening layer as well. His fingers looked as if they were gilded.

"Programming glitches can occur and mutations can always occur, Paolo," he replied. "The NNTR made that clear from the beginning. The city council assessed the risk and agreed. Didn't it?"

"The city council," one of the patrons snorted disdainfully. "That pack of good-for-nothings!"

"All bought by the Japanese," another grumbled.

"The Japs shouldn't even bother to show their faces around here. I'll throw them out," the owner asserted.

"They have no business here. That's the truth," someone said, and several others expressed their support: "Absolutely! You're right, Paolo!"

"Don't be unfair, people," said Frans. "The scientists are doing their best. The water of the lagoon is still quite dirty. Things like this can happen. It's unavoidable. Most of the mutants are harmless, but there are now and then aberrations—"

"Aberrations!" The old man with the white mustache snorted angrily; he turned around to his wife over his shoulder and grumbled: "He said 'aberrations,' did you hear?"

"—which are capable of turning a healthy lucerna into a polymeric imitation wood."

"Or worse!" grumbled the old man, defiantly striking the floor with his cane.

"Enzo," his wife admonished softly.

"Polymeric imitation wood," murmured the owner, poking the fish, which despite its opened abdominal cavity was still writhing sluggishly. "If only it were real gold. I paid cash for it."

"The fish dies of internal ossification," Frans told me. "While its body goes through an astonishing transubstantiation from a living organism into a practically indestructible artifact."

"Then bring this artifact to the Japs, so that they can break their teeth on it," said Paolo.

I remembered the paperweight I had seen on Falcotti's desk at the university in Rome. Hadn't he said that a friend had brought it back for him from Venice?

"And what was with that boy in the spring?" the old man asked; he raised his voice and struck the table leg with his cane. "Did he undergo an astonishing transubstantiation too?"

"Enzo," his wife moaned. "Please!"

But he continued undeterred and snorted: "The little one was dead in an hour!" His wife placed her hand calmingly on his arm, but he shook it off. "That's a load of crap!"

"That was a real killer," Frans conceded. "It took the boy's life."

"Yes, that's right," the old man said to me. "That's exactly right."

The waitress peered with horror over three tables at the fish, whose mouth opened and closed in slow motion. Frans wrapped it in the napkin and pushed it aside.

"And who will pay me for it?" asked the owner, gesturing to it with a nod.

"The NNTR will pay you ten times what you paid for it," said Frans.

"I don't want anything from them."

"Be sensible. It's important for the research, so that at least this mutation doesn't occur again in the future."

"Then take it with you. I'll give it to you as a gift."

"And tell those Japs, young man, to make sure that face no longer appears over Murano," said the old man with the mustache. "Why do they do that? The Austrians won't stand by and watch much longer. They'll bomb us."

"Come now, Enzo."

"They've bombed Venice before," he snapped at his wife. "They were aiming for Santa Lucia. Did they hit it? Of course not. Instead of the train station those idiots damaged Gli Scalzi."

He pursed his lips as if to spit.

His wife grabbed him by the sleeve and tried halfheartedly to pull him away, but he stood like a statue.

"The Austrians won't put up with that indefinitely. Take it from me. They won't hesitate for long. With that monkey making grimaces at them, that grinning gook? They have air sovereignty over Venice. Yes, they do. They already fly their stupid airships much too low over our city as it is. That *Prince Eugene* and the *Archduke Maximilian Franz* and the *Empress Maria Theresia* and the *Archduchess Maria Amalia*"—and with each name he struck the table leg with his cane—"and the *Grand Duke Leopold* and the *Kaiser Joseph* and the *Archduke Leopold Wilhelm* and the *Kaiser Franz* and whatever the names of all those Habsburg cretins were . . ."

"Enzo," his wife pleaded, tugging at his sleeve, but he seemed to be firmly embedded in concrete next to our table.

"They don't do that for fun," he asserted emphatically. "They want to humiliate us once again. You don't believe it, young woman? Let me tell you: That ridiculous face over Murano has got to go! Or else we'll all pay the price."

He slammed his cane into the cement floor and trudged with a grimly raised chin to the door.

"Tsk, tsk, tsk," his wife whispered apologetically, hurrying after him.

We watched the two of them leave, and when the door had closed, everyone burst out laughing. People turned back to their tables.

"That's Enzo," said the owner, wiping the tears from the corners of his eyes.

The tufts of thick hair sprouting from his shoulders and from the pale skin of his neck shone like black steel wool. He smelled of grilled fish, garlic, and sweat.

"I'm sure Paolo also has fish that have not yet turned into artifacts," Frans said to me, running his finger down the menu, which lit up at his touch and showed underwater pictures of fishing grounds.

"I'll just have a salad," I declared hastily.

As Frans carved up his grayling and drizzled lemon over it, he gestured with a nod to my salad, in which I was poking around, and said with a smile: "That won't protect you from breaking your teeth—on the contrary. The nanos were actually developed for plant tissue, to turn decaying wood into synthetic resin."

I put aside the utensils. "Do you want to completely spoil my appetite?" I asked him.

"Sorry. That was thoughtless of me. You need not be afraid, Domenica. Gastric acid destroys them. It's even more harmful to them than coldness."

"Is that why that ice barrier was built around the city?"

Frans nodded. "So that the fish in the Adriatic don't all turn into plastic. But seriously. Only with those tailor-made little machines can this city be saved. With them the millions of tree trunks that were rammed into the caranto are to be turned into solid synthetic resin pillars, which will last for a few millennia. If the experiment fails, Venice will go under."

"Apparently, that comes at a price."

He shrugged and looked around uneasily.

"What was the story with the boy?" I asked.

"That happened over in the Giardini," Frans explained in a soft voice. "The boy was about twelve. He had gotten something in his eye while swimming and cried out in pain. Then he lost consciousness. Before they had gotten him to the eye clinic in Vicenza, all that was left of the eye was slime, and before they had prepared him for emergency surgery, the boy was dead. When they opened the skull during the autopsy, the brain was nothing but a crumbly mass—like old Stilton cheese. That mutant had multiplied explosively in the vitreous and had entered the brain via the tissue of the optic nerve. They immediately cremated the corpse and quarantined everyone who had had anything to do with him. The whole area was in a state of agitation. Thank God nothing like that has happened again since."

"There's one thing I don't understand: These nanos are machines. How can they mutate?" I asked.

"Don't be fooled by the term 'machine,'" Frans explained. "At this scale, organic and inorganic structures behave the same way. It's a sort of molecular mechanics on the basis of electric charge distributions; the functions are identical in both cases—and the malfunctions too. That's why it would be a catastrophic mistake to use nanos in the radioactively contaminated areas of Central Europe, as people are always demanding. It would be an absolute disaster! That would result in more than just a few plastic fish. Killer mutants would burst forth and run amok, which we would be powerless to oppose." He drained his glass. "The NNTR is in the process of developing improved emergency brakes, but there are limits to that. And with such programs malfunctions can occur. Matter is simply something elastic, mutable. And that goes even more for living matter, or else there would be no life. But I don't need to tell you that."

I pointed to the napkin with the dying fish.

"What does such an emergency brake look like in this case?" I asked. "After all, you have to be able to pull it before an afflicted organism escapes into the oceans."

"A suicide program. A sort of apoptosis, programmed cell death."

Frans placed his wrist flat on the table and slid back the protective cover of his Scarabeo, opened a program, and turned on the holoprojection.

"Here you have the record of an emergency braking," he explained, as a small chart appeared and filled up with signs. "In purely statistical terms, between a thousand and ten thousand mutations occur per second in a cubic yard of water. Depending on environmental conditions."

"So many?"

"That's a very low percentage. You have to consider that in a cubic yard of lagoon water, about sixty to eighty billion lins are active."

"Lins?"

"Long-term stable intelligent nano structures, as the techs call their fancy little machines. The mutation is expressed in faulty readings during the structure recognition in the molecular architecture. The breakdown is caused by toxins in the water: industrial effluent from Mestre, fertilizers, herbicides, pesticides, plasticizers, detergents; on top of that, there's solar radiation in the UV range, penetrating cosmic rays, radioactivity.

"Here you can identify an emerging mutant. First error clusters form: the tector, the little nano machine, no longer clearly recognizes its tectoplast— what it is supposed to reshape. Here you see the error accumulation shooting up—exponentially. The error clusters expand explosively. It has mutated to the extent that it mistakes an incorrect tectoplast for the correct one and reshapes it—as in the case of our fish. That's why, before it reaches that point, the suicide program must be activated. Schematically, that looks like this."

In the holograph appeared a bright red scrolling script.

⇐ *TECTOPLAST NEGATIVE*
→ *ERROR*
⇒ *TECTOPLAST NEGATIVE*
→ *ERROR—ERROR*
⇐ *TECTOPLAST NEGATIVE*
→ *ERROR—ERROR—ERROR*
⇐ *TECTOPLAST NEGATIVE*
→ *ERRORCLUSTER—ESCAPE!*
⇐ *TECTOPLAST POSITIVE NEGATIVE POSITIVE*
    NEGATIVE
→ *ERRORCLUSTER EXPONENTIAL—ESCAPE! ESCAPE!*
⇓ **ESCAPE**
⇓ **EXCAPE**
⇓ **EXIAPE**
⇓ **EXIAUS**
⇓ **EXITUS**

⇓ *EXIT*
⇓ *EX*
⇓ ...
⇐ *REPROGRAMMING?*
→ *FAILED*
⇐ *EXITUS*
→ *POSITIVE*

"That's the schema, but of course this dialogue is conducted in the molecular language of chemistry. That alone is comprehensible to the tectors," Frans explained.

In the meantime, the restaurant was almost completely full. Some patrons were looking over at us with curiosity. Frans turned off his Scarabeo and lifted the napkin in which the mutated fish was wrapped. The mouth was still opening and closing as if in extreme slow motion. You had to look really closely to perceive the movement. The golden shimmer now covered almost the whole body. Only the ugly head still had its reddish color. Even the shed blood had a golden finish.

"In this case the suicide program failed," I noted.

Frans shrugged and replied: "The mutant would still have to surmount the ice barrier and the floodgates of the lagoon to make it into the open sea."

"Is there a danger that it could succeed?"

"The chances are extremely slim. The alternative would be a comprehensive killing program. That would mean destroying quadrillions of good hardworking nanos that had done nothing wrong. Mass murder. And the project would be set back months. The fishermen should finally stop casting nets in the lagoon. The city rented expensive fishing grounds beyond the litorali to compensate them."

Paolo, who was just passing the table after taking an order, stopped. He must have heard what Frans had just been saying, for he pursed his lips with amusement, gestured with a nod to the fish in the napkin and said: "I'll bring you a clean plastic bag in a moment. Then you can take your gift with you. I forgot to tell you, my friend: It was caught south of Sottomarina, below the third sluice, near the mouth of the Adige."

Frans glanced at me and puffed out his cheeks. "Oh, shit," he whispered.

When we left, the grandfather clock still indicated that it was a quarter to six.

"It stopped," I said.

Frans cast a glance at it. "Yes, but that was a hundred years ago."

ON THE RIALTO dock, Frans fished a pair of rolled-up plastic boots out of his shoulder bag and pulled them over his shoes and pants.

"You have to get these," he said. "The most important piece of equipment here. At night, the streets are usually flooded."

"Despite the Lido Dam?"

"For more than fifty years the system of locks has been a matter of dispute. At the same time, the level of the Adriatic has been continuously rising for a hundred years. *Acqua alta*—the people here have learned to live with that. But it's getting more and more dicey. The Gibraltar Dam Project was vetoed by Indonesia and Japan, and ever since the south of Bangladesh and the Maldives had to be evacuated, it hasn't had a chance of even making it onto the global political agenda. So the hydraulic engineers here are running out of time. At the same time, the lagoon is equipped with an ingenious system of gates, the so-called Moses Project. It dates back to last century, in the eighties. The lagoon can be sealed off automatically from the high waters by remote-controlled modules, but it has to be regularly flooded, or else it would die away, and Venice would be swamped with rot and muck. *Acqua alta* or *acqua morte* are the alternatives. So the attempt is being made to maneuver between them. And the opening to the Adriatic holds its dangers, as you can see." He raised the plastic bag with the fish. "A filtration system for nanos—such a thing will never exist. They're too small for that. Only the chemical cudgel. And that often strikes the ones nearby too."

Campo San Bartolo was knee-deep under water. Frans stuffed the plastic bag into his shoulder bag, grasped me around the waist, and lifted me onto the wooden walkway that ran along the facades of the houses and on which people could reach Calle Stagneri without getting their feet wet, as he sloshed through the water next to me.

FRANS HAD A tiny apartment on the second floor of a house on Rio di Sant'Agostin, directly in the shadow of the brick toad of San Lorenzo.

"What was that old man actually talking about with the face that supposedly riles the Austrians so much?" I asked.

"Haven't you seen it yet?"

"No."

"It's the master himself. Professor Ishida as a cherub—only his head and his odd beard. As large as San Michele, it sometimes floats over the northern lagoon. Until now no one has figured out how he does it, no one can understand how it works. Probably it's a holograph for which he uses the humidity, as it can be seen particularly clearly in hazy weather."

"And why does he do that?" I asked.

Frans shrugged. "Ishida is simply an eccentric fellow—and also terribly vain."

"That hasn't escaped my notice."

"By the way, you can now buy the Ishida cherub as glass art. A student he failed commissioned it in Murano and sent it to physicists all over the world."

"That must have rankled him."

"Not in the slightest! In the meantime, he sends out the thing himself. It promotes popularity, he says."

BEFORE FALLING ASLEEP, I wondered how that fish experienced its gradual ossification. It must have been like a sort of time dilation. The environment must have accelerated nightmarishly, while time for it slowly came to a standstill.

When I thought he had long been asleep, Frans suddenly asked: "Do you know where I get the wood samples from?"

"From the foundations."

"Oh, what the heck. If you don't tell anyone, I'll reveal it to you."

"I'll be as silent as the grave."

"From the past."

"You screwball."

He didn't respond to that. From his breathing I could tell that he had fallen asleep.

The death of a fish and the death of a nano. Both had disappeared from our universe. Their event horizon had closed around them.

FRANS WAS A tender lover, but not a very attentive one. He always seemed to be preoccupied with something, even when we were together. Often he was nervous, stressed, and sometimes completely drained. He constantly shuttled back and forth between the NNTR and the city authorities, often sat for hours with Ishida and his assistants or had things to do in the studio, where he advised the technicians during the construction of simulations, which were worked out holographically with computer support down to the minutest detail.

"Why go to such trouble to create artificial realities?" I asked him.

"It's an age-old dream, Domenica. People are prepared to invest a great deal if given the chance to visit a longed-for world that lies beyond the realm of their experience. It need not even be real; it must merely appear sufficiently real to them. The brain lets itself be deceived easily. And that would hardly be the case if it didn't want to be deceived. Nothing is more appealing to people than roaming other worlds."

"Other worlds? Most people can barely cope with the one they live in."

Frans laughed. "That's exactly why."

"So it's pure escapism."

"No, Domenica. It is done out of entirely practical considerations."

"To earn money?"

"That too. But not only. It's a multibillion-euro market. And it has huge potential for growth. It began with a well-told story. Today you can literally depart your reality. Technology makes it possible."

"But that's all just trickery."

"Not trickery, but simulations, which can no longer be distinguished from reality. At least not by the human senses. At this point they go far beyond the optic and acoustic. The problem of olfactory components has been solved as well, and in the haptic area we have already made some progress with the help of nanotechnology. Think of Kazuichi's finger and Ishida's hands."

"You said: 'But not only.'"

Frans nodded and scrutinized me.

"That has to do with addressing," he explained. "We Dutch stumbled on it. Through extensive correspondence, realities can be linked across time."

"So then, when you suggested that you got the samples from the past . . ."

"Yes."

VI

The Astronaut

The ability to perceive or think differently is more important than the knowledge gained.

DAVID BOHM

Of course SimStims already existed back then," Heloise Abret said. "Without them I would have gone crazy. I would have died like Chris, except that I would have died of boredom. — Abe, lift me up a bit, I can barely breathe. Don't you see that? How am I supposed to speak like this? Yes, thank you, that's good. — What were we just talking about? Oh yes, right. My favorite was bird flight, naturally. Besides, it can be simulated ideally in a state of weightlessness, without technical effort.

"Children, I'm telling you, it's magnificent. To soar in the morning at sunrise over a river, which rolls and whirls along just below you, as the morning mist lifts, the sky becomes golden—endlessly gliding along close to the surface of the water. The reflections of light make you high, flickflick—flickflickflick. I've flown for hours with wild geese, fished with them, mated with them. Of course, that was all still a bit primitive back then, thirty years ago. In the meantime, a lot has been accomplished in that field.

"Do you know how it all began? The American philosopher Thomas Nagel provided the initial stimulus. Last century, in the early seventies—I think it was in 1974—he wrote an essay for *The Philosophical Review*: 'What Is It Like to Be a Bat?' That was an interesting challenge for neuroscientists and cognitive scientists. In any case, the idea never lost its hold on them: 'Interspecies Transcription of Mental Models of Reality' is what it's called today, if I'm not mistaken.

"In a very confusing way sense impressions of the external world mingle with deeply dormant emotions—that I can assure you. For a lot of people it was a curse, as soon became apparent. Like a drug. For us astronauts, though, it was a blessing. It helped us chip away at the enormous mountain of time that had suddenly risen up before us. It opened up to us—cooped up as we were in that tiny cosmos, in that cramped capsule, in which we had to endure—realms of experience, expanses of space."

Heloise spread her hands, and her eyes followed the sickle-shaped black shadows of the swifts, which plunged from the massive brick tower of Santi Giovanni e Paolo and shot through the afternoon sky. Her small, wrinkled face stretched into a happy smile.

"The flight of a bird. That glorious feeling of gliding. You feel every feather that stands up or bends—how it reaches into the air currents and slices through them, how the interplay of forces is transferred to the body, how it reacts to them with economical countermovements, how it tilts and twists, straightens and tautens. True, all this can be expressed mathematically and represented by vectors, but you have to feel it—experience it!

"The bath of a swallow early in the morning in the cool, clear water of an oasis, before the animals are led to the water and the palms gather up their shadows for midday. When your breast plows for a brief moment through the water, it's . . . it's like a ringing—a high, piercing sound that flings you up and carries you into the day.

"I see I'm going into raptures, girls. Forgive an old woman. But Heli, I said to myself again and again in those days, this is your only chance. This is the only way you can hold out. And that was the truth too. Wasn't it, Abe?"

"Yes."

"He says yes and has no idea. Or do you have any idea what four years of weightlessness mean? Of coldness and loneliness? No one who has not experienced it firsthand has any idea. At the time, I was the same age as you are now, girls. 'Where did you find the strength?' they asked me. 'I have strength,' I assured them. 'I simply didn't give up,' I said. In the end—well—then it was hard. I slipped into the plumage of an eagle that had to survive a hard winter. That made it a little easier . . ."

Heloise's gaze got lost in the distance, and her small delicate hands lay motionless in her lap. Her fingernails were unusually long, like talons.

"I glided along over snow-covered forests, over glaciers and white slopes, over icy peaks under a black sky, observing the course of the distant sun. NASA had done all that was humanly possible for us. But the best idea was to send us those data packets. The transmission of a single-hour SimStim program lasted several days. Masses of data. We erased from the computer's memory everything that had become superfluous with the failure of the mission, and loaded it up with SimStim. We stored a lot, for the ship computer was equipped with millipede nano memory storage, which had been developed shortly before the turn of the millennium and could hold incredible amounts of data."

Heloise waved her hand and said, "Abe, I would like to lean back a bit. I'm exhausted. Yes, that's good."

She was silent for a long time. I thought she had fallen asleep and asked Renata with my eyes whether we should discreetly withdraw, but then she went on: "Humanity grows with each technological adventure, even with a failed one. Only I have shrunk."

She chuckled.

"TODAY I'M VISITING an old friend. Would you like to join me?" Renata had asked me.

"Sure. As long as I won't be intruding."

"Does the name Heloise Abret mean anything to you?"

The name sounded somehow familiar to me, but I couldn't remember in what connection. I shook my head.

"Do you remember the failed Mars mission in 2022?"

"I remember *only* failed Mars missions," I replied.

"I mean the manned one, which didn't return for four years, because the spaceship first had to fly a good distance toward Jupiter and then take a huge detour before it came back into the vicinity of Earth."

"That was before my time."

"Heloise is the only survivor among the six participants in the mission. I met her when I worked here, before I went to Rome to study. She had chosen to spend her old age in Venice, and lived here in the Ospedaletto. I attended to her."

"You worked as a nurse?"

She nodded. "I was active for STOP at the time, but that didn't earn me any money; it was volunteer work. I needed a job on the side. So I became a geriatric nurse."

"What was STOP?"

"Save Terra from Overpopulation."

"Never heard of it."

"Condoms for the world. Websites in all the languages of the Third

World about family planning and contraception. Didn't do much good. But, we told ourselves, at least the children have their fun blowing up the condoms into balloons."

"And you lived here in Castello?"

"Yes, I had a room in the Ospedaletto. It's very close to here. I'll show you."

We walked down Calle Barbaria delle Tole toward Campo de Santi Giovanni e Paolo, but turned right shortly before it and entered a building, quite inconspicuous-looking from the outside, right next to the grandiose baroque facade of the Chiesa di Santa Maria dei Derelitti.

"The Ospedaletto used to be an orphanage," Renata explained, "but it was famous for the musical performances in the Sala Musica on the second floor. To this day there are concerts there, but unfortunately only rarely."

Then she showed me an architectural feature: a winding spiral staircase made of large stone slabs in a round tower at the back of the building.

"That's the chiocciola. The former owner of this building impressed his guests by appearing on horseback on the fourth floor after having his horse climb that spiral."

The tower and the surrounding buildings now housed an old people's home, which was affiliated with the nearby Ospedale Civile. The wings of the building surrounded a spacious inner courtyard, in which a cafeteria had been set up.

"Let's sit down. She'll come soon," said Renata. "When I worked here, they washed corpses and put them in coffins in this courtyard. The residents could watch from the window when one of their fellow residents departed this life."

"Horrible."

I looked around. At the center of the cobblestone courtyard was a marble pozzo with a rusty lid. It stood on a low octagonal marble step and was crowned with a wrought-iron decorative arch, from which a lantern hung. Under the white sun umbrellas stood wrought-iron tables with heavy white marble tops. The north side of the courtyard was flanked by four stone figures. Three of them depicted, it seemed to me, the pleasures of life, while the fourth, on the outer left, in the shade of a cypress, was probably meant to be an allegory of arrogant erudition.

Suddenly a scraping and dragging could be heard above us that I could not place. Was it some sort of road sweeper or a cleaning robot? The sound lasted about ten minutes and seemed to be coming closer; then the strangest object I had ever encountered appeared at the entrance to the tower. It looked like an armchair spun out of strong silver wire, or rather a wicker beach chair, which with the undulating movements of its wire bristles or tentacles or whatever the winding, surging, thin tendrils of flexible steel wire should be called, made that scraping, scratching sound.

Embedded in the center of this cocoon was—like an egg in a nest—a tiny, dainty figure in pale blue coveralls. At first glance she could have been mistaken for a doll. She looked terribly frail and feeble, until she raised a finger, pointed to us with an energetic gesture and commanded:

"There!"

The wicker chair directed the optic cell at its upper end at us, tautened its wire bristles, and began to move toward us.

"Renata," she exclaimed, "how lovely to see you again! How have you been, child? I see you've brought a friend with you."

"Domenica Ligrina. She studied with me. Both of us finished this spring."

"Biology, if I'm not mistaken."

"Botany."

"How wonderful."

"I'm the only living person who has been beyond Mars," said Heloise Abret, holding out her hand to me. It felt like a tiny, shy animal, and I let go of it immediately for fear of hurting her. She gestured over her shoulder. "Abe, my life companion."

What did she mean by that? No one was standing behind her. Did she mean the extended camera eye of her mobile chair, which rose over her head and was directed at us?

In her dark eyes flashed energy, while her body, worn down by the long period of weightlessness and dried up by the hard radiation like an autumn leaf, hung limply in the tender embrace of the machine.

"How are you, Heli?" asked Renata.

"NASA provides for my well-being," she said, baring her false teeth. "Whether it wants to or not. It has no choice. — Don't let me sag like this, Abe! I can't breathe."

Abe whined and straightened up with a scraping sound. With trembling hands, Heloise opened the zipper of her coveralls a bit. I had never before seen such an emaciated human body. Her skin was almost black and riddled with pale spots where the pigment was destroyed.

"What would you like to drink, my dears?" she asked. "It's all on NASA.

It owes me my life. But I don't want to complain. Considering the circumstances, I'm doing excellently—and the same could certainly not be said of the space agency." And patting the fine mesh at the edge of her seat hollow, she added: "And Abe takes good care of me. What brings you to this beautiful city? Is Rome already being evacuated?"

We told Heloise about our contracts with the Rinascita Project and that we were to undergo training with the NNTR here in Venice.

"But they haven't told you anything concrete yet." She nodded and chewed on her lower lip. "Probably there are still aptitude tests to be given. Medical examinations. We astronauts often didn't even know yet the evening before takeoff whether we would really be on the mission."

Heloise was silent for quite a while, and then she said: "It must be something completely new. The Holy See, the NNTR, the CIA, the CHI, the Pope, and Ishida in one boat—what an unholy alliance! Those are extremely unusual connections. Entirely new dimensions are opening up there! Would you have thought it, Abe?"

"No," said Abe.

She closed her eyes and sank back in her lined nest of steel wool.

"Come on, Abe," she said. "I'm exhausted. Good-bye, you two. And visit me again soon."

Abe rose and began to move, dragging and shuffling. For several minutes, the sounds could still be heard on the stone slabs of the spiral staircase, until they went silent up on the fourth floor.

"SEPPIA D'ORO," THE "golden ink" is what the Venetians called the nanos.

At noon the lagoon lay black under the sun when they swarmed and multiplied. It must have been quadrillions by now. The surface of the water shimmered gold. In the north was San Michele, the great death raft of the city, where tens of thousands of bodies waited for Judgment Day embedded in cold mud or in stone troughs and acacia-shaded niches.

What would happen when the teeming mass engulfed them and the great transubstantiation of the corpses began?

During the day, when the wind blew in from the ice dams, it was pleasantly cool in the city, and the residents opened windows and doors. In the evening, when it came from the mainland, it sometimes bore swarms of biting flies and mosquitoes from the countless canals and estuaries. Then the street cafés would close early and no one stayed outside unless it was necessary. There were screens in all the doors and windows. They'll save the city and lose it to malaria, I said to myself. Or they'll devise new nanos to turn those insects into diamonds, simply by transforming their exoskeletons into crystalline carbon.

In the morning, the coral reefs of the Tethys Sea were enveloped in haze, while Ishida as a cherub hung over the water beyond San Michele. The *Prince Eugene* flew through the face as through a cloud, and for a minute the eyes of the professor could be seen sliding back on the outer shell of the balloon and undulating from the turbulence of the engines, before they found their way back to their proper place. Then he looked down again, smiling like a satisfied God the Father, who after completing his work on the seventh day surveyed his Creation.

"A CALL FOR you, Domenica," said Luigi.

"Who is it?"

"Keller, Bernd."

"Okay, yes. — Hello, Bernd! What a surprise!"

"Same here, Domenica. So you still dwell among us."

"What do you mean by that?"

"Not yet sent through space and time?"

"What's that supposed to mean?"

A bee landed on the rim of my glass and crawled along the curve. I jumped up and accidentally knocked over my chair. The patrons at the next table gave me a startled look. I took a few steps out onto the square. The owner of the Cavallo raised his head questioningly. I signaled to him that I was on a call.

"Don't play dumb, Domenica," said Bernd. "There have been some rumors about the activities of that fabulous Istituto della Rinascita."

"Such as?"

"They use tunnels through which you can crawl into the past."

"Crawl? That's the first I've heard of it. So you know more than I do," I replied.

"You're not permitted to talk about it. I get it."

"Of course I can talk about it. I just wouldn't know what."

Didn't he have anything more to say to me? The conversation was getting on my nerves. I couldn't focus on his words.

"Because you've been brainwashed."

"Listen, Bernd . . ."

"You probably didn't even realize it."

His sly intonation and his know-it-all manner bothered me. Why should I argue with him about this at all? He had chosen to back out. That had been his decision. Or rather, his sister's. So then what did he want? I didn't feel like discussing this subject with him anymore. I didn't want to discuss it with anyone. It made me nervous.

"Is that why you're calling me, Bernd? I don't really understand what you want. Do you want to warn me about something, or . . . ?" I asked him.

"Yes . . . that is, no. It's completely your own decision. That's how it has to be."

"You told me that once before, but I still don't understand what you mean."

My impatience was growing.

"It's better that way. You won't get lost like so many others. You'll come back. I'm now completely certain that you don't have an older sister. It's you yourself. I ran into you," said Bernd.

"Where?"

"On the train station square. In front of Termini."

"When?"

"On June twenty-second. I called you that day."

"I remember your call. It seemed pretty confused to me," I replied.

"Yes. I was pretty flustered at the time. You had given me quite a scare, for you were completely changed—older. And you had said such strange things. But since then I've put one and one together . . ."

"And hopefully gotten two."

"I don't think so."

Both of us were silent. So I would meet him at some point on Piazza dei Cinquecento, because I had met him there. That was absurd and yet entirely logical.

"How are you doing? How's Birgit?" I asked.

"We're doing well."

"Did you find a job?"

"Not yet. I'm doing another voluntary semester, to the extent that's even still possible. The department is in disarray, but they granted me another scholarship. Birgit has a job in a café on Piazza della Rotonda," Bernd replied.

I nodded. The same old story.

"Say hello to her. And take care of yourself, Bernd."
"Take care of yourself too, Domenica."

THAT NIGHT I heard screams and the sound of people running in the streets. Thousands of black bodies had crawled ashore from the lagoon and were trying to surmount the old brick walls that line eastern Castello and the arsenal. Some had already made it into the city, before they were discovered and slain. They looked like human-sized black slugs, and many of them wore decomposed shreds of clothing or rotten shrouds. No sooner were they slain than those creatures turned into puddles of stinking black slime, the surface of which shimmered gold.

An enraged crowd had gathered in front of the institute and was trying to smash the windowpanes with cobblestones, but the windows kept disappearing, and the stones crashed ineffectively against the bare masonry.

Later that night a hailstorm fell. The hailstones sprayed over the roofs and amassed in the streets and on the squares. In the light of the full moon they flashed like billions of diamonds.

When I awoke, rain was pelting against the windowpanes. I opened the screen door to the loggia, stepped out, and took a deep breath of the cool, damp night air. In the east the lightning flashes of a departing storm could be seen. The clouds broke. A waning moon had ascended to its zenith and hung small as the skull of a cat between three solitary stars. The lagoon appeared as if it had been filled with tar, and the reefs of the Tethys Sea shimmered on the horizon like the bones of the dead. The walls of San Michele rose like a dark fortress, lined with vigilant cypresses.

I shivered and fled back into the cozy security of my bed.

VII

Solitons

Therefore, the object of every cognitive power can be only equality itself, which can reveal itself in its likeness. Hence only equality is the object of perceptual knowledge as well as of imaginative and intellectual knowledge. By nature the power knows its own object. But knowledge arises through likeness. Hence the object of all cognitive powers is equality, whose likeness actualizes all cognitive powers . . . But every likeness is a form or sign of equality.

NICOLAUS CUSANUS

In fact, it's not hard at all to carry out an air braking in the high atmosphere of Mars. Much easier than in the Earth's atmosphere. Imagine an insect that has to fly through blinds to get into a room: It has to go at a very particular angle through two slats. Whereas on Earth the slats of the blinds have only a small gap between them, on Mars they are far apart, so form practically no obstacle. — Massage my back a little bit, Abe. But be careful. My spine is extremely tense. Yes, that's good. — Where was I?" said Heloise Abret.

". . . so form practically no obstacle," said Abe.

"What?"

"Whereas on earth the slats of the blinds have only a small gap between them, on Mars they are far apart, so form practically no obstacle," repeated Abe.

"Thank you, Abe. — I'm exaggerating a bit, my dears. But the scale height of the atmosphere is much greater in the case of Mars. That is, the atmosphere of Mars is much thinner than that of Earth, but due to the lower gravity it extends much higher into space. Its density is reduced by half only every six miles, instead of every three, as in the case of Earth. Besides, the atmosphere of Mars has triple the molecular weight, because the proportion of heavy gases is higher. So downright — not so hard, Abe — downright ideal for an air braking and another one — *Touché! Touché!"* said Heloise, cutting at an angle with her mother-of-pearl-covered pocket-knife, on which a little silver chain dangled, into the peel of the orange she held in her left hand.

"And then we should have glided down on our beautifully tiled belly like a bar of soap in the bathtub. But we didn't manage it and spun on an erratic course like bolas whose cords had gotten tangled—literally. For when we were about to jettison the cable that connected us to the ascent stage—the 'tether,' they call it at NASA—it didn't go *bang*, but only *plop*. And when we had finally gotten rid of our counterweight, we went into such a spin that the computer was incapable of getting the situation under control before the first braking and of bringing the heat shield into posi-tion. 'You're looking really good,' Houston still assured us, when hell had already broken loose among us ten minutes ago. When the time-delayed reaction of mission control finally reached us, panicked cries of terror sub-sided into horrified silence. There was nothing they could do to help us, sitting there on their asses; they lived hopelessly in our past. Then we flew into the dead zone, and contact broke off completely.

"We had to abort the approach. Of course. With a little bit of luck we would have just scraped along the outermost atmosphere and remained on an open return course. You always approach an outer planet in its direction of motion on the night side. If things go wrong, then PAMAO. That sounds like a tropical vacation paradise, doesn't it? In NASA lingo it stands for Passing Mars Abort Option, and means a hellish version of Apollo 13. But anyway: You get a push, which carries you back into the inner Solar Sys-tem. But we didn't get lucky. We ricocheted off the atmosphere like a pebble on a pond; that is, Mars dealt us a blow that threw us off course, hurling us into the outer system. That meant that Mars and the sun had to take over the braking, and that took a miserably long time."

Heloise looked into the distance. The mother-of-pearl handle of her pocketknife sparkled, the little chain flashed.

"The Valles Marineris drifted by below us. It looked like a terrible ax wound in the skull of a slain warrior. We were supposed to have landed down there, between the western commencement of the rift valley and the foot of the Tharsis ridge with its monster volcanoes. The scientists of the Geological Survey anticipated interesting findings there. It was a rather controversial hypothesis among areologists, but still: It was well suited to attract private investors, and NASA desperately needed the money for the Mars missions. There was speculation that the Hellas Basin on the opposite side of Mars was the impact crater of a large planetoid, which, I don't know"—she stabbed her forefinger into the fruit—"a few hundred million years after the formation of the planet broke through the crust and penetrated deep into the mantle. The shockwaves of the impact, according to model calculations, had propagated straight through the planet and raised a plume of core matter. This ultimately caused the Tharsis ridge to bulge out and the gigantic shield volcanoes to rise up across it." Heloise turned the orange around and looked at it from the other side.

"Through those volcanoes, the proponents of this theory surmised, some material from the core must have been carried up to the surface—a lot of heavy elements like uranium, platinum, gold, and rare ores, which would be of the utmost significance for a settlement of Mars and the construction of an aerospace industry in situ. Gigantic lava caves full of vast treasures, well hidden from views from outer space. All we would have had to do was gather them up and bring them to Earth.

"Oh well, nothing would come of that now. Mars—adieu! We flew by and out into the night and the cold far from the sun. Half the distance to the asteroid belt lay ahead of us before we would reach our turnaround point, before our speed would be used up and we would fall back into the inner system.

"The cosmic rays lashed us so hard in the face that we almost lost hope of ever getting home alive. We had to do without artificial gravity once we had separated from the ascent stage. Mission control calculated and calculated. They didn't dare to tell us the results, for all they could have presented to us was a depressing pattern chart of Hohmann ellipses: far outward, then deep inward and past Venus—so that it would take more than three years before we came close to Earth again. Right, Abe?"

"To be honest, Heli, such calculations far exceed the computing capacities for which I am designed."

"Why should you burden yourself with stuff like that?" she said with a good-natured wave of her hand. "The technicians in Houston, by the way, quickly found the error that had led to the failure. It would have been easy to avoid its occurrence, but technical processes that have been computer-simulated a hundred times are considered sound. Around that time I discovered the blessings of SimStim; I flew with the wild geese and the swallows and in the end with the eagles. But times were tough, my dears. Horribly tough."

Heloise slit open the fruit with her fingernail and inserted a segment into her mouth.

"Rations were reduced to the absolute minimum. It was barbaric. And the taste of recycled water can be conceived only by someone who has tried it. — Won't you get rid of these peelings here, Abe?"

Abe extended two tentacles, gathered up the orange peelings, and disposed of them somewhere inside his wire-mesh body.

"Yes, that's how it was, my dears," said Heloise, fiddling with the little chain on her knife, lost in memories. "Mars turned into a crescent and the sun got smaller and smaller. It was depressing. That pale, weak little light was supposed to be able to stop us and bring us back? Perhaps we were simply drifting despite all laws of physics into the interstellar night? Sometimes, when I lay awake in the darkness, I thought I could already hear the rumble of the crushing storms on Jupiter.

"Finally we were only creeping along—another light-second and another. The turnaround point was like a winter solstice: The farthest point had been overcome, but the long, cold winter still lay ahead of us. Around that time, Chris discovered the melanoma on his shoulder. He just went out, outwitted the airlock-spacesuit security, and disembarked. 'Farewell and get home safely,' he left on the screen. He traveled seventy-five million miles at our side—until the first course correction for the Venus swing-by. That's where he left us."

Heloise shaded her eyes and looked into the sky over the Ospedaletto, which was dominated by the massive tower of Santi Giovanni e Paolo. In the merciless autumn light her face was like an ancient land fissured by the erosion of time, emaciated by deprivation and aridity—an epidermis turned into dry valleys and dunes. But her smile cast all ugliness aside. Cheerfully, she said: "He's still up there somewhere, perhaps for another hundred thousand years. — Abe, what are you doing? Have I asked you for something?"

"Sorry, Heli. I have moved you into the shade."

"Thank you, Abe. That's very thoughtful of you. — Well, one less nose breathing and one less mouth eating, that was to our benefit, of course. And we did ultimately make it. But there weren't many of us left when they picked us up with a shuttle five light-seconds from here. We had to hold out another six months on Earth's doorstep, on the old, never completely finished ISS, until we had learned in the centrifuge to sit upright in a wheelchair, until we had enough strength that our heads didn't sink to our chests at half a g," she said with a sigh. "In the meantime, they've all died: Natasha and Caroline, Brad and Raphael. Brain tumor, anemia, bone cancer. We are simply not optimally constructed for something like that. Or not yet," she added.

"But I'm alive!" she exclaimed, banging her small fist on the armrest so that Abe straightened up in surprise. "I got off lightly. Irreversible atrophy of the muscles and advanced osteoporosis. Abe has to transport me like a porcelain doll, right, Abe?"

"Oh . . . hm. If you say so. To be honest, I have never been confronted with the problem of transporting a porcelain—"

"Never mind, Abe. We don't need to delve deeper into the matter."

"If you say so."

With her thumbnail she slit additional segments of the fruit, pulling apart the rest of the orange.

"So now they will send people not only through space, but also through time," said Heli.

"Hey, watch out! Is there a short-circuit here somewhere, or what?" Renata cried, raising her head; she sniffed and scrutinized the metal mesh around the cushioned seat hollow. "For a moment I thought something had caught fire."

Heloise had paused in her movements and looked at her.

"Everything's fine, sweetie. You don't need to tell me anything. Nothing at all. The same goes for you," she said to me. "Perish the thought that something here should really catch fire or something even worse should happen"—chuckling, she inserted an orange slice between her shriveled lips and nibbled with a smirk—"I know how these things are done. It's harmless. You've been taught to hold your tongues."

Renata and I exchanged a glance.

"Time always seemed to me to be something immense, something unconquerable. Like a bulldozer that pushes us with unrelenting cruelty into the future. Sometimes agonizingly slowly, as in my case." She shook her head with a smile. "Now it too has been conquered. Or can't one put it that way?"

"It's probably only the beginning," I was about to say, but it was as if my throat were constricted.

"Are you afraid, girls?" Heloise suddenly asked.

"Yes," said Renata.

I nodded.

"I was afraid back then too. Extremely afraid."

"Things don't always go wrong," said Renata in an upbeat voice; the fragments of amber in her eyes flashed cheerfully. "In the meantime more than a hundred people live in Port Abret alone."

Heloise gave a dismissive wave. "They could have spared themselves the trouble of naming a settlement after me. An undeserved honor. After all, I never set foot on Mars. What do you think about that, Abe?"

"Nothing," replied Abe.

"You're right as always, my treasure," she said, raising her chin. "As for these time travel experiments, I've known for years that something has been going on there. There have been plans for a long time. I had enough free time to delve into the mathematical works of Hla Thilawuntha, who is regarded as the reborn Ramanujan, the self-taught Indian mathematician who came to Cambridge at the beginning of the last century and astounded the world—which, by the way, is not at all such an absurd idea, when it comes to time travel."

I saw a bee land on the back of her hand. Heloise and Renata seemed not to notice the insect. I was sure that it existed only in my imagination, but the urge to drive it away was nearly overpowering, and it cost me a great deal of effort to remain calmly seated.

"This Frans," she said, "whom they supposedly send to get wood . . . I've wondered for years where the building plans of one or another palazzo that have turned up recently have suddenly come from. They were considered lost for centuries. I couldn't make sense of it. You, Abe?"

"No," said Abe.

Her hands had sunk into her lap, and her gaze rested on me. I don't think she even blinked. Her dark eyes, usually so lively, were completely fixed. It seemed to me as if all the sounds around us had died away and time had slowed down. Nothing seemed to be moving. Even the light seemed to have somehow grown fainter, as if an invisible haze were enveloping us. Fear overcame me.

Suddenly she raised her small, clawlike hand and pointed at me with her knife. The mother-of-pearl handle sparkled, and the dangling little silver chain flashed.

"Nothing will happen to you," she croaked, "as long as you do not stray too far from yourself. It won't always be easy, but you can return to your world. You only have to want to. Look at me, I did it too. The same goes for you, Renata. Keep that in mind."

She closed her eyes and sank back into her cushioned seat hollow, as if that advice had completely exhausted her.

"Come on, Abe," she said softly, "bring me upstairs."

Abe rose and headed, rustling and scraping, toward the entrance to the stairwell.

"WE'RE CONCERNED SOLELY with addressing here, ladies and gentlemen," said Ishida, leaning back in his seat at the front of the old lecture hall and folding his hands behind his head.

The four of us sat in a light-flooded semicircle, feeling somewhat lost in the ascending benches. The professor wore a ceremonial robe in classic Japanese style made of heavy dark blue material with silver edging and had taken a seat with his legs crossed on a snow-white tatami.

"These addresses consist of data packets, each of which reproduces a sufficiently accurate scene from the past of a specially selected place: the target point in time for the traveler. I emphasize 'sufficiently' as opposed to 'exactly.' An exact copy is in principle impossible, but also unnecessary, as it has turned out. It's not about the production of *identity*, but rather the production of *equality*, or to be precise: the production of *association*. Association—as in art—is the connective element. Above all—but not only—it's about optic correspondence. This is achieved through holographic and other simulation techniques. To put it crudely: We produce the match, which aligns the here and now with the there and then—from a purely technical point of view.

"In the case of a sufficient *association*, a sort of entanglement occurs between the two space-time states, the simulated state and the real one. Regardless of the temporal and spatial distance between the two points, a connection is produced that we have learned how to use—even if we don't understand how it arises. This connection can be compared to an EPR Bridge, or an Einstein-Podolsky-Rosen Bridge, which occurs in the subatomic realm. Einstein, incidentally, called the phenomenon spooky action at a distance—and far be it from me to contradict him. Before Hla Thilawuntha no one suspected that a similar phenomenon could be possible in the macroscopic realm as well."

The tatami had risen from the focal point of the hall and had come to a standstill halfway up.

"The optic correspondence or *association* seems to be the most important precondition for this bridge, which allows the traveler to reach the selected place at a selected time. The importance of the optic correspondence might be due to the fact that photons stand in an instantaneous relation to each other. That is, for them time does not exist. The structural similarity of optic scenarios leads—according to the hypothesis—to the quasi-suspension of the time in between.

"This theory is based on a tradition that goes back to Leibniz and Mach, Boltzmann and Barbour. It rejects the hypothesis of a Newtonian 'flow' of time, which one-dimensionally follows a time-arrow, and defines time as sequential similarities in the arrangement of matter in the universe, as structural associations. Imagine a mountain of moments layered like rock strata. Those moments are not units of time, however, but rather, so to speak, snapshots of the same landscape from different perspectives. Each snapshot is thus a description of the state of the universe, which contains the respective coordinates of all the particles in this universe in their relation to one another—seen from a particular angle. Those coordinates form structures that adjoin according to their similarity. Their sequence is interpreted by human consciousness as a time 'flow,' but they are only paths that consciousness clears for itself through the mass of sense data, that is, through the mountain of coordinates. There are, however, a great number of such paths through the mountain landscape. Our job here is to search for the shortcuts and make them traversable."

Ishida raised his hands in a balancing gesture. His palms shimmered in the colors of the rainbow.

"This theory is controversial," he went on. "Most brane physicists flatly reject it and cling to Einstein's conception of the classic space-time continuum. They trace the phenomenon of the transition from here and now to there and then back to a side effect of the passage of so-called time solitons; those are wavefronts that, at irregular intervals, pass through our present toward the past and future, thereby deforming space-time. Those deformations produce so-called gap junctions in the p-membrane enfolding our universe. Thus they break open the boundary layers of the here and now and make them permeable for a brief time—both toward the temporal dimension and, perpendicular to that, into the so-called Everett worlds, that is, into the parallel universes that are constantly emerging and accumulate at the periphery of our reality like the molecules of growing crystals. The representatives of this theory imagine the movement of the time travelers as a sort of surfing on these solitons and indeed regard our work here as nothing but addressing, so that this mysterious delivery service knows on what beach to drop off the surfer.

"Probably both hypotheses contain part of the truth. In any case, the works of the Burmese mathematician Hla Thilawuntha, which appeared in the twenties on the Web and caused a stir among experts, can be interpreted in both directions."

Ishida rubbed his hands together. He was now floating above us and looking down at us. We looked up at him raptly.

"At bottom, all this is of course pure speculation, for we don't know how the transition technology we use—or rather: in the use of which we are permitted to share—works, for it was not developed in our present, but rather in the future. Probably in the distant future, to stick to the classic parlance, or, to be syntactically consistent: It *will be* developed.

"Its use extends to our present and to the past. By chance we discovered the possibility of the transition and learned to avail ourselves of it. Thilawuntha's mathematics provided the key to that. So basically we are the beneficiaries of a foreign technology that we do not yet grasp in all its particulars. That is by no means unusual: For centuries we have made use of electric energy without yet having totally unraveled the nature of the electron. I mention that merely as an aside."

Ernesto laughed. We laughed too. Ishida waved his iridescent hand.

"Our knowledge of the transition technology is, as said, pretty sketchy, but what we've figured out about it is extremely complicated. I won't delve into those theoretical explanations. You—or at least the physicists among you—will learn enough about that at the CIA, the Hendrik Casimir Institute for Quantum Gravity and Multidimensional Boundary Layer Studies in Amsterdam, and at the Christiaan Huygens Institute for Temporal Stratimetry and Structural Virtuality in The Hague, where you will have your practical training. There you will become acquainted with Kaku's quantum mechanical spaghettini and Ed Witten's cat's cradles, with string loops smaller than protons but with the mass of suns and other monsters of quantum gravity. You will also be tortured . . . with the calculation of the past endpoint of a null geodesic of the universal hyperbolicity, the development of a future Cauchy horizon, and with terminal indecomposable past sets. The pleasure, ladies and gentlemen, will be all yours."

Laughing, he raised his chin, and the ruffled-collar beard gleamed in the backlight like a halo that had slipped out of place.

"Nor do we know anything about the inventors and operators of this future technology. There are time travelers who claim to have encountered on their excursions strange beings from the distant future, but let us consider that those people were usually under extreme stress. So let's take their words with a grain of salt when they speak of angels and talking rats.

"Why don't we travel into the future to clarify things? Quite simple: The future is not accessible to us, because we do not possess any corresponding optic coordinates there. It is impossible for us to simulate a sufficient *association*. So we simply don't know who these future dwellers are who grant us a free ride—whether they are distant human descendants or aliens, whether they are cyborgs or supercomputers, intergalactic intelligence clusters or merely an automatic repair program of the multiverse for the self-preservation of the future, constantly at work on its optimization. Professor Auerbach in Amsterdam will eagerly explain that to you, and Professor van Waalen will elucidate the fabulous 'brushing out' theory of the multiverse he has come up with.

"But what we do know—and this is important for our practical work—is the strong interest of the, let's call it—whatever it may be that's sitting there in the future—ENTITY in a fundamentally undisturbed course of history on this Earth, with tolerance for deviations within a certain margin—which indeed suggests a sort of self-acting repair program. That is, if a time traveler intentionally or inadvertently precipitates a change of the established historical reality that goes beyond the fixed margin, the transition into the past does not take place, even if the rest of the preconditions have been met. The logic is clear: A parallel universe comes into existence, in which the transition ensues. The undesired result occurs; it is rejected post factum; in our universe the transition ad hoc does not take place.

"Nor does the transition take place if we make a grave error during the addressing of the spatiotemporal target coordinates or if the person who is to be transported has not been sufficiently fit into the target point in time. The same logic comes into action: parallel world / assessment of the situation post factum / rejection of the result / denial ad hoc.

"Borderline cases might be interesting, in which an oscillation in the border area of the fixed margin might occur. That could lead to a repeated emergence of parallel worlds. However, up to now we have not encountered such a case. That's all for today. I thank you, ladies and gentlemen."

Ishida spread his hands and disappeared in a violet flash of light. A gong sounded as in a Shinto temple, and suddenly it smelled like incense.

"Was he never even here?" Renata asked in amazement.

"It's all part of the show," Ernesto asserted.

Marcello chuckled and said, "And I was wondering the whole time how he does that with the levitation."

"Joking aside," I interjected. "Did you understand that?" My head was spinning.

Ernesto shrugged. "Did you have problems with that? It wasn't so hard to understand."

"Well, I expect that from you," I said. "Can you explain to me what a soliton is?"

"Send your Scarabeo to dig it up, Domenica," he urged me.

"Okay, I'll do that. But I have to listen to all that closely again."

"That couldn't hurt."

"Stop being such a know-it-all, Ernesto," Marcello snapped.

"Okay, okay."

"That seems absolutely unreal to me," Renata said, shaking her head. "You go into a sort of holoshow, then a wave comes and washes you into the Middle Ages or wherever."

Ernesto gave her an appalled look. "Do you have any idea how much lies behind all that? How much math? And brane physics? And cosmology?"

"But that's what it boils down to. She's right." I came to Renata's defense. "We surf into the Middle Ages, pick a few flowers and collect seeds from plants that no longer exist in the present, wait for the next wave in the opposite direction, and surf back. Show's over."

Ernesto eyed me reprovingly. "You'll be surprised, my dear," he said. "You might be in for some nasty shocks."

I could not have suspected how right he would turn out to be.

"What's going to happen, when a dozen first-class scientists are sitting at the monitors watching over you?" Marcello said airily.

"They can watch over you for only so long, as long as you're still here," Ernesto replied. "The moment the transition has taken place, you're completely on your own. Then you're stumbling around in the seventeenth century . . ."

"I'm supposed to go to the eighteenth century."

"All right. Do you think that's better?"

"No time is easy," I broke in.

"But some are really bad," said Renata.

How right she was.

"I don't envy all of you," Ernesto asserted. "But, thank God, that's not my job."

"Oh, come on," said Marcello. "Do you want to frighten us? I'll look for a job as a court jester and give my master wise counsel, maybe play the prophet a bit and without much trouble prove right. In short, be indispensable to him. Or I'll tour Europe as a dottore, as an herbalist . . ."

"Specialist in love potions," I suggested. "Dangerous! Dangerous!"

"Don't get involved with alchemy! You can easily lose your head with that," said Renata. "And keep your good advice to yourself. In the royal courts of that time, paranoia reigned. You could easily come under suspicion of being a spy. They made short work of them."

Grabbing our hair, Marcello pushed Renata and me ahead of him through the corridor to the exit.

"You're no longer allowed to cut your hair, my dears, or else you'll arouse suspicion," he said.

"How come?" I asked.

"They sheared the heads of witches and sinners."

I tousled his black ringlets. "And what about you? Will you get away with this?"

"They'll put a powdered wig over his head," declared Ernesto.

"As behooves a man of the world and esteemed scholar," replied Marcello, raising his chin arrogantly. "Jealous?"

"Don't make me laugh. At that time every puny village schoolteacher walked around with one of those lice-ridden things on his head."

We were meanwhile walking along the Fondamenta Santa Giustina to our accommodations. It was a warm, late-autumn day. The sun was shining.

"What did the professor mean when he said that time didn't really exist?" I asked Renata. "I get older every day, damn it!"

"Probably that's just a bad habit," she replied with a laugh.

"Luigi."

"Yes, Domenica."

"Wake up our Scarabeo."

"That is not necessary. It is always in standby mode."

"What does it do the whole time?"

"It tests servers, checks its connections to data storage devices, follows links and organizes them into priority hierarchies; it also assembles expert programs and keeps them up to date. As a SuperGrid browser, it has access to the Grid, of course, and because it is a level-four AI, it makes independent decisions regarding the weeding out of unimportant data."

I detached the device from my wrist and placed it on the table.

"A diligent little guy," I noted.

"One can put it that way, Domenica."

"I have a question for it: What is a soliton?"

"The word designates a solitary wave. The term stems originally from fluid dynamics. In the seventies of the twentieth century, it was imported into particle and quantum physics and at the beginning of this century into boundary layer or dimensional brane physics and redefined accordingly."

"I would have liked to know more about it."

"The Scarabeo asks whether it should present the data in infotainment, high, or top."

"It should just show me something."

I put the audiovid band over my eyes and leaned back on the sofa. Formulas and three-dimensional graphics immediately stacked up in my field of vision and scrolled down.

"The form of a soliton is optimal when the sum of potential and kinetic energy is smallest, and it is smallest precisely when the curve crosses the wave crest at an angle that lies exactly between the extremes. The equation says that for any value phi of the field you get the internal energy by squaring the sine of phi. A field that satisfies this equation is called a sine-Gordon field. Transferred to quantum physics, this means that in a matter field coupled to a Yang-Mills field, three-dimensional solitons can be generated as well. Four-dimensional solitons emerge when—"

"Stop! — Well, I'm reluctant to admit it, but I don't understand a word. I need a little bit of basic knowledge. When was the soliton discovered? Where was it? What does the thing look like? Try it with infotainment."

The graphics and equations dispersed and trickled away before my eyes like ice chips evaporating in an instant. Mist rose, enveloping a flat landscape. Poplar alleys, willows, alders. It was early in the morning. At first the bumpy visual field confused me, until I realized that I was sitting on a horse and riding at half-gallop on a path along the right bank of a canal or a diked small river.

In the murky brownish water next to me I saw an odd phenomenon: a single, roughly knee-high wave, moving along soundlessly at a speed with which my horse, despite its brisk pace, could scarcely keep up. The strangest thing was that this swelling of the water glided on and on, without even a suggestion of gradual flattening or flagging—as if it were kept in motion by a mysterious force emanating from something racing along below it on the bottom of the canal. The movement was completely soundless; only when an irregularity interrupted the smooth course of the banks could a soft burbling or lapping be heard. The snorts and coughing gasps of the horse, which seemed to be at the end of its strength, sounded all the louder. I reined it in. The wave glided on and disappeared from my sight.

"The phenomenon was first described in 1840 by the hydraulic engineer John Scott Russell," explained a male voice-over, "who regularly inspected the Glasgow Canal and the Ardrossan Canal in Scotland. 'I was watching the motion of a barge,' he reported, 'which a pair of horses was pulling at great speed along a narrow canal, when suddenly the barge stopped sharply. But the mass of water it had set into motion in the canal was by no means stopped. Violently seething, it began to gather around the prow of the boat, and then suddenly, abandoning the boat, it rolled off ahead with tremendous speed, having taken the form of an isolated large mound—a roundish, smooth, and sharply outlined mass of water which continued its path along the canal without any noticeable change of form or slackening of speed. I rode after it on horseback and when I caught it, it continued to roll forward at a speed of eight to ten miles an hour, preserving its initial form in the shape of a figure about thirty feet long and one and a half feet high. The height of the water gradually decreased, and after pursuing it for one or two miles, I lost it in the windings of the canal.'"

The horse had suddenly disappeared, and I was looking down from a helicopter at the delta of a river.

The voice went on: "Since then the phenomenon has often been observed. It occurs primarily in funnel-shaped estuaries in connection with a large tidal range. These waves, known as tidal bores in hydrodynamics, can surge upstream unflaggingly for hours and wreak considerable destruction; examples are the mascaret in the Seine, the pororoca in the Amazon, and the enormous bore in the Qiantang near Hangzhou. Aerodynamics too is acquainted with solitons; around the beginning of summer a powerful bore regularly forms in the atmosphere of Mars over the Tharsis ridge in the early morning hours.

"From the perspective of particle physics or quantum physics, the soliton is an energy packet that can travel but cannot disperse in space, because its vacuum states are arranged topologically such that its field cannot be extended to a single vacuum value consistent everywhere in space. The result is a stable field perturbation. Understood in these terms, it has the character of a particle.

"In the year 2024, the concept of the soliton was also applied for the first time to boundary layer or brane physics by the Burmese mathematician Hla Thilawuntha. He used the term to designate disturbances of the flow of time that had not been detected up to that point, because they can only be demonstrated indirectly. Only on the basis of his theoretical work and predictions did Folkert Jensma and Koos van Laere the following year at the Christiaan Huygens Institute in The Hague prove the existence of so-called time solitons, which Thilawuntha had predicted. These disturbances traverse the flow of time in both directions, that is, they bring about with their passage momentary damming and acceleration in the temporal dimension. They thereby deform the structure of space-time, but are eo ipso not directly detectable by an observer situated within this structure—that is, within our universe. Their existence can, however, be indirectly demonstrated, because their passage is accompanied by gravitational waves of various strength.

"What these disturbances are—whether a transformation by another, hidden temporal dimension or an artificial manipulation, possibly carried out through deliberate use of superstrings—is a matter of controversy. According to calculations, the passage of every soliton is associated with amounts of energy in the peta and exa-electron volt range. The mass equivalent is thus several times the mass of our universe."

WHAT ARE THEY talking about? I wondered. It seemed to be a heated discussion, for I saw them intensely raising and lowering their hands. Why were they speaking so softly? They were murmuring and whispering. Did they not want me to hear? But damn it, this involved me too!

What had happened to the horse? It was surely grazing somewhere nearby. I must have dozed off. It had gotten cool. Something was tickling my chin. I swiped at it. The audiovid had slipped off my face. Dazed, I sat up. No one was there. The heated discussion was being carried on by the *Caprifoliacea*, which was rooted in the flower box on my balcony and had covered the white plaster of the wall and ceiling with a confused pattern of dark formulas. The hand-shaped leaves, stirred by a breeze; their continuous rustling and scraping against the wall had led me to believe I heard whispering voices.

The tiles on the balcony were cold. The sky had darkened. Clouds from the north lay like coal seams over the autumnal faded blue.

. . . the passage of every soliton is associated with amounts of energy in

the peta and exa-electron volt range. The mass equivalent is thus several times the mass of our universe.

I shivered. I closed the balcony door.

Was it Dottore Ercole Mondoloni's language implants that so exhausted me? That fragmented and scattered my thinking? During the day, I was often dog-tired; lately I had also been sleeping poorly and having strange dreams. You have to eat a sufficient amount, the doctor had impressed on me. Your gray cells are working hard. There are billions of new links to install.

Sometimes I felt as if at night unbidden guests were making themselves comfortable in my brain, shamelessly taking advantage of my absence to misuse it for their purposes. Was that part of our conditioning too? Or was it the countless nanos that you took in with each breath here in Venice, which unloaded their chemical instructions before they died? The air was heavy with that tiny mechanical pollen, which drove the sunlight from the surface of the lagoon and swirled up like fine dust. Frans laughed when I brought it up with him.

"Think of the countless microorganisms in the biosphere, which infiltrate your respiratory passages every second," he said.

All right, but the oxygen breathers had had 250 million years' time to come to terms with them. I thought of the little boy whose brain had within an hour turned into crumbly Stilton.

Questions.

"Can one imagine these solitons as waves that flow along the temporal dimension or the space-time continuum, deforming it in the process? Please don't look at me so condescendingly, Frans! I'm trying to grasp this phenomenon. I actually always got good grades in physics."

"I'm not looking at you condescendingly," he replied.

"So when this soliton comes closer, time passes faster—or slower? Fine, I understand that. I'm not unfamiliar with the feeling, depending whether I'm bored or in a hurry. Still, I know that my clock always runs at the same speed. Right? But that's not what you mean."

Frans nodded with amusement.

"Then tell me, how do you detect whether a soliton is coming? It must be with clocks somehow . . . atomic clocks or something," I added helplessly.

He made a face as if he had bitten down on a piece of shell in a nut croissant, and shook his head.

"No, Domenica. Even with the most precise clock it could not be measured. Our space-time continuum is a closed system. We and all our clocks are situated on the inside. If time flows faster or slower, our clocks run correspondingly faster or slower, atoms vibrate faster or slower. You have no independent standard by which you can measure that. We would have to leave our universe and view it from the outside to detect those irregularities."

We sat in Il Cavallo on the south side of Campo Santi Giovanni e Paolo, at the feet of Colleoni, less than two hundred yards from the Ospedaletto where Heli Abret lived. She had traveled farther than anyone before or since. She had flown with the birds over the sea and had now finally come to rest in the arms of Abaelard.

It had gotten cold. Only at Il Cavallo were there still tables and chairs outside. We were the only patrons; both of us had turned up the collars of our jackets and were defiantly holding out.

"So then how do you know when a wave is approaching?"

"There's an indirect sign: We detect an increased presence of gravitons—a gradual and then an ever-steeper rise. Those are virtual particles; they indicate masses of quintillions of electron volts, which interact with the real gravitons."

"But the mass of a graviton is tiny, if I remember correctly."

"A thousandth of an electron volt."

"Then where, for heaven's sake, are those gigantic masses?"

Frans shrugged. "They are their twins in parallel universes, which come into contact with them. Gravitons seem to be the only particles for which the boundary layers of the universes do not constitute an obstacle. They can shift between the membranes in which the universes are embedded, appear in ours, and vanish again. That happens above all during the passage of solitons. Whether they are secondary effects or directly related to these waves, we don't know."

"Hm. You don't actually know much about the things you're playing around with."

"We're learning more. We can roughly estimate what amounts of energy are moving along the temporal dimension. They're gigantic. They are powerful tsunamis, which suggest deeper underlying convulsions."

Frans pushed aside our cups as if he wanted to make room for one of those surges and added: "They have so much energy that they can obliterate whole universes."

"Or create new ones."

He looked at me with surprise and nodded. "Or create new ones."

"And we don't notice a thing, even though they pass through us?"

"Some time travelers claim to sense when they're coming," he said.

"Not you?"

"I'm not sure, Domenica. Your perception can easily play tricks on you. They certainly flood through every atom of your body, through every neuron of your brain. But then I think: That's utter nonsense. How can you sense what's going on in the atoms of your body? Or even in the subatomic realm? That's absurd. We have no sense organs for that. But still—" Frans sighed. "All this is nothing but speculation, my dear."

"But it works when you use them to transfer masses, to transport them through time."

"With their immense energy they deform the membrane that contains our universe, our space-time continuum," Frans confirmed. "They open for a brief moment the here and now and allow access to other spaces and times."

I looked up at the tower of Santi Giovanni e Paolo.

"I always thought that the edge of our universe was far out there, fourteen billion light-years away from us."

"Not at all, Domenica. It's only a tiny fraction of a millimeter away."

"Where?"

He spread his hands with a smile. "Everywhere. The membranes that form the multiverse are tightly packed like cells in an organism. Each is a world unto itself, but the exchange of messenger substances between them seems to be vital. The passage of solitons makes this exchange possible. To stick to the image, it makes the cell walls temporarily permeable."

I felt the coldness creeping into me. A coldness that wafted toward me as if from shadowy abysses.

"The idea somehow frightens me," I confessed.

"Oh. The membranes protect us. We are safely ensconced in our dimensions."

"Let's go," I said. "I'm cold."

He paid via his ICom, and we stood up. I burrowed deep into my jacket. The sun was gone. From Rio Medicanti fog was coming in. The membrane of reality dissolved, and Colleoni rode through.

VIII

The Serenissima

> The Turing principle says that a universal virtual-reality generator can be built, and could be programmed to render any physically possible environment, so clearly it could be programmed to render any environment that did once exist physically . . . Accuracy, in virtual reality, means the closeness of the rendered behavior to that which the original environment would exhibit if the user were present in it. Only at the beginning of the rendering does the rendered environment's state have to be faithful to the original. Thereafter it is not its state but its responses to the user's actions that have to be faithful.
>
> DAVID DEUTSCH

I remembered a dream that had often haunted me when I was a teenager. It was a passionate sexual dream in which a lover visited me in the darkness. His body was familiar to me, his voice, his touches, his caresses, with which he brought me to climax—all this suggested an extremely intimate familiarity. But I never saw his face. He entered my room in the dark, came into my bed and embraced me . . . And when I awoke, he was gone.

Those nighttime experiences were so realistic that in the morning I checked my body and the bed for traces of my amorous adventure—without finding anything, of course. But sometimes I doubted my sanity and caught myself eyeing men on the street or in a café who might have been secret nightly visitors.

A typical young-girl dream, certainly—teenage longings, wishful sexual fantasies—but for me it was a highly unsettling experience that repeatedly made me feel ashamed. I had never told anyone about it. It felt eerie to me that I was so naturally intimate with a man about whom I knew nothing—not what he looked like, what his name was, or where he lived. Sometimes I had the suspicion that he crept in from a parallel world and after our secret tryst stole away from my reality to lead his life in his world, perhaps by the side of a woman with whom he lived or to whom he was married.

Or did a different version of me live in his universe, with whom I occasionally exchanged selves? Who let me participate in her life, in her happiness? Did she, this other self, do that knowingly? Or was I a sort of nocturnal vampire, secretly battening on her pleasure, only to creep back into my world in the morning—sated and full?

That feeling, which I thought I had overcome many years earlier, that at once cozy and scary feeling of familiarity, which should not actually have been possible, was suddenly back the first time I slept with Frans. He was, in an eerie way, physically familiar to me, as if I had known him for years. He had unexpectedly behaved so familiarly toward me when we had met on the piazzetta. Had that been the trigger for the return of that strange, unsettling feeling? And that familiarity had increased frighteningly the first time we were intimate.

Did that feeling emanate from him? Was I so familiar to him? My body? But how was something like that possible?

"You puzzle me, my dear," I said to him.

He furrowed his brow questioningly.

"You act with me as if you'd known me for years. But we saw each other for the first time only recently."

He looked at me for a long time, then stroked my hair.

"I don't know," he said. "Sometimes that's the way it is."

"Do you feel like going for a ride on the vaporetto?" he asked me casually one morning. I had spent the night with him, and we were putting the breakfast dishes in the dishwasher.

"Where?"

"Canal Grande," he said. "I have to pay a visit. To a woman."

"Then you'd better go alone."

"First of all, it's an old woman; secondly, a sick woman; and thirdly, it could be interesting and enlightening for you."

"If you insist," I replied.

I quickly went home, and we met half an hour later in his office at the institute. He wore an elegant, light gray jacket and a tie with a red paisley pattern. Over the back of his chair hung a dark blue cashmere coat.

"Hey!" I exclaimed. "You should have said something. Look at me! Can I even go like this?"

I looked down at myself: gray sweater, black corduroys, my old green anorak.

He was about to spray his face and hands with smartdust.

"Why not?" he asked with surprise.

"You've gotten so dressed up."

"That's part of our routine. The woman expects that from me."

"Not from me?"

"Hm," he said uncertainly. "No."

He handed me the spray bottle with the red-gold liquid and nodded encouragingly.

"Is that necessary?"

"It would be better. At least your palms. As a precaution."

"Precaution?"

"Yes. It's safer. If you touch something."

Shaking my head, I sprayed my palms. The cool feeling on the skin disappeared in an instant. It iridesced and looked as if it were lightly oiled, but didn't feel greasy. It was more as if it had tautened and had become more sensitive to touch.

"Are you ready?"

I nodded.

We walked through the studio toward a side door. A technician sitting next to the exit had directed his eyes to a monitor on which Frans and I could be seen. I saw Kazuichi sitting behind the glass pane in the control room at the main console. He gave a thumbs-up. Frans waved to him.

"One moment," said the technician next to the door, raising his hand. According to the sticker on his breast pocket, his name was Kenichiro Akabane. The young man did not look at us but kept his eyes fixed on his monitor. Then he reached for a pair of data glasses and put them on.

The light over the door turned from red to green.

"Okay," he said, lowering his hand. "Ready to go."

We went through the door and walked along a dim corridor illuminated only by emergency lighting. A heavy steel door opened automatically and we stepped outside.

It was a hazy winter day. Not really cold, but damp and unpleasant. I plunged my hands into the pockets of my anorak and tramped alongside Frans. Heading down Calle Sagredo, past ugly gray apartment buildings, which were largely unoccupied and would soon have to make way for an additional complex of the institute, we reached the station—a light blue box on a pontoon at the end of a floating dock, rolling on the standing waves. ACTV CELESTIA was written in black on a yellow background over the large, smeared windows. The vaporetto approached and moored with a terrible grating noise. The boat woman looped the rope around the H-shaped iron bars and slid open the railing made of metal tubing. A woman in a fur coat with a shopping bag waddled off the boat, and three boys wearing garishly colored school bags on their backs ran across the dock, jostling each other.

We went aboard. Frans made no move to enter the passenger cabin and stayed outside. All right, I thought with a sigh, pushing my fists even deeper into my jacket pockets and involuntarily rubbing the coating off my palms.

The rope was unfastened, the electric motor whined, and we rode along the long blackened brick wall of the Arsenale. A stiff north wind drove the waves forward, which slapped against the foundations. Strangely, it could scarcely be felt, though we were standing outside. Nonetheless, Frans turned up his coat collar.

The water was choppy and sprayed up over the railing, but the boat didn't rock, moving astonishingly smoothly and evenly. The boat driver sat motionless on his raised seat in the stern—his red cap pulled down low over his forehead and a black scarf wrapped around his head, leaving an opening only for his eyes. The passenger room was empty except for a young couple in an oblivious embrace, occupied with their caresses.

The boat made a loop until the traffic light over the flat arch in the crenellated wall turned green and we could pass through the entrance to the arsenal. To the left, small boats bobbed in the spacious halls of the former shipyards. Some of the facades had been covered with glass and equipped with large rolling doors; on others rotten nets hung from bars that had been inserted across the arches. Between the buildings we saw the massive bodies of old military facilities soiled with bird droppings and the truncated cones of ammunition bunkers discolored by the rust of their half-eroded metal parts. In between were wildly growing bushes and pines, an unadorned flat building to the right, and a representative building with elaborate masonry over the entrance.

I had never taken this route before and looked around with curiosity. We passed the twin towers of the main entrance. The three clocks of the tower on the right displayed three different times. At the Tana the young couple got off. The woman was very small, and I noticed that she was wearing laced boots with abnormally high platforms, with which she could hardly walk.

Then we rode through under the low arched bridge and in a wide right turn out into the Bacino di San Marco. Suddenly the sun broke through for a moment in the southeast. To the right, near the bricole of the southern harbor entrance, toward San Servolo, a flickering and flashing could be seen on the water, and out of the fog emerged, crowded together, masts and superstructures—pennants and standards of blue silk, shiny brass fittings, narrow galleys next to bulkier chelandia with catapults on the high deck and gatti with covered siege towers—and in their midst, with its huge baldachin, the bucintoro of the admiral.

"Are they shooting a film here?" I asked.

"A film?" Frans replied with surprise. "In this weather?"

"Yes!" I exclaimed. "Looks like the whole fleet has been raised."

"Where?" Frans asked, turning his head. I pointed, but the ships had vanished. The screen of fog in the harbor entrance had closed again.

"I just thought I saw the Venetian fleet."

Frans gave no reply, looking silently straight ahead again. I eyed him from the side; he looked very focused, as if he himself had to steer the boat through the fog.

A large ship blasted its horn nearby. The dark, indistinct silhouette of a car ferry drifted by.

"I thought large ships are no longer permitted in the lagoon," I said.

The vaporetto lurched in the bow wave and turned right toward San Marco.

Frans shrugged and replied, "There are often exceptions. You need a special permit."

The sound of an organ came from the shore. From Santa Maria della Pietà? A boys' choir took over the melody. Voices of an almost painful clarity and freshness.

In front of the Danieli a fairground was set up—a children's carousel and several booths. The short-winded blare of an old barrel organ could be heard, and the flat claps of air rifle shots. Two days earlier I had walked by here. The pier had been empty then. But that didn't mean anything. Showmen often set up their attractions overnight.

A strange daze overcame me. I grasped the railing—and drew back my hand in shock. It had felt warm and soft like skin, as if I had inadvertently touched an arm or a leg. I eyed the railing mistrustfully—it looked like a completely normal, white-painted metal tube. Had I been mistaken? Carefully I reached for it again. I must have been mistaken: It felt cold and hard, like a completely normal metal tube covered with a thick layer of white paint. I held on and took a deep breath. The air suddenly seemed warm and stuffy to me, but immediately improved when we had passed the Palazzo Ducale and entered the Canal Grande.

"Strange weather today," I said.

Frans raised his head and looked up as if he were searching for the sun. But it was nowhere to be found. He nodded at me encouragingly. "We're almost there."

The boat seemed to be making faster headway now. We passed under the Rialto Bridge and got off at Ca' D'oro. Frans pressed the white button in a round, brightly polished brass bowl next to a heavy dark wooden door with massive wrought-iron fittings. It unlocked with a soft click and swung open soundlessly. There was no one in sight.

We entered a small inner courtyard tiled with old marble slabs. In the center stood a beautifully hewn pozzo made of pale stone. An old, well-trodden staircase with a carved banister led along the wall of the house to the second floor. The lower end of the railing was guarded by a small bronze lion. Its head had been ground down into a shiny sphere by the touches of hundreds of thousands of hands. Frans led the way up the steps.

He pulled on a brass stirrup hanging on a thin chain next to the door. No sound could be heard, but the door was opened immediately from inside. A young, dark-skinned woman in a nurse uniform silently invited us in.

We entered a high-ceilinged anteroom. From the artfully decorated stucco ceiling hung two magnificent glass candelabra. The floor was carpeted with a floral pattern in light blue, tobacco, and saffron. On the walls to the left and right hung large paintings in massive dark blue wooden frames, but the varnish was so darkened that you couldn't make out anything that was depicted in them. To the right against the wall stood a dainty old gold-lacquered table with curved legs, on it a medium-sized bell jar sheltering a Madonna in a blue robe. Strangely, instead of the baby Jesus she was holding a sheaf of grain in her arms.

We stepped out onto a spacious terrace, which was open facing the Canal Grande, with a floor of red and black marble slabs, spanned by airy openwork arches. The ceiling of massive, darkly stained wooden beams, whose edges were trimmed with a cable pattern, sagged under the weight of the upper stories. Through the side windows made of leaded bull's-eye panes of varying thickness and curvature, the sunlight cast a variegated pattern on the curtains of pale raw silk. The sun seemed in the meantime to have fought its way through the fog, for the water of the canal glittered and painted trembling reflections in the intrados of the arches.

The nurse signaled to us to wait a moment and slipped through a door. It was flanked by two stone lions, which denied admittance with wide-open mouth and raised paw.

A minute later the door was opened.

"The signora has gotten up and will see you now," said the nurse.

We entered—and I faced the strangest female figure I had ever encountered. She was—bizarre.

Supported by two strong young male nurses, the old woman stood in front of us on legs wrapped with terribly thick bandages. Although she must have left the sickbed just a few minutes earlier, she was fully dressed. She wore an ankle-length blue brocade dress, which despite her disability had a slit all the way up to her thigh and on which golden star patterns were embroidered; over it a wide fur shawl with dangling white . . . yes, it actually must have been ermine! Her long, dark blond hair was piled high and pinned with mother-of-pearl combs. Falling curls framed a majestic face that must once have been very beautiful and seemed to belong to a far younger woman than the frail body suggested.

"Spola!" she cried, joyfully surprised, raising her heavily painted eyebrows and spreading her arms.

Frans approached her and she pressed him to her with excessive warmth.

"How are you doing, my boy?" she asked.

"I'm doing well, signora. You too, I see. You look dazzling!" he replied, beaming. "May I introduce Signorina Domenica Ligrina," he added somewhat lamely, pointing to me.

How embarrassing, I thought, involuntarily curtsying. But the signora had only an imperceptible nod to spare for me, as she took Frans's offered arm and supported herself on it.

While she chatted with Frans, I felt terribly superfluous. I regretted having come along. It was hard for me to conceal my displeasure about the disregard with which this decked-out matron treated me.

I looked around the room. It must once have served as a salon, but had been converted into a sort of intensive care unit, with a modern functional sickbed flanked by two mobile stations full of electronic monitors, with which the nurses fiddled.

I looked into one of the tall, narrow mirrors on the wall. It was so deformed and murky that it reflected only shadowy images, but by some effect of doubling and redoubling every movement was reproduced so many times that it was as if with each gesture whole hosts of specters were roused, which scattered away through milky, cloudy corridors into infinity.

I felt an increasing unease in my chest and would have liked nothing more than to escape onto the terrace, but politeness forbade it; so I tried to calm down and grazed a bouquet of yellow silk roses with my hand. The flowers felt almost insubstantial, like flaky ashes. Nonetheless, they did not crumble at the touch. When I inadvertently ran my knuckles across the rim of the porcelain vase that contained them, I felt such a sharp, aggressive vibration that I recoiled in shock. But when I touched it cautiously with my fingertips to find out what that could have been, it felt cool, smooth, and completely normal.

A small glass vase with lilies of the valley stood on a shelf under one of the clouded mirrors. Lilies of the valley at this time of year? I took them in my hand and sniffed the flowers. They had an intense scent, so were actually real. As a result of a clumsy movement, three or four of the panicles slipped over the edge of the vase and fell on the floor. I was about to bend over and pick them up—but they were gone. I could find them neither on the carpet nor on the floor tiles. The vase in my hand suddenly lost its substance, becoming slippery, as if it were made of a soft water-filled film. Shocked, I balanced the wobbling container with the liquid and the remaining lilies of the valley between my two palms and tried to set it down on the shelf, but the slippery vessel would not part from my hands, it seemed to be stuck to my skin. I began to panic, but gradually it reverted to its original form and I could finally return it to its place. What sort of strange material was that?

In the meantime, the nursing staff had escorted the signora back to her bed, but made no move to extricate her from her ostentatious regalia of brocade and ermine. As Frans took his leave with a bow, I murmured a good-bye and fled through the exit and down the stairs.

I heaved a sigh of relief when we were finally in the open air again, waiting for the vaporetto. The sun had evidently not managed to prevail; Santa Maria della Salute was enveloped in fog and could scarcely be made out. All around us the purring and chugging of boats could be heard as they glided by like shadows.

My mood was at a low point. I felt imposed upon by Frans taking me with him on this excursion. I remained stubbornly silent, but he seemed not even to notice it. I gazed at the strong hands of the boat woman as we docked at a station; with practiced movements she looped the rope, which creaked from the burden, around the belaying pin and then unfastened it again. With what simple elegance, precision, and efficiency she performed her work. I smiled at her, but she did not return the smile. She looked at me—no, she looked through me, as if I were invisible to her.

The clocks on the twin towers of the Arsenale still indicated the same times, none of which could be correct.

"What time is it, Luigi?" I asked.

He did not respond. I flicked the microphone bud on my lapel with my finger.

"It's eleven fourteen," said Frans.

"Something's wrong with my ICom."

"Yes," he replied, as if that were the most obvious thing in the world.

I was about to snap at him angrily, but his smile disarmed me.

"Strange, the dense afternoon fog today. A little while ago, I thought the sun had broken through."

"It seemed that way to me too."

"Peculiar pet name that odd bird gave you," I said. "Spola."

"You think so?"

"Yes, I do. For a man, in any case. Unless . . ."

I paused, for the implications were too grotesque.

Frans shrugged and said, "Oh, I do a lot for her. Am at her service."

He grinned challengingly.

You idiot, I thought, I won't let myself be provoked by you.

"I hope she appreciates that."

"Oh, yes."

The fog lifted somewhat as we walked down Calle Sagredo to the rear entrance of the institute.

"Who is that bizarre signora anyway?" I asked him.

"You didn't recognize her?"

"No. Am I supposed to know her?"

Frans stuck his key-chip in the automatic mechanism of the steel door. "There are dozens of representations of her."

Someone above us called: "Sequence three four three six eight—concluded."

I looked up, but saw only the facade of the institute.

"It was the signora herself who received us," said Frans.

He opened the door. I pushed against it with my elbow, but felt no resistance and saw with horror that half my arm had sunk into the steel and had disappeared, while several inches away my severed forearm stuck out. With a cry I broke free and pressed my arm against my body. I felt no pain; my arm seemed unscathed. The walls of the corridor in front of me suddenly had the consistency of spiderwebs, which disintegrated within seconds and dissolved into nothingness.

Frans put his arm around me and patted my shoulder reassuringly.

"Don't worry, it's completely normal," he said.

Kenichiro Akabane was still sitting in his seat next to the entrance, had the data glasses over his eyes, and was touching illuminated fields on his control panel. The steel door dissolved in a crackling shower of sparks, which immediately died out. I stared uncomprehendingly at the photosensor-covered wall of the studio.

"You've been better, boys!" Frans called to the control room.

Kazuichi in the glassed-in cockpit shrugged and spread his hands regretfully. Akabane pushed the data glasses up on his forehead and rubbed his eyes. He seemed to have been on duty at the control instruments during the whole period of our absence, for he looked overtired and had trouble finding his way back into the reality of the studio, which was now superimposed over the fading contours of cyberspace on his retinas.

"You can now use your ICom again, signorina," he said, giving me a friendly nod. "Sorry, I had to block it for the duration of the simulation. It interferes with the signals of the holoprogram, you understand."

No, I did not understand.

"We conduct simulations here on various levels of abstraction," Frans explained. "Up to the structural level."

Gradually it dawned on me what had played out here.

"She . . . the signora was a *simulation*?" I asked, taken aback.

Akabane looked at me with surprise, then laughed. "You didn't know that?"

"It was a test," explained Frans, and turning to me, he went on: "She was the Serenissima, the city itself, Domenica. The sensory representation of billions upon billions of facts related to this city. A computerized avatar, so to speak."

"And I was angry about her bad manners. Was even a little bit jealous. Of a *simulation*!"

Frans grinned. "It was all a simulation, Domenica: the boat ride, the palazzo . . . only the two of us were real. Everything else was holographic projections—of very high density, to be sure—and other sensory stimulations. We never took a step outside this studio."

I couldn't believe it. But there had been moments . . .

"Sometimes I had such a strange feeling of unreality. As if something was somehow wrong with my perception."

"Oh, your perception is excellent. I observed you closely. You passed the test brilliantly. When you came across gaps in the simulation—there were several—you closed them immediately. Your gift for synesthesia and confabulation is excellent."

"Hey! I'm a botanist, not a psychologist."

"Hm," he murmured, pursing his lips. "It's like this"—he tapped his temple—"the human brain constantly produces a model of the environment, which it updates every three seconds. If dubious data arrive from the sense organs, the top priority is completing the model under all circumstances. What does the brain do? It cheats a little bit by correcting the sense data, and it deceives itself by inventing some just so everything fits together believably. Hearing steps in for seeing and vice versa. That's synesthesia, and it has evidently stood the test of evolution. Better to cheat than to doubt. It seems to facilitate our survival, in any case."

"And confabulation?"

"Another deceitful trick to fill gaps. Here we invent additional things we never perceived at all."

"Even a mentally healthy person?"

"Yes, indeed! You can observe it in yourself."

"I wouldn't know how."

"An example. Every evening you see a television anchorwoman behind her desk. She's pretty, has a nice figure . . ."

"Okay."

"One evening, the news is over, the camera stays on her. She doesn't get up to leave the room; an assistant hurries over to help her. He pushes her in a wheelchair out from behind the desk. She's a leg amputee. You didn't know that. For her—or rather, for yourself—you invented legs evening after evening. You can't say whether fat or skinny legs, but legs. It hits you like a shock that there aren't any there."

"Hm. Got it. I think I'm going to throw away my Scarabeo. You do that much better," I said.

Frans laughed. "You would have found the simulation even more convincing if you had sprayed yourself with smartdust not only on your hands;

then your haptic and your optic sense perceptions would have been better correlated, and you would not have had the feeling of uncertainty and unease that occasionally overcame you."

"Was that noticeable?"

"I noticed it."

I looked down at my iridescent palms. "So I could have been duped even more effectively."

Frans sighed.

"I simply find the idea of billions of robots scurrying around on my skin creepy, I'm sorry," I said.

"It's merely a matter of getting used to it, Domenica. More microorganisms settle on your skin than there are human beings on Earth. You know that better than I. Do you ever give it a second thought?"

"Excuse me, I wash my hands regularly and shower every day."

"You know what I mean."

"Yeah, you smarty-pants. You're right."

"By the way, that involuntary collaboration of the human brain is essential to such simulations. They would not even be possible without that notorious human tendency toward self-deception."

"Is that an insight of the wise Toshiaka Ishida?" I asked.

"No, that was already figured out when the first VR programs were written. The problem with cyberspace is the so-called combinatorial explosion. In order to realize a genuine smello-feelo SimStim, the volume of data grows astronomically. Despite data compression and prefabricated senso components, it would not be manageable even with state-of-the-art optical computers. Without the helpful support of the fastest computer in the solar system, things would look pretty gloomy for Ishida's little magic tricks."

"My brain?"

"Our brain, yes. It's eager to fill the gaps that our technology has to leave open due to a lack of capacity."

"*My* brain. We were talking about *my* talent for synesthesia and confabulation."

Frans laughed. "All right. *Your* brain."

KAZUICHI OPENED THE door of the control room and hastened over to us. Beads of sweat stood on his forehead. He was straining to listen inwardly; probably his implant was chattering.

"About an hour ago the ESA received a signal from LISA; in the meantime, LIGO and VIRGO have reported the approach of a soliton as well. Amsterdam has just confirmed it."

"When will it pass through?" asked Frans.

"Around zero-two-three-zero. Maybe somewhat later."

He seemed stressed, and I noticed that he had bad breath.

"Then I don't have much time left for the preparations. See to it that as of two-three-zero-zero someone from makeup is there. The same tour again: end of the tunnel?"

"Fifteen seventy-two. We've already begun the construction. The simulation should be up by midnight. San Francesco. On the big stage."

"Excuse me please, Domenica. I have to go," said Frans.

"You're being sent . . . on a trip?" I asked.

"Yes."

"May I . . . may I watch?"

Frans looked at Kazuichi questioningly. He shrugged and said, "Why not?"

"What do you have to do?"

"Get wood," said Kazuichi.

Both of them laughed.

Like little boys, I thought.

THAT AFTERNOON I roamed the city—aimlessly. A few times I had to sit down, because I felt really sick with anxiety. I had a stomachache, and I suddenly realized that I hadn't eaten anything since morning. So I bought a sandwich in a café, but didn't get a single bite down. Finally I fed it to the fish in the Giustina.

Shortly after midnight I went to the studio, where I was assigned a seat. When Frans came out of makeup, he looked like an extra in a Hollywood movie from the sixties of the previous century. He wore tight pantaloons, pointed shoes of soft leather, a wide raw linen shirt laced across his chest, and a broad leather belt; over it the cucullus, the gray cowl. So that was what a mid-sixteenth-century Venetian looked like who could loiter in the harbor, snip off wood samples, and make inquiries and observations without attracting attention. I eyed him from top to bottom.

"Is that all you need for the trip?" I asked him.

"Everything I need I carry in my head. I couldn't take much more with me, or else no transition would occur," he replied.

One might have thought he was putting out with fishermen who disapproved of wasting space in the boat with personal belongings.

"Aren't you afraid?" I asked, irritated by the tinge of disquiet in my voice.

"No," he said, briefly pressing me to him and giving me a kiss on the forehead.

My lips sought his mouth, but Frans was not as affectionate as usual; he was inwardly tautened—inattentive. As if he were already on his way.

"When are you coming back?"

"Soon, I hope," he replied. "But it's impossible to predict where the returning soliton will drop one off, sooner or later. It can take two or three days, but just as likely two or three weeks."

"Damn, Frans. I'm fond of you. Take good care of yourself!"

He smiled and stroked my hair fleetingly; inwardly, he had already departed. "I'll be back soon."

I noticed that my fingers had dug into the linen material of his jacket. I had to force myself to extract them. Frans turned away and walked through the gate in the transparent partition that divided the rest of the studio from the simulation stage.

On the other side, morning dawned over a monastery garden—about fifty feet by fifty feet. Gradually, the colonnades of the cloister emerged from the darkness. A fountain burbled in the middle distance; it was new. The brick pedestal in the center of the inner courtyard was freshly laid; the statue of San Francesco had not yet been erected. The grass was trampled, almost completely hidden under building rubble and garbage. In the corner was a heap of broken bricks; scrap wood lay around. Palladio's facade of San Francesco della Vigna had just been finished. An important time marker for travelers, Frans had explained to me: the year 1572. The monastery courtyard had served for years as a storage area for the carpenters and stonemasons. After completing their work, they were in the process of cleaning it up. The labor dragged on. Over the unadorned single-story building of the monastery, the studio ceiling flashed like a diamond crust of laser muzzles, reflectors, and filters.

The studio was filled with whispering and buzzing, which was transmitted over the monitor speakers. It sounded as if dozens of beehives were getting ready to swarm. The sound made me even more nervous than I already was. Involuntarily, I scratched my forearms.

Frans strolled across the inner courtyard and entered the dark cloister. In the simulation itself he could no longer be seen, but on the monitors, which showed a contrast-enhanced image, he was visible. He stood in the shadows with his arms crossed and looked toward me. Could he make me out through the partition?

I waved; he did not react.

I had never before seen so many technicians, engineers, and assistants in the control room. There were fourteen or fifteen sitting at the consoles and at least another ten standing around. Kazuichi had taken a seat at the mission controller's console, flanked by two assistants. Why wasn't Ishida present? The trips had become routine, it had been explained to me, and it was now the middle of the night.

"Another five minutes to transition," a technician said over a loudspeaker. Frans stepped out of the shadows, walked to the middle of the inner courtyard, and placed his hand on the empty pedestal of the monument. He really did not seem to be afraid. It was his sixty-third trip, he had told me. He nodded to the control center and signaled with his hand that he had understood the announcement. He was not permitted to carry any electronic devices on him.

The tension in the control room grew, though everyone was acting with studied calm.

Someone shouted something in Japanese—terse and severe. It sounded like a command to fire. Kazuichi nodded and keyed something into his console. A monitor showed a light blue graphic, a curve shooting steeply upward. The wave was approaching. I thought I heard a rumble that shook the foundations, but no one seemed to take notice of it. The morning light over the simulation had brightened. In the monastery courtyard all the details could now be made out.

Frans stood in the midst of the broken and discarded building material and debris. Tools leaned against the walls, along with boards, half-hewn stone moldings, primitive hoisting equipment with coarse hemp rope.

Over the loudspeaker came the countdown: ". . . twelve . . . eleven . . . ten . . . nine . . ."

The roar of the wave swelled. I covered my ears. It seemed to me as if the image of the simulation were becoming distorted. At the center of the stage I perceived a blurring, as if I were looking through a transparent plastic sheet deformed by the wind. But it was probably due to my overtired eyes, which had been staring for too long at the holograph. And I didn't

hear a rumble, only the voice of the technician and the chirping and clicking of the instruments from the control center.

Frans gave a thumbs-up and nodded.

". . . two . . . one . . . zero!"

A gong sounded.

Where Frans had stood, about two or three paces from the brick pedestal
of the monument, a dust cloud surged up as if someone had knocked away a
cricket ball, as if a small whirlwind were plucking at the leaves of the bushes.

"We've caught the curl!" a voice cried triumphantly. A jumble of voices
arose, relief, cheers. The faces of the technicians lit up with joyful excitement.

Kazuichi came out of the studio, wiping the sweat from his forehead.

"The transit worked," he said.

"Where is he now?" I asked him.

"At the destination, I hope," he replied, exhausted. "If everything went
according to plan, the soliton dropped him off in the monastery garden on
a summer morning of the year 1572."

"He's already there? I mean . . . he's not still on his way?"

"Time is not a road, Domenica. Time is a threshold. A nothingness."

"On a . . . summer morning?"

The Japanese man looked up at the studio ceiling as if he were checking
the brightness of the sky. Time seemed suspended. It didn't get lighter. Not
a leaf or a blade of grass stirred.

"The simulation is now frozen. It stops until he enters it again. On another summer morning. Three or four days later. Maybe in a week or in two
weeks. As long as he needs. But not too long. It must not change too much,"
he said, pointing to the debris lying around in the monastery garden.

"Then he reappears."

"He can reappear at any moment. The length of his stay has no influence on the time of his return. It is solely dependent on where the soliton
that brings him back drops him off. That can be in a few hours or tomorrow
or in a week. Whenever a soliton coming from the past passes through on
its way into the future."

I suddenly found it hard to breathe. The air in the studio was stale and
stuffy. In the transept of the monastery a choir could be heard faintly.
Monks who had gathered for morning prayer?

"Turn off the radio!" Kazuichi shouted into the control room. "Sorry,"
he said to me, patting my arm. "Don't worry, Domenica, we'll get it done.
We'll bring him back to you."

I was in a hurry to get out of the studio. In the anteroom technicians crowded noisily around a vending machine. It smelled like cheap instant coffee.

The night was clear and cold. I walked along the Fondamenta Giustina and tried in vain to fathom the depths of time that now separated Frans and me.

Time is not a road, Domenica. Time is a threshold. A nothingness.

From the balcony I looked out over the city. Venice slept. Beyond the Lido the Milky Way poured into the sea; light that had traversed the abysses of centuries reached its destination—at exactly that moment.

The campanile of San Francesco della Vigna projected like the pointer of an astrolabe vertically into the dark vastnesses of the night somewhere between Sirius and Tureis, into the billion-years-deep abysses from out of which, invisible to the human eye, fossil light trickled. I stared upward and tried to comprehend that I was looking across the sea of time at archipelagoes that were decades, centuries, millennia apart and combined into constellations—a mosaic of time snippets.

Suddenly I grasped what Ishida had meant by the arranged photos that lead people to believe in the course of time. The past is a collage, a gallery arranged in layers, which is projected onto a two-dimensional screen. The photos are copied over one another on a single film. The dimension of depth is blocked out. It's not the planimetric projection that fools the mind, but its own conception of depth. You have to negate the dimension of depth, and the spatially staggered distances arrange themselves on the surface like terrain formations on a topographical map. The sky is a gigantic screen on which the history of the universe is displayed: a synopsis of all events that have ever taken place in it, from the beginning. Our cosmos presents itself to us as a user interface. Similar photos are dragged over one another with the cursor. Then the negated dimension is reopened. The transition has taken place. That's how the universe of photons is constituted, which can bridge billions of light-years and have already reached their destination before they set off. That's how the trictrac game of space and time works. It was fantastic.

Hla Thilawuntha had figured out those rules and opened up access to all this with his mathematics. Only in reality the game was played in higher dimensions. We primates with our savanna brain could intuit it, but not really grasp it. Frans had indeed only taken a step over the threshold— but that threshold existed outside our everyday reality.

IX

The Garden of San Francesco della Vigna

For the rest of my life, I will reflect on what light is . . .
—Fifty years of intense reflection have not brought me closer to
the answer to the question "What are light quanta?"

ALBERT EINSTEIN

The soliton had passed through, heading toward the past. It had rolled down from the future, had with its universe-crushing power touched us so gently that we were able to detect its proximity only indirectly. It had washed around the membranes of our reality and made them permeable for a moment, had surged through us, as the physicists asserted, because it traversed all dimensions, the unfolded ones as well as the ones curled up in Planck space—however many that might be. It traveled farther into the depths of the past until after 15 billion years it would reach the beginning and cross the nadir of the continuum, as a swell crosses the North Pole, maintaining its direction of movement unchanged and yet inverted 180 degrees in the opposite direction, only to seek its way up into the future, to the end of time; there, perhaps—no one knew—streaming through a high gate, it was turned around in a similar way and headed back down into the past, driven by unimaginable forces. No one knew how long it took one of those strange cosmic tsunamis to travel along the surface of space-time. Perhaps the question was senseless, for it moved outside the continuum, as an electron moves along the surface of a conductor.

Nor did anyone know how many of those inconceivable energy packets were out in the cosmic ocean and whether there was any connection between them. From their movements it could be inferred that there was no interference between them. They seemed not to touch when they encountered each other—indeed, they did not even react when one glided through the other, just as a neutrino doesn't react to the Earth and passes through it when it crosses its path.

One of those waves would carry Frans back into my present. But no one could tell me when that might happen. Day after day I went to the studio and stared through the glass wall at the stage on which the simulation had been frozen: the monastery courtyard of San Francesco della Vigna on a summer morning 480 years earlier shortly before sunrise—a sliver of time, cast in glass in order to survive, captured by the computers in the control room, whose displays glowed patiently in anticipation of the moment that the spell would be broken and time would begin to move again.

Sometimes it struck me that only a few paces away the monks of the monastery were immobilized in the midst of their morning prayers as in an old painting. And then, when I closed my eyes, I thought I could hear their singing again, the lauds penetrating upward from the depths of the centuries as from dark vaults.

"When will he return?" I asked Kazuichi whenever I saw him, full of impatience, even though I knew that the question was senseless. "You promised me you'd bring him back."

"With the next passage upward," he replied with a laugh, for in the beginning it was more a game, "or at the latest the one after that."

"When will the next one be?"

"Hard to say. Sometimes we have three or even four a week, sometimes none at all."

"And how many have there been since his departure?"

Kazuichi raised his hand and extended his fingers. "Five," he said. "Up to now, he has always managed it quickly. Sometimes only a day passes, or a week; sometimes it takes a bit longer. You won't be an old woman so soon, Domenica."

He chuckled. But I wasn't in the mood to laugh.

"Don't worry. It's completely normal, believe me," he said, nodding at me encouragingly.

"How many of these tunnels are there actually?" I asked Ernesto.

"As far as I know, four. And another twelve are in the works. The longest is in Amsterdam; then comes the Venice tunnel. In Oakland and Johannesburg they have not yet advanced far. Into the nineteenth century or so, if I've been accurately informed. You only find this out on the sly. The Americans in particular shroud it in secrecy. Every scientific publication must be approved by a special committee made up of representatives of the government, the military, and the intelligence agencies, who have no clue about Thilawuntha's complex mathematics. Their institute in Oakland resembles a fortress and is more heavily secured than the Pentagon, the Dutch scientists who were permitted to visit it told me."

"They probably have to keep the militant creationists at bay," I surmised.

Ernesto nodded. "The military and the intelligence agencies guard the institute with grim determination. The thought that some rats could gnaw in the catacombs of the past at the foundations of the United States is unbearable to them. They regard it as an unforgivable error of judgment on God's part that he did not bestow the invention of the time tunnel on them but on the Dutch instead. Meanwhile, they had been spying on their studies from the beginning, but had long dismissed them as crackpot ideas."

"The Americans have always had a somewhat problematic relationship to reality."

"Yes, because they confuse reality with their way of life. Their worldview has been influenced more by the wishful and anxious fantasies served to them by Hollywood than by the facts of the reality in which they live—to say nothing of the reality of the world outside the United States."

I thought of Sarah. "That's not completely true, Ernesto."

He waved dismissively. "I know, there are exceptions. Especially among the scientists, but most of them, above all the politicians, really do seem to live in another universe."

"Do you have any idea why the Rinascita Institute wants to send us through the Amsterdam tunnel?"

"That I can tell you. First of all, it extends farther into the past; secondly, they have the most experience there with trips; and thirdly, it's the best developed. That is, they've stationed their own people along the route, who can help the travelers if they run into trouble."

"Which is not the case here in Venice."

"In more recent times, it is, but the tunnel construction into the sixteenth century is dragging on. Frans can certainly tell you something about that."

"But he doesn't. That's why I'm asking you."

Ernesto smiled, flattered. "Well, this is how it is: Here in Venice they have a few well-documented places. Such as San Francesco della Vigna. They know quite precisely what changes in the courtyard of the monastery from week to week, sometimes even from day to day. All the details are stored and can be retrieved and holographed as needed. That allows a precise targeting, of course. The traveler arrives at the aimed-for point in time—to the week, even to the day. But the whole thing has one serious drawback: Incredible amounts of data must be stored. The position of every stone someone heedlessly plunked down in the monastery courtyard, every board that was leaned against the wall, every tool a tradesman forgot somewhere in the area—everything must be documented and retrievable in order to construct the simulation in the studio. You understand?"

"Yes, I understand."

"In Amsterdam they can do that with considerably greater ease, especially when it comes to the simulation of a medieval scene. The southern shore of the Zuiderzee was a godforsaken area into the late sixteenth century. Hunters wading around in the mud in search of ducks, occasionally a fisherman inspecting his traps, now and then a few peasants cutting fresh reeds for the roofs of their houses. Otherwise not a soul far and wide. There you can tunnel to your heart's content, of course. But there's also a disadvantage: It's immensely difficult to aim. It can even happen that the traveler is dropped off a year earlier or later." Suddenly his ICom chirped. "Excuse me," he said, then stood up and went to the window to carry on a conversation in a low voice.

The institute's cafeteria was on the second floor of the old wing, where there were real windows. Beyond the Fondamenta Nuove, San Michele could be made out, looming closer in the clear autumn midday light. The cypresses stood like a cordon along the southern enclosing wall, as if they had to guard the dead and prevent them from breaking out again at night.

Ernesto brought back two espressos from the vending machine when he returned to the table. The brown sludge smelled disgusting, as always at the institute. Why did people put up with that? Were they so accustomed to simulations that they no longer even recognized the smell and taste of real coffee?

We work on real reality—don't make me laugh!

"Thanks," I said. "So you've stored the past on a computer, if I understood that correctly."

"Not exactly," he replied. "More along the lines of . . . well, how your life is stored in the photos that have been taken of you since your earliest childhood. Those photos are the tunnel."

He scratched the sugar out of the paper cup and licked off the plastic spoon.

"The pictures that you need are brought back for you by the travelers."

"Exactly. No photos, of course—at most a charcoal or red chalk draw-ing. The transition won't work if you try to take a camera with you into the past, because that could possibly change the world."

"Change the world? I keep hearing that. What does that mean?"

Ernesto sighed. "Yes. That's the way it is. New parallel universes are constantly arising. Saint Everett help us. You'll learn all this for yourself before you're sent off."

"And who determines what gets through as luggage and what doesn't?" I asked.

"No one knows exactly. Falcotti would probably say that God ordains it. Professor Auerbach from the CIA thinks it's a sort of supercomputer with a self-preservation program of the future that decides. But it was soon discov-ered that there is in any case an iron law: No technical artifact can be transported toward the past, lest anachronisms occur. No cameras, no mod-ern weapons, not even details of clothing such as snap buttons or zippers."

"The future of the universe hinges on snap buttons and zippers? You must be kidding."

"I'm afraid not, as experience has shown. We are reliant, and indeed ex-clusively, on what the travelers can transport in here." He tapped his temple.

I nodded and discreetly pushed aside the cup of coffee, which had got-ten cold.

"It works like this: Take Amsterdam, for example. A traveler returns from the end of the tunnel. Together with the visualists he constructs an image of what he saw in the year twelve so-and-so—that's how far the people from the CIA have ventured by now. He travels once again, carefully seeks contact with inhabitants of that time and inquires: Was a tree cut down near here last winter? Where exactly? Aha. That hut over there, it's new, isn't it? Since when has it been there? It was built last autumn? Have there been any other changes here? No? With that information he returns. The simulation is reworked. The tree is restored to its place, the new hut re-moved. And again the journey is taken to the thirteenth century. Indeed! There stands the old tree; the hut, on the other hand, not yet. Another half a year done. Next jump . . . That's the job of the tunnel diggers, Domenica. In that way they burrow farther and farther. Sometimes it goes faster, some-times slower. Sometimes they manage forty or fifty years per year. And eventually the Amsterdam people will stumble on a sign that says: Day of Creation. End of the road."

Ernesto chuckled, folded his arms behind his almost bald head, and
stretched his long legs out in front of him.

"I didn't imagine it being so arduous."

"Arduous? That's child's play! Here in Venice it's arduous. There were
years when they barely managed to advance another month into the past.
In a whole year! That's real backbreaking work. The visualists are often in
complete despair, there are so many details to take into account. It's a constant back and forth."

"But I haven't gotten that impression at all."

"You mean because of Frans?"—He gave a wave of his hand—"That can
happen. A question of accuracy of aim. Don't worry."

"Damn it! Everyone here tells me not to worry, but the more I delve into
the technical principles, the more my head spins at the thought of what
thin ice you're all treading on."

Ernesto puffed out his cheeks and nervously rubbed his forehead below
his receding hairline.

"I don't deny that there's still a lot to do."

"Just that you're sitting comfortably in a chair in front of your monitor in
the control room while Frans creeps around the sixteenth century and risks
his neck."

"The travelers need us. Have to be able to rely on us."

"That's certainly clear. And I hope you do a good job, Ernesto."

FOR DAYS I avoided the studio. I didn't want to see the image of the simulation anymore. It paralyzed me, for it hadn't changed for twenty-three days.
Then I ventured there again after all and cast a glance into the shadows of
the cloister. Nothing. Not the slightest movement. In the control room a
solitary technician was listening motionlessly to the whispering of his cranial implant.

"Has he ever been gone this long before?" I asked Kazuichi.

"Yeah, yeah," he declared, smiling. "He's been gone for a whole month
before. The return trip didn't work right away because he had something
bulky with him."

"Something bulky?"

"Copies of building plans for some palazzo. I don't remember which it
was."

"Do you think that this time too he . . . ?"

"No, no. He's had a lot of experience since then," Kazuichi tried to reassure me.

THIRTY DAYS HAD now gone by and four more solitons had passed through heading upward, I heard, but none of them released the courtyard of San Francesco from its stasis. It seemed to me as if Kazuichi looked somewhat worried. That Japanese man's expression was so hard to read.

Any number of things could have happened to Frans. I had questioned my Scarabeo about 1572. What an unquiet and dangerous time! In the Arsenale there had been a fire in June of 1569. Four almost-finished galleys went missing; more than a dozen ships were damaged. Arson was suspected; a heightened state of alert was decreed. An eye was kept above all on strangers roaming around in the vicinity. In 1570 Cyprus was lost. The humiliation of Famagosta still inflamed passions. After being betrayed and captured, Marcantonio Bragadin, who had audaciously led the defense of the besieged city, was publicly flayed by the Ottomans. In the meantime, satisfaction had been attained and the disgrace avenged at Lepanto by sinking the Ottoman fleet, but the foreboding that this might have been the last stroke of the paw of the lion of San Marco and the star was irrevocably sinking nonetheless spread a sense of nervousness and insecurity. The Signoria resorted to a policy of "bilancia," of subtle balance. A shameful policy of rotten compromises with the Sublime Porte, said many patriots. "The powers that be in the Palazzo Ducale bow and scrape as if our fleet had been defeated at Lepanto," they murmured, watching with mistrust the coming and going of the papal and imperial delegations, which haggled for money and support, reasserted claims to power, and strove to increase their influence—attracted like hyenas scenting the approaching death of a fat prey. The city was teeming with spies, informants, and denouncers, snooping around on the squares and in the palazzi, in the taverns and the brothels, and the judges in the Purgatorio and the Inferno made short work of anyone on whom even the shadow of a suspicion fell.

How easily Frans, as a stranger, could get caught between the millstones, when so many inhabitants of the time were ground between them. Spies were executed by the sword. Or had they been hanged? Broken on the wheel? Drowned? Or simply left to waste away in the lead chambers?

I slept badly.

* * *

LUIGI HAD A surprise for me. He reported a positive change in my account balance. A five-thousand-euro "monthly training grant," retroactively effective as of July. The money had been transferred by a company named Timelink Manpower in The Hague via Banca Ambrosiana, which had been resurrected as if by a miracle under Paul VII. I had a twenty-five-thousand-euro fortune in my account! Nothing like that had ever happened to me before in my whole life!

"Shall I invest it for you?" Luigi asked helpfully.

"You can do what you want with it, just don't squander it."

"I'll manage it for you, Domenica. But we have to save and submit an authorization."

"You're getting on my nerves."

"I'm sorry, but it is my duty to call your attention to this."

"Take me out to eat instead."

"You mean you would like me to make a reservation for you?"

"Yes, and a date with all the Romans who are still here. My treat."

"Incidentally, an invitation has arrived."

"From whom?"

"From Ernesto Caputi. He is taking his leave."

ERNESTO WAS TO depart for Amsterdam on December 12. He would receive his further training there at the Hendrik Casimir Institute, the former workplace of the legendary Hla Thilawuntha from Burma.

"I'm looking forward to it," said Ernesto, his eyes shining.

"There's no missing that," Renata mocked.

Ernesto looked around blankly as we all laughed, and then he laughed with us.

He had invited us to a good-bye meal at the Madonna, an old restaurant rich in tradition on a covered side street southwest of the Rialto Bridge. It consisted of a dozen interconnected dining rooms and exuded an intimate ambiance.

The fish soup was excellent, as was the orate, and the house wine, a dry Prosecco from Valdobbiadene, was top quality. Still, things never really livened up. Perhaps I was to blame for that, because I had infected all of them with my worries and my gloom. But Marcello too was gazing sadly at his plate and had scarcely said a word.

"What's the matter, Marcello?" I asked. "I've never seen you like this."

"His hormones are a bit off-kilter," Renata interjected. "I think we'd better leave him alone."

"Is he in love?" I asked.

"He's always in love. No, he's fallen into the hands of the doctors. They're adapting him for the eighteenth century. They've injected him with buckyballs full of nanos—that affects his spirits."

Marcello gave me a suffering look with his dark eyes.

"That lies in store for the two of us as well," Renata declared.

Ernesto didn't let anything interfere with his excited mood. He had blissfulness in his eyes and beads of sweat on his forehead below his receding hairline as he raved about "CIA Mission Control," which could oversee the activities of two dozen time travelers at the same time.

"Hey," said Renata, "keep your feet on the ground! You watch freeriders jump onto a train passing through and hope they catch a train coming in the opposite direction that will eventually bring them back."

"Well, that's not exactly true," replied Ernesto. "Professor Ishida is just prone to little jokes like that. Isn't that right?"

He looked at Kazuichi in search of support, but he only grinned inscrutably.

"That's true," I said. "You'll never believe how funny I find those little jokes."

"Okay, stop," said Renata. "It's my fault. I was talking nonsense. Forgive me. It's his party."

She gestured with a nod to Ernesto, who was looking somewhat uncomprehendingly from one face to another.

"Let's hear it for Mission Control!" I exclaimed, draining my glass—and then another . . . and a few more.

I didn't recall exactly how we had gotten home. I could remember only the dense fog, deserted streets, and pools of light on damp cobblestones. And that, giggling, we had puzzled over Kazuichi's compass finger, but couldn't make sense of its directions, because the Japanese man was just as drunk as the rest of us. Ultimately, we had gotten lost and, staggering arm in arm, stared aghast from a narrow step into the black water of a canal that had suddenly opened up in front of us. We had come within a hairsbreadth of stumbling into it.

DECEMBER 18. FRANS still had not returned. For thirty-two days he had now been away.

That morning I had brought Renata to the train station. She was traveling via Milano, Domodossola, Bern, Basel, and Cologne to Amsterdam, because she was with certainty on the wanted lists stored in the Austrians' computers. Somewhere in a train station, in a pedestrian passage, or on a busy square, one of the ubiquitous surveillance cameras would be able to identify her face in the crowd and trigger an alarm.

We took the vaporetto to Santa Lucia. It was a clear morning. The colors of the faiences on the facades of the elegant palazzi along the Canal Grande gleamed in the rising sun. The gold in the frescos glowed, faces of saints came to life, eyes unexpectedly returned the viewer's gaze. But the signs of decay, of shabbiness and decline, were unmistakable in the unsparing light of the still-low sun.

In the large glassed-in cafeteria of the train station was a noisy school class. About thirty twelve-to-fourteen-year-olds in ugly ocher school uniforms with red piping were flopped, slouching, on the benches, waiting for their departure. The obligatory Venice trip was over. Anoraks and caps were piled on the floor. Smart travel bags lay in a group like a herd of garishly colored seals, huddled together anxiously in an unfamiliar environment. Their chips were programmed onto the IComs of their owners, so that they could not get lost or be forgotten. They began to move halfheartedly whenever their owners changed seats or went to one of the kiosks. Almost all the schoolchildren wore sensoelectronic BioPets on their chests or their upper arms, where they clung, whimpering and begging their masters for food and affection. But like all sentient beings they had to bear the torments that their merciless gods inflicted on them.

Some of the boys and girls had interconnected their game modules into small holovid arenas in which they pitted animals against each other. King Kongs, Godzillas, giant scorpions, roaring brontosauruses reared up and stomped toward each other. Cherry-red fountains sprayed into nothingness; severed body parts whirled away and disappeared on the periphery. It smelled like warm blood.

"Always the same cruel crap," Renata said crossly.

The rudimentary AIs of the pets panicked. The half-creatures wriggled, tugged, and screamed in utter confusion. I watched with fascination. Emotions escalated. Some travelers turned to the schoolchildren and scolded them. The saleswomen at the counter of the cafeteria were shouting something that was lost in the tumult.

"Stop!"

Like an almighty supreme deity, the resolute face of the teacher suddenly appeared on the holostages, shut down the game programs, put an end to the carnage, and swept the chimeras into nothingness.

The hysterical whimpering and squealing of the pets abated only gradually. They had to be soothed by stroking and coaxing.

"Let's go! Get ready!"

I turned around, but couldn't find the original of the forceful woman anywhere. Perhaps she was supervising the excursion from her desk in Turin or Bologna and directing her swarm of schoolchildren via satellite.

The schoolchildren sullenly pulled themselves together, fished their jackets out of the chaos, and put on their caps. The herd of travel bags grew agitated; it electronically picked up a scent and began moving, pushing and shoving, toward the exit. One of them let out a sobbing bleat, because it got wedged between a chair and a table leg. A kick from a young man freed it from its unfortunate situation and it hurried to catch up to the others.

I took Renata in my arms, glad that most of the people had in the meantime left the room, for I couldn't hold back tears.

"Have a good trip," I sniffled. "See you in Amsterdam."

She nodded. I felt her digging her mutilated fingers into my shoulder.

"Take care of yourself, Domenica."

"Yes, you too," I replied.

When I kissed her on the cheek, I noticed that she was crying too.

"Hey!" she said, running the back of her hand over her lips and nose. Then she fastened her wooden clasp tighter in her hair and grinned at me bravely. At that moment I realized how fond I was of her.

"Give Frans my regards. I'm sure he'll be back soon," she said, giving me an encouraging poke. "Oh yeah, I almost forgot. Would you be so good as to look in on Heli at the Ospedaletto?"

Renata fished out of the pocket of her anorak a small square package, which fit in the palm of her hand, wrapped in gold paper and adorned with a red ribbon.

"Give this to her, please. It's a Christmas present for her. I found it by chance, but didn't have time to bring it to her myself."

"What is it, if I may ask?"

"It's a small piece of Mars."

"That will definitely make her happy."

"Yeah, I think so too."

I waved to her for a long time as the train left the station, heading out onto the embankment toward Mestre.

ON THE WAY back I went to the Rialto market. Next to the traghetto pier, a float rocked in the canal on which a nativity scene was being set up— apparently the Adoration of the Magi.

Afternoon was approaching, but the fish market was still bustling. Gulls squawked. They demanded their due, pattering by the dozens on the ledges, crowding together in the warm spots on the roofs and besieging the chimneys. On the splashed ground were heaps of discarded greasy white Styrofoam containers with the remains of blood-speckled crushed ice. Oily zinc tubs on wooden stands, half filled with gray-blue clouds of cuttlefish, coiled together like excised brains full of dark memories. Fish guts were scraped off slippery wooden boards. Broad blades glided through light red gaping tissue, scraped emery-rough fish skin, crunched through cartilage and fish bone. Cut-up bodies, tossed briefly onto the scale, slithered into transparent plastic bags. On the edge of a fillet board, upright chopped-off swordfish heads were lined up into a picket fence.

Whenever I came here, I observed with a mixture of horror and fascination the killing all around. The transformation of living things into food, discreet, clean—apart from a few blood spatters. The opening and emptying out of abdominal cavities, the expert, exact mutilation. When I closed my eyes, I heard whispering at the edge of the audible. White noise? Little screams? Or was it only the roar of my own blood in my inner ear?

I noticed a young man with a shaved head looking around uneasily. A salesman handed him a bulging plastic bag full of fish from behind the counter, which he quickly slipped into his shabby duffel bag.

"Is the signorina looking for something in particular?" the salesman asked me loudly and somewhat too forcefully. "Bronzini, mormore, dendici? Completely fresh. All caught last night."

In the lagoon?

He wore a black wool cap and a new red plastic apron, which was sprinkled with fish scales as with mother-of-pearl sequins. I had stared at the plastic bag for too long. It did not contain dead fish; I had recognized the sluggish movements immediately. They were paralyzed specimens infected by nanos gone haywire. "Golden fish"—oros, which were in the meantime worth their price among collectors.

With a heavy blade as wide as a hand, the merchant hacked off a ray's fin edges and tossed the mutilated body onto a heap of half-prepared fish in which there was still life, which shuddered with pain.

"Here!" cried the merchant, throwing a severed fin toward me. But he had feinted; it landed a few yards next to me on the ground between the Styrofoam containers. A gull with a hunched neck and large as a goose grabbed the piece, fluttered ungracefully into the air with the spoils, and dragged its large yellowish red feet behind it like rags. The fish dealer guffawed at the successful joke and, with a sniffle, wiped his nose on his sleeve. The sellers at the surrounding stalls grinned. The young man with the duffel bag had disappeared into the crowd.

I shivered. It became clear to me that the scientists had long since lost control. Those nano-contaminated things had long since passed from hand to hand; they ended up in souvenir shops, on shelves and in display cases, as wall decorations in living rooms all over the world—and on Falcotti's desk in Rome. And I doubted whether in their isolation measures they had also considered the birds, which caught their prey in the lagoon and dragged it God knows where. Or had they been fully aware of the risk they were taking? An unashamed large-scale field experiment? It was in any case clear that nothing and no one could stuff this genie back into the bottle.

X

Sand from Mars

If we indeed live on a brane in a spacetime with extra dimensions, gravitational waves generated by the motion of bodies on the brane would travel off into the other dimensions. If there were a second shadow brane, gravitational waves would be reflected back and trapped between the two branes. On the other hand, if there was only a single brane and the extra dimensions went on forever . . . gravitational waves could escape altogether and carry away energy from our brane world. This would seem to breach one of the fundamental principles of physics: the Law of Conservation of Energy. The total amount of energy remains the same. However, it appears to be a violation only because our view of what is happening is restricted to the brane. An angel who could see the extra dimensions would know that the energy was the same, just more spread out.

STEPHEN HAWKING

At the institute I noticed that in Studio Two an additional simulation had been generated and in Studio Three a third was being prepared. Were those emergency measures?

The second stage also showed the frozen image of the monastery courtyard in the morning light, but some details had changed. The stones and broken bricks were gone, as were the scrap wood and tools. The grass patches between the cloisters had recovered; the grass had grown. What did that mean?

Kazuichi had explained to me that the arrangement of the target point was left unchanged in order to ensure the "association." It was required for a safe return. Now they were apparently trying to simulate the same target point at a later time—the image of the monastery courtyard in late summer or autumn of the year 1572, which was stored in the computer as a result of a previous trip—to create an emergency entrance into the tunnel for Frans, if he had been delayed for some reason or prevented from a timely return to the target site. A "virtual fan" had been opened, as one of the technicians present explained to me, a young freckled Dutch woman. She was tall and lean, almost bony, but had strikingly large breasts. Over the right one, on her light blue coveralls, was a white sticker on which RIET SWEELINCK was written in red. The computer, she explained to me, was now constructing a series of various eventualities of later, well-documented points in time and offering them to the traveler.

She denied my objection that that was a pure game of chance. The original point in time was still being maintained, she argued, and Mr. van Hooft had the alternative points in mind. On top of that, a second site was being prepared. She pointed to the stage in the third studio, on which there was not much to see, however—nothing but an unoccupied, half-ruined, single-story building, whose window frames had been torn out and whose roof trusses had apparently been destroyed by a fire. In front of it, a strip of land overgrown with weeds was taking shape.

"Where, for heaven's sake, is that?"

"That's the monastery on the island San Francesco del Deserto south of Burano, abandoned in the fifteenth century," she explained. "Not until the nineteenth century did monks resettle there."

"Why aren't the travelers sent to that inconspicuous place right away?"

She shrugged. "How are you going to pinpoint a target when nothing changes for years?" she asked me with a laugh. "Mr. van Hooft would first have to inquire in what century he had landed. Besides, how would he get away from there without attracting attention? The fishermen would capture him and turn him over to the authorities in the hope of snagging a reward. Bounties are put on spies' heads. With the time-natives it's not so simple here, I can tell you that. We have it easier in Amsterdam. Our tunnel is secured by our own people, deep into the Middle Ages. Someone is always nearby."

She gestured with a nod to the half-ruined monastery building in the simulation and added: "For a return the place is ideal, however. That's why we have it in reserve."

"Do you know Marcello Tortorelli?" I asked the Dutch woman.

"The guy with the black curls who came here from Rome this fall? Yes, I know him," she replied, turning red.

Look at that, I thought. That rascal.

"He's going to work here as a tunnel guard, he told me. In the eighteenth century," she said tersely.

An interesting job, no doubt, I reflected, but probably not simple. Marcello would have to learn to rein in his temperament. To have all that knowledge and not be permitted to use it would be particularly hard for him. Occasionally he would travel home to the twenty-first century to let off steam and also present the fruits of his botanical excursions to the Rinascita della Creazione.

What would my job look like? I wondered. Probably not so different. Just three hundred years earlier.

"I see that you like him."

The young technician looked at her worn-out sneakers and smiled. "He's good-looking, yes," she said with a shrug, adding a bit snippily, "but he still has a lot to learn."

"Will Frans come back soon?" I asked.

She looked at me with surprise.

"He won't get lost," she replied with a laugh. "Not him."

"Hello, Mama! *Buon Natale!*"

"*Buon Natale*, child! Where are you?"

"In Venice."

"What are you doing there? Why aren't you spending the holidays with us?"

"I have things to do, Mama. I've accepted a job. I'm being trained for it here in Venice. How are you doing, Mama?"

"I have a lot to do too. If I didn't have Chalid . . ."

"Who's Chalid?"

"A charming person. He's staying with us. We're now renting rooms in winter too. To extended-stay guests, you know? Otherwise, there's not enough money. And Chalid helps me a bit in the café. He's such a kind person."

"How's Grandma doing?"

"Oh, she's doing fine, but she leads a more withdrawn life these days. She prefers to be in her room."

"Aha."

"She doesn't like Chalid that much, even though she has no good reason not to. But you know her prejudices. A bit pigheaded, you know. And she's not the youngest anymore."

"Give her my regards. I wish her all the best."

"Yes, my child. A lot has changed here in Genoa . . ."

So it seems, I thought.

"You should see it. The old town here is half underwater, despite the dam they built last summer along the harbor promenade. You remember where we used to have the café—no, you were still too little back then—down on Piazza Caricamento. Now there's an antiques dealer in there. Everything destroyed. All the old furniture and pictures. But we don't have to worry about that. There hasn't been a flood like that in their lifetime, the people say. Probably it's due to all the refugee ships in the harbor—so they claim anyway. The whole gulf is full of them. Where are they all coming from? Mainly Moros, of the inferior sort. Chalid is completely different."

"Where's he from?"

"Oh, he's Italian. Though your grandma has somewhat different views. His parents come from Benghazi. But he was born and raised here. A typical Italian man. So friendly and helpful. I don't know what I'd do without him. It all depends on me now."

Did this Chalid sit at the cash register? Or on the high seat next to the espresso machine, in front of the warmly soaked drawer giving off the scent of coffee, on the edge of which, day in, day out, Grandfather had knocked countless batches of coffee dregs out of the metal filters? I closed my eyes, heard the dull beat of metal on damp wood and smelled the scent, which spread immediately when the steam was pressed with a stifled sigh into the metal cylinder packed with ground coffee, saw the darkly stained leather apron he had draped over his shattered knees.

". . . to me at all?"

"Yes, I am, Mama. I'm listening to you. I wish all of you a happy holiday . . ." Oh, what the heck? I said to myself. Grant her the little bit of happiness with her Chalid! ". . . and give Chalid my regards too, even though we haven't met."

"I'll do that, child. And you have a wonderful holiday too, if you really can't come."

"Another time, Mama. *Ciao!*"

IT WAS CHRISTMAS; forty-eight days had passed since Frans's departure, and the efforts at the institute to bring him back had so far come to nothing.

"We've never had as few passages as we do at the moment," Kazuichi said in a troubled tone when I ran into him on the way to Mondoloni's language laboratory at the institute. "In December we had only eight altogether—five down into the past and just three upward. Going by experience, a phase of increased activity should now follow."

But his optimism was less convincing than usual. Or was I only imagining that?

IN THE LATE afternoon I went to the Ospedaletto to visit Heloise Abret and deliver Renata's Christmas gift to her. As I walked down the corridor through the housekeeping wing toward the cafeteria in the back, Abe approached me—empty.

"Hello, Abe," I said. He stopped.

"Please forgive me, but I should know you, right?" he said softly. "I'm afraid that not much was invested in my optical recognition system. Regrettably, I therefore cannot . . ."

"I'm Domenica Ligrina. I've visited Madame Abret a few times."

"Now I recognize your voice, Signorina Ligrina. More care was taken on the audio system."

"Is Madame Heloise here?" I asked him.

"I'm afraid I don't know. She was taken away, and since then I have had no more contact with her."

"Are you familiar with that thing?" asked someone behind me. I turned around to face a short, stout man in a black suit.

"What thing?" I asked.

"The handicap chair." He patted the wire mesh of Abe's backrest.

"No," I said.

"It's been shuffling around the house for three days. No one dares to switch it off for fear of breaking something. The thing is outrageously expensive, I've been told, and I have impressed on everyone to keep their hands off the electronics, for heaven's sake. Someone from NASA is supposed to come and pick it up, but that can take weeks."

"To my knowledge, Madame Abret relies on it . . ."

"No. Not anymore. She died yesterday. For two days we had her in the intensive care ward over in the Ospedale. Heart failure. Did you know that the woman had scarcely half of her bone mass? She almost crumbled through our fingers when she had to be moved to another bed. The poor thing screamed her head off before the sedation kicked in. Well . . . anyway. Are you a family member? My condolences. — No? Well, her suffering is over. But I ask you: Does it have to be on Christmas of all times, when all hell breaks loose here? Please excuse me, signorina," he said with a wave, hurrying away.

Abe had heard our conversation, but had apparently not entirely comprehended it.

"When will it be possible to resume contact with Heloise?"

"That will . . . I'm sorry, Abe, but that will probably no longer be possible."

"Oh . . ." said Abe. "But she needs me."

"I'm afraid . . ." I could not go on.

When I stood later in front of the portal on Barbaria delle Tole, tears came to my eyes and my hand clenched around the small gift packet in my jacket pocket. What stupid questions that robot had to ask!

At home I untied the ribbon and unpacked the gift. It was one of those small plastic half-spheres that used to enclose a little house in a wintry landscape. When you shook it, thick snowflakes came down from the sky. This one was different: A few elongated drop-shaped buildings that were half embedded in the ground of a barren, rust-brown landscape. When you shook the half-sphere, its interior became opaque with surging red dust, which only slowly sank down. PORT ABRET was written on a little label on the wooden base, and SAND FROM MARS—with a guarantee of authenticity from NASA.

IN THE AFTERNOON I made a pilgrimage to Santa Maria Gloriosa, my favorite church. What large-hearted patrons the friars must have had in that greedy, stingy society!

I entered the vast nave. The Titian altar shone under the chancel screen. The Assunta's garments were in flames, seemed to fly blazingly upward. I walked toward her under the beams that had been stained by the light into silvery silk and slid my hand over the polished wood of the Coro dei Frati. In the high window over the altar six stars twinkled green, blue, and red in the light of the low sun like the pattern in a kaleidoscope.

"Please," I said silently. "Protect him and bring him back."

I hadn't prayed since my father's death—out of protest, for I had never forgiven God for that. Now I'd come crawling back and felt like a traitor. I looked around. Numerous people absorbed in prayer. All women. Some were weeping.

"Please," I whispered.

In a side chapel I lit candles: one for Frans, one for Renata, one for Heloise, one for Abe, and one for me.

I WANDERED ON to Campo San Giacomo dall'Orio. The Uncino, where I had been with Frans, was closed until January 6. I peered through the glass entrance into the empty restaurant. The hands of the large clock in the rear of the establishment still stood at a quarter to six. Behind me a dog growled. I spun around in alarm, but it was not a modified animal; rather, it was a completely ordinary, self-important little yapper bothered by my presence.

When I left the square, the window of a tiny stationery shop happened to catch my eye; it displayed postcards of the city from the nineteenth century. Suddenly I recognized Frans in one of them. I caught my breath in astonishment. It was a photo of a scene on the harbor. Under the mast of a fishing boat, three fishermen were sitting and crouching, sorting their catch into shallow woven baskets. One of the men stood at the mast and with his left hand held on to the hanging ropes of the rigging—Frans! His head was bowed—he was watching the others work—so that only his foreshortened profile was visible, but by the casual, somewhat stooped posture, the height, and the hand holding the bundle of ropes I had recognized him at once. It was clearly Frans! He wore fisherman's clothing, coarse striped pants, reinforced in front by strong cords, tucked into thick knee-length socks made of white wool, a vest buttoned up halfway, a long jacket of soft, light gray material, and on his head a pointed wool cap with a thick pompom that hung down to his chest. Like the other three men, Frans too had a long thin meerschaum pipe between his teeth.

The door of the stationery shop was locked. It was a holiday. The moment I turned around to move on, the door of the café on the opposite corner opened, and a pale, elderly man came shuffling across the street. He fished a key from his pants pocket.

"Can I do something for you, signora?" he asked.

He smelled of peppermint liqueur.

"I'd like to have that postcard," I said.

The man unlocked the door and we entered the tiny shop—it was packed to the ceiling with merchandise, and it smelled overpoweringly of mothballs. He fetched the card from the display window.

"What are those photos?" I asked.

The stationery seller examined the photo as if he were consciously seeing it for the first time and tried in vain to scratch off with his fingernail a few specks of fly excrement that were stuck in the laminate. It must have been holding out for years in the window waiting for me. He turned over the card.

"*Archivio Filippo. Vecchie immagini di Venezia*," he read from the back. "A historical photo of the harbor. Hm. Fishermen," he said, shrugging.

I bought the card from him.

KAZUICHI SMILED WHEN I showed him the photo later.

"I remember," he said. "He brought back one of those pipes for each of us back then. At the time in which he had work to do they were very popular. Must have been around 1896. A shipment of sepiolite had just arrived on a freighter from Bursa. The best meerschaum comes from there; it's mined in Eskisehir. Frans had two dozen of the things made by a Nuremberg pipe carver, which he brought back and gave away at the institute."

"What are those cords in front of Frans's fly there? I can't make sense of them. Is that a cage?" I asked.

Kazuichi took a look at the detail. His eyes narrowed to slits and he let out a brief, shrill chuckle. "Perhaps a security measure. You have to ask him that."

"Easier said than done," I sighed, and then both of us were silent for quite a while. "Fifty-eight days have now passed. I don't know what to think anymore. Has a traveler ever been gone for so long?"

Kazuichi gave me an uneasy look. "Not here. But in Amsterdam they once had a case—it was a long time ago—in which a traveler came back only after a year. They had long since given up on him, but left the simulation as it was to be safe."

"A *year!*"

Kazuichi nodded.

"Three hundred and forty-two days. But subjectively he had aged only two weeks. He had stayed in the past only that long."

"And the rest of the time?"

"Destination-time presence and the span between the transitions are not proportional."

I looked at him inquiringly.

"The time spent subjectively in the past and the time span that opens up in the here and now between the departure and the return are not congruent."

Kazuichi swept one hand in a wide arc over the other, which lay motionless on the table.

"Someone can stay a day in the past, and he is gone for a year," he went on. "Someone else is back the next day and has gotten a year older, because he spent a year in the past. There's no connection there. That's what makes the traveling so difficult and nerve-racking."

"I've come to know that."

Kazuichi nodded.

"So keep waiting."

"Yes," he said.

He closed his eyes and ran both hands over his face. I had never looked at it consciously from such close proximity. His lashless eyelids were shaped like egg cowrie shells, gently rounded and smooth as porcelain. He seemed exhausted. His beardless face was sunken, and from up close he looked older than usual. Over the corners of his mouth, wiry black hairs sprouted from a dozen deep follicles, hanging down like the barbels of a catfish. Did they enable him to detect patterns of cosmic order in the mud of reality?

"There's really very little we can do, Domenica," he said in an unusually soft voice. "We shouldn't deceive ourselves. Ultimately, we're dogs that have learned to ride the subway. We have no idea about the schedules or the route network; we don't know what drives the trains or how they are steered. We know only that we have to board when the doors open and that by doing so we can get to places that would otherwise be unreachable for us. Our activity is purely parasitic."

His black eyes flashed at me from under his heavy lids.

"What we can do—and what we do—is the following," he went on. "We minimize the details. They're important for the accuracy of aim during the journey there; for the journey back, however, they're more of a hindrance. The traveler does this—to the extent it's feasible for him—on his side, on-site. On our side we make the corresponding changes in the simulation. The steps of the detail reduction are precisely arranged in advance. They facilitate the alignment, the association. It can, of course, occur that something in the target site unexpectedly changes that we know nothing about and that he cannot influence. If it is for some reason impossible for him to make it to the target site, he has to find his way to another prearranged site that we keep open for him as an emergency exit."

"And if that possibility is barred to him as well?" I asked worriedly.

"Then things get somewhat more difficult. If an undocumented change has occurred at the target site, there's a danger that he could slip into a reality that is not our past. That would involve an Everett deviation, an offshoot of our universe, a developing parallel universe. That used to signify a theoretical solution to the quantum paradox. In the meantime, we know that those deviations are reality—even if not our reality."

"If he has ended up there, then he's lost."

"No. No traveler has ever gotten lost before. More than two thousand transitions have been successfully carried out to date. All the travelers up to now have returned to our universe. Those Everett deviations are subject to a regression. That is, they are reintegrated, so to speak, into the main strand, when the alternatives that have arisen are not so grave that they retain their own weight. Imagine it like this." He cupped both hands and placed them together. "You have two soap bubbles that are stuck together. Suddenly the dividing membrane between them disappears. They have united. There seems to be a force inherent to the multiverse that counters Everett inflation. Dorit van Waalen hypothesized as early as in 2028 that solitons bring about that effect. He called it '*Uitborstelen*,' brushing out. In any case, all travelers who had slipped into a clearly deviating reality were borne home by the solitons to the here and now."

"But there's no guarantee that it couldn't happen at some point," I insisted.

Kazuichi shrugged. "Guarantee? — No. There's none," he said, sticking out his chin confrontationally. "But it might be the case that his trip went off without a hitch."

"*Went* off? Did I hear you right: *Went* off?"

"You heard me right. He has long since returned, only the soliton carried him some distance into the future and dropped him off there. That's exactly what I've been trying to explain to you." He blew air out of his broad nose, causing his barbels to flutter. "Destination-time presence and the span between the transitions are not proportional."

"Are you saying that he . . . that he might now be living in the future?" I asked.

Kazuichi let out his shrill laugh. "No, Domenica. He isn't *living* in the future. Rather, that means that he will appear in the simulation when we will have reached the point in time when he was dropped off. Granted, it's difficult to understand. The grammar of our language is ill-suited to express such matters. You have to imagine it visually."

"That he has overtaken us, who are on foot, or—in a way—flown over us?" I asked.

Kazuichi nodded. "Exactly! He is in the process of surfing over us, so to speak." He once again swept one hand in an arc over the other. "Frans is describing a curve in a higher dimension, before he lands again on our familiar one-dimensional timeline. Right now he's somewhere up there, over us, in a sense. Somewhere out there. No problem."

I took his hand between both of mine and squeezed it. "It's sweet of you, Kazuichi, to try to bolster me up, but I can tell by looking at you that you're really worried."

"No, no, no," he protested vehemently, and his barbels bristled as if he were picking up a scent.

Dogs on the subway.

THE WHOLE MONTH of January went by. Frans did not turn up. February began.

I now visited more and more often the garden of San Francesco della Vigna, the real one. I always faced Saint Francis. Flanked by two old cypresses and oleander bushes, he stood in his hooded robe on the high brick pedestal and prayed. Sometimes I joined in his prayer.

Occasionally I felt as if any moment Frans would step out of the semi-darkness of the cloister, the pompom cap on his head and the meerschaum pipe between his teeth. I was jittery with anticipation—ready to jump up and rush down the gravel path to him. But no one appeared, not even tourists. They were denied access to the monastery courtyard. The sexton let me in, because he knew me. I had told him I was waiting here for someone. He had furrowed his brow thoughtfully and then nodded sympathetically. He thought I wasn't quite right in the head, but took pity on me.

What had Renata said about the bells of the campanile of San Francesco della Vigna? They tolled on Ash Wednesday? That night, I told myself, I would be out. Perhaps under one of the masks that were traditionally removed at midnight Frans's face would appear.

No, it did not appear. The bells had faded.

XI

Death Raft

Time forks perpetually toward innumerable futures. In one of them I am your enemy.

JORGE LUIS BORGES

R enata called. She liked it in Amsterdam, she said. There were a lot of really nice and helpful colleagues at the CIA. As soon as her medical conditioning was completed and her wardrobe was finished, they would perform the first transition test with her. A leap into the middle of the fifteenth century and back. She was pretty nervous, she confessed. Now she was calling all her friends one more time, because soon her ICom would be shut down and she would be elevated to NEA status.

"I never would have thought that I would one day be granted this privilege," she said. "Not to be electronically reachable, like a celebrity or an important politician. I'm simply no longer reachable, No Electronic Access, no security snoop can scan my personal data anymore. Quite a nice career for a former terrorist, Domenica. Don't you think?"

I told her that Heloise Abret had died on Christmas.

"Did you give her my gift?" she asked.

"No, I have it at home."

"Would you like to keep it?"

"No," I said. "Maybe we should give it to Abaelard as a memento."

"He must have long since been reprogrammed. He probably can't even remember her name," she said.

"Then we should keep it as a memento of her. I'll bring it with me to Amsterdam."

"When are you finally coming? I'm looking forward to seeing you again."

"As far as I know, soon, but I haven't been given an exact date."

"How's Marcello doing?" asked Renata.

"He has a girlfriend here. A nurse, I think. He shows his face only rarely."

"Things are similar with Ernesto, but he has a relationship with his computer at Mission Control."

Both of us laughed.

"Frans still isn't back, right?" Renata asked after a pause.

"No," I replied, and had to pull myself together to keep from crying.

"Sorry to say this to you so bluntly, Domenica, but it's not good in this job to get into committed relationships."

"You mean because it's easy to lose someone," I replied.

"Yes, but not in the sense that you might mean. Frans will return eventually. Up to now, no one has gotten lost yet, as far as I know. No, that's not it. But here in Amsterdam I've heard troubling things about travelers. They don't only visit a strange time, but also enter a strange world; they see incredible things, terrible things, which they could often prevent through their knowledge, but they are not permitted to intervene. That turns them into different people. You don't have a guarantee that the person who returns is still the same one who parted from you—even if you've known him for so long. That has led to tragedies."

I was silent.

"Think about it," she implored.

"Stay the way you are, Renata, for heaven's sake. No matter where they send you. I don't want to lose you too."

"I'll try my best. Do you remember the advice Heli gave you? She said: 'Nothing will happen to you, if you do not stray too far from yourself. It won't always be easy, but you can return to your world. You only have to want to.' And she knew what she was talking about. She got through the longest and farthest journey ever undertaken by anyone."

"Yes. I remember."

"Good luck, Domenica."

"Good luck to you too, Renata."

On a foggy morning in late February, I rode across to San Michele, driven by a vague presentiment and inner unease. It was damp and chilly; a cold spell had put an end to the dreams of an early spring. The bridges on the Fondamenta Nuove were covered with frost, the planks of the pier slippery. The ferry appeared out of nowhere; the navigation lights were surrounded by halos.

Venice disappeared behind us, and ten minutes later we moored at the pier of San Michele. The cypresses rose into the fog; their tops were invisible. For over an hour, I walked along graves and studied the names: the last resting places of the Caragianis, the Zorzis and Brazzoduros, the Saccomanis and the Pasinetti-Zanchis. None of the names meant anything to me. How alike the bearded faces looked—well nourished, the brow righteously raised in civic pride and self-satisfaction. The salt dealers and confectioners, the hosiers and silk merchants, notaries and bankers, all craving a small piece of immortality.

Among the simpler gravesites in the east, three gravediggers were sitting on a board and an overturned wheelbarrow next to a small excavator. They were eating bread and salami and drinking hot tea with rum from a large thermos. The scent of the alcohol was strong.

"Can we help you, signorina?" one of them asked, standing up.

"Are there graves somewhere around here from the sixteenth century?"

All three shook their heads.

"No," said the one, "the oldest are from the end of the eighteenth century, up near the chapel."

"Are you looking for the grave of a particular person?" asked one of the others.

"Yes, the grave of a Dutch man. He was named Frans."

"I know that one," said the third man. "It's a pretty new grave. Very close to here. I'll show it to you, signora."

He led the way.

What nonsense, I told myself. Why would he be buried in a new grave?

It was a fresh grave with a wooden cross and a small plaque with simple official letters that read:

FRANS VAN DEN BOOGARD
03.06.1998–11.08.2052

The man had died the day Frans had departed.

"No, that's not him. I'm looking for a Frans van Hooft."

The gravedigger self-consciously shuffled his rubber boots in the frost-covered grass and hunched his shoulders as if he had to apologize for failing to come up with the sought-after grave.

"I might have been mistaken," I said. "I was probably mistaken. Please forgive me. Many thanks for your help."

The man's wrinkled brown face stretched into a smile.

"Maybe he's still alive," he said with a shrug. "Those declared dead live longer. Isn't that what they say?"

ON THE WAY back the sun had broken through the fog. The gray of the lagoon was marbled with streaks generated by the currents between the countless shallows. I never ceased to admire the hydraulic engineers of previous centuries, who had developed with inflated pig intestines and pieces of wood instead of with computers and flow diagrams a perfect system of supply and disposal.

Venice once again looked the way Turner had painted it, in dissolving colors and forms, suffused with a golden light that cast no shadows but rather seemed to emanate from the objects themselves.

As I strolled down Rio dei Mendicanti, the fog thickened again. The crews of the ambulance boats with their yellow-green and orange SANI-TRANS uniforms stood on the dock and smoked. One of them whistled at me; the others laughed. The water in the canal smelled fresh, as if the city had taken a deep breath that night and flushed its gills with clear water.

Half frozen, I entered the Cavallo; it was full of noise. Half the district seemed to be flocking there, but I managed to get a seat at the counter. I ordered an espresso macchiato and then another. Fabrizio poured a cognac as well and put it down next to my cup. I knocked it back. Gradually I was getting warmer.

"Is your flying Dutchman still not back? He hasn't shown his face for ages. Away on travel, I heard!" Fabrizio shouted to me over the noise.

I nodded.

"I bet he comes back today. I just have a feeling!" he exclaimed.

"I don't find those little jokes particularly funny, Fabrizio."

Someone covered my eyes from behind and growled into my hair: "Guess who."

I spun around. *"Frans!"*

"Hey! You're strangling me."

"Where have you been for so long? You were gone for over three months!"

"For me it was far more than three months, my dear. The ascending soliton carried me out quite a ways beyond the target."

"And today I was looking for your grave."

"*What* were you doing?"

"I was over on San Michele, checking the gravestones for your name." Frans didn't laugh. He nodded.

"I know the feeling," he said in a low voice, more to himself. "But now it's time to celebrate!" he announced, and then whispered in my ear: "I have to make up for Christmas and New Year's Day."

I do too, I wanted to say, but I was silent.

THERE WAS A hint of hardness and bitterness around Frans's mouth that I didn't remember. Had I overlooked it before? I sensed a tinge of strangeness about him after he had returned, and I thought about what Renata had said about travelers who came back from the past and had trouble dealing with their own past.

Had he met another woman where he had been?

I wasn't sure. But a certain distance had arisen, which both of us sensed, but which I could not pin down. When he was affectionate toward me, smiled at me, that bitterness disappeared from his eyes, and I was almost certain that I had been mistaken. But then there were again moments when I sensed that we were drifting inexorably apart. Moments I resisted acknowledging, because I loved him.

"How are the women—back then?" I asked him, and my throat constricted.

"Back then?"

"Where you were."

He looked past me into the distance. "Strange," he said. "And a bit unreal. Because you know that in the meantime they are long dead."

"Are they beautiful?" I asked.

"Yes," he replied, "some are. But you look at them differently. Like flowers shortly before the frost."

"How elegiac."

Frans gave me a thoughtful look and nodded. "Time is a wilderness, Domenica. You'll see."

I didn't ask any more questions.

* * *

"WHAT'S THIS?" I asked, placing my finger gingerly on the freshly healed scar under his left collarbone. I felt him slip out of me without either of us having climaxed. Frans lifted his head from the pillow and opened his eyes.

"Some guy tried to kill me," he said.

"A jealous husband?" I asked.

He sighed. "A patriot who thought I was a spy."

"So you were in trouble. The whole time you were away I had a bad feeling that something had happened to you. Why didn't you tell me about it?"

"I've been conditioned too, my dear. Don't forget that."

I slid down, stroked his taut flat belly, and took his member between my lips. But all effort was in vain.

"What's going on with the two of us, Frans?" I asked, sitting up.

He shrugged. "Forgive me," he said. "I'm not in a good mood at the moment."

I didn't want to press him further, stroked his chest and fingered the soft, puckered tissue of the scar.

"Was it a stabbing?" I asked him.

"With a dagger, yes. But my nanotects helped the wound heal quickly. No infection. Nothing."

"*Your* nanotects? Do you have that stuff inside you too?" I asked, disgusted.

"Every traveler has them inside him. What do you think, with all the pathogens you encounter? The filth everywhere. The decay. Without nanos you wouldn't have much chance of surviving if anything serious happened to you. They definitely helped me get back on my feet fast," said Frans.

"So why don't you let them help you up some more?"

"I love your sarcasm, Domenica."

"Oh, I mean it entirely seriously."

He reached for my hands and held them tight.

"What's wrong?" I asked.

He sighed. "I'm afraid the psychologists always seem to end up being right."

"No committed relationships for the responsible traveler."

He nodded.

I tried to wipe the tears from my eyes with my bare shoulders. I failed.

"I thought it would be different with the two of us. I had so wished it. And I was even quite certain, but . . ."

He averted his face.

"Why, for heaven's sake, would it be different for the two of us, of all people, than for everyone else?" I asked him.

"Because . . ." He broke off. "One day you'll understand."

Book

THREE

I

Highgate

If the recollapse were to happen before stars had all expired, our remote descendants could find themselves in a universe where cosmic
and local arrows of time pointed different ways.

MARTIN REES

He was always happy to return to Highgate, the man some time-
natives who had encountered him on his distant travels called the
angel. He was fond of this world, because it was ancient and mysterious—
full of interesting phenomena. He liked it best of all the worlds he had
seen, and in his life he had indeed seen a great many.

Early in the morning, when the vegetation took a deep breath once
again and loaded the air with quadrillions of chemical messages before it
closed itself off and braced itself for the onslaught of light, he loved to roam
the high-built cities and the castles striving toward the heavens and to fly
through the artfully ornamented arcades. Like finely spun lace of stone and
glass, they presented themselves to the rising sun and broke its light into
multihued fans, filling the shadowy interiors with fleeting colors. He had
discovered a hall in the airy Palace of Karabati where the frescos had regen-
erated and regained their original magnificence. They were rendered in
the style of a very early epoch of this planet, as returning time travelers had
described it: two-dimensional images of astonishing expressiveness, in
which a world was reawakened that had been gone for billions of years. He
often lingered there and viewed the artworks, studied the intensity of the
colors in varying brightness and the nuances of their expiration when shadows fell over them.

Plants climbed up the arabesques of the palace's arches and towers; they
turned autumnally sienna and crimson, only to green anew when the tides

changed. Then the colorful flowers returned, borne back by the wind, and gathered like swarms of butterflies among the fresh foliage before they folded into buds and withdrew into youthfully contracting vines.

For millions of years, buildings had been erected on Highgate. Young architects from all parts of the galaxy had realized their visions—or found them realized, for many an architect who had arrived and moved out into the wilderness intoxicated with genius to seek in the vast plains or on the massive remains of former mountains a location for his ambitious buildings had returned disheartened to the capital and had reported despondently that he had seen his plans realized by a stranger's hand—long since carried out in all their particulars and already marked by decay. The unhappy ones had beaten their heads bloody in despair against overgrown walls and recounted in confused words how their visions had changed strangely into memories, how in their dreams images haunted them of collapsing scaffolding, of bitter sacrifices they made, of triumphs and outrageously daring solutions with which they overcame seemingly insurmountable problems. Over wine they brooded about the years that they had unexpectedly lost, while others had somehow mysteriously taken possession of their ideas and their lives and realized their plans.

They encountered the cosmologists who had come to Highgate specifically to study the conditions along the temporal fault lines. Skepticism and opposition stirred in them when the cosmologists tried to explain to them that due to the muddled time patterns on this planet it might have been they themselves who had erected those buildings at some point in the future.

Some who heard that tapped their foreheads and asked with a laugh: "How is that possible?"

An older scholar, however, who had already lived for many centuries on Highgate, raised his hand and said, "The scientists are right. We have to learn to tell of the future as if it had been, or else the world will slip away from us."

"But we can tell only of the past," someone countered. "Of what has happened. What we have experienced."

The old scholar reflected on this objection for a while, and then shook his head resolutely.

"What do you really know about the past?" he asked. "How can you know what really happened? Are you so certain of what you have experienced that you can say: 'Thus it truly was and not otherwise'? Think hard about it! I assert that only what is told is real. And even that for only a brief time."

THE MAN SOME time-natives who had encountered him on his travels called the angel also loved to fly over the dry white floor of the vanished ocean. Sometimes, while doing so, he saw one of the brains, those soft, semitransparent forms, which had at some point found the strength to rise into the air—huge gelatinous creatures that consisted of millions of individual beings. Since primeval times they had populated the seas of the planet, and as the water grew increasingly nutritious due to the proliferating life on land, the creatures multiplied and multiplied, until finally whole bays and ocean basins were filled with monstrous masses of their soft, beautiful protoplasmic bodies. Herds of whales ate their way through them in rapturous orgies until they suffocated in them and, engulfed in billions of tons of protein, found no way out.

Around that time the planet had long been regarded as uninhabitable, and its original population had abandoned it. Only a few had remained, as some always remain and hold out, no matter what might happen. And soon visitors appeared—descendants of those who had left—to dig for the traces of their ancestors. But they too left again, for the past had turned to dust, and the wind, which unrelentingly ground down the stranded continental shelf, had long blown away all traces.

And finally came the architects, who were always in search of places of dwindling gravity, where they could erect the boldest of all buildings and realize their ambitious visions—but that has already been recounted.

Only the mollusks remained and took advantage of the conditions in their way. Over millions of years they had merged into monstrous creatures: the brains, which were capable of considerable intellectual performance. They drifted over the continents, resembling balled masses of clouds, milky white, semitransparent forms, domed by red-veined cranial roofs protecting them against the rays of a sun that had become merciless, burning furiously through a thinned-out atmosphere. At the same time, however, the sunlight was their nourishment: it gave them the strength to rise and maneuver sluggishly to avoid dangerous gravity depressions. Millions of visual organs had gathered in their nadir and formed there a large, dark eye. Imperturbably it stared down, on the lookout for the last damp hollows that might serve as a laying place and settlement area for their spawn—their young, which for a while led a life of their own before they rose and, seeking shelter, attached themselves under the cranial roof of the mother body.

Sometimes, when the setting sun shone through the huge body of the brains, one or another encapsulated whale herd could be seen, which had been buried in it for many millennia. They were mummified, some claimed. But there were scholars who were firmly convinced that those primeval mammals were only frozen in a long-lasting sleep and would one day awake and burst forth, when the sea returned, in order to plunge into their ancestral element. Some of those scientists thought that they had occasionally registered movements suggesting that the enclosed creatures were already eating their way through toward the forehead, in order to spring from it one not-too-distant day—and fertilize the world with new life, for in their genes, those scientists asserted, they bore the inheritance of the planet's entire ecosphere.

Sometimes one of the brains was stranded; it stumbled into gravity depressions and was forced to the ground. When it no longer found the strength to rise, it collapsed under its own weight. It did not take long for sun and wind to erode it. What remained were deposits of a tough glittering substance that had hardened and turned into an island of brownish mirror shards—and in it were hills of white, interlocked, impacted whalebone.

Highgate was regarded as the strangest world in the old galaxy. Scientists who had traveled there from afar regarded it as the world in the universe on which signs could be discovered that time had fulfilled itself and was preparing to change direction. It was as if the universe had reached its greatest expansion and in some border regions the fractal pattern of the cosmos seemed to have paused in the process of unfolding and expansion that had lasted for billions of years, only to turn around hesitantly and sink back into itself, while the arrow of time, like a compass needle over the magnetic pole, pointed without orientation vaguely in this or that direction.

Highgate was in one of those regions on the outermost edge of time where solitons swung around to plunge back into the past. There were on the planet chronotopes, in which the flow of time was jammed or came to a complete standstill. Those were areas in which, according to reports, the sun had not set for years but moved on an erratic course this way and that and kept stopping indecisively, where its light lay like a honey-colored haze over the land and covered the rock masses with a brown glaze, where nature froze in dreamy immobility. Elsewhere the living world seemed already firmly resolved to reverse, the plants gathered up their leaves, trees withdrew overnight into the soil as if in the face of imminent disaster, and the fledglings in the nests spat the food into their parents' beaks and shut themselves up in the fragments of their eggs as if they were already tired of the world at first sight. This, in any case, is what the scholars reported who believed they had observed such things. They also told of bizarre rites that the people who lived in those areas celebrated—such as the resurrection of their dead or the homecoming of those whose lives had been fulfilled into the bodies of their mothers, where they saw the light of the world go out behind them and curled up, only to be immediately absorbed into nothingness. Those natives told the visitors in an exceedingly strange way of the future in all its particulars, as if they had vivid recollections of it, while they had only rough ideas of their past, as if they had completely lost the memory of what had been reality and what had not. Such accounts were sneered at by only a few, for on Highgate everything was possible.

Native prophets also emerged regularly announcing a return of the moon. Highgate once had a large moon, the astronomers had claimed for a long time. But it had left its orbit and was eventually attracted by the sun and consumed by it. It would be reborn from the sun, declared those who remembered the spectacular event in the future. It would rise, ablaze, from the sun and, after it had sufficiently cooled, reclaim its rightful place in the sky. It would also soon resume its reign over the tides, for the sea too would return. First a haze would accumulate in the high atmosphere, gradually condense and then descend, and eventually the enormous hollows that had once been oceans would refill with water. People believed those prophets as people always believed prophets—only half and not without mockery and yet with a secret spark of hope and a tinge of fear.

Thus it was on Highgate, and the man some time-natives called the angel loved this world, which, as he knew firsthand from many travels, was the oldest of all human worlds. And he lived there with his friend Don Fernando, who chose to remain in the form of a large rat, a *Papagomys*. From an early age, this had been his wish, for he enjoyed being hated by idiots and hounded by prejudice and leading a life characterized by resourcefulness, courage, quick-wittedness, and decisiveness.

IT WAS MIDDAY on Highgate, the time when the blaze reached its zenith. Light burst forth from the sabkha, a sharp, bitter light—like the evaporites of the dried-out ocean itself—which corroded the edges of reality, dissolved them, and assembled the fragments into trembling chimeras that seemed to float on pearly puddles before they melted and seeped into the sand.

The man some time-natives who had encountered him on his travels called the angel loved this hour. He sat in a rocking chair on the shady porch and gazed into the distance. Sometimes, but only rarely, a shadow dimmed the landscape, when a brain passed over it, staring down indifferently with its eye.

He enjoyed resting on this narrow seam between all-crushing light and the icy emptiness and darkness into which the bright vast sky imperceptibly slid not far above him. He knew that he found himself in the unsecured no-man's-land between chaos and entropy, but could life ever have had a greater chance? Here it had emerged. Here it had unfolded. Here it had endured, thanks to its characteristic tenacity and its inventiveness.

He closed his eyes and yielded to the feeling of fragile security. He heard Don Fernando's cry and directed his eyes upward.

The sky burst, broke open, as if a frozen-solid hatch had been pried open. Chunks of ice broke off and plummeted. Cold air wafted in his face. A flower shattered and trickled down like broken glass.

Over the horizon a second sun had appeared, gleaming blue-white but as weak as a star that was light-years away. Wind swept over rippled snow-fields, and the man who seemed to be coming straight out of the distant sun cast a long, thin shadow—as did his companion, the wolf.

Pale phantom suns illuminated the broken-open world; from their edges sprayed electric discharges, overlapping with those of Highgate.

"I suspected it," Don Fernando sighed, scurrying back and forth on the polished stone tabletop. "I suspected it."

They waited silently until the two figures had approached and stopped. The man from the ice, whose cowl extended over his nose, opened the fastener of his robe and took out a tied-up bundle he had carried against his chest. Snow sprinkled off his clothing. His eyes smoldered from under the frost-covered hood like dim protosuns clouded with dust and haze. He tossed the bundle onto the table.

The wolf growled. From his belly fur hung beads of ice, which now thawed.

"Don't start peeing now too," said Don Fernando.

"Shut your fresh mouth, you lousy rat," the wolf growled, "or else . . ."

"Yeah, come up with something new, for a change, you mangy mutt," Don Fernando said in a bored tone.

The wolf snapped at him, but with a single bound Don Fernando had escaped onto the angel's lap.

"Did you see that?" Don Fernando asked indignantly. "He has taken this nasty form for so long that he behaves like an animal!"

"Nasty? That's coming from you, you vermin!" the wolf grumbled.

"Hey! How dare you? You've gotten so stupid that you can't even piss your name in the snow," Don Fernando jeered.

"Stop!" said the hooded man, pushing back his cowl and wiping the thawing frost from his eyebrows. "It seems that the improbable case of an oscillation has actually occurred." His voice sounded muffled through his wool-lined mask.

"I have to see that," said the man some called the angel. "A further variant, I assume."

The man from the cold nodded. "Come, Sir Whitefang!" he said to his companion, the wolf. "Let's not be tardy."

Don Fernando watched with fascination as the man from the ice and his companion, the wolf, walking backward, receded. As they did so, they effaced their own tracks, for the wind-rippled snow was untouched as soon as the next step had been taken. They tramped away across the ice field; their shadows grew longer and longer, as the weakly gleaming sun withdrew toward the horizon and slowly set.

Chunks of ice formed from meltwater, left the grass and rose from the bushes, shot up and froze solid at the edges of the sky, as it closed with a crunch. The crack lapped by blue electric discharges merged with the evening sky, in which a few veils of clouds glowed and then dissipated.

"Show me," said Don Fernando, making himself comfortable on the shoulder of the angel.

The angel untied the damp bundle and smoothed out the pages.

"Let's take a look at this variant."

Writing rose before them.

II

The Cusan Acceleratio

Whoever possesses the sense of possibility does not say, for example: here this or that has happened, will happen, must happen; but he invents: Here this or that might, could or should happen; and if he is told that something is the way it is, then he thinks: Well, it could probably also be different. Thus the sense of possibility could be defined, at heart, as the ability to imagine everything that could just as well be and to give no more importance to what is than to what is not.

ROBERT MUSIL

There is a certain irony in the attempts that have been made to elevate Nicolaus Cusanus, the papal legate and personal friend of Pope Pius II, into the guardian and protector of Western science in the face of a Church hostile to enlightenment and progress, as if there had ever been tendencies of that sort on the part of the clergy. Certainly, there were at times differences of opinion and disputes over technical questions of astronomy and cosmology, but those debates are the expression and sign of a vibrant scholarly life—indeed, its precondition. After the decline of the Roman Empire, who else but the Church carefully preserved over many centuries the treasures of Greek, Roman, and Oriental erudition? Who reproduced and disseminated the inestimably valuable works of our forebears? Who studied, interpreted, and taught their content? In the Church, there is a long, unbroken, venerable tradition of scientific inquiry into Creation. It required no Cusan and no "Acceleratio" to, as Diderot wrote, "clear a path for science" and "pave the way for technological progress." That is, if truth be told, a historical fiction, as in those virtual historical constructions that are increasingly in fashion nowadays, which proliferate more and more but serve only to obscure the facts and distort the view of reality.

Let us consider the facts: two letters penned by the cardinal, both written on March 12 of the year 1452 during a brief stay in his former parish of St. Florin in Koblenz. One to Dietrich von Moers, the archbishop of Cologne, advising him to request papal support in a trial in which a woman of unknown origins is accused of heresy. Another to Pope Nicholas V, proposing the founding of a scientific academy by the Holy See dedicated specifically to unusual natural phenomena.

What mysteries have been read into those last February days, which the cardinal, coming from Brussels via Leuven and Maastricht, spent in Cologne, to open there a provincial council! There is talk of a "Paul experience" (as if he had ever been a Saul!); of strange letters delivered to him by a scholar shrouded in mystery; of an encounter with an enigmatic beauty from a distant land who beguiled him and foretold the future to him.

Indeed, as a papal diplomat and traveler in matters of restructuring and organization of the Church, Cusanus had up to that point—most likely for reasons of time alone—not devoted much attention to the promotion of the sciences, had in fact been unable to do so, although he was, as we know today, ahead of his time in questions of astronomy and cosmology, practiced experimental physics, and was the first to seriously deal mathematically with the concept of infinity. But for his efforts to strengthen the institutionalization of scholarship and instruction on the part of the Church, neither mysterious scholars nor beguiling sibyls were required. It was a demand of the time, and the cardinal from Kues on the Moselle was certainly only one of many who knew how to interpret properly the signs of the time. The Cusan Acceleratio, as Leibniz postulated it, is a chimera. The claim that it was Cusanus alone who "awakened a sleepy Church in conflict over ridiculous matters of faith," as Voltaire put it, is a fiction. The thunder of modern artillery, which Sultan Mehmed II mounted outside the gates of Constantinople the following year and against whose firepower the West was defenseless, was loud enough to shake from its slumber the entire Occident—and finally to unite it.

THOUGH THIS INTERPRETATION cannot be regarded as the official position of the Vatican in the rekindled scholarly debate over the so-called Cusan Acceleratio, it would undoubtedly earn its approval. It is the duty of the chronicler to record the most important facts of the past five centuries, which have helped shape the present state of the world, in particular of the West.

Here they are:

1460   On behalf of Pope Pius II, the papal legate Nicolaus Cusanus and Julius Pomponius Laetus found the humanistic research institute Accademia Romana.

1461   Johannes Regiomontanus is appointed head of the Accademia.

1462   At Nicolaus Cusanus's suggestion, Johannes Regiomontanus conducts a "measurement of the world." The results confirm the data of Eratosthenes of Cyrene (276–195 BC), who calculated from the divergent shadow lengths on the meridian arc between Syene (Aswan) and Alexandria a circumference of the Earth of 40,000 kilometers.

1463   Death of Pope Pius II and Nicolaus Cusanus in Todi, Umbria, while preparing for a crusade to retake Constantinople.

1467   Pope Paul II, successor to Pius II, pursues the closing of the Accademia Romana, which, for all his sympathy for the revival of the humanist heritage, he regards as a heretical secret society. Julius Pomponius Laetus is accused of blasphemy; another member, Bartolomeo Platina, is tortured. Johannes Regiomontanus and some of his colleagues manage to escape to Milan, where the Sforzas shelter them.

1470   Leonardo da Vinci becomes a member of the Sapienza, as the former Accademia Romana has been called since its exodus. It is known as a center of humanist education and research and becomes the destination of numerous scholars, craftsmen, and students from all over the world.

1475   Introduction of the lodestone on the ships of the Italic League.

1476   Following the death of Johannes Regiomontanus, Leonardo is elected head of the Sapienza.

1478   Invention of the "burning spinner" in the Sapienza by Corbinian Seeshaupter, a gunsmith from Salzburg. Initially fueled with naphtha, later with petroleum and its derivatives, the spinner constitutes a sort of turbine, which is soon employed as a "mechanical slave" in all fields, whether to power vehicles or pumps, in agriculture as well as in industry and increasingly in transportation.

1480   Renewal of the Italic League between Venice, Milan, Florence, Naples, Montferrat, and Savoy for another twenty-five years. Genoa joins.

1481   First performance of Alberti's *Song of the Mechanical Slaves* in Milan.

1484   Pope Sixtus IV declares that there must be undiscovered lands in
        the western sea. A contrary view, as disseminated by some mis-
        guided scholars who believed that toward the west Marco Polo's
        legendary Cathay was separated from our world only by an ocean,
        would presuppose an imbalance of Creation. That would be un-
        christian, heretical.

1486   Giovanni Caboto, sent by the Signoria of his hometown of Genoa
        in search of new lands in the western part of the world, reaches on
        St. Christopher's Day (July 25) the mouth of the Delaware. On his
        second expedition (1488–1490) he explores the coast between the
        mouth of the Savannah and that of the St. Lawrence. On the third
        journey (1492–1495), which serves the construction of fortified
        bases and trading stations and on which his son Sebastiano accom-
        panies him, he meets his death during an armed confrontation
        with indigenous people of Terranova. He is buried on Capo
        Caboto, which was named for him. His son Sebastiano success-
        fully completes the expedition.

1489   While the galleons of the Grand Duke of Tuscany explore the
        mouth of the Mississippi and the coast of Yucatán, Venetian
        trading captains establish at the behest of their Signoria fortified
        trading posts on the northern coast of southern Terranova, which
        must increasingly fend off rapacious attacks by Portuguese and
        Spanish seafarers, after the tidings of abundant troves of gold have
        reached Europe.

1492   First successful firing of a "Milan," also known as a "firefly," a mis-
        sile propelled by a "burning tube." Produced in the smithies of the
        Sapienza and launched by a catapult at a steep angle, the projectile
        covers a distance of twenty stadia or two and a half Roman *milia*
        and carries a *bomba* with a mastello of naphtha to the target.

1494   Invasion of Lombardy by King Charles VIII of France on the way
        to Naples. On September 23, encounter in Ticino. The united Ital-
        ian army under the command of Francesco Gonzaga deals the
        French a devastating defeat. The Florentine statesman and histo-
        rian Francesco Guicciardini writes in his *Storia d'Italia*:

        "The so-feared modern French artillery was taken completely
        by surprise. The infernal shriek of the Milanese fireflies, which
        raced through the sky, spraying naphtha fire and in a few minutes
        engulfing the battlefield in smoke and flames, hurtled like the

wrath of God into the enemy ranks, whose march soon lacked any battle order. When the horn sounded for the cavalry attack, the horsemen were helplessly dispersed, and the peasants in Savoy abandoned their fields to capture widely scattered saddled horses and sell them everywhere for good money at the markets.

"Francesco ordered the beautiful new French cannons, not a few of which had not managed to fire a single shot, brought to Milan, to have them examined in the foundries . . ."

1510   Copernicus declines an appointment to the Sapienza.

1512   Michelangelo: "Everywhere in the provinces one hears day and night the hissing and buzzing of the burning spinners. Gone is the bucolic peace of our country. The air is full of smoke and the stink of burnt naphtha. Over the floodplains lies an unhealthy fog, a miasma that takes one's breath away."

1576   Giordano Bruno is elected president of the Sapienza.

1613   Johannes Kepler manages to escape the pursuit of the Counter-Reformation in Germany. Together with his mother, he travels via Vienna and Venice to Milan.

1614   Not Galilei but Kepler becomes Bruno's successor as head of the Sapienza. Galilei demonstratively leaves the academy and retreats to his villa in Arcetri.

1620   Decisive failure of the Counter-Reformation in Europe. Banning and expropriation of the Dominican Order.

1626   Protestant troops unsuccessfully besiege Rome. The Pope flees via Budapest to Krakow.

1627   Defeat of the Nordic army, decimated by epidemics, in the battles of Orvieto and Bologna. Return of the Pope to Rome.

1630   End of the religious war in the Peace of Prague. Reordering of Europe.

1672   Leibniz coins the term "Cusan Acceleratio" of the sciences. Construction of the first functioning mechanical calculating machine.

1674   Naval battle of Chalcis. Liberation of Greece.

1676   Reconquest of Constantinople.

1682   A mercenary army under the command of Condottiere Alessandro Tarvisio defeats the Turks at Tarsus and Mersin. Liberation of Aleppo, Damascus, Jerusalem, and Cairo in the Second Holy War. Securing of the petroleum wells in Mesopotamia.

1705   Completion of the Suez Canal.

1708 Occupation of Oman and Jask on the Strait of Hormuz by an Italian/German/British expeditionary army in order to secure the shipping lane to the petroleum ports in the Persian Gulf.

1710 Increased construction of ships with powerful burning-spinner motors, in particular seaworthy petroleum freighters, by the European great powers.

1712 For "security reasons," the military Signoria of Cairo permits only motor-powered ships to pass through the Suez Canal. Sailing ships are forced to take the arduous journey around Africa.

1715 The burning of the petroleum freighter *Amalfi* reduces Piraeus to ashes.

1720 Sinking of the petroleum freighter *Haven* in the Gulf of Genoa. Fish and crab stocks are wiped out in a wide radius. The old town of Genoa must be evacuated for several months.

1738 Construction of the first hydrogen-inflated airship by Ian McInnes.

1752 The *Glory of Glasgow* under Captain Seamus Shaw is the first airship to successfully cross the Atlantic.

1758 Ludwig Euler publishes his pioneering work *Calculations for Reaching Outer Space by Means of Reactive Flying Machines.*

1763 First successful flight attempts by George Rauschle with the motor-powered airplane *Skylark of Massachusetts.*

1780 The states of New England win the war of independence due to the air superiority of their maneuverable *Arrow* motor-powered aircraft, designed by Robert Fulton, over the heavily armed but vulnerable battle cruisers of the Royal Air Navy. Bombing of Boston and Norfolk. Destruction of Philadelphia by air-to-surface missiles with phosphorus-naphthalene warheads. Devastating defeat of the British in the air battle over Long Island.

1795 First regular transatlantic air service between Amsterdam and Boston as well as between Rome and Genoa Nova via Ponta Delgado and Bermuda.

1814 Flood disaster in Holland claims over one hundred thousand human lives.

1819 The German North Sea coast is beset by storms with a wind force of up to twelve. Dams broken over a distance of twenty-five miles. Hamburg must be evacuated due to flooding. Holland too is again hit hard. Plans for a joint Northwest European dam project founder on the immense costs.

1822   An estimated one million dead in the worst typhoon within living
        memory in Bengal. Three million people flee the flooded areas.

1825   A worldwide rise in the sea level registered. Scholars are baffled.
        Some of them predict a "tropical eon" marked by higher tempera-
        tures and stronger air currents in the Earth's atmosphere. Joseph
        Louis Gay-Lussac, the renowned French atmospheric scientist
        from Saint-Léonard-de-Noblat, advances the hypothesis that there
        could be a causal connection between the excessive burning of
        petroleum over the previous three hundred years and the change
        in the global climate.

1830   *Orbital Trajectories in Planetary Space*, by Carl Friedrich Gauß and
        Heinrich Olbers, appears.

1845   The computer language ADA, invented by Ada Lovelace, the
        daughter of Lord Byron, helps the electric Pascal calculating ma-
        chines achieve a breakthrough. The age of so-called data pro-
        cessing begins.

1854   Publication of the Gauß-Riemann General Theory of Gravitation,
        which postulates a space-time continuum geometrically deformed
        by mass.

1866   The last stronghold in the sultanate of Malé must be abandoned.
        The evacuated occupants receive settlement rights on the Coro-
        mandel Coast.

1871   After the monsoon storms at the beginning of the year, the pilots of
        the Durban-Bombay Line report the flooding of the last Maldive
        Islands.

1873   Discovery of the mass-energy principle by William Clifford.

1878   First supersonic flight of a rocket-powered clipper from Savannah
        to Sydney in less than six hours.

1881   First orbital flight with circumnavigation of the Earth by Major
        Brian McLaughlin with the rocket plane *Thunder*.

1883   Approximately half a million dead in the vast and populous vaca-
        tion areas along the coasts of Sumatra, Surabaya, Siam, and Malay-
        sia due to a catastrophic flood of indescribable magnitude, caused
        by the eruption of the Krakatoa volcano in the Sunda Strait. Rich-
        ard Burton, the famous British explorer and man of letters, who was
        staying in Bandung at the time and the next day traveled by heli-
        copter to the southern coast of Surabaya, present-day Java, and took
        a direct look at the disaster area, wrote in the face of the immense

destruction: "It was as if the fist of a wrathful God had swept across the land" (*London Times*, Thursday, August 30, 1883).

1886   "Inexhaustible Energy out of Nowhere," announces the April 28 edition of the *Washington Post* on the occasion of the opening in New York of the first electricity-generating station powered by the Maxwell forces dormant in matter. Thomas Alva Edison, the builder of the facility, was honored with the Thomas Jefferson Award by President of the American Federation Grover Cleveland, the highest distinction for a scientist.

1897   The states of the North American Federation, with California leading the way, complete the construction of numerous Maxwell power plants, with the help of which gigantic irrigation projects are to be undertaken in order to counter the increasing dryness in the agricultural areas of the continent.

1899   Catastrophic drought in India. For the third year in a row the monsoon rain doesn't come. Sixty million people flee the country. Aid deliveries from all over the world prove unable to ease the hardship. In the face of deaths in huge numbers, the World Confederation compels by force of arms the opening of the borders to Burma and Siam.

1906   Earthquake in San Francisco. Two Maxwell power plants heavily damaged. Samuel Ruben, the president of California, declares a national emergency and asks the neighboring states for help.

1907   A mysterious epidemic spreads from west to east across the North American continent. The midwestern states close their borders and adopt rigorous quarantine measures after the prohibition of the transport of livestock achieved no effect. The epidemic causes illness and deformities not only among animals, but also increasingly among plants and even among people. Scientists are baffled.

1908   Ernest Rutherford, professor in Manchester, who until recently taught at McGill University in Montreal, is awarded the Nobel Prize for chemistry. Rutherford claims that there must be a direct connection between the radiation released by the destroyed Maxwell power plants in San Francisco and the occurrence of deadly illness among people and animals as well as deformities among newborns and plants; that the affliction is thus by no means an infectious disease, but rather a "radiation sickness," which, though it remains medically unexplored, is in no way contagious. Nonetheless, in rural areas pogroms are repeatedly directed against the sick and dying in the guise of "protective measures."

1909   "Political Gambit or Technical Breakdown?" asks the October 26 edition of the *Manchester Guardian*. "The German moon expedition ended in disaster. The launch of the *Helmuth von Moltke*, prepared in secret for months, apparently went off according to plan. After a three-day flight the spaceship touched down in one piece in the Mare Imbrium, but a return lift-off to Earth either was not attempted or failed. Suspicions of some foreign experts who claimed that bringing back the four moon voyagers had never been planned in the first place— indeed, that it had scarcely been technically possible—were sharply countered by the German Admiralty and the Imperial Naval Office. Political observers likewise assume a technical breakdown and regard the speculations as absurd. They believe that the risk was criminally underestimated because no one dared to argue the Kaiser out of this propagandistic technological undertaking. The unexpected resignation of the Imperial Chancellor Prince Bernhard von Bülow certainly shed no light on the dubious 'conquest of the moon by the German Empire,' heralded with aplomb by Kaiser Wilhelm II but shamefully executed. From Potsdam itself no comment has been forthcoming."

1914   Famine refugees from Africa and Asia stream into Europe. Italy and Spain appeal to the remaining European states with an urgent request for help. First Pan-European Conference in Geneva.

1915   Despite strong protests by the World Confederation, intensified regulations on foreigners in the European countries. Increased deportations; closing of the external borders. Pogroms against illegal immigrants, particularly in Austria, Germany, France, and Switzerland.

1917   Second Pan-European Conference in Vienna. Common immigration policy decided. Exemptions only for "homecomers" from the states of the former North American Federation and the South African Republic, who are classified as racially and genetically unobjectionable. Concrete plans for a unified economy, currency, and defense. Decision to erect a North Atlantic dam.

1918   Third Pan-European Conference in London. Winston Churchill acclaimed as the "Unifier of Europe." The demand of the World Confederation for a relaxation of European immigration regulations is unanimously denied, the proposal "oil for immigration" rejected as an extortion attempt.

1923   During an anti-European rally in Munich, an armed confronta-
        tion takes place between militant nationalists, the so-called
        Kampfbund, and law enforcement officers. The ringleaders of the
        radicals, Erich Ludendorff, Max von Scheubner-Richter, and Adolf
        Hitler, meet their deaths.
1924   The Fourth Pan-European Conference in Berlin adopts autarky
        measures. The Berlin resolutions outline plans to build a fleet of
        orbital power plants in order to secure the energy supply and to be
        armed against "extortion" on the part of the World Confederation.
1925   Founding of Eurospatial in Paris. Decision to build the first per-
        manently manned orbital station.
1933   Formal signing of the charter of the United States of Europe in
        Versailles.
1936   Withdrawal of the "volunteer" forces under General Francisco
        Franco from Ceuta and Tangier and the troops of Field Marshal
        Benito Mussolini from the Mezzogiorno. Erection of a "Secure
        Border" in central Italy (Gaeta-Termoli line), which is later moved
        to the southern edge of the Po Plain (Abruzzo Wall).
1937   Extension of the Bastion Midi along the Spanish-French-Italian
        Mediterranean coast, of the Southern Atlantic Wall and the San-
        tiago Wall along the Portuguese and Spanish west coast, and of the
        Eastern Wall between the Adriatic and the Gulf of Finland
        (Trieste-Lemberg-Helsinki line).
1944   Erection of a floodproof Atlantic dam along the edge of the
        European continental shelf between Bilbao and Kristiansund,
        past Brandon Head and Erris Head, enclosing the Hebrides
        and Shetlands, completed after a twenty-five-year period of con-
        struction.
1945   President of Europe Charles de Gaulle declares the Old Continent
        an "impregnable fortress." In his official speech, he calls Europe
        an "ark that will bear our Western culture into the future."

DON FERNANDO DIPPED his paw in the ashes to which the notes had been
reduced. He sniffed at the gray flakes and licked them off his claws.

"Real paper," he said appreciatively. "What an odd bird!"

The man some time-natives called the angel brushed his hand across
the table. The wind carried the ashes away.

"We'll have to return again," he said.

"Probably several times," said Don Fernando. "It's as if I smelled it."

The man some called the angel leaned back in his rocking chair and closed his eyes. "We have to proceed carefully," he said. "The fabric is very thin at that point."

He sensed the approach of a soliton and turned his head.

"Are you ready?"

"At all times," replied Don Fernando.

THE OCEAN HAD returned. A wave washed against the beach. And the next was already raising its head, rising, inclining its crest in order to break, but it didn't crash down. It stopped. It was as if it had suddenly decided to change its state; it became viscous and congealed into a shape that was frozen in time, as he had seen in one of the replications in the Palace of Karabati. The wave, which had paused in its movement, now threw back its mane and sank backward into the sea from which it had risen.

The coast was marshy and covered with reeds. The sea, now farther away, rushed weakly toward the shore. It was a cold sea. The air too was cold. Poured out over the sky were stars, strange constellations. A thin fog lay over the inland valleys. Somewhere a wolf howled.

"Carry me," requested Don Fernando.

The angel picked him up and held him against his breast.

The dull sound of hooves on soft ground could be heard, then the anxious snorting of a horse. A white horse. Two boys sat on its back; they had reined it in and were staring. Again the wolf howled, this time closer.

"Old monster," hissed Don Fernando.

"Stop scratching my chest with your cold wet paws, Fernando," said the angel.

"Forgive me."

The white horse flailed its head and turned to flee. The boy riding it tightened the reins; the other held on to his companion and looked mistrustfully over his shoulder.

"Don't be afraid!" the angel called to them. "We have arrived," he then said to Don Fernando.

"I should hope so."

They approached the hut. The hooded man stepped out and pushed back his cowl.

"Welcome," he said.

III

Padania

Turn the key the other way, and the dancers would dance backward,
the music play backward, vanished nights reappear.

GENE WOLFE

My departure was set for April 17. I was to go to Salzburg first. Falcotti would be there and would personally deliver and explain to me the final instructions of the Istituto della Rinascita for my mission. That had to be done in private, the e-mail indicated.

Frans brought me to Santa Lucia. He stowed my luggage and sat down opposite me.

"I'd like nothing better than to go with you," he confessed. "Sometimes I get a bit homesick. My contract here expires in the middle of the year; then I'll come to Amsterdam and show you a few tricks you can use to get primed for a transition."

I had trouble "getting primed" for the departure. The train was about to leave, and Frans had to hurry to get out of the car in time. As the train slowly started to move, he knocked on the window from outside, but it wouldn't open.

"See you in Amsterdam!" he shouted.

I read his lips. The train accelerated. Frans trotted after it a bit, then remained behind.

Beyond Mestre began old cultivated land. Old farmsteads rolled by; umber brick buildings with caved-in roofs, between them modern factory farms. Cypresses lined driveways to country houses and villas, screened by walls and parks. Old willow trees stood along winding brooks, clad in fresh green and gilded by the spring sun. Then the flashing, dead-straight canals of an unbroken irrigation system appeared more and more often, between them fields of turbo rice, intensively applied genetics, quadrillions of tiny nanomachines, which spun sugar out of water, air, and sunlight—each a submicroscopic robot-mechanic dismantling and reassembling molecules in its own way.

On the outskirts of the cities from Padua through Verona to Trento were thousands of stacked-up container homes full of refugees from Alto Adige. Air-supported domes had been erected between them. Grapevines with tendrils reaching upward like columns of the desperate lined the railroad embankment. The visions of Padania had been dashed—a distressed area, beset from the south and from the north.

Beyond Trento the world narrowed.

A group of four lattice towers stood, painted red and white and pressed close together, on a rocky ledge above the valley; it seemed to me as if they had escaped there during a flood and awaited rescue. I thought of angels plunging into the valley spraying sparks like Lucifer, and of Renata's mutilated hand.

The train slowed down. We were approaching the border. In Bolzano I had to change trains. The Austrian magnetic levitation train was enthroned on an elevated platform. Everywhere were the flags with the red, white, and red stripes and the emaciated eagle. They should have exchanged their eagle for that of the Germans a long time ago, Renata had once said mockingly. The fat bird would have suited them better by now.

BOZEN. On the painted-over station signs the old BOLZANO showed through.

The inspection of IComs, travel documents, and luggage took its time. The older official with his gray uniform cap nodded at me with a smile when the papal visa appeared on his screen. My luggage was brought over. It had obviously been examined more closely. An official in civilian clothes placed the paperweight with the Mars sand on the counter.

"What's this?"

"It says on the label," I said brusquely.

The border official reminded me of my geography teacher in high school, whom I could never stand. The same arrogant type: slender, short gray hair, gray-streaked mustache, mocking blue eyes. And just as vain. He flicked the bottom of the paperweight with his finger. Red sand flew up between the domes and clouded the sky over Port Abret.

"Pretty," he said, putting the half-sphere down on the counter; his fingernails were very well tended.

"A souvenir," I explained. "A gift."

"From Renata Gessner?"

Oh, damn! Damn! Damn!

"Tissue traces from her skin," he said, pursing his lips, and added with casual condescension, "We have our smart nanobots too."

I felt that tingling in the muscles at the back of my thighs that always overcame me in panic situations. A flight reflex? What could the guy do to me? I hadn't committed any crime just by having that thing in my luggage. Still, I felt cold inside. He enjoyed my shock reaction and watched me mockingly.

"We haven't heard from Frau Gessner in a long time," said the border official. "Is she doing well?"

"Yes, she is," I stammered, intimidated. "I don't think she'll cause you any more trouble," I added stupidly, hating myself for it.

"Trouble?" Under his mustache he twisted his mouth into a mocking smile. "I doubt that, Fräulein Ligrina. Have a pleasant journey!"

The border official turned away and disappeared through a glass door.

Fräulein. I hastily pulled the zipper of my travel bag; it got stuck. The kind older official helped me force it closed. Then I hurried to the escalator that led to the platform of the Austrian State Railroad.

THE EXPRESS MAGNETIC levitation train to Salzburg was luxurious and spacious. The dove-blue upholstered seats could be converted into lounge chairs. On the screen in front of me appeared a route map indicating times and distances.

Austria-Hungary had become a great and wealthy land; there was no reason to hide the light of national pride under a bushel. Ever since the withdrawal from the EU and the annexation of Hungary, Slovenia, Friuli, and South Tyrol under a liberal regime, things had been going uphill. Vienna had managed to leapfrog a century and a half and connect to the dubious glory of the old imperial monarchy—indeed, as some believed, even to the glory of the Holy Roman Empire of the German Nation.

We plunged into a tunnel and reemerged from it, shot up a slope and soared into a mountain panorama. Ten minutes later we stopped in Brixen.

The railroad line ran straight through the city. The new train station floated like a blimp high above the houses between the cathedral and the monastery. I looked down at glistening wet slate roofs and the countless sooty mouths of the chimneys. The shadows of the clouds scudded across them. It was a small world: the streets and squares, the monastery, the cathedral. A gusty northwest wind swept down over Monte Quaira and tugged at the cables of the train station. For a moment, I felt dizzy. I felt like an insect caught in a spiderweb and looked around involuntarily as if a spider were about to come scurrying from somewhere to kill its prey.

Very nearby tolled a clock—a single ringing stroke. The air had a different taste here, raw and yet smooth and cool like a blade. Was it due to the altitude? A zeppelin, the *Archduke Ferdinand,* had moored between two futuristically styled pylons made of carbon fiber composite materials and lowered its passenger gondolas onto a platform. The laser-guided airscrews fought with the wind, constantly changing the number of revolutions to keep the airship in position. Its shadow fell onto the eastern bank of the Isarco. The platform was already teeming with people, and still more followed through the connecting tubes to the train station.

Beyond the great valley basin stretched vineyards on the southern slopes. They looked like vigorously and crudely crosshatched black-and-white drawings. The sunlight was pale, unable to ignite any colors. Wood stained silver by sun and snow. Defiant houses, huddled, turned inward. Here reigned narrowness and rejection. In this basin the world passed through; it never came here. "Here we are," said the inhabitants of these valleys. "Strangers, stay out, stay strangers."

Nicolaus Cusanus had been confronted with this narrowness, as I had learned. He, a man of the world, farsighted and full of transgressive ideas, had been the first modern thinker to reflect on experimental science, on mathematical infinity and that of God, on the infinity of the world and the nature of time and eternity. With these people here he did not get along. He, the intellectual, exhorted them to practice a Christian lifestyle, tried to force them to do so with ecclesiastical penalties. He, the theorist, failed to grasp that he was not dealing with Christians, that their crosses, their processions and pilgrimages were only a veneer, varnish on heathen, militant traditions thousands of years old.

They didn't like him, that—German?—Roman? A stranger, in any case! That supposed friend of the Pope. He thought too much for them, knew too much, saw through too much, expected them to think about things they did not even grasp, did not even wish to grasp. They defied him, ignored his instructions, sabotaged, deceived, and denounced him. They preferred to make common cause with his opponent, the Habsburg duke, whom they actually hated even more, but whose greed they nonetheless comprehended, whose tricks they could calculate, because his imperious and quick-tempered style corresponded more to their nature. The Cusan remained incomprehensible to them, unsettling, uncanny. He lived and acted in a world whose horizon lay far beyond their mountaintops, behind which the sun set for them each day.

Still, he held out here for seven years as archbishop and consumed his energies, because he could not set aside any problem unsolved. Here he had failed until his friend, Pope Pius II, showed understanding. In 1458 he summoned him to Rome and assigned him tasks more worthy of his genius than the trivialities of provincial ecclesiastical administration.

The train had glided on as I listened to the scholarly chatter my Scarabeo had compiled. A desolate, ignorant bunch you're descended from, Renata, I have to say!

BEYOND BRIXEN, HEADING north, I had the strange feeling that I wasn't approaching the main ridge of the Alps but was coming out of the mountains. But the impression was deceptive. Franzensfeste remained a symbol of narrowness and isolation, the ideal bottleneck for military officers and highwaymen. All that was needed to make the valley impassable was to squeeze in a plug. Walls of stone masonry, punctured by embrasures and cannon ports, had been wedged between the narrow rock faces like the locked jaws of attack dogs, which cannot be wrenched open even in death. Franzensfeste—a monument to the fury and idiocy of bygone wars.

FORTEZZA could still be vaguely discerned under the new blue paint on the signs.

A border policeman in civilian clothes walked through the car, his eyes focused on the electronic display of his Wristtop. He was again scanning the IComs of the travelers, and absurdly that aroused in me a feeling—no, not really of fear, but rather of indeterminate guilt.

The world became even narrower and darker. The train moved over short stretches like a bullet through the barrel of a gun. Suddenly I saw for the first time in my life real snow! Like opaque white paint it clung to the northern slopes of the precipitous peaks.

A gong sounded. The chief steward, a pleasant young man in a tailcoat who introduced himself as Magister Bosnitschek, appeared on the screen at my seat. He addressed me personally by name and invited me to dinner in the dining car. His Italian was not "piped in," but it was passable, and I automatically thanked him for the kind invitation. But then I noticed that by a trick of the computer system the same honor of a personal invitation was bestowed on all my fellow passengers in their respective native languages.

There was *Fiakergulasch* with *Semmelknödeln, Tafelspitz* with *Apfelkren* and *Erdäpfeln,* as well as Viennese *Vanillenbraten* with *Häuptel-* and *Paradeisersalat.* For dessert he recommended *Topfenobersnockerln, Marillen-Palatschinken,* or *Liwanzen* with *Obers.* What did all that mean? Signore Mondoloni, I thought, you supposedly taught me perfect German! But now I didn't understand a word! Nonetheless, it tasted heavenly.

As we flew down the west-east transverse line from Bregenz to Budapest between the mountains, I had trouble coping with the main points of the menu before the train slowed down in the approach to Salzburg. Even the espresso was perfect—a *kleiner Brauner.* The waiter assured me, however, that the name did not imply racism or even resentment toward us Moros.

A ROOM HAD been reserved for me in the Hotel Altstadt. At the train station it was impossible for Luigi to get a taxi.

"We've had a construction site here for about a century," a helpful older man told me, "and ever since the Vatican took up residence here too, with God's help it's gotten even worse. Your ICom, or whatever that device is called, you're better off throwing away here. Most Austrians already disposed of the thing with the withdrawal from the EU. We still have telephones. Or we have them again, depending how you look at it."

"And how do you prove your identity?" I asked him.

He laughed sardonically. "Everyone doesn't need to know everything," he replied. "But let's not talk about that."

He raised his cane and hailed a taxi. *"Droschke!"* he shouted commandingly. *"Subito!"*

The taxi driver, a bulky, bull-necked, middle-aged man with a double chin and greasy blond hair, smelled overwhelmingly of garlic, sweat, and a synthetic patchouli with which he evidently doused himself as a deodorant. To no avail.

"Where to?" he wheezed while looking over his shoulder.

"Hotel Altstadt."

"Rudolfskai. Not the worst address," he murmured appreciatively.

"What do you mean?" I asked him.

"Something is offered there, my dear lady. At least to the Texans and the gooks, people say," he said with a chuckle. "People say."

We drove down a street lined with banks and expensive shops.

"Where are you from, ma'am?"

Again he twisted his neck to look at me.

"Europe," I said assertively.

And turn around right now, for heaven's sake! I pleaded silently, holding my breath.

"Europe," the taxi driver snorted. "Are you pulling my leg, ma'am? Euroland has burned down." With his thick hand he slapped with pleasure the sheepskin-covered steering wheel.

"But you do take euros, right?"

"Of course," he wheezed. "I take everything except marka bavarese and Bohemian crowns. Those not even the peddlers will take. Play money."

Cursing, he stepped on the brake as a horse-drawn coach burst from a side street. "Now, come on!" he shouted.

Finally I managed to roll down a window. Cool, damp air streamed in, with a whiff of horse dung. We drove across a rapidly flowing gray-green river in the evening light, then turned left onto a narrow street running along the high bank. After about two hundred yards we stopped.

Under an arch with an ornamental wrought-iron gate yawned a dark cave opening. Over the inelegant, massive substructure rose a light-colored four-story building. On its facade hung long red, white, and red flags. The driver didn't make a move to get out, so I lifted my suitcase and travel bag on my own out of the trunk, in which all manner of junk rolled around. A young hotel employee came hurrying from the entrance to help me. He wore a moss-green apron under a black vest. Had he been summoned from working in the garden before he had time to change?

"Thirty euros," the driver demanded.

"Quite a lot for the short distance," I said.

"It's standard," he countered. "You're in Salzburg, young woman, *and* in the Vatican too. What more do you want? Give me a break!"

The scene seemed to be embarrassing for the young man. His Adam's apple jumped up and down nervously, but he didn't say a word. I handed the driver the money through the window.

"Many thanks for your help."

He laughed, unmoved. "Have fun!" he said, and drove away.

A carpeted stone staircase led steeply up into a treasure chamber of dark wood—an ambiance in a solidly made imitation of rococo.

"Roblacher. — Welcome, Fräulein Ligrina," said a young, well-nourished man in a dark suit at reception, briskly extending a short-fingered hand across the counter and offering me a businesslike winning smile from the corner of his mouth; from the other he rasped toward the bellboy: "Four hundred and eight."

The gangly boy nodded assiduously and led me across expensive carpets past lime green laquered display cases and green-and-orange-striped armchairs to an elevator lined with impressively sparkling punched brass. Signore Falcotti seemed to want to put the Vatican to great expense for me.

On the anthracite-colored floor mat in the elevator was the word "Wednesday."

"Is that changed every day?" I asked my escort.

"Of course. After midnight."

"May I ask your name?" I asked him.

"Janez." The acne on his pale cheeks flared up.

"You're not Austrian."

"Yes, I am. From Marburg," he replied. "Marburg an der Drau," he added.

"Maribor?" I asked.

He shrugged and looked up at the ceiling.

We got out under a glass roof from which birdcages hung. It spanned the stairwell and seemed to have been added later, for the stairs ascended along the external wall of a house punctured by windows that looked as if they had once faced out to the street. On the opposite wall hung a pious image that, judging by the form, must have previously been part of a winged altar. In the center was a monstrance over which God the Father floated in the clouds. A baroque Eucharistic representation, probably made by a local artist.

In one of the cages a macaw uttered a deafening squawk.

"*Sie Hai!*" it shrieked.

"What's that about?" I asked with amusement.

Janez gave me a disconcerted look. "That's our Joseph," he explained.

"What a plain name for such a vibrantly colored bird."

"Most people find it funny," he replied indifferently.

"Aha."

My accommodations were next to the "Kaiser Suite," as I gathered from the large brass letters on a marble plaque. Room 408, however, was rather small, but cozy, apart from the massive dark beams, which loomed on the ceiling, especially as they were borne by an even more massive crossbeam, which ran across the head of the double bed. The bathroom was an extravagant luxury in gold, marble, and fluffy white terry cloth. I indulged in it and changed my clothes.

When I came out of the bathroom, I suddenly noticed that someone had inadvertently opened a door that led into the Kaiser Suite next door. Beforehand I had not even realized that there was a direct connecting door. Voices could be heard, a subdued giggling and squeaking and soft music. Definitely Mozart—I thought I recognized *Così fan tutte*. Presumably someone had moved in, perhaps newlyweds spending their honeymoon here, and they had opened the inadvertently unlocked connecting door. I wanted to close it softly, but couldn't resist casting a brief glance into the suite.

It was a spacious bedchamber with a huge square bed on which, with lifted skirt and spread legs, a buxom young woman was lying. Her face was heavily painted and adorned with artificial beauty marks. On her head she wore a white powdered wig. Her genital area, which she presented invitingly, was shaved and seemed to have makeup on it as well. It looked like a slit gaping in the white flesh between her thighs.

At the foot of the bed a young man, also wearing a wig and a red tailcoat, was performing a toe dance—a sort of ballet in step with the music. From his open pants jutted a long, thin member, swinging back and forth like the tongue of a hungry anteater. The dancer had closed his eyes and was moving his arms, completely abandoned to the music, as he approached his partner around the foot of the bed. Finally, he sank with a cry of joy into her arms and merged with her as the music soared to a climax and then went silent.

The next moment I could not believe my eyes: The copulating couple was suddenly gone, the bed immaculately smooth. With embarrassment I noticed that I had not been the only witness to this erotic performance. At least six other guests, equally curious, had been peering through half-opened doors into the Kaiser Suite. Men, women, mainly tourists—some only half-dressed or in a terry-cloth robe with the emblem of the hotel on the breast pocket. All of them were now anxious to withdraw as hastily and discreetly as possible.

"Dear guests and friends of the house," cooed a women's voice with silky sensuality from a hidden loudspeaker. "Welcome to today's Amadeus party. That was a small sample of our interactive performances. The actual event begins at ten in the evening. To get to know each other, we will meet half an hour beforehand in the rococo hall for an informal drink on the house. Everyone is cordially invited. See you then!"

And a male voice, in which, for all the effort at a velvety timbre, I recognized that of the brusque head of reception, added: "Participation costs ten thousand schillings per person. For an additional charge we will gladly provide you the necessary VR equipment on request, ladies and gentlemen."

I wanted to close the door completely, but my hand touched only the cool plaster of the wall.

Oh, God! Frans was right: It was a multibillion-euro gift Toshiaka Ishida and company had bestowed on humanity—the gift of turning any desirable possibility into physical sensation, into a realistically experienceable surrogate for reality. I remembered Richard Fortey's book on the development of life: "Although nature is full of camouflage, we are the first animal ever to deceive ourselves."

I sat down on the bed and asked Luigi to activate our Scarabeo. Then we took a tour through Salzburg and its history. We visited the former salt and slave markets, the palaces and houses, the fortress and the catacombs. I became acquainted with the imperious, vain archbishops with a passion for splendor, who built themselves fantastic castles and whose mistresses bore them dozens of children. And then Mozart, always Mozart: Mozart the Father, Mozart the Son, and Mozart the Holy Business-Savvy Ghost.

Later that night I heard beautiful music resounding somewhere in the house, heard the giggles and lustful cries of women wearing powdered wigs and artificial beauty marks on their painted faces, and I dreamed of an anteater hungrily darting its tongue in and out as it foraged for prey in a cracked-open pomegranate. And again and again I heard the mad laughter of Tom Hulce in Milos Forman's ancient film *Amadeus*, which my grandfather had loved so much that he watched it whenever he found time.

IV

The Salt Caravan

There is no especially prominent and extraordinary state of the past . . . but rather a vast number of pasts, all of which possess their particular incomparable significance . . . And any moment of time, however briefly we may hold it, is split in the course of events and forks like the trunk of a tree into two individual, related but diverging branches.

ANDRÉ MALRAUX

The window of my room faced the old town: Judengasse, I read. Over the green dome of the cathedral, the fortress stood out against a slate-colored, rainy sky. It was far from as imposing as the travel guide accessed by our Scarabeo would have had me believe. I did not at all perceive it as a symbol of dominance over the land, but more as the image of a precipitate escape upward—a fluttering-up in the face of a threat from below, like a shoddily nailed-together coop meant to protect the poultry from predators.

When I left my room, Joseph scurried in alarm to the far end of his perch and eyed me mistrustfully. I looked out a window across the Salzach to the Kapuzinerberg: a landscape that appeared embossed in lead; soft contours on which the eyes found nothing to hold on to; a light that seemed to seep through a gray ice floe. The air tasted clammy, as if infused with the stale dampness of just-hung laundry, with the addition of chemicals. A feeling of trepidation overcame me. How could the Pope move his seat from Rome to *here*? I asked myself. How could Mozart compose that heavenly music *here*? This was an ambiance for brass bands and orchestras in traditional costume.

At reception I took one of the umbrellas provided in abundance for the guests of the house in a massive container made of wrought brass and set off to explore the old town on foot.

The cathedral—destroyed by bombs in the Second World War and, as the travel guide put it, "resurrected in uncompromising simplicity." Well, did it have to be the simplicity of a riding arena, I wondered, as I looked at the nave from the fountain on Residenzplatz. But when I stepped onto the cathedral square and saw the facade, I was actually quite impressed.

Soon I also discovered the exceptionally beautiful sides of Salzburg. In the middle of the city I found under a rock face a small cemetery with trees, old houses, and a little church as if in a remote mountain village. Next to it I then stopped in at a massively built tavern with cozy rooms, where I had an excellent lunch. Completely blindly I ordered *Salzburger Nockerln* for dessert, because I found the name so funny, and was then confronted with a mountain range of frothed-up, baked egg white, in the face of which I had to capitulate after the first peak. The waiter, who could have been Janez's brother, assured me that the establishment had been called St. Peter for more than a millennium and that the name had nothing to do with the Holy Father recently moving in. The house wine reconciled me completely with the city.

The rest of the afternoon I continued to roam the streets of Salzburg, but could not bring myself to set foot in the famous festival hall. The cavernous interior, half hewn into the rock, scared me off. Bernd had once told me that the Nazis had been partial to having their terrible war weapons produced in cave systems. Thousands of prisoners of war had lost their lives there in a horrific fashion. I cast a glance into the darkened foyer, in which holographs of stage scenes had been constructed—a ghostly array of unmoving figures in gloomy dungeons. I turned away with a shudder. What nonsense, I chided myself, but the sense of unease would not abate.

Later I sat on a bench in front of the Residenz palace and watched the coachmen and their horses; the fine rain unrelentingly dripping on them they seemed not even to notice. Then a call from Falcotti in Rome suddenly reached me. He was still held up, he explained, and seemed to be in a hurry. He would not be in Salzburg until Monday to have a conversation with me. I was fine, I assured him; Salzburg was a wonderful city and an extended stay would be really nice for me.

One of the coach drivers, an old man wearing a green loden jacket and a black felt hat like the ones the Roman Hobbits wore—with a thick tuft of chamois hair on it—gave me an antagonistic look. Did my Italian bother him? He held a cigarette in his cupped hand and drew on it while with the other he fed an apple to his small shaggy coach horse.

On an impulse, I called Renata. She had NEA status, her ICom notified me.

"Is she traveling?"

"I'm afraid I cannot provide any information about that, Domenica. Would you like to leave a message for her?"

"Give her my regards when she returns. Is she doing well?"

"If you would like information, I can relay your questions to Hendrik Casimir. I am at present under the control of the institute's AI and have only limited decision-making authority. Shall I connect you, Domenica?"

"No, thank you. Over."

Frans too had NEA status.

"Is he already traveling again?"

"No, but he does not want to be disturbed," his ICom informed me.

"Tell him that it's me, Domenica."

"I am aware of that, but he does not want to be disturbed by anyone. I'm sorry, those are his instructions."

"Well, then I really don't want to disturb," I said crossly and broke the connection.

The coachman had given up hope of customers and climbed onto the coach box. "I've had it for today," he said to his neighbor, a robust younger man with a coarse red face, swung his whip, and drove away.

"*Sie Hai!*" the macaw squawked at me as I stepped out of the elevator.

I knew *Hai* meant "shark" in German. "One day," I snarled at it, "when the Salzach floods, one will come swimming in here and devour you, you stupid creature!"

IT MUST HAVE been after midnight. The last elegantly dressed visitors to the festival hall had gotten into taxis or fetched their cars from the underground garage and had gone home. The gates had been closed, the lights extinguished. The sky had cleared. A bright moon bathed the street in light and made the rock face appear even darker. A cold wind descended from the mountains. I was freezing. If only I had dressed more warmly.

I had huddled in the darkness of a house entrance with half a dozen well-trodden stone steps leading up to it and stared across the street. There was no one to be seen. At any moment it would be time.

And indeed, it then began. It was as if the gray stones of the facade morphed and took human form. They separated from the walls of the festival house, were gray as the stone—gray shoulders, gray faces, gray arms.

Emaciated, ragged figures, ten or twelve chained together, they separated from the rock and shuffled, staggering with exhaustion, across to the horse fountain, soundless, in ghostly silence. Only the water burbled. They washed themselves, drank out of cupped hands. Then they were again led away, through the stone. They disappeared into the rock, while the next column was led to the fountain.

I trembled from the cold.

Suddenly I felt a hand on my shoulder. I spun around.

"Did you seriously think you could hide from us?" my geography teacher, whom I had encountered at the border, asked me.

He lifted the small half-sphere and shook it. It was full of darkness.

I awoke with a scream.

THE NEXT DAY started off with a radiant morning. I looked out the window down into Judengasse. The first few people were out. I watched a scrawny old man with a beige sarong flapping around his calves. On his head a brown turban was enthroned, and over his shoulders he had wrapped a worn gray wool blanket. Supported by a long walking stick, he took measured steps from Waagplatz, accompanied by a dark-skinned, perhaps twelve-year-old boy, who was hauling with both hands a tied-up, suitcase-like piece of luggage made of wood. It was so heavy that he had to put it down repeatedly. The old man pointed with his stick to a spot next to the entrance to our hotel and watched the boy untie and open the object. It seemed to be a sort of bed. Was the old man intending to camp there in the middle of the street?

As I stepped through the green lacquered door, the old man was resting on his bed, which—I could not believe my eyes—was covered with closely packed nails. The blanket lay folded up under his head. His ribs stuck out from his torso under the skin like the frame of a fish trap, and his scrawny legs looked as if they had been rooted in dry earth for decades. He looked at me with extremely sad tobacco-yellow eyes, as if he had lain down to die.

"My goodness, the fakir is here!" said Roblacher, our concierge, who had come through the door behind me. "How are you, you old rascal?"

The old man made a weak gesture toward the boy, who was crouching next to the bed, and uttered a sound as if he were too exhausted to speak.

"He says he's not doing well," said the boy.

"That means," said the concierge, "if I understand correctly, you haven't had breakfast yet."

Both nodded.

The boy looked at me with dark eyes and pushed a shallow little basket imploringly toward me. I rummaged in my handbag and threw a two-euro coin into it. The concierge reappeared and handed each of them a croissant.

"There you go," he said.

The old man reached out his hand commandingly and the boy obediently handed him his share. Both croissants disappeared under the old man's yellow-flecked mustache.

"Are they gypsies?" I asked the concierge.

He shook his head. "No, Bangladeshis," he said. "They've come with the salt caravan."

"Salt caravan?" I asked, perplexed.

"Yes. The salt caravan comes every year at this time. These people hold a market on Residenzplatz. You should have a look at it, young woman. They offer pretty things: pottery, baskets, carvings, but especially seeds and seedlings. They know something about that. First-rate quality. And they're artists too."

"But why salt?"

"With the proceeds they buy salt. Guaranteed pure salt, with the papal seal, the tiara, which they then sell in Bohemia and especially in Poland. It's a wonderfully healthy salt, young woman, you can take it from me," he declared with a laugh. "Miracle salt, so to speak, against all afflictions. Even against radioactivity. The people in the east are wild about it. Especially the Polacks. They'll pay any price for it."

"And where do these people come from?"

"Where are you from?" he asked the boy.

"Saxan Analt," the boy said softly.

"These two here come from the region between Halberstadt and Quedlinburg. They live there in fortified villages, because of the Nazis, the Asens, and Kicobs. The UN resettled them there. Thuringia, Saxony, the Ore Mountains. The contaminated areas from which the residents have fled."

"I thought those regions were uninhabitable," I said.

"These people manage astonishingly well, it is said. See for yourself. Radioactively contaminated land is better than none. For their homeland is underwater." Roblacher chuckled.

"I know."

"Well, then. Petroleum deliveries only in exchange for taking in refugees. You know the motto of the UN. What else is it to do?"

"And here in Austria-Hungary?"

The concierge held up his hands. "We're overflowing with Slavs, young woman, if you will pardon me. The Bangladeshis are still my favorites."

With measured movements the old man brushed the crumbs from his mustache. He belched and closed his eyes. The nails seemed not to cause him particular torment. I saw that they were not very sharp.

The satyr head over the entrance gate looked down at us, grinning.

RESIDENZPLATZ WAS UNRECOGNIZABLE. At the fountain stood about two dozen camels, snorting as they drank from plastic tubs. Along the facades of the carillon tower and the cathedral, large army tents adorned with pennants had been pitched; in front of them were market stalls from which Asian vendors dressed in colorful sarongs offered wares. Between the fountain and the Residenz palace, men wearing turbans and baseball caps erected a large stage from prefabricated parts.

Two city officials in white protective suits, the yellow propeller-like hazard symbol for radioactivity on their backs, walked around between the market stalls, running their measuring gloves over the displayed items and reading the data from the small monitors on the backs of their hands. They seemed not to have any complaints. At the corners of the square stood squad cars of the gendarmerie, which were there to nip in the bud assaults by militant racists—in order to gain attention, they seldom missed such events. I was, of course, interested above all in the offering of plants. It ranged from flowers through seedlings, ornamental plants, vegetables and fruit, to culinary herbs and spices; native species as well as exotic ones, which they had evidently brought with them from their homeland, but also strains and mutants with which I was unfamiliar. Probably genetically engineered creations.

I listened to customers comparing notes on their experiences with previous purchases and expressing their satisfaction—indeed, their enthusiasm regarding the yield, the taste, and the resistance to pests and diseases. It did not take long for me to realize that I was looking at products by experts here, by artists of haute couture in the field of botanical genetics.

I plucked a blade from a pinnate plant that looked like a variant of watercress. However, it belonged to neither the *Nasturtium officinale* species nor the allotetraploid form of *Nasturtium microphyllum*; nor was it related to the triploid *x sterile*, as was cultivated in England and on the other side of the Atlantic in Virginia. I crushed the blade between my fingers and sniffed it; it emitted a strong, sharp smell. It was definitely watercress, but this form was unknown to me.

"Is this found in the region where you live or is it tailor-made?" I asked the woman at the stall.

"Those who look for it find it," she said dismissively, pulling her chador over her mouth; her cheeks were fissured with radiation acne.

But I did not retreat, plucked a sprig and scrutinized it. It bore six pairs of pinnae instead of four.

"Have you heard of Dreienbrunnen?" she asked. "Near Erfurt? That's Dreienbrunnen watercress, young woman, if you want to know exactly."

I shook my head. "Not this form," I said. "I just wanted to know whether this plant is a genetically engineered product or a mutant from the plutonium fallout."

"What are you talking about? Do you want to drive away our customers?" she hissed indignantly. "Our goods are officially inspected. The authorities have checked and found no cause for complaint. So stop asking questions like that!"

"Sorry," I murmured.

With a friendly smile, she turned to a customer.

"Do you know something about genetics?" a male voice asked behind me.

I turned around. It was a middle-aged man with a pale, doughy face and thinning blond hair. His stomach was kept in check by wide leather suspenders with cross-braces, from which gray-brown buckskin breeches hung. A gruesome bundle of yellow teeth, antler tips, and claws protected his fly. He self-consciously turned a flat black felt hat in his hands, on the double cord of which billowed the hugest tuft of chamois hair I had ever seen.

"Depending how you look at it," I said carefully. "I'm a botanist."

"Ah, I see," he said, disappointed. "I heard you saying something about mutants."

His gray cable-knit jacket with clasps made of carved tusk smelled intensely like a pet shop. He seemed well-off, but made a somehow helpless impression on me.

"What do you want to know about?" I asked.

"It's more about animals," he replied. "Birds, to be precise."

That explained the smell.

"I don't know whether I can help you with that."

"Too bad," he said. "I need some advice. I thought that maybe you . . . You see, I'm a businessman. My shop is very nearby, on Goldgasse."

"You have a pet shop," I surmised.

He gave me a sad look and asked with a sigh, "You can smell it, right? Yes, there's not much that can be done about that."

"Hm."

"No, not a pet shop, my dear lady. It's a leather goods store and specialty store for hunting and forestry accessories. A traditional shop—family business for generations . . ."

Before I knew what was happening, I was walking across the square at his side and we were turning onto Goldgasse. The man stopped in front of a glass door and unlocked it laboriously. In the display window hung wide leather belts embroidered with edelweiss and ostentatious handbags with sewn-on silver coins and silver-mounted deer teeth, as well as hand-sized, heart-shaped containers equipped with snap hooks, the function of which was impenetrable to me.

"You're a foreigner, right?" he asked, opening the door.

"That's a matter of opinion," I replied. "I'm from Rome."

He nodded. "Then you probably won't be able to muster much interest in this. It's more of a . . . a national, historical matter."

"Now you're making me curious."

Inside the shop a flood of folkloric showpieces surged over me: powder horns for snuff, more Alpine-hunter-style handbags, even more deer teeth in silver, more fashionably spruced-up death for atavistic tendencies of either sex—whole display cases were full of it. And on the walls dozens of antlers in a double row, peruke, cross, and corkscrew antlers, in the dim background whole heads, luxuriously prepared, with alertly gazing glass eyes: deer, sows, eerily grinning pikes, a courting wood grouse, flanked by two pheasants.

I followed the owner to the back. As he opened a door, the smell that came pouring out took my breath away. I saw an incubator on which small red and green indicator lights gleamed. Next to it stood a sturdy mesh cage in which a feathered something could be vaguely made out.

"Recently I've gotten into something that has already cost me a lot of money," he confessed, slipping on a leather glove. "But it doesn't yield anything, even though I have customers who would with pleasure count out a hundred thousand schillings on my table to be able to show something like that to their party guests. But it doesn't really work."

I gave no reply, taking care to breathe through my mouth and pressing my nose into the crook of my anorak sleeve. The man opened the cage and at first I thought he was pulling out a voluminous bird skin, but the thing unfolded strong wings and let out a pitiful squawk. I saw a milky nictating membrane, which slid aside to reveal a shiny, imperiously gazing eye. It was a young golden eagle, a real *Aquila chrysaetos*, but something was wrong with it. On its neck a lump had formed—a growth like the bib of a turkey, swinging limply back and forth. The neck . . . Suddenly I realized it: That was no lump. It was a second head, underdeveloped and feeble, hanging down and trying in vain to erect itself—with the beak opened to scream. That was what was letting out those weak squawks.

"I obtain the fertilized eggs from a genetics laboratory in Klagenfurt. It's the double-eagle, the original imperial eagle. And the scientists in Carinthia assure me—"

I was no longer capable of responding. I pressed my fist to my mouth to keep from vomiting over the display cases full of corpse parts and ran out into the street.

AFTER SUNSET THE performers began their acts on Residenzplatz. On the stage appeared acrobats who juggled plates, spat fire, and pushed long swords down their throats. Slender-limbed children in colorful bodysuits were hurled up with a seesaw and formed a living pyramid. A beautiful young woman in a glittering costume and with a fantastic headdress made of glass and little mirrors stood on a camel draped with mulberry- and tobacco-colored rugs. She rode around and held up a neon sign on which each coming attraction was announced. A band played Bengali music: tabla rhythms and sitar sounds—a trancelike endless loop.

At dusk a tightrope walker came down as if from the heavens on a rope that had been stretched on a slant between the carillon tower and the fountain. He had not yet descended halfway when a shot rang out. A moment of breathless silence and anxious horror—but the frozen figure on the rope, though it teetered, did not plunge to the pavement. A few seconds went by, and then he tentatively placed his right foot forward and moved on. At the ends of the balancing pole a red and a green light glowed alternately. A gasp of relief went through the audience. Was the shot part of the show?

There were many people on the square, not just pilgrims and tourists, but also numerous residents of the city and families from the surrounding rural communities. As night fell, a striking number of young men appeared who had been drinking liquid courage in the bars and seemed to be on the prowl for one of the exotic young women who had mingled among the spectators in small groups. Again and again I saw two or three of them get into a taxi with men and drive away.

Only three coaches stood at the passage to the cathedral square. The horses were nervous due to the proximity of the camels. They grew even more anxious when an older little man, who was dressed in a brown cowl but seemed to be neither a monk nor a priest, climbed onto a coach box and began to sermonize with a shrill voice about the immorality of the youth.

"Do you not grasp," he shouted, tearing desperately at his beard, which hung sparsely down to his chest, "that they are only after your most valuable possession, that they are seed robbers, that they steal your seed, plunder your genes, and make off with them?"

"Bet you'd like to get plundered a little too, eh?" exclaimed one of the coachmen good-naturedly.

The onlookers laughed.

"But the bells never move when you pull on the rope!" another exclaimed, cracking his whip so loudly that the horses shied and the preacher almost fell off the coach box.

"Do you know what they're doing in their secret laboratories with your seed?" he continued to shout, undeterred, as he held himself steady. "Chimeras and monkeys and demons! That's what they're making out of it!"

Well, certainly not that, I thought, but there's something to be said for the concept.

"They go, our young men, unknowing, stupid, and blinded, and let those . . . those . . . *monkey women* fuck them."

"That's enough!" exclaimed the coachman, pulling him off his vehicle.

The preacher staggered and fell to the pavement on his behind.

"Fuck them!" he shouted again with all his might, bristling his beard and breathing with a hiss through his teeth.

"Get lost already!" the coachman snapped at him, raising his whip.

"Let him be," said his neighbor, grasping his arm.

It was the one with the coarse, chubby-cheeked face who had also been standing here the day before.

IN CAFÉ GLOCKENSPIEL I bought ice cream to go and took it with me to my hotel room. The bed of nails had been folded and tied up. The boy was sitting on it and guarding it. He looked hungry. Full of sympathy I handed him the ice cream.

"You eat that now!" I said, when he hesitated.

As I turned to the door, I saw that he was greedily spooning it. Probably he had held out all day at the old man's side and gotten nothing.

At the hotel bar the fakir sat with Roblacher, holding a large cognac glass in his hand and smiling somewhat absently. His eyes shone. The turban had slipped down over his forehead.

The porcelain figures with their rococo costumes in the showcases along the corridor, which had that morning still exhibited innocent bucolic revels, had evidently been switched in order to put the guests in the mood for another wild evening. The scenes now had a completely unambiguous erotic character, and some of the figures displayed monstrous priapic attributes. Out of the corner of my eye I thought I glimpsed sexual movements. Indeed! My newly trained eye caught in the almost imperceptibly flickering edges of the colors that these were mobile holographs staging a computer-operated orgy. Mozart trickled faintly from hidden speakers: *The Marriage of Figaro*.

NO SOONER HAD I fallen asleep than I was awakened by shots. But this here wasn't Rome. From afar I heard a dull pounding, but it wasn't the drumming of the Hobbits. I wasn't in Rome here, but in Salzburg. And the sounds were coming from the other side of the river, from the Kapuzinerberg. I opened the door of my room and looked through the glass dome. It was fireworks—the screeching and buzzing of rockets and other pyrotechnic devices. Multicolored fans sprayed upward, dandelion heads bloomed in the sky and showered the city for a few seconds with unreal light.

In the hotel things seemed to be quite lively, but it didn't sound like a Mozart party downstairs in the rococo hall. Rather, the shouts and laughter penetrated from the Kaiser Suite next door. Champagne corks popped, glasses clinked against the wall. What nerve! It was now past midnight.

The entrance to the Kaiser Suite was opened; a loud hubbub, laughter, and a gust of smoke- and alcohol-infused air wafted out. A waiter in a tailcoat walked backward out the door; he had a tray with dirty glasses in his hand and a napkin over his arm. Then he bowed to the guests inside the suite and underscored that gesture by striking the heels of his shoes together with a strange scissorlike movement of his feet, making a hard clicking sound. An expression of politeness? A submissive gesture? A courtship ritual? I couldn't interpret it. Then he closed the door and turned to me. I didn't know him, had never seen him in the hotel before. A tall, thin, bald man, whose head shone waxily in the light of the stairwell—probably a temporary worker hired for a private party. His narrow face looked sickly pale. He raised his eyebrows when he noticed me. Then he eyed me up and down, as if he disapproved of the fact that I was wearing a bathrobe and slippers, and asked: "Is there something I can do for you, Fräulein?"

"May I ask what's being celebrated so boisterously here?"

His eyebrows rose even higher. "You're not German, are you?" The waiter pulled at the napkin hanging over his arm.

"No," I said. "But what does that have to do with my question?"

"Today is April 20."

"Was the foundation stone laid for the Vatican?"

"The *what*?" He leaned forward and tilted his head as if he had not heard correctly.

"Over on the Kapuzinerberg. I was told that they were going to lay the foundation stone for the construction of the new Vatican one of these days."

Now he seemed really dismayed. "Over on the Kapuzinerberg?" he repeated.

Then he threw his head back and let out a whinnying laugh that almost made him drop the tray.

"That's the best joke I've heard in a long time," he gasped. "The Vatican!" He shook his head as if he had to struggle for composure. "They are going to tear down the Gauhalle and the Gauhaus with it and demolish the Gauforum to build the *Vatican* there! The two Ottos are turning over in their graves."

He closed his eyes and doubled up with laughter.

"That's good! I have to tell them that!" he said, gesturing with a nod to the door of the Kaiser Suite. "No, Fräulein, today is the Führer's birthday."

"What Führer?"

The man suddenly became serious.

"Now hang on," he said sternly, looking down at me reprovingly. "You're

Italian, right? The Führer has been dead for over a hundred years, but we preserve his memory. He means something to us Germans."

Suddenly I felt dizzy. Amid shouts, glasses again shattered against the wall in the suite.

"*Sie Hai!*" squawked the macaw.

The waiter turned to the cage. "That's our Joseph. What did the old boy once say? 'Our end will be the end of the universe'—a bit grandiose as always. Who knows what he meant by that?" He bared his long yellow teeth. "Did you know that the old stallion could look down on more than a hundred children and grandchildren when he died? There's a photo of him and his whole clan on his ninety-ninth birthday. He's in the middle, in a wheelchair, surrounded by a brood of diligent bucks. That was his universe." The man flicked the bars of the cage with his finger. "*Sieg Heil!*" he said, again making that strange clicking sound with his heels, the meaning of which remained impenetrable to me.

V

The New Vatican

Is the universe in the end nothing but a gigantic computer, which permits reversible and irreversible time evolutions?

KLAUS MAINZER

Well, it's not exactly a pilgrims' hostel, I admit," said Falcotti, smiling at me from under the brim of his panama hat, "but I hope you've nonetheless slept well."

"I've slept badly and had even worse dreams," I replied. "Though I'm not even entirely sure whether they're dreams."

He leaned forward with surprise. Was there worry in his eyes?

"What do you mean?" he asked.

"I can't quite classify it," I confessed. "Was it a sort of waking dream? In any case, I thought shots woke me in the middle of the night. But it was fireworks."

"Fireworks? I didn't see or hear anything about fireworks."

I looked at him aghast. "There weren't any fireworks last night? Over there, above the Kapuzinerberg?"

"Not that I know of."

"Then I must have dreamed that too. But that was only the beginning of a weird experience I can't make sense of."

I told him about my nighttime encounter with the ghostly waiter, about the Nazi celebration I believed I had witnessed. I described to him my confusion when I complained in the morning to the hotel management about the disturbance and was told with a shake of the head that there had been no party in the Kaiser Suite that night. Roblacher, the man from reception, had taken the elevator up with me, and I had cast a glance into the rooms. I really must have dreamed it. Nor was there a waiter in the house who

would have fit the description I provided. Roblacher had given me a disconcerted look and shrugged helplessly.

Falcotti listened to me with growing concern.

"Only that Joseph, the *'Sieg Heil'*–squawking macaw, scurried fearfully
away from me on its perch in the cage as I approached. You see, Signore
Falcotti, that's a point I don't comprehend: How did I suddenly know that
'Joseph' was an allusion to the Nazi Joseph Goebbels? And suddenly I also
understood *what* that wretched creature was screaming. I can't remember
anyone in the hotel hinting that to me—besides that waiter who supposedly
doesn't even exist. Is it possible to dream something like that? But it can't
be. I really don't know how to explain it."

Falcotti thoughtfully bit his lower lip, stared across the square, and
pushed his VR glasses back and forth on the table. The two flip-down dark
screens looked like small blinders.

"There's another thing that's odd. A Gauforum, you said?" Falcotti
asked.

"The waiter mentioned not only a Gauforum, but also a Gauhalle and a
Gauhaus. And he said the two Ottos would turn over in their graves."

"That's really strange. For there actually were plans of that sort for construction on the Kapuzinerberg more than a hundred years ago, during the
Third Reich."

"That was the time of that Führer?"

"Yes. Adolf Hitler. The so-called Third Reich. The Nazi era. And there
was at that time a detailed plan to build on the Imberg. I've seen a model.
The plans were designed by"—he closed his eyes—"by an Otto Strohmayr
and an Otto Reitter, if I'm not mistaken."

"The two Ottos!"

Falcotti nodded and gave me a serious look.

"Those plans—they were never realized, though," I said, shrugging uneasily.

Falcotti shook his head, reached for his cup, and took a sip of his *großer
Brauner,* which had in the meantime gotten cold. "No, thank God! They
were supposed to be impressive monumental structures. They would have
given Salzburg a completely different face. That architecture had something . . . something bombastic about it. The planned buildings exceeded
all human measure, but nonetheless lacked any grandeur." He carefully
put down the cup. "But tell me, Domenica, have you ever heard of those

architectural projects or seen any photos of the models, in a museum here, in a travel guide or a city history?"

"No."

"Or did you consult your Scarabeo?"

"I did, but I neither saw nor heard anything about such planned structures," I said.

"Are you completely certain?" asked Falcotti.

"Absolutely."

His eyes wandered to the gables of the houses on the other side of Makartplatz, over which the slope of the Kapuzinerberg rose, as if he had to make sure that the small monastery really still stood there. He was visibly nervous.

"Is something bothering you?" I asked him.

He puffed out his cheeks, shrugged, and replied: "Indeed."

"Do my dreams give you cause for concern?"

"If they were dreams—no. But I'm afraid, Domenica, they weren't."

"What do you mean?"

"Do you remember the game we played together in my office at the university? The *globus* game?"

"Yes, I remember. The Cusanus game with the crazy balls."

"You are apparently on a rather erratic course, Domenica."

"Heading where?"

"No one knows. But it frightens me a little."

"Frightens you? Why?"

Falcotti spread his hands. "Have you ever heard of the so-called Goldfaden-Hargitai effect?" he asked.

I shook my head. "What is it?" I asked him.

"A quite peculiar psychic phenomenon. A sort of empathy. It used to be considered a strange form of schizophrenia, and to this day many psychologists mistake the effect for heautoscopy. But it's not a projection of one's own body outward, as is usually the case with doppelgänger appearances. Heautoscopy frequently occurs at times of intense stress and in states of anxiety and exhaustion. It can originate in physical defects: lesions in the right half of the cerebral cortex, tumors on the hypophysis, or temporal lobe epilepsy. But with GH all this is not the case."

"I'm afraid I don't understand much about such illnesses," I admitted.

"Excuse my psychologist Latin," said Falcotti. "GH is not a dissociative disorder, as André Goldfaden and Urban Hargitai already proved in the second half of the twentieth century, but a rare ability, which . . . Well, it's hard to explain. It's the ability to establish contact at certain moments with one's doppelgängers in parallel universes, to participate in their experiences, so to speak, or even to exchange one's consciousness with them."

I shook my head incredulously.

"You're looking at me skeptically, Domenica, but these are facts. The effect often causes us a lot of trouble during time travel. When travelers, as a result of multiple transitions, are close to their doppelgängers or even encounter them, that can become an unbearable psychic strain, for interferences occur between their brain functions."

"But what does that have to do with my experience last night in the hotel?"

"A temporary exchange of perceptions might have taken place between your self here and another that lives in a parallel temporal dimension—a universe in which the history of National Socialism and the Second World War took a different course."

A shiver ran down my spine. So there was a version of me that had to live in that terrible world. Did she feel the same way as I did? Did she share my perceptions as well? I remembered the disturbing dream with the unknown but strangely familiar nocturnal visitor, which had often haunted me as a teenager. Had I partaken in the pleasure of a doppelgänger?

"You need not be afraid, Domenica. You'll learn how to deal with these unusual experiences," said Falcotti. The cross in his temple pulsed. He flicked the handle of his cup with his forefinger, then said with a shake of his head: "Perhaps our difficulties are due to the fact that you possess an extraordinarily strong GH talent. The conditions for it are present in you. If I remember correctly, your right temporal lobe is quite highly developed."

"How would you know that?" I asked.

"During the preliminary medical examinations of the candidates, things like that are already taken into account. Highly developed visual memory and things of that sort."

Falcotti lifted his hat and rubbed with his fingertips the temple in which he wore his cross implant.

"You spoke of difficulties, Signore Falcotti. Do they concern me or my planned work?"

He shook his head slowly. "There's no reason to keep it from you. During our preparations for the Rinascita Project we have recently stumbled on a few facts with which the technicians in Amsterdam have problems. For

historical and geographical reasons, we chose northwestern Europe around
the middle of the fifteenth century as the field of operation for you botanists. The destination time is after the great plagues and before the excessive witch-hunts, which, as we have come to realize, pose an extreme
danger to time travelers in the sixteenth and seventeenth centuries. There's
also the fact that around the middle of the fifteenth century an unadulterated European flora can still be found: The age of exploration has not yet
dawned; from Asia barely any species have been introduced, and from
America none at all. We have envisaged a topographic profile from the
marshes of the North Sea to the higher regions of the Eifel and the low
mountain ranges: a rather unadulterated ecology. On top of that, the area is
politically tranquil. From the perspective of Ghent or Cologne, the fall of
Constantinople might as well have taken place on the moon—and still,
with transitions to that destination time, we keep running into difficulties,
which the Amsterdam tunnel technicians can't explain."

"But what does all that have to do with me? I haven't traveled yet," I
said.

He smiled indulgently. "Oh yes, you have, Domenica. You've done so a
long time ago—from a chronological perspective. If everything proceeds
according to plan, you have already existed before in this universe, six hundred years ago—and perhaps more often in the time that has passed since
then. You've done important work to secure the future of this world."

I looked at him in confusion. But . . . of course. What he said was completely logical—and nonetheless inconceivable. But what did it mean? I
shook my head.

"Then it's not even necessary to send me to the fifteenth century anymore, if I . . . I mean . . ."

It dawned on me that the objection I was about to bring up was absolutely
senseless, and I broke off. I would have to travel in order to . . . Falcotti's
smile had vanished.

"That would be theoretically possible, but then the two of us would now
find ourselves in another universe. A universe that might not last."

"And what sorts of difficulties have come up, exactly?" I asked.

"Again and again, well-conceived and meticulously prepared transitions
turn out to be unrealizable or fail to achieve temporal precision. Either the
tunnel doesn't open at all, even though all the settings appear to be correct,
or the travelers return and report that they missed their target by years. It's
as if the destination time of 1450 were a 'sophisticated area,' as the tunnel

technicians call it. It's a mystery to the theoretical physicists at the Hendrik Casimir Institute. The computers are working on dozens of simulations to figure out the cause."

"And I could be the cause of those difficulties, you think?"

"That can't be ruled out," Falcotti replied with a shrug. I had a feeling that, even though he was concerned, he was somehow proud of me. "A lot of this is still uncharted territory, Domenica. About the Everett multiverse there are countless speculations. Each of us seems to live in many, probably very many parallel universes at the same time. These universes are probably only nanometers apart, and the membranes between them are perhaps only Planck lengths thin. And yet for most people contact with their other consciousnesses, which exist beyond the barriers, is impossible. There are, however, people—"

"Like me."

Falcotti nodded and went on, "GH talents, who can penetrate those barriers, mostly in dreams, but sometimes also in reality—if the concept of reality still makes any sense here. They seem to somehow disturb the symmetry of the multiverse. Certainly, it could also be something entirely different causing the technicians difficulties: historically important events in parallel worlds that cannot be registered in ours but bring about turbulences in it. But it could also be events of historic significance that have happened at some point in our universe but were subsequently corrected and therefore never happened, were never recorded, or have disappeared from our records."

"That's over my head, Signore Falcotti," I interjected. "I'm sorry but I don't understand a word of what you just said. How can something disappear from historical records? Does a section suddenly go missing from a text or a whole page from the books?"

"It's much more complicated," he replied. "But basically it's like this: The past is not set in stone, Domenica. We have to learn to grasp it as a living, breathing organism, which changes, regenerates, and constantly sprouts branches. We're part of a multiverse that grows through space-time like a plant, a tendril or liana. Some cosmologists compare it with a coral reef, which stretches over hundreds of miles but every centimeter of which forms an independent biological realm with a complex architecture, which is continuously built on."

Falcotti fiddled with his glasses and turned his eyes once again to the green summit of the Kapuzinerberg, on the slope of which the red roofs of the small monastery were now bathed in sunlight.

"I can no more imagine a Gauforum or a Gauhalle up there than I can St. Peter's," I said with a sigh.

He nodded. "But as for the New Vatican: The foundation stone was supposed to have been laid already on Easter. Now the date has been set for Pentecost to give all the cardinals enough time for the journey. It will be a big ceremony. The Holy Father wants it that way. He wants to show that the Church lives and is not bound to Rome."

"Hm."

"And the next day the earth-moving will already begin. The whole hill is to be hollowed out in order to accommodate everything. There was a long debate about whether a replica of St. Peter's should be erected here. But after careful consideration the Holy Father decided against it, and now a modern solution has been agreed upon: It is to be an open center of faith, a meeting point for all who seek God, wherever they come from, from the earth, from other worlds, or from other times. Nor will it be called St. Peter's. St. Peter's will remain reserved for Rome, especially as there is already a long-standing church here by that name."

"And a long-standing tavern," I interjected.

Falcotti laughed. "That would be too much of a good thing," he said, pushing his empty cup into the middle of the table. "Probably we will break completely new ground. You must have heard of the St. Matthias Pilgrimage."

"The St. Matthias Pilgrimage? I only know that many people come here to visit his shrine in the cathedral."

"His bones rested for centuries in Trier. That's in the middle of the worst contaminated area. A few courageous believers from Westphalia made their way from Belgium to Trier. They managed to overcome all barriers and security measures. They sacrificed their lives in that brave act; two years later all of them were already dead. But they managed to bring the shrine to Paderborn. Because the authorities in Brussels pressed the city government to surrender the radioactively contaminated relic and even threatened to confiscate it and permanently dispose of it in a salt dome in Gorleben, it was secretly brought to Salzburg. There have always been very good connections between Paderborn and Salzburg. Now the apostle Matthias rests here in the cathedral in a double-walled lead sarcophagus. He will—as we all hope—find his final resting place in the New Vatican. Pilgrims are already flocking here today from Europe to pray at his grave. Admittedly, malicious tongues claim that they are coming in droves to

Salzburg not only because of the apostle. Well, in any case, each week it is now more than used to make a pilgrimage to Trier in an entire year. He is now also regarded as the patron saint of the victims of radiation sickness and genetic disorders and enjoys a lively stream of intercession."

Falcotti put on his data glasses and stood up. "Domenica, I'm afraid I must go back to my office. I've had your travel chip sent to your hotel. I can't imagine that anything else could go wrong, but should there be unexpected problems at the border, your ICom can reach me at any time."

"Thank you, Signore Falcotti. And thank you for the conversation."

"Maybe we'll see each other in Amsterdam before your assignment begins."

"I'll keep an eye out for you on the Noordermarkt square."

"This time I won't come as a clown," he said with a smile, raising his hand in parting. "Have a good trip, Domenica. God be with you."

I HADN'T RECOGNIZED Falcotti at first glance when I met him. He looked as if he had traveled south on vacation instead of north to work. He wore a broad-brimmed straw hat; a wide, light gray pair of pants; and a dark blue blazer with a breast pocket handkerchief—a bit old-fashioned, I found. I had liked him better in his casual outfit at the university in Rome. And what most astounded me was the fact that he was smoking! He was puffing on a long, thin cigar, which looked like the withered tendril of a viorna, a *Clematis vitalba*. I could barely make out his eyes, because he was wearing a pair of those dark VR glasses, which had small screens that could be flipped down over the eyes. Immediately after his arrival in Salzburg he had contacted me, and I had offered to come the next day to the papal residence in the Mirabell castle.

I walked across the Makartsteg into the new town, passed the Landestheater and Hotel Bristol and entered the papal district, but the palace was closed off. At the entrances stood pairs of Swiss Guards. In their colorful uniforms they looked like extras in a pageant, but when you stood directly opposite them, you became aware that they were pros: cool-headed men in peak condition, trained in close combat, who could take swift, drastic action and could undoubtedly even kill if the situation required it.

I was forced aside from the main portal with the stream of believers and saw that there was no way through. So I instructed Luigi to coordinate with Falcotti's ICom and waited under the trees at the portal of St. Andrew's. Ten minutes later he stood in front of me. Falcotti spread his hands apologetically as he noticed the surprised look with which I eyed his elegant appearance.

"I almost didn't recognize you," I confessed.

"The Holy Father desires somewhat more southern European flair in this city," he said.

"Certainly couldn't hurt," I said. "But I see you're indulging in a vice that is hardly ever seen anymore nowadays." I gestured with a nod to his cigar.

"An unsavory one, I know. That's why I take advantage of the opportunity when I happen to be outside," he confessed, gazing at the Havana in his hand. "Would it bother you if I . . . ?"

"No, please, go ahead. I find it interesting. My father smoked those things too. Perhaps only because he could rile my mother that way."

"I simply can't resist, and enjoy it," Falcotti confessed, lighting it with some difficulty with a match. "Ever since the Austrians extended their tentacles to Central America and the Caribbean and invested in Havana to restore it to its old splendor, excellent cigars have been available here. Imported originals. Also the best rum and the finest hats." He tapped the brim of his panama.

We strolled eastward and entered the Mirabell garden. Visitors crowded on the gravel paths and on the grass in front of the fountain, behind which a flexomon had been mounted in a gigantic frame. The screen was flanked by muscular marble men dragging off overweight Sabine women. Under the blooming chestnut trees on the left side a youth orchestra in traditional costume gave a promenade concert. About thirty boys and girls in light green loden jackets and flat black hats sat on aluminum folding chairs around an older conductor and played a grave, solemn melody.

We entered a small park on the west side of the castle, which was closed to visitors as well. The guard at the entrance let us pass after he had glanced at the monitor on his wrist. A stone dwarf with a spiked helmet, in a mixture of reproof and disgust, held the ruined globe out to me with his left hand. His right arm was sheathed up to the armpit in a dangerous-looking armor, with which he, in his impotent rage, visibly would have liked to strike.

"You gave me a terrible scare in that Amsterdam simulation, Signore Falcotti," I said.

"With the bees crawling around on my arm?"

"Yes. I have a phobia of those creatures."

He flicked the ashes from his Havana. "Then that was probably intentional, Domenica."

"It was part of the conditioning, I assume."

Falcotti nodded. "We psychologists are monsters."

For a moment we had sat down on a bench. The misshapen dwarves had encircled us—and I shivered.

"It's still too cold to sit here in the shade," Falcotti said sympathetically, standing up. "Let's go to a café on Makartplatz, as long as people are still waiting for the Holy Father's appearance. Afterward, everything will be packed."

The Swiss Guard at the entrance was a giant, and his face looked as stony as the faces of the dwarves under the trees. We walked through an arbor overgrown with honeysuckle, which was ingeniously designed to create the optical illusion that it stretched several hundred yards into the darkness.

The orchestra in traditional costume, which had in the meantime segued to more lively tunes, suddenly stopped playing. The people jostled their way to the grass in front of the monitor, on which the Holy Father could now be seen: a small agile man with black eyes and animated gestures. He raised his hands in blessing and nodded with a smile. Some of the visitors sank to their knees before the screen.

We strode to the entrance of the park. More and more people streamed in, and it was difficult to get through.

"Your train departs early tomorrow morning, Domenica," Falcotti informed me.

"May I ask why we have to take the elaborate journey by train across Europe? By plane it would be under two hours to Amsterdam and by airship four or five. Is it because of the costs?"

He shook his head. "That's part of the conditioning as well. The committee has decided that all candidates of the Rinascita Project are to travel through the ravaged areas so that they see what was done to God's Creation there. In this way, your mission is vividly brought home to you."

We found a free table in the café of the Hotel Bristol and both ordered a *großer Brauner*.

Falcotti flipped down one of the small screens on his glasses over his eye; on it a pinhead-sized light blinked.

"Excuse me, please," he said, then stubbed out his Havana in the ashtray and pressed his forefinger to the small cross in his temple.

"That looks good," he said after a while. "Thank you."

He took off the glasses and put them down on the table.

"Have you ever traveled before?" I asked.

"To Amsterdam?"

"No, in time."

He scrutinized me for a moment before he answered. "Only when it's absolutely necessary. But I shouldn't talk about it any more than you should, Domenica. I too have been conditioned. Let's talk about something else instead. How do you like Hotel Altstadt?"

I told him.

I HAD TO be at the train station before dawn. A sleepy Janez brought my luggage from the room to the taxi that Luigi had scared up after a long back-and-forth. He had to gain unauthorized access to a local network and connect with the city's central exchange. In Austria nothing seemed to proceed via international satellites anymore.

Joseph Goebbels gave me the cold shoulder. I knocked against the bars of his cage.

"No parting '*Sieg Heil*'?" I asked the bird.

He did not deign to answer.

A bus brought the two or three dozen passengers who had gathered to the border. At the customs office at least a hundred trucks waited to be cleared for departure; in between stood buses full of pilgrims who wanted to return to Germany.

"What smells so strongly of burning here?" I asked my neighbor, a young man who was on his way home to Munich. He wore his ICom as an earring.

"That's the sawdust," he explained. "Whole mountains of sawdust over there at the old container terminal. They've been burning for years. Some claim the Bavarians intentionally set fire to them by shooting flares. But it was probably kids playing with fire."

"Why doesn't anyone put it out?"

"It can't be extinguished. Or at least they've tried several times unsuccessfully. Deep inside the embers keep smoldering, and it smokes and stinks horribly. During *föhn* winds you can smell it as far as Lake Chiem."

I looked out the window. Morning seeped through a leaden cloud layer, which hung low over the city and had gotten caught between the mountainsides like a dirty ice floe in a ravine. It cut off the top part of the panorama. The upper half of the mountain with the Hohensalzburg fortress had disappeared; the chicken coop had been raised. Of the Kapuzinerberg only the lower part could be seen. The summit—with the Gauburg or the Vatican—was separated by a membrane. It was as if the city had been punched out of a nightmare. Half an hour later we crossed a bridge. On both sides stood watchtowers with LasGuns.

"Take a look at that," said my neighbor. "Razor wire all the way into the water on both sides of the Saalach, mobile mines, automatic laser-firing devices. It's hard to believe that fifteen years ago you could cross back and forth here as you pleased. When I was little, I often went fishing with my father at this spot. No one knew that there had once in the dim and distant past been a border here. Now it's again as it was in the Stone Age. That's really sickening."

"I always thought the Bavarian and Austrian conservatives got along so well."

"Well," he sighed, "there used to be something to that. But it was like a spontaneous engagement in a beer tent. When sobriety returned and it came down to it, that was the end of the solemnly sworn Alpine alliance. Bavaria was jam-packed with four million nuclear refugees from Thuringia and Saxony. Do you know what that means?" He spread his arms and puffed out his cheeks. "They offered the Austrians a few contingents of them, but they declined. 'Keep away from us with those Germans! We're already saddled with a million Slavs and half the Balkans, despite the Klagenfurt resolutions and an intensified repatriation decree. More are coming in than we can repatriate.' So they closed the border between Bregenz and Passau."

My neighbor made a dismissive gesture and stared sullenly out the window.

"Italian?" he asked suddenly.

"Yes."

He snapped his fingers. "Beautiful."

"That I'm Italian or that you guessed right?" The question was on the tip of my tongue. "Or do you think *I'm* beautiful?" But I kept my mouth shut. I had learned from experience that such mocking counterquestions confused some men.

So I said, "Thank you," and gave him a smile.

The man smiled back.

On the Bavarian side even more pilgrim buses sat in traffic, lined up for half a mile before the approach to the bridge.

"So much piety?" I asked at random.

My neighbor gave me a meaningful look.

"St. Matthias!" he snorted. "Nothing but pack rat pilgrims! Austria is a rich land. Here you can buy all the things that have not been available in Bavaria for a long time."

"But not for marka bavarese," I quoted the taxi driver on my arrival.

"That might have been our state government's greatest idiocy, to reintroduce the mark by referendum. Outside Bavaria no one accepts them, not even the Albanians. How could anyone be so stupid?" He tapped his forehead. His ICom swung on his earlobe.

"Pack rat pilgrims. Such masses every day?"

"Of course," he replied. "That's the blessing of St. Matthias and the Holy Father. You can't deny a pious person access to the sites of his faith. But you can take him for a ride and relieve him of his money. That's always been the case, hasn't it?"

"I think so."

In Freilassing a modern express was waiting for us, a streamlined articulated train, painted pine green and fawn brown, with the white and blue Bavarian state coat of arms on each car and the inscription BAVARIAN STATE RAILROAD—FREE STATE OF BAVARIA. Despite the streamlined outfit it somehow made a quite dignified and immensely traditional impression.

Although the train had only first class, it was completely packed. On the luggage racks and in the aisles were piles of cartons, baskets, and bags belonging to the pack rat pilgrims. I saw containers of olive oil, plastic bags with boxes full of spaghetti and other pasta, canned meat and fish, coffee, cane sugar, bananas and oranges, palm butter—yes, and alcohol: rum, slivovitz, grappa.

Many of the travelers spoke a German I had trouble understanding. Some gave me dirty looks when I claimed my reserved seat. They displayed a mixture of satisfied greed and grim readiness to defend—their fingers tightly clutching their possessions on their laps. I looked around in vain for holy water and devotional objects. More pack rats than pilgrims.

The landscape rolling by looked very fertile. Lush shades of green, meadows, pasture. I had always wondered why green has a soothing effect on us, why the sight of an open verdant field fills us with a feeling of calm and peace. Is it the genes in our chromosomes that we have in common with grazing animals that signal to us: Take it easy, everything is absolutely fine, there's food in abundance?

But the first impression deceived. We were passing through a battlefield: decline everywhere. Overbred monoculture in dissolution. Ecological disasters. There were more and more stretches where on both sides of the railroad embankment the vegetation had been scorched, trees cut down, and massive amounts of herbicides and fungicides employed. It looked terrible and yielded nothing. The native flora fell by the wayside. The mutants rose again, regrouped.

For the first time I glimpsed *Clematis vitalba nigra*, the blackish green variant of the common clematis, which after the plutonium accident of Cattenom had first appeared on the Middle Rhine. I knew that the "viorna," as we Italians called it, had already completed its triumphal march across Europe before the turn of the millennium and had colonized almost all the railroad embankments between the Kattegat and the Strait of Messina. Many called it "gray claw" because of the gray-bearded claw-shaped inflorescences that survived the winter. "Old man's beard," the British called it—and, curiously, "traveller's joy," although it offered anything but an uplifting sight. The *nigra* variant surpassed even the original form in robustness and growth. It overran the other vegetation and pressed it to the ground with its sheer weight. "Death cloak," some people had therefore recently begun calling it, or—erroneously—"black ivy," and it had not confined itself in a long time to the slopes on both sides of the railroad lines. Unstoppably, it penetrated orchards, mixed forests, river meadows, and fallow land to bury and smother everything under it.

The train passed through shafts made of concrete components that had been mounted in metal frames. They too had long been conquered and overgrown by the climbing plant, and when the view opened up onto the landscape, I saw in the meadows tall-growing variants of the *Urticaceae*, the black stinging nettle, and in the depressions cohorts of huge *Heracleum mantegazzianum*, the giant hogweed, which assembled like units of elite troops for an assault.

But worst of all was the invisible enemy, which had infiltrated long ago and now exercised its power: the spores of mutant, aggressive fungi, which were spread through the land not only by the rail and road transport but above all by the wind. I saw cornfields in which the seedlings, scarcely two handbreadths tall, had already become withered and brown, and winter wheat rusting in the spring sun. The grass still seemed largely unscathed, though densely starred with the magnificent yolk-yellow of the dandelion—a sign of ruined soil due to overfertilization and a genetically overbred and weakened vegetation.

The farms bore witness to the pride of their former cultivators. Their descendants seemed to have less cause for it. At the hearts of the villages crowded broad, sturdy houses, which displayed wealth with ornate wooden facades and ostentatious balcony architecture. Toward the outskirts cheap prefabricated houses predominated. Bavaria had seen better days. Here too livestock death had repeatedly wreaked havoc.

A shower between two sunny stretches. Thin rain crosshatched the window, drew speed diagrams. The dashed lines became more and more vertical—the train stopped.

Rosenheim. A gorgeous name! But there were no roses in sight far and wide. Ugly square troughs cast in river gravel and concrete were lined up on the platform. In them were mountain pines that had perished from air pollution and rust fungi; the bare spots in the soil between them were planted with pansies—exposed in autumn, frozen in winter.

Alongside the tracks clustered dreary low buildings in red and yellow, from which the paint peeled; crumpled blinds in the windows. A rusty metal bridge on thin concrete stilts spanned the tracks and platforms; on both sides of the steps stood filthy dumpsters spray-painted with radical slogans of the Asens and Kicobs and surrounded by hundreds of greasy bottles and blue garbage bags. On the next track a freight train with tanks that were covered with camouflage tarps was shunted.

We rolled on.

The small houses were built much too close to the tracks; kiddie pools, plastic-covered porch swings in tiny front gardens. I could imagine the desperate defensive battles of the owners, how they took a stand with poison and garden shears against the onslaught of vegetation. But probably they had long been overrun by hyperactive ants, which marked their trails through living rooms and bedrooms and plundered provisions, by roundworms and earthworms, millipedes, centipedes, and pauropods, by spiders and other insects, springtails and diplurans, woodlice, which, crowded together in damp darkness, waited for their hour, by adapted termites, which invisibly ate away at the house over the heads and under the feet of the occupants.

Long before the arrival in Munich I noticed the sprawling city: container homes, stacked up triply, even quadruply in rows—the upper ones reachable by external stairs. Between them dead-straight camp roads stretched to the horizon, lined by streetlamps and makeshift sidewalks. Bus stops, playgrounds, air-supported halls. Train stations: Eglharting, Zorneding. Placards were stuck to the walls along the tracks: WE CENTRAL GERMANS PROTEST AGAINST THE SELLING OUT OF OUR HOMELAND and THE EU BETRAYED US. WE DEMAND OUR RIGHT TO A HOMELAND. Bridge piers, concrete walls, and dumpsters were spray-painted with graffiti, ugly and aggressive: ASEN—the raised fist. KICOB—the hurtling-down short sword.

"Don't be fooled by the view," said the young man from the bus, who was suddenly leaning in the doorway of the compartment. "Munich is still better than Calcutta or Mexico City. At the moment we may be somewhat inundated with Saxons, but in the meantime they've already learned to speak some German."

Among the passengers in the compartment there was loud protest. The man winked at me; only now did I notice that he was missing an incisor. Probably he said things like that often.

"Do you hear that?" he asked with a grin, holding his hand stagily in front of his mouth. "They already understand me really well. They're diligent, these people. We're going to manage. Have a nice trip!"

He gave me a thumbs-up in parting and got off. The signs said MÜNCHEN OST. Then we rolled on and, shortly thereafter, crossed a shallow river glistening in the sun.

"Isoh," declared the woman in the window seat opposite me, giving me a somewhat reserved but not unfriendly nod.

IN NEU-ULM THE passengers from Württemberg had to wipe their feet. They went through a hall from which foul-smelling chemical fumes emanated. BAVARIAN RED CROSS said a large sign in red letters. Underneath in threatening black: DISINFECTION FACILITY. NO ADMITTANCE. ENTRY ONLY BACKWARD.

I did not really understand the sign, but the conductor informed me that, because I was a south-north traveler, as opposed to the north-south travelers, it did not apply to me, but that I could go directly through to the other part of the train station.

"Forward?" I asked, to make sure.

He seemed not to understand me, but nodded.

So I left the fawn brown, pine green train of the Bavarian State Railroad and proceeded to a yellow and black one, which was indistinguishable from it, except that it belonged to the BADEN-WÜRTTEMBERG STATE RAILROAD and on its coat of arms bore three lions facing left. Shortly thereafter, we rolled across the Danube. To the right over the city rose the cathedral in the midday light; a tower that looked as if it were made of pleated lace, stiff and gray with old age.

Two different states, but to me the same image presented itself: abandoned small businesses in all stages of decay, overcrowded tower blocks, rotary clotheslines made of wire and plastic in front of the windows, peeling facades on which old-fashioned antennas grew rampant like tree fungi. Stacked-up container homes with off-white plastic coating, stained brown by sewage and rust, calcified pipes and corrugated hoses, ladders on which playing children clambered around.

The train snaked down into a narrow valley. On the slopes fresh beech green below a crystal-clear sky of a refreshing light blue. Strange quaint names, as in a fantasy game: Geislingen, Süßen, Eislingen, Uhingen, Plochingen, Untertürkheim, Feuerbach, Zuffenhausen, Pforzheim . . . finally: Heidelberg—end of the line.

For a long time the outpost of the human-inhabited world at the border of the death zone, the "unsettled area," as the authorities officially called it. "Unsettled" it would undoubtedly remain for the next twenty or thirty years, even if the decontamination continued to proceed according to plan and the required expenses of approximately five trillion euros were met. "Unsettled" for the next twenty to thirty thousand years in the core zone between Saarbrücken and Erfurt, according to pessimists.

"Heidelberg," said the voice on the loudspeaker. "Final stop. Everybody off!"

VI

The Octopus

History itself and how magnificently far we have come we owe, after all, to the fact that the right side has always won, the right decisions have always been made, the right people have always lived. Gloria! Victoria! Historia! To wish to rethink all this—is that not an unwarranted and wanton ingratitude toward the Norns? . . . Only a concept of history pruned of its most fruitful part contents itself with reality. If the point of history is to free us from the prison of the present, then it does something more by teaching us to look out of the narrow world of the real into the great space of the possible. Here there is a whole dimension to be gained.

ALEXANDER DEMANDT

Still more cadavers—fourteen or fifteen, Fingerhut counted. They lay on a pasture along the stream. Senselessly picked off. Dark brown heaps of fur, hooves, and bared teeth.

"Why do they kill the camels?" Fingerhut shouted over the rotor noise.

The pilot turned to him. "Those are animals that don't belong here!" he shouted back. "They say that they're unnatural, completely degenerate animals."

"Do you believe that too?" asked Fingerhut.

The pilot shrugged.

Fingerhut checked on the monitor in front of his left eye whether the free-flying camera drone following them had a good view of the dead camels. He grabbed his steering collar and zoomed in on one of the cadavers.

"They seem to have set their sights on exterminating those animals."

"And their owners right along with them," the pilot added with a laugh. "Listen, mister, I'll drop you off now somewhere around here."

"You will fly me to the meeting point," Fingerhut replied firmly. "When we receive the arranged signal, we will land. That's the deal."

"Just a second! There was mention of Wettin, just beyond the autobahn between Löbejün and Lettewitz," the pilot countered. "The autobahn is the border for helicopter flights. Meanwhile we have passed the Saale and are almost within range of Eisleben. There in the south I already see Lake Süßer. I'm not permitted to fly farther west. Besides, it hasn't rained for weeks. The rotor is whipping up so much radioactivity that the Geiger counters between Oslo and Helsinki are ticking. I'm not crazy!"

"I've paid you a lot of money to take me to this area," Fingerhut said threateningly.

"Money! Money!" moaned the pilot in a Saxon singsong. "I'm risking my license, mister. I can't afford that."

Fingerhut flicked the microphone in front of his mouth. "Dear viewers, you've heard it for yourselves. We're now flying over a heavily radioactively contaminated area. We're in the so-called death zone. The pilot refuses to penetrate deeper into the restricted area; it's too risky for him. He doesn't want to jeopardize his health. He's young. He wants to father healthy children. That's an argument that we can understand and that we should respect."

"I only said that I don't want to jeopardize my license. I didn't say anything about health," the pilot protested crossly.

But Fingerhut had turned down the external mike so far that the objection could not be understood, and went on: "Nonetheless, tens of thousands of people are living in this area by now, refugees from Bangladesh, Indonesia, and Sri Lanka, from countries whose coastal regions were destroyed in recent years by the rising oceans—from Micronesia and from the Maldives, which have in the meantime sunk in the sea. They have volunteered to come to Central Europe in order to fight here against the radioactivity and defeat it. They've knowingly taken the radiation risk and have dared to brave the cold climate of this region, unfamiliar as it is to them. As I have already shown you, my viewers, these courageous people cope astonishingly well with these challenges. The worst enemy opposing them here, however, is neither the cold nor the radioactivity, but people with extreme racist attitudes, who take intensely brutal action against them. These are small paramilitary units, first and foremost the ASEN, the Aryan Sons of the European North, and the KICOB, a radical international splinter group of the resurgent Ku Klux Klan in the United States, which exhibits its goal in its name: Kill the Colored Breed. They receive financial support from international racist organizations and—though it is denied despite overwhelming evidence—from the Central German refugee associations."

The pilot flew in circles and strained to keep a lookout down below. He was beginning to get rather nervous.

"If everything goes according to plan, you, dear viewers, will get to know some of these defenders of their race and their fatherland and possibly witness a conversation with one of their leaders."

"Do you see that over there?" shouted the pilot. "They're burning down a village."

The helicopter flew over destroyed greenhouses. The plastic coverings were slit open; laser guns had burned large holes in them, the black shriveled edges of which looked like the gaping mouths of corpses.

"Closer!" commanded Fingerhut; he fiddled with his steering collar and corrected the course of his drone.

"I'll drop you off here. If they're engaged in combat, I'm at risk of getting hit by a surface-to-air missile. They're all crazy. They're sick, I tell you."

"Did you hear that, dear viewers? We are in danger here of getting hit by a surface-to-air missile . . ."

"That's what I just said."

"What do you mean by sick?"

"That virus they've been infecting each other with, those idiots. During sexual intercourse or their crazy rituals. Blood brotherhood, loyalty unto death . . . What do I know? That's what people say anyway."

"So you believe that these people have been infected?"

"I'm getting a signal!" the pilot shouted; his thin face in his black full shell helmet was pale.

"Good," said Fingerhut, pointing downward. "Land!"

"I see movement over there." The pilot gestured to a group of trees.

"That must be the commando. Give the arranged sign."

"I already have."

"And pick me up here again in three hours," ordered Fingerhut, looking at the monitor on his instrument collar. "Six thirty P.M. Okay? Later the light can no longer be used. Six thirty. Do you understand?"

"Understood, mister."

No sooner had Fingerhut climbed out than the pilot again put the helicopter into a climb and accelerated.

It was two boys, no older than fifteen or sixteen. They wore green and brown camouflage suits and black ski masks with the balled fist, the ASEN logo, on the forehead. Each of them had a LasGun lying in the crook of his arm. They signaled to the reporter with a nod to follow them. The camera drone hovered indecisively over them. Having noticed the buzz of the minirotors, one of the young men looked up and raised his weapon.

"No!" Fingerhut howled.

The boy lowered the weapon.

"Dear viewers . . ."

"Shut up!" said the other one.

"Listen . . ."

"I said *shut up!*"

Fingerhut spread his hands. "Okay, okay. Take it easy, gentlemen," he murmured.

THE PACK LEADER shoved the toe of his boot under the hip of the corpse and turned it onto its back. The bony chest of the man was a charred, shriveled-up mass. The laser must have been fired at him from up close. The eyes of the dead man were wide with terror. The mouth, opened to scream, suggested the man's horrible pain. He had several missing teeth; his long yellowish brown incisors jutted out almost horizontally under the dark, leathery upper lip. Probably he had been the village elder or spokesperson for the settlers. The sign of his position, a long, carved staff, he held in his hand even in death.

Fingerhut zoomed in on the wound and then panned to the face. He bowed his head and clenched his teeth in order to hold steady the targeted sensor of his shoulder camera. He refrained from commentary. The images spoke for themselves.

"You wanted an action interview, if I understood you correctly, Herr Fingerhut," said the pack leader with his high, youthful voice. He emphasized the name, seemed to find it funny.

"Do you have a name too, Herr Pack Leader?" Fingerhut asked, annoyed that under the strain his voice sounded somewhat shrill, almost a little squeaky. Like a beginner, he said to himself. Like a damn beginner! But the guy really did frighten him. Unpredictable. A psychopath.

"That's irrelevant here," said the pack leader. "We all serve a greater task."

His gaze was directed into an indeterminate distance. Fingerhut had him very close and in profile. He had a soft, almost beardless face, deeply suntanned skin, and extremely short-cropped curly hair—dyed light blond.

The pack leader gestured to the almost-burned-down houses all around. It was windless. The smoke rose almost vertically. The wood of the collapsed roof beams crackled.

"We're the purifying fire," he said in his drawn-out way of speaking, as if he were on drugs, but his eyes flashed coldly and alertly, and his gestures were smooth and precise. "We exterminate the rank growth, the inferior. We eradicate the superfluous, the worthless."

"Ah, I see. And you decide what is of value and what is expendable."

"It's providence that gives us the knowledge. The great ones above have chosen us to prepare the earth for their arrival. You have, I see, no idea, Mr. Fingerhut. From the ashes the new will emerge, a new, greater world. Have you ever read Blavatsky? Helena Petrovna Blavatsky? Or Gurdjieff? Never heard of them, huh?" He nodded mockingly. "But Aleister Crowley you must have heard of, at least. Or Bulwer-Lytton. Englishmen like you. You are English, right? Or are you American?"

"American."

"Get rid of him!" the pack leader shouted to the two young men and pointed to the corpse. Only now did the reporter notice that the man was wearing elegant gloves made of fine dove gray suede. Why is he wearing gloves? Fingerhut wondered. Is he loath to touch this world before it has been purified of all that is "inferior"? Blavatsky. Gurdjieff. Oh yes, he was acquainted with them. Not their works, but their names. And their paranoid ideologies. Von Sebottendorf, Jörg Lanz von Liebenfels, Guido von List, Hanns Hörbiger, and whatever the names of all those protofascist mystics of the superhuman and World Ice Theory were, who at the beginning of the previous century not only fogged the small minds of a Hitler or Hess, but also polluted all Europe with the haze of their abstruse ideas. Had they risen from the grave here and now?

Two of the young people grabbed the dead body by the feet and pulled it across the street. It was as if the old man, in a last surge of protest, were shaking his head as he was dragged across the asphalt.

In a front garden they had dug a shallow grave with a bulldozer. "Dear God," Fingerhut whispered in horror when he saw that thirty or thirty-five corpses were lying in it—old people, young people, men, women, children, probably all the residents of the small settlement. His knees shook as he aimed the camera at the dead. He brought the drone into position at a height of ten yards and checked the wide shot on the monitor.

The pack leader watched him with a smile. He was not a tall man, but unusually slender, and the tight black uniform with the silver fists on the collar patches made him look taller. The uniform jacket he wore unbuttoned over the black shirt. In his waistband he had an old handgun with which explosive ammunition could be fired. He's proud of that vulgar SS image, Fingerhut said to himself, that cliché of a Nazi henchman we've provided him from Hollywood.

In front of a nearby shed stood the yellow-painted bulldozer with which they had excavated the mass grave. The building was the only one that had not yet been burned down, but the thatched roof was already smoldering. From inside screams could be heard. So they haven't killed everyone after all, Fingerhut said to himself. Perhaps they've spared a few of the children.

"Are they not yet done with them in there?" called the pack leader.

There was anger and contempt in his voice; he made a dismissive hand gesture. "Bring them out already and finish up!" And turning to Fingerhut he said: "Young wolves sometimes have to be given flesh to tear, or else they'll lose their natural instincts."

Three young men pulled two girls outside. The clothes had been torn from their bodies. Blood stuck to their thighs. They dragged the girls over to the edge of the mass grave. Both of them were too weakened and dazed to grasp what was happening to them.

Fingerhut was trembling all over.

"Don't do it!" he cried with a sob. "Please, don't do it! I'll turn off the cameras. Dear God, don't do it!"

No one paid attention to his protest. Two of the young men held the girls while the third unblinkingly pumped the LasGun, held it to the back of their heads, and pulled the trigger. First the one, then the other. The skull seemed to glow from within before it exploded in a fan-shaped rush of steam and the beheaded body plunged into the pit.

The stink of burnt hair reached Fingerhut's nose. His stomach rebelled. He clenched his teeth but could not prevent vomit from pouring out of his mouth and soiling his instrument collar. He wiped it away with his hand and swallowed convulsively. He was in danger of fainting. Staggering, he turned around and noticed that the pack leader was eyeing him with a smile.

"You forgot to turn off your cameras, Fingerhut," he said sarcastically, the corners of his mouth turned down. "I see that you too fulfill your duty with . . . passion."

"I abhor you, Commandant. And I abhor deeply what your people have done here. I hope that you are caught, brought to The Hague, and put on trial by the International Court of Justice. Half a billion viewers all over the world are tuned in to my satellites. All of them are witnesses to these two murders, this appalling bloody deed, and they will testify against you. For that reason—and for that reason alone—I haven't turned off the cameras . . ."

"Don't talk nonsense, Fingerhut! That's not the reason you kept your cameras running, but because you know well that you might now be able to reckon with a billion viewers. And the same goes for me. Of course, you have to act outraged now in front of your viewers. But you understand nothing, Fingerhut. Do you seriously believe that this bloody business is *fun* for us? It's a disgusting and dirty *duty*!"

The gloves, thought Fingerhut. He wears elegant, soft, dove gray suede gloves. Clean and immaculate.

The pack leader put his arm around him in a friendly manner.

"Fingerhut," he said. "A strange name."

"You mean . . . funny?"

"I mean . . . Jewish."

"My ancestors were Germans."

The pack leader squeezed him tighter and murmured, "Amazing what passes for German these days."

And he led him to the edge of the mass grave. Fingerhut could not prevent himself from trembling uncontrollably in the man's embrace.

"You wanted to know what message I have for the world? Here, Fingerhut, zoom in on the faces—to the extent they even still have any. How many viewers, did you say?"

"Half a billion worldwide."

"Wonderful. Maybe there are already two billion by now. Show them this! Show them what awaits them if they come here! And show them who awaits them! This is our message."

And with his immaculate glove the pack leader gestured all around.

A mass grave full of corpses. Burning huts in the background. In front of them, young men, practically children. A wretched bunch, dressed up in martial garb, aping pathetic clichés. The terrible banality of violence.

"This is our message," repeated the pack leader, pulling his pistol out of his waistband and shooting Fingerhut in the back of the head. The explosive bullet exited at the right temple and tore a fist-sized breach. He held Fingerhut by the instrument collar. The green LEDs indicated that the lenses and the transmitting computer were still working, while the body of the reporter danced two or three steps in place and then went limp.

The pack leader shoved the pistol back into his waistband and with his fingers pulled the steering implant out of the reporter's temple wound. It seemed to want to escape back into the protective cavity of the skull. The pack leader yanked out the object. Silver tentacles moved, winding around his wrist. He sniffed it, hurled it with disgust to the ground, and trampled it with the heel of his boot. The indicator lights on the instrument collar, which had turned red, went out. The pack leader let go of Fingerhut, and the reporter's body plunged headfirst into the pit.

The camera drone, which up to that point had been working soundlessly at a height of about ten yards, seemed to suddenly have trouble controlling its gyroscope. With a dangling lens it buzzed back and forth like a furious hornet until it finally plummeted with a shrill screech and buried itself in the heap of corpses.

A few of the young men laughed. Then they threw wood, straw, and broken furniture into the pit and set the heap on fire with a few laser shots. Dark smoke welled up. The pack leader held his blood-smeared glove over his mouth and nose and ordered a withdrawal.

The police did not appear until an hour later. Although a wide perimeter around the area had been closed off, the ASEN commando managed to escape. Long before the arrival of the police, curious onlookers and a few journalists had come; they had followed the murder of the well-known TV reporter on television via satellite. They made holos and videos of the ruins of the village and the half-incinerated corpses and greeted the police with whistles, jeers, and laughter as the squads jumped out of the helicopters in radiation suits, drove back the onlookers, and cordoned off the area with red and white plastic tape. Shortly thereafter, four fire trucks arrived; the firemen unrolled their hoses and sprayed the last smoking beams with water. The collection of evidence had to be broken off when darkness fell.

When the collection of evidence was completed the next day, a special commando recovered the corpses and packed them in gray plastic bags, which were brought with a helicopter to the forensic institute in Magdeburg. Not much was left of Fingerhut, but his mortal remains could be identified on the basis of the instrument collar of his TV equipment. In the late afternoon two trucks with loading arms appeared and collected the cadavers of the killed camels. They were brought to the rendering plant in Dessau, where they were cremated.

Neither the police and forensics officers nor the men from the relief agency noticed the young man who had been surveying the site since morning, taking precise measurements of the various crime scenes, and by means of a Wristtop constructing an exact outline of the course of the massacre. And it would have been hard to notice him, for he was an octopus. He wore a camouflage suit of the special response force from the Amsterdam tunnel, clothing coated with optical microelements that had been developed by the NNTR laboratories in Kobe. They automatically took on in color and structure the appearance of the background against which their wearer stood. He could have been in front of a house wall, a tree, or a fence two yards away from a passerby who was looking in his direction, and he would have been completely invisible—except for his eyes, of course, which had to remain uncovered for his orientation. But who is on the lookout for eyes in the plaster of a house wall, the bark of a tree, or the posts of a fence? If he had moved rapidly, an attentive observer would have noticed a sort of streaking effect, a minimal blurring of edges in the form of a wandering wave, caused by a tiny delay during the image construction in the simulation of the background by the optical system.

Because the men of the task force from the AT could work exclusively alone, this camouflage was indispensable. Completely on their own and frequently confronted with a well-armed and numerically superior enemy, they had to be able to strike practically out of nowhere. They had the additional advantage of knowing exactly their enemy's intentions. That was the case, of course, only for the first move, the gambit, for the second already took place in a changed world, an alternative world that had come into being as a result of their intervention. Therefore, the gambit had to be planned meticulously and the first strike had to be carried out as decisively and precisely as the first cut with a scalpel in a surgical procedure.

Old Dorit van Waalen at the Hendrik Casimir Institute for Brane Studies called these activities "*Uitborstelen*," "brushing out," "grooming"—brushing history against the fur, "*tegen de haren instrijken*." That sounded almost tender and corresponded only rarely to the reality. Most of the time, it was an invasive operation, during which blood usually flowed immediately.

Hla Thilawuntha himself had proposed these short-term interventions in the past before he returned to his native country. Most of the scientists at the CIA had been skeptical that under such circumstances transitions would open up at all. Let's just try, Thilawuntha had suggested, and they had tried. It had turned out that interventions in the immediate past, when they were prepared with sufficient exactness, could be carried out more easily than those in the more distant past.

The boundary layer theorists at the CIA saw an explanation in the fact that the membranes between parallel worlds that had not yet diverged widely were more permeable than those between worlds that had existed for a longer time side by side or had already diverged more widely. And those who were more inclined to think in botanical categories, such as Dirk Straets, said, "Clearly, a fresh shoot can be clipped more easily than a full-grown bough."

So the response force of octopuses was formed.

"IF YOU WANT to cut off a new growth, you first have to take a close look at the branch," his teacher Dirk Straets had impressed on him during his training, "and indeed from all sides. Then you have to determine where to cut. Take your time with that. Time is absolutely not an issue for us, only the right point in time. That's the decisive factor. And the right place, of course. The right spatiotemporal point. Then you prepare, calmly and coolly, and then—boldly and resolutely: *snip!* That's how it's done."

So the octopus took his time with the development of his plan. He thoroughly studied Fingerhut's recordings: stop, play, slow motion, rewind— over and over again; above all the wide shots the reporter had taken with his camera drone. Then he set to work developing his strategy and an exact timetable.

A month later he submitted his outline to the commission for review. Another month later he was summoned. His plan was explained in detail; objections were raised, improvements suggested, and finally his proposal was approved. The prospects for a transition were judged to be favorable.

The fortified village had been taken because the residents had been tricked by a simple ruse. The ASEN commando had ambushed three girls; after lunch break they had returned without armed escort to their work in the greenhouses, where they were to prepare seedlings for transport south by caravan. Two of the girls were killed, the third had been allowed to escape, and she had as expected run back to the village. The enraged farmers had then set off, armed, toward the greenhouses, leaving the village unprotected. The pack had attacked the mostly unarmed residents who had remained home—women, children, and old people—and massacred them. Hearing the noise, the farmers had turned around and hurried back. But then they fell victim to an ambush.

The octopus's actions thus had to be deployed in a synchronized fashion over an extensive area. The first step was to save the girls from death, thwarting the ASEN commando's plans, without their knowing exactly why their operation did not go according to plan. He then had to take advantage of the moment of uncertainty and regrouping and eliminate the pack leader. Finally, with the help of the alerted village residents, the rest of the pack would have to be subdued. To avoid being seen by the time-natives, he had—in addition to his personal operation—to take control of the incident in order to redirect the course of events.

And then—*snip!*

"No ASEN PACK has passed through here!" the pilot shouted over the rotor noise.

"How do you know?" Fingerhut shouted back.

"Those strange creatures there," the pilot replied, pointing down below. "They would have done them all in."

Fingerhut looked down. On a meadow along the bank of the stream, shaggy dark brown camels nibbled on the dry grass from the previous year. Along a hedge hay had been scattered for them, because they could find barely any fresh food, but they preferred to scavenge in the brown tufts for fresh shoots.

"Why would they kill those animals?" asked Fingerhut.

The pilot turned to him and replied, "Those are animals that don't belong here. They say that they're unnatural, completely degenerate animals."

"Do you believe that too?" asked Fingerhut.

The pilot shrugged.

"The guys who do that are sick," he remarked tersely.

Fingerhut checked on the monitor in front of his left eye whether the free-flying camera drone following them had a good view of the grazing camels. He grabbed his steering collar and zoomed in on one of the animals.

"So they seriously kill those camels because they don't belong here? You've got to be kidding."

"And their owners right along with them," the pilot added with a laugh. "Listen, mister, I'll drop you off now somewhere around here."

"You will fly me to the meeting point," Fingerhut replied firmly. "When we receive the arranged signal, we will land. That's the deal."

"Just a second! There was mention of Wettin, just beyond the autobahn between Löbejün and Lettewitz," the pilot countered. "The autobahn is the border for helicopter flights. Meanwhile we have passed the Saale and are almost within range of Eisleben. There in the south I already see Lake Süßer. I'm not permitted to fly farther west. Besides, it hasn't rained for weeks. The rotor is whipping up so much radioactivity that the Geiger counters between Oslo and Helsinki are ticking. I'm not crazy!"

"I've paid you a lot of money to take me to this area," Fingerhut said threateningly.

"Money! Money!" moaned the pilot in a Saxon singsong. "I'm risking my license, mister. I can't afford that."

Fingerhut flicked the microphone in front of his mouth.

"Dear viewers, you've heard it for yourselves. We're now flying over a heavily radioactively contaminated area. We're in the so-called death zone. The pilot refuses to penetrate deeper into the restricted area; it's too risky for him. He doesn't want to jeopardize his health. He's young. He wants to father healthy children. That's an argument that we can understand and that we should respect."

"I only said that I don't want to jeopardize my license. I didn't say anything about health," the pilot protested crossly.

But Fingerhut had turned down the external mike so far that the objection could not be understood, and went on: "Nonetheless, tens of thousands of people are living in this area by now, refugees from Bangladesh, Indonesia, and Sri Lanka, from countries whose coastal regions were destroyed in recent years by the rising oceans—from Micronesia and from the Maldives, which have in the meantime sunk in the sea. They have volunteered to come to Central Europe in order to fight here against the radioactivity and defeat it. They've knowingly taken the radiation risk and have dared to brave the cold climate of this region, unfamiliar as it is to them. As I have already shown you, my viewers, these courageous people cope astonishingly well with these challenges. The worst enemy opposing them here, however, is neither the cold nor the radioactivity, but people with extreme racist attitudes, who take intensely brutal action against them . . ."

The pilot flew in circles and strained to keep a lookout down below.

"If everything goes according to plan, you, dear viewers, will get to know some of these defenders of their fatherland and possibly witness a conversation with one of their leaders."

"No ASEN have passed through here!" shouted the pilot. "Everything looks completely peaceful. No smoke, nothing."

"Are we really in the right area?" Fingerhut asked with chagrin.

"What do you take me for, mister?"

"Hm."

This was turning out to be a flop—and he had been making big announcements about the report for days. Damn it!

"Are you still not getting any signal?"

"No, I'm not getting any signal. But something seems to be going on in the village over there."

"What do you mean? What do you see?" asked Fingerhut.

"The farmers aren't doing their work, but are standing around in the road. And there are a few figures lying on the ground, maybe injured or dead people. Something must have happened there. I recognize a helicopter from the rescue service that has landed on the village square."

"Then fly me there already, for heaven's sake!" shouted Fingerhut. "Land on the village square or somewhere nearby. Hurry up!"

When the helicopter landed, it was instantly surrounded by half a dozen dark-skinned young men. Shotguns and drawn crossbows were aimed at the cockpit. The people all seemed to be very upset and were all shouting at once. The village elder—as a sign of his status he bore a long, carved staff—gestured to the pilot to stop the engine.

"Who are you?" he shouted, raising the staff over his head. "What do you want?"

He bared his long yellow teeth, which stuck out horizontally under his upper lip.

"My name is Fingerhut. I'm reporting on the situation here. Worldwide. Via satellite."

"Yes," said the old man. "Yes, do that. We were attacked."

"By whom?"

The old man spread his arms.

The roof of the house had obviously been on fire, but it had been extinguished. People had also been wounded; they were attended to by the emergency doctor and his two assistants. Fingerhut saw among the village residents a few bad laser burns. He pushed his way forward with practiced movements and zoomed in on the injured, while he monitored the drone's wide shot out of the corner of his eye.

"Tough luck, Mr. Fingerhut," said a hoarse voice beside him.

On the stretcher in front of the ambulance helicopter lay a slender young man in a black uniform. He had extremely short-cropped curly hair, dyed light blond, and a thin, suntanned face, which looked gray from the pain he was suffering. He was attached to the drip of a blood bag. The breast of his uniform jacket and black shirt had been cut away and his chest covered with compresses to stanch the bleeding; between them protruded the shafts of two metal arrows, which had pierced his lungs. His narrow rib cage rose and sank in violent spasms. His breath rattled.

"I had promised you an action interview for your viewers," he gasped, "but it seems to have come to nothing."

"Please don't speak with him," said the young doctor, trying to drive Fingerhut back, but the reporter, his neck drawn into his instrument collar, stood as if rooted to the spot and did not budge a millimeter.

"I just have a few questions," he insisted.

"I'm sorry. I can't allow that."

"Let him be, Doctor. I promised him," said the pack leader. "And what do I have to offer him now? Not even a heroic death."

He chuckled. Foamy blood oozed out of the corner of his mouth. With a dove gray suede glove he wiped it off; then he held the glove in front of his face and gazed in astonishment at the smears of blood on it.

Why is he wearing gloves? Fingerhut wondered, taking a close-up of them. He saw that the light was fading and the color temperature was no longer quite right. The dove gray had a bluish cast, and the bloodred had a tinge of black. He hated these technical deficiencies.

"I don't even have a dead camel to offer your viewers," said the pack leader.

"Why do you kill those animals?" asked Fingerhut.

The pack leader laughed and gasped in pain as his chest moved. "I'll reveal it to you. Have you ever taken a close look at the physiognomy of a camel or dromedary, Fingerhut? They are said to be the descendants of the Jews who didn't leave with Moses, because they had their reasons to stay in Egypt."

"Funny."

"I didn't make it up. A thing like that only a Jew could come up with," murmured the pack leader; he closed his eyes for a few seconds and breathed shallowly.

"Please leave him alone. He's very debilitated," said the doctor. "I can't remove the arrows. He will lose even more blood. We don't have any more blood bags for him, because he has blood factors that are rarely found here in northern Europe. We have to bring him to the hospital in Magdeburg. I've requested a helicopter."

"Did you see the moon last night, Fingerhut?" asked the pack leader. "It got bigger."

"It's a full moon."

The pack leader raised his hand weakly. "No, you don't understand. It got bigger. It's getting closer to the earth. A new era is dawning. The era of the high moon is over. Now space must be made for the new man, a new human race. The little things all around have to go. We ASEN have been chosen to prepare the ground for the new race."

Blavatsky, Gurdjieff, von Liebenfels, von Sebottendorf, Haushofer, Crowley, Bulwer-Lytton—he's up to his neck in that mystical swamp of World Ice Theory and the superhuman, thought Fingerhut. Those crazy fantasies, over and over again.

"You haven't grasped a thing, Fingerhut," hissed the pack leader, raising his head. "Admit it. Not a thing."

"What haven't I grasped?"

"That we're only dirt on the boots of those who will come after us. You—and I."

"He's hallucinating," said the doctor.

"He's not hallucinating," Fingerhut replied with a sigh.

"I tried, but against an octopus you have no chance," said the pack leader.

"Against what?"

"He knows your intentions exactly. He's a step ahead of you. But only one. With the second you already have a chance—theoretically. You might be able to catch him and defeat him. But you need a lot of luck."

"He's hallucinating," said the doctor.

"I don't know," said Fingerhut.

"What's he talking about?"

Fingerhut spread his hands. "A legend," he said.

"Not a legend," whispered the pack leader, exhausted. "They come from the future."

"I thought the future belonged to the supermen," Fingerhut remarked.

The pack leader furrowed his brow and gave Fingerhut a dull, somewhat feverish look. He seemed to be straining to think.

"That's what confuses me," he said softly, and after a pause he went on, "Goebbels said our end would be the end of the universe. If we die—we, who believe in the supermen—then the universe has no future. They need us to pave the way for them."

"I wouldn't want to live in that universe," said the reporter.

The pack leader laughed and screwed up his face in pain. "I would have relieved you of that concern, Fingerhut." He wiped his forehead with the bloodstained glove.

"Please leave him alone now," said the doctor.

"Do you see the eyes over there?" cried the wounded man, pointing to the wall of the house; his feverish gaze darted back and forth. "He's moving."

Fingerhut and the doctor turned around but couldn't make out anything.

"The octopus," groaned the pack leader. "He can't fool me. He's nearby. I sense him."

The doctor loaded his injection gun, held it to the pack leader's neck, and pulled the trigger.

"I'm sorry," he said.

"WHAT'S THE DEAL with that illness the ASEN are supposedly afflicted with?" asked Fingerhut, as they walked along the row of prisoners who had been chained up in the grass on the roadside. The ski masks had been pulled off their heads. Under them the faces of children had been revealed. Some were completely apathetic; one wept; another spat defiantly at the camera. For that he earned a kick from one of the farmers guarding them.

"You mean the Fenris virus?" asked the doctor. "Some call it an indoctrination virus. I regard that designation not only as misleading but also as dangerous. We still know too little about it. It's similar to HIV, the immunologists from the Charité say; same ways of spreading: blood, sperm. It could be a genetically engineered product, tailored very deliberately. During the so-called blood rites, they consciously infect one another with it. Loyalty among comrades, blood brotherhood . . . they've been taken in by that mystical nonsense."

"And the symptoms?"

"The virus surmounts the blood-brain barrier and afflicts the caudate nucleus and the hippocampus. It has a paralyzing effect on the amygdala, the anxiety module in the limbic system. The consequence is fearlessness. That is, the fear threshold is lowered and social patterns of behavior are suppressed. The result is blind obedience, defiance of death, and a horrible mercilessness."

"Who, for heaven's sake, would release something like that into the world?" asked Fingerhut.

The doctor shrugged. "Certain circles of the military must have been delighted about it."

"Is there a treatment?"

"It's at a primitive stage, at best. No medication so far—it's going to take time. We're working, so to speak, with a sledgehammer. Burning it out, literally. The infected person has to be kept for at least eighty hours at a body temperature of 108 degrees. That kills most people. But the boys here"—he gestured to the row of fettered prisoners—"seem to be strong and healthy. A few will surely survive it."

The sound of an approaching helicopter could be heard. It came in for a landing next to the two others. The cockpit was painted with a red cross. Two men jumped out and slid the stretcher with the pack leader in. The doctor hurried over and gave them instructions. Then three men and a woman from the village who had suffered burns boarded.

When the helicopter had taken off, the doctor returned to Fingerhut.

"A tangential remark," he said, "if it interests you."

"Everything interests me."

"The blood analysis of that patient . . ."

"The pack leader?"

"Yes. His alleles, the form of his HLA genes for immune defense, indicate a rare genetic enzyme deficiency. It's known as Mutation A of the G6PD gene."

"And what does that mean?"

"The man's racial roots clearly lie in southern Africa. Herero, I would say."

"Oho! I thought it was a suntan."

The doctor smiled triumphantly. Fingerhut saw that he was older than he had assumed at first glance.

"Maybe German Southwest Africa," he said.

Fingerhut nodded. "It happens."

THE STREAM GURGLED. Long gray grass from the previous year hung from the banks. It was still early in the year, but the last remains of snow in the shady spots had disappeared. The alders and poplars were still dreaming, held captive by winter. Only the willows gleamed in faint gold, as if it had wafted over from the fleeting shores over the southwestern horizon, in which the sun sank early.

The octopus looked around. The camels snorted and rumbled; they scavenged between the trees for the first green and ground the hay that had been strewn for them. Occasionally they raised their heads and looked over at him. But their reaction did not suggest that they were aware of him, that they glimpsed anything but an old willow by the stream. Why shouldn't a pollard willow have eyes in a lumpy face under the growths of its forehead? A magpie flew up with a squawk and darted away. Had it sensed his presence?

It had again been a clear day. Rain had not come. In the evening there would be fog. It had also been a successful day.

Then the octopus sensed the soliton approaching. He felt it like an almost inaudible crackling in his body, as if an electric current had accelerated the molecules in their movement. The crackling swelled to a roar. When it was really close, he shut his eyes. And a fraction of a second later, only the willow remained.

VII

Princess Brambilla

For us believing physicists, the separation between past, present and future has only the significance of an illusion—though a stubborn one.

ALBERT EINSTEIN

A re you sure this isn't a prison?" I asked Luigi, as the gate in the high chain-link fence sprang open in front of me.

"It's the Bahnhofshotel, Domenica," he explained to me in his humorless manner.

That was also what an elegant brass sign next to the entrance said.

Apparently my personal data had obtained admittance for me. My travel chip in my ICom had signaled my arrival. But the hotel seemed more like a row of lockers for bulky luggage, for it consisted of a collection of white-lacquered container homes arranged side by side. A second level accessible via metal steps and walkways had been stacked on top.

"Is there no reception here?" I asked anxiously as the metal door shut with a resounding *clank*.

"No, but I am in contact with an AI; it performs that function," said Luigi. So I was dealing with one of those high-tech shelters with which the Chinese inundated the world. Here you encountered at most other guests; there was no staff. I already longed to return to the Hotel Altstadt on Rudolfskai and Herr Roblacher, even though the ghosts of Salzburg were still breathing coldly down my neck.

Number 024 was on the second "floor." I had to lug my two smart travel bags up myself, for they weren't among the all-terrain models. My concern about feeling confined in the tube turned out to be unfounded. The bright colors, indirect lighting, and ingeniously positioned mirrors counteracted any hint of claustrophobia. I had the impression of being in the cabin of a modern cruise ship. The accommodations were spacious. I had a living room, a spacious sleeping berth for two people, and a bathroom.

"Is there anywhere to get something to eat around here?" I asked Luigi.

"There's a service through nearby restaurants. May I order you something?"

"Never mind, Luigi." To be safe, I had bought a few sandwiches in Ulm; that was all I needed for the evening.

IN THE MIDDLE of the night I was awakened by a sound as if someone were climbing around on my lodgings. Were burglars attempting to break into the containers and rob the guests? Was it mutants from the restricted zone, about whom ghastly rumors were spread, or wild animals that had escaped from the zoos because during the precipitate evacuation the people had not managed to kill them all?

I asked Luigi to contact the AI. It assured me that its motion detectors had not been set off, that the sounds were completely natural, caused by temperature differences between day and night in the suspension of the containers and in the supply and drain lines.

"Can I trust it, Luigi?"

"I think so."

I listened anxiously to the thumping and creaking around me, but didn't dare to look out the windowpane on the door or even to unlock it to take a peek around. Eventually I must have fallen asleep again.

The AI woke me with the music of a local station. Outside on the metal walkway clattered footsteps; then something was pushed into my door slot. I got up and looked through the tiny lens that allowed a wide-angle view. It was already daytime. I saw a man in a white uniform wearing a yellow crash helmet with a dragon emblem—a dark-skinned man delivering breakfast packages. He got into the electric vehicle and drove along the road in front of the containers. Outside the chain-link fence jostled begging children in ragged clothing. The man paid no attention to them. A baton dangled from his hip. Probably he had to defend his cargo when he left the enclosure.

I took the cardboard carton from the slot. It contained a self-heating drinking nut of miserable coffee, a limp croissant with packaged "Butter-fäßle" brand butter, "Sonniges Reichenau" apricot jam, and a paper napkin printed with an imposing castle ruin and the inscription "O Heidelberg, dear city" and "We wish our guests a pleasant meal." Who was "we"?

I poured the remainder of the coffee into the sink, stuffed the drinking nut into the carton with the other things, and after a shower headed to the train platform. Luigi had in the meantime settled the bill with the AI.

No sooner had I walked through the gate than I was surrounded by a horde of children. I handed them the breakfast carton. A small boy snatched it from me and ran away quick as a flash. A whole pack charged after him, screaming. But some had stayed behind and stretched out their hands toward me, whimpering grovelingly. Farther away a few older children gave me furtive looks. They were all terribly dirty and unkempt, had long tousled hair, and some of them displayed physical defects from genetic disorders. The death zone was close.

"Hey! You can earn some money if you carry my luggage to the train," I called to them. They did not react, merely stared at me uncomprehendingly.

"Or not. Maybe it's better that way," I murmured, turning off the servos of my travel bags and grabbing them with a firm grip by the hand straps.

HEIDELBERG HAD BEEN a border city for twenty years and was often embattled. Plunderers would penetrate into abandoned Mannheim and the region on the left bank of the Rhine in the belief that after their raids they could plunge back into the streams of refugees and, without being identified, bring their spoils into the unrestricted areas. Upon being discovered, they would frequently take hostages and engage in shoot-outs with the border troops. The structure spanning the tracks had been destroyed by grenades and replaced with a makeshift bridge made of carbon-fiber-reinforced plastic. All around the train station ruins could be seen, buildings gutted by fire, which had not been restored.

On the walkway and the platform, scores of young beggars roamed around, stretching out their hands toward me and exhibiting their deformities. A small girl held out her hand to me. From her right wrist sprouted another tiny hand, bent and black like a talon.

The train was to depart at seven o'clock, but the passengers had to be there by six to take their reserved seats. RHEINEXPRESS was written on the cars of the sleek gray articulated train, the paint of which was badly scratched. The electric current collectors of the two power cars were folded down. At the back and front a diesel locomotive was attached.

First class was barely occupied as the passengers crowded into the remaining cars. Sitting in the window seat in my compartment was a delicate older woman, who greeted me with a nod and a brief scrutinizing look. She wore a light blue linen suit over an openwork white blouse, and had on a broad-brimmed dark blue hat, the band of which was studded with little metal plates the size of a one-euro coin. From her ICom, which she wore on her wrist, hung half a dozen special modules like piglets from the teats of a sow. The woman was electronically armed to the teeth. That might have indicated that she was a photojournalist or filmmaker, also because she didn't conceal her lavish equipment, though she apparently unintentionally spread her light gray shawl over her hand, which rested in her lap. I furtively eyed her profile as she looked out the window.

She had on glasses adorned with little round mirrors, equipped with flip-down monitors and barely balanced on her small snub nose. The tale of Princess Brambilla came to my mind, who, with her magic glasses that enabled her to look behind reality, set off in search of her Assyrian Prince Cornelio.

The woman turned to me and asked in a friendly tone, "How far are you going?"

"Amsterdam," I said, not particularly eager for a conversation that early in the morning.

"A beautiful city," she sighed. "I used to go there often."

"Not anymore?" I asked, for the sake of politeness more than anything.

"What do you think? It's no longer so simple for us Germans to get a visa."

"As a German you need a visa for the Netherlands?"

"Germans need a visa everywhere. They could be illegal immigrants, after all, or looking for work without permission. Besides, there are health policy concerns—genetic problems. We Germans are regarded as genetic cripples. For marriages with foreigners we need a whole sheaf of medical certificates. In most countries a German can't get a marriage license at all."

"I didn't know that."

"You're Italian, right?" asked the woman.

"Yes," I said. "From Rome."

"How I'd love to go to Italy again someday. Rome, Naples . . ."

"It's not without danger," I said.

She nodded. "I follow it in the news. It's terrible. But at least Venice," she said longingly.

"I've just come from there."

"How interesting! Is it true that it will soon shine again in its old splendor?"

"Oh, I think that's still going to take a while."

"Is it still so difficult to get a visiting permit?"

"For you as a reporter that can't be a problem."

"Reporter?" she asked, frowning.

I gestured with a nod to the equipment on her wrist.

"Oh, I see," she said with a smile. "In the old days, yes . . . Everyone finally seems to have gotten on. So we have the compartment all to ourselves," she said, turning to look outside. "They've begun sealing it off."

Workers in bright orange clothing, with breathing masks and yellow hard hats on their heads and knapsacks on their backs, filled the cracks around the doors with foam. There was a sharp smell of solvent.

"They do that because of the radioactive dust raised by the wheels," said Princess Brambilla.

Dirty children's hands slapped against the panes. The children knew it was their last chance to get hold of something before the passengers were cut off.

"I thought the disaster victims and their surviving kin were being provided for," I said.

"They're provided for. These children have run away. They don't want to be confined in homes; apparently they prefer to roam around."

The small hands left smears on the pane.

"Many of them aren't right in the head," she added after a pause. "Malnutrition, genetic defects. They're like animals. Speechless. You can't talk to them. They don't understand you."

A small agile man in white pants, a red uniform jacket, and a red cap inspected our travel chips. RHEINEXPRESS was embroidered in golden letters on his breast pocket.

"Windows and doors are not to be opened during the journey," he explained. "Getting on and off at the stations is permitted only via the marked door in the middle of the train and under the supervision of the train personnel. For the duration of the journey you will be provided with drinks and meals. The cafeteria is located in the middle of the train. In first class there is also service in your compartment. You need only instruct your ICom accordingly. I wish you a pleasant journey."

A few compartments down a brief dispute seemed to flare up between the conductor and a passenger. He came down the aisle with a scowling man.

"I'm sorry, but your indicated birthplace seems to be incorrect," said the conductor. "I have to check that."

"But that's nonsense," the man said angrily. "I'm not from here."

"Because of the birthplace?" I asked the princess, shaking my head. "What's that about?"

"People who were born in the death zone do not receive travel permits," she explained to me. "Probably he tried to obtain one fraudulently. That often happens."

"Yeah, and if he did?"

"There have repeatedly been dangerous incidents in which defiant people pulled the emergency brake and tried to leave the train in order to return to their original home. They endanger all the other passengers, of course, when they smash windows or break open doors."

"And why do they do that? I mean, that's extremely dangerous for them too, isn't it?"

"Some underestimate the danger. Believe it has passed by now. They want to see what's left of their belongings or their parents' property. Often valuables or cash were left behind. They want to get it before it falls into the hands of plunderers or the cleanup workers pocket it."

It was seven o'clock. The train promptly started moving. The children ran alongside the train as if they were still hoping for gifts. Then they remained behind.

Along the route stretched rusty tracks; barbed-wire fences were overgrown with *Clematis vitalba* and blackberry vines. Between them garbage, broken-open abandoned pieces of luggage in all stages of dissolution, rotten dolls, children's toys, household items—probably all this had been weeded out as radioactively contaminated and discarded by the border guards. Battered signs warned urgently with the symbol for radioactivity and the inscription

ATTENTION!
END OF THE SAFETY ZONE
NO ADMITTANCE!
DANGER OF DEATH

Behind the barriers I saw more destroyed and burned-down buildings. To the left of the tracks rose a brick tower with a flat copper roof, the facade scarred with gunshot holes. From a man-sized round opening, which had apparently once contained a clock, jutted the remains of a heavy laser weapon.

Here at the edge of the death zone the bitterest battles had been fought, my fellow passenger told me. Many people from the surrounding regions viewed the demarcation of the border as arbitrary, as official harassment. And those scarcely contaminated areas had, of course, particularly attracted plunderers, and thus very rigorous measures had been necessary to clear them of their residents, because they did not understand why they should leave their houses while others, a few blocks away, were allowed to stay.

Dilapidated watchtowers, an abandoned, half-overgrown hut camp stretching over several square miles. Here the streams of refugees from the west had been received and filtered. Here a selection had taken place. Those who were heavily exposed to radiation were transferred to the field hospitals in Karlsruhe and Rastatt, "permanent disposal sites" for those who were—how had Birgit put it?—hopelessly poisoned by radiation. The others were permitted to travel onward to the safe south and southeast.

"Terrible things happened here," said the princess. "Families had to part from their more severely afflicted members, had to leave them behind. Can you imagine that?"

I nodded. Could I really imagine it?

The train rolled through a monotonous flat landscape. To the left I glimpsed a tall building with a pyramidal roof. A peeling facade with the remains of a painting announced: BADEN WINE, PAMPERED BY THE SUN. On the left appeared a high-rise, rammed into the ground like a double-edged blade, then on the right a huge palace of rust-brown sandstone with triangular gables over the windows and a stone balustrade on the roofs of the massive towers on both sides. The white around the windows shone freshly.

Spray-painted on the concrete walls along the tracks were francophobic slogans:

MAY GOD PUNISH YOU, YOU GALLIC FROGS!
YOU TOO WILL SOON GO TO THE DOGS!

And:

TO THE VILE FRENCH WE OWE THE FATE
OF OUR LOST PALATINATE

It had been a calamitous chain of unfortunate circumstances, everyone knew that. Negligence, perhaps—but never intentional. Hate had nonetheless burrowed deep, especially into the hearts of those expelled from their homes. And the extreme right knew how to instrumentalize it and channel it into their propaganda mills. Again and again on the bare concrete: ASEN—the balled fist; KICOB—the hurtling-down sword.

"Such nonsense," said Brambilla. "The fatal batch came from Germany, from Hanau. It had been incorrectly declared, claimed the French. But Berlin denied it. Said that no transport had ever gone from Hanau to Cattenom, but exclusively to La Hague." Princess Brambilla shrugged.

"One good thing came out of the catastrophe, though: The belief in cheap nuclear energy was buried once and for all. But do you know what the craziest thing is?" she went on. "People are suddenly clinging to those awful ruins. They protest against demolishing them. Apparently there are in all seriousness efforts to elevate the horrible concrete sarcophagus of Chernobyl into a world heritage site! Can you imagine that?"

"No," I replied. Actually, I could imagine it.

On the left I glimpsed an up and down of elevated roads and underpasses. And frequent signs painted over in red: CLOSED! CLOSED! CLOSED! Then the train rolled onto a bridge: the Rhine.

A freighter, deep in the water, pushed a large bow wave in front of it. On the opposite bank stretched industrial plants; between them stood apartment blocks and office buildings converted into lodgings. Laden clotheslines protruded from the windows like flagpoles.

After twenty-five years, the authorities had allowed Mannheim a resurrection. I saw repaired roofs, newly paned windows, curtains, flowers on the balconies, and, in the front gardens, playing children. Cars, buses, people at bus stops, occupied parking spots. Many trees had been freshly planted, particularly plane trees and fast-growing eucalyptus trees. Here and there I saw newly planted groves—particularly *Picea omorika*, the Serbian spruce, which was more resistant to environmental toxins and coped better with the increasing warming than its sister, the *Picea abies*.

Life was returning.

The train stopped between stations. From outside penetrated the muffled twittering of birds.

"Do you hear that?" asked my fellow passenger. "That's always a good omen. For twenty years, they could no longer be heard here. Songbirds are a reliable sign. Where they appear, people can live too. If you see dead songbirds, it's high time to leave the area. Miners already knew that a long time ago. Birds sense disaster."

Canaries have always been a reliable indicator of mine gas. With radioactivity, however, that would hardly work. They don't have an organ for that any more than people do.

"With ravens it's different. The radiation doesn't seem to bother them. I know that from experience," she said, and looked out the window, lost in thought.

The train rolled on—out into the region on the left bank of the Rhine. The border was not marked, but it was unmistakable. It wandered; each day a step, or ten . . . The land was suddenly deserted.

Two rows of electricity pylons from which the lines had been removed stood around indecisively, robbed of their task. They spread their arms regretfully like discharged servants. To the right and left of the tracks stretched allotment garden colonies flattened and pushed into piles by bulldozers. Yellow tank trucks with the inscription DÉCONTAMINATION were parked in the bare terrain. Long-legged, spiderlike robots stalked through the landscape as in H. G. Wells's *War of the Worlds*; remote-controlled, they sprayed with their long thin swiveling snouts aerosol carpets, until they returned to the tank truck to suck themselves full like monstrous insects.

"You won't believe it," said Princess Brambilla, "but ever since the French have been decontaminating the area here on a grand scale, the real estate prices in Hessen and the Rhineland-Palatinate have shot up tenfold. I know what I'm talking about. I live off it."

"Are you a real estate agent?"

"No, not that, but thanks to my work, the interested parties no longer have to jeopardize their health and that of their fellow human beings. With my drone I shoot any desired picture for them. I travel the route twice a week. My transmitter has a range of about thirty miles. Between Pirmasens and Kassel I photograph any hovel they wish and send the image data via satellite directly to my computer at home."

She handed me a small card: *IPMAS – Image Provider and Mapping Service, Margit Bodmer.*

"My name is Domenica Ligrina. I'm a botanist."

She nodded gravely. "Then brace yourself for something terrible right up ahead."

"That's the purpose of my journey."

"A research expedition, so to speak?"

"Yes. For my work."

"Then take a close look. It's bad. Really bad."

VIII

The Inner Circle of Hell

No star, and no vestiges
Of the sun, even low in the sky,
To illuminate these marvels,
Which shone with their own fire!

And over these moving wonders
Hovered (terrible novelty!
All for the eye, nothing for the ears!)
A silence of eternity.

CHARLES BAUDELAIRE

I looked out the window of our compartment. The land was literally stripped bare, its green skin peeled off down to the debris of the Rhine's gravel tongue. Huge bulldozers pushed the farmland in front of them like brown waves. Belching black diesel smoke vertically into the sky, they lifted the soil onto gigantic trucks, which then dumped it into cube-shaped concrete containers. Sealed, these were transported across France to the coast, where the contaminated earth was used to build the new Europe Dam.

There was not a human being in sight far and wide. The drivers of the earth-moving machines sat in their fully air-conditioned cockpits as if in space capsules, or they operated them by means of telepresence from the safety of their mobile control centers.

Occasionally I glimpsed on the side of the tracks or in a hollow a few trees—alders, ash trees, maples, poplars, or willows—but despite the advanced season they bore no green. Their bark was blackened. They were dead. The fruit trees were systematically leveled, shredded, and amassed into piles of wood chips. I saw barriers as high as houses made of heaped-up grapevines; gnarled, bent wood, waiting to be pushed into the gaping maws of the shredders. It had to be buried very deep and turned into peat, for if it were burned, the radioactivity would be in the air again and descend somewhere else.

Miles-long scrap heaps were lined up along the tracks: cars piled up in stacks of six or eight; trailers, tractors, harvesters, buses, and streetcars; remnants of white, turquoise, and lime green paint. The rust had only partly effaced the advertisements. I still saw the numbers, the names of city districts where no one lived anymore. Complete, state-of-the-art urban transport fleets were discarded there—radioactive scrap. Railroad cars, Eurotrans containers, tank cars, forklifts, machine tools, parts of building cranes, antennas, lawnmowers, cut-up pipes, torn-out heaters, metal frames of roofs and greenhouses, and between them frequent dunes of shattered glass.

Suddenly my gaze fastened on a dismantled children's carousel, the colorful coaches with horses, double-decker buses, boats, a swan—the sections of the crown painted with giraffes, camels, hippopotamuses, and dolphins. That broken children's world made me sadder than the rest of the destruction all around.

Everything was lined up along the tracks for transport. Probably it would eventually be compressed and, loaded onto trains, roll toward the sea, to be permanently disposed of under the concrete sheath of the Eurodam, where it could exhale its radioactivity over the next several million years. The Eurodam as the sarcophagus of cutting-edge European technology, a memorial for eternity.

To the left on a hill two churches rose into the sky, one of them gutted by fire. The redbrick tower was half collapsed. Most of the houses in the village had been blasted by cleanup crews. Everywhere were heaps of rubble, on which black weeds had shot up, monstrous coltsfoot, thistles as tall as men. OPPENHEIM I read on a rusty sign.

The sky was almost cloudless. The sun was shining, but the light was strangely hazy, too dim to cast shadows. Things were without contours, drab and gray. Birgit had tried to describe this to us: The contaminated areas had turned into an indistinct shadow realm, over which the powers of darkness seemed to have spread their cloak.

Suddenly the river reappeared to our right: rank riverside meadows, cutoff bends, silty pits in which boats rotted, fallen trees, caved-in huts. We overtook a military convoy—cleanup equipment in front, behind it a dozen trucks in Euro-white; the drivers and passengers wore goggle-eyed face masks. They looked over. One of them waved. I waved back, even though he probably couldn't see me through the tinted windows.

Suddenly Luigi chirped.

"Yes?"

"Please use the earpiece," he said at a minimal volume.

I detached the receiver from the clasp and pressed it into my ear.

"Very nearby a strong transmitter has begun operating. I have substantial disturbances in communication."

I looked over at Brambilla. While I had been staring out the window, IPMAS had been activated. She had flipped down the monitors in front of her eyes; on her wrist in her lap glowed green and amber lights. Her fingers performed steering motions with an invisible joystick. She looked really grotesque: the delicate figure, the slim stockinged legs, the knees close together, the elegant suit, the medium-length blond hair under the hat brim, the dark squares in front of the glasses, and the mechanically jerky hands.

"*Tutto bene, Luigi,*" I whispered.

"If you say so, Domenica."

The train stopped, but I saw no station. Next to the tracks stood an ugly, completely graffiti-covered building with a flat, hole-ridden roof. In the east a railroad bridge made of simple latticework spanned the Rhine. The segment on the opposite bank had collapsed; overgrown with dense bushes it projected partway into the river.

"The bridge was blown up because plunderers from France were constantly coming over to Mainz," Brambilla, who had paused in her work, suddenly remarked. "Frankfurt was never successfully evacuated. The residents didn't even let the military intimidate them. 'Kiss our ass!' they wrote on bedsheets, and hung them out the windows." She laughed.

"Are you already finished with your work?"

She had flipped up one of the monitors and was scrutinizing me with one eye.

"My computer takes care of it. I set the flight path of the drone beforehand so that it heads for the pinpointed objects. Sometimes a bit of precision work is necessary to choose the correct angle, but direct steering by telepresence is impossible—for one thing, because of the many tunnels here."

The train slowly rolled on. The ramp onto the bridge was guarded by two round brick towers. The tracks on the railroad embankment, which ran between them to the bridge, were nothing but rust marks on concrete ties, between which tall grass grew. A swarm of mosquitoes hung over them like a smoke cloud.

"Frankfurt had also taken far less of the brunt than this region here. Do you know how it happened?" Brambilla asked me.

"Only what I've read about it."

"Then let me tell you." She looked out the window and flipped up the other monitor on her glasses. "July 28, 2028, was a hot day. A slight west-southwest wind blew, which later turned southwest and finally south-southwest. Around ten o'clock, when the contamination cloud from Cattenom arrived here, the Rhine Valley had not yet heated up much. So there were downdrafts. The stuff came down, and most of it landed on the eastern bank, here between Oppenheim and St. Goar. Mainz got the worst of it."

"Is this here Mainz?" I asked.

"Yes, we're just outside of it."

"Frankfurt is very close to here, isn't it?"

I remembered Birgit's story about her excursion into the death zone in search of her parents.

"It's about twenty miles northeast of here. When the cloud reached the Frankfurt area around noon, there was fortunately already a strong thermal over the city. It drew the fallout up like a chimney. It first came down again more heavily between Fulda and Leipzig, contaminated a roughly one-hundred-and-twenty-five-mile-wide swath between Potsdam and Karlsbad, and thinned out gradually on its way to Posen," she said, shaking her head. "I've never forgotten it, after all these years."

"Did you live here?"

She nodded. "In Gießen. Fortunately, many people had gone away on vacation at the time, and we were among them. Lots of children, in particular, for they had school break; otherwise there would have been even more victims."

"And those who had stayed home?"

She gave a wave of her hand. "Don't ask me about them."

"They died."

"It was terrible. Many didn't die right away. Only later in the reception and transit camps on the periphery: Heidelberg, Schweinfurt, Osnabrück, Braunschweig, Magdeburg. There were many dead in particular among those who had followed the evacuation orders too late. They were not even brought into safe areas anymore. The condition of most of them was hopeless. The worst affected, however, were those who had simply stayed home, mostly older people who did not even grasp what was going on. For a while, there was still electricity, gas, and water. 'We have a right to assistance,' they told themselves. 'After all, our whole lives we worked, paid our taxes, our insurance, our contributions. So eventually someone has to come, damn it—from the fire department, from the relief agency, the Red Cross, or some other emergency service.' So they remained in their armchairs in front of the television, but soon they no longer fully understood the broadcasts because of the headaches, the nausea, and the general weakness in their limbs. 'Nothing but boring movies about refugees somewhere and medical emergency treatment, one special after another about radioactivity and that plutonium dust from France. Who cares? And that—what awful program-ming everywhere—on all the channels.' They didn't grasp that it was live and affected them too. And so they died, remote control in hand—if they were lucky. For those who weren't lucky things got completely surreal. First came the flies, attracted by the smell of blood flowing from their orifices and lymph seeping through their brittle skin. Progressive radiogenic fibro-sis. And then, at some point, came the rats . . ."

I cringed with horror. Suddenly branches and foliage scratched and grazed the car. The train pushed its way through a tunnel in the vegeta-tion. It got darker and darker. A tunnel? The grinding and grating stopped. Again a stretch of half-light—like a clearing in the jungle. I had never before seen the *Clematis vitalba nigra* from so close. Its dark claws slid hungrily across the window; it was feeling the train, searching for a crack, a way in. Again it got dark. The train rolled at a crawl. The window was soiled with chlorophyll slime, white secretion from spurges, and mashed black leaves. For a moment I thought I saw the scurrying movement of something furry—the face of a lemur.

Once again the train entered a tunnel; this time it was a longer one. Then came another jungle clearing, which gradually took on the form of a train station. Behind it was a row of half-overgrown flat-roofed buildings. Through the window on the other side I saw a former parking garage full of dark, abundant vegetation. Was that mutant ivy? I had never before seen ivy with such large leaves. On the concrete ribs grew tree fungi like stacked-up dish antennas made of rotten flesh. Above it rose a round, smashed glass tower like the dome of a greenhouse, from which rubber trees gone mad had broken free in a vegetal eruption. Between them *Rafflesia* had spread its three-foot-wide white-starred dark red cushions. The train stopped.

MAINZ.

On the next track were two hitched-together diesel locomotives, in front of them a flatbed equipment carrier with two contra-rotating rotors, higher than a train. A sort of high-performance shredder. The thing had apparently cut a path for us through the vegetation. The locomotives were covered with shredded plant parts and a slimy green foam of chlorophyll. Clusters of branches had gotten caught in the protective bars in front of the viewing windows; in them hung the remains of birds—and the severed arm of a monkey. I observed the vegetation all around and felt as if I had been transported to a strange planet.

Some of the plants had forgotten the art of photosynthesis—their fundamental vital function for more than three billion years. They incorporated into their protein molecules elements that blocked large areas of the spectrum to them. In their abnormal hunger for light they searched for a way out in gigantism and ever-larger leaves, only to be smothered in a genetic chaos of diversity and formlessness.

At the main entrance to the train station building, which was sealed off with plastic and foam, an accordion-like object unfolded; it grew straight across the platform toward our train and docked with it. Two bulky figures with knapsacks on their backs trudged through and sprayed the sealant of the door to the car. A few minutes later six distorted dark gray figures strode across through the ribbed plastic corridor. Shortly thereafter, two women and four men walked through our car in search of their compartment. Their light gray papertex coveralls rustled and gave off an aseptically fresh scent. The smell of soap wafted toward my nose. The young people seemed to have scrubbed themselves thoroughly. They were unusually pale and had acne on their necks and cheeks. All of them had dosimeters hanging around their necks.

"There are still idealists," said Brambilla, nodding approvingly. "They come from all over the world to help—most of them from France. They wish to make amends. The 'month in hell,' they call it. They get a medal for it, which is recognized worldwide as education credit. So there is something to be gotten out of it. But they are certainly well advised to have stem cells and sperm or eggs frozen as a precaution."

"Do many come?"

"Yes. Even though they have to put up with getting spit on by some Germans."

"I've read those stupid slogans."

She shrugged. "They're not assigned the really hard tasks. For those there are specialists: forensic scientists, military doctors, pathologists. They deal with one house after another, floor by floor, apartment by apartment, photographing the skeletons and the mummies and whatever the rats have left, taking DNA samples, collecting and bagging them. Awful work. The authorities keep the records under wraps. But I've seen a few photos. I can tell you . . ."

I shivered.

"The volunteers are assigned mainly to the decontamination work. A month in a protective suit," Brambilla went on, gesturing with a nod in the direction the young people had gone. "They're done with it."

"How long will it take before the decontamination is completed?" I asked.

"Estimates range between thirty and three thousand years," replied Brambilla. "I've often wondered whether they shouldn't team up with the Asians. I heard they have a plant that removes the radioactive contamination in a harmless fashion. A papyrus or something like that from India. It has those fullerenes in its cells, in which the radioactive material is enclosed as in a cage. When the plant decomposes, it's washed away. Harmless. They've supposedly been using it for years along the Saale. As a botanist, you should actually know more about that than I do."

"I've never heard anything about it before."

I would have to look into that miracle plant. Probably it was a rumor. Wishful thinking. On the other hand, I knew that the Asians conducted their research at the Botanical Institute in Gardelegen with great success.

A buffet cart was pushed through the car: sandwiches, tofu with rice, and drinks were included in the train fare. And there were drinking nuts with that miserable coffee I had already loathed in Heidelberg. For such spinoffs we truly did not need space travel.

Suddenly I spotted a fly on the edge of my plate.

"Take a look at that," I said to my fellow passenger.

The princess took her glasses off her nose and leaned forward.

"A fly."

"Yes, but take a closer look."

Despite the shielding, the insect had made it onto the train with the young people: a large black blowfly with a green metallic shimmering abdomen. But the front limbs looked strange to me; dark, pearl-shaped outgrowths dangled from them.

"It has an extra pair of eyes on its front legs," I observed.

The insect tried repeatedly to raise the mutant pair of legs over its head in a cleaning movement. To no avail.

"Oh, there are worse things, young woman."

I was aware of that—and involuntarily I thought of CarlAntonio, the Siamese twins, and of the little girl on the platform in Heidelberg, from whose wrist sprouted a small black talon.

A howl approached from behind. The two diesel locomotives with the shredder rolled by on the next track. The rotors spun threateningly. So a swath would have to be cleared for the continuation of the journey northward as well. Finally the train moved on. To the left of the tracks I saw five-story houses from the beginning of the previous century. Gutted by fire. Black window holes. To the right rose two tower blocks built very close together—twenty-seven or twenty-eight floors high, with panoramic windows like embrasures. Most of the windows had been broken. Ivy and wild vines had already made it to the fifteenth floor and had penetrated inside through the openings. I pictured scenes inside: the residents sitting dead in their television chairs, entwined by *Parthenocissus tricuspidata*, their bony temples adorned with blooming *Hedera helix*, and eye cavities in which spiders nested.

Thousands of ravens flew over the roofs, swarming here and there.

"Do you see the ravens?" asked Brambilla. "You have to be careful around them. They hunt animals in huge swarms. They've grown fiendishly intelligent, perhaps because they've battened on human flesh. They originally came from the east, from Poland and the Baltic states, people say. Then they stayed here. No wonder, with the abundant food supply. The woods and fields were littered with animal carcasses. Who wanted to collect them all? It had not been possible to bury and cremate even close to all the dead people. And those birds have multiplied incredibly here, despite the radioactivity."

"Like the rats."

"Like the rats," she confirmed, nodding.

The tracks now ran along the river. A passenger ship lay with its bow half on the embankment—the *Princess of Rhine-Hesse*. The stern was missing. What jutted into the river had been severed. The ship rested high up on the bank. So the water level had dropped significantly, probably because of the melting of the last glaciers in the Swiss Alps.

"Those ships were the first to pass through the death zone," said my fellow passenger. She told me that between Mainz and Koblenz more than thirty sunken passenger ships had blocked the channel. They had been stormed by refugees and had gone under. "It took over a year before the river was navigable again. Now it has been open again for twenty years, but there are still some ship owners who don't dare to operate on it. Superstitious people; they're afraid of ghosts—Loreley and such . . ."

Brambilla smiled; then, with a jerk, she flipped down both monitors in front of her eyes.

"Damn beasts!" she hissed. "They're attacking my drone again."

"Who?" I asked, perplexed.

"The ravens," she said through clenched teeth. "But feathers are going to fly." Her fingers twitched back and forth.

Brambilla seemed to be completely preoccupied with her reconnaissance work. I looked out the window. It was already late afternoon. One abandoned village followed another. Hotels, boarding houses, restaurants, boat docks—run-down, decayed. Rotten fences, caved-in roofs. Fire had raged unopposed, spreading from one house to the next and eating its way through whole lines of old half-timbered houses. The black roof beams rose from the rubble like the ribs of large, half-incinerated monsters.

Occasionally I saw special ships spewing riverwater in high arcs over buildings and the streets to wash away the fallout. Probably remote-controlled; people were nowhere to be seen.

The base of the tracks was so bad in places that the train wobbled like a large animal ponderously plodding along.

Again we stopped. Probably the tunnel cutter made only slow progress. The vegetation of the riverside meadows had begun to storm the railroad embankment and had in places overrun it. Fallen trees lay on both sides of the train, buried under the shroud of the ubiquitous *nigra*. BINGEN, I read. On the hill of the opposite bank stood a huge dark bronze figure, its fist raised threateningly to the west.

The valley narrowed. City ruins lined the river, beyond them rank vineyards, collapsed walls, breaches from mudslides. The streets were impassable due to mud and drift sand, in which blackberry thickets welled up. The late-afternoon light, which broke through gaps in the clouds in the west, revealed details on the eastern slope: here a castle ruin, there a hotel, a porous rock face, a house, a hole-ridden slate roof.

Suddenly I glimpsed in the middle of the shallow riverbed a water castle. It was freshly whitewashed, and the roof had been covered with new wood shingles. The shutters were painted red, light blue pennants hung from the bay windows, and the main tower wore a fresh, red-gold, sparkling copper hood. Was this the first sold real estate?

"What's that?" I asked my fellow passenger.

"That's the Pfalzgrafenstein toll castle. It belongs to a Chinese ship-owner from Singapore. Filthy rich. He had the castle renovated. By Asian guest workers."

"Can people live here then?"

"Some like it hot," she said with a shrug.

The island was besieged by driftwood, on which dense bushes grew rampant. It looked like *Sorbaria*, but I couldn't identify it with certainty. The pinnate leaves ranged from dark green to black—a landing force that had formed a beachhead.

OBERWESEL. The view of the river was obscured by dense woods. The valley made a ninety-degree turn to the right. The eastern slope had gotten it worse than the western. The steep terrain was crosshatched by dead vines—contorted as if they had died in pain. The lichens, on the other hand, had experienced an unexpected evolutionary boost. In some places they formed large, continuous, reddish brown splotches, as if a giant had vomited over the slopes.

HOTEL LORELEY, I read in the dim evening light. A Disneyland of the dead.

Dinner was served. Poultry salad with peas, corn, carrots, and mayonnaise. Turkey? Chicken? Or something in between?

"Biotech muck," Brambilla grumbled with disgust, but ate nonetheless.

I longed for *Tafelspitz*, for *Vanillenbraten* and *Fiakergulasch*, for the *Salzburger Nockerln* at St. Peter, of which I had had to send back a double peak. In one gulp I emptied a bottle of mineral water before I even got down a bite. I felt as if I had ashes in my mouth, as if I had to wash down the plutonium dust in my throat and the effluvium of an unrestrained vegetation that had settled on my mucous membranes.

Gloom sank over the landscape. It was the minute after sunset, in which the last light of day seems to suck the colors out of things and smear them across the sky, before everything is melted into darkness. The train now moved faster. Night fell. Outside emptiness, no people, no movement, no cars, no illuminated windows. Only the reflection of the train windows dragged like a pale chain along the railroad embankment; sometimes it jumped up onto a wall, then rushed again along the sides of the tunnel.

The land on both banks of the Rhine, a settled area for thirty thousand years. Here light had burned from time immemorial; campfires had flickered, around which people sat. Now it had plunged back through time into deep prehistoric darkness. Only occasionally pale red and green lights appeared on the river, ghostly, as if from time-ships seeking their course through the abysses.

A SCRAPING AND pattering, hissing and pounding woke me. Had we gotten stuck in the wild vegetation? Were the locomotives trying with futile thrust to free the train from entanglement? Were the branches and vines already breaking through the windows to seize us? The panes were opaque, covered with a white foamy smear. Rotating brushes wiped it away. Our train was passing through a carwash; the radioactive fallout stuck to it was being cleaned off. Hard jets of water lashed metal and glass, thundered from below against the undercarriage.

I looked at my watch; three o'clock in the morning. Outside it was pitch black.

"Is this Koblenz?" I asked.

"We were in Koblenz shortly before midnight. You were fast asleep, my dear. Now we're almost in Cologne."

My God! I had slept through Koblenz! But I had been so curious about the city, the towers of St. Florin, where Nicolaus Cusanus had been dean.

"You didn't miss anything," said the princess. "Koblenz is still an empty city. Cleaned up to a large extent, but it will still be a few years before people can live there again."

I looked out and saw portal cranes on which spotlights blazed, containers, freight trains. KÖLN EIFELTOR was inscribed on the cranes. A troop of workers with breathing masks sprayed solvent on the sealant of the doors.

"Cologne too had to be abandoned for ten years. Do you know how many rats were collected after the gassing of the houses? Over two million! Can you imagine that? The radioactivity hadn't afflicted them—on the contrary. Barely any sick specimens. The scientists think that the ones that fell ill had been devoured by the healthy members of their species. Only the best and healthiest survived. But there had been horrible mutants among them, people said. Large as beavers and fiendishly intelligent. The future belongs to those beasts, my dear. Not us."

"Let's wait and see."

"Wait? For what? For a sign from God?" she asked, shaking her head. "If *that* wasn't a sign, young woman!"

Brambilla was right. Satisfied, she pulled the modules out of the contacts on her ICom and stowed them in her handbag.

"Have you put the ravens to flight?"

"Certainly. I have a few tricks up my sleeve. Laser flashes. They still have respect. But for how long?"

We stepped out onto the platform. The air was fresh and cold. I shivered.

Tracks stretched into the darkness. Spotlights cast a radiant glow over stacks of containers. Cranes hummed and whirred. And from all sides I heard the groaning and screeching of metal scraping against metal. Brambilla held on to her hat as an electric cart rushed by us with a whine. Nearby the whistle of a locomotive could be heard.

HALF AN HOUR later we were instructed to board a new red-painted commuter train that was to bring us to Cologne. The upholstery was new and gave off the slight ammonium chloride smell of fresh synthetic fibers.

When we reached the Cologne central station, morning was dawning. Despite the early hour, the platforms were teeming with people. There was almost no way through. A din of voices, mainly French. Tour guides tried with shouting and pennant waving to hold their groups together and conduct them through the crowd.

"What are all these people doing here early in the morning?" I asked my companion.

"Those are Ursuline pilgrims. Some have just arrived, the others are returning home. Every day more than a dozen special trains are running."

"Ursulines?"

"Don't you know the Ursula legend?"

"Yes, I do," I said, remembering the paintings by Carpaccio I had seen in the Accademia. "The one who set out for Cologne with her eleven thousand virgins, where they were all massacred by the Huns."

"That's the medieval legend. But there's a new one, according to which the first people who around 2035 dared to return to the city found the saint praying in her church before the altar. She prayed for the souls of all who had died in the disaster and for the souls of those who had through their negligence and carelessness brought disaster upon the people."

"The French . . ."

"A hysterical need for atonement arose, which set off a wave of deep religiosity in France. This gives those people an outlet for their excessive guilt. Do you see the vials some of them wear around their necks?"

I noticed that many of the departing pilgrims had small glass containers hanging around their necks, which looked like closed test tubes and contained something black, a dark liquid or dust.

"You won't believe it, but those people take a tiny sample of contaminated soil home with them."

"That can't be true!"

"Oh, yes, my dear. And that serves everyone well. Every pilgrim can get the feeling of a martyrdom in miniature. They dispose of dangerous waste according to the supposed polluter pays principle and bring a little bit of the fallout outside the country. And don't ask me how much money those who had this fantastic idea make from it."

"But the Church . . ."

". . . undoubtedly has a considerable share in the business. You need only take a look at the cathedral. It shines in new splendor."

"Can you see it from here?"

"Poorly. Even though it's located directly next to the train station. But when you cross the Rhine later, take a look back."

We had descended the stairs to the spacious floor below the platforms. Here it was even more densely crowded—and it smelled like all the snack bars of Asia. The food service industry all around was indeed firmly in non-European hands: Thailand, Vietnam, Cambodia, Pakistan, India, and Indonesia had established their culinary consulates. A Turkish and a Greek place had claimed their territory. Only the brewery business seemed to remain in European hands.

We managed to get a place to stand and a hot noodle soup, which tasted of ginger, lemongrass, and fresh coriander. I eyed suspiciously the chunks of meat floating pallidly between the noodles.

"You can safely eat that," the princess assured me. "It's flapo."

"It's *what*?"

"Flat pork. It's real. Though it didn't grow on bones, but on nutrient film. The Belgians do a good job of that."

Brambilla gestured with a nod to a poster in the small, steam-filled kitchen, in which two dark-skinned cooks toiled. It showed a cheerfully smiling pig about ten yards long with a four-leaf clover in its mouth, a dozen pairs of legs, and a curly tail at the end. *Brussels Pigs* was written above it. I tasted the meat cautiously. It was somewhat spongy, but it really did taste like pork. The genes seemed to be right. I spooned hungrily.

Suddenly a melody, flashing and sharp as a knife, cut through the din of voices and the air laden with the smell of spices and cooking. Bach? Four young people had positioned themselves in the middle of the crowd and let flutes, clarinets, and trumpets sound. The conversations went silent; everyone listened. At the end applause thundered, and the coins jingled in the instrument cases.

"Give my regards to Amsterdam," said Princess Brambilla in parting.

"I'll do that," I replied. "Thank you. You've told me a lot about your home."

"I'm always happy when I find someone who listens to me. Journalists are like that."

Without her high-tech glasses she seemed like a nice grandma. I had the feeling we liked each other.

HALF AN HOUR later I sat on an express train of the Nederlandse Spoorwegen and finally drank a palatable coffee. The cathedral on the opposite bank looked unreal in the morning light—somehow delicate and brittle. I was overcome by a strange unease, however, at the sight of the pointy twin towers and the huge nave, and I was glad when the trees lining the railroad embankment hid it from view. What would await me on my journey into the past, if I visited this city long before the cathedral had been even halfway erected?

An hour later the train reached Holland. On the meadows lay rafts of mist, in which black-and-white-spotted cattle stood, sunken to their bellies. Lush pastures steamed in the morning sun. After that journey through the apocalypse it was agreeable to finally see unscathed nature again. Falcotti had been right: You had to have seen with your own eyes how endangered Creation is—how terribly simple it is to open the door to darkness.

I knew, of course, that appearances deceived. Here too there had repeatedly been extensive killing, when the food chain, tugged back and forth by rapacity and greed, had gotten hopelessly entangled and had had to start afresh, to the extent that was even still possible on the narrow genetic basis after decades of reckless and irresponsible monoculture.

After the hopes of breeding back had gone up in smoke, the geneticists seemed to be at a loss. Under the pressure of selection, the animals had apparently developed some tricks of survival that were stored *not* in their genes but in their mitochondria, in the internal ecology of the maternal organism or even outside the phenotype in the social behavior of gregarious animals. Only an unrealistic dreamer could assume that a living creature could be pulled out of a test tube and could be expected to develop in a vacuum, so to speak, into a self-sufficient organism capable of survival and reproduction. Gradually the whole terrible magnitude of the species annihilation that had been so carelessly carried out became clear. Diversity was gone, obliterated, irretrievably lost. That was where our task began and that of the Istituto Pontificale della Rinascita della Creazione di Dio, San Francesco, for suddenly an opportunity had unexpectedly presented itself. Evidently, life itself had at some point in the future found a way to take action across time in order to secure its own existence and with recourse to the past launch a self-repair program—and we were its instruments.

It was not about traveling to the fifteenth century to obtain a few seeds and tissue samples of extinct species so that the desolate landscapes could again be adorned with little flowers. It was about a mission that, if successful, would secure the continued existence of life on earth. Only at that moment did the whole scope of what Falcotti had meant when he took us into his confidence reveal itself to me. The vision was overwhelming.

IX

Message from a Cologne Witch

The whole of physical reality, the multiverse, contains vast numbers of parallel universes.

DAVID DEUTSCH

The cardinal counted the leather containers that were attached to the packsaddles of the beasts of burden. In Brussels he had managed to acquire state-of-the-art astronomical instruments and in Leuven several scholarly manuscripts, which he had had carefully packed for the journey. He reassured himself that everything was still there.

The morning dawned.

"Get up!" the captain of the city guard shouted.

Three darkly dressed figures, who had been cowering next to the landing, rose. Their clothing was dirty; their sidelocks curled from under their hats and hung down to their chests. The three men had been bound together with thin chains, the older one between the two younger ones. They wore wretched footgear; the toes of one of the men peeked out from his shoe. Two officers of the city guard drove them from behind with their pikes. The three prisoners eyed the weapons silently and impassively. They shivered in the morning cold.

"They've known for more than twenty years that they are not permitted to stay in the city at night," the captain declared to no one in particular, as if he had to excuse his official act, "but they try again and again." When no one paid attention to him, he barked: "Move! Or do I have to make you?"

"You don't have the say around here!" exclaimed the ferryman. "This ferry is from Deutz. We ferrymen are not subject to the city council of Cologne, but to the archbishop. Bear that in mind. Remove the chains from those men!"

At that moment, a rat crawled out from between the planks, an enormous animal of an unusual color—more grayish white with reddish spots than grayish brown. Sniffing, it scurried along the edge of the dock. One of the officers jabbed at it with his pike—playfully, more to scare it away than to impale it. Like lightning, the rat had jumped on the weapon, had climbed the shaft in no time, and stood a handbreadth from the officer's face. The rat then made a noise that sounded to the cardinal, from where he was standing, almost as if it had spoken, hissing a warning. But that was nonsense, of course.

The man recoiled in fright and threw the spear away from him. "The devil!" he cried, pale with horror, took a stumbling step back, and fell on his behind. "The devil!" The pike clattered to the ground, and the rat disappeared between the planks over the water.

The cardinal turned with surprise to the man, who sat on the ground and gawked around, his eyes wide with terror. "The devil?" the cardinal asked with curiosity, scrutinizing the man.

"Apologies, Your Eminence," said the captain, signaling to the officer with a brusque hand gesture to pull himself together and get up from his undignified position. He then got to work unlocking and removing the prisoners' chains. He threw them grumpily over his shoulder. Then he turned away and spat in the river.

Nicolaus scrutinized the prisoners, who seemed not to have even noticed the incident with the rat. They made an apathetic impression as the officers drove them onto the ferry with their pikes. He had endorsed the expulsion of the Jews from the city, but the measure had not brought about the hoped-for solution. The conflict between the council and the archdiocese continued to smolder, and Hussite-influenced preachers constantly rekindled the acrimonious atmosphere between the denominations and religious currents. For many, Rome's word carried no more weight. No one seemed to want to obey. The world was in a state of dissolution.

The cardinal nodded to his groom to lead the horses onto the ferry. Their hooves clip-clopped on the planks, and the man tethered the four animals to the railing side by side. They were uneasy and eyed anxiously the foaming dark water of the river. The ferryman shouted a command, and the ungainly, heavy vessel cast off. With their long oars the oarsmen pushed it off from the rocking, wooden dock. It started to turn. The river was already swollen, even though it was only mid-March. In the Black Forest and in the Vosges, the thaw had probably already begun.

"Row!" the ferryman shouted at his oarsmen. "Or do you want to dock in Düsseldorf instead of in Deutz? Row!"

The cardinal turned to his young companion, who wore a blue beret on his thick, shoulder-length hair, on which he had boldly stuck three quills as a sign of his occupation.

"Well?" asked Nicolaus, resuming the conversation that had been broken off for a while. "What else happened?"

"If I may, Your Eminence, since when does much happen in Cologne?" asked Geistleben, taking his knapsack off his shoulders and dropping it next to him on the floor. "A handful of little Roman monks arrived who fled from Constantinople, because the Turk is approaching the gates. They moan and ramble on about the end of the world and scrounge and beg for benefices. Oh yes, and a little witch is about to be put on trial. But you have surely heard about that."

"Not a word," Nicolaus replied, shaking his head with displeasure. "Is it spreading here too, that awful folly of torturing women and putting them to death?"

"Yes, certainly. It is getting worse everywhere. People are afraid of the spawn of the Antichrist, who gnaw at the limbs of the Church and eat their way deeper and deeper into its heart."

"What sort of talk is that, Geistleben? It is not the Antichrist who gnaws, it is greed that gnaws, it is vanity that gnaws, it is lust that gnaws in the flesh of our brothers and sisters."

"Well, indeed, that is your affair, noble lord. You undoubtedly understand more about it . . ."

"Quite true."

"But the East will fall, Your Eminence. Half the Empire—"

"What else was to be expected? I saw it with my own eyes, Geistleben. Catacombs full of writings, accumulated for centuries, with the knowledge of millennia from all over the world. But no one reads it; no one can even sort through it! Schemers and empty-headed scholars swarm over it like rats. Everyone gnaws at everyone else. Often at their own flesh. No wonder, then, the enemies are lurking. That's how it is everywhere. Here in our lands too. It was often painful, what I saw on my journey to Flanders and the Netherlands. It fills me with bitterness and rancor. As for the archbishop, however—we spoke daily during the concilium, but he did not mention a word about planning to hold a witch trial."

"Well, Your Eminence, he seems to be not at all so certain. He doesn't want to make any mistakes. Once before he has been at odds with the Pope, old von Moers. After almost forty years in office—simply excommunicated."

"That was Pope Eugene. He held it against him that he had voted against him at the Council of Basel."

"But that was a deep shock for him in his old age."

"Pope Nicholas reinstated him. He won't want for anything."

"Certainly not."

"When I stayed here on Christmas and New Year's Day, I heard rumors of a woman who had been found with a strange collection of herbs. Is she the one?"

"Yes, she is."

"And she is to be put on trial?"

"The archbishop has sought advice and support from the highest authority. A commission is to come from Rome, to investigate the case, whether devil's work is actually involved . . ."

"Why wasn't the woman forced to renounce all vengeance and banished from the city, as usual?"

"There were inflammatory speeches. A young priest was very active, a zealot from Swabia, Bartholomäus von Dillingen is his name—he is a preacher at St. Maria im Kapitol. People call him 'Witch Bart.' If I may, Your Eminence, an evil snooper. He watched her every step for weeks. After his sermons, an angry crowd always proceeds to the Old Market square and demands that she be made short work of. She was ultimately turned over to the episcopal judge, for the archbishop is insisting on the main jurisdiction, as the law would have it. He had her interrogated. She was found guilty, but he isn't doing anything. He's biding his time."

"What were the results of the interrogations?"

"A serf who encountered her in the summer on the Moselle testified that, without touching him, she used devilish powers to cast him to the ground with such force that he was black and blue all over his body and felt pains in his chest for weeks. He heard laughter that sounded like the bleating of a goat and could smell the definite stink of sulfur. A citizen with whom she lodged testified that she told her that one could fly from Cologne to Rome in an hour. And under torture she spoke heedlessly. She confessed to having flown through the air herself. It was the herbs, though, that determined the outcome."

"How so?"

"Over the whole summer she had gathered a collection of seeds—kernels from grain and fruit, blossoms from all sorts of flowers and plants. For medicinal purposes, she claimed. These seeds were sorted neatly into little canvas pouches and labeled and inscribed with Latin words. But these words were incomprehensible. A sort of secret system of classification, Your Eminence, which . . . well, so it seemed to me, is strangely coherent, but of which no one has ever heard, as the professors of medicine brought in from the university confirmed. This system points to heretical, arcane knowledge and cannot possibly be of godly origin . . ."

"Of devilish origin, then . . ."

"The commission of professors came to that conclusion. The young woman lied through her teeth. Went so far as to claim that the Holy Father himself sent her to collect little seeds and flowers."

"The Holy Father?"

"Yes, in order to save Creation, she asserted."

The cardinal shook his head. "She is surely confused. An unfortunate creature. The woman should not be treated this way. Such a thing is shameful."

"Verily, I look at it the same way. Especially as she has more education than can be ascribed to the devil, or—if I may—to the archbishop, for that matter."

"How so? Is she a nun? From what order?"

"I don't think so. It's odd . . . no one who has sworn a vow of humility would speak like that. And her Latin, oh my . . ."

"A noblewoman then?"

"Not a chance!"

"A simple woman? You are making me curious."

"You will be even more surprised, Your Eminence, when I tell you that she wrote you letters. It emerges from them that she seems to be quite well acquainted with you."

"What do you mean, she is acquainted with me? Is she from here? From Koblenz? From the Moselle?"

"No, certainly not. No one really knows where she is from. Some claim that she comes from Amsterdam, others that she is from Sweden, was the assistant of a court physician there. Her appearance, her speech point more to a Roman, perhaps Florence, Siena . . . who knows? But definitely not from the countryside. By no means. She is educated. Knows things even I have never heard of. At times, I think she came . . ."

"Yes?"

". . . from another world."

"You mean, from distant lands?"

"Very distant lands, Your Eminence. Of which we still know nothing."

"A sibyl perhaps, from the Orient?"

The scholar shook his head hesitantly. "Those prophetesses speak obscurely. She speaks more with the light of certainty. It seemed to me—how should I put it—as if the darkness were in our heads more than in her words, if you understand what I mean, Your Eminence."

The cardinal lowered his gaze thoughtfully. "From where might she know me? Has she ever crossed paths with me? Has she spoken with me? In Rome perhaps? But I don't remember ever having met a woman of that sort . . ."

"It does not seem so. I don't think she knows you by sight. It is more— how should I put it—as if she were acquainted with your writings and with you as a very famous man."

"You're speaking in riddles, Geistleben. How could she be acquainted with my writings? And me, a very famous man? That I am not, God knows. She must be confused."

"It would indeed be no surprise. She has, after all, spent months in the dungeon. The icy cold has afflicted her. She is sick and desperate. Without friends or acquaintances."

"Did she confide in you personally?"

"No. I caught only fleeting glimpses of her now and then, when she was brought to an interrogation. I read the transcripts."

"You were permitted to see them?"

"Well . . . as a scribe in the chancery of the archbishop I could not help taking notice of them. I worked for him for almost a year. I write quickly and largely flawlessly, you should know. But now boredom drives me onward."

"The letters to me . . . ?"

"Are in the records for the commission from Rome. They will—I assume—eventually be delivered to you, as soon as the case is concluded. But so that you would not have to wait too long, I took the liberty of copying for you one or two letters that came into my view, Your Eminence."

"So you copied documents that are under lock and key and—I presume—classified . . . ?"

"Well, apparently not so classified. Far more than that, they are incomprehensible, mysterious—but extremely remarkable."

"You are carrying the copies with you?"

"I'm afraid not. I wanted to fetch them from the hiding place when the synod members set off and your departure too was approaching. I hastened after you to be on the ferry and present them to you. But the copies were gone."

"How did that happen?"

"I don't know exactly, but I suspect a novice. A fellow who plays dumb but seems to me quite cunning. He is smitten with the woman, loiters around wherever she is, and stares at her slobberingly. But the fellow has a face—if I may, Your Eminence—like a wild boar under its tail. It's abysmally ugly, and if you ask him something, he only grunts and crawls away like a rat."

"Could it be that he has informed the archbishop? Then you would be in serious trouble, as you well know. Now courage has abandoned you and you are absconding at the crack of dawn."

"You are probably right. I cannot discount the possibility that he has denounced me. But it is also possible that he so reveres her that he makes do with anything her hands have touched, especially what she has written down. For the rags she wore on her body before she was given a fresh robe for the interrogation have disappeared as well. Perhaps he has hidden the stuff in the straw in which he sleeps, the fellow. Well, be that as it may, it seems to me time to set off. I would like to finally move on. First Strasbourg, then Paris, to study there the Lullian art of which I have heard."

"You mean that Majorcan's art of creating knowledge by means of a little mechanism—click, clack—without exerting the mind and calculating—from one to two to three—the wisdom of God's Creation?"

"If I may, Your Eminence, it might, I think, be the true future of all philosophizing: counting, measuring, weighing, calculating. Not the errors, superior attitudes, and disputes over authorities of the past and present. Computing! The little witch writes it at one point: You will one day be credited with having advanced this very thing."

"Me? That is as bold as it is incredible, Geistleben. True, I have—it was a long time ago, I think it was in the year '26, when I was still Giordano Orsini's secretary—examined the work of Raymundus Lullus. While rummaging around here in Cologne, I found it among many other writings. The cardinal pointed out to me that there was an extensive, almost entirely unexplored library here. He had a nose for such things."

"I too discovered it here. It intrigued me."

"I made excerpts back then, but I never found time to devote myself seriously to that *Ars Magna*, as its creator so vainly called it. Only I have reservations about ceding the practice of philosophy to the mechanics and clockmakers. Although . . . Well, indeed, at the Camaldolese monastery Val di Castro, after a dispute with Toscanelli, I wrote down a few thoughts on weighing, which . . . I will delve deeper into it, when time permits . . . But no, how would that woman . . ."

"Does anyone know what the future will bring, Your Eminence? Besides God, perhaps the devil . . . and a little witch now and then?"

"What else did she write in the letters?"

"She asked you to exert your influence in high places. I assume she means the Holy Father himself."

"He has, God knows, other things to do than to concern himself with the confused remarks of a woman who is suspected of witchcraft in distant Cologne. What else did she write?"

"You should protect Accademia Romana . . ."

"Accademia Romana? Never heard of it."

"Its founder is . . . What was his name? Pomponius Laetius or Laetus . . ."

"I don't know who he is."

"She wrote of a Regiomontanus who was supposedly summoned to Rome."

"A scholar? From Königsberg? He is unknown to me."

"Nor have I heard of a scholar by that name."

"What else?"

"Well, as far as I can remember, many confused things. In particular of a place where a terrible plague breaks out, on the upper Moselle."

"On the Moselle? Did she mention the name of the place?"

"Cattelon . . . Cattenom, or something like that."

"Cattenom . . . It is possible that I have heard of a place by that name before. A plague, you say?"

"From which the earth turns black, deep into Bohemian, indeed, into Polish regions, which ravages man and beast, and poisons and spoils tree and bush so that people can no longer live in that land."

"So a sibyl, who, like Cassandra, of whom Aeschylus tells, sees what will come?"

"Will you intercede on her behalf, Your Eminence? It might well turn out that the city court condemns and burns her for witchcraft. Knowing the archbishop, he will not lift a finger."

"I will write Dietrich a letter, from Frankfurt, where I must journey in a few days. I will speak with Tilman in St. Florin, although we are not on the best terms . . ."

"Provost Tilman Joel von Linz?"

"Yes. He has been an adviser to the archbishop for many years."

"I had the honor of meeting him, Your Eminence."

"Moor the vessel!" the ferryman shouted to the oarsmen.

On the riverside two young men had hastened over and caught the lines that were thrown to them. Horses were harnessed, a dozen or more, to tow the heavy vessel upstream to the upper dock, for the leeway was surely three thousand feet. The breath of the animals steamed in the cool morning air. Up on the bank Jewish children stood in the wet grass. Wrapped in rags— barefoot. They followed the horses at a proper distance, for the towing men swung their whips widely. A pale sun rose between cloud banks and turned animals and people into gold-enveloped silhouettes.

"I hope to be in Rome again by summer, Geistleben," said the cardinal. "If your wanderlust should lead you there, you would be a welcome guest."

"You are too kind, Your Eminence. I am honored by your offer."

"You would then have to tell me about the Lullian art, if it has been taught to you in Paris."

"It will be my pleasure, Your Eminence."

The groom led the animals by the reins up the dock, held the stirrup, and helped the Cusan mount. The cardinal raised his hand.

"Thank you!" he called to the scholar, who had shouldered his knapsack. "God bless you."

"Farewell, Your Eminence."

"We set off," the cardinal commanded, taking the reins. "I want to be in Heisterbach with the Cistercians for sext and in Andernach for vespers. The day is short, and I hate journeying in the dark."

The groom nodded, leaped into the saddle, and fastened together the reins of the pack animals. Then they rode off, leaving behind the voices of the children ringing out in the cool morning air.

A couple of geese flew low over the reeds along the river. The heavy, rhythmic beat of their wings sounded like the lusty moans of two lovers. The groom turned his face away and grinned.

Book
FOUR

I

The New Dam

I like to think of space and time as analogous to the ocean, and changes in it as analogous to waves on the surface of the ocean, but those waves, of course, don't show up when one is miles above the ocean. It looks flat. Then as one gets down closer to the surface one sees the waves breaking and the foam. I see no way to escape the conclusion that similar foam-like structure is developing in space and time.

JOHN WHEELER

In the changing room it smelled like damp, sun-warmed wood and urine. As I turned around, I saw a wide-open eye in the hole a voyeur had drilled through the wooden wall.

"Hey, you little rascal! This isn't a peepshow here!" I shouted, slapping my wet bikini top against the opening. A moment later, I heard the running feet of two boys on the boardwalk behind the changing room.

Renata was already dressed and sat at a table under a sun umbrella of the adjacent cafeteria. I strolled over to her. From the Old Sea a pleasantly cool wind blew in; the heat that had shimmered all day over the pale, broad, sandy beach was becoming more bearable. My skin burned from the saltwater and the impact of billions upon billions of photons that had rained down on us unfiltered through the huge ozone hole on that summer day.

Renata had already headed out to Zandvoort the day before and had spent the night at Grit's. Grit had already completed half a dozen missions in the fifteenth and sixteenth centuries; she was to advise and help us as soon-to-be travelers.

"Too bad Grit couldn't come with us," I said.

"She has visitors this evening and still had some things to buy and prepare."

Two boys, perhaps twelve or thirteen, had stopped at some distance, were sucking on their popsicles and staring over at us. I raised a finger threateningly, but that only elicited a grin from them. One of them stuck his thumb between forefinger and middle finger and shook his hips.

"Look at that little bastard!"

Renata looked around bemusedly, then smiled faintly. She seemed exhausted, and I hoped that the sea air did her good.

"So Frans isn't coming," she remarked.

"He extended his contract in Venice. They need him badly, he told me. Actually I had expected it. Just after his return from his last trip I already sensed that he had grown distant from me. And I had been so worried about him and was so happy when he finally returned."

Renata nodded. "I warned you, Domenica. With time travelers you shouldn't get into committed relationships or expect them to last. Travelers live in their own universe; they move on erratic courses. When they get close to you, it's as if on a parabola. There's a point where they are very close to you, but then they're carried away again," she said, resting her hands on mine. "The same thing will probably happen to us. On top of that, there are those mysterious temporal effects. When they go through the transition today and return after a few days, they've often spent weeks, months, sometimes years in the past. Sometimes they've gone through terrible things and seen even more terrible things, and they might, despite all their resolutions, have gotten into relationships wherever they were staying. When they then return, they are immersed in a world that has become strange to them, in which everything they have just known or loved has changed or even disappeared. They lead a literally fractured life. Their biography is full of rifts and abysses. How can you expect continuity from that?"

"I never really realized that," I replied.

"You probably didn't want to. But it has to be that way. Some have broken down from it and lost contact with reality. You need to have a thick skin, as Frans does, to keep up a life like that for years."

I nodded. "I'm starting to come to terms with the fact that I don't have the best luck with the men I'm attracted to."

Renata laughed. "With your looks? — Come on, take the handkerchief and wipe away your tears, for God's sake!"

"My mother wants to remarry, by the way. A real Moro," I said, eager to change the subject.

"How nice for her. When?"

"At Christmastime."

"By then, both of us will probably have been back a long time. Then we'll take a vacation in Italy."

"Bernd and Birgit are planning to begin studying psychology, by the way. They were awarded some grant for orphans."

"That won't hurt them. And if we suffer a breakdown"—she tapped her forehead—"we can fall back on them."

"It would be better not to."

"Do you still keep in touch with them?"

"I quickly made a last round of calls before I had to send Luigi into temporary retirement," I said.

"So you too now enjoy the privilege of NEA status. Unreachable by Tom, Dick, and Harry."

"Hm."

"I've come to appreciate not being reachable by anyone—like my ancestors, when they were cut off from the outside world in winter in the mountains. In the beginning, I found it harder than I had expected. You get used to effortless data acquisition. We'll miss that, of course."

"Do you think our mission will be hard?" I asked Renata.

"Yes, I think so. We'll be transferred to a world stranger than Mars. But we'll make it. We've got what it takes and have certainly been tested long enough."

"Last week I went to a fortune-teller," I confessed. "On Sint Annenstraat."

"I had no idea you set any store by things like that," said Renata.

"I don't. It was a spur-of-the-moment impulse."

"And what did she say?"

"She looked at my hands, did some hocus-pocus with a crystal ball, and said, 'I see you standing before a mirror, but . . .' Suddenly she paused in horror. 'What is it?' I asked, and she whispered, 'There's no reflection in the mirror. It's empty!' Then she stared at me and screamed: 'Leave! Leave right now!' And then she practically threw me out. She even refused to accept any money."

Renata shook her head. For a long time we sat there silently. Far out on the horizon rose a vague contour: the crown of the New Dam, which had been erected northwest of Terschelling past Texel to Westgat and which would one day extend from Cherbourg to the Skagerrak. The "Atlantic

Wall," some quipped, while others called it the "sarcophagus of the European nuclear industry," but the mockery was lost on most people in the face of the onrushing floods in spring and autumn. The water in the oceans rose unrelentingly, and all Holland was now below sea level. The Dutch had lived for centuries with that threat—often they had compared themselves with the chosen people of Israel, who, putting their trust in God, had crossed the Red Sea. One thing was clear to everyone: If the Northern Association, the so-called Rump EU, would not undertake massive efforts and invest more than two hundred billion euros annually in the New Dam project, which would by the turn of the century extend from Normandy to Jutland, the North Sea would soon be sloshing into the Cologne Bay.

In Zandvoort the Old Sea, as it had become known, lapped the broad, flat, sandy beach with small waves. The children could splash around in it without danger, and the water in June was already as warm as in a bathtub. Indeed, due to the elevated horizon formed by the structure growing into the sky, when you looked west in clear weather you felt as if you were on the bottom of a massive bowl; along its rim crawled ceaseless columns of army ants—the remote-controlled one-hundred-ton robotrucks, transporting their cargo to the construction sections and unloading it there.

When our training left us enough time, Renata and I usually headed out to Zandvoort. Sometimes Grit came with us too. Then she would tell us about the experiences she and others had had on their travels through time.

"Can I treat you to a port wine?" I asked Renata.

"No, thank you, Domenica. That's sweet of you, but I don't want to drink any alcohol. The medical treatment is having a worse effect on me than I expected. I feel as if I were coming down with the flu. I have splitting headaches."

"Is that normal?"

"Nothing out of the ordinary, according to Dr. Hekking. I'm having an intense reaction, but that's all right. I'll be glad, though, when I've finally gotten it over with."

"When?"

"If everything goes according to plan, I'm supposed to attempt my first transition on August 18. There and immediately back. That's in two weeks," replied Renata.

"And that's the reason for the whole ordeal?"

"No, the medical conditioning lasts for the rest of your life. You just mustn't forget on your return to take the necessary medications right away so that you're armed against infections."

"If I understood Grit correctly, the danger comes from us," I interjected.

"That's right," said Renata. "They can't simply send us into the past in our normal condition. For people in the fifteenth century we'd have the impact of bioweapons, according to Dr. Hekking. We have the plague on board—the measles, smallpox, scarlet fever, and God knows what else. But all those vile pathogens are so surrounded by defense units that they can't harm us. People in that time, however, don't yet have those antibodies. They would be defenseless against those pathogens, like the Indians in the days when the European conquerors came, and even more so when the black slaves came from Africa. We would cut a swath of death, the doctor explained. So we have to be disarmed, as it were. The immune system is shut down. But that means that after our return we're as vulnerable as people infected with HIV, whose immune defense has to be supported."

"I had no idea you were so well versed in immunology, Renata," I remarked.

"Didn't I ever tell you about that? Before I got the job at the Ospedaletto on Barbaria delle Tole, I had worked at the infirmary of a refugee camp near Verona. At one point a strange strain of flu surfaced there; it afflicted mainly undernourished children who had a very particular genetic makeup. There were suspicions that it came from a laboratory, but no one could prove it. I had helped identify the at-risk children to be vaccinated. I learned a lot about infectious diseases from that. I would have liked to study medicine, but my grades were too poor," she said with a smile. "For botany they were good enough."

"The idea of the medical conditioning unsettles me. Honestly, I don't like when people fiddle with me."

"But it's in the small print of our contracts, Domenica: 'The best possible medical monitoring and attention shall be provided.' Dr. Hekking will explain all that to you when you're lying in his ward for a few days. It's not at all threatening. I have the sense that the doctors at the CIA have things well in hand. After all, they look back on more than twenty years of experience with time travel," Renata reassured me.

"I'm going to order myself a port wine now anyway," I said. "What would you like?"

"I'll have a bitter lemon or a tonic."

"Okay. My treat."

Renata nodded. Her cheeks were flushed. Was it from the sun or did she have a bit of a fever?

"Ultimately, it's all even far more complicated," she went on, after the waiter had brought the drinks. "Between the destination time of 1450 and the present there are almost exactly six hundred years. For the pathogens that's a time period of several billion generations. They've gone through many mutations since then. As a traveler you encounter, so to speak, the stegosauruses among the plague bacilli and the archaeopteryx of the small-pox virus. Dangerous, but not particularly refined. That's different now. The pests have learned new things. In their genome they've accumulated experience. On top of that, they increase in number every year. They come from destroyed biospheres and from laboratory blunders. At present our organism is threatened by more than a hundred and fifty different pathogens, most of which surfaced only in the past two hundred years. That's the greatest challenge the human immune system has ever faced in its millions of years of evolutionary history. Without modern nanomedicine things would look pretty bleak for humanity. We need mercenary forces. Without the refined nanotects in our cells and in our circulation our chances of survival would not be particularly good."

"And you've been pumped full of such nanotects."

Renata rubbed her forehead. "Yes, I now have a billion firefighters on board, looking out for me, keeping my cell armada on course and making sure I don't turn into a bioweapon. A guard regiment at each pore."

I thought with a shudder of the diligent nanotects that had run amok on the boy in Venice and turned his brain within an hour into Stilton. Suddenly I had the overwhelming need for a hefty sip and emptied my wineglass in one gulp.

"My God, Renata, what have we gotten ourselves into?"

She smiled and patted my hand. "Don't worry," she said. Her skin felt hot and dry. "Dr. Hekking says sooner or later all humanity will have to be reequipped in this way if it wants to survive. We're just the avant-garde."

A supertanker came out of the High Sluice near IJmuiden and glided south toward Rotterdam through the evening sea as if on a runway made of jade-colored light. It was one of those massive old ships that had been chartered by Caritas and Bread for the World and sailed under the flag of the United Nations. The deck looked as if it were encrusted with clay, as if sediments had been deposited on it, from which withered brown undergrowth grew. It was a slum. Between pipes, pumps, and ventilators lived four or five thousand people. They were climate refugees, mostly from Bangladesh, Indonesia, or the Philippines. The tanks were released for unloading only once the immigrants had been brought to the camps of Landsmeer and Monickendam; from there, after their identity check and a medical inspection, they were brought to the sufficiently decontaminated areas of Central Europe and settled there. Oil for immigration quotas—that had been the motto of the UN since it had been dominated by an angry majority of developing countries, which were literally up to their necks in water. The tanker was escorted by three EuroForce combat helicopters to protect the people on deck from terrorist attacks by the KICOB and other militant racist groups.

"You know," said Renata, "I have the feeling that the gigantic self-repair program of the universe, which Auerbach is convinced exists, is beginning to take effect. And it doesn't surprise me at all that it's happening in our time, of all eras."

The huge ball of the sun rested on the crown of the New Dam; it seemed to collapse under its own weight and disperse. The heavy robotrucks crawled across the fiery river like an endless chain of ants. A streak of trembling red-gold lay over the water, as if applied with a thick paintbrush.

The whipping of the helicopter rotors had meanwhile gone silent. Shadows fell over the Old Sea. A thin crescent moon stood like a trophy over the sarcophagus. The army ants now bore lights in front of them. The sand was cool under our feet as we walked across the beach to the train station.

At the Centraal Station we had to transfer to a bus. Even before we had reached Java, Renata was asleep on my shoulder. I brought her to bed.

"That thing with the mirror," she said, without opening her eyes, "does that frighten you?"

I shrugged. "No, not really."

She nodded, satisfied, and immediately fell asleep again. I placed my hand on her forehead. She was hot. I sensed millions of guards swarming out and attacking my palm with concentrated defensive fire. Then I looked for a blanket and prepared a bed for myself on the sofa. I toyed with the idea of going home again for a little while—I lived on the same block, in the Archimedes House, while Renata's apartment was in the Diogenes House—but I couldn't bring myself to do so. I felt the effects of the wine. I undressed, lay down next to her, and nestled against her.

"We shouldn't get into such close relationships, you know?" she said, laughing softly.

"I know," I said, pressing her to me and enjoying the warmth of her body.

"Hold me tight," she whispered. Then she fell asleep again.

The night air blowing in from the IJ was pleasantly cool. On the opposite bank of the river, in Noord, the brightly illuminated buildings of the CIA, which extended into the riverbed, could be seen. Supposedly, a refinery had once stood there, but it had been shut down and demolished when oil became scarcer. I looked out for a long time into the dark water, on which the reflections of the many lights were in constant motion, and abandoned myself to the hypnotic effect of that dance.

Suddenly the water became choppy. Straggly patterns formed in the chaos of the reflections. A ship passed by, shadowy, almost soundless; its machinery could be felt more than heard, like the pulse of a large animal.

When I finally fell asleep, I had a strange dream. I was at the edge of a sandy desert. The dunes stretched to the horizon. It was an ancient, dead world. I stood on the ridge of a dune and looked down on a small oasis—a tiny blot of green in the terrible emptiness. It was on the shore of a dried-out sea, which fell away sharply and got lost in depth and darkness.

The gigantic blazing ball of the alien sun sank toward the horizon. The steep slopes of the canyon, black rock faces many thousand yards high made up of petrified sediments on which mats of pale drift sand hung like dead lichens, were covered with a soft pink. The shadow tide rose. In the depths it was already darkening. Could lights be seen down there between the salt domes on the bottom of the sea? Were they reflections on the last traces of water on this old world? Had its inhabitants burrowed deep down in order to huddle against the dwindling warmth at the heart of their cooling planet? Or had they long ago set off for the stars? Was this the Earth in the distant future?

The sun had set. A cold wind stirred. The stars burned over the desert. In the oasis there wasn't a glimmer of light to be seen. No moon.

I awoke. Renata was fast asleep under the protection of her bodyguard regiments. In the west a lone deep ship's siren sounded. Two or three higher-pitched ones answered.

TWO DAYS LATER I stumbled unawares into a demonstration on the Dam. I had bought a few household items in the large department store Amsterdam residents amusingly call De Bijenkorf, the beehive, and had allowed myself time to stroll through the floors. When I stepped back out onto the street, more people than usual were on the large square. They were all shouting at once, excited, though not in a hostile mood, but rather in high spirits. In front of the royal palace a few hundred seniors had gathered, holding up banners with inscriptions:

WE REFUSE TO BE SHUNTED ASIDE!

GRATIS CYBERSEX VOOR BEJAARDEN!

YOU WON'T WIPE US OUT!
WE KNOW HOW TO DEFEND OURSELVES!

I had repeatedly heard about attacks on old people's homes by young rowdies. There was talk of fatalities. A vial of Legionnaires' disease bacteria in the air-conditioning and the old people coughed and gasped themselves to death.

From the Damrak the rumble of heavy motorcycles could be heard. Oh God, I thought, so they're already here too, the Praetorians. No, it was a mixed bunch—a march of mainly dark-skinned youth. Most of them came on foot, with a few Harleys protecting the flanks and with threatening background music. In front banners were carried:

CROAK ALREADY, YOU OLD FARTS!

DISPOSE OF YOURSELVES! WE CAN'T STAND YOUR STINK!

YOU TURDS, DO YOU WANT TO LIVE FOREVER?

On the other side intense indignation vented itself when the seniors in the front rows were able to decipher the slogans. At the head of the crowd I saw a dense phalanx of rolling walkers; involuntarily I thought of siege machinery. They were pushed by women with gray ringlets and grimly determined faces. Motorized units flanked the contingent—they were electric wheelchairs. Their drivers wore petrol-colored baseball caps and vests of gray-green Kevlar.

The banners billowed toward each other; the confrontation was unavoidable. From Rokin and Raadhuisstraat police sirens could be heard. I walked to the left and rounded the massive national monument of pale stone. It looked to me like an oversized fertility symbol, adorned with escutcheons and guarded by two young men with raised hands whom a vandal had beheaded.

Suddenly a police van came speeding from Warmoesstraat and stopped with squealing brakes. Police with man-sized shields, rubber batons, and flipped-down visors jumped down and charged across the square to throw themselves between the fronts. The people all around me began to run; I was carried along by the tide toward the Grand Hotel Krasnapolsky.

"Come in, young woman! Hurry, hurry!" the doorman called to me when I hesitated at the steps—a tall, robust man whose midnight blue suit stretched over his chest and belly.

I fought my way through to the revolving door as a security screen unfolded with deafening rattling and hissing at my heels, pushing back the pressing crowd. They hammered furiously with their fists against the springy plastic segments, which had been fully inflated with a gas mixture and made opaque. The shrill voices of the passersby who had escaped into the lobby were quickly hushed in the light of the elegant, air-conditioned ambiance. A liveried bellboy directed us into a tiled corridor with seats in front of a glass wall surrounding a winter garden. The few benches were occupied in no time by agitated people, mainly tourists, who complained and chattered into their IComs because they had been separated from their family, or bemoaned the failure of the police. They calmed down when two bellboys appeared with trays and served water and fruit juices—on the house, they assured everyone, which drew a jostling crowd, especially among the locals, it seemed to me.

I seized the opportunity to look around a bit and entered a gigantic dining hall decorated entirely in lime green with dozens of tables laid with damask and silver and surrounded by palms in large pots. Over the hall vaulted a glass roof; from its girders hung large art deco chandeliers. I looked to the left and saw myself reproduced a hundred times in mirrors reflected in endless illuminated rows.

When I went out into the street again an hour later through the massive revolving door, the protective screen was retracting with a sighing and scraping into its slot in the ground. The doorman greeted me with a friendly nod. I thanked him; he nodded again, but seemed not to remember me.

Water cannons had apparently been used, for the pavement of the square was wet. The national lingam was covered with yellow foam, which also wafted onto the spread arms of the decapitated young men. The tattered banners had been heaped up next to the monument. . . . WIPE US OUT! I read. GRATIS CYBERSEX and . . . LIVE FOREVER? The wreck of a rolling walker lay nearby. A sweet smell hung in the air; probably one of those designer psychopharmaceuticals that were sprayed as tranquilizers during riots. I saw a fleet of a dozen electric wheelchairs with seniors hurtling at breakneck speed across the pavement and disappearing in orderly formation on Rokin.

"They can take care of themselves, the old people," said the doorman, nodding confidently; he bowed in perfect form as an older couple went outside through the revolving door.

"What's that smell?" asked the elegant old woman, who despite the warm weather wore a mink, with a shrill note in her cracking voice. She stopped and craned her wrinkled neck uneasily. Her companion, a trench coat over his arm, a cane with a silver knob in his hand, raised his white mustache to sniff the air.

"Vanilla," he remarked with surprise.

"But Ragni!"

The man opened and closed his fist in front of his nose as if he were pumping a rubber ball. "I'm telling you, princess, it's vanilla!"

"PLEASE UNDRESS, Ms. Ligrina," Sibyll van Campen instructed me.

"Completely?"

"Yes, completely. But if you wish, you can keep your underpants on. We'll be able to imagine them away. In the future you'll have to do without them, there's no way around that, my dear. But I can assure you—it's a *liberation*! I haven't worn them for years."

No, Sibyll van Campen didn't wear any underpants, but a see-through one-piece suit oscillating between silver and violet, which she could not possibly have put on in a normal way. Perhaps it had been sprayed on or somehow secreted through the skin like a film of sweat. In any case, it was on so tight that her shaved genital area showed clearly underneath. Her head of tousled red curls was gathered and pinned into a tuliplike shape, and over her surgically relentlessly lifted cheeks sat boldly curved glasses adorned with glaring holograms, behind which two extraordinarily alert green eyes flashed.

Sibyll van Campen was a star designer of orbital significance, a world-renowned expert on the fashions of all countries and times. She was director of the legendary Gillian Vogelsang Institute for the History of Textiles and

Dress in Leiden and the highest authority for historical productions on all the great stages of the world and the studios of the entertainment industry from Hollywood to Mumbai. For the CIA, as she assured initiates, she worked out of passion and of course without remuneration. Every transition was an honor for her and a validation, because if there were even the slightest discrepancy in the outfit with respect to the material or the accessories, a transition would not be achieved.

She circled me on her long, somewhat too-thin legs like a spider surveying its prey.

"Hmm," she said, sticking her long, aubergine-painted claws in the padding that had in recent years settled around my waist, pursing her lips, grasping me under the breasts and holding them up with a scrutinizing gaze. "Hmmm."

Sibyll van Campen nodded. "Go over there," she commanded.

Suddenly my body was covered with red meridians crossed by green circles of latitude.

"Please turn. Yes, and now in the other direction. Now all the way around. Yes, good. Now two long strides"—she demonstrated them for me—"*yooob, yooob*. And now please take short, rapid steps: *tap-tap-tap-tap-tap!* Good. Now please a curtsy to the left—knees bent—yes, now please the same thing to the right. Thank you. You can get dressed again now."

When I came out from behind the folding screen, I stopped with surprise, for I saw myself standing stark naked in the room. Sibyll van Campen circled my holograph and ran her claws over the touchscreen of her Wrist-top, which she wore like a pincushion strapped to her wrist. And suddenly my holographic avatar was covered with a sacklike linen garment held together by a narrow band between chest and waist.

"What's that?" I asked, taken aback.

Sibyll eyed me over her glasses with a schoolmarmish, reproving look. "A basquine," she said, as if it were the most obvious thing in the world, "though made of simple material, without lace."

"Sleepwear?"

She closed her eyes and raised her fingertips to her temples as if she were struggling to maintain her composure. "Where you're going, young woman, people sleep naked, with whomever—in any inn, any lodgings. Three, four, five to a bed. People will immediately assume a stigma or an illness if you sleep clothed. This here is a simple basquine. I cannot dress you as a woman of rank, or else an identity would have to be created for you.

But something like that is easily verifiable. Nobility is out of the question—though a country girl is too. You'd be in too much danger, my dear. Every cart driver, every charcoal burner would reach under your skirt. We'll fashion something in between: young widow on a pilgrimage, runaway convent girl, nun of better stock on a mission on behalf of her order—something along those lines." Oh God! My spirits sank. I watched myself curtsying. An openwork breast cloth lay over my bosom; then it disappeared again.

"No, that shows too much, is at most for special occasions, celebrations and the like. Perhaps a plastron?"

An embroidered front piece took shape.

"Not bad. Yes. But in everyday life it would be better not to be so revealing."

A modest bodice covered my nakedness; a blouselike top followed, an ankle-length skirt, a smocklike overgarment, another skirt over the first one.

"For the cold season," explained Sibyll.

A cloak appeared on my shoulders, dark, heavy, with cords and clasps as fasteners. A bonnet, another bonnet—and a third. For home, for the walk to the market, for traveling, a firm winter bonnet made of felt, almost a helmet.

"So, my dear. How do you like yourself?"

"I . . . well, I think, I . . . look enchanting."

"Sarcasm is out of place here, child. Listen to me carefully! Enchanting would be completely wrong. Mysterious—okay. There can be no objection to that. Everyone at that time signals their social status through clothing and is obligated to do so. Down to their hairstyle. You see? Also their regional background. That's the point of dress, understand? But you're traveling. You have no geographic place. You come from afar, so cannot be clearly classified. But under no circumstances should you appear too foreign, understand? The xenophobia threshold is low. On top of that, there's envy. So be careful! Still, some intimidation never hurts. Not everyone's—not every man's—prey. But not lofty either. That attracts sycophants, scroungers, parasites, thieves. There's cheating and stealing. We've learned that the hard way. Don't worry, you'll be taught how to deal with that. But for the interior the psychologists are responsible; I provide only the outward appearance. Next week, Ms. Ligrina. Everything has to be sewn by hand, after all, with special threads and yarns, of course," said Sibyll van Campen.

"Please no wooden shoes!" I pleaded; my toes still hurt from the attempt to walk in Grit's clogs.

Sibyll gave a wave of her hand. "Too peasantlike. Besides, you'll be traveling to Germany, I was told. There only the very poorest wear clogs. There's enough leather."

I was relieved.

In parting she held out her aubergine claw to me. I grasped it vigorously and gratefully, for I knew I was in good hands. I valued her competence.

"Bye-ee!" Sibyll sang, baring her teeth.

"Thanks," I sputtered, intimidated. "Thank you, Ms. van Campen."

"THE FILTH IS the worst. In the beginning, I found it hardest to sleep with complete strangers in one bed—naked!" Grit said with a chuckle, wrinkling her nose. "They're unwashed and never brush their teeth. They stink of sweat and I don't know what else. They fart and grope around on you, groan and screw next to you, and when there's finally peace and quiet, then come the fleas, the bedbugs, and the lice. But the most astonishing thing is—you somehow get used to it. It's really strange, hard to explain; somehow a sense of security, of coziness sets in, being among other people at night. You move close together, cling to each other. Outside is the wilderness— and it's really still a wilderness! Inside people snuggle up to each other like puppies."

"Or like piglets," said Renata.

We laughed. Grit liked to laugh and did so often, even though she had gone through a lot on her travels. As one of the first researchers, she had conducted fieldwork in the late fifteenth century. Grit was among the pioneers; as a historian and sociologist, she was predestined. In the 1490s, she had witnessed several witch-burnings in Trier, Aachen, and Worms and had herself only narrowly escaped prosecution for witchcraft. In Mainz she had been forced to renounce all vengeance and then leave the city in which she had been based. After six missions Grit had entered the training cadre of the CIA and was now charged with advising and educating us beginners.

Grit was a small, energetic person; she was strong and had become somewhat plump with age. As she lived in Zandvoort and often spent time on the beach, she was suntanned. She wore her gray hair short.

"Originally there were attempts to make provisions for the travelers not only temporally but also spatially. There were thoughts of inns, hostels, and the like, to offer at least a minimum of comfort. Even the founding of an order with the papal blessing had been considered, but after several simulations the idea of creating havens outside the destination-time stations was discarded. For such establishments soon attract whole flocks of needy people—among them beggars, vagrants, thieves, and all sorts of rabble. As a result, they come under the scrutiny of the authorities and quarrels must be adjudicated. Inevitably, investigations take place, questions are asked. In short, it's too risky to operate undisturbed in hiding."

"So only the people in the destination-time stations of the tunnel are a help to us as well as the trustworthy time-natives they work with," I concluded from what she had said.

"But what about the other travelers?" Renata interjected.

Grit shook her head. "No, my dear. The missions usually last only one or two months, half a year at the longest. Among the few travelers spread across the fifteenth century, you can reckon that they won't exactly be tripping over each other's feet. It can happen, of course. I've heard about it, in any case."

"Have you never thought about staying there?" asked Renata.

Grit shook her head. "Never!"

"And why not?"

Grit thought for a while, then said: "For two main reasons: First of all, there are so many illnesses, so much misery, so much brutality and indifference toward fellow human beings, so much know-it-all arrogance—and all that stems from the terrible ignorance. And you're standing there with your knowledge advanced by centuries; you could help, could save lives—and are not permitted to."

"And the second reason?" I asked, when she did not go on.

"Yes," she continued, bowing her head, even more bitterness in her voice. "It's an unfinished world. A world in a raw state. Just one example: I love music. I think that music is capable of warming the world—makes it more inhabitable. Where you're going, there's barely any music. There are the simple prayer songs of the monks, the ecstatic warbling of nuns. Granted, I encountered a few minstrels—entertaining, bold, and brilliant in their way—but the prismatic clarity of Bach, the solemnity of a Gluck or Handel, the brightness of Mozart, the pathos of Beethoven, and the pomp of Bruckner—all that lies in the distant future. That makes that world so impoverished, so cold, so cheerless . . . In any case, that's how I experienced it. I practically froze. It was like sensory deprivation. I could never feel at home there."

"With painting it's no different," I said, remembering the wings full of Madonnas from the Middle Ages in the Vatican Museums through which my father had led me before I saw the painting by Peter Wenzel, *Adam and*

Eve in the Earthly Paradise, which had appeared to me as a child like a revelation.

"That's probably true," said Grit, "but I'm not as well versed in painting as I am in music."

"It liberates," I said. "It gives the world color. And the colors are the place where our brain and the universe meet. That's how Paul Cézanne felt."

WHEN THE SUN broke through, the auditorium was interlaced with nets of white light, made by the water of the IJ on the glass roof. Auerbach looked up, frowning as he contemplated a school of fish moving westward at a leisurely pace, heading downstream with the outgoing tide. The professor, like everyone in the hall, had an unhealthy complexion from the filtered light.

"None of you are physicists," he told us, "but all of you probably know what a world line is, which every body—your body too—describes through the space-time continuum. It's the trace of its existence. In a similar way"—he drew a horizontal line across a touchscreen on his lectern, which appeared on the wall monitor like a vapor trail—"the multiverse as a whole can be depicted schematically as a sort of rope made up of countless thin, intertwined fibers, each of which represents the world line of an individual, self-contained universe. In contrast to a rope made of synthetic or natural fibers, however, we're dealing here with an active, virtually living material, which constantly buds, sprouts, and branches."

He provided the line with tendrils on both sides, until it resembled a bristle worm.

"This rampant structure unfurling offshoots extends from the beginning of time"—he wrote an alpha on the left end—"that is, from the Big Bang, to its end . . ." He drew an omega on the right end.

"The time waves or solitons are undulations that pass through this structure. They move from alpha to omega and back again—back and forth, incessantly. The rope is thereby shaken, so to speak. Through that process, the individual fibers are constantly tested for their durability. Only the strongest—that is, the established realities—withstand the strain. The branches that cannot stabilize themselves are broken off. They rot, collapse, curl up into Planck dimensions, and disappear. That holds in check the rank growth that for most physicists made Everett's quantum interpretation—the theory of realities splitting off at every moment—into a nightmarishly elaborate, not to say ridiculously overblown hypothesis, with which every theoretical physicist always felt decidedly uncomfortable. Old J. S. Bell"—Auerbach bared his teeth—"known for his understatements, called it 'extravagant' when he heard about it."

He drew a structure on the touchscreen that looked like a fertilized egg cell in advanced mitosis.

"Everett's multiverse is often compared to bath foam, with the bubbles that are formed representing parallel worlds. The foam structure grows and grows as long as enough water is flowing in. If you turn off the faucet, the foam gradually collapses. With a particular influx of water, the formation and breakdown of bubbles balance each other out. The process of breakdown becomes clear when we recall how we sent soap bubbles on their way as children. Often there were double bubbles, at times triplets, and not infrequently even quadruplets—bubbles that clung to each other by adhesion, separated from each other by internal membranes. These structures tend toward fusion—that is, the membranes disappear. Quadruplets turn into triplets, triplets into double bubbles and ultimately single ones."

"If they haven't burst beforehand," said someone in the auditorium.

Auerbach looked up and squinted.

"Objections?" he barked.

No one raised objections.

"I know the comparison with the soap bubbles is feeble," Auerbach declared gruffly. "But everyone can picture it in their mind's eye, right? That's my point." He nodded emphatically.

"Who, or what, you will ask, causes these undulations along the temporal dimension?" He moved his hands as if he were pulling on both ends of an elastic band.

I was having more and more trouble following him. My eyelids sank. The constantly moving, flickering light had a hypnotic effect on me. I saw that it affected the other listeners the same way. Neither the city planners nor the architects had considered that when they had made the bold decision to build parts of the Hendrik Casimir Institute on the north shore of the IJ underwater. The optical effect from the south, seen from Java, was impressive. The glass facade of the building slid like a glacier tongue from the shore down into the water and glowed at night like an undersea palace, which delighted tourists, but brought the users as well as the Amsterdam city fathers nothing but chagrin and immense maintenance costs.

". . . is it a sort of cosmic entity that"—Auerbach drew a circle around the omega—"sits at the end of times and tugs and shakes at the rope? An unimaginably sophisticated supercivilization, which must fear for its existence if its past crumbles, frays, is beset by Everettian division, and splits apart? Why does this entity nonetheless allow our activities, which are liable only to tangle up the fibers even more, sow disorder, and possibly weaken the sensitive structure? Why? We are permitted activities the consequences of which we cannot assess and the meaning of which remains hidden to us, but which must in some way have a positive impact. Perhaps our blind interventions usher in important new growth processes with which weak points are removed, the architecture improved, and the structure optimized. Might we through our doings unconsciously be improving its condition? Yes! We believe that we can proceed on that assumption."

Auerbach snorted.

"Now, my colleagues Surtees, McFarlane, and Beltrame go a step further in their interpretation. They see in the multiverse"—he thickened the bristle worm with decisive strokes of his data stylus—"a living creature, whose evolution is not yet complete. They regard it as a multidimensional spatiotemporal body in which billions upon billions of universes like ours are incorporated like the cells in an organism. In this body new cells are constantly being formed. The body selects those that are conducive to its well-being and promotes their thriving, while it destroys those that diminish its well-being. Is the adrenaline molecule aware of its function? Does the endorphin have any idea of its effect? Does histamine comprehend its task? Does testosterone know what it is capable of? Those are their questions directed at us. Our travelers, in their view, are assigned the role of such messenger substances. The solitons, which form the vehicle and in the multiverse body perform the function of the blood circulation, wash them to the points where they can best carry out their work. If by chance or mishap more harm than good is done, if the initiated, planned development goes off course, then—to stick with the metaphor—a cancer cell emerges. At that point, other messengers are sent to provide on-site damage control and cut off the unwanted development."

The sun disappeared, and the lecture hall now seemed like a marine aquarium darkened by algae. The main problem of the underwater buildings was the uncontrollable algae growth, which of course especially thrived in those areas where the sunlight was meant to stream in. In response, our marine biology colleagues had introduced a species of snail that had been developed by Konuki Genetics and that bore the designation Noboyushi

Number Twelve. The Japanese had supposedly had the best experiences with it in their undersea airport buildings in Tokyo Bay. Resettled in Dutch waters, however, the small, unsightly creatures displayed an entirely different behavioral repertoire. Instead of grazing the algae growth from the glass surfaces with their tiny radulae, they spurned the food supply. Were they homesick? Did they not like the taste of the water? In any case, they seemed to have lost their appetite. They conglomerated into ugly, lumpy settlements in the corners of the clerestories, wasted away, and ultimately turned into a black sludge that plunged corridors, lecture halls, and offices into gloom and darkness. Now nanobots—also a Japanese creation, from the laboratories of the NNTR in Kobe—were supposed to finally bring about a change to brightness and cleanness, but they mysteriously seemed to stay away from the sunlit areas, either because they were driven by sheer survival instinct to avoid the bombardment of intense radiation or because the algae had in the meantime developed an active agent that struck fear into the tiny machines. The nanotechnicians were still puzzling over it.

"As impressive as this SMB interpretation—the explanation offered by Surtees, McFarlane, and Beltrame—might be," Auerbach went on, "to my mind—and not only mine—it's too biologistic. To presuppose that their conceptions, derived from the model of earthly life, would have validity in the whole universe—indeed, in all universes—is an anthropocentrism blown up to absurd proportions. But the idea that these processes involve a mechanism of self-correction, of self-preservation, or self-defense is undeniable. Imagine"—now he was even soaring into pathos, which rarely happened with him—"the multiverse as a gigantic data processing network! As a supercomputer on which a cosmic repair program is running, if you will, with which all possible developments are simulated and the unwanted are eliminated . . ."

With decisive blows, Auerbach cut clusters of bristles off his projected bristle worm.

"Though we are unable to say so conclusively, it is possible that a permanent revision takes place, with the goal of an optimally edited universe, an evolution from labile to more stable states in all regions of the cosmic chronology."

He now drew a curved arrow above and below the bristle worm.

"Mockers call it cosmic fitness training. They're not even so wrong. Professor van Waalen, on the other hand, speaks of 'brushing out.'" Auerbach bared his teeth in a disparaging grin. "As for that, it should be noted that our colleague van Waalen is a practicing Methodist and on top of that a cat lover. He imagines the dear Lord tenderly brushing his Creation. But I will permit myself to paraphrase a famous saying of our esteemed colleague Einstein"—and he raised a finger—"God—does not—brush!"

"HE'S PARTIAL TO the soap bubbles for the osmotic tendencies of parallel realities. I don't find the image helpful at all," Ernesto said after the lecture. I had asked him a few questions because I did not fully grasp some of the hypotheses Auerbach had hurled at us. "With a simple experimental design, a parallel universe can be produced for a short time by means of a laser and a semipermeable mirror, only to disappear the next instant—or, to be precise, both universes merge again into one."

"That may well be. But it's still not clear to me how that's supposed to work," I replied.

"It's not easy to understand," Ernesto confirmed. "But it's a fact that the realities that arise from an Everett split, when they differ only marginally, have the tendency to reunite—with interesting uncertainties in the data, as we are familiar with from quantum mechanics."

The shadow of a ship passed over us. I looked up. The streams of bubbles generated by the turbines dispersed, sparkling in the sunlight.

"The multiverse seems to be as frugal as a Dutch housewife," I stated, completely exhausted.

Ernesto laughed. "You could put it that way. That has to do with the fact that it always strives for the state of maximum stability attainable at a given amount of energy."

"But those energy amounts must be gigantic."

"Certainly, but apparently a constant exchange with other universes is taking place. There must be an immense energy pool available, which can be drawn from for the formation of new universes," Ernesto explained.

"Which the energy flows back into when two universes fuse again," I added.

"Exactly, because the energy pool of the multiverse, as vast as it might be, can't be infinite," Ernesto remarked.

"It strives for maximum order, you say. I always thought the opposite was the case—that entropy leads to chaos."

Ernesto shook his head. "No. It leads to maximum stability at minimum energy gradients. At the end would be a cosmos full of iron atoms, if things went exclusively according to the laws of physics. But apparently the multi-verse develops according to the laws of life."

"That sounds good."

"Well, I don't know. If it's actually a living organism, then . . ."

"Then what?"

"Then it's much more incalculable. We wouldn't be able to explain it."

"This adhesion of the universes—does that have something to do with the Goldfaden-Hargitai effect?"

Ernesto shrugged. "The membranes are permeable for some physical phenomena, such as gravitational waves. Some claim for other signals too. There are apparently empathic people who claim to be able sometimes and under very particular circumstances to share in the thoughts of their dop-pelgängers in a neighboring reality. As a physicist, there's not much I can say about that. Something like that has not so far been measurable, but I wouldn't rule it out."

"Why are you smiling? That doesn't seem so farfetched to me," I asserted.

"You seem to possess that ability yourself."

"Who says?"

"Falcotti hinted at it. I met him recently at a conference in The Hague. He was quite taken with your talent. He seemed to be really proud of having discovered you."

"I have no idea why. I told him about my nightmares; that's all this dubi-ous gift has brought me up to now."

Ernesto furrowed his brow. "Maybe you belong to the new generation of time travelers that has been rumored to exist. They supposedly no longer need us scientists and technicians."

"What am I to make of that?"

He nodded gravely. "Wait and see, Domenica."

In my wildest dreams I never would have been able to imagine what that fate meant.

II

The Eye in the Sky

What is has already been, and what will be has been before; and god brings back what is past.

ECCLESIASTES

The waiters—tall, robust fellows in white shirts, colored pants, and long, dark blue aprons—had freshly stocked the three massive steel rims with candles; then they had lit them and hoisted up the wagon wheels one by one on chains hanging from the ceiling. It was about 4 P.M. The barroom of the Waag was empty; in the hot weather the patrons preferred to sit out front on the square under the large sun umbrellas. I enjoyed the peace and quiet that prevailed in the high-ceilinged, shadowy interior, the massive beams of which were now illuminated by soft candlelight.

Renata and I had picked up Grit at the institute, and then we had taken the tunnel train under the IJ to the city center to have a beer in the renowned restaurant where you often met people from the CIA. We had just sat down and placed our order when a loud male voice called over our heads: "Hey, Grit!"

Startled, I looked up. On a gallery over the open kitchen stood a broad-shouldered man who had stepped through a curtain as if onto a stage. In his right hand he held an almost-empty glass mug, while with his left he clung to the heavy burgundy material.

"Hello, Leendert!" Grit called up to him.

She did not seem particularly enthusiastic about the encounter.

"Are those the two fledgling papists you told me about?" he asked with a loud voice.

Clearly the man was tipsy. The waiter who brought us the beer looked up with a disapproving frown. Grit's acquaintance pulled the curtain completely open, revealing a room with a wall occupied by overstuffed book-shelves.

"Are you three coming up to my study or shall I come down?" asked Leendert.

"We don't want to disturb you at work," answered Grit, but he would not be gotten rid of so easily; carefully he held on to the railing, tottered down the steps, and came to our table.

"Another for me too," he said to the waiter.

Leendert wore baggy overalls and a coarse-checkered shirt. On his left temple I noticed a deep scar, which ran from his cheekbone across the corner of his eye to the top of his head and gleamed through his bristly gray fringe of hair. An accident? The scar seemed rather to suggest a saber cut. The lid of his left eye drooped and almost completely closed the eye when he looked down.

"Leendert de Hooghe," Grit introduced him. "A former colleague."

The corpulent man nodded to us and ran his fingertip over the scar. Then he sank down into a chair and, breathing heavily, drained his mug.

"What are you studying here?" asked Renata, gesturing with a nod to the gallery.

"History," he said.

"His hobby," explained Grit with a shrug. "Leendert searches for temporal paradoxes; he scours all the historical writings he can get his hands on to find evidence for the intervention of time travelers. A hopeless undertaking, but he refuses to accept that."

Leendert leaned his head back so that he could lift the drooping lid and look at her with both eyes. "Oh, Grit," he said with an indulgent smile, "old girl. We'll probably fight about this till kingdom come."

He removed his gold Rolex from his wrist and laid it on the table. "For more than ten years, ever since they've been digging their own tunnel, the Americans have been trying to undo the 9/11 catastrophe, the attack on the World Trade Center and the Pentagon at the beginning of this century. Through the intervention of a time traveler, that event is to be prevented. Look at this watch. It belonged to a man who died in the terrorist attack in New York. The man disappeared. His molecules entered the hard core of Ground Zero—that baked mass of dust, glass, plastic, and metal that was produced under heat and pressure during the collapse of the towers. As if by a miracle this watch survived." He tapped the glass over the watch face with a fingertip. "This watch got scratches and nicks, but it escaped the destruction. It works to this day. Souvenir hunters chiseled it out of the rubble or sifted it out of the debris at Fresh Kills Landfill on Staten Island and sold it like so many other macabre finds—rings, tie pins, cuff links, and writing utensils. My father bought this watch in 2002 in New York. He was proud of the thing. Some of his friends envied him for it; others regarded it as tasteless. Be that as it may. I've been wearing the thing for many years now."

He threw his head back and looked from one of us to the other.

"I ask you: What will happen to this watch if the Americans realize their plan? Will it leap back onto the wrist of its former owner?"

"Then your father will not have bought it in 2002 from an obscure souvenir hunter but in one of the luxury boutiques on the ground floor of the World Trade Center," Grit replied with a sigh.

Leendert snorted. "This watch bears a serial number and was sold before September 11, 2001, Grit. My father would not have *been able* to buy it the following year."

"Then he would have bought a different one."

"With a different serial number?"

"Of course. And you would never have known any other serial number. And the attack never would have taken place. Leendert, you overestimate the weight of the factual."

He shook his head. "No, my dear, you underestimate the weight of the factual."

"The Americans will never succeed in eliminating that fact," Renata broke in. "Just as all attempts in connection with Cattenom have failed."

Suddenly I remembered what Princess Brambilla had called it.

"A sign from God," I interjected, instantly regretting having said it.

Leendert curled his lips mockingly. "A lofty phrase," he declared with amusement. "The writing on the wall, when Belshazzar gave orders to bring the golden vessels from the temple in Jerusalem so that his whores might drink from them. '*Mene, mene, tekel, upharsin.*'" His beer belly shook with laughter.

"In any case, there seem to be things in this universe that cannot be changed, as terrible as they might seem to us, because they steered history at pivotal points in a very particular direction," Grit asserted.

"Things that Auerbach's automatic repair program doesn't want repaired no matter what," Leendert replied with a grin; he reached for his watch and brushed it over his strong suntanned wrist. "The Americans will continue to agonize over that damn 9/11/01 and I get to keep my watch. What more could I want?"

"You don't believe in God, Mr. de Hooghe," Renata interjected.

He turned to her.

"Young woman," he said in a pointedly matter-of-fact tone, "I give you credit for the fact that that wasn't a question but a statement. If you'd asked me that as a scientist, I would have felt insulted, for it would have amounted to the question: 'Do you have the courage to be honest, or are you only a hypocrite like most of the others?'"

Renata shook her head and replied: "I certainly didn't intend to insult you."

"Okay, forget it," he said crossly.

"Leendert, is that really—"

"Grit, I said it's okay. But you know my position. I find it not only questionable but also extraordinarily dangerous that the CIA has thrown in its lot with the Pope and is sending religious people to that particular destination-time. Everyone knows that at that time after the Council of Constance the situation in questions of faith resembles a powder keg."

"Leendert, stop—"

"No, damn it!" he cried, his face turning red. "You know how often I have warned of this collaboration with the papists. I've stated my reservations to Auerbach as well as van Waalen and Surtees. Oh! I've implored them. But those naive theorists refuse to acknowledge what we might wreak."

"You're seeing ghosts, Leendert. You know that I don't share your reservations. No one shares them," Grit said, growing agitated.

"Oho!" he exclaimed.

"If anyone tried to travel to the fifteenth century with the intention of exacerbating or even changing the fronts in matters of faith, the transition wouldn't work. And if, contrary to expectations, it were to succeed, then sooner or later the ambitions for power would again come to a stalemate with which the basic structure of history would be restored."

"I envy you your confidence."

"We weren't recruited for any sort of missionary work," I broke in.

Leendert made a dismissive hand movement.

"I don't mean the two of you personally. But you know what memes are, right? And religious memes are extremely dangerous. They're monsters with contempt for humanity. They're selfish and parasitic—obsessed with power and bent on absolute domination. They'll take advantage of any opportunity to expand their power, cost what it may. They're programmed to. They can't help it; they have to gain an edge. But it's high time that those Furies from dark times in which people could not yet understand the world finally departed. They've brought nothing but disaster upon the earth. But no, now a saving back door is literally being opened for them. Feedback processes are negligently being facilitated from which they can only emerge stronger to sow further disaster in the world."

"It doesn't have to be that way," Renata objected.

"But that's the way it is," Leendert replied scornfully. "Belief spawns monsters. I know what I'm talking about." He ran his finger over the scar on his temple.

"Unbelief too," I asserted. "Think of the Nazis."

"Those weren't unbelievers," he replied, shaking his head emphatically. "They had their belief system. Only it was so ridiculous that one can't even bear to think about it."

"But effective," I said.

"Of course it was effective. To be successful, a religion can never be ridiculous enough. Look at the belief system of Islamic fundamentalists, that monotheism reduced to washing instructions and degenerated into gymnastic exercises—misogynistic, self-righteous, and incomprehensibly stupid in its conceptions of the afterlife. But efficient! A clever instant religion, hatched by Salafi cynics and delivered by Wahhabi lay preachers in easily comprehensible form to the—both economically and intellectually—less-endowed people of this earth who sense their lack of sustainability and hurl their hate at the trash of the globalist Western credo."

"Or airplanes at skyscrapers," said Renata.

A rolling laugh from the depths of his throat. Leendert glanced at his Rolex. "Those were direct hits," he remarked. But then his brow darkened again, and he bellowed, "There you see what explosive power religious memes can unleash."

Angrily he pushed his empty beer mug back and forth on the table with his forefinger. "Those archaic relics are the true scourges of humanity. They produce brainless religious zealots practically choking on their self-righteousness, the certainty of their faith, and their sense of mission. And those people rant not only in Cairo, in Baghdad, in Qom, or in Islamabad, but just as much in Washington, in Warsaw, and in Vilnius."

"God knows, yes. And yet those memes seem to be important for the course of history," Grit noted.

"Yes," he said, and it sounded almost like a sob. "Like so many other monstrous things. What sort of universe is this?"

"We have only the one," said Renata. "We have to live in it. And if we are only determined enough, we'll improve it."

"If we are only determined enough . . ." he mimicked sarcastically.

"What's wrong with that?" I asked.

His right eye scrutinized me. It was a surprisingly light blue. The lid of the other one drooped limply, and for a moment I thought he was winking at me mischievously, but in his look there was no trace of cheerfulness.

"Because that's a foolish idea," he snorted. "Free will is one of the strangest illusions human consciousness has created. It's a scientifically untenable assumption, a self-deception, but it's essential for survival, that's undeniable."

"Why should it be an illusion? I can decide one way or another," I objected.

"No, you can't, young woman. Not within one universe. There you make only one decision."

"Then I make the other in another universe."

"Oh yeah? Good old Everett says hello. Here a universe in which Hus wasn't burned at the stake, there one in which Luther didn't nail up his theses, or even one in which Catholicism is swept away—wonderful!" he said excitedly, and pointed up with his thumb over his shoulder. "I've been searching for years for clues, for discrepancies in the source material, where contradictory facts might have been rearranged. Auerbach takes the easy way out. His double soap bubbles go *plop* and are one again, and van Waalen brushes his cat's fur when it's shedding. But things aren't as simple as those gentlemen think. I don't receive messages from parallel worlds."

"I do . . . sometimes," I claimed bravely, and felt Grit's and Renata's eyes turning to me. "But I . . . I'm not sure."

Leendert threw his head back and stared at me. "So you're the one," he murmured thoughtfully. "Van Waalen mentioned that. He was beside himself. 'If only Hla Thilawuntha were still among us!' he cried."

I shrugged and looked to Grit for help. She nodded gravely.

"We should go," she suggested.

"Are you familiar with the memoirs of Urban Hargitai?" he asked.

"Goldfaden-Hargitai?"

"André Goldfaden was his grandfather. He was a doctor and psychologist—a Hungarian Jew who practiced in Vienna. Later, when the Nazis came to power, he went into exile in London. His grandson published his notes at the beginning of this century. Pretty odd stuff."

"Thilawuntha believed in it," said Grit.

Leendert gave a wave of his hand. "Thilawuntha believed in all sorts of things."

"And most of the time turned out to be right."

"No one can deny that," he conceded. "He was a true genius. A shame about him. Would you like something else to drink?"

"We're leaving now," Grit said assertively.

Leendert beckoned to the waiter. "Put it all on my bill," he said. "And bring me another beer."

"Thank you," I said.

"It was a pleasure to meet the two of you."

At the door I looked back. Grit and Renata had already gone out. Leendert was sitting at the table and staring with bowed head at his freshly filled glass mug; then he rose decisively, grabbed his beer, and tramped up the stairs to the library.

"Is something wrong?" asked Grit, who had been waiting outside for me with Renata.

"What a poor, bitter man," I said.

"Well, Leendert has always been a contrarian, but not so intolerant," Grit sighed. "He used to travel as well, to the 1560s. He experienced terrible things there. At that time, the Spanish had depopulated whole villages around here. He had joined a small troop of peasants who encountered Alba's cavalry near Haarlem. He was the only survivor of the bloodbath. Sometimes, it seems to me, the injury gets to him."

IT WAS A hot day, and the air-conditioning at the institute wasn't working. I had been summoned to the medical wing. I had hoped the appointment would be canceled, but when I called, a woman's voice declared sharply that a bit of heat wasn't going to make her throw out her schedule.

I showered for the second time that morning, but no sooner had I taken a few steps than my T-shirt clung to my body.

"I'm supposed to see Dr. Hekking," I said with slight annoyance. "Do you know where he is? Dr. Willem Hekking."

A massive black man looked up from the monitor and scrutinized me silently. The whites of his eyes were shot through with yellow as if he were feverish. Beads of sweat covered his broad nose and the area above his thick upper lip.

"I've been summoned to Dr. Hekking; it's about my medical conditioning. Is he here?"

"Then your name is Domenica Ligrina."

"You know about this?"

"Of course I do."

"Then would you please . . ."

The man held out his hand to me, which was as large as a shovel and surprisingly dry. "Hekking," he said.

"Please forgive me, Doctor," I sputtered, "but with the Dutch name I'd—"

"I am Dutch."

"Oh . . ."

"As an Italian you wouldn't know, but Dutch people come in all colors— black, yellow, brown, and a few whites as well."

Dr. Hekking opened his large mouth like a yawning hippopotamus, and burst into riotous laughter. "My grandparents were from Suriname, but I was born in Duivendrecht."

He turned back to the monitor.

"Will it hurt?" I asked him.

"I will tear you to pieces and leave your remains to the nanos." His hefty belly shook cheerfully. "But you won't feel anything, that I can assure you. Despite my physique I have a reputation as a gentle doctor. Besides, we'll begin very carefully. Today I will merely take some of your blood so that I have a basis for mixing the cocktails with which I will pump you up and for programming the computer. I'll be ready for you the day after tomorrow. Prepare to be stationary for about a week."

I didn't even feel the prick.

TWO DAYS LATER I lay on a mobile sickbed. Needles were stuck in the crooks of my arms and attached to plastic tubes. The computer-operated apheresis apparatus next to me clicked and snapped, sucking blood out of my right vein like a high-tech vampire, infusing it with chemicals and nanotects, and then feeding the mixture into the left arm vein. Out of the corner of my eye I saw the measurements on the monitor. My entire blood volume was being sent through the labyrinth of the machine and returning into my body. Eventually the soft pumping sound must have lulled me to sleep.

I awoke in a darkened sickroom.

"You'll stay here a few nights so that we have you under observation," a woman's voice said softly.

I nodded and drifted off again.

The days that followed largely escaped my memory. Afterward I didn't know whether I had gotten anything to eat or had been fed intravenously. The humming and clicking of the apheresis apparatus accompanied me. At times I saw the face of Dr. Hekking over me like a dark heavenly body, then an unknown light-skinned face again. In my arm veins I felt the slight pressure of the needles, which were left in place between the treatments.

Confused dreams haunted me, but only one remained in my memory, because it terrified me. I dreamed again of that old desert world, of the oasis on the shore of the dried-out sea with its precipice that got lost in dark depths. I stood on the ridge of a high dune under a gigantic hazy sun and looked down to the oasis. I thought I saw a movement, but it might have been an illusion.

Suddenly a shadow fell over me. I looked up—and directly into a gigantic eye hovering in the sky, half filling it and staring down coldly at me. My heart stood still. I tumbled backward into the sand, and at that moment I thought I heard a shout and laughter. I awoke and listened anxiously into the darkness. No shout, no laughter. Only the soft hum of the monitoring instruments and the dull reflection of their illuminated displays on the ceiling and walls.

I couldn't stop thinking about the dream. Had I looked into the eye of God? It had stared at me so pitilessly and indifferently. I shivered.

A CRASH OF thunder woke me. When I opened my eyes, I saw Renata sitting at my bedside.

"What happened to your hair?" I asked her in confusion.

She laughed. "Nothing. A storm. It's raining. I got wet. How are you doing?"

"I don't know. I had bad dreams. I looked into the eye of God."

She nodded. "And I saw Amsterdam, six hundred years ago."

"And?"

"It was actually exactly as I'd imagined it. A filthy little dump with terribly pious residents." Renata gave me a radiant look.

"You're looking forward to going to the Middle Ages, I see."

"Yes," she said, stroking my hot forehead. Suddenly she recoiled and stared at me wide-eyed.

"What's the matter?" I asked, now frightened myself. "What did you just see?"

She had turned pale.

"Your face . . ." she whispered. "It looked as if it were burnt . . . My conditioning—it's somehow gotten stronger. I don't know."

"Forgive me, Renata. I didn't think of that. I won't ask any more questions. You came to say good-bye, right?"

She nodded.

"When do you depart?"

"Tomorrow."

I felt for her hand. "I'm sure we'll find each other," I said.

"Of course," she said. "I'll keep an eye out for you."

"Then—see you soon, Renata!"

SUNLIGHT SPARKLED ON the water.

"I'm Nurse Sietske," said the woman, pulling open the other half of the curtain at the terrace door. "May I bring you breakfast?"

"Yes, please," I said in a daze.

Through the open door I looked out at the shimmering IJ and made out the familiar contours of Java and behind it the bizarre skyline of Zeeburg. After a while I looked at the crooks of my arms. The bandages had apparently been removed earlier; the puncture points of the needles were barely visible.

Nurse Sietske was my age—full-bosomed, with a round, good-natured face and a soft rosy complexion that promised tenderness and warmth.

Gradually my head cleared. I felt energetic and full of anticipation. It seemed to me as if my senses had sharpened, as if I had gained a greater distance from my body. I had the strange feeling that I could operate it by remote control in a subtle fashion—as if I were standing behind myself and directing myself with telepresence equipment, which enabled me to speed up and slow down my physical movements. That phenomenon was completely inexplicable to me.

"That's one of the effects of the nanotects you now have on board look-ing out for you," Dr. Hekking explained during his final examination. "In a sense, an additional subsystem has been inserted in your consciousness that intensifies or dulls external stimuli—depending what sort of attention you want to give the relevant details. We call it the distance mode. It's a sort of anosognosia. The nanotects are concentrated in depots. You can mobilize them by an act of will. I'll show you what exercises you can use to do that. The nanos then colonize the ventromedial cortex and the somatosensory cortical fields in the right hemisphere. Some of the neurotransmitters are thereby blocked. At the same time, the release of adrenaline and cortisol by the adrenal glands is reduced. The main effect is as follows: Pain tolerance is heightened, without influencing the remaining sense perceptions. That's associated with a certain flattening of affect. The nanos buffer you against the external world. In other words: You will from now on be able to ap-proach with considerably more calm many things that might previously have caused your heart to race."

"Sometimes I like it when my heart races," I replied.

Dr. Hekking ran his massive paw gently over my cheek. My whole head would have fit in his cupped hand.

"You don't need to give that up, my dear. On the contrary. But when you don't want it, it will not come into play. That has its advantages. Not only where you're going."

I nodded.

"You're protected from infections, and if you should suffer injuries, you'll recover faster. On top of that, for the duration of your operation, you will be unable to conceive, so you won't menstruate."

"So you've completely disarmed me biologically."

"As a bioweapon, yes. But apart from that . . ." He let out his riotous laughter. "Ms. Ligrina will be staying with us another two days," he said to the nurse. "I still have to perform a few examinations."

"Have there been any complications?" I asked, when he had left.

"Don't worry," said Sietske, stroking my temples with her soft hand. "Everything is absolutely fine."

But my sharpened perceptiveness told me that she was somehow unset-tled.

WHEN I MET Ernesto at the institute, I asked him whether everything had gone according to plan with Renata's transition. He shrugged. "I wasn't there myself, but I heard that she caught a powerful soliton, a real energy monster. It might have carried her somewhat farther than to the year 1450."

"What does 'somewhat farther' mean?"

"Maybe 1448 or 1445. It's not possible to say exactly. But someone is on site—at the target point in time, I mean. He'll send her back if she should be too wide of the mark. So don't worry," Ernesto reassured me.

Renata didn't reappear. At least not in the weeks that followed. So I dared to heave a sigh.

III

The Papers of Dr. Goldfaden

A radiolarian, in a drop suspended,
Said wouldn't it be truly splendid
If other worlds existed
In which radiolarians subsisted.

For that he earned only taunts and jeers,
As has many a dreamer through the years.
Ridicule and laughter were especially inspired
By the thought of the volume of water required

To pour out a universe so immense.
Ergo, said detractors, it's common sense
That there's only this world, no others around,
For where should so much water be found?

À LA CHRISTIAN MAYER

Christian, who knew Urban Hargitai from his university days with Professor Pfleiderer in Innsbruck, had invited him to Dornbirn for his birthday. "Urban," he had said, "don't tell me you have no time. In August there's not much going on in the software industry, is there?" Not much had been going on all year, and there was so much sarcasm in the question that it hurt. Christian knew, of course, that he hadn't had much success yet and, sensitive as he was, he quickly added: "I haven't sold my new novel yet either, but we'll ce-celebrate anyway. A few interesting people will be there, among them many colleagues. You're going to co-come, right?"

Swayed by Christian's expression of solidarity in failure, Urban Hargitai had accepted the invitation to travel to Vorarlberg on the weekend of August 12–13. It had indeed been a lousy year, just like the previous ones.

After completing his studies in mathematics—and on the side in astronomy—he had managed to get a job at Erste Bank, where he toiled as a programming slave, but the night work, which was necessary in order to get the crashed programs running by the next morning, had worn him out. Then, like at least ten thousand other computer specialists in Vienna, he had come up with the idea of going freelance. URBAN HARGITAI: SOFTWARE CONSULTING—blue on silver. The business card was impressive, but apparently only to him. The market was saturated with inexpensive special programs for any conceivable need. Things were moving only sluggishly, and the frustration gnawed at him . . . If his mother hadn't repeatedly sent him some money . . . But they would celebrate anyway . . .

Friday was hot and muggy. Hargitai hadn't felt well the day before. Probably a cold, he thought, one of those nasty summer viruses that gum up your brain until you're no longer capable of thinking clearly. But somehow he had the need to leave Vienna as quickly as possible. The city was stifling, loud, and full of sweaty tourists pushing their way noisily through the streets of the center and overcrowding the cafés and taverns.

As a precaution, Hargitai bought a flask of rum and a pack of tissues at the kiosk in the train station hall. Thus armed, he boarded the IC-566 Lower Austrian Tonkünstler Orchestra, which would arrive in Bregenz at 7:30 P.M. Christian had promised to pick him up. In the second car he found an empty compartment. Contrary to his expectations, the train on that Friday afternoon was only sparsely occupied; most of the Viennese were on vacation.

In St. Pölten he already regretted having taken the trip. He broke out in a sweat all over his body, and his headache intensified. When the buffet cart passed through, he ordered a tea, mixed in a substantial amount of rum, and drank the whole cup with slow sips. Then he poured what remained in the flask into the cup and drank the rum straight.

In Wels an older German married couple clattered into the compartment with three suitcases. The man held the reservation under his nose and informed him that they had a claim to the window seats. The two of them eyed him with disgust as he sipped his drink and blew his nose into tissues. Was he supposed to apologize to them for having a cold? Dark thoughts loomed in his brain: Perhaps he would manage to infect the Germans. He blew his nose copiously. In Salzburg they got off.

Around that time Hargitai felt increasingly drunk. But at least the headache had subsided, he said to himself, putting his feet up on the seat across

from him and closing his eyes. He must have fallen asleep shortly thereafter, for when he looked out the window he saw that the train had already
reached Innsbruck.

The sky in the west toward the Arlberg was black; the mountains seemed
to Hargitai to be flooded with sulfurous light. He took his backpack and
stepped out onto the platform. He was met by a hot, gusty wind, which
raised dust and scraps of paper. In the north rumbled thunder.

From that point on, his thoughts became confused.

Hargitai got back on the train, closed the compartment door and the
curtain, and lay across the seats in order to sleep through the last stretch of
the journey as well. In Bregenz I'll be sober again, he told himself.

A loud crash of thunder woke him. Rain lashed the window. He sat up
and looked out. Lightning flashes bathed the steep wooded slopes in chalk-
white light. The train was moving downhill and braking before the bends
in the tracks. It was not completely dark outside; the lights were on in the
car. He peered out through the rain-streaked window—and suddenly for a
fraction of a second lived through a nightmare: The front locomotive was
heading in a curve toward a ravine that a bridge should have spanned. But
the bridge was gone. The railroad tracks jutted, bent downward, into emptiness, and ended in midair.

That same moment he heard a shrill screech. He was hurled out of his
seat. His knees struck the seat on the opposite side, and his face smashed
into the headrest over it. The front part of the car reared and doubled up
like a caterpillar. The roof buckled and rippled with a creaking groan; the
windows burst, and a hail of glass shards sprayed over his head and back.
The lights went out. Passengers screamed. From outside dim light seeped
in. Water rushed loudly nearby.

For a moment the car remained in its slanted position; then, with scraping and squealing, the end he was in sank lower. Directly before his eyes
the upholstery suddenly opened, and through the fabric pierced the end of
a dark iron beam. He tried desperately to throw his head back—and realized with horror that the compartment had folded up in such a way that he
was clamped between the facing seats. Ice-cold water foamed through the
crumpled window opening onto his face and the iron beam, which had
stopped just before his eyes but protruded threateningly toward him. Suddenly the car collapsed further in on itself and the metal began to move
again. That was the last thing he was aware of.

*   *   *

THE COLDNESS WOKE him. Hargitai was soaked and freezing. All around was darkness. Somewhere nearby a woman was whimpering. He felt something mushy in his lap and between his fingers. Mud? Torn leaves? His whole body hurt, because it was wedged in that contorted position. His legs were numb from the knees down. When he tried to move his shoulders, he felt a fierce pain in his forehead, which the icy water had numbed. He cried out and tried to touch his face with his hands—to no avail; they were stuck. He lost consciousness again.

A LOUD NOISE brought him out of his unconsciousness. Rattling chains struck the car. He heard a male voice shouting orders. Winch engines whined, cables grated, and with a groaning creak the car was lifted up. Suddenly he could move his head again and his hands were freed.

"Hey, there's another," said a male voice nearby.

He turned his head with difficulty in the direction of the voice, but couldn't make anything out.

"Oh God!" said the voice.

HARGITAI GOT TO his feet and groped his way to the bathroom. He turned on the light and looked in the mirror. His face above the mouth was covered with a flat, sticky mass out of which two dead eyes looked at him as if out of a ski mask. His legs buckled, and whimpering with horror he sank down onto the toilet seat. He felt his bladder emptying, though he hadn't had the strength to pull down his pajama pants. There was something comforting about the warmth streaming down his thighs. He yielded to it and felt it carry him away into the darkness.

WHEN HARGITAI CAME to again, days seemed to have passed. That train wreck . . . He had been rescued. He was injured, but he experienced no pain, felt strangely removed, as if the accident hadn't befallen him personally. He was lying in a bed. Was he in a hospital? Somewhere a regular electronic signal could be heard. Was he in an intensive care ward? Perhaps he had been brought to Innsbruck by helicopter. His hands lay on smooth sheets. Darkness surrounded him.

His face . . . His fingers felt bandages. So it was actually true. Carefully Hargitai stood up and groped his way to the bathroom. But it was his bathroom . . . his bathroom in his apartment on Wiedner Hauptstrasse! He turned on the light and plucked at the bandages. They came apart like cobwebs under his fingers. But what was revealed was not a face at all, but a rosy oval surface with no hint of eyes, nose, or mouth. What had they done to him? What had they done with his face? He ran his fingers over the strange skin. It appeared smooth, but had a distinct texture; it felt like hand-made paper, hard and yet soft. Had he undergone plastic surgery? Had his face been covered with artificial skin? He stared at the reflection. How could he see it in the mirror at all without eyes? Did that texture consist of sensors that sent nerve impulses to his brain? Was he still a human being?

Hargitai doubled up and vomited into the toilet bowl until the bilge of his stomach made his mouth bitter. He wiped his mouth with the back of his hand; his lips were dried out, hot and chapped. Had software been pro-grammed into the artificial head, leading him to believe he was still him-self?

Then he straightened up and looked in the mirror. But he saw only the white door behind him, on which his blue bathrobe hung; apart from that, the mirror was empty. Had he become invisible? An error in the software?

"What's wrong with me?" he whimpered helplessly.

Hargitai opened the door—and stood in his bedroom in his apartment.

"It went on like that for three days," said Hargitai. "Over the whole week-end. I had a fever and horrible headaches. Probably I was hallucinating."

"Why didn't you call me?"

"I'm sorry, Mom, but I was completely out of it. The telephone must have been ringing incessantly. The answering machine was full. Christian called a dozen times. He knew I'd been on the crashed train. But I must have gotten off in Innsbruck. I don't know why. Maybe I wanted to buy an aspirin or another flask of rum. When I got to the platform, the Intercity was gone. I saw only the taillights of the rear locomotive. How I got back to Vienna and to my apartment I can't say for the life of me. I have no idea. How lucky I was that I missed the train became clear to me only when I glanced at the *Standard* on Monday."

He pushed the newspaper from August 14 across the table.

Vienna/Bludenz—"This is the horror vision you have sometimes," said Martin Purtscher, the governor of Vorarlberg: A train is flung into a ravine by a collapsing bridge. The crushed cars lie below like Legos. Strewn around them are the dead and severely injured.

Friday, just before 7 PM. A violent thunderstorm unleashes a mudslide. The masses of mud and debris cause the Masonbach Bridge to collapse. At that very moment the IC-566 Lower Austrian Tonkünstler Orchestra Vienna-Lindau with 200 passengers on board has reached the bridge. The express train plunges with the locomotive and three cars about 130 feet into the depths. The fourth car is derailed and suspended over the abyss. The eight cars behind it are stopped by the wedge. 17 people are severely injured. The locomotive driver, a 26-year-old woman from Vorarlberg and a six-year-old boy from Lower Austria lose their lives.

Hargitai's mother cast only a fleeting glance at the newspaper page. Her mind seemed to be elsewhere. He was surprised that she didn't show more sympathy. Finally, he said: "I don't know how to explain it, but I *experienced* that crash, literally right in front of my eyes. My face was maimed. It was exactly as it's described here. I *saw* it! I *felt* myself get injured and stuck in the car! How is that possible?"

His mother only nodded. He looked at her in astonishment.

"Well, it was only a dream, of course," he said dismissively, a bit disappointed about her seemingly indifferent reaction.

He watched her furtively as he cut up the apple pie with his fork and ate it. She had turned sixty in March but was still an attractive woman. Her short black hair showed the first gray strands, which actually looked elegant. Her dark eyes were lively as always; time had engraved itself only in the area over her upper lip and on her cheeks over the corners of her mouth, a waffle pattern forming where there had previously been mocking dimples.

After a while, his mother put aside her pastry fork, gave her son a serious look, and said softly, "No, Urban, it wasn't a dream. I had hoped that you would be spared this, because I had never noticed any trace of it in you. But you seem to have inherited the Goldfaden gene after all, with which your grandfather and his father and his father as well were afflicted."

"Goldfaden gene?" Hargitai asked uncomprehendingly.

The tall clock out in the corridor rattled as it struck. It was two.

"You know that your grandfather was known as the dream doctor," she went on.

"I remember Dad sometimes making fun of that."

She raised her head and stuck out her chin. "Your father made fun of many things. For him it was all just crazy talk. He had other interests—God knows! Let's not talk about that." She drained her cup. "Do you want another piece of pie?" she asked her son.

"Yes, please. But what's the deal with the gene?" asked Hargitai.

She didn't respond to his question.

"You were only ten when Grandpa died. You were entering Gymnasium. I had put away his things and packed everything in the suitcase in which he kept his notes. At the time I decided not to tell anyone about it. Not you either. Especially not you. But now the moment seems to have come for me to explain to you about that damn family inheritance."

"What are you talking about, for heaven's sake?"

"It's the gift of seeing things that haven't occurred but might well have occurred," she said emphatically.

He looked at his mother wide-eyed.

"I've often had such strange dreams, but . . ."

"They're not *strange*, Urban. God knows," she said with a bitter laugh. "They're *horrible*. They shattered your grandfather's mind. Back in London. The Nazis, the bombings. I was still little; there was a lot I didn't understand. Father had fled with Mother to England in 1937, eluding the Nazis' clutches. But that decision didn't do him much good. He had physically escaped the torments of the concentration camp, but in his dreams he suffered them, was there night after night. He had tried laudanum, sleep deprivation, later morphine."

"But they were just dreams. Nightmares . . ."

"He didn't think so. He regarded it as a form of empathy. He believed firmly that he had a doppelgänger, who had to suffer for him, in his place, the agony and death he had avoided by fleeing. That doppelgänger, he was convinced, possessed the power to exchange souls with him in dreams."

"I'm sorry, Mom, but that's a completely outlandish idea," Hargitai broke in.

"No. Grandpa wasn't only a doctor; he had also always been interested in psychology. He was familiar with several cases. He had taken notes on them—patients who had similar dream experiences. I still remember Joshua Seidenspinner well. He often came to visit us, because he had no family. Josh was a gangly young man, who could make wonderful paper cuttings. I was fascinated by his dexterity. In a matter of minutes, he would snip whole garlands of rabbits, horses, birds, lizards, flowers, or faces out of blackout paper. He too suffered from that empathy, had the same nightmares as Father. One day in early May—the war in Europe had just come to an end—he stood in the doorway, pale and trembling. 'We died, André,' he said to Father. 'The dreams have stopped.' Father nodded. 'Don't say such things!' cried Mother. But Josh would not be deterred. He was out of his mind. He pulled a copy of the American magazine *Life* from his coat pocket, in which for the first time photos of the German concentration camps were shown, horrifying photos. He opened to a page and laid it on the kitchen table, pointing with a trembling finger at the picture of a man who had squeezed halfway out from under a wall made of boards and met his death. 'That's Daniel, my friend. We were together until the end, when they locked us in the barn and set it on fire. He said we would make it. I was close behind him. But we didn't make it.'

"Mother had glanced at the photo, grabbed me by the shoulders, and pushed me out of the room. Scarcely had the door shut behind us when I heard a scream unlike any I ever heard again in my life. Half an hour later they took Joshua away. I never saw him again, and my parents never mentioned him again. What remained of him were rabbits, horses, birds, lizards, flowers, and faces made of blackout paper. Mother eventually burned them, when we packed our things and returned to Vienna. She believed firmly that those horrors were over, a thing of the past . . ." Hargitai's mother broke off. After a while she then said softly, "But they weren't over. No, they weren't over."

"The concentration camp dreams?" asked Hargitai.

"There were different ones. The Americans, Father claimed, had dropped the Bomb on Vienna. He was out night after night treating the mutilated and radiation-poisoned, providing relief to the dying and bringing the dead to the Franz-Josephs-Kai, where they were cremated before daybreak."

"I'm sorry, Mom, but that's completely crazy," he blurted out.

"You're saying that after describing your completely crazy experiences to me?" she replied vehemently; she pressed her napkin to her mouth and wiped away her tears.

"Well, the train crash really did happen. But the Americans never dropped an atomic bomb on Vienna. That's a difference, isn't it?"

She shrugged. "And if there weren't only one reality?"

"But, Mom, that's absurd."

"Oho! No, my dear, there you are mistaken. There's an entry in your grandfather's notes that he regarded as very important. It was an experience that seemed to have been a revelation for him. That was why he recorded the scene in detail. It was a conversation with his friend Samuel Lieber-mann, who had returned from exile in the United States. Both of them had attended the Albertus Magnus Gymnasium in the eighteenth district and knew each other well from there. After his return in the late fifties, Lieber-mann had a lectureship at the University of Technology. He was a theoreti-cal physicist—quantum physics, if I remember correctly. They often met at the upper end of the Naschmarkt for a glass of sparkling wine and a few oysters. Grandpa had his practice a few paces around the corner, on Getrei-demarkt. Liebermann was a funny bird who enjoyed a drink, was witty and full of unconventional ideas. Grandpa liked him."

"Do those notes still exist?"

"He had kept all the notes in a suitcase. After the funeral I put it in the attic and never touched it again."

"Can I take a look at it?"

With a deep sigh Hargitai's mother stood up. "I had always hoped I wouldn't have to show it to you. But it's probably better that I do, so that you know what you have to contend with."

They climbed up to the attic. Under the roof of the single-family house, summer had nested. Hargitai's mother carefully lifted a bald, dusty cellu-loid doll from a medium-sized brown cardboard suitcase with reinforced corners and pressed it to her chest.

"This is Liz," she said. "A real Schildkröt doll. I brought her back with me from London. Liz and I told each other stories during the nights in the air-raid shelters. Long stories, for we believed firmly that nothing could pos-sibly happen to us as long as a story had not yet been told to the end—no matter how many bombs the Nazis dropped on us."

She placed Liz in a beige wicker baby carriage and blew the dust off the suitcase lid. *Dreams* was written on the taped-on yellowed label with a broad fountain pen, in that old German script that only few could still decipher, and underlined twice. The clasps were rusty and gave way grind-ingly. In the suitcase were several sheaves of preprinted yellow patient cards, which were folded into pockets in DIN-A5 format, as doctors had used them before the advent of computers. They were arranged in blocks and held together by pale rubber bands, which had become brittle and so greasy with age that they stuck to the box like limp worms.

"Are you taking it down with you?" she asked.

"I'm just going to have a quick look at it."

His mother left him alone.

He began to rummage through the documents. Most of them were dream logs of patients in alphabetical order. Some bore in the margins the note "probably fabrication," others "correlation possible." Attached were newspaper clippings, mostly reports of accidents, of shipwrecks, names marked with crosses on casualty lists. The relations of the facts to the dream descriptions appeared quite vague to Urban; sometimes he couldn't discern any connection at all. One of the sheaves contained his grandfather's records of his own dreams. Some of the texts were harrowing, images of awful, unimaginably brutal events, which had haunted him for months and years. He also came across a copy of *Life* magazine. It was the issue of May 7, 1945. It was folded open to page 34. Among other things, the page displayed the photo of a young man who had squeezed his head, shoulder, and left arm out from under a wall made of boards—indeed, had literally tunneled through the hard ground in his mortal fear before the flames had overtaken him nonetheless—Joshua Seidenspinner's friend Daniel.

Another sheaf contained theoretical considerations. Urban hadn't known that his grandfather had had a twin brother who had died on the day of their birth. For a long time, the idea seemed to have preoccupied him that that brother had not really died, but lived in a sort of intermediate world, from which he made contact with him in dreams. *I'm firmly convinced*, he wrote at one point, *that there are perhaps not many, but nonetheless a considerable number of people who possess the gift of communicating with dream worlds in which things take a different course than in this our world, dream worlds in which a divergent fate befalls their doppelgängers.*

Urban raised his head and closed his eyes. The interplay of sun and cloud shadows was chanted by the metallic creaking of the gutters expanding and contracting in their attachments. The slavery of matter under the inexorable laws of thermodynamics, a constant senseless back-and-forth of energy, which obeyed the thrust toward entropy. Those were calculable and comprehensible physical facts, but what sort of laws would enable the human brain to depart the limits of its reality and perceptually infiltrate other realities?

Finally he came across the notes on the pivotal conversation with Samuel Liebermann.

At that time I had lapsed somewhat into parapsychological speculations, studying the life courses of identical twins who had lived apart for a long time, but I had the sense that this wasn't getting me anywhere.

I had once again met Sam for lunch at Strandhaus; we had drunk a fresh Chablis and were in a cheerful mood. As we strolled toward Karlsplatz, I noticed that one of Sam's shoelaces had come undone and was dragging through the puddles.

"Your shoelace is untied, Sam," I said.

Sam stopped and looked down at himself thoughtfully. Then he scratched his side-whiskers and shook his head.

"The price of tying it would be too high," he said.

"What do you mean?"

Sam made a theatrical gesture that encompassed the silhouette of the city before us. "A new Karlskirche, a new Secession—even if unfortunately still without the golden head of cabbage—a new Stephansdom, a new Vienna along with its environs, a new Austria—God forbid!—a new Europe, in the end a new solar system, not to mention the galaxy and the universe. Tell me, André, doesn't that sound somewhat too costly to you too? Well, then."

He shuffled on impassively, the open shoelace trailing behind him.

"Are you crazy?" I asked.

"Not at all," Sam replied with dignity. "That's what it would indeed amount to."

"If you bent down and tied your shoelace?"

"That is correct," he replied.

"Would you allow me to tie it for you?"

"Please. In doing so, you would relieve me of the great responsibility, my friend, of having doubled the world—no, the universe."

I kneeled down and tied his shoe.

"All right, seriously now," I groaned, as I stood back up. "What do you mean by all this?"

"That the world reproduces itself with every decision made."

"And you believe that?" I asked him.

"I haven't completely made up my mind yet, but the idea is remarkable. An extremely interesting interpretation of quantum theory. Elaborate, yes, but substantially more simple than the Copenhagen interpretation, which not even Einstein understands—or rather doesn't have a high opinion of, because it presupposes that the human mind can through a mental effort force matter in a mystical fashion to arrive at a decision."

"And I don't understand you."

"Hugh Everett is my colleague's name. A fabulous man. I know him personally. He wrote his dissertation under Wheeler in Princeton. I wouldn't have thought him capable of it. But his idea is really ingenious. I agree with him, although the united physics community will come at him with Ockham's razor and tear him to pieces," said Sam.

"And what does this boy wonder claim?"

"Nothing less than the following," said Sam, raising his sidewhiskers toward new horizons. "Every decision made brings into being a new universe—whole, complete. A universe with untied shoelaces and one with tied shoelaces. You've actually made things even more complicated, because you relieved me of the decision. Probably we're now dealing with one or two additional universes. But a couple more or fewer don't matter anymore at this point."

"Are you serious, Samuel—I mean, as a physicist?" I asked.

"Absolutely serious."

"Does that mean that universes are constantly coming into being in which the same people live as here?"

"Similar people, André, not the same, for they decided differently a moment before. And from that moment on they diverge from each other," Sam replied.

"That's the solution! But where could those parallel worlds be?" I asked him.

Sam shrugged.

"A hairbreadth to our right, to our left, above us or below us. A millisecond ahead of us or behind us . . . Who knows?"

"You're frightening me terribly, Samuel," I said. "It takes my breath away. I'm carrying my doppelgänger around with me like a Siamese twin. What am I saying! It's not only one twin. It's many of them. One weighs on my chest, another I bear on my back, they walk to my right and left, cling to me and encumber me."

"You can't feel them," he said reprovingly.

"Oh, yes, I feel them, God knows!"

"That's nonsense, André. The alternatives have split off from our reality. They're inaccessible to us."

I shook my head. "That's where he's wrong, your friend Hugh Everett. The borders of reality are not impermeable—at least not for everyone."

"What are you saying?" asked Sam.

"*I've experienced it myself with great suffering, all my life. I experience it again and again.*"

"*Oho!*" Sam replied, raising his eyebrows and pointing to me. "*The dream doctor. Am I right?*"

"*Yes,*" I said, grabbing his arm. "*And perhaps I'll be able to prove it one day.*"

"*Be careful, André Goldfaden. You're on thin ice. I can assure you that Everett would not exactly be pleased with your interpretation of his interpretation.*"

It's true, Urban Hargitai's grandfather had written under this. *This theory has something monstrous about it. It's repellent in its unrestrained extravagance, in its boundless inflation. But it's the only plausible explanation of what I repeatedly experience. Still, when I really try to grasp it, all logic melts away.*

Well, thought Hargitai, it might have seemed that way to him. His grandfather, like many scientists striving for truth before him, still thought entirely in the categories of Aristotelian logic and according to the biblical imperative: "Let your word be 'Yes, yes' or 'No, no.'" But in the face of quantum phenomena, those rigid intellectual templates no longer got one anywhere. Hargitai's grandfather had ultimately given up and packed the results of his research in a cardboard suitcase and stuck a label on it, on which he wrote *Dreams* with a fountain pen, thickly underlined twice.

URBAN HARGITAI TOO had to face the fact that with his mathematical skills and with the help of sophisticated programs he didn't get much further. He had systematized the dream logs and entered them into the computer in order to correlate them with events that had occurred or had been narrowly avoided such as thwarted bomb attacks, near-collisions of airplanes, and similar things. Correspondences emerged. Sometimes it seemed, according to the dream logs, that in neighboring realities such events had not been successfully avoided. Here and there probability clusters formed, but they were hard to interpret. Hargitai could superimpose the framework of virtual realities on the texture of reality and slide it back and forth as much as he wanted, but no matches could be determined. Again and again new intermediate layers appeared that could not be integrated.

He tried the matrices developed by Bernard de Vyse for the programming of computer strategy games. But he had to capitulate in the face of the nodes, for chains of events proceeded from them that led through various reality planes, over which probabilities of event patterns again smeared.

It was clear to Hargitai that an event could take place simultaneously in several—indeed, in a great many realities: The train crash on the Arlberg could not possibly have taken place only in this reality, but at least in numerous others as well. He had—if his vague memory did not deceive him—boarded the train going in the opposite direction in Innsbruck. But he might just as well have boarded it in Wörgl and returned to Vienna—or already in Salzburg, in Attnang-Puchheim, in Wels or Linz—or even already in St. Pölten or in Hütteldorf. He might have declined Christian's invitation and not taken the journey to Bregenz at all. Or Christian might have forgotten to invite him or decided not to have a party in the first place. In all those virtualities the train crash would have occurred on the evening of August 11, 1995, and in 10^{100} universes in addition.

Urban Hargitai realized that polyreal mathematics was beyond his abilities. He packed his grandfather André Goldfaden's documents back in the old cardboard suitcase, put his CDs and disks in with them, used scotch tape to stick the yellowed label with *Dreams* written on it back on the lid, and pushed it under his bed.

A FEW WEEKS later he received an e-mail from a Dr. Misrun Ardita, who was staying in Vienna for a conference.

Dear Herr Hargitai,

In a roundabout way it has come to my attention that you are the grandson of Dr. André Goldfaden and are in possession of the research notes of the deceased. In insider circles—I too work in the field of extradimensional empathy—your grandfather is regarded as a pioneer, even though he never published his findings. I am also aware that you too have become active in the field. As I am currently staying in Vienna, I would very much welcome the opportunity to meet you and speak with you. Please suggest an appropriate place and time.

Many thanks in advance for your kind response.

I'm looking forward to our conversation with great interest.

With best regards,
Dr. Misrun Ardita

Urban Hargitai wondered what sort of "roundabout way" that might have been. After all, his mother had said that her father had spoken only within his closest circle of friends about his gift and his inquiries into the phenomenon of parallel world empathy. And that was even truer in his case. His curiosity piqued, he agreed to the meeting.

URBAN HARGITAI AND Dr. Ardita met on a warm spring day at Café Schwarzenberg. The weather permitted them to sit outside. Dr. Ardita was a Dutch man of Indonesian descent, about thirty years old, and had an engaging, straightforward nature that instantly won over Urban. He wore a brown-and-red-patterned sarong and a blousonlike white shirt. His thick black hair fell over his ears. He had drawn one leg under his behind, a common sitting posture among Asians. Several patrons as well as the waiter seemed to find that somewhat too casual, but Dr. Misrun Ardita ignored their disapproving looks and spooned a cup of chocolate ice cream with whipped cream. On the chair next to him was a travel bag made of a colorful exotic fabric. Dr. Ardita jumped up and greeted Urban Hargitai like an old friend. Hargitai placed the cardboard suitcase on the table and snapped open the locks. Dr. Ardita flipped through the material and read one page or another. The chocolate ice cream melted.

"Most of it I've transferred to disks," declared Hargitai.

Dr. Ardita nodded. "That's very helpful," he said. "How would you feel about publication?"

"I've spoken to my mother. She can't decide whether to give her consent regarding the personal . . . well, experiences of her father in the concentration camp."

"I understand. But they are, of course, of particular relevance. Your grandfather had—in my view—a remarkable narrative talent. May I ask you to speak with your mother again about that point?"

Out of the corner of his eye Urban caught a movement in the travel bag on the chair between them. He turned his head and glimpsed an unusually large spotted rat that had climbed halfway out of the bag, its front paws resting on the zipper. It sniffed in his direction and scrutinized him with intelligent eyes.

"Beautiful day today," it said.

Urban Hargitai very nearly dropped his cup.

"Allow me to introduce," Dr. Ardita said, without looking up from his reading material, "Don Fernando."

The rat had withdrawn again. None of the patrons seemed to have noticed anything.

"Did you train the animal?" Hargitai asked in shock.

Dr. Ardita raised his eyebrows. "Don Fernando is no animal. He's my friend and partner."

"You're joking."

"That's no joke," replied Dr. Ardita, laughing cheerfully.

Urban Hargitai wasn't completely certain, but he thought he heard a chuckle from the bag.

IV

The New Clothes

Visitors from the future cannot know our future any more than we can, for they did not come from there. But they can tell us about the future of their universe, whose past was identical to ours.

DAVID DEUTSCH

The delivered clothes had a strange charm—hard, durable, a bit cool and rough on the skin, but well made and of a simple elegance.

I wore them in my apartment in order to get used to them. Without underpants, however, I felt like an exhibitionist—a bit perverse and shamelessly accessible. Not even two or three skirts helped with that; nor did a cloak. I simply felt naked. The basquine was slit open in front. It slid down on its own when you undid the band under the chest. What refinement! Sleepwear with a quite special attraction! But I would have to remove it, and it would take a tremendous amount of willpower for me to sleep with three or four completely unknown naked women in one bed. The thought alone already plagued me.

A skirt made of fustian, one of wool, one of calico—all earth-colored, brown, gray, discreet. The cloak was made of dark brown wool, cut wide, roomy; it felt almost like a dwelling and was lined with rabbit fur for the cold days. "Just in case the transition doesn't work out in a punctual fashion and you arrive in winter," Grit had said. "But what's a botanist supposed to do in winter? If everything goes according to plan, you'll simply take out the fur."

The boots too were lined with rabbit fur. The stockings scratched. They felt somehow greasy. Sheep's wool. Had the beasts rolled in thistles before being sheared to take revenge?

"You'll get used to it," Grit reassured me. "And always keep a close eye on your clothing! Make sure no one steals it from you! The people at that time steal like ravens."

Yes, the ravens! They particularly enjoy eating the eyes of the hanged, sprang to my mind. As I gave vent to my unease, Grit warned me again: "It's better not to get too close, if you see gallows—or even a gallows tree, from which they hang by the dozens in all stages of decomposition. It's not only a horrific sight; feral dogs often prowl there, which can be rabid."

A wave of dizziness came over me. I would have so much to get used to. Oh God, what had I gotten myself into?

THAT NIGHT I was again visited by the frightening dream. I stood on the high dune in the endless desert. I looked up. The sky was empty and illuminated by the first glow of dawn. Below me, in the oasis on the shore of the vanished sea, a light could be seen. There must have been people there.

Suddenly a roar rose behind me. When I turned around, an arc of fire burst from the sand, a vaulting eruption. Lava flowed from the gaping opening and spread to both sides; it flooded the dunes and buried them underneath it. And then the edge of a massive sun ascended over the horizon, threatening to fill the whole sky. The photon storm of its light lashed the dune ridge, dispersing the sand like smoke. I felt the impact of the solar wind on my skin like a sudden hot gust. Horrified, I turned away and stumbled down the flank of the dune toward the oasis.

"Help me!" I shouted. "Oh God, help me!"

But I saw no one and heard no reply.

ON ONE OF the days that followed I had spent the morning at the Botanical Institute on the Nieuwe Keizersgracht. At noon I had called it a day and walked toward the Centraal Station to have chili con carne at the Havana Social Club on Geldersekade.

I had just taken a seat at a table under a sun umbrella on the sidewalk and ordered a soda when three electric wheelchairs turned from Prins Hendrikkade onto Geldersekade—an assault squad of militant seniors. Something must be in progress again, I thought. They were the spearhead of the senior movement, the grays, as they called themselves. Often they were veterans with war experience from UN operations in crisis areas around the globe.

At breakneck speed they hurtled—almost soundlessly; only the soft whine of the electric motors of the wheelchairs could be heard. Shortly before the club the formation dispersed. One of them came shooting toward me, whirled his vehicle around 180 degrees next to my chair, and stopped.

The two others took position nearby. He communicated with them via his ICom, which dangled next to the corner of his mouth; meanwhile he was listening to some sort of radio device.

The old man turned his face to me, bared his implants, and tapped his petrol-colored baseball cap with his finger. DEATHHUNTER BRIGADE was stitched onto the brim in large red letters. He wore a bulletproof vest of gray-green Kevlar. FUCK YOU! was written on the back. Like a thin brush his bristly white hair stuck up horizontally in the back between the edge of the cap and the elastic band. He must have been eighty-five, maybe ninety.

"What's going on?" I asked.

"Ha!" he croaked. "A whole lot."

I couldn't believe my eyes when he folded back the checkered blanket on his knees. I knew that these militant seniors were frequently armed—gas sprays, flash grenades, electric batons, so-called stunners—but what he had lying on his bony thighs was a short double-barreled pearl ceramic shotgun. He fished large shells out of the breast pocket of his vest, snapped open the barrels, and loaded the two chambers. SLAAPSCHROOT was written on the bright yellow cartridges.

"What's going on here?" I asked, taken aback.

"Don't worry, young woman," he replied with a grin. "Everything's under control."

"Pray tell!"

"First of all, today a few suspicious young people entered the city," he said, counting off on his fingers. "Obviously something preconcerted. But it's not directed against us this time. No matter. Fascist riffraff. There are Belgians among them, Germans too. Second"—he raised his forefinger— "refugees arrived in Rotterdam yesterday. Six thousand. On a tanker. And they're going to fly them up to the camp in Landsmeer. The flight heads directly over the city—just about right here." The old man stuck out his chin combatively. "One and one . . . Aha! Something's up here, right? Some misdeed by the KICOB, no doubt."

He twisted his leathery neck, looked searchingly up to the sky, and hid the shotgun under the blanket with a sly sidelong glance.

Suddenly a large silver jeep turned from Prins Hendrikkade onto Geldersekadel; slowly it rolled up and finally parked on the bike path under the trees on the canal. The driver ignored the ringing bells of the bicyclists, who had to swerve onto the street and the sidewalk. The bed of the jeep was covered with a blue tarp. At the wheel sat a man with a pale helmet; through the tinted window he could scarcely be made out.

Two minutes later, two heavy Kawasaki motorcycles appeared from the other direction, from the Waag. The drivers wore mirrored black helmets.

"They intend to use the vehicles to escape, wanna bet?" the old man croaked with a grin. "Ha, we'll foil their plans." His teeth clicked nervously. Might he have been afraid? I felt more and more uneasy as I heard in the distance, in the south of the city, a dull pounding sound growing gradually louder.

"What do they want? Are they planning an attack?" I asked the waiter who brought me my drink. Frowning, he looked over at the motorcyclists, who were now blocking the promenade along the canal as well. He made a worried face as he opened the bottle and poured the foaming bitter lemon over the ice cubes in the glass; then he shouted something in Spanish into the establishment. The owner, a tall black man, appeared in the entrance.

"*Merde.* I'm calling the police," he murmured, disappearing inside the club.

The motorcyclists had dismounted when the door of the jeep opened and the driver climbed out. He wore a white EuroForce steel helmet and mirrored sunglasses. Slowly he walked around the jeep and folded back the tarp on the bed. I couldn't make out exactly what was under it; it looked like a bunch of thick gray pipes. The thundering in the air got louder and louder. Suddenly the two motorcyclists had automatic weapons in their hands. At that point, the old man folded back the blanket on his knees.

"*Verdomme! Jullie fascistische klootzakken!*" he bellowed, firing both barrels.

I couldn't tell whether he had hit them. The old man grabbed my wrist with unexpected strength. With a jerk he knocked over his wheelchair, tearing me from the chair. As I was falling, I saw one of the men swing his weapon toward us, but suddenly he was holding up only a bloody arm stump, while the severed hand flew through the air. I didn't know whether we'd been fired at, for the noise in the sky was now infernal. I felt no pain apart from the viselike grip of the old man clasping my wrist. And then I watched as one of the motorcycles suddenly disappeared in a fireball. The other motorcyclist staggered away with burning uniform from the exploded vehicle down the bike path and plunged into the canal, while the third man, the one with the white steel helmet, kneeled in front of the bed of his jeep and slowly sank forward.

All around people were running away, tables were overturning, dishes and glasses were smashing on the pavement. The sound in the sky was approaching with immense shock waves.

"Halt! Halt!" the old man shouted loudly. "There's an octopus here. I sense an octopus!"

"Let me go!" I screamed at him, but he held me with an iron grip.

Above us a gigantic transport helicopter appeared; its shadow swept across us. It flew so low that you could make out the dark faces crowded together behind the windows of the passenger cabin. Their eyes wide with terror, they stared down at the burning motorcycle.

From the chaos of smoke and flames on the bike path a face emerged. It was absolutely surreal, as if it had been cut out of a backdrop—no, as if it had glided across it, as if it had moved in front of a screen on which a film was projected.

It was a hard, young face, and it wasn't bodiless. I registered a low wave, which slightly shifted the background, as if a large fish were moving under the surface of a still stretch of water. He must have been wearing a camouflage suit, which adapted to the background in a split second, like the skin of certain fish—or an octopus.

Finally the old man let go of my hand. I stood up halfway and groped for my overturned chair. The face was approaching me. It grew larger, more distinct, but it was impossible to gauge the distance. At that point I felt a light touch on my cheek, the touch of an invisible hand. Then, from one second to the next, the face had vanished. The rotor noise receded slowly northward and ultimately died away.

"Won't you help me up?" the old man asked with a chuckle.

He was lying next to his vehicle, quite helpless and also rather pale. I stood his wheelchair on its wheels. The waiter helped me lift him up and heave him into it, and handed him his shotgun. The old man snapped open the barrels and took out the empty cartridges. Meanwhile the other two seniors inspected the jeep.

"Surface-to-air!" one of them called over. "Quite a nice caliber. They wanted to blow the refugees down, in the middle of the city."

"They did blow them down," murmured the old man.

"What do you mean?" I asked him.

"Haven't you ever heard of an octopus? They're emergency helpers, but they come only—how should I put it—when something has already occurred, a catastrophic event. Then they turn back the clock a few seconds and intervene so that the event doesn't take place." He turned his turtlelike neck and looked at me. "Strictly speaking, that octopus didn't save our lives but raised us from the dead. Probably all of us here were dead. Otherwise he would not have had the authorization to strike so hard. Those vile fascists were firmly resolved to make a big mess—a really big one."

From Prins Hendrikkade the wail of sirens could be heard; police and rescue vehicles turned with squealing tires onto Geldersekade, followed by fire trucks. The seniors made a retreat.

"Time for a beer in the Waag," my aged protector said with a wink and a grin. "Was nice to be raised from the dead with you, young woman."

I wasn't in the mood to laugh.

The burning tires of the destroyed motorcycle gave off greasy black smoke. Foam extinguishers hissed. The fire fighters cordoned off the street with orange and white plastic tape. Smoldering rubble was heaped up.

"Are they dead?" I asked the waiter.

"I don't think so. The two of them are apparently still alive. The old man seems to have flattened the man with the steel helmet with his tranquilizer ammunition," he said with a laugh. "They'll fish the third out of the canal soon. If they immediately pump out his stomach, he might have a chance to survive . . . None of those fascist dirtbags would be a great loss. In a few weeks they'll be free again."

More vehicles arrived—officers in uniform and in civilian clothes.

"You're not wearing an ICom, young woman?" one of them asked me with a glance at his Wristtop.

"I'm wearing an NEA chip."

He nodded and moved on.

So that's a "*Uitborstelen,*" as Professor Dorit van Waalen so wittily calls it, I thought; so that's how the great beast that is our universe is groomed. But it seemed to me more like the brutal stroke of a bullwhip to keep yoked animals on course.

"So THERE'S A universe in which I'm no longer alive right now."

Grit scraped out her pipe over the light blue bowl she used as an ashtray.

"There must be a great number of those," she replied. "And there's a universe in which that terror attack succeeded."

She lifted the lid of a porcelain pot, plucked tobacco out of it, and stuffed the pipe. A pleasantly sweet, aromatic scent reached my nostrils.

"Probably there were hundreds of victims," Grit added. "As many as two hundred people fit in a Colossus 6006. And if it crashed down in the middle of the old town . . ."

"Does that universe still exist now, or was it . . . brushed out?" I asked her.

Grit shrugged and lit her pipe. "Maybe not. We don't know."

"What did you actually smoke when you were in the fifteenth century?"

She took the pipe out of her mouth and looked at me. "Believe me, I would have liked nothing more than to set off and discover America myself. I had tried all sorts of things—yarrow, whatever, and burned my tongue. I had even smoked the stem of *Clematis alba*."

"Yuck."

"Oh, we used to do that as kids, until we got an upset stomach and had diarrhea. There's no substitute for tobacco. And cannabis is different. You can't just get stoned all the time. On top of that, you can smoke only secretly at that time, or else people will think you're a fire-breathing dragon or even the devil himself and run away screaming."

For a while we were lost in our thoughts.

"Why can't terrorist attacks like that be prevented in a less violent way?" I asked.

She exhaled a cloud of smoke. "That's not so simple. History is a chaotic system. It requires astronomical processing power to calculate only a few steps. The critical event knot would only be displaced and tied elsewhere. Not to mention the side effects that you can inadvertently set in motion. You kick a pebble loose somewhere and in the blink of an eye it turns into an avalanche."

"But those three people yesterday . . . they could have been arrested for illegal possession of firearms."

"Yes. But if no crime was committed, they would be out again after a few days and would plot a new attack. The octopuses act post factum: They intervene in a universe in which unwanted developments have been set in motion and try to cause it to collapse. Often enough, however, the intervention isn't even possible. The Cattenom disaster, for example, which ravaged Central Europe. How many attempts do you think there have already been to prevent that catastrophe? But no one has come even close to that date. No one knows why. In the run-up to the disaster, a few clever people gave propaganda a try. Stood in marketplaces, sermonized and distributed leaflets. People laughed themselves silly at the supposed crackpots. Check out their reports at the institute. No one believed a word they said. People tapped their foreheads when they even listened. Those voluntary saviors felt like weeping. And you can also get to the time after the accident, though you can travel to the immediate vicinity only clandestinely and at the risk of your life due to radioactive contamination and the barriers. But the event itself—the catastrophe—stands there like a mysterious dark fortress, impregnable. And there are unfortunately a lot of those enigmatic bulwarks in the timestream."

We were sitting in Zandvoort in her living room. Grit had invited me to visit her over the weekend. Outside it was getting dark. She now placed her finished pipe in the porcelain bowl.

"I remember my first tentative steps," she went on wistfully. "Back then Hla Thilawuntha was still at the institute."

"The inventor of time travel?"

Grit shrugged. "You can't actually call it an invention. It's more like something handed down."

"How so? Was there already in the past—"

"Well," she interrupted me, "time travel has by definition always existed. It was, so to speak, imported from the future. Thilawuntha created the mathematics that gave us access to the mysterious transport system."

"What sort of person was this Thilawuntha actually? Did you get to know him personally?"

"Yes, of course I knew him. He was a very gentle, kind, modest person. Everyone liked him. But he was rather shy and didn't talk much. His language was mathematics. Some regarded him as a reincarnation of the legendary Ramanujan."

"Ramanujan?"

"A young man who in the early twentieth century came from India to Cambridge with a notebook in his bag in which he had written the most important proofs from three hundred years of mathematical history. He had produced them himself and didn't have the slightest idea that they had already been established by the most famous mathematicians of Europe. He had on his own accomplished what had taken the greatest minds in the field centuries. And Hla Thilawuntha was an even greater genius, for what he provided were answers to questions that had not even been asked previously. He was sometimes incredible."

"He was Burmese, right?"

"Yes. His elaborations first appeared on the Internet under the initials H.T.—and caused a stir among specialists. It took years before people found out who was hidden behind them. Hla Thilawuntha declined an invitation to MIT. He went to Bangalore and later came to Amsterdam. In the early forties, he returned to his country, supposedly because his father had died and he had to take care of his mother. There his tracks were lost. In Burma at the time there was civil war. It's assumed that he died in 2043 in the massacre at the University of Yangon."

"Has no one tried to find out more precise details? Why wasn't an octopus sent there?" I asked Grit.

"His friends and colleagues had at that time exhausted all possibilities but found no trace of him. That has contributed a great deal to the formation of legends."

"Legends?"

"There are some time travelers who claim to have encountered him and his talking rat on their journeys to other centuries," Grit replied.

"The talking rat . . . I read about that."

Grit nodded. "Yes, that's part of his legend. It's said that he kept a rat as a pet. I never saw it, but it was supposedly a real *Rattus papagomys*, a gigantic spotted animal he had brought with him from his country. Many people assert that he would talk to it about mathematical problems."

"He must have been talking to himself."

"There are people at the institute who swear that the animal answered him," Grit maintained, stuffing her pipe again.

"Maybe he traveled to the future and brought the secret of time travel back from there," I said.

"No one can travel to the future, my dear. We can only travel to places that can be simulated. The future can't be simulated. It's unknown to us."

"But when you returned from the fifteenth century, you traveled to the future."

"True, but that future was known to me."

"Couldn't future situations be extrapolated from the present?" I asked.

"In a chaotic system? Domenica!"

"But if someone who comes from the future describes it to me, provides reference points . . ."

"From which future? There are countless ones."

Silence spread between us. I ruminated, but I felt like a hamster on its wheel.

"How did this Thilawuntha come up with the idea in the first place that something like time travel might exist?" I asked.

"I assume he derived it from his mathematics," Grit replied. "But the idea is not that much of a stretch. He proceeded from the hypothesis that time travel would someday be discovered—whether in a thousand, in ten thousand, or in a million years. Given that, it's presumable that such journeys, when they lead to the past, must traverse our present. So there must be, so to speak, under our feet—or over our heads, behind our backs, what do I know—a higher-dimensional tunnel system in which those movements take place. If there were a way to plug into that transport network, we would be able to use it."

"As freeriders, so to speak. And he found one of those tunnels?"

"He discovered the principle of the tunnels and figured out how they can be used."

"Dogs on the subway," I remarked in passing.

"What did you say?"

I explained to her what Kazuichi had meant by that when I was waiting for Frans's return.

"We have no clue. We don't know the route network or the schedules, don't understand the technology, and are completely in the dark about the terms of transport. Yes, that's right on the mark." Grit struck a match and lit her pipe again.

"Maybe he didn't even come from Burma, but from the future," I remarked.

Grit paused; then, as the match threatened to singe her finger, she blew out the flame. She shrugged and sucked on her pipe. "The legend claims as much. He himself never commented on it."

"I've read the Hargitai biography by Imre Enyedi. In it there's a scene in which Urban Hargitai meets a man in Vienna around the turn of the millennium who persuades him to publish his grandfather André Goldfaden's notes. He introduced himself as Dr. Misrun Ardita and claimed to be a Dutch man of Indonesian descent."

Grit pursed her lips and formed a few smoke rings.

"The description could apply to Thilawuntha," I went on.

"At that time Thilawuntha wasn't even ten years old."

"They sat outside in front of Café Schwarzenberg, Imre Enyedi writes. Between them, on a chair, was an open travel bag. For a brief moment Hargitai thought he perceived a movement in it out of the corner of his eye, and when he turned his head, he glimpsed the intelligent eyes of an unusually large spotted rat."

"Yes," said Grit. "And what do you conclude from that?"

"Thilawuntha is a traveler. He came from the future."

Grit nodded.

I WAITED FOR my assignment. Gradually, summer turned to autumn. I spent the beautiful sunny days at the café of the Hortus Botanicus, in the shade of a sprawling *Quercus x turneri* next to the greenhouse of the orangery. There I sat between a veteran of evolution, a *Podocarpus macrophyllus*, which had unflaggingly held its ground for 290 million years, and a gently fragrant little lemon tree, which was spending its last sunny days outside, and recalled the forms and colors of those species I was to search for, which would be in my care, because they hadn't managed to survive: the umbellate wintergreen, the spring pasque flower, the bug orchid and the early spider orchid, the dwarf water lily and feather grass, northern running pine and stag's horn clubmoss, the ghost orchid, the autumn lady's tresses and the pheasant's eye—all of them wiped out over the past hundred years, gone.

DON FERNANDO RAISED his nose to sniff the air.

"She's in the dunes," he said. "At some point we have to bring her in. So that we don't lose her."

The man some time-natives who had encountered him on his travels called the angel said, without opening his eyes, "I know. But it's still too early. She still thinks she's dreaming, because the things she touches appear so fleeting to her. She is not yet able to recognize that she's gliding through strange, remote realities. But she'll learn. She has the ability."

His rocking chair moved back and forth, softly creaking. Don Fernando scurried restlessly across the dark polished stone tabletop and finally plumped down with a sigh.

"Yes," he said, "she's still a bit naive, but she has kindheartedness and sympathy—and she is a really extraordinary talent. Only she still knows nothing of it. It frightens her."

The man some who had encountered him called the angel said with a smile, without opening his eyes, "She's won your old rat heart, Fernando, admit it!"

Don Fernando rose and again scurried back and forth and forth and back, and finally he said, "Yes, you're right. I'm fond of her and I'm going to look after her."

V

Transitions

It is not the present which influences the future, thou fool, but the future which forms the present. You have it all backward. Since the future is set, an unfolding of events which will assure that future is fixed and inevitable.

FRANK HERBERT

Was I through?

I looked around. Was I still in the simulation? Dr. Coen was nowhere to be seen. I couldn't detect any difference in the immediate vicinity. The air was damp. The man-sized rushes rustled in the wind. Nearby I heard the surge of the sea. I stood in a clearing in dry grass bleached by the winter cold.

I looked up at the sky—pale blue. The position of the sun had changed. It was lower in the southwest, veiled by thin, high fog—as if it were cocooned in copper wire. And it was noticeably colder, I realized. In the studio it had been warmer; there it had felt like an early spring day. What surrounded me here felt more like a late afternoon in February. I pulled the cloak tighter around my shoulders and was thankful for the lining of rabbit fur.

A slight wind came from the lake. I had studied old maps and knew from them that after the St. Elizabeth's Flood of 1421 in the southwest the Zuiderzee reached almost as far as Amsterdam. If the transition had worked and I was in the year 1450, the city was less than a mile west of me—or rather, it was more a small market town, covering an area of perhaps a square mile.

It would be easy for me to orient myself spatially and temporally by the church towers, Dr. Coen, my head of operations, had assured me, showing me the panorama in the simulation. The Nieuwe Kerk had been built in

1408, but burned down during the great conflagration of 1452. The Oude Kerk, already erected at the beginning of the fourteenth century, had been spared by the flames, and in 1452 the construction of a bell tower had begun there—recognizable by the temporary wooden cap from which a crane jutted. Thus I had committed it to memory: If I didn't see the Oude Kerk in the west as a construction site with wooden cap and crane and if I saw to the south of it the not-yet-burned-down Nieuwe Kerk, then I had reached my target time period: 1450 or earlier. If I saw a ruin destroyed by fire and to the north of it a construction site with wooden cap and crane, then I had arrived in the year 1452 or later.

But I saw nothing at all. In the simulation the rushes had been far from as high. Here I couldn't see beyond them; no building or church tower could be made out far and wide.

The sun descended and spun itself deeper into its cocoon. Fog spread. It got colder. It smelled of mold, of peat, of rotting vegetation. Had the smell grown stronger? The surf louder? The air tasted of salt. Was the sea getting closer? Would the land on which I stood be flooded when darkness fell? No, said the botanist in me. The vegetation testified against that. But the roar of the sea was damn close.

I didn't dare to take even one step, stood as if rooted to the spot where I had been dropped off and trembled more with fear than with cold. Someone would be on site to take care of me on my arrival, Dr. Coen had promised me, but I saw no one far and wide. Had something malfunctioned? Had they misplaced me somewhere in time and were now having trouble finding me? Had Dr. Coen, as nice as he was, perhaps lacked the competence he so casually flaunted? Did I have to brace myself to spend a night, several days, or even weeks here, before they tracked me down again?

In the southeast there would be a mighty ash tree, easy to spot, he had assured me. There I would—only in the event that, contrary to expectations, something really went awry—come upon a log road. It would lead to a hut, where our man on site resided. But I saw no ash tree. Had it since been chopped down? I saw only *Cyperaceae*, which towered over me by more than a head. Should I simply march off toward the southeast? But then would I be able to find this spot here again, from which I could be brought back? The landscape was certainly rather uniform; there were undoubtedly other clearings of this sort, which would be hard for me to tell apart. Here, where I stood, I was in the safety of the area that was simulated in the studio. If I were to move outside it, I would be in another world. Six or eight paces away began the wild. I shuddered at the thought of wading in unknown terrain through bog and cold water. I cursed the tunnel builders of the CIA, who were unable to choose a drier location for their outposts. But perhaps there was no such thing in the Netherlands of the fifteenth century.

Was it already getting dark? The fog had definitely thickened. Were predators to be expected here? Probably not. But damn it, I was cold. How long would I have to stretch my legs here before a soliton picked me up and carried me back to the warm, comfortable world of Amsterdam in the summer of 2053?

Which way was southeast? In February—if it was February—the sun in these latitudes described only a shallow arc over the horizon. So it was rather low in the sky all day. On top of that, it was barely visible, almost completely obscured by fog. Indecisively, I grabbed my woven suitcase—and despondently put it back down. My feet seemed to have turned to lead, my knees to jelly. In the meantime I was trembling all over.

"Is anyone there?" I called out, startled by my thin, squeaky voice, which got lost hopelessly in the expanse.

Suddenly I heard the whinnying of a horse and the dull clatter of hooves on a log road. A large white horse appeared among the rushes and stopped. Two boys sat on its unsaddled back, the one in front perhaps twelve, the other ten years old. They stared at me. They couldn't possibly be from the tunnel outpost. The older boy shouted something. I didn't understand him and took a few steps toward him. The horse shook its head and snorted.

"Did you come from the heavens?" the older boy called in Dutch.

"I feel that way!" I shouted back. "Could you help me?"

He turned the horse. The smaller boy clasped the bigger one with both arms and looked back anxiously over his shoulder. The bigger boy kicked his bare heels into the animal's flanks and the next instant they had vanished in the fog.

"Damn it!" I cried, running after them, but tripped after a few steps and fell flat in the grass, which felt surprisingly supple.

Sobbing, I didn't get up.

"You're back already!" Dr. Coen exclaimed, parting the rushes with his long arms. In one hand a paper cup of coffee, in the other a poffertje, he hurried over to me.

"Did you hurt yourself?" he asked, shoving the poffertje in his mouth, licking off his fingers, and helping me to my feet.

"No," I said, brushing my hair and my tears from my face. "Help me find my suitcase. It must be lying around here somewhere if it came with me."

He finished his cup of coffee, crushed it, and stuck it in the pocket of his lab coat, looked around and lifted my suitcase out of the grass.

"I didn't expect you back yet at all. You must have only just arrived in the destination area when the next soliton seized you from below. Did you have any contact with our man on site?"

"I only saw two boys passing on a white horse. I stood around for hours and—"

"For hours?" he repeated, stopping his chewing. "Hm. Yes. Here not even ten minutes have passed since you—"

"I stood around for hours and froze my feet off!" I replied indignantly. "I saw neither an Oude Kerk nor a Nieuwe, burned down or not burned down, Dr. Coen. And no ash tree, because the *Cyperaceae*—"

"The *what*?"

"The rushes! They were so tall that I couldn't see beyond them," I declared angrily.

"The rushes too tall," he murmured thoughtfully, nodded, and looked down at me with concern.

He was two heads taller than I was. His prominent Adam's apple rose nervously and sank again. He looked up and gazed into the distance.

"I see the problem," he said.

PHYSICISTS ASSERTED THAT it was impossible to sense the approach of a soliton. The positive or negative gravitational waves—depending on the direction of the passage—accompanying the phenomenon could, in their view, be registered only with highly sensitive laser interferometers like VIRGO in Pisa, GEO in Hannover, LIGO in Hanford and Livingston, or the LISA satellites in orbit. The human organism, they said, could not perceive those minimal fluctuations of gravitation passing through our membrane. Nonetheless, many travelers claimed to have sensed the approach of the wave. Grit said she had always felt it as an inner tension, which built up for several minutes beforehand and peaked in a feeling of liberation when the transition occurred.

"I know that the physicists scoff at our feelings, but I'm more inclined to think they're at a loss and have no explanation for it. They claim that it's a physical phenomenon, a stress symptom. I don't think so. We travelers have to possess that sensitivity. Sometimes your life depends on that intuition, when you're in the area of the reference point that corresponds to the simulation. When you're in danger, you have to know whether a way home is going to open up or whether you'd better get to safety in the terrain by hiding or fleeing."

THE FIRST TIME I sensed nothing. But I was also much too excited to pay attention to my inner state. So I listened inwardly when the second trial transition was approaching. Of course, the tension grew during the countdown, but I didn't feel the wave itself coming closer. Only when I caught the soliton did it seem to me as if an irresistible but gentle force had touched me, seized my body, and lifted it up imperceptibly—as if I had stumbled unawares into emptiness.

I found myself in the same clearing as last time, but, at odds with the simulation, it was a clear, cold winter day. The sky was cloudless; a pale, weak sun shone low over the horizon, even though it seemed to be late morning. "Memorize every detail at the reference point, so that you can identify it later, when you arrive for the return," Dr. Coen had impressed on me. Easier said than done in this monotonous landscape. "Above all, keep in mind the cardinal directions." Yes, the churches and the ash tree. This time I could orient myself, for the reeds ducked whisperingly under an icy easterly wind, revealing the view. "Turn slowly around your axis and take in your immediate surroundings like the illuminated area in the beam of a flashlight. That's the entrance to the tunnel for you. Should it be inaccessible due to unfortunate circumstances, stay nearby and keep calm. Someone will come and help you." Would I meet the man on site this time? "Leave the reference area this time, so that the next ascending soliton doesn't wash you back again right away."

And again that unease seized me and constricted my throat—the fear of leaving the familiar terrain from the simulation. It was as if I had to slide over the edge of a life raft into the water and swim out into a boundless ocean.

Suddenly I heard a shot, then a shout and a dog barking. Minutes later a rider burst from the reeds. He wore a white sheepskin jacket and on his head a wool cap like a ski mask, which covered his nose and chin. He had three bloody birds hanging from his saddle, black-tailed godwits with long pointy beaks. There was a primitive shotgun in a holster next to the saddle.

A large, light gray dog appeared. A wolf? Another shorebird hung between his bloody jowls. He put the bird down next to the horse's hooves and moved slowly toward me. My heart stood still. He sniffed at my cloak. Did he smell the rabbits that made up the lining? He scrutinized me with eyes like glacial ice, intelligent and alert. I felt as if at any moment he would say something to me, but he was obviously not a modified animal. In the fur on the top of his head and on his throat were no visible scars.

The rider dismounted, picked up the bird, and pulled the wool cap off his head.

"Give me the suitcase," he said, and fastened it to the back of the saddle.

Then he swung himself back up and held out his hand to me.

"Mount!" he commanded curtly.

"How do you suggest I do that with the cloak?" I replied uncertainly.

The rider leaned down, I grabbed his hand, and he pulled me up with a strength I wouldn't have expected even from a fellow of his size. The horse snorted and made agitated movements, but he held it in a viselike grip with his thighs. I ended up sitting crosswise in front of the saddle, the heels of my boots resting against the shot-down birds. I held on to the light brown mane with one hand and to his jacket with the other. It smelled of wood smoke and damp sheepskin.

"First trip?" asked the man.

"Second."

He nodded.

"On my first you seem not to have been home."

The man laughed. He was younger than he had seemed at first glance due to the short gray hair and the stubble on his face—maybe in his mid-forties. He spurred the horse on with his heels. We trotted across a dead straight embankment made of thin birch trunks; the gaps between them were filled with peat and rushes. We passed a tall, leafless ash tree and reached a reed-thatched hut, built in the style of a log cabin and caulked with grass, peat, and clay.

The man dismounted and lifted me off.

"I'm Wouter," he said.

"Domenica Ligrina."

"Welcome, Domenica," he replied, handing me my suitcase.

Wouter threw the birds to the ground. Coagulating blood hung like little rubies in the mane and the fur of the brown horse. He tethered it to a pole next to the door. The dog lay down next to its forelegs and scrutinized me alertly with his glacial eyes. Again I had the feeling he would say something to me at any moment.

"What's his name?" I asked.

"That's Sir Whitefang."

The hut was more spacious than it had appeared from outside. And it was pleasantly warm inside. In the brick fireplace glowed a fire of heaped-up peat bales. At the table sat the two boys I had encountered on the first transition. The older boy fished greasy chunks out of a bowl with his fingers and chewed them noisily. It was probably eel—that must have been available here in abundance. The younger boy drank milk from a dark wooden bowl. Two trickles ran out of the corners of his mouth, because the vessel was too big for him; they had converged into a drop on his chin and fell into his lap when he turned to me.

I greeted the two of them, but they had eyes only for the third person at the table. He was apparently visiting, a dark-skinned young man who wore a loose white shirt in an Oriental cut with an embroidered collar. He had stuck a hand into the open shirt and was stroking his chest. Or was he carrying an animal around with him that he was petting?

"This is Wim and Joop," said Wouter, gesturing with a nod to the two boys. "They're time-natives. Their parents drowned in the last flood. They live with me and lend me a hand."

The two boys stared with fascination at the visitor, who returned their gazes with a smile.

"And this is . . ." Wouter began, raising his chin toward the man. "Who are you anyway?" he asked him.

The young man turned to us. The dull winter light falling through the parchment-covered small windows illuminated his handsome profile. He had medium-length black hair; a round, well-nourished face; strikingly long, dark eyelashes; and jet-black eyes, which flashed with amusement as he drew his hand from his shirt and spread his arms as if in apology.

"Some call me the angel," he said with a shrug.

"Angel," the smaller of the two boys whispered, awestruck, raising the milk bowl, which he had put down, back to his lips.

Oh God, a madman, I thought.

"If you're really an angel, then you must have wings," said the older boy.

"I have wings," asserted the visitor.

"Then let's see them," the boy demanded boldly, wiping his greasy fingers off on his jacket.

The visitor opened his shirt and pushed it back over his left shoulder. I couldn't believe my eyes: He exposed the edge of an immaculately white wing.

The little one dropped the bowl. It clattered on the table; milk sprayed in his face and on his chest. Both boys stared at the angel with a mixture of awe and horror.

"How did you do that?" I asked him incredulously.

The visitor turned to me and in the dull winter light his eyes suddenly seemed to light up honey-colored from within, the way the eyes of aliens in silly Hollywood movies sometimes do. Was he wearing tinted contact lenses?

"I have to continue on my way," he said.

Casually he buttoned his shirt; then he rose and put on his cloak, which had lain beside him on the bench—a white traveling cloak, which he wrapped around his shoulders. He raised his hand in parting and went out. Hesitantly, the dog took a few steps toward the door and then let out a growl. Outside someone then uttered a shrill laugh.

Wim and Joop had hurried out to watch the stranger. As I stepped outside with Wouter, they had untied the horse and the older boy had already mounted. The embankment was empty.

"Where'd he go?" I asked.

"Into the heavens," said the boy on the horse, leaning down to help his brother up.

"That's the best explanation," Wouter murmured behind me. "Anything else would only confuse the time-natives. They don't understand what the future means, let alone that it already exists."

I turned to him. "Is he a traveler?"

Wouter nodded vaguely. "He comes here often."

"From what time?"

Wouter shrugged. "Once he mentioned Highgate. Wherever that may be."

He raised his head as if he were picking up a scent and grabbed my suitcase. "We have to go," he said. "I'd better bring you back now. The boys took the horse. Can you walk there?"

"It's not far."

Sir Whitefang got up to accompany us.

"Didn't you have a white horse too?" I asked Wouter, as we walked down the log road.

Wouter gave me a sidelong glance.

"No, but I'm planning to buy one at the horse market on St. Valentine's Day. I've already looked at the animal. It's for the boys, to pick up our visitors. And I'll take the brown for hunting."

"You enjoy hunting."

"Yes. It's the only variety—apart from the visitors."

"It's boring here, isn't it?"

"Not at all. I love this life. I couldn't stand it anymore where you come from."

"What's the date today?" I asked him.

"Candlemas."

"And what year?"

"1449."

"Then I'll be back soon," I said with certainty.

I SENSED NOTHING of the approach of the soliton, but Wouter seemed to know that an ascending wave was nearing, for no sooner had I entered the reference area than it was as if the cold wind had been cut off, and Dr. Coen was clearing a way through the rushes.

"With this one you took your time," he said.

"I was there for less than two hours," I replied.

"We sent you off two months ago. Today is October 26," he replied.

I looked at him in amazement. "You see, Dr. Coen, I still can't get my head around the thing with the divergent courses of time, even though I should have gotten used to it a long time ago, God knows."

He furrowed his brow with concern. "Did you injure yourself?" he asked. "You have blood on your cloak and boots."

"Shorebirds," I said. "Our man on site seems to be an avid hunter."

"We've got some strange ones."

"Last time you greeted me, you had a coffee. I could use one. It was terribly cold."

"Did we inadvertently send you into winter?"

"February 2 . . ."

"My goodness! Come with me!"

"Is RENATA NOT back yet?" I asked Grit.

She sat in her office at the institute. She was rarely to be found there, because she hated the "aquarium," as she called it.

"No. When do they send you on your mission?"

"On November 19, if all goes according to plan."

"I hope both of you are back by Christmas so we can celebrate together. I'll get a goose in time."

"Do you think that's possible? I mean, that both of us are back by Christmas," I asked her.

"You can stumble around for two years in the past and still be back after two hours. I've experienced that often enough."

"I understand it intellectually, Grit, but it confuses me anyway."

"It confuses everyone. It has destroyed many people, especially when they're in love. I know a case like that. There was once a woman who brought her boyfriend to the institute and said good-bye to him; he departed. She then went home and had scarcely closed the door when the telephone rang. It was him; he had returned. She went back to the institute, still completely filled with the emotions of a loving good-bye that had taken place not even two hours before, beside herself with joy that they would be reunited after such a short time—and encountered there a man who had spent three years in another time, a terrible time . . . That's a devastating experience. The two of them never found their way back to each other."

"Leendert?" I asked softly.

She nodded and wiped tears from the corners of her eyes. I took her in my arms. The undulating streaks of the November sun on the water of the IJ enmeshed us in a net of light.

"I promise you I'll be back by Christmas," I said.

But then I remembered that Mother was planning on getting married at Christmastime, and had to disappoint Grit.

"I'm really sorry," I said to her, "I made her a definite promise."

"Where's the wedding going to be held?"

"In Genoa."

"Then we'll just roast the bird earlier. As travelers we have to be flexible about time. I always stuff it with apples and chestnuts," she replied, somewhat apathetically.

I kissed her on both cheeks. "By the way—I absolutely have to tell you: On my second leap I met an odd person—if he was a person at all. He had such strange eyes. I met him in the hut, where Wouter, our man on site, lives."

"Who was he?"

"I don't know. He was a good-looking guy. He looked somewhat Oriental. Wouter seemed to know him, but he gave no name—though he hinted that he was a traveler."

"What a coincidence. Travelers rarely encounter each other," Grit said with a frown.

"And you know what? He had an animal with him. He carried it around with him in his shirt."

"Are you sure?"

"Absolutely. Could that have been Hla Thilawuntha with his rat?"

Grit shook her head. "That can't be ruled out."

"He looked it, but . . . tell me, Grit, was Thilawuntha a human being?"

She shrugged. "We never found out."

THIS TIME I sensed the monster approaching. I felt it in every fiber of my body—a vibration, then an inner flash, as if the first molecules of a strong drug had reached my brain. A feeling of clarity, of euphoria, which swept me up and flung me into chaos.

I was surrounded by acrid smoke; hissing flames soared several feet high where the reeds were ablaze. Shouts over the crackling of the fire, the anxious whinnying of a horse.

"Here!" cried a male voice. "Someone must have arrived. Over in the clearing. I can't get through from here."

"I'm here," I called; then a cough choked off my voice. A boy emerged from the smoke. Joop, the older one. His face was blackened with soot, his hair full of ash flakes. Two blue eyes flashed at me as if out of a mask. He held a damp cloth over his mouth and nose.

"Here she is! I found her!" he exclaimed with a rasping voice.

Joop took my suitcase from me and grabbed my hand. "Hurry!" he said to me, handing me the sooty, damp cloth.

The smaller boy appeared—Wim, just as covered with soot and ash, his legs encrusted with mud. He took the rest of my luggage, a basket. Then the two of them pulled me deeper into the bog. I saw open water in front of us; already I had sunk into it up to my knees. It was ice cold, and my boots got sucked into the mud. I was afraid of losing them and hitched my skirts up over my hips to avoid tripping. The boys tugged me into lower water, slipping barefoot through the bog and heading from one shallow area to another, to a point where the fire had already burned down the rushes. The stalks were still smoldering. The air hung full of yellow-brown smoke clouds in which sparks swirled. Glowing pinnate panicles rained down. Countless roused birds flew away above us. The sun sailed like a bronze eye blinking angrily through the ash-clouded sky.

We got lucky; the wind drove the fire past us. By a roundabout route we reached the log road that led to the hut. Horse hooves clip-clopped toward us on the damp wood.

"Somewhat exciting, the reception today, huh?" Wouter exclaimed, swinging himself off his saddle and lifting me up.

The horse rolled its eyes, which were wide with fear, and tried to swerve sideways. I held on with both hands to keep from sliding down. Wouter led it by a short rein, placed a hand over its nostrils, and kept talking soothingly to the animal.

"I see you've bought the white horse," I said with a rasping voice. "So I've arrived at the right time."

"It's 1451, if that's what you mean. Next week is Easter," he replied.

The sky in the southwest was brown with smoke. Flocks of birds were still flying over us: coots, snipes, avocets, tufted ducks—I had never seen such diversity before.

"The birds are flying away from you," I said.

Wouter eyed the withdrawing fire front. "In a few days they'll be back," he asserted. "They haven't brooded yet. It's still too early. Good thing the fire came so early."

"It almost got me, but I agree."

He laughed and lifted me out of the saddle. I looked down at my skirts and boots. They were so sodden and mud-covered that Sibyll van Campen would no longer have recognized her creations.

"We'll fix that," he reassured me when he noticed my horrified look. "You can wash up in the hut. Fetch water!" he commanded the boys. "And clean yourselves as well."

Later we sat together in the main room of the hut—I at the open fireplace, wrapped in a wool blanket, he at the table, a tub of hot water next to his chair.

"Tell me, Wouter, has Renata been here? Renata Gessner?" I asked.

"Yes, twice. During her trial transitions." He dunked the tufted duck in the steaming water and began to pluck.

"Not a third time?"

"On her mission?" He shook his head slowly and raised his hand covered with red-gold feathers. "That must have been before my time," he said in passing.

"How long have you served here?"

"Since the summer of 'forty-four."

"Continuously?"

"Certainly."

"And in those seven years, she's never showed up."

"That's what I'm saying."

I shivered. It wasn't the cold. The glowing peat bales in the fireplace emitted enough heat.

"They must have slipped up with the destination time," Wouter remarked.

"Slipped up?"

"Yes, that happens sometimes. It doesn't always work the way the physicists at Casimir reckon. Sometimes the scattering is greater than calculated—when the soliton is very energy-rich and breaks through the membranes more forcefully. That's the way it is."

Ernesto had mentioned something about a powerful wave that had passed through during her departure.

"That would mean that she arrived here before 1444."

Wouter nodded. "Or she is about to arrive. Though that strikes me as less probable."

"Are there notes? Your predecessors might have—"

"Nonsense," he replied brusquely. "No notes are taken. The tenth commandment for travelers: leave only unavoidable traces. That was hammered into you during the mission preparation, wasn't it?"

"Of course."

Wouter nodded and dipped the tufted duck into the tub.

I recited:

1. Keep a low profile.
2. Act naive and slow-witted.
3. Make as few contacts as possible.
4. Ask questions only when absolutely necessary.
5. Avoid disputes and quarrels.
6. In word and deed, use only means native to the time.
7. Carefully consider the unleashing of possible consequences before you act.
8. Keep away from all VIPs.
9. Beware of polluting historical sources.
10. Leave no traces apart from the unavoidable ones of your stay.

"I find those rules somewhat excessive," I said, "for if history were seriously violated or the source material were even changed, a transition would not be achieved in the first place."

"Aha. Would you like to put that to the test? I'm warning you, Domenica. A few stupid blunders, and you'll come back here and find nothing left—not me, not the hut, perhaps not even solid land, because you'll have ended up in another universe, in which perhaps no one ever tunneled."

The wet gray and red-gold feathers of the tufted duck clumped between his boots into unsightly heaps. The bare pale yellow skin of the bird was revealed, darkly speckled by the remains of the plumage.

"What actually became of your predecessor?" I asked Wouter.

"No idea. One day he was gone. Maybe he died. Maybe he went to the Reich to make his fortune."

"To the Reich?"

"To the Kaiserreich, up to Germany. Or maybe a time-native turned his head and he moved somewhere with her. Who knows?"

He laid the bare bird carcass on the table and dunked the second duck in the tub.

"And you?" I asked. "Will you return to the future?"

He shook his head. "I don't think so. I like living here. You know a lot more than the people. That pays off."

"The sixth commandment . . ."

He blew a few feathers off the back of his hand and grinned. "You have to proceed carefully, as when you're stalking an animal."

"You like to hunt, don't you?"

"Yes, I like to hunt," he replied.

Wouter went on silently with his work. Eventually he threw the two bare carcasses on the table, washed the feathers off his hands in the tub, and drew a short curved blade from his belt. With a quick cut he opened the body of the bird and disemboweled it. Then he got to work on the second one. Finally he decapitated both birds. The blade forced its way with a crunch through the vertebrae. The two beautiful golden-feathered heads with the long beaks he brushed thoughtlessly off the table.

VI

A Spring, a Summer . . .

But what prevents the good, corporeal and existing infinite from being equally acceptable? And why should not that infinite which is implicit in the absolutely simple and individual first principle become explicit in his own infinite and boundless image, quite capable of containing innumerable worlds, instead of within such narrow bounds that it appears shameful not to think that that body which seems to us so great and vast is in view of the divine presence a mere point, even a nothing? . . . For I believe that there is no one so stubbornly perfidious as to deny that, because space can contain infinity and because of the individual and collective goodness of the infinite worlds that can be contained in it no less than this world which we know, each of these worlds has a proper reason to be.

GIORDANO BRUNO

I t's possible to get to the Rhine from here via waterways?" I asked with astonishment. "I thought I'd have to go by land to Utrecht or by ship to Rotterdam . . ."

Wouter shook his head. "After the great flood of 1421 the Rhine dug itself half a dozen outlets toward the northwest. Even the IJ and the Amstel were for many years among its branches, and to this day there are connections that can be navigated with shallow boats if you know exactly where to enter. Kapitein Mulder is a good, knowledgeable boatman. He goes up to Cologne three or four times a year and knows the through routes. He knows exactly where he has to be careful. You'll be safe with him, and you can trust him. On top of that, he has a crew who know how to use their fists and if necessary a knife. He pays his people well. They stay loyal to him."

We rode off before daybreak, Wouter leading the way, my horse on a long rein. We followed the system of embankments and ditches south

through man-sized reeds. Fog hung over the plain. Finally we reached a
cart road, which followed an open stretch of water westward.

"Is that the IJ?" I asked.

Wouter reined in his animal. "Yes," he said. "And that's Amsterdam."

In front of us a river flowed from the left into the IJ. The Amstel? The
sun broke through the fog. Ducks and geese floated on the water. Pigs
soiled with black filth rooted around and wallowed on the muddy bank.
Cows grazed the withered grass on the slope. On the river a few boats
could be seen.

I straightened up in the stirrups. Beyond the mouth of the river I spotted
on the heaped-up embankment stabilized by logs a row of houses with
reed-thatched roofs. In front of them stretched gardens, enclosed by fences
made of brushwood and woven straw, which were probably meant to keep
pigs and cows away from the beds. Over the roofs an imposing new building could be seen—built out of clay bricks and with numerous gables punctured by large arched windows. That must have been the Oude Kerk.
Finally I was setting eyes on it. The massive rectangular bell tower I had
seen in the pictures was not yet there. It would only later be erected. About
three hundred yards to the west of it, the new construction of a second
church could be seen. The narrow nave was overarched by a temporary
wooden roof from which two building cranes jutted.

"That over there is the Nieuwe Kerk," explained Wouter, as he steered
his horse down to the dock. "It will burn down next year. A great fire will
break out. The houses you see there will all be destroyed. Only the Oude
Kerk will be spared by the flames."

Wouter said that with equanimity, as if it had all happened long ago and
were inevitable. Had it happened long ago? My eyes darted involuntarily to
the east, toward Java, where I would live, and to the northeast, where the
building of the Casimir Institute would be. I saw only water. In the west too,
where the Centraal Station would be built in half a millennium—nothing
but water. The mighty IJ, streaming along imperceptibly, dammed up by
the rising tide of the nearby sea.

Two large, shallow boats were moored to the dock. Both belonged to
Kapitein Mulder, a stout, thickset, middle-aged man, who stuck out his reddish blond beard pugnaciously. With a loud voice he gave orders and struck
with a short braided leather whip against his boot shafts when he found no
other target nearby. Wouter spoke with him and then came back to me.

"He won't ask you a lot of questions, and you will speak as little as possible," said Wouter, carrying my suitcase and the basket with my belongings on board, along with a bundle of provisions and the bare necessities for a traveler: a blanket, a pot, a cup, and a knife.

"Keep an eye on the money I gave you. Have you memorized the value of the coins?" he asked me.

"I've written it down and memorized it. The Rhenish guilder is worth about fifty euros," I recited. "The stuiver corresponds to roughly two euros, and there are twenty-four stuivers to a guilder. The albus, the Rhenish white pfennig, comes to two and a half stuivers, or five euros. Right?"

"Good," he whispered. "You're carrying two hundred guilders with you. That's a fortune. Until autumn that will be more than enough. You won't need to worry about earning anything and can devote yourself entirely to your mission. Don't let anyone steal it from you."

I felt for my belt. The rest was sewn into my cloak. If I fell in the water, I would drown.

"Make sure you're back by the end of October. The winters come earlier at this time than they do in the twenty-first century, and they're colder. We're at the beginning of a little ice age. Branches of the Rhine can freeze already in November. The boatmen want to be home before that happens."

"The autumn is of course the most important time to collect seeds," I pointed out.

Wouter nodded; then he walked to his horse and swung himself into the saddle. He raised a hand in parting and rode away. I suddenly realized that that introverted, somewhat grumpy, even unfriendly man was the last link to my world, to my civilization. Now that connection had been severed. From now on I was completely on my own. My throat constricted. I suddenly had trouble breathing. I would have liked nothing more than to run after Wouter. But he didn't even look back. To be marooned on a desert island in the ocean couldn't have been worse. I hid myself away in the round hut made of woven rushes in the middle of the deck. As a woman traveling alone I was permitted to stay in it. Usually pigs were transported in it; the smell was distinct, although it had been rinsed and scrubbed. I sank down onto the sack stuffed with hay that was to serve as my bed and indulged in self-pity. I was afflicted by profound homesickness for my world. I wiped the tears from my face. Dozens of women and men had taken this on before me and gotten through it. I thought of Grit—and of Renata. She was some-where in this world, possibly for many years already. She hadn't returned to Amsterdam, or else she would have showed up at Wouter's. Could something have happened to her? Had she gotten into trouble? She would be able to fend for herself—I was certain of that. Perhaps I would manage to find her. I would keep an eye out for her and ask after her wherever I went, for she had been assigned fieldwork in the same area as I had: From the Cologne basin we were to head south and, along the tributaries on the left bank of the Rhine, penetrate into the Eifel and the Hunsrück and, on the right bank of the Rhine, into the Siebengebirge, the Westerwald, the Taunus, and the Odenwald.

IN THE COURSE of the morning the wind from the west strengthened and dispelled the fog.

Kapitein Mulder gave the order to cast off. The yard with the large square sail was hoisted up the mast. It billowed. The second boat followed us at a distance of six to eight lengths. Amsterdam fell behind us. We sailed eastward up the IJ, hugging its southern shore. Rushes as far as the eye could see. In the north the shore receded; it opened to the Zuiderzee, which had formed in the heart of the land during the great flood on St. Elizabeth's Day in the year 1421. Half of the inhabitants of this region had died in the flood.

In the afternoon we turned southeast into one of the numerous branches the Old Rhine had split off into before it finally headed south. Mulder must indeed have been an experienced boatman, for there were no landmarks, no docks, no villages, no signs by which he could have oriented himself. But I had watched him repeatedly inspecting the water and checking its hue, having his people bring samples aboard in a small wooden bucket, sniffing it, tasting it, and swishing it around in his mouth before spitting it out. In some places the water level was so low that Mulder had the sail taken in and the boats propelled with poles until the shallow area had been overcome and the sail could be set again.

In the evening there was cooked eel with pearl barley. I wolfed down the greasy porridge voraciously, for I had eaten nothing all day but a bit of cold poultry early in the morning, shortly before we had ridden off. The boatmen were quite simple fellows. They ate and drank raucously, farted audibly, and laughed a lot, but they obeyed Mulder's every word. They cast timid glances at me out of the corners of their eyes. Probably their Kapitein had given them specific instructions and held out the prospect of a thrashing with his riding crop should they pay me undue attention. He brought me a wooden bucket, and I nodded to him gratefully, for I wouldn't have known how to use the railing to relieve myself; the boatmen had it easier and urinated uninhibitedly into the river. Might Mulder have transported passengers who had come from the tunnel inland before?

"Has a young woman named Renata ever traveled to Cologne with you?" I asked him.

The Kapitein thought for a moment, then shook his head. "When would that have been?" he asked.

"Seven or eight years ago. Or maybe nine or ten."

"My father was still sailing at that time. But I was usually there. No, I can't remember any Renata," he replied.

When it got dark, I retreated into my woven hut and spread my cloak out on the mattress. Cold crept up from the water. I wrapped myself in the thin blanket and all the clothing I had with me. No question, I would have to buy myself a sheepskin.

In the middle of the night I was awakened by angry shouts. It was Mulder's voice; he was quarreling with someone on the shore and swearing at him. I stuck my head out of my dwelling. The boat had stopped; the sail had been lowered. On both shores were torches, and men with long knives in their hands. An attack? Mulder stood in the bow and swung his horsewhip threateningly, but his adversaries didn't seem particularly impressed. Next to him crouched one of his men, aiming a crossbow. I withdrew my head, although it was clear to me that the woven rushes didn't offer me the slightest protection if the opposition was similarly armed. To the extent I could follow the confrontation, however, it seemed to be more a matter of threatening gestures and concrete haggling. Our passage was barred by a chain, and the men on the shore wanted to collect a toll, which Mulder first considered unwarranted and then completely excessive. The highwaymen demanded for each boat a cask of Vinho de Lamego, the Portuguese sweet wine from Oporto, and a barrel of Spanish olives. Finally they agreed to half. The chain was unhooked and lowered. It scraped along the keel, and the journey went on.

After five days we reached the main current, but then the wind abandoned us. Towing was out of the question, for there was no embankment. All around was nothing but forest, impassable flood areas, cut-off stagnant water, bog. Mulder had to moor the boats on a sand bank, perhaps in order to be safe from attacks from the shore. That had the advantage that you could disembark, lie down in the sand, and sunbathe. At night, however, it was bitterly cold. The boatmen caught fish and roasted them on sticks over

the fire, which made for more varied meals; since Amsterdam they had in-
variably consisted of eel and greasy pearl barley.

I gratefully seized the opportunity to escape the stink of the cargo for a
few hours, which consisted—along with barrels of whale oil, wine, Portuguese salt, and Spanish olives—of wheels of cheese sealed in beeswax and
bedded in straw and a few dozen barrels of salted cod. No one but me
seemed to notice the pungent smell. Well, I told myself, these people grew
up from childhood in this stench. I would just have to get used to it. It was
simply an epoch that was not marked by pleasant aromas, and the cities,
Grit had assured me, were worst of all in that respect.

I realized that the people here had a completely different relationship to
time. No one was impatient or nervous, not even the captain, although the
quality of his merchandise over the days we were stuck wasn't getting any
better. Day came and went—we waited. Eventually the wind would turn
west again. The men slept or fished or played dice. At night I gazed at the
starry sky and tried to make out the constellations Grandfather had shown
me, but in the incredibly bright swarm they could be found only with difficulty.

I practiced diary writing, as Grit had taught me. With the spatula-
shaped end of the wooden stylus I smoothed my wax tablet, then wrote
down my impressions, visually memorized what I'd written, and smoothed
the tablet again for the next page.

After four days the weather changed abruptly. It was still dark when
shouts and general commotion woke me. The sky was overcast. Torches had
been mounted, blazing and hissing in the gusty wind as if the flames were
tugging furiously at the oil-soaked tow. Their unsteady light illuminated
the faces of the boatmen and the leafless trees and bushes on the shore.
In the east the day dawned. A rain shower approached from the northwest
over the water. The men had already raised the mast; the lines were unfastened, and the sail had been hoisted. It filled with a flapping sound. Rigging creaked, and damp wood rubbed together with dull groans. Commands
were shouted back to the second boat behind us; it too set off. The vessel
rocked and gathered speed, was pushed off the sand bank with long poles
and steered out into the river.

A rain shower lashed the deck. The sky was full of dark frayed clouds;
the Rhine resembled a scarred leaden expanse between nothing and nowhere. We hugged the shore, where the current wasn't as strong. In the bare
branches of the trees hung driftwood and half-rotten grass from the last

flood. Here and there a half-decomposed carcass of a drowned sheep, a goat, or a dog had gotten caught. It smelled of putrefaction and decay.

Boats came toward us and passed. Sometimes they reminded me of junks in Chinese pen-and-ink drawings: men in rush cloaks and rush hats huddled dripping wet on deck or on the heaped-up cargo, which consisted mainly of timber. With loud shouts messages were exchanged and usually answered with obscenities and laughter. The voices carried far over the water. Occasionally sudden sleet showers deluged the sluggishly rolling river and covered it with a pearly shimmer.

But spring wouldn't be long in coming. In sheltered hollows I spotted wood anemones, snowdrops, daisies, and spring snowflakes, and here and there the first green tinge on the willows. Sometimes I saw a fish attempting in vain to get to another universe.

On the eleventh day the current became perceptible and too strong to sail against. On the embankment horses and towing men stood ready. Lines were thrown aboard and fastened; then we were towed.

On the thirtieth day we finally reached Cologne. From afar I already heard the dull rumbling and crashing and pounding of the fulling mills along the shore, the creaking and squealing of the cranes, and the ringing of countless church bells.

GRIT HAD ADVISED me to ask first thing on arrival in a city for lodgings in a monastery, perhaps even to find a residence for the duration of my stay, which would enable me to take excursions from there with light baggage and safely deposit my collection. In Cologne I had no luck; wherever I asked, I was coolly refused, in one case even brusquely. Was it due to my southern appearance? That could well have been. For I soon learned that fear and growing unruliness were spreading throughout the convents on the Lower Rhine. Rumor had it that Rome had called for stricter compliance with the rules and was prepared to enforce them. Powers were to be cut back and visitations were in store to uncover irregularities and find legal bases for reshuffling personnel. Thus unknown travelers were eyed with particular suspicion and turned away at the door, because they could easily have been snoopers at papal behest.

On the whole, the atmosphere in Cologne was poisoned. For decades the conflict had been smoldering between Dietrich von Moers, the archbishop of Cologne, who insisted on ancient rights and as a cunning tactician aspired to expand his position of power, and the city council, the representatives of a prosperous and self-confident citizenry, which sought to shake off old constraints and refused to be dragged into legal matters. It practiced its own politics and strove to prune back the privileges of the clergy.

That created legal uncertainty and an inauspicious aggressive attitude among the citizens, which often erupted in fierce quarrels and outbursts of violence. On top of that there was a latent hysteria, particularly among the simple people, who took their lead from the scholars. Cologne wasn't Paris, but here too scholastics of various stripes met for their tournaments in shadowboxing and hairsplitting. Even though it had been almost two hundred years since the two Dominicans—Albertus Magnus, the great "doctor universalis," and Thomas Aquinas, the great "doctor angelicus"—had taught and been active in Cologne, their authority had in the meantime grown even stronger. "The two great windbags of their century," Leendert de Hooghe, Grit's acquaintance, had derisively called them. That was certainly unjust and couldn't be upheld so sweepingly. They had made substantial contributions to ancient knowledge and, in the case of Albertus, in the observation of nature as well. I was acquainted with his *De vegetabilibus*, for that time a remarkable book on botany, with many precise descriptions. But both had also wreaked much havoc with their tracts on the power of the devil on earth and spawned many disciples in spirit who pedantically discussed the matter of magically induced impotence, the flight of witches, and the different possibilities of sexual intercourse with the devil, whether "incubus" or "succubus"—that is, whether the devil incarnate was on top or bottom during coitus. It was a pernicious seed that had fallen on fertile ground, and it would sprout horribly, when in the 1480s Pope Innocent VIII would issue his bull *Summis desiderantes affectibus*. But the terrible events were already being foreshadowed now. People feared devilish powers and the dark machinations of his minions. All this presaged the excesses of the witch-hunts that would soon take place in Cologne and its environs. There was a prevailing climate of suspicion, of mutual spying and denunciation that I found oppressive. I decided to leave Cologne as soon as possible and begin my fieldwork.

IT WAS ON the fifth or sixth day that I witnessed a gruesome execution. A man had robbed a cloth merchant and, when the victim resisted, stabbed him and his twelve-year-old son to death. He was condemned to be quartered.

From the early morning on, spectators had converged on the market-place, among them many women, youngsters, and children. They mobbed the execution site as if a circus performance were taking place. For me the butchery—even in nanotechnologically achieved distance mode, into which I had prudently fled—was a harrowing experience. In my era—at least in Europe—killing, even the slaughter of animals, had been moved behind the scenes, so to speak. Here it happened conspicuously—and people enjoyed quite unself-consciously the torment of the creature, when that poor human being was reduced with a few strokes of the ax to flesh and blood, bones and brains. It was a scene of profound horror: the bloody cadaver, the bowels pouring out and bones shattering as the joint capsule was hacked with the ax and the ligaments severed, as the executioner took on the spine from the anus upward, cleaving the pelvis until the body lay in four gro-tesque parts, each with a limb, on the blood-spattered wooden stage; and then a mouth that wouldn't stop screaming and was still rattling in agony until a final blow opened the skull.

I felt paralyzed as the people all around cheered and rolled their eyes enthusiastically. Small children were held up so that they too could see the spectacle, and youngsters vilified the dismembered corpse and spat on it. They would have seized the body parts and dragged them in triumph through the streets if they had not been driven back with truncheons by the officers in the service of the criminal judge.

I stole away quickly and vomited in an alley. I was trembling all over. At a fountain I rinsed out my mouth and washed my face as if that could rid me of the ghastly images. I tried desperately to get it through my head that in my native world similar mutilations occurred during wartime events, terror attacks, or traffic accidents and plane crashes, but the media, under pressure from the public, largely refrained from showing them. Here the cruelties were a public entertainment, a macabre spectacle. Were these people more animalistic, more indifferent, more insensitive to suffering—the suffering of others and also their own distress in the face of it? Could there really be something like an evolution of civilization, a slow—much too slow—emergence of humanity from barbarity, or did we only increasingly develop the art of cosmetics, in order to offer a more pleasant sight when we looked in the mirror?

Was it the ubiquitous, naked reality of a terrible death that so fortified the belief in the immortality of the soul among the people of that time? The soul was the invulnerable and indestructible pillar to which they attached their hope. It was the guarantor of an existence beyond death. With it every single individual, however insignificant and unworthy, was personally involved in the history of the world and salvation. The soul could not be lost, for on Judgment Day it had to be called to account before God. In all perils and in the face of death, that belief provided the certainty of being more than a vulnerable body. That certainty had gone missing for many of us members of future generations. I sought in vain within myself for that consolation, that assurance.

I was in shock and lay awake all night. Again and again the dreadful images appeared before my eyes. I stared at the dark ceiling, listened to the scurrying and squeaking of the mice and the rustling and crackling of the cockroaches. Gradually I became aware that I had arrived in a strange world, that I had reached my destination planet—far from the sun, gloomy and overcast. Yet I had set out in search of brightness, the untouched and unscathed.

Stick those dreams in your botanical specimen case, I told myself, when morning finally dawned. Wherever human beings had gone, those unpredictable and fiendishly intelligent apes, they had spread filth and death— but always also carried around with them a spark of hope for a better world. I had come here to lend that hope more weight, to salvage and reintroduce some of what indifference and greed, the two worst scourges of our species, had destroyed.

I HAD FOUND lodging with a widow on Holzgasse, in a shabby half-timbered house with an overhanging story. On the ground floor it had once contained a bakery, which was why it was teeming with mice and cockroaches, which must have still ferreted out leftover flour under the floorboards. The baker's widow was named Lena: she was a gaunt person who had a swift and sharp tongue, but she treated me from the first moment on with friendliness, even warmth. She was quite active—not so much in her household as in her bed, as I gathered from the nightly noises in her bedchamber next door, and it was not only one lover who enjoyed her favor and offered her comfort in her widowhood, but half a dozen, if you sorted them by temperament and vocal register. She might have gained many a white pfennig mounted at night that she could scarcely have earned during the day at the market, where she sold the bread of a master baker who had his bakery a few houses down. She spent the money lightly on beer and pretty clothes. A few days after I moved in with her she began to give me gifts; she insisted on brushing my hair, plucked at me, and stroked my clothes. I sensed that she might not be exclusively fixated on the opposite sex and that an indulgence of her intimacies could bode disaster.

So I decided to keep the period of "acclimation" insisted on by mission control to a minimum. I commissioned from a coffin maker a lockable chest reinforced with copper. In it I stowed my things that I didn't necessarily want to drag along with me on my excursions and gave them to Lena for safekeeping. At the livestock market I bought a donkey, which cost one and a half Rhenish guilders—an already somewhat aged animal, which nonetheless was still steady on his feet. He had a shaggy, gray-and-black-patterned coat and a funny crease in his left ear. I named him Buridan, and he became my patient companion.

I roamed the Cologne Bay and the bordering mountainous area to the extent the terrain allowed it, spending the nights in small villages and on isolated farms, where I slept on straw, and presenting myself as an herbalist in the service of an apothecary. I scrupulously took notes on the location of various plants in order to collect their seeds at the end of the summer. In the cities the people dwelled in oppressively cramped quarters; everywhere was overcrowded. The countryside, however, was devoid of people, frequently uncleared and inaccessible; parts of it were even dangerous, because bears and wolves made the forests unsafe. And people.

At times the stillness overwhelmed me, particularly at midday, when the birds went silent or only a cuckoo called in the distance, when the air was laden with tons of pollen, filled with olfactory mating calls and chemical longings, wasteful abandon and sweet vanquishment, charged with quadrillions of messages in unimaginable redundancy—tiny modular probes, which, jam-packed with blueprints and assembly instructions, expert programs and data files with material requirements, set out in search of their addressees, the specific docking sites of their genetic counterparts. It was a universe of puzzle pieces striving toward one another—in short: springtime.

I kept an eye out for the daisy-leaved toadflax and the Parnassus-leaved water plantain, for the waterwheel plant and the dragonhead, the whorl-leaved waterwort, the saltmarsh sandspurry and the garlic pennycress—all of them creatures that would no longer exist in my century. Sometimes I wished I had Sarah by my side. She had always been absolutely certain of what location she had to survey in order to track down a particular plant. I came across species I couldn't identify, which I had never before encountered in any index, which had perhaps never borne a name, because they had vanished before they could catch the eye of an interested scientist—plants that had at some point silently taken leave of Creation from one spring to the next, because they had had to make room in the world for other forms.

I was surprised by the abundance of types of grain. There were dozens of different barleys, ryes, and wheats, for which I knew no name—I decided simply to number them. They usually had a low yield and pitiful growth, but what a wealth of uncharted genetic traits and possibilities! My collection might not be comparable with the treasures of the famous Saint Petersburg archive, but my samples would be alive and germinable, not dusty mummies.

The labeling of the samples caused problems. I had used the ship voyage to cut and sew little pouches of thin canvas, which Wouter had provided me, but it was difficult to write on the material. Grit had recommended using black lead—which wasn't actually lead but graphite—obtained from England. But in Cologne I hadn't been able to get hold of any. No one had ever heard of black lead. Probably traders first brought it to the mainland in the second half of the century. The silver styluses I found—actually a mixture of tin and lead—turned out to be too hard and brittle, and inks, even applied very thinly, ran into the material. So I cut labels out of Italian paper, which was quite expensive but good—the far cheaper Lüneburg paper was too soft and came apart when it got damp. I inscribed the labels with quill and ink and sewed them on when I sealed the canvas pouch with awl and thread.

Occasionally I returned to Cologne to buy things that were only available in the city, like cheese, raisins, dates, figs, and—if you were lucky—a lump of cane sugar. What a sour, salty, bitter time it was for someone like me, with a sweet tooth spoiled by the twenty-first century! For sweetness you might at best now and then manage to get some honey, and that was often inadequately spun and full of wax. Still, I devoured it voraciously.

I also never forgot to stock up on salt at the market: coarse-grained bay salt from Normandy, which usually looked gray and smelled stalely of the pig blood and tasted sharply of the alum added during boiling. It could be traded with farmers, who used it to preserve meat, for eggs, bread, nuts, smoked bacon, or lard. For myself I always tried to get Portuguese salt from Setúbal, which, dried in the southern sun, was snow-white and looked appetizing—but cost almost twice as much. And I never neglected to have my little clay jug filled with spirits at the apothecary on the Old Market square, the owner of which was one of the few in the city with a mastery of the art of distilling.

I would visit my room in the house on Holzgasse to store my collection in the chest. Lena always greeted me like a dear family member who comes to visit much too infrequently, but never forgot to remind me about my rent for the shabby little chamber. The baker's widow might have been avaricious and licentious in her moral conduct, but she cooked the best blancmange I had ever eaten. She prepared the pudding with grated almonds, rice flour, white wine, lard, chopped-up chicken breast, and sugar. With my eyes closed I would often recall the heavenly taste of that delicious treat.

OVER THE SUMMER I extended my excursions up the Rhine. I proceeded up the Lahn and Main valleys, through which the much-traveled road to Nuremberg ran. But that by no means made it safe—on the contrary: robbers and highwaymen expected richer loot there.

It was best, I soon realized, to journey as a lady of rank, if you wanted to progress quickly and unharmed—on horseback and with escort, equipped with titles and thalers, with letters of reference and signets as well as a lot of luggage and servants. But for the likes of us that was out of the question. The nobility were acquainted with one another, and if they didn't know much else, they were aware of every bastard and every branch of the clique. And for a botanist it was all the more unthinkable, for why would a noblewoman care what her mount ate or what her dogs pissed on at the roadside, whether they were daisies or coltsfoot?

Grit's advice to join traveling nuns might have been worth following in subsequent decades or in the sixteenth century, but in the year 1451 this offered, according to my observations, not the slightest protection—on the contrary. The morals of those godly maidens were so loose that cart drivers and grooms were partial to small groups of traveling nuns, because they knew their intentions wouldn't meet much resistance when they stormed the chambers in the hostel with crude laughter. If a strapping fellow unsheathed, they usually willingly stuck out their little boots toward him and with much squealing, fervent prayer, and exaggerated wriggling let him overcome them, as if it were an unexpected gift from God.

So, I thought to myself, hire a strong donkey driver to protect you from such harassments; but on that very same day, I saw that I had let the fox guard the henhouse. Though well paid, he demanded that evening a ride as a bonus, as if it were the most obvious thing in the world, like a ferry fare or bridge toll. I managed to keep him at bay only with the riding crop, and had to strike him a few times before he grasped that he was picking on the wrong person.

But one day I would be caught off guard.

On a hot July day—I had journeyed up the Moselle—I reached Kues. The second mowing on the meadows along the river was over; the after-grass hung, heaped up into fragrant cones, on erected poles. The river flowed by calmly and gurgled softly in the hollows of the embankment. I was less than fifty yards from the house where Nicolaus Cusanus was born. It stood raised above the riverbank of the Moselle, was built broadly and solidly out of stone, with large windows on the second floor—the most impressive building in the area. It was the house of a wealthy man, the river boatman and wine merchant Johan Cryfftz, the birthplace of the famous cardinal. Directly to its right, somewhat set back and adjoining, rose an older, even taller building, through which an archway led into the village of Kues. This must have been the house his father had bought in addition when Nicolaus came into the world.

A wide vessel was tied to the dock in front of it, a ferry that crossed to Bernkastel on demand. In the garden next to the house a woman was hanging laundry on the line. A housekeeper? His mother was by then long dead. Was the father still alive? If I remembered correctly, he had died around the middle of the century.

Here Nicolaus had played as a child; here he had walked to school on the path along the river, on which a flock of cackling geese was now heading toward the water, and had helped his father with the ferry service. From here he had accompanied him on his trading voyages up the Moselle and down to Koblenz.

A middle-aged man stepped out the front door. He wore black breeches and, despite the warm weather, a black cloak. He walked past me and gave me a sullen look. His doughy face looked unhealthy; thin dark hair hung over his forehead. Was he Nicolaus's younger brother, Johannes, for whom the cardinal had obtained a parish church in Bernkastel and who would supervise the construction of the foundation Nicolaus would establish here? A certain resemblance was discernible: the broad face, the narrow nose, the prominent chin. The man was heading toward the village along the riverbank path. I followed him at a slow pace to the stone to which I had tied Buridan. The church bell began its midday chimes.

I had a young man bring me across to Bernkastel and rode down into the valley. The air was muggy; hungry mosquitoes assailed Buridan and me. I had not yet reached Zeltingen when a storm reared its head over the mountaintops in the west; its brow and temples quickly darkened. I drove my mount to hurry and kept an eye out for shelter. Soon I found a barn; its double doors opened, and I pulled Buridan in. Just in time, for heavy wind was already blowing the treetops, and the first thick drops struck the slate roof. I looked around in the semidarkness and saw a handcart. A load of hay was heaped up right next to the threshing floor of stamped clay. On the wall hung two flails and a rake; a few sickles were hacked into the beams. Suddenly I heard the clatter of hooves. A rider swung himself off his horse, opened the barn door wider, hesitated when he saw me, and then pulled his animal in and tethered it up.

"Would you permit me?" he asked.

I shrugged. "The barn doesn't belong to me," I replied.

The man nodded.

A downpour began, and it rang as if a thousand tiny fists were pounding on the slate slabs of the roof. Thunder rumbled. The wind moved the cobwebs on the roof beams.

The rider reached into the feedbag on the saddle and pulled out a handful of oats, rolled the grains between his palms, blew away the hulls, and offered me the kernels.

"No, thank you."

He tossed them into his own mouth and began to chew.

Lightning struck in the meadows on the riverbank, less than a hundred yards away. A crash of thunder followed. The rider scrutinized me. He wore a gray felt cap with two flaps that hung down over his ears.

"Where does that come from?" he asked.

"What?"

"A lightning flash like that."

"From the sky," I said with a shrug.

"That's what I said too, when the scholar I recently rode with asked me. Do you know what he replied?"

"How would I know that?"

"He said, 'Of course it comes from the sky, or rather from the clouds, but what cause might it have?' — 'If you don't know, my lord, how should I know?' I replied."

The rider stopped chewing; hulls hung in his dark beard.

"Do you know what he said to that? He said, 'Might it not be the case that a balance of light is necessary? When the clouds absorb the light of the sun and withhold it from the earth, don't they then, in order to avoid an imbalance, have to pass it on to the earth?' — 'But some lightning bolts jump from cloud to cloud,' I pointed out. 'And some have been seen that flare up to the sky.' — 'Yes, indeed,' he replied. 'Balance is always necessary, so that equilibrium is maintained in Creation. Wherever you look, balance is being established between oppositions.' — 'Your Eminence,' I ventured to interject, 'for a simple man it's better not to think about such things. It could be that they are not pleasing to God. I take Creation as it is. God has certainly done everything right, Your Eminence.' He then gave me a serious look and said, 'Indeed he has, but why should it not please God when we reflect on his Creation and examine it more closely in order to grasp its meaning and understand the many wonders in which it reveals itself to us?'"

"Your Eminence?" I asked.

"I beg your pardon?"

"You called him 'Your Eminence.' Was the man you rode with a cardinal?"

"Yes, indeed. Our cardinal. He goes by Nicolaus the Cusan. Born very nearby. In Kues. Son of old Cryfftz. He has a high office in Rome. Six years ago he journeyed a lot here on the Rhine and Moselle. Preached a lot. He's a good preacher. People like to listen to him, even if they don't always understand everything he says," the man replied.

"You know Nicolaus Cusanus personally?"

"Everyone here knows him. You don't know him?"

"How should I? But I've heard of him."

"I thought you were from here."

"No."

"I've ridden with him twice. From Cologne. But that was a few years ago. This autumn he will be here again, I heard. A synod is to take place in Cologne."

Another lightning bolt lit up the semidarkness of the barn. A blast of wind slammed the door. The horse shied; the rider yanked it toward him by the rein and tethered it to the handcart. Buridan, who had been plucking at the hay, recoiled in fear and pricked up his ears. The rain, which had in the meantime abated, resumed with renewed violence.

Suddenly an arm wrapped around my neck from behind, choking me. I cried out in shock and tried to wrench myself away, but the fellow squeezed even tighter. He was strong; I had no chance against him.

"The oats make me ardent," he hissed into my ear. "You won't regret it."

He smelled of horse sweat and oiled saddle leather.

"Let me go!" I gasped.

The man pulled my arms behind my back and held them with an iron grip. He drove me to the haystack, pushed me down, flung up my skirts, and forced my legs apart with his knee. I felt his hard member scraping along my thigh, seeking entry. The fellow must have had experience in raping, for I could do nothing against his oppressive weight and his cruelly hard grip, no matter how much I squirmed. He kept his face out of reach of my teeth and with each of my movements came closer to his goal.

Suddenly the weight bearing down on me was gone. Someone must have grabbed the scoundrel by the nape of his neck and flung him off me, but I saw no one. I rolled over in a hurry and got to my knees. Then I saw the groom getting to his feet four yards away, drawing a long knife from his boot and charging with a cry of rage. I tried desperately to get under the handcart; but then I noticed that the attack wasn't directed at me, but at someone who must have been by the door. The horse reared up in terror and was jerked back by its short rein. Its front hooves thrashed against the wheel of the cart right next to me. And the next instant I saw the groom, knife in hand, with outspread arms, fly five yards through the air and land with a nasty sound on his back on the threshing floor, where he remained lying motionless.

At the door I saw a fleeting movement, but could make out nothing and no one. I seized the chance as long as the nefarious fellow was out of commission—may he have broken his neck or skull—untied Buridan, and pulled him out of the barn.

There was no one in sight far and wide. The rain had darkened the stone walls of the vineyards. The slopes on the right and left of the river now appeared threatening. The air suddenly smelled like autumn. In the east, in the Rhine Valley, where the storm had moved on, distant thunder still rumbled. I drove Buridan to hurry and kept looking around anxiously, because I thought I heard hoofbeats, but no rider was following me.

Had the scoundrel really ridden with Cusanus? Or was he only trying to put on airs and impress me? On the other hand: Could a groom make up such dialogues? Probably not. But would a cardinal have to travel in such company? Probably he had had no idea what a good-for-nothing had been provided him as an escort. Would I encounter the Cusan in Cologne? He was to come in autumn. Would that mean: in October? Perhaps shortly before my departure back to Amsterdam? The chance to encounter the living Cusanus, face-to-face—the man whose cool grave slab in San Pietro in Vincoli I had so often sat on over that hot summer?

The next evening I arrived in Koblenz. The squat tower caps of St. Florin shone in the evening sun.

VII

An Autumn . . .

Would you render vain all effort, study and toil on books . . . over which so many great commentators, paraphrasts, glossators, compendiasts, summists, scholiasts, translators, questioners and logicians have racked their brains—on which profound, subtle, golden, magnificent, unassailable, irrefutable, angelic, seraphic, cherubic and divine doctors have established their foundation? . . . Should we cast them all . . . into a latrine? Certainly, the world will be well governed if the speculations of so many and such worthy philosophers are to be dismissed and despised.

GIORDANO BRUNO

In August and September I brought in my "harvest." I visited the places I had committed to memory and filled little canvas pouches with seed samples, leaves, bits of roots, as well as fruit and grain kernels. Having labeled them, I stowed them in the saddlebags. The collection was more extensive than I had hoped. I had managed to gather more than six hundred plant species and their variations, and most of them I'd been able to identify. About three dozen I had had to inscribe with a question mark, because I hadn't been able to classify them. In any case, with the roughly two hundred canvas pouches already stored in my chest in Cologne, I had compiled almost a thousand samples. It was a beautiful collection. Many of the species and subspecies were already thought to be extinct in the twentieth century and even more in the twenty-first, above all after the Cattenom disaster, which had led to unparalleled species annihilation throughout Central Europe, eliminated countless biotopes, and truncated long evolutionary lineages.

I was quite satisfied with my mission when I returned to Cologne at the end of September. I planned to stay in the city for only a few days and find

a good home for Buridan, of whom I had grown fond over the months. After that I would keep an eye out for a passage downriver in order to be in
Amsterdam at some point in October and visit Wouter and finally the reference point for my return home.

When I arrived at the house on Holzgasse and unsaddled Buridan,
Lena appeared in the doorway and I knew immediately that something
unpleasant had happened. She received me with a shrill lament and accused me of betraying her trust. She forbade me to set foot in her house. I
had no idea what Lena was talking about, for what she spewed hysterically
was so confused that I turned to the neighbors standing around us for
help—nice, friendly people with whom I had spent many an evening in
conversation. But now they turned away from me, and some of them even
assumed a threatening attitude. A few times the word "*herbaria*," herb witch,
was spoken, and once I heard from the background a woman snarl "*striga*,"
which could only mean I was suspected of witchcraft. I couldn't figure out
why. Had someone incited these people to turn against me?

"All right," I said to Lena, "if you won't let me enter your house, then
give me my chest and I'll move on. You'll never see me again."

"I don't have your chest," Lena replied.

"What's that supposed to mean? Did you sell it?"

"I had no idea what witchcraft things you had hidden in there. And under my roof!" she cried, crossing herself.

"What do you mean by witchcraft things, for heaven's sake?"

"Black magic materials. Pernicious herbs to corrupt animals and people
or the seed. Leaves to set on fire and make storms!" shouted the surrounding people. "We won't tolerate anything like that here. Begone!"

"Where's my chest, Lena?"

Suddenly she burst into tears. "The officers took it away."

"Where was it brought?"

"Where you'll be brought too, you foreign witch," said a woman. "To
the tower."

"You've betrayed our trust, you witch," sobbed Lena.

Shocked by the violent reaction and the spitefulness confronting me
all of a sudden from people I had experienced on my arrival in spring as
friendly and helpful, I was at first too surprised and confused to grasp the
whole significance of their accusations. *Herbaria*—well, all right, that was
what herbalists were called. I would speak before the city council and ask
for the return of my belongings, would serve up my story about the apoth-

ecary in Amsterdam in whose service I collected seeds and herbs for medi-
cines and tinctures. But the word *"striga"* had been uttered. To be accused
of black magic was a massive and serious charge. Who had put that word in
the mouth of those simple people? Who had confiscated my chest and for
what reason? I had to sort this out immediately.

I lifted my saddlebags onto Buridan's back and was about to head to the
city hall when two officers showed up to arrest me. Either word had spread
quickly that I had returned to the city or a denouncer had rushed straight to
the authorities to inform them. I was brought to the Trankgasse gate and
taken into custody. My belongings and my mount were confiscated.

I gave Buridan a pat.

"Find a good home for him," I implored them.

They pulled him away.

I was permitted, at least, to wash up and pick out fresh clothing from my
bundle and have a meal. After that I awaited the next day with confidence.
It would surely be easy to clear up the misunderstanding. My departure
would scarcely be delayed.

But the next day nothing happened, nor the day after and the one after
that. I received my meals—for which I would have to pay in the end—and
waited with increasing impatience for someone from the city council to
deign to summon me. I assumed that the reason for the delay was that they
were snooping through my botanical samples and examining them before
my interrogation—and were puzzled by harmless rye, barley, and wheat
kernels, flower and grass seeds, dried blossoms and rootlets. That ought to
have proved my innocence, but things did not seem to be going my way—as
indicated by the fact that on the fifth day I was brought from the Trankgasse gate to the prison tower known as the Frankenturm.

"Tri-ti-cum di-coc-con," stammered the short, particularly zealous
expert, shaking his head. "Wheat? That's no wheat!"

"You know it as emmer," I replied. "Emmer is a type of wheat."

"Never!" he cried, giving his colleague, who was one and a half heads
taller than he, bald, and pale-complexioned, a questioning look.

I gave no response, for it was hopeless.

"Sor-bus do-mes-ti-ca. What is that supposed to be?" he asked, sniffing
the brown seeds.

"It's also called a sorb tree," I replied.

"Ha! *Sorbus* designates rowanberries. The fruit of the mountain ash."

"The sorb tree is related to the mountain ash . . ."

"Related? What's that supposed to mean?"

"They're very similar, even though the fruits look more like small, mealy pears. They have a common ancestor. That's why they're related. They're cousins, so to speak."

The expert frowned at me as if he suspected me of pulling his leg; then he burst out laughing.

"Have you ever heard such rubbish, Herr Collega?" he asked the bald man, who screwed up his face and shrugged.

The short man turned back to the table and my collection.

"These are fava beans. Quite clearly," he said, shaking them back and forth in his cupped hand and then bending nearsightedly over the label. "Vi-cia fa-ba. *Faba*—yes! But not *Vicia*, not vetch!"

"It's a species of vetch . . ."

"So you claim. But that's simply nonsense."

Anger welled up in me in the face of so much ignorance and smugness.

"What's this here? Phy-sa-lis al-ke-ken-gi," he read off the label. "Unquestionably a cherry."

"Here it's known as Jews' Cherry."

"Correct. So what's with the silly Latin double name?" he probed.

"It serves the purpose of classifying the plant precisely."

"Ha!"

"Classifying?" asked the other expert, bowing his bald head; for the first time he showed mild interest.

"And what's this here supposed to be?" cried the short man, yanking open another canvas pouch and strewing the contents—spikes with tiny pale violet flowers—carelessly across the table. "An-arr-hi-num bel-li-di-fo-lium?"

"The plant is also known by the name daisy-leaved toadflax," I informed him.

The short man ground one of the spikes between thumb and forefinger, sniffed it, and nodded pompously.

"And what do we have here? Dra-co-ce-pha-lum ru-yschi-ana?" he sounded out, picking out another pouch from the heap of my samples. He then yanked it open and scattered small wilted bluish purple petals across the table.

"Dragonhead, as the name says, sir. As a doctor or apothecary you must have a command of Latin, I assume. And please don't pour the seeds on the table. You're mixing up my samples."

He paused and looked at me, taken aback by my presumption, with narrowed eyes.

"And what does *ruyschiana* mean?" the bald man rasped.

"That must be the name of the discoverer, I assume."

"Of the *discoverer*?" he repeated uncomprehendingly, shaking his head with bewilderment.

"Ridiculous!" the other seconded caustically.

Oh, holy Carolus, help me! So these were the authorities of the local university. What boastful arrogance, what know-it-all ignorance! The self-importance of these pompous "experts" disgusted me. But, I said to myself, how could these people have an inkling of the ingenious system of botanical classification that Linnaeus would not develop for another three hundred years?

"You were asked a question," the tower master bellowed, looking up for the first time. "Kindly answer!"

"I already said: The name of the discoverer of the plant. And please see to it that these gentlemen don't make a muddle of my plant samples. I've spent the entire summer collecting and identifying them."

"Identifying?" asked the short man. "What is there to identify?"

He went on yanking open my pouches, sniffing the contents, and strewing them across the table.

"With all respect for your erudition, Professor, you don't seem to understand that much about plants."

"It . . . it is *incredible*!" he cried, trembling with rage.

"Another insubordination and I'll have you locked in irons!" the tower master grumbled.

The bald man gave an impatient wave and asked again, "What sorts of designations are those? Who taught them to you?"

"Where I come from, they're common. That's where I learned them."

"And where is that?"

"Rome."

"Rome? Never! I would have heard of it. Besides: In your so-called botanical collection are plants that no one in Rome, or anywhere south of the Alps, could even know about, because they grow only here in the north."

Oh, holy Carolus, he's right, I said to myself. But why shouldn't anyone know about them there? Just because they don't grow there?

"She's lying!" said the short man.

The tower master nodded gravely and gave the transcriber a sign. The quill scratched across the paper.

The bald man disregarded his colleague's interjection. "There seems to be some system behind it," he murmured thoughtfully, placing his forefinger to his lips.

Yes! I would have liked more than anything to shout. An ingenious system! *Fundamentum botanices duplex est: dispositio et denominatio*, gentlemen. But I am not permitted to explain it to you!

"Who devised it?"

"Carolus Linnaeus."

"Never heard of him. A Jew? A Muslim?"

"A Swede."

"A Swede? Impossible! A physician?"

"A quack," the short man broke in.

"No, a royal physician."

"She's lying."

"Young woman, if this were a Christian system, I would know about it," the bald man declared with dignity.

"I'm of the opinion, Herr Collega, that it is an unchristian one. Possibly a devilish system. Witches' secrets . . ."

The tower master nodded. "My lords, I'm breaking off the interrogation," he said, furrowing his brow morosely. "If a suspicion of that sort exists, then a theologian or a lay judge of the archbishop must be present."

THE PRIEST WHO attended the next interrogation two days later was an unappealing young man with close-set eyes, which excluded the possibility of farsightedness for optical reasons alone. He was dean at St. Maria im Kapitol and obviously a zealot, probably a fanatical adherent to the doctrines of Albertus on witchcraft. I could tell by the hate-filled gaze of his dark little eyes that he already saw me branded as a *striga*. My spirits sank as I became aware of what a dangerous situation I was on the verge of sliding into.

"What were you planning with the herbs?" he asked slyly with his drawn-out Swabian dialect. "Black magic? To poison the fields and the livestock? To brew pernicious potions, or what?"

"A great deal of the collection consists of rye and barley kernels; the cores of apples, pears, and other fruit; seeds and blossoms of all sorts of flowers; and the like," the bald professor corrected him. "There are a few herbs as well, but I cannot find any with which any damage could be done."

"We will soon determine that. She will certainly reveal to us what mixtures can be prepared from them that take diabolical effect under a magic spell," the priest replied.

The physician gave an impatient wave.

"Nonsense," he murmured. "Will you allow me to continue the questioning, dean? You can interrogate the woman later, if you harbor further suspicion."

"Certainly."

"You claim that this system according to which you have arranged the plants was devised by a Swede."

"Carolus Linnaeus is his name, royal physician in Uppsala."

"Where did you meet him? Where did he teach you this system? Are you traveling at his behest?"

"No, I never met him. I'm traveling . . ." I began, and taking a deep breath I went on, "I'm traveling at the behest of the Holy Father."

The dean started like a roused cobra. "She's lying! She said at the time of her arrest that she was traveling at the behest of a physician in Amsterdam. That's in the transcript."

"The physician in Amsterdam serves the Holy Father as well," I asserted.

"What incredible infamy!" he said venomously. "The Holy Father would never take anyone like you into his service and charge them with the task of rummaging around in God's Creation, where everything has its fixed place in accordance with His wise will. Why should anything be rearranged that the Lord long ago arranged splendidly? That's a blasphemous presumption! A heresy!"

"Oh, no! You're mistaken. It's about the knowledge of the order in God's Creation," I replied.

"You're better off leaving that to the authorities who understand something about it."

"Well, the Holy Father has enlisted me to work for a Rinascita della Creazione—"

"What a brazen affront to His Holiness!" cried the dean, his face red with anger. "She is an impudent, lying whore. She is of the devil!"

"Control yourself!" the professor barked at him.

"Calm down!" admonished the tower master, realizing with annoyance that this case was becoming too much for him.

Why had I played that card? What was I expecting it to achieve? What was I hoping to gain? Perhaps I wanted everything of relevance to my case to become too much for them, so that they wouldn't dare to pass judgment and I would buy time. I had brought the highest authority into play—and yet told nothing but the truth.

AGAIN DAYS UPON days passed without anything happening. In the meantime, it must have already been November. Finally I was again brought before the tower master.

"Further incriminating factors have come to light for which the council lacks authority," he informed me, looking at me grimly. "Your case has been taken over by the episcopal judge. Should the suspicions be confirmed, things look bad for you, young woman. Because of your herbs and the magic potions that might be prepared from them, I would have condemned you as a *venenata*, a maker of poisons, or as a *lamia* well versed in black magic, forced you to renounce all vengeance, and banished you from the city. But now there is evidence that you are capable of entirely different things as well."

The tower master crossed himself.

"What things?"

He ignored my question. "You are herewith transferred to the jurisdiction of the archbishop and the episcopal prison on the cathedral square. There you will be dealt with further." The tower master gave the cancellarius a sign to conclude the transcript with that remark, and then pure fear overcame me for the first time.

"What sort of evidence is it?" I asked.

But the judge had already turned away and left the room. The officer, who had up to that point been taciturn toward me but not unkind, now seized me with a firm grip, turned me around, and led me out.

THE HATE-FILLED DEAN of St. Maria im Kapitol, whom I had already met in the council's court, seemed now to have set himself up as prosecutor. The episcopal judge, a corpulent gray-haired clergyman enthroned behind him, seemed more interested in his fingernails and the heavy ring on the middle finger of his left hand than in my case. His assistant, a young clergyman of about thirty, displayed a simpler nature but abject servility, and he was—in a manner that bordered on miraculous—capable of anticipating the reaction of his master instinctively or perhaps based on his body language and of nodding or smiling a split second before the man himself. Thus he secured the advantage of agreement.

"*Incipit confessio strigae*," said the dean to the cancellarius.

The judge raised his eyebrows with astonishment, for it was up to him to officially open the trial, and not the task of the prosecutor.

"A question, Reverend Father," I broke in. "The prosecutor calls me a witch. Have I already been found guilty of witchcraft?"

"That won't be long in coming!" the dean cried spitefully. "You're as good as convicted."

"Oh?"

The judge nodded to the cancellarius and opened the questioning. "We shall now hear the confession of Domenica Ligrina, born by her own account in Rome, suspected of witchcraft, black magic, and preparation of poison as well as knowledge of the future, witches' flight, and liaison with the devil."

I was dumbstruck. How did they arrive at those crazy suspicions? On what did they base those accusations? Did they plan to extract a confession through torture in order to "prove" the outrageous claims? That had indeed been the method of some inquisitors in later eras. The middle of the fifteenth century was, according to Falcotti, a safe, tranquil time—at least he had assured me of that. The great plagues were over, and the witch-hunts still lay almost half a century in the future. The *Hammer of the Witches*, the *Malleus maleficarum* by Institoris and Sprenger, would not appear until the end of the century, but that ill-fated specter was apparently already stirring in the heads of the zealots and agitators. It would take little more than an order from on high to unleash them and sanction their rage. The seed that had been carelessly sown was sprouting.

"You seem to have been rendered speechless," the dean said triumphantly.

His little eyes, between which his narrow nose barely found room, flashed maliciously. What had I done, for heaven's sake, to incur his hatred?

"You do believe that witches exist, don't you?"

That was, of course, a trick question: To dispute the existence of witches was already regarded as heresy and was thus punishable by death.

"I have never seen one before," I replied.

"We didn't ask you whether you've seen one, but whether you believe in witchcraft or not. Answer the questions you are asked!"

The judge nodded.

"People have convincingly assured me that things of that sort exist. However, no one has ever revealed themselves to me to be a witch or a wizard," I replied.

"You must think you are one of the especially clever ones?" the dean asked angrily. "Who taught you such rhetorical tricks?" he went on slyly. "Other witches . . . or . . . perhaps even . . . ?"

If he expected that to fool me into unthinkingly uttering the word "devil," then he was mistaken. I wouldn't let this religious hothead outwit me.

"I don't know any witches. I said that already," I insisted.

"Always flew alone? Never in the company of other witches? That's unusual."

"Flew?"

The dean unrolled a document. "This is the statement of a respectable, devout, God-fearing woman of this city. Her name is Lena Bittner. She is the widow of the former master baker Gotthelf Bittner, residing on Holzgasse. During her interrogation she testified that you told her it was possible to fly in two hours from here to Rome," he said, presenting the document pompously to the judge.

Oh, Lena! I might have guessed that she had been pressured and threatened with the dungeon or worse. At some point I had blabbed over a beer. When she learned that I was from Rome, she had longingly confessed to me that it was her greatest wish to make a pilgrimage to the holy city, but the journey was arduous and took a whole year. And unthinkingly I had mentioned that in five hundred years people would be able to fly from Cologne to Rome in two hours.

"Well?" my inquisitor asked sneeringly. "Do you wish to dispute that?"

"I never said that I had flown from Cologne to Rome, but that in a distant future—perhaps in five hundred years—people might well be able to fly from Cologne to Rome in two hours."

"In five hundred years!" repeated the dean, cackling with pleasure and casting a glance over his shoulder to the judge, who for the first time showed mild interest.

"Supposing," said my prosecutor, "that the world still exists for that long—which is most unlikely, for our Lord God will not let the souls of the dead languish in purgatory for centuries—how can you see such a thing? Is it magic potions that turn you into a sibyl? Hemlock? Spurge? Black grain?"

I shrugged. "I don't need a potion for it. Such visions appear to me in dreams. It's . . . it's like a memory of another time that still lies ahead of us."

"Confess it: Do such . . . memories come to you during liaison with—"

The judge raised his hand. "How can you be certain that these dream images are visions of the future and not confusion, lies, and deceptions insinuated by the devil?"

The assistant and the dean nodded in unison.

"I don't know," I conceded.

"Oh, she will reflect on it and reveal it to us," declared my prosecutor. "She will—"

The judge interrupted him impatiently. "And how will people fly? What do your visions show?" he asked me.

"With machines that can take off into the air like birds. Mechanical birds."

"Machines? Not with the power of the mind?" he asked.

I could tell by his face that his interest had faded.

The dean unrolled another document. "This is the statement of Sebastian Melker, a groom in the service of His Excellency the archbishop of Cologne. He reports on an event on St. James Day of this year near Zeltingen on the upper Moselle, of which he was witness and victim. 'It was a cloudless, sunny day when suddenly in the clear blue sky a storm appeared. My first thought was that it must have been a weather spell, for the occurrence was inexplicable and quite violent. I sought shelter for me and my horse in a barn in the open country and found there a young woman who upon my entrance furtively slipped some herbs into the saddlebag of her donkey. I suspected at once that she was a witch, who had through the burning of certain herbs performed a weather spell in order to ravage the fields and particularly the surrounding vineyards with hail. I detected the smell of burning, but intermingled with a much fouler stench of rot and flatulence and other disgusting vapors. It was immediately clear to me that I had disturbed someone here in the midst of a liaison. And with those infernal effluvia that could mean only one thing: I had surprised the witch and the devil in flagranti. I looked around and indeed at the barn door I caught sight of a dark-skinned figure with a snoutlike face and a goat's hoof. I prayed to the Almighty for support and bravely charged at the figure, but before I reached the door, I felt a blow to my chest from an invisible hand, which flung me back five or six paces. I drew my knife and bravely charged a second time at the unearthly figure. Once again I was pushed back by an invisible hand, and this time so forcefully that I fell down and lost consciousness. When I came to, my head hurt, for I had hit it against the threshing floor, and in my chest my breathing stabbed me so sharply that I could barely keep myself in the saddle and for two months was incapable of doing my duty in the stables of His Excellency. Both the dark figure and the witch with her donkey had vanished from the barn when I regained consciousness. I recognized that young woman. She is a vagrant known in the city as the Roman woman and had previously lodged with the widow of the master baker Bittner on Holzgasse. I testify to that before God, our heavenly Father. Amen.'"

That mendacious, sanctimonious scum!

"Do you confess that you were the witch referred to in the statement, whom the groom surprised during liaison with the devil?" asked my prosecutor.

"I'm not a witch, and that incident occurred completely differently!" I exclaimed indignantly.

"But you admit that you are the person who was found in the aforementioned barn."

"Yes. But the incident happened completely differently. That perfidious scoundrel of a groom—"

"You're speaking of a faithful servant of the archbishop, a righteous, pious man. Mind your words! We will have you flogged if you make defamatory remarks."

"—attacked me and wanted to do violence to me. Someone else came—"

"Aha! And that someone—"

"—came, thank God—"

"Careful what you say!"

"—to my rescue. I didn't see him. I don't know who he was."

"Did you smell, or at least . . . sense him?"

The judge, who had sunk back into his lethargy, straightened up and announced with his soft, hoarse voice, "I order an examination in search of *signa diaboli* by *doctores medicinae* of the local university."

The dean eyed me scornfully. That young man had a merciless self-righteousness that nothing could challenge, and at the same time a narrow-minded and know-it-all ignorance, with which the most pious among the pious are often afflicted. It gave him deep satisfaction to humiliate me, to injure me, even to annihilate me. And all the while he apparently still had the feeling of doing God's work.

So I would be strapped down naked on a table and searched for *adventi- tiae mammae*, for superfluous nipples, so-called witches' tits, with which I nursed my offspring spawned in liaison with the devil. I would be pricked with silver needles in every birthmark, in every wart, to find out whether blood flowed. My genitalia would be examined to determine whether wounds or scars indicated violent or perverse intercourse—*succubus* or *in- cubus*.

Usually that *majus argumentum et satis firma probatio*—in Albertus Magnus's terms—which permitted the conclusion of a successful possession by the devil, was produced the night before the examination by the respon- sible torture master and his servants, who were granted the rough fun of doing it like the devil—thus creating a fait accompli.

The triumphant grin of my prosecutor, the hoarse drone of the judge, and the scratching of the cancellarius's quill were the last things I was aware of. As the officers pulled me up and turned me around to lead me back to the cell, I blacked out.

FROM THAT POINT on my memories became blurry; I had the sensation that they encompassed disparate strands of events. My experience branched off, so to speak, as a photon can split when it is both reflected and absorbed by a semipermeable mirror and exists simultaneously in two universes; when two paths open, a shadow brother rushes to its aid, so that both uni- verses can be traveled.

At first I thought I had triggered a sort of enhanced distance mode by activating my depots of nanotects in order to dull my perception of pain and alleviate the emotional burden, but it went beyond that. It was some- thing else. It seemed to me as if a shadow sister were rushing to my side and taking it upon herself to go down the difficult path that had actually been intended for me. As a little girl I had already occasionally had the feeling that I had a dream sister, a consubstantial doppelgänger, but I had never had the courage to tell anyone about it—for fear of being thought mentally ill. Ever since I had delved into the biography of Urban Hargitai, I knew that there were other people who in dreams or under special circumstances had contact with their alternate selves—with shadow beings who live be- yond the boundaries of our reality in parallel universes in which events take a different course. I understood what Urban Hargitai had gone through when his shadow brother lost his eyesight in the train crash. I could empa- thize with what his grandfather André Goldfaden had gone through when his other self was at the mercy of the concentration camps. Even on the safe shore of another universe they were not spared the torments.

OF COURSE THEY came that night. They were drunk and, in their coarse way, cheerful. I didn't feel them. I saw their faces close above me, always a different one, goggle-eyed, the gaze turned inward; even that mendacious groom was among them. Grinning, he showed his satisfaction that he now got to take his pleasure after all. I heard their grunting and panting, the shouts of encouragement from the others, who crowded around the table on which I was bound; I smelled their disgusting breath, which struck me in the face, their sweat, their unwashed bodies. But I felt no physical pain, no emotion—nothing.

For the examination in search of *signa diaboli* the nearsighted little pot-belly in a blue doublet who had inspected and made a mess of my botanical samples was present. His diagnosis regarding a successful possession by the devil I didn't hear. But I would often think back on his long, dirty finger-nails and on how many women would still have to die in childbed before Semmelweis taught these self-important filthy pigs that a doctor should occasionally wash his hands.

IT'S ASTONISHING HOW much neglect a person can bear. The farmers strewed their animals' bedding each night to keep them clean. I, on the other hand, received fresh straw only once a week, and it was already swarming with vermin on the second or third day. I was surprised that no rats had shown up yet.

"I keep them away from you," I suddenly heard a voice say.

I turned around in fright, for I had heard neither the grind of bolts nor the creak of the door. Above me, in a recess in the wall, sat the biggest rat I had ever seen—a monster of a rat, neither black nor gray or white, but spotted, with a thick coat of russet, umber, and ocher like a cat. Its long bare tail hung down over the beam on which it had made itself comfortable. With its tongue it salivated on its front paw and cleaned its face. Then it looked down at me with its eyes reminiscent of black beads.

"Before you turn away with a shudder or even scream, I tell you that the first impression is deceptive," it remarked with a reassuring voice.

"You can speak?" I asked in amazement.

"Of course."

"Are you a modified animal? Where I come from dogs are bred that way. Their intelligence is elevated and they're given a little bit of linguistic ability."

"To sic them on people more successfully without getting one's hands dirty. I know."

"But rats . . ."

"I'm not a rat, young woman."

"But not . . . a human being?"

"Oh, that's a difficult question." The rat raised his snout and bristled his whiskers. "I certainly have a great many human genes in me . . . No, I've chosen this form of existence."

Was this a dream? I sensed that I was still deep in distance mode due to the shock of the rape, that a state of anosognosia flattened my perception, but that could not be connected to hallucinations.

"*Rattus rattus* is a downright optimal life form," the animal went on. "It's ubiquitous wherever human beings have set foot and left behind their muck. For many millions of years it has been native to the time and therefore inconspicuous; on top of that, it's robust and resilient—almost impossible to kill."

"Who are you, then?" I asked.

"Pardon me, I forgot to introduce myself. My friends call me Don Fernando," replied the rat.

"Don Fernando? And you keep the rats away from me?"

"At least the four-legged ones, and the—"

The rat suddenly fell silent, for at that moment the young man who for several days had been bringing me my food entered my dungeon. He seemed not even to notice the rat on its perch. The fellow was remarkably ugly. His shaggy black hair hung over his eyes, and his mouth was surrounded by a frayed sparse beard. And what a mouth! The upper and lower teeth stuck out almost horizontally, as if when he was a small child a piece of pipe had constantly been shoved down his throat through which food had been poured into him. That deformity magically attracted my eyes. Again and again I caught myself staring at that grotesque set of teeth, over which his lips could not close.

"What's your name?" I asked him.

The fellow emitted a whining wheeze and pointed to his open oral cavity. It was empty; his tongue had apparently been cut out. He was one of those poor creatures to whom the torturers could assign base tasks. They couldn't divulge anything, couldn't communicate—mute and stupid as they were.

No, this one here wasn't stupid. Winter was approaching. It was cold in the dungeon; the straw was damp and smelled putrid. He brought fresh straw and a wool blanket. Gratefully, I stroked his cheek. He grunted and his eyes shone. Who gave attention to such an ugly creature? For hours he sat on the steps outside the door and stared down at me. Might he desire me?

In the meantime, it must have been December. Nicolaus Cusanus was expected in the city. Wasn't it true that he was staying in Cologne shortly before Christmas, before traveling on to Leuven and Brussels? I wasn't certain. Why hadn't I studied the sources more thoroughly when I still had my Scarabeo at my disposal?

Then I had a sudden inspiration. Might I be able to escape my cruel fate with a petition to the cardinal? But how was I to appeal to him? How could I attract his attention?

"Can you get me paper and writing implements?" I asked the poor fellow.

The mute looked at me and shrugged. Again days passed. I repeatedly looked at him questioningly when he brought me the food, emptied my bucket, and swept the cell. Had he even understood me? Probably my request exceeded his capabilities. He had to fear punishment, after all, if he smuggled things in and out. So why should he risk it? But eventually he came and fished paper out of his shirt—a handful of sheets, an inkwell, quills, and a small knife. I was overwhelmed, pressed him to me and gave him a kiss on his disheveled hair. No, he wasn't stupid, he was lovable—and cunning.

What should I write now? *To His Eminence Cardinal Nicolaus of Cusa. Your Eminence . . .* But would the letters be sent on to him? Or would my prosecutors file them away sneeringly to increase the burden of proof against me? But what could make my situation any worse? Wouldn't it be better to risk an attempt, as slim as the chances of success might be, and take the bull by the horns? Reveal myself to be from the future, traveling in the service of the Curia as he was? Simply tell the truth?

East of Cattenom, I wrote, *the land is black, deep into Bohemian and Polish regions, as can seen from orbit . . . This happened in the year of our Lord 2028 . . .*

I gave the letter to the mute, asked him to pass the paper on to someone who could deliver it to the cardinal when he was in the city. He nodded and hid the letter in his shirt.

MEANWHILE, THE INTERROGATIONS continued. My prosecutors wanted to know which witches had instructed me in magical practices. I didn't know any names to name, even though they now subjected us—my shadow sister and me—to the torture of the *curlo,* hoisting up and dropping by the hands, which were bound behind the back. Hoisting up—for the span of a *Paternoster,* a *Salve Regina,* and a *Miserere*—dropping; hoisting up—a *Paternoster,* a *Salve Regina,* a *Miserere*—oh, how horribly long—dropping; hoisting up—*ter squassata,* three times in a row.

Do you have any ideas, sister? I don't know any names to name. They think we're being obdurate. The shoulder pains are growing intolerable. We try to endure them together. Hekking's little sorcerers help us. I bear the magic invisibly within me for which they're searching so frantically, but they won't find it.

Those were my thoughts, the thoughts of a tortured woman accused of witchcraft, stranded five hundred years before her time—and her shadow sister.

No mention of the letters. Had the mute managed to smuggle them out and place them in the hands of a trustworthy person who had access to His Eminence? I was relying on it.

So I wrote: *You were the first to have the courage to look infinity, eternity in the eye. You tried to conceive of it, whereas others uttered the word as unthinkingly as if it were only the time until St. Bartholomew's Day next year.*

I wrote: *You explained, "Nothing is found in time except an ordered present. The past and the future are the unfolding of the present. The present is the enfolding of all present times, and the present times are its serial unfolding."*

And I wrote: *You explained, "Just as in matter many things are possible that will never happen, so, by contrast, everything that will not happen but could happen, if it is in the providence of God, is not possible but actual. But it does not therefore follow that those events actually are."*

And you explained further, *"Thus the infinite providence of God encompasses both what will happen and what will not happen but could happen, as well as the contrary, as the genus encompasses contrary differences. And what God's providence knows, it knows not with the difference of time, because it does not know the future as future nor the past as past, but knows them in an eternal way and thus knows the mutable in an immutable way."*

And I wrote on: *You explained, "If someone did not know that the water was flowing and did not see the shore while he was on a ship in the middle of the water, how would he recognize that the ship was moving? And because it always seems to each person, whether he is on the earth, the sun, or another star, that he is at an immovable center, so to speak, and that everything else is moving, if he were on the sun, the earth, the moon, Mars, and so on, he would certainly always set new poles in relation to himself. The structure of the world is therefore as if it had its center everywhere and nowhere its periphery."* You can hardly imagine, Your Eminence, what you anticipated with those ideas, not only philosophically, but also mathematically and cosmologically. Not until more than four hundred years from now will people grasp them and take them up.

In addition, I wrote: *You recognized that reality, the* actu esse, *and virtuality, the* posse esse, *possibility, are entangled, form a unity.*

What could better characterize our situation, shadow sister? Finally I wrote: *Beware of Todi.*

THEY WANTED TO break my obstinacy. The Holy Tribunal had decided to forcibly pour into me a brew of wormwood, aloe, and rue, so that the devil would come out in *flatus, stercus aut utrumque in corporis excrementa*—in winds, feces, and other bodily excretions.

Three days of diarrhea and vomiting. I was exhausted and at the end of my strength. I felt boiling heat in me, while at the same time I was freezing. My nanotects were on highest alert; they swarmed into action. My teeth chattered. The mute brought fresh straw, another blanket, and a warm beer. The bells had often tolled in recent days. Christmas must have been over and the cardinal long since departed for the Netherlands. He had given me no sign. Had my letters not reached him? Perhaps, I thought, at least my warning had reached his ears. If he heeded it, he would escape the epidemic in Todi and continue to do beneficent work for many years.

Don Fernando visited me.

"You know what those letters could bring about, Domenica."

I looked up to the beam on which he was enthroned, fat and well nourished in his warm coat.

"Yes, but I don't really care."

"History could take a different course," he pointed out.

"Maybe a better one. A world without witch mania, a brighter, more rational world—one that is more receptive to the sciences. Maybe it would be good enough to be included in the corpus of the multiverse," I replied.

Or were those vain hopes, which would soon founder on the inertia of history, the inertia of humanity? Don Fernando didn't give me an answer.

THAT NIGHT I dreamed again of the deserted world. This time no eye hovered over me. The sky was empty and nearly black, though the sun still shone over the horizon. The dunes cast long, sharp shadows. I stood on the shore of the dried-out ocean, in the depths of which night gathered and rose like black water. Beyond the abyss, along the murky gray precipice, the wind wafted clouds of smoke, which seemed to rise from burning underground coal seams.

"What's that?" I asked Don Fernando, who was by my side.

Don Fernando raised his head and sniffed the air.

"There," he said, "lie the ashes of billions upon billions upon billions of chronicles of possible worlds that failed."

VIII

...And a Winter

In one inconceivably complex cosmos, whenever a creature was faced with several possible courses of action, it took them all, thereby creating many distinct temporal dimensions and distinct histories of the cosmos. Since in every evolutionary sequence of the cosmos there were very many creatures, and each was constantly faced with many possible courses, and the combinations of all their courses were innumerable, an infinity of distinct universes exfoliated from every moment of every temporal sequence in this cosmos.

OLAF STAPLEDON

W itches must be burned in winter," my inquisitor from Swabian Dillingen, the dean of St. Maria im Kapitol, had explained. "Then their ashes cannot wreak havoc in the fields. They will not poison the crops or the grass for the cattle."

Candlemas. It was a windy day; the cold spell had broken. The clouds scudded across the sky so fast that it could make you dizzy to watch them. Gusts tugged at the banners and pennants adorning the gallery from which the archbishop intended to follow the spectacle. He washed his hands in innocence. His judge only carried out the investigations and handed down the sentence. The execution fell under the jurisdiction of the city council.

The stake had been erected. The crowd flocked to the square, but it was silent. No high spirits were perceptible as at the execution of the murderer I had witnessed in spring. Worried looks were directed at the sky, in which light and shadow alternated as the wind shook the shutters and roof hatches of the tall houses. Would the *striga* take revenge in her hour of death with flying sparks and conflagration? Would the devil rise up with a fiery wind, fluttering as a red cock from gable to gable? His Excellency the archbishop too looked up to the sky with a scrutinizing gaze; the pale, sagging face of the well-nourished old man seemed beset by doubt.

The executioner ordered his assistants to set up buckets filled with water around the execution site and to dampen the brushwood so that the flames wouldn't blaze up too fiercely. That made it easier for the condemned woman: She wouldn't feel the angry bites of the flames but would perish beforehand in the smoke.

She had been clothed in paper, and a paper cap had been put on her head on which herbs, mandrakes, lightning bolts, and eyes had been drawn. Last rites were administered to her. The bells of St. Martin nearby were silent. This soul did not need to be announced to heaven; it would go straight to hell. Then the bundles of straw were kindled and thrust into the brushwood all around. In no time the execution site was surrounded by a dense cloud of smoke. Coughing, the executioner's assistants backed away, and hesitantly flames surged up.

Thus things took their course. I remember nothing. With whose eyes was I to see? I knew how the terrible event unfolded. Images were engraved in my mind—of simulated fires, of the corpse burnings on the ghats of Varanasi. As execution by fire typically takes place standing at a stake, gravity takes on a substantial share of the destruction of the body. When the fatty tissue of the breasts is completely ablaze, the temperature reaches over a thousand Kelvin. The face is quickly consumed down to the skull and teeth. Ears and nose smolder away and disintegrate in a matter of minutes. The steam buildup from the boiling brain fluid escapes through the nasal cavity and eye sockets and turns the inner ear inside out. Then the neck vertebrae lose their connection; the head sinks forward onto the chest and finally falls off. The abdomen bursts and the seething bowels plummet along the legs, which have been burnt into sticks. The intestines drag the other internal organs down with them into the embers. The exposed blackened ribcage is scarcely distinguishable from the burnt pieces of wood. The spine and pelvic bones hold out the longest, are ultimately shattered by the assistants with pokers, pushed into the embers, and covered with the rest of the wood while the servers collect their equipment, pull the cloth from the makeshift altar, and fold it up, while the executioner wipes his heated face with a handkerchief and drinks the longed-for sip of wine from the tin jug handed to him.

*　*　*

DID SHE STAY by my side after her death by burning, my shadow sister? Did the molecules of my body still exchange subatomic particles with her incinerated body? Was she still bound to me by the entanglement of matter? Was I from that moment on clad in a shimmering cloak of appearing and vanishing particles from her universe—in a drift of chance and nothingness? No. Her state had changed. Her world line, which had previously run parallel to mine, was frayed and severed. A part of her body had entered the matter of this world; it had become part of the crust of this planet and its sea of air. Another part had turned into light, into photons, which in their peculiar timelessness and ubiquity have been rushing through the cosmos ever since and will do so for as long as it exists, a tiny bundle of radiation that illuminates the darkness between the stars. At the same time she had become part of me, a remembered image, spreading across the memory fields of my cortex. She had found a refuge and home in me, in my inner self, which she had saved by taking on the terrible alternative, so that I could reach the safe shore of a world in which I was not condemned as a witch to be burned at the stake. Only, where was I living? In the world from which I had formerly come, or had I strayed into an alternate one?

THE JUDGE HAD me brought to him and informed me that His Excellency the archbishop had decided to suspend the sentence and postpone the execution. Questions, particularly with respect to visions of the future, had arisen in my case that might be of significance in high places. Advice had been sought in Rome and the sending of an investigative commission had been requested. The request had been granted, and now the arrival of scholars and clergymen was awaited. That was, however, not anticipated before early summer, for the noble lords could not be expected to take the journey across the Alps before the thaw or to entrust themselves to a ship during the winter storms. For that time, it had been decided, a stay in the dungeon was advisable, but under eased conditions.

Had my letters reached their addressee after all? Had Nicolaus Cusanus intervened on my behalf?

"Is the cardinal in the city?" I asked the mute. He nodded.

"He is departing tomorrow bright and early," said Don Fernando, who was again crouching on his beam.

Then he had certainly not received my letters. Even a very busy man such as he would have been curious and would have had me brought to him to question me and to form an impression of a woman who had appealed to him in that way and demonstrated knowledge of his works. Probably the judge had confiscated the pages and added them to the trial records. Or . . .

"Admit it, in reality you never passed on the letters," I said bitterly to the mute.

"Which reality do you mean?" asked Don Fernando.

THAT NIGHT I dreamed of the stake. But instead of me being burnt, it was Falcotti. As his head leaned forward, his temple burst, and the silver cross he had worn under the skin flowed like a bright rivulet down his blackened cheekbones.

Someone shook me awake. It was pitch-black in the dungeon. I heard the moaning whine of the mute nearby. Again he reached for my shoulder. I brushed off his hand and stood up.

Above me I heard a scurrying. Was it Don Fernando?

"Come on," he said. "You have a visitor."

"The cardinal?" I asked anxiously.

Don Fernando chuckled. The mute opened the dungeon door; from outside candlelight fell in.

"I thought I heard voices last night," I said. "Has the commission from Rome arrived?"

It seemed to me as if I had heard Falcotti's voice behind the door. Or had that been part of my dream?

"No. It is not to be expected before May or June—if it sets off at all," said Don Fernando.

"Who is it?"

"Come on already!"

I felt my way up the stairs.

The air was cool. It was early in the morning, shortly before daybreak. No one was out, but somewhere nearby a horse snorted. The mute blew out the candle. I vaguely made out three riding animals in the street and a man holding the reins.

"What's this about?" I asked suspiciously. Was I going to be eliminated?

"I'm taking you away from here," the man replied. He was short and wiry, as far as I could tell in the first daylight. He wore a pointy felt hat with a feather on it, breeches, and thick knitted socks. His jacket was padded and had many pockets. He had a weather-beaten, friendly face. When he briefly smiled, I noticed that two upper incisors were missing.

"Who are you?" I asked him.

"Whoa!" he exclaimed, reining in the shying horses as Don Fernando crept by them, heading toward the river.

The man noticed that my teeth were chattering with cold. He pulled a cloak from one of his saddlebags, wrapped it around my shoulders, and with strong small hands buttoned it over my chest. I noticed that his left hand was mutilated.

"We have to hurry," he said. He swung himself into the saddle, reached out his hand to me, and pulled me onto the horse behind him; then he spurred the animal and rode across the cathedral square toward the gate.

The man had gathered his long gray hair into a sort of ponytail and fastened it behind his head with a pin in a wooden clasp. I stared at the clasp. It was old, and the blue paint had worn away, but in some places I recognized contours of gentians and edelweiss. Was I dreaming? What a wonderful morning! I balled my hand into a fist and punched the back in front of me one, two, three, four times . . .

"Renata!" I cried. "Renata!"

"Hey! Hey! Stop beating on my back!" she shouted back.

A wave of joy washed over me. I buried my face in her padded jacket, embraced her with both arms and felt under my hands her small breasts, which had grown thin.

"Renata!" I sobbed.

The gate was already open. A group of Jews was being led down to the first ferry, which would bring them to Deutz. They were chained together; probably they had been apprehended in the city after nightfall. Other passengers were already on board, among them a clergyman wearing a broad-brimmed hat and his groom. The packhorses were laden with cumbersome containers and carefully sewn cases of hard leather. Suddenly two officers barred our way and leveled their pikes at us.

"Take the reins!" said Renata, handing me the straps of the packhorses plodding along behind us. "For God's sake, don't let go. In their packs are the results of more than twenty years of fieldwork. And hold on tight!"

Renata steered the animal toward one of the guards.

"What is it?" she shouted.

"Who are you two?"

"I'm afraid it would take somewhat too long to tell you that," she declared with a laugh, kicked the spurs into the horse's flanks, and simply rode over the man. The pike rattled on the pavement. The other, who was rushing to help his companion, she lashed across the face two, three, four times with the riding crop, until he could no longer hear or see and tumbled backward. Then she drove the horse down to the dock. I clung to the reins of the packhorses and pulled the shying animals along behind us, while clutching Renata with the other arm.

We clattered across the planks of the floating dock and onto the ferry, which was ready to cast off. Renata fished a handful of coins out of her jacket pocket and slapped them into the ferry master's outstretched hand. "Cast off!" she shouted to him.

He raised his eyebrows when he saw the amount in his hand.

"Row!" he commanded loudly. "Row!"

Bracing their long oars against the dock, the oarsmen pushed the vessel off into the current.

"Halt!" cried the leader of the guards.

"Are you out of your mind?" the ferry master called back. "We're already in the middle of the river."

"You'll pay for this!" the officer shouted furiously.

"Control yourself! We Deutz ferry masters are not subject to the Cologne council. Bear that in mind!"

"Halt!" the clergyman now exclaimed as well, raising his hand; he pointed to a figure wearing a knapsack and rushing from the gate down toward the dock waving both arms. "Isn't that one of the archbishop's scribes?"

"I beg your forgiveness," said the ferry master. "As much as I would like to do it for you, noble lord, we are already too deep in the current. Even if we tried with all our might, we couldn't return to the dock. The scribe will have to take the next ferry. It departs before midday."

The clergyman gave an understanding nod. The young man with the knapsack stopped running and spread his arms in resignation. From under the dark damp planks of the dock a loud squeal rang out.

"Don Fernando," I said.

"Who?" asked Renata.

"The rat who kept me company in my dungeon," I replied.

"A *rat*?"

"An educated rat, with whom I had many stimulating conversations."

"I don't remember you being so funny, Domenica," she said, wrapping her strong arms around me.

The dimples in her cheeks had grown deeper. She looked tough and wiry, but had grown thin and—terribly old. And as if she had overheard my thoughts, she said, "How young you've stayed."

"And yet it was a hard year I went through here. A wonderful summer, a bitter autumn, and a horrible winter."

"A year! I've been here for twenty-three years," replied Renata. "Our friends sent me to the year 1429 by mistake. But I don't want to complain. It was a glorious time."

"Why didn't you return sooner?"

She shrugged. "Should I have? I like it here. I kept putting off returning to Amsterdam. Besides, I'd promised to keep an eye out for you. And as it turns out, it wasn't for nothing."

"How did you find me?"

She rummaged in her jacket pockets and pulled out a torn piece of paper. *Come get me,* was written on it. *Prison on the cathedral square in Cologne, on March 10, before daybreak.* It was my handwriting.

"I didn't write that," I said.

Renata wrinkled her forehead.

"Then you will write it at some point. As a traveler, God knows, you have to get used to paradoxes like that."

The ferry master joined us. "You were in quite a hurry, it seems to me," he said.

Renata raised her hand. "We haven't done anything wrong, master," she replied with a gap-toothed grin. "More like a private feud with the authorities."

"You've spent a good bit of money on it, huh?" He laughed. "But it's all the same to me," he assured us, jingling the coins in his jacket pocket.

"Who's the noble lord?" I asked, gesturing with my chin to the clergyman with the broad-brimmed hat, who stood with his groom near the horses at the railing and looked across to the eastern riverbank.

"That is Nicolaus, the son of old Krebs of Kues, a river boatman like me," he declared proudly. "His boy has amounted to something in the service of the Church. The Pope appointed him cardinal."

My knees grew weak. Less than ten paces from me stood Nicolaus Cusanus. Should I go to him and reveal to him that it was I who wrote him letters from the dungeon? But perhaps he had never received them. He might think I was trying to put on airs or was not quite right in the head. I didn't dare.

"Your favorite philosopher, I remember. You sat every day on his grave slab in San Pietro in Vincoli. Now he's standing in front of you in the flesh. What a stroke of luck! But you don't look exactly delighted. You don't have the courage to speak to him, do you? It's a strange feeling, I admit. I don't know whether I'd do it. 'Keep away from all VIPs.'—eighth commandment," Renata reminded me.

"I wrote him letters from the dungeon," I confessed.

"Are you crazy? 'Beware of polluting historical sources.' Did you forget that? You can easily set off a new universe that way, on which you would then drift away as if on a broken-off ice floe. Incidentally, that was my greatest fear when I first realized that I had ended up twenty years farther in the past than planned. I feared drifting off due to carelessness and wrong decisions into a universe that had no connection with our future. Perhaps that was the true reason I kept putting off my return to Amsterdam," Renata said, rubbing her forehead. "I was simply afraid of finding nothing and no one there. No tunnel . . . But gradually I began to feel at home in this world. And now I've found you. So I can't have drifted far."

She brushed a gray strand of hair from her forehead.

"And did he answer you?" she asked, gesturing with a nod to the cardinal.

"No."

"Many admirers of great men have fared no differently," Renata remarked with a smile.

"You know, I thought it was my last chance."

We reached the eastern bank and docked. Renata untethered the horses before the oarsmen had moored the vessel and slid the gangplank to the dock. She led the animals ashore and up the bank. The breath of people and animals formed steam clouds in the cool morning air. Behind her the cardinal's groom disembarked from the ferry with the two riding horses and the packhorses. The cardinal brought up the rear. His eyes wandered intently over the strange cases and leather containers. Might he be carrying astronomical instruments with him? I followed him with a hesitant step. Should I pluck up my courage after all?

The groom had stopped and readied one of the riding horses for him. Bowing respectfully, he looked down to the ground as he held the stirrup. The cardinal grasped the pommel and raised his foot to insert it in the stirrup—then lowered it again, while the groom remained in a stooped position.

I too had stopped and looked at Nicolaus Cusanus: the broad face and forehead were familiar to me—only the wrinkles over the corners of his mouth were not yet as deeply engraved as in the bas-relief by Bregno in San Pietro in Vincoli. He actually had markedly peasantlike features, except for the narrow, crooked, aristocratic nose: the large ears; the completely attached earlobes; the prominent chin; the expressive mouth; and the large, strong, and yet slender hands.

"Did you wish to speak with me?" he asked in a friendly tone, nodding to me encouragingly.

His blue-gray eyes scrutinized me intently. I must have looked horrible: my nose reddened by the cold, my matted hair, my dirty bare feet. My throat felt constricted.

"N-no, my lord," I sputtered in a near-whisper.

"Don't you know whom you have in front of you?" hissed the groom, his face averted, his eyes directed submissively at the ground.

"Let her be," the cardinal said calmly, but with a voice that was accustomed to issuing orders.

"Forgive me, Your Eminence," I managed to get out. "I didn't mean to . . ."

He waited patiently, but I had become tongue-tied.

"I had the impression you wanted to say something to me," he encouraged me with a smile that deepened the wrinkles on his cheeks. "What's your name?"

"Domenica, Your Eminence."

Nicolaus Cusanus nodded. "The day of the Lord. May the Lord bless you and keep you, Domenica," he said, raising his hand.

Then he reached for the pommel, inserted his boot toe in the stirrup held by the groom, and swung himself up. Tall as he was, he cut an impressive figure on horseback.

"We set off," he commanded his escort, who had swung himself into the saddle as well. The cardinal knotted the chinstrap of his hat and took the reins. "I want to be in Heisterbach with the Cistercians for sext and in Andernach for vespers. The day is short, and I hate journeying in the dark."

At that moment the groom turned his face to me. It was the scoundrel who had tried to rape me the previous summer and then made the false incriminating statements against me before the council. Behind the back of the cardinal he now spat in my direction and with a grin looked out at the river, where two wild geese flew upstream low over the water. The beat of their wings sounded like a rhythmic moaning.

"You miserable bastard!" I shouted after him, but my voice was drowned out by the rattle of the chains and the crack of the whips of the towing men, who were harnessing their animals to tow the ferry to the far southern dock, from where it would cross back to Cologne.

In the meantime, I had lost sight of Renata. She was standing with her horses next to a man on the summit of the embankment and was waving to me with both arms.

"Look who I found, Domenica!" she exclaimed elatedly, pointing with her horsewhip at the lanky young man standing with crossed arms on the embankment—surrounded by barefoot Jewish children, who had fled up the slope from the towing men's long whips and had taken cover near him. The sun had just risen; his red hair gleamed, and he looked at me uncertainly. It was incredible—a morning full of miracles!

"Frans!" I cried. "Frans!"

I started to run, slipped on the wet grass, and fell down. I then got to my feet, gathered my cloak, and continued to run. He gave me a disconcerted and flustered look. Did he not recognize me in my awful getup? Joyfully, I spread my arms and he caught me.

"Oh, Frans," I sighed.

"Have we met?" he asked.

I pushed him away from me and stared at him aghast. How young he looked!

"You don't recognize me?"

"I'm sorry. You two are"—he made a vague gesture—"travelers?"

Renata suddenly chuckled and held out her hand to him.

"I'm Renata," she said, taking off her hat, unfastening the wooden clasp, and shaking out her gray hair. "And she"—pointing with her thumb toward me—"is Domenica."

And turning to me, she went on, "My dear, what we have here is apparently a very early version of Frans. You haven't met him yet."

"Indeed," he said, frowning and a bit unsettled, "this is my first journey so deep into the past."

I eyed him with growing horror. "And Venice?" I asked, almost desperately.

"Venice?"

"All that still lies in the distant future for him," explained Renata, and the fragments of amber in her eyes flashed. "How nice for him. We will meet him there in our youthful innocence."

"So you haven't come looking for us?" I asked Frans.

My words condensed in the cool morning air. The wind carried them away. Uncomprehendingly, he shook his head. "No, I've been assigned to determine the exact state of the construction work," he replied, gesturing with a nod to the unfinished cathedral building on the opposite bank. "I'm an architect."

"Yes, I remember."

"What do you mean?" he asked me.

"Oh, it's not important," I replied with a sigh.

"In the time he comes from they don't even know our names yet at the CIA," Renata explained. "Still, the young man can make himself useful. We need accommodations where we can make ourselves somewhat presentable, and then a passage downriver."

When we had told Frans the circumstances of my liberation, he thought it advisable for us to abscond to Düsseldorf in order to be safe from the officers of the Cologne city council and the archbishop's henchmen. We rode for a day down the Rhine and sought lodgings. Renata sold her horses, and I helped her sort and repack her botanical collection. The results of her fieldwork exceeded all expectations. Frans roamed around the harbor and finally found a boatman who was heading to Utrecht. It was a barge full of timber from the Eifel. On his northwest journey he docked for a few days in Duisburg to load ironware.

Due to the thaw, the current was quite strong. It took us less than a week to reach Utrecht and from there a day on horseback to Amsterdam. We were almost home.

"Today is the beginning of a new era," said Frans, as we rode through the reeds.

"For us?" asked Renata.

"For the world," he replied with a smile. "Today is the day Leonardo da Vinci is born."

"Oh my! I beg your pardon, Your Eminence. We were not expecting you. We thought you were still staying in Cologne. Oh God, I was planning to go to the market tomorrow morning to buy some things to which you are partial, as I know from the past. Oh, Your Eminence. What am I doing standing here before you? Please . . ."

"But Katrin! Are you seriously going to sink to your knees before me?

Stand up and let me embrace you. And don't call me 'Your Eminence'! What did you always call me when I was still dean at St. Florin?"

"I wouldn't dare."

"Nico, you called me, and you were like a mother to me. Let us stick with that, Katrin."

"But you have become such an exalted man. You come right after the Holy Father, says Helwicus."

"Well, isn't it so?" the dean broke in. "It is said that Pope Nicholas is your friend and values your advice."

"Indeed, we see eye to eye in many respects."

"What am I doing here?" the old housekeeper lamented, spreading her arms. "Completely unprepared. I can offer a chicken, roasted in butter and rosemary, but cold. The bread is fresh."

"I'm not hungry. We did not set off from Andernach until after lunch today. In the morning I had to dictate an urgent letter to the chapter of St. John's in Osnabrück. But I'm thirsty. I could certainly do with a glass of wine."

"Wine from home?"

"Yes. Do you have some from my father's vineyards?"

"Indeed, we do. Every year your brother Johannes sends us a tun down the Moselle. It is the best wine far and wide."

"Then bring me a flagon of that, Katrin, so that I may at least taste a mouthful of home."

"You mean, you're not going to ride up to Kues?" asked the dean.

"I would be delighted to, but I don't have the time, Helwicus. I'm expected in Frankfurt. And next month I shall be in Brixen once again. I would have liked to ride up to Kues to check on things and see how far the plans for the foundation have come to fruition, but I have trustworthy people under my brother's supervision who are advancing my cause and managing it well."

"I heard the same."

"Did you also hear about the witch they plan to bring to trial in Cologne?"

"Yes, but only vaguely. There are many rumors going around in Cologne. I think it will turn out the same way as in the year '46 with that sorceress. The city council had her banished. A lenient sentence for the woman."

"I hope that they proceed the same way in this case."

"I hope so too. Only there was once again conflict between the city council and the archbishop. A little witch like that could easily get caught between the millstones if one side is keen to make an example."

The housekeeper brought a roast chicken and a flagon of wine.

The cardinal filled the glass and drank from it in small, sampling sips. "It's good," he said, nodding appreciatively. "That reminds me: There is a gift of wine on its way from Brussels. Dietrich von Xanten will arrive here next week. Take it for yourself, Helwicus, for your hospitality."

"That is too kind, Your Eminence."

"I need the wine neither in Frankfurt nor in Brixen. And traveling isn't good for it. Wherever I go, I receive gifts of wine as if I were St. Florin himself," he said with a laugh. "As if God had not sufficiently blessed me with my own vines."

The dean joined discreetly in his laughter.

"And it is the best," Katrin declared emphatically, and withdrew.

"May I withdraw as well?" asked the dean. "I still have preparations to make in the church for tomorrow. Will you give the sermon again, as always when you're staying in Koblenz?"

"It's always a pleasure and an honor for me to serve God in St. Florin. *Beati, qui audiunt verbum Dei et custodiunt illud* is the subject I've chosen."

"It is a great pleasure and honor for all of us as well, Your Eminence." The dean bowed and turned to leave.

"Helwicus," said the cardinal. "Have you heard of a place named Cattenom?"

The dean stopped and turned around. "Oh, I believe there is a hamlet by that name up at the top of the Moselle, in Lotharingia, not far from Metz. I'm not certain, but Adrien, the fisherman who brings us his catch every Thursday evening, comes from that area. I will ask him."

"In Lotharingia?" the cardinal repeated reflectively. "East of Cattenom the land is black . . ."

"I don't understand."

The Cusan sighed. "Nor do I. Forgive me. Sometimes strange thoughts come into one's mind. God be with us."

Where had that name come from? Where had those dark words come from? he wondered. Was it an inspiration? A sign from God? He saw before his eyes the face of the young woman he had encountered the previous day on the ferry. The look in her eyes had been so frightened—and so knowing.

It was pointless to lose himself in such speculations. He prayed; then he broke the bread and the joints of the chicken, separated the light meat from the breast and the darker meat from the wings and legs. Slowly he ate, and with relish; only once did he stop.

"Todi," he murmured, and was seized by a shiver. "What made me think of Todi?"

The Cusan stepped to the window and looked out over the meadows around the mouth of the Moselle. They stretched almost down to Andernach—a vast wetland from which myriad mosquitoes swarmed up in the summer. It was a nuisance for man and beast, as he recalled. What a carefree time that had been, when he had still performed his duty as a dean here at St. Florin!

Mist rose like smoke from cold fires. An army camp of ghosts, which had moved on through time.

"Lord," he prayed. "Blessed are they who hear your word and keep it. You alone know the course of the world. Protect us from affliction and sorrow. Have mercy on us, Lord, and on all your creatures . . ."

Book

FIVE

I

Crossroads

Furthermore, I say that this infinity and immensity is an animal, although it has no determinate form nor perception of external things; for it has all soul in itself and embraces all the animate and is all this.

GIORDANO BRUNO

Now I realize, of course, why Frans already knew me when we met back in Venice. I mistook it for a come-on. And yet there's one thing I can't explain: When I first saw him, I had the strange feeling that I had known him for a long time. It's still inexplicable to me. I thought at first that it had been a sort of déjà vu, but . . . well . . . And at the time he knew exactly what was in store for me, everything I would have to go through. He didn't say a word to me about it! Frans was very close to me. I still love him. And he knew exactly what awaited me in Cologne . . ."

Grit, who had up to that point listened silently, took her pipe out of her mouth and shook her head.

"No, he didn't know that," she said firmly.

Light and shadow alternated. Sleet showers lashed the Old Sea, which rolled white-headed toward the shore against a dark sky. The New Dam was obscured by clouds—invisible.

"Everything that can be *is*—somewhere," she went on. "No traveler will ever tell another anything about their future. He can't. How is he to know which future he has seen?"

We were silent. Sleet pattered against the windowpanes. Finally Grit laid her pipe in the ashtray and turned on the floor lamp.

"*Posse esse* and *actu esse*. They are one," I said.

"Quantum mechanics?"

"No—Cusanus."

"Really! Incredible," Grit remarked, shaking her head in disbelief. "You met him, Renata told me. Did you speak with him?"

"She was tongue-tied," Renata explained with a smile.

Tooth embryos grown from stem cells had been implanted in place of her missing incisors. She had gotten a haircut and had her hair dyed—dark blond with highlights. She now no longer looked like an old woman, but like a lively, pretty woman in her mid-forties.

"Maybe it's better that you didn't speak with him," said Grit. "How easy it is to unleash a universe in situations like that."

"That might have happened anyway. She wrote letters to the cardinal and mentioned future events," Renata remarked.

"He never received them," I replied. "I'm absolutely certain of that. He would definitely have reacted in some form."

"Maybe not the Cusanus you met," Grit interjected. "And you liked it there, Renata?"

"If I were offered an attractive task, whether in botany or another field, I would be delighted to travel to that time again. I think I did a good job, as the people from the Hortus assure me. I brought back hundreds of plants that had gone extinct, among them a few dozen we had had no idea existed. That will enormously enrich the All Species Foundation, they told me. Some of them are interesting evolutionary missing links. They want to name them after me—*renata*. I will only agree to that if they name the most beautiful among them *domenica*. You can't help it that the learned *doctores* in Cologne confiscated and ruined your collection."

"That's nice of you, but it's my own fault. I was too reckless—too naive. And I didn't exercise the necessary care."

"You're both back. That's the most important thing," said Grit, lifting the carafe from the warmer and filling up our glasses with mulled wine. "And in time for Christmas."

Renata had returned on November 26, exactly a week after my departure. The ascending soliton had dropped me off on December 18. At that point, the institute was practically abandoned; most of the physicists and technicians had already gone on Christmas vacation. Only Dr. Coen was still on duty. He had definitely expected a return before the holidays and kept his eye on the simulation. As a precaution, he had equipped it with numerous motion sensors, which would notify him if someone appeared in the scene.

"I assume Frans returned to the time from which he had come," I said.

"Yes, to the year 2045, I presume," Grit confirmed. "If I remember correctly, he went to Venice the following year, when the Japanese began the restoration project. They were seeking travelers with architectural knowledge and had recruited him."

"My God, at that time I had just been cramming for my university entrance exams," I said.

"What will you do now, Domenica?" Grit asked me.

"No idea. I doubt they'll have any more use for me after that failure."

"You never know."

"Please, Grit! I almost ended up burning at the stake for my stupidity. I bungled everything."

Grit shook her head. "No, your transition worked—despite everything."

"And what does that mean?"

"That your journey had a point, or else it never would have taken place; the transition would not have opened."

"Oh, what point could all that have had?"

"You should have asked Don Fernando," Renata broke in.

"Yes. If it hadn't been for him . . . I don't know whether I would have made it through the winter in the dungeon."

"They'll find a job for you," said Grit. "The institute needs travelers with experience."

"Experience!"

"Didn't Falcotti ask you during the job interview what you would like to do if you could turn back time?" asked Renata.

"Yes. I had said I would go back to September 2039 to prevent my father from boarding the ill-fated train in Naples. He died in the attack. Do you seriously think . . . ?"

"Perhaps your wish will be granted."

"You mean an octopus operation?" Grit asked, sipping her mulled wine.

"No. It's enough for Domenica to go up to her father and say, 'For heaven's sake, do not board that train,'" Renata suggested.

"How do you imagine that, Renata? Tell me, how do you imagine that? I step in front of him on the platform and say, 'Listen, Papa, I have a strange feeling. Please don't get on that train. Something might happen.' He sees a twenty-eight-year-old woman in front of him, puts his hand to his forehead, and says, 'Signora, are you all right?' After all, I was only twelve at the time, Renata!"

"A bomb threat," Grit mused. "You could spread the news that a bombing is planned. Call the police."

"Oh, that can be damn dangerous. I know that from experience," said Renata. "They'll find out like lightning who you are. And if the train is then actually stopped, if they search it and find a bomb, then you're in for it."

"But you would have saved not only your father's life, but also the lives of hundreds of people. If it's a constitutive event, however, you'll never reach the year 2039," Grit pointed out. "But the commission has to decide on that anyhow."

"I would have a different suggestion, Domenica," Renata interjected with a smug smile. "You make a pass at your father in the hotel before he goes to the train station. You make eyes at him, let him treat you to a drink at the hotel bar, go with him to his room, and see to it that he misses the train."

"With my own father? You're indecent!" I replied indignantly.

"You don't have to go all the way, sweetie," Renata went on teasingly. "You can ask him for a favor. My goodness, you'll think of something! You can always lock yourself in the bathroom if things get too dicey for you."

Grit laughed out loud and slapped the table with her palm. With a loud crack the carafe shattered on the warmer; the wine extinguished the candle and spread in a red pool across the table. Grit jumped up in shock, hurried into the kitchen, and came back with a roll of paper towels.

"How could that happen?" she asked. We helped her wipe up.

"When are you leaving for Genoa?" Grit asked me.

"Nothing came of that," I sighed. "Of the wedding, I mean. Chalid, the splendid groom, eloped with a younger woman."

"So you're not going."

"Am I supposed to spend the holidays listening to my forsaken mother's laments? Not after this year! Her call was enough for me."

"Ah, wonderful," said Grit. "Then the three of us will celebrate Christmas together—as planned. The goose has been ordered. I'm going to stuff it—"

"—with apples and chestnuts," I said. "I'm looking forward to it."

"THIS IS INDEED puzzling," said van Waalen.

He worriedly puffed out his cheeks and furrowed his brow. The jacket of his dark blue double-breasted suit stretched over his belly and there were white hairs stuck to the lapels and the sleeves. Angora? He loved cats, I recalled. Next to him stood Jörn Auerbach; his mouse-gray suit, which would have fit a man fifty pounds heavier, hung loosely on his emaciated figure. He sucked in his hollow cheeks even more and pursed his lips skeptically.

"But please, sit down, Ms. Ligrina," said van Waalen, gesturing with his plump hand to a chair opposite the table at which both directors now took their seats. Suddenly I felt as if I were at an oral exam. Dr. Coen hurried in with an open lab coat, took a seat, and placed his documents and his Palmtop on the table in front of him. He gave me a friendly nod.

Just come right out and say it, I thought. I failed across the board. You have no more use for me. I'm fired.

Auerbach, who sat in the middle, cast a questioning glance to his left and right, then brought his terribly scrawny freckled hands together into a gable and rasped in a harsh Baltic accent, "There's probably no rule of self-consistency that you haven't violated, Ms. Ligrina. I have to assume that someone familiarized you before the start of your mission with the ten laws to which a traveler must adhere."

He cast a sidelong glance at Dr. Coen, who seemed not to notice it, because he was consulting his Palmtop with the utmost concentration.

"Of course I was instructed to that effect, director. I'm sorry I failed to exercise the necessary care. I'm aware that I've made big mistakes."

"Catastrophic ones," said Auerbach.

"Still," van Waalen broke in, nodding at me benevolently, "the transition to the past went off according to plan and without a hitch. That's the astonishing thing. You seem to have powerful supporters."

"Supporters?" I asked, perplexed. "Where?"

He shrugged his massive round shoulders and pointed with his thumb to the ceiling. "Maybe up there," he said.

Auerbach let out a brief laugh that sounded like a stifled sneeze. Then he laid both hands flat on the table and stared sternly ahead as if he urgently had to demand scientific discipline. Dr. Coen turned with a smirk to face the window and looked out at the IJ and the silhouette of Java, behind which the Amsterdam skyline rose in the pale January light. Always the same amusing little games between the two factions of the CIA, he seemed to be thinking.

"Ms. Ligrina," Auerbach said in a matter-of-fact tone, "the self-repair program of the multiverse is evolutionary—that means it has the inherent tendency to revise itself constantly and optimize its objective. It is therefore always trying out different possibilities. If no improvements arise, those alternatives are rejected and erased. The problem is that the virtual universes are indistinguishable from the real ones. Quantum cosmology grants equal rights to both—and theoretically infinite—variations."

"Only according to your theory, my esteemed colleague," van Waalen broke in, smugly brushing his mop of white hair from his forehead.

"According to the Advanced General Brane Theory of Hla Thilawuntha," Auerbach corrected him with a withering sidelong glance.

"According to your interpretation of that theory," van Waalen replied with a self-satisfied smile. "There are others."

"As for the case of Ms. Ligrina . . ." Dr. Coen ventured to interject, but fell silent when he saw the reproving looks directed at him by the two professors.

Auerbach cleared his throat and adopted a formal tone: "As for the case of Ms. Ligrina, it is to be feared that her activities have caused drastic fractures in the historical texture. That applies in particular to the letters to the cardinal Nicolaus Cusanus—an incredibly reckless act, a catastrophic intervention in the source material, the consequences of which cannot even be estimated. A contamination of unprecedented magnitude."

"I feared for my life, Director. I saw it as the only chance to save . . ."

He gave me a look of consternation as if a mouse he was about to dissect had cried "Mercy!"

"I'm sorry, but we're talking here about the existence or nonexistence of universes, young woman," he said.

"Every human being is a universe," van Waalen interjected in a solemn tone, folding his hands in front of his chin to conceal his faint smile, as if he had only been waiting until his rival ventured so far out onto thin ice that he could enjoy watching him fall through.

"Yes, yes, my esteemed colleague," Auerbach snorted, throwing up his scrawny arms. "Not a single sparrow will fall to the ground without . . . and so on. Only you know as well as I do that the same person is present in countless universes."

"But that doesn't make the person a negligible quantity," countered van Waalen. "In each of those universes the individual is a vulnerable creature, afflicted with pain and mortal fear. It's about the human beings—in every single one of those universes."

Auerbach sank back in his chair, drummed his fingers on the table, and looked up to the ceiling.

"As for the case of Ms. Ligrina . . ." Dr. Coen made a renewed attempt.

"As for the case of Ms. Ligrina," van Waalen declared forcefully, "her violations of the rules of self-consistency—for which I, incidentally, have complete understanding—were not only permitted, but also might even have been provoked by the . . . um . . . self-repair program or whomever. There's no other way to explain the course of her mission. It is not possible for us to extrapolate the historical ramifications she might have brought about. But I submit that they might have been desired. They were taken into consideration and—we'll never know—ultimately accepted or rejected."

"Brushed out," Auerbach sneered, baring his teeth.

"Brushed out," van Waalen replied emphatically, plucking a hair from his lapel.

"But why, actually?" Auerbach objected, tracing a question mark in the air with his scrawny finger. "Theoretically, it's entirely possible for such alternatives to coexist in the multiverse."

"But it could just as well be the case that a better variation was found and that the days of this our universe are numbered," van Waalen countered.

Suddenly I saw again the smoking seam beyond the abyss—the ashes of the chronicles of countless worlds that had squandered their chance.

"Then it's only right and proper," said Dr. Coen, "that Ms. Ligrina be given the opportunity to improve the chances of this our universe in the cosmic contest of alternatives."

Frowning, Auerbach looked first at me, then at him. "Do you think she is capable of that?" he asked.

"I do," Dr. Coen said emphatically.

"That's not for us to determine," declared van Waalen. "We can, as in every case, only make a preliminary decision and approve the mission or not. The ultimate decision lies in the hand—"

"Please!" Auerbach said sharply. "The ultimate criterion is the question of whether the transition will open for this plan or not."

I was taken aback. Apparently I really did have powerful supporters—wherever.

"Am I to understand," I asked, "that I am being permitted . . ."

The two directors exchanged a glance. Dr. Coen nodded.

"Yes," said Auerbach, clearing his throat. "The commission has agreed to approve the experiment and to allow you, Ms. Ligrina, to attempt to travel to the year 2039 and save your father from death in the train disaster near Naples. However, we make no secret of the fact that the majority of commission members do not endorse averting the train disaster, because it might be a constitutive historical event. I do not share this opinion; I regard the event as marginal."

How sensitive, I thought. For me it wasn't marginal at all, no more than it was for the many other people who lost their family members in the horrible attack. In any case, I would try to save at least my father. That was my objective, because I would otherwise not reach the year 2039.

THERE WAS, OF course, an abundance of reference points stored in the CIA archive from the decades since the founding of the institute. I asked Dr. Coen to select for me a day in late August or early September. The construction of the simulation was a matter of a few minutes.

Dr. Coen led me into a spartanly furnished office, which could have been anywhere in the institute; in it were two chairs and a desk, on which there was an old-fashioned push-button telephone with a small screen. Through the window I saw the silhouette of Amsterdam beyond the IJ in the simulation of 2039. Some of the prominent buildings were missing from the skyline; they had been erected only later.

"We have to naturalize you appropriately," he said, handing me a Europass, as had still been customary fifteen years earlier. My birthdate was indicated as May 25, 2014.

"I look pretty old," I said.

"It's unavoidable if you are to pass as a time-native," replied Dr. Coen. "Those are difficult years. The Cattenom disaster is only a decade in the past. Europe is increasingly breaking up. The political situation is fraught; numerous refugees are on the move. The authorities are mistrustful and cracking down hard. We don't want to lose you."

I pocketed the unfamiliar document.

"I'm afraid you can't use a credit card, but we're giving you enough cash. And come back safely," said Dr. Coen.

"When will the soliton arrive?"

He looked at his watch. "I think I'd better leave now. It can't be much longer."

He hurried out of the room and closed the door, over which a little red lamp burned. I waited for the wave, but nothing happened. Had the transition failed? I tried to open the window to check, but it was sealed shut. When I turned around, I saw that the little lamp over the door had changed color.

At that moment someone knocked, and a young woman stuck her head in. She had a friendly, open face with dimples in her cheeks. Her chestnut brown hair she had pulled back into a ponytail.

"I had a feeling someone had arrived," she said with a laugh. "Welcome to the year 2039! I hope that's where you wanted to go. You're looking at me with such dismay."

"The transition . . ." I stammered. "I didn't feel anything."

The young woman shrugged and replied, "The physicists claim it's impossible to feel them."

"Opinions are divided on that."

She looked at me sympathetically. "The journey seems to have taken a lot out of you. Why don't you come to my office first and have a coffee with me?"

My gaze fell on the identification she wore on her light gray blouse; I caught my breath. GRIT HAAS was written on it. Oh, God! How young she was! Dear Grit, how many long years you will have to spend in the past! She had never told me that! In a daze, I followed her into a room decorated with posters of art exhibitions. Stedelijk Museum. Rijksmuseum. Van Gogh Museum. Rembrandthuis.

"You love art?" I asked.

"I don't know much about art history, if that's what you mean. But I hate having bare walls around me," she said. "We're housed here only temporarily, until the new institute building is finished. We're even supposed to get underwater offices, which I think is a harebrained idea."

I nodded and smiled at her.

"You shouldn't contaminate me," she said, handing me a cup and pouring me hot coffee from a large thermos.

"Contaminate?" It was meant to sound casual, but didn't succeed.

"You're looking at me as if you knew me well. Since I've never seen you before, I have to conclude from that that we will get to know each other better at some point. I find that reassuring."

"Reassuring?"

"Well, it proves to me that I have a future and will return safely from my travels, for which I'm currently being prepped. And as a result, I'm already contaminated. That's what they call that, right?"

A handsome young man entered the office. He was a robust, athletic-looking guy and wore his blond hair down to his shoulders. He greeted me with a nod and asked, "Are you coming along, Grit?"

She looked at her wristwatch. "I'll be off in half an hour, Leendert. Then we can head over, okay?"

He nodded and left.

Leendert de Hooghe. I clenched my teeth when I thought of the embittered man with the wounded eye I had met in the Waag, and of the painful fate of these two people who faced the future so nonchalantly.

"Thanks for the coffee," I said, and hurried out.

THE CITY ITSELF hadn't changed much in the fifteen years. Some of the high-rises in the southwestern port area hadn't been built yet. Around the Centraal Station bicycles still predominated; the Lectrics were in the minority.

The flight offerings were, compared with those in the middle of the century, still abundant. But oil was already beginning to grow scarce. The first light-clippers were flying by then on the long-distance routes around the equator, and everywhere magnetic levitation catapults were being built for the hydrogen boosters—including in Schiphol.

The fateful political developments in the Middle East still lay several years in the future: the Saudi Revolution; the Jahiliyah Massacre in Riyadh; the Hormuz disaster, in which the United States suffered a catastrophic defeat; the British-Italian North Africa adventure; the Caucasus War; and the Aegean War. Those conflicts would result in the final drying up of the crude oil streams and thus the end of unrestricted mobility, of private car traffic and traditional civil aviation. Not to mention the consequences of that development for the market economy: the collapse of the auto and aircraft industries. Relying on its military superiority, Western civilization would attempt to secure the extraterritorial basis of its existence by force, but would fail miserably. The terror organizations would deliver the beloved oil to their doorstep, hundreds of thousands of barrels in the harbors, on the beaches—burning. All later attempts, above all by the Americans, to avoid the consequences of their disastrous policies retroactively and undo them through octopus operations would come to nothing. Those historic events would prove to be constitutive and thus inexpungible facts of this universe like September 11, 2001, and the Cattenom nuclear disaster. They were the ugly dents that helped shape the face of recent history.

ROME IN 2039 was still a different city. It was the city of my childhood—full of life, full of people, full of cars and motor scooters—not the frontline city in which I would pursue my studies ten years later. I got a room in the Vatte, a small hotel on Via Cavour near the train station and the metro. San Pietro in Vincoli was only a few paces away.

I strolled across Piazza Navona and Campo de' Fiori, but this time, un-like during my—later—university years, I took a deep breath to catch a molecule of the ashes of Giordano Bruno—and sucked in the sharp fra-grance of the first late-summer flowers—of gladioluses, asters, phlox, and dahlias, which were offered at the stalls. It occurred to me that here too a small part of the body destroyed by fire had turned to light that illuminated the darkness between the stars.

In "my" apartment on Via Garibaldi lived someone named Bartocelli. A bus with a tour group was arriving at the convent across the street. The pilgrims rolled their suitcases across the cobblestone street and through the archway into the convent courtyard; in the process, they held up all the traffic with their clumsy operation of their remote controls. There was a concert of honking and much shouting. To put an end to the obstruction, the tour guide promptly seized two of the wayward suitcases to carry them out of the roadway—at which point they began to shriek loudly, because their theft alarm had been triggered. Finally, the last pilgrims had disap-peared into the inner courtyard, and the cars clattered bumper to bumper over the cobblestones down to the bank of the Tiber. I had forgotten how many cars had still been out on the streets back then.

The university had sunk into the deep sleep of summer vacation. I turned the corner onto Piazza San Pietro, climbed the steps, and entered the spacious, cool nave of the church. Several times I had to wrap my head around the fact that my memories of that familiar place were memories from the future, that everything that connected me to it had not happened in the past, but was still to come. I gazed at the impressive crayfish in the net made of twenty thick red tassels on the shield under the relief by Bregno. Now that I'd met Nicolaus in person, I could better judge his re-semblance to the depiction. The deep indentations over the corners of his mouth must have engraved themselves during the bitter years he had spent in Brixen. Next to the entrance I lit three candles, one for Renata, one for my shadow sister, and one for me; then I stepped out onto the sunlit square.

It was late morning and I decided to visit the Vatican Museums, for around that time the crowds were lightest. Most of the tourists were on the way to their hotels to have lunch. But there were still far too many visitors there, and the guards channeled the stream of people upstairs and downstairs through the building and the Sistina. I knew a few shortcuts and reached the hall with the maps, globes, and atlases, at the end of which, if I remembered correctly, almost directly before the exit in a side room on the right, hung the great painting of Paradise by Peter Wenzel, which had so inspired me as a child with its colorfulness and its wealth of animal and plant forms.

Too late I noticed my growing dizziness as I turned the corner and entered the room. There I saw a dark-haired girl of eleven or twelve, with faded blue jeans and a light blue top. She was in the company of a man of around forty, who was dressed with striking elegance. In one hand he held a panama hat, with which he was fanning himself, in the other a tightly rolled-up newspaper, with which he was impatiently tapping his leg.

I froze. It was like déjà vu—only from a different perspective. I saw the girl in profile, enraptured by my favorite painting. But she must have noticed my entrance, for she glanced briefly in my direction. Suddenly she raised both hands to her temples and began to whimper. At that same moment I knew that I had committed an unpardonable error.

"You . . ." I began, but then I couldn't get another word out. *No! No! No!* I gasped for air, because a stabbing pain in my temples almost robbed me of consciousness. Then I sought support on the wall and groped with my eyes closed toward the exit.

"Is something wrong, young woman?" the man asked me. "Do you need help?"

"I've made a terrible mistake," I murmured. "Please forgive me."

The girl burst into tears. The man turned away from me in dismay, hurried to the little girl, took her in his arms and asked her worriedly, "Are you okay, *cara*? Sit down for a moment."

"I'm leaving," I asserted hastily, shaking my head to dispel the piercing pain. "I'm leaving . . ."

A guard came rushing over and supported me; sympathetically, he offered me his chair and was about to call for help via his walkie-talkie.

"Please don't," I said. "I'm feeling better already. It must be the heat."

The guard led me to the exit; outside I then sat down on a bench for a few minutes and took deep breaths.

"How's the little girl doing?" I asked him.

"You mean the girl who was here with her father? The two of them left, I assume," he replied.

Soon thereafter I left the building, for I was aware that only one thing helped during such attacks: to create spatial distance between yourself and your alter ego. The scientists warned sternly against risking such encounters. In the consciousness of the two parties interferences could occur for which there was no neurological explanation. They were superimpositions that might be conditioned by identical structures, the psychologists asserted. The neurologists, on the other hand, ruled that out, for according to them the brain was in a state of constant flux; with each sense perception, with each thought new neural structures were created and old ones modified or dismantled, they argued.

Whatever the case might be, it had been a sudden pain that had flared up behind my temples. And now I again remembered that incident from the point of view of my younger self, on that day when I had been with my father in the Vatican Museums and had seen the painting *Paradiso Terrestre*. It had been that magical moment that I had destroyed through my blundering entrance. I myself had been the dark-haired middle-aged woman who had stumbled in back then, giving me a headache and making me nauseous, and then departed, murmuring, on the arm of a guard. The human organism replaces itself completely in a period of fifteen years—exchanging itself gradually, molecule by molecule, for new material from the environment, giving the "worn-out" and "used-up" material back to it—but memory remains stored.

What had I seen this time? A pretty, slightly chubby girl in designer jeans, with a stylish cutoff top and white and blue sneakers. Obviously spoiled and a bit vain. And my father? Strangely, I had remembered him differently. He had always struck me as tall and handsome, elegant in appearance and always impeccably dressed. But he was actually a shorter man who made up for his lack of height with markedly upright posture and high heels on his expensive suede shoes. Even for a sales representative in select fashionable textiles and knickknacks ranging from trendy to brazen, a tad too extravagantly dressed, almost a little—well, dandyish.

In retrospect, his death had set off a strange coping process in me. As a child you experience the loss of a loved one not as a shocking, agonizing bereavement. It's more of a strange mixture of sensation and disbelief. I had been the only student in my school who had lost a family member in the Mondragone terror attack—and not just any relative, but my father. Secretly I had even enjoyed being the center of attention among my schoolmates, for the event had for days flooded the newspapers and television with horrible images. It had been more embarrassing for me than anything else when I came home and Mother sat apathetically in her black dress like a crow in the living room, in the kitchen, or on the terrace—with a pale, stony face, as if she wanted to put the dead man on trial because he had done this to her and escaped responsibility. Only very gradually did I grasp that a void had opened up in me that would never, never close again. It opened painfully on the weekends when Father suddenly no longer returned home with his sample cases—those cases in which he had always brought back beautiful clothing for Mother and me as a surprise, mostly display items or floor models from fashion shows. And for me always a special surprise: a VidClip or HoloClip, earrings, a bracelet or a necklace. The closets overflowed, but my mother made little use of the treasures he unrelentingly amassed. She didn't like that sort of clothing. I wore them, and what didn't fit me or didn't look good on me, I gave away to my friends to buy their sympathy and secure their loyalty.

That had been my father as I remembered him. In the subsequent months and years I dreamed of him often. I loved him, I idealized him— built an altar for him in the void he had left behind. I suffered from the deprivation of his closeness, his attention, and his care. I missed the hand that gently stroked my hair and caressed my cheek, the scratch of his thin mustache on my nose, the touch of his puckered lips.

Now I had encountered him; I had seen him as he had actually been, with the eyes of a grown woman. It hadn't—I confess—moved me deeply. Was it due to the circumstances of the meeting, the shock of the unexpected encounter with myself? Was it due to the nanotechnological armoring of my inner self, which was still operative and shielded my heart as well? The distance that separated me from him disturbed me. His leering, appraising gaze at my figure had not escaped my notice any more than the impatience with which he reprovingly took note of his daughter's lingering in front of the painting as she imbibed the minutiae of forms and colors, and the suppressed irritation with which he slapped the tightly rolled *Corriere* against the side of his knee because she couldn't get enough of the diversity of plants and animals.

ON THE WAY back to the hotel I bought a train ticket to Naples and made a reservation for September 15. I would go to Naples and try to find a way to stop my father from boarding the ill-fated train. I would not prevent any constitutive fact of this universe in Professor Auerbach's sense, but a constitutive fact of my universe, as marginal as it might be. I would save him from death. My father would keep coming home on the weekend with his surprises for me in the sample cases. Nothing would change for my mother and me. Life would go on. What would become of me in that case? Where are you, my other shadow sister, who grew up sheltered with Mommy and Daddy? Did you dutifully fulfill your university entrance requirements and study botany as well—did you follow in my footsteps? Or did you pursue completely different paths, which led to completely different universes? Would I ever find out?

II

Forking Roads

At the heart of everything is a question, not an answer. When we peer down into the deepest recesses of matter or at the farthest edge of the universe, we see, finally, our own puzzled faces looking back at us.

JOHN WHEELER

I lowered the book when the express entered the tunnel under Monte Mássico. At that exact point a bomb would go off the next evening on the train traveling in the opposite direction, the Naples–Rome express, killing more than five hundred people. My father would, if my plan succeeded, not be among the victims.

I looked at my reflection in the window of the car. I still had no idea how I would manage to stop him from boarding the train. I would somehow have to draw his attention to me, somehow head him off, on the square in front of the train station, in the ticket hall, at the latest on the platform—speak to him, urge him, implore him . . .

We had a long stop in Casoria. The reason for that, we learned later, was unrest around Napoli Centrale, as a result of which the train station had to be temporarily closed. Some passengers had chosen to get off in Casoria and take the city buses or a taxi to their destination in order to avoid being held up in the city center. It was already night when the express finally reached its last stop.

The city was seething. The people reacted with protest rallies to Rome's decree that those residing south of a Gaeta-Termoli line needed special permission to travel north. Many people, particularly refugees from the south and illegal immigrants, tried to cross the border before the official measures took full effect, and everywhere I sensed anger and aggression.

I had reserved a room in the Grand Hotel Terminus on Piazza Garibaldi, a building of solid elegance but with affordable prices, in which better-off business travelers apparently often stayed. My room in the rear faced east and offered a view of Mount Vesuvius. On the left side stretched the brightly illuminated skyline of the Centro Direzionale with its modern high-rises, which had been built around the turn of the millennium.

After I had checked in, I took another walk down Corso Umberto Primo to Piazza Nicola Amore, followed Via Duomo toward the port, and headed past Castel Nuovo to Piazza Trieste et Trento. Things had not yet reached that point, but in four or five years those two cities would be officially known as Triest and Trient, and beyond the borders in Slovenia, Friuli, and South Tyrol, signs bearing the old Italian names would be nowhere to be found.

It was a warm evening; though it was already almost midnight, the thermometer still read eighty-two degrees. The sidewalk cafés were packed with theatergoers from the Teatro di San Carlo, who had gathered for a drink after the final curtain and were discussing the performance with loud voices and eloquent gestures. They were predominantly well-dressed young people from wealthy families. I saw the first IComs dangling as pendants from necklaces or bracelets. They were still ridiculously large. It was the time when they were gradually replacing the "Universals," the all-purpose super cell phones. The name ICom, which accurately characterized the function as an identification and communication device, caught on only later. In the beginning they were called "partners." You still had to operate the super cell phones yourself—the new devices operated for you. They possessed perfect voice recognition, obtained any desired information from the Nets, carried on telephone conversations independently in accordance with instructions, and made appointments; they monitored bank accounts, paid bills, and maintained constant contact with the smart chips in the immediate vicinity in order to stay apprised of supply inventories and necessary purchases or repairs.

Only a few paces from the elegant cafés, begging peasants from the south sat on the sidewalk; Africans had spread out mats on which they offered carved wooden statuettes and leather goods. You could tell by looking at them that they were suffering hardship, and I knew that much worse was still to come.

On the way back to the hotel I saw a holominiskirt in the display window of a boutique on Corso Umberto Primo. Father had been interested early on in the animated textiles from the Far East, because he expected to make a great profit on them. The chip was turned on and showed a pornographic sequence: a dark-skinned hand ran down the belly of a fair-skinned woman and thrust between her legs, where it made stroking, masturbating movements, until it slid back up—only, following the program on the chip, to slide down once again.

A group of young people crowded in front of the display window, boys and girls clinging excitedly to each other and reacting with squealing, whistling, and laughter when the hand slid between the thighs. My father's calculations had clearly been correct . . .

That would be the appropriate eye-catcher, I told myself. If he saw me in one of those animated miniskirts, which he offered as a sales representative, he would definitely take notice of me and speak to me. I didn't know whether the first models were equipped with different programs, but I assumed they were. That pornographic sequence was suitable for bedroom fun or at best for a party gag, but not for public view. But you could also turn off the program as needed, and then the flexomons printed on the skirt filled with funny patterns. I decided to buy a holominiskirt the next morning.

It was stuffy in the room. I pulled up the blinds, opened the balcony door, and stepped out. Not a breeze stirred. The guests next door seemed to be indulging in a very private pleasure. A brightly lit room was reflected in the half-open glass door. There was a champagne bucket on a serving cart next to the bed, and on the bed itself passionate copulation was under way. A man lay on his back, and over his loins crouched a dark-haired woman, bouncing lustfully up and down and accompanying the rhythm with sharp cries.

I retreated to my room and turned out the light. Strange, how the thought came into my head, but somehow the man, even though I had seen only his legs, reminded me of my father. Could that woman . . . ?

No, never! I told myself.

Hadn't Renata advised me to come on to my father and go with him to his room? Gradually I truly seemed to be losing my sense of reality.

THE WHISTLE OF a locomotive woke me. I heard voices out in the hallway and the closing of the door to the next room. I stood up quickly, opened my door a crack, and peered out. Two people were walking down the hallway to the elevator: a short man wearing a natural linen suit and a panama hat and next to him a dark-haired woman of my height and about my age in a light red minidress with a straw hat hanging over her arm.

The lovers from that night were apparently checking out; they entered the elevator. Inside it the rectangular mirrors set in polished brass moldings reflected a distorted image, so that I could not make out the faces. Please don't turn around, I pleaded. My prayer was answered. The two of them turned their backs to me as the elevator door closed. I think I would have died if I had looked into my own face.

THE OWNER OF the boutique was a good-looking, slim woman in her late forties. She had medium-length black hair and blue eyes, as are frequently found among Neapolitans—undoubtedly an inheritance from the Norman conquerors.

"I'm sorry," she said. "I sold the last of those skirts fifteen minutes ago. It was the only one I still had in—" Taken aback, she broke off and put on her glasses, which hung around her neck on a little silver chain; then she eyed me from top to bottom.

"Are you pulling my leg, young woman, or am I hallucinating? Wasn't that you who just bought the last holominiskirt from me?"

"Certainly not, or else I wouldn't be here. You must be mistaken," I asserted.

The saleswoman did not seem convinced. "Personally, I don't much like that sex kitsch from Korea, to be honest, but the young girls are totally nuts about it. I could sell two or three dozen of them a day. Yesterday the sales rep was here. He left me two—because we're old friends. I had ordered a hundred, but he told me that at short notice he could deliver to me at most ten. The whole world is crazy for those animated textiles. The manufacturers couldn't produce them fast enough, he complained."

"Do you know where the sales representative can be reached?"

She pulled a card from the drawer of her imitation Biedermeier secretary.

"His name is . . . one moment . . ."—she put back on her glasses— "Jacopo Ligrina, lives in Frascati. Do you want his address or his number?"

"No, thank you."

"When he's in the city, he usually stays in the Grand Hotel Terminus. That's right around the corner, by the train station. He used to invite me there sometimes . . ." she went on, tapping the card wistfully with her glasses. "For a business meeting over a glass of wine. We always got along well. He helped me a lot when I took over this shop. But that was already a few years ago," she added with a sigh.

"I'll try to reach him there," I said.

"Not a bad idea. Maybe you can wangle one of those miniskirts out of him. He likes pretty young women," she replied, a trace of bitterness creeping into her voice. "I'm sorry, but I would have bet anything that a short while ago you—"

I shook my head. "Anyway, thanks for the tip."

I RETURNED TO the hotel. Shouldn't I call the police after all and warn them that an attack on the train was planned? The transition had gone off without a hitch. Wasn't it then at my discretion . . . ?

I dialed the number of the police. When headquarters answered, I said, "I happened to overhear a conversation. An attack is going to be committed today on the express train to Rome that departs here at 4:49 P.M. There was talk of a bomb."

"Listen, signora, we've been on heightened alert for days because of the unrest at the Centrale," replied an irritated voice. "We already have enough problems. This is the thirtieth anonymous call about all manner of attacks on institutions and people, acts of revenge, death threats . . ."

"But I know for sure. In the first car there's going to be—"

"Signora, we pursue all leads, of course. Please tell me your name."

"I don't want to get involved in this," I protested. "These are ruthless killers. The train will be blown up near Mondragone. From a viaduct located shortly before a tunnel, they're planning to detonate a bomb that will be planted beforehand on the—"

"My good woman, please! You're calling from the lobby of the Grand Hotel Terminus, I see. Please tell me your name."

I hung up.

I might have failed to undo the disaster, but I would definitely stop Father from boarding the train. Should I, as Renata had suggested in jest, come on to him and let him drag me to his room? Me, his own daughter? Well, I could prevent him from getting intimate with me, but I somehow had to detain him long enough for him to miss the ill-fated train. That had to be doable. But where was he?

I looked at my watch.

I LOOKED AT myself in the mirror over the sink.

"But we know each other," he had said.

"I've never seen you before," I had insisted.

"Yes, yes! It must have been only recently. I don't forget the face of a beautiful woman so easily. And definitely not yours."

"I can't remember us ever meeting anywhere."

"Well, then it's high time to deepen our acquaintance and get to know each other better," he had said with a smile.

I felt hot and cold all over. I glanced at my watch. There was no way he would make the 4:49 train. I washed my hands. They were trembling so much that the drops sprayed off before I could dry them.

When I stepped out of the bathroom, he lay naked on the bed and had draped the sheet over his hips. He must have undressed as fast as lightning; he had thrown his clothes over the armchair.

My father looked at me with surprise in his brown eyes. "Aren't you getting undressed?"

"No, I'm not going to do that."

He folded his hands behind his head and asked with a smile, "This can't be the first time you've gotten involved in an affair like this?"

"What is it I'm getting involved in?"

"Now don't be like that! When someone lets herself be persuaded after a glass of champagne to come with a man to his hotel room, then it's obvious that . . ."

With a twinge of disgust and unease I noticed the erection that showed under the sheet.

"Now come on, girl! You'll have fun, wanna bet? I'm no beginner."

I stared at him in shock.

"You can't have had a sudden fit of remorse," he sighed, swinging his legs over the edge of the bed. "Then I could have just taken the earlier train to Rome."

He looked sullenly at his wristwatch and stood up. As the sheet slid down, I turned away quickly.

"Or am I too old for you?" he asked challengingly, looking at his slim figure in the tall mirror of the wardrobe, running his hand over his belly and stroking his stiff penis.

"You're not old," I said.

"Still, I could be your father."

"Yes," I sobbed, grabbing my handbag and rushing past him so that he wouldn't see my tears. Hastily, I opened the door and ran down the hallway to the elevator.

No, I told myself. You have to put those daydreams out of your head, or else you'll go crazy. Such a confrontation would rob me of what remains of my illusions and cost me my self-respect. I had to find another way. Somehow I had to get to the platform and attract his attention.

I HAD NEVER before been wedged in by so many people. An attack of claustrophobia seized me; I could barely breathe. Sweat poured down my body. Ultimately, I managed to fight my way to the ticket hall, but it was impossible to get through the barrier to the platform.

"Please, let me through," I pleaded. "My father is on the platform. I have to get to him."

"Don't talk nonsense!" gasped the young policeman.

His face was red with strain; he was sweating even worse than I was in his bulletproof vest and helmet. He angrily pushed me back with his transparent plastic shield; the scratched surface was right in front of my eyes.

"Back!" he roared. "No one's getting through here!"

The crowd behind me surged unrelentingly forward like a swell; it pressed me against the shield and squeezed the air out of my lungs. The people shouted and loudly gave vent to their rage, but they couldn't break through the cordon. The police officers had interlocked the edges of their shields. They formed a springy but impenetrable wall. I was glad that they weren't equipped with living shields, as would be used against demonstrators a few years later—stuck-together thin layers of calcium carbonate connected by muscles. Those muscles grown from mussel genes reacted to pressure with powerful countermovements. A group of police officers armed with such shields could clear a path for themselves through the densest crowds.

"Last call," boomed a voice from the ceiling loudspeaker. "Passengers to Rome with valid travel documents, please proceed to the passage next to counter one. I repeat: last call . . ."

The remaining words were drowned out by a bang followed by clinking, screams of pain, and cries for help. One of the huge glass walls at the entrance to the ticket hall had burst from the onslaught of bodies. Again the swell surged forward and drove the air out of my lungs. I couldn't even have screamed, but only gasped for breath. I was beset by the labored panting of the people; I felt their hot breath on the back of my neck and my ears, smelled their sweat and the exhalation of their fear pheromones. My travel bag hung somewhere between my knees. I couldn't even bend over to reach it.

Then I saw Father. He was walking along the platform with his two sample cases.

"Father!" I cried. "Father!" But I produced only a croak, which was hopelessly submerged in the tumult.

Up front by the train stood a young woman who hurried to him when she saw him. She was wearing one of those miniskirts made of animated textiles that I had tried in vain to buy that morning. But my father didn't even notice her. Before she reached him, he boarded a car in the middle of the train. A conductor lifted his cases to him through the door, and he tipped his hat in thanks. The woman stopped, and her hands sank to her sides. Then she too got on.

Who was that woman who had been waiting for him, of whom he took no notice? Had he not seen her? Unlikely, for there weren't many people on the platform. No one had been permitted to accompany the passengers, and they had apparently chosen in the onrush to take their seats on time.

Shortly thereafter, the doors closed and the express began to move. Now fate would inexorably take its course. With tears in my eyes I stared at the red lights of the rear locomotive.

The pressure of the masses of people behind me had abated after the train was gone. The tumult had moved onto Piazza Garibaldi. Stones flew; swarms of police officers trotted, armed with shields, their visors closed, across the square to the next operation. An overturned police car burned, and black smoke rose into the sky. Nearby the sirens of fire trucks and ambulances could be heard, but the vehicles had great difficulty reaching the piazza through the congested streets. The police had to beat open a lane for them. I remained at the entrance to the ticket hall. Broken glass crunched under my soles. I felt like crying. I couldn't believe that I had again failed so miserably. Now, as soon as an opportunity arose, I would return empty-handed to Amsterdam and report my defeat. I had achieved nothing. In half an hour my father would be dead.

I turned to the left, where the wild dogs of the city lived between the ugly concrete columns under the train station overhang. They seemed to be only moderately impressed by the people's excitement and were indifferently watching a water cannon attempting to extinguish the burning police vehicle. A big gray mongrel—spotted, almost without fur, with fearsome yellow fangs in his ugly snout and drooping ears ragged from countless battles—stood up from his spot and approached me with measured steps to sniff my hand. The dog wasn't modified—there was no such thing yet at that time—but his beautiful brown eyes, the most beautiful thing about him, had an alert intelligence and looked at me encouragingly. His stumpy tail twitched in a friendly way.

I crouched down and fished a bar of Belgian chocolate from my travel bag. It had gotten soft. In Schiphol I had in a fit of ravenous hunger bought half a dozen bars after I had been forced to go without sweets for a year. He ate the soft mass out of my hand without even touching me with his dark jowls. As his companions stood up and approached, a glance out of the corner of his eye and a warning growl were enough to send them back to their spots. They watched him and drooled as he licked the last remains from the tinfoil.

I noticed that my hands were trembling. In these minutes it was happening; in these seconds. The animal looked at me intently. He sensed my tension. Did he feel sympathy? I closed my eyes and could no longer hold back the tears. The express had reached the space-time point of its doom.

What a failure I was, damn it.

TWENTY-FIVE MINUTES AFTER the departure from Napoli Centrale, rounding the northern part of the city in a wide curve, the express reached the bend at Villa Literno and entered the first high-speed stretch toward Rome. Within five minutes it accelerated to 220 miles per hour, which it reached near Falciano. Shortly thereafter, it crossed under the viaduct of the road from Carinola to Mondragone; then it shot in a low concrete trough across the Fontanelle and sped toward the tunnel through Monte Mássico.

The bomb the terrorists had planted in one of the compartments of the car directly behind the front locomotive was probably detonated from the viaduct. The blast pressure built up to its full strength when the head of the train had entered roughly sixty to eighty yards into the tunnel tube. The front locomotive was blown off and raced on; it was, however, lifted off the tracks by the explosion and shot, rotating like a projectile in a rifle barrel, through the tunnel until the friction with the walls stopped it after about five hundred yards and it came to rest lying on its side.

As the explosion tore apart the first car, the second was pushed into it, followed by the third and fourth. In fractions of seconds they became wedged and plugged the tunnel. The kinetic energy of cars five to eight and the massive rear locomotive pushing from behind, functioning like the piston of a scrap metal press, compressed the agglomeration of matter even more and brought the core area to a temperature of over thirty-five hundred degrees. Sealed off from air, the train and its passengers were baked into a compact mass of metal, plastic, leather, textiles, and human flesh. None of the passengers escaped with their lives. The total number of people who met their death was never determined. The authorities spoke of 412 victims, but those were only the ones who had valid travel documents and reserved seats. Many suspected that it was over five hundred, for some people had managed despite the barriers to make it onto the train.

I STARED DESPONDENTLY into my wineglass. How could I have approached my plan so stupidly and rashly? It would have required more thorough research, precise planning, and refined strategy—the way the octopuses prepared themselves for their operations. I hadn't expected it to be impossible to get to the train, even though I might have guessed as much.

Who had the woman on the platform been, who had been waiting for my father? That should have been me. She had been in the exact situation that would have been useful to me for my plan. Might it have been me? Had I returned a second time from the future to carry out my plan? Nonsense! The woman had boarded the train. Had she died with him? Inevitably. I had never seen her get off again.

When I entered the hotel half an hour later, a woman came plunging out of the elevator, distraught and teary-eyed, and rushed past me. For a moment I thought I was looking into my own face. Was I seeing ghosts?

The waiter replenished my glass. I looked around the lobby. On a deep sofa upholstered in natural silk, a middle-aged man and a young black-haired woman sat side by side under a huge gold-framed painting that showed a deer crossing a forest path. Both were sitting with their back to me, but in the mirror off to the side behind them I could make out the man's profile. If I hadn't seen with my own eyes my father board the train, I would have bet that I was witnessing one of my father's "business meetings." Of course, I was mistaken, but I wished it had been him, for at that moment he was already dead. Deep apathy overcame me. I couldn't bring myself to stand up and walk around the pillar to make sure.

An old woman sat down at the table next to me. From her handbag she pulled out an orange and peeled it. I looked at her thin, liver-spotted hands. In her scrawny fingers she held a small mother-of-pearl-covered pocket-knife, on which a little silver chain dangled. "Nothing will happen to you," Heloise had said, "as long as you do not stray too far from yourself. It won't always be easy, but you can return to your world. You only have to want to."

I stared at the knife with fascination. The mother-of-pearl handle sparkled, and the little chain flashed.

"Is something wrong?" the old woman croaked.

"N-no, no," I said, averting my eyes. "I'm sorry. For a moment I wasn't completely with it."

"That happens," said the old woman, "but actually you're still too young for that."

She laughed with a rattle, slit the fruit with her thumbnail into its segments, and inserted them one after another in her mouth.

I was exhausted from the events in the train station and depressed about my failure. Ultimately, I had let it slip through my fingers, squandered my chance to make the pick-up sticks of reality fall only a little bit differently. I wanted to be alone. I asked the waiter to bring the rest of the wine to my room. I didn't want to watch when the first news of the terror attack came on television.

In the next room a frisky pair of lovers seemed to have nested again. I closed the blinds on the balcony door, finished the bottle of wine, showered, and soon thereafter went to bed. The next day I would try to get to Rome somehow, in order to book a flight to Amsterdam from there. The planes departing from Naples were undoubtedly all booked up.

IN THE MIDDLE of the night a rumble woke me. I reached for the light switch, but apparently there had been a power outage. Another rumble. Was it a storm? Was it an earthquake? A volcanic eruption? Somewhere a loud clinking sound could be heard, as if a large painting or a mirror had fallen off the wall and shattered. Something trickled on my face. Had the ceiling burst? Was plaster falling down? I stood up quickly and opened the door to the corridor. There was no light on outside either. I pulled up the blinds on the balcony door and peered out. It was long before daybreak. Over Mount Vesuvius hung a cloud of smoke in which lightning flashed. Or was it the reflection of volcanic eruptions? On the dark slopes of the volcano hung frayed clouds. Were they effluvia? Poisonous gases, as had beset Pompeii? In the distance the wail of police and rescue vehicles speeding through the streets could be heard. There seemed to be a mist over the city, approaching from the sea. Domes rose out of it, and slender towers that looked like minarets. The high-rises in the northeast were no longer there; the whole skyline of the Centro Direzionale was gone. Nowhere was a light to be seen. Had the whole city been affected by the power outage? I looked down. The train station was gone. I thought I made out in the dimness a vast square overgrown with weeds, on which there were scattered half-demolished and dilapidated market stalls. Everywhere were heaps of trash and half-decomposed carcasses of horses and dogs. Were there also human corpses among them? The area resembled a battlefield, and the flickering red reflection that poured out over it reinforced the impression that the fallen had been flayed. The sky was mirrored in black puddles. The smell of putrefaction filled the air.

Far to the south, near the port, I spotted scattered lights and thought I saw ships: dhows, three-masted vessels . . . above them more lights in a break in the clouds. Were they airplanes? Satellites? No, they were standing still. A chain of balloons? No, they were stars—a striking constellation. The Corona Borealis? Impossible. I didn't know this constellation; I had never seen it: a red supergiant like Rigel—but brighter than Sirius or Capella—in the center, surrounded by a semicircle of seven bright young stars, which it wore around its neck like a sparkling piece of jewelry.

I went back to bed and stared into the darkness. Where was I? Was I being fooled by a tenacious dream? Or had I ended up in another universe? Stranded in a parallel world? Perhaps in a distant time? I shouldn't stray too far from myself, Heli had warned me. I was as helplessly at the mercy of the gravity centers of the courses I was traveling as she had been when she had to follow a long detour to return to earth.

Suddenly the light came back on. A bare lightbulb hung on a wire from the burst, stained ceiling. I closed my eyes. Nearby a muezzin sang the subuh, the first prayer of the day. What a horrible, godforsaken place—and yet its residents praised the Almighty.

I felt dizzy. I opened my eyes. Darkness surrounded me. Then I heard nearby the whistle of a locomotive. The train station—I must have returned.

WHEN I WOKE up, it was broad daylight. The sun shone over the eastern flank of Mount Vesuvius. Shouts rang out from the street. On the sidewalk stalls had grown out of the ground overnight like mushrooms after a summer rain. The umbrellas stood close together, and traffic struggled through a jumble of parked delivery vans and two-wheeled carts that were being unloaded. The glass facades of the Centro Direzionale glistened, and on the square and in the train station itself crowds were already gathering. Where were these travelers heading? The route to the north would be impassable for months. The trains had to be diverted to the east coast.

I heard voices out in the hallway and the closing of the door to the next room. I stood up quickly, opened my door a crack, and peered out. Two people were walking down the hallway to the elevator: a short man wearing a natural linen suit and a panama hat and next to him a dark-haired woman of my height and about my age in a light red minidress with a straw hat hanging over her arm.

The lovers had apparently not departed yesterday after all, but had spent another night in the next room. The two of them entered the elevator. Inside it the rectangular mirrors set in polished brass moldings reflected a distorted image, so that I could not make out the faces. Was it the couple I had seen sitting in the lobby the previous evening? Had another version of me, one of my shadow sisters, had fewer scruples in another universe and . . . ? No, I told myself. I would never stray so far from myself.

"*BUON GIORNO, SIGNORINA,*" the young man behind the counter greeted me as I passed reception on my way to breakfast. My gaze happened to fall on the calendar on the wall. It showed the date to be September 16.

"The calendar . . ." I said, and stopped.

"The calendar?" he asked. "What about it?"

"Today is the seventeenth . . ."

"I'm sorry, but you're mistaken," he replied kindly but firmly. "Today is the sixteenth."

"Is that really true?" I asked.

Frowning, he looked at me over his narrow glasses, then pushed the latest newspaper across the counter to me and pointed to the date. I cast a timid glance at the headlines. Not a single one mentioned the terror attack on the Rome express. Not a line about the more than five hundred victims who had met their death in the tunnel. Nothing about the Mondragone disaster . . . Of course not, if today was only the sixteenth.

"I must have been mistaken," I said tonelessly.

Dizziness overcame me. I held on to the counter and took a deep breath.

"Are you all right, signorina?" the receptionist asked with concern.

"I'm fine," I assured him, even though my legs almost gave out.

What had Ernesto said to me? "You might be among those who no longer need our technology." But, for heaven's sake, how could that be possible?

The reaction of the boutique owner . . . And then the woman on the platform . . . Father was still alive; he was out there somewhere in the city.

All the people who had boarded the train were still alive. I had a second chance! A world opened up before me, a new day, a new universe! I could have cheered with relief. So I still had more than seven hours. This time I would set to work more carefully . . .

On the spur of the moment I decided to skip breakfast. I hurried to the boutique on Corso Umberto Primo and bought the miniskirt I had noticed the previous evening in the display window. It was the last one.

"I admire women who have the courage to wear something like that," the owner said with a smile that turned somewhat wry.

"I know it's terribly tacky. It's intended as a party gag," I replied.

"Then have fun with it!" she purred, puttering around busily.

I returned to the hotel, put on the skirt, and looked at myself in the mirror. No way! I quickly took it off again, grabbed my travel bag, and paid my bill. One night less was listed on the bill—a night that had gotten mysteriously lost. I then strolled to the train station and took a look at the places where I had failed on the first try.

As Napoli Centrale is U-shaped in front, the stream of passengers moving in from the spacious Piazza Garibaldi was first pooled as if by the grating of a weir, then channeled together into the ticket hall through funnel-shaped openings between large glass facades, and from there relayed to the platforms. That structure was functional and undoubtedly worked flawlessly at normal crowd levels; but when the onrush increased and greater masses of people tried to get into the building and to the trains, that design was disastrously hazardous. The funnels between the glass facades formed dangerous bottlenecks, which could provoke panic. When those confined spaces were cordoned off as well, in order to prevent people from reaching the ticket hall and the platforms, the concentrated onslaught would surge against those very glass walls, which were not shatterproof. Panic among people who felt helpless and driven into a corner and injuries from the bursting of the panes were thus preprogrammed. In addition, one floor down there was a quite similar system of funnels from which stairs and escalators led up—the metro in the underground level and the connection to the Circumvesuviana—which doubled the pressure on the entry points to the ticket hall.

So far the police had withstood the onslaught of travelers who wanted to leave the city, but the glass panes had not. There had been dozens of injured. But even passengers who had permission to travel north, I learned in the hotel, had been unable to reach the passages designated for them, because they had been wedged in by the surging crowd. This had apparently been going on for days. For glaziers, business was booming.

Shortly before noon I managed to enter the ticket hall. I inquired about the possibility of getting a seat on the Rome express at 4:49 P.M. It was hopeless, even though I had a valid return ticket. The train had been booked up for days. I mustered all my charm—to no avail.

Somehow I had to get onto the platform, but a glance at the grim faces of the police officers controlling access told me that there was no way through there. They were young men who were highly motivated but a little bit anxious. Pale, they stared out from under their visors and put up with the abuse with which people bombarded them.

I returned to the piazza in front of the train station, where the wild dogs, unmoved by all the excitement, lay in the shade of the concrete columns of the entrance area. I saw the large gray dog in his spot. He raised his head and looked at me with his beautiful brown eyes, while his gnarled tail stump tapped on the asphalt. Hey, I thought, how do you know me? We never met before. Or do you live a little bit in my crazy world too? Do I remind you of the taste of chocolate? He stood up slowly, stretched, and shook out his frayed, drooping ears. He approached me and sniffed my hand, then walked past me, stopped after a few steps, and turned around to look at me, as if to say: "Well, come on!"

The dog trudged ahead, and I followed him. He pissed casually on the post of a no-stopping sign and turned around again as if to make sure that I was still behind him. He approached a gate at the east wing of the train station; behind it were a small yard and a counter for freight and express goods. He sniffed at the gate and waited until I was beside him. I tried it; the gate opened with ease. He looked at me with his gentle brown eyes. "There you go," he seemed to be saying. "And thanks for the chocolate."

I squeezed through the gate and closed it behind me. The gray dog stayed outside and gazed after me. The entrance was indeed unguarded. Three railroad employees sat in the area behind the counter, watching a bicycle race on television. They were talking loudly and took no notice of me.

I was in the train station! Now I only had to make it through the time until the Rome express was ready. I was glad that I had at the last minute decided against the miniskirt, which would have attracted all eyes to me. Why had I bought that tacky thing in the first place? I wondered in confusion. Okay, the idea of arousing his attention with that skirt had become fixed in my mind. But I knew that plan would fail. Yesterday my father hadn't taken the slightest notice of the young woman on the platform.

Soon more and more passengers crowded onto the platform, and finally the express was ready. I noticed a young man who lifted a heavy aluminum suitcase from his luggage cart and got into the first car. A few minutes later he came out again—without the suitcase—and took a seat on the local train on the opposite track, which departed shortly thereafter. I stepped into the car and searched it, but couldn't find the aluminum suitcase anywhere. I walked through the whole car twice and looked in every compartment. Some of the passengers eyed me suspiciously. No trace of the suitcase. Had he lugged it into the second car? I couldn't find it there either.

"Did you lose something?" the conductor asked me.

I told him what I had observed. He gave me a troubled look, but nonetheless took on the task of checking with me once again in every compartment, on every luggage rack, and even under the seats. We found nothing. By the third car it finally became too much for him.

"You must have been mistaken, signorina," he said with a shrug, when we were standing again on the platform.

"Wouldn't it be better to alert the security authorities?" I suggested.

"Mother of God," he murmured, rolling his eyes; then he gestured with a nod to the police barrier at the access to the platform and the pushing mass of people behind it. "They'd be all we need. Besides, we're departing in five minutes."

Suddenly I saw Father all the way at the end of the platform. He had loaded his sample cases on a luggage cart, which he was pushing in front of him. On his arm hung a young woman wearing one of those animated Korean miniskirts. Both of them boarded in the middle of the train. The conductor helped them lift the cases into the train. Father tipped his hat in thanks.

We departed on time.

In the first twenty-five minutes the high-speed Naples–Rome express set only a moderate pace. It rounded in a wide curve the northeastern outskirts of the city: Casoria—this time it didn't stop—Frattamaggiore, Aversa, San Marcellino, San Cipriano d'Aversa. I had in the meantime fought my way through the third car and looked in every compartment—without any result. The train was full; passengers stood in the aisles; luggage was piled everywhere. Many people had managed to board without a reservation, even though reserved-seat tickets had been mandatory. Well, I had managed it too.

Mothers with children sat tightly packed in the compartments. The men stood in the aisle, smoking, debating, and only grudgingly making room.

After the bend at Villa Literno began the first high-speed stretch toward Rome . . .

I squeezed through the vestibule to the fourth car . . .

The express now accelerated within five minutes to a speed of 220 miles per hour . . .

. . . the second, the third, the fourth compartment, mistrustful, hostile looks . . .

. . . which it reached near Falciano . . .

. . . the fifth, the sixth compartment—nothing. In front of me a pile of suitcases and tied-up boxes, on which children clambered around. There was no way through.

Shortly thereafter, the train crossed under the viaduct . . .

Shouldn't I pull the emergency brake? But to do that, I would first have to get to the end of the car.

. . . the viaduct of a road from Carinola to Mondragone . . .

"Please let me through!"

. . . then it shot in a low concrete trough . . .

The door to the next compartment was open . . .

. . . in a low concrete trough across the Fontanelle . . .

There I saw the large aluminum suitcase up on the overhead luggage rack. Next to it two sample cases . . .

. . . and sped . . .

In the window seat sat a middle-aged man in an elegant natural linen suit with a bow tie and opposite him a dark-haired woman in her late twenties. They were holding hands, and both of them stared at me silently.

. . . sped toward the entrance of the tunnel through Monte Mássico . . .

Struggling for breath, I stood in the doorway and looked into strange faces. It was as if time were standing still, as if I had before me an old photo that had captured a moment long past. A chance constellation of frozen movements, a stochastic pattern, burned in by the photon flood of a flash washing back. Fossil time.

Aghast, I retreated into the aisle. The end of the car was still two compartments away. I would no longer make it.

"Please let me through!"

Suddenly the four or five men who had blocked my way and, burning cigarettes in hand, turned around questioningly toward me, flew away from me down the aisle. I was swept off my feet and plunged after them, clinging to pieces of luggage, which were sliding as well in the direction the train was moving. Suitcases and bags tumbled from the luggage racks. People flung up their arms to protect themselves and screamed. The chaos culminated in an infernal screech, which penetrated from outside. Suddenly there was darkness, as bursts of sparks streamed past the windows. Finally, after seemingly endless minutes, the train had stopped. We were in the tunnel. Deepest darkness. This was the moment when the explosion occurred. But nothing happened—silence. The people were in shock. Then I heard the weeping of children. Names were called. Worried voices. Agitated voices. Outraged voices. Loud tumult. Finally the emergency lighting came on. It smelled of charred plastic and hot metal.

"Please accept our apologies," said a voice straining for calm from the loudspeakers. "We had to carry out an emergency stop."

Not a word of explanation. The outrage grew.

My God, I thought, there's a universe in which all of you are at this moment nothing but a hot sludge of coal tar. I don't know why, but you escaped that fate by a hair—the all-scorching lightning that would have brought about your transubstantiation.

TEN MINUTES LATER the train began to move backwards; at a crawl it rolled out of the tunnel tube into the concrete trough across the Fontanelle and stopped. The sun shone low in the west. Helicopters circled the train at a low altitude. The men of the antiterror unit, who were combing the terrain along the railroad line and had taken position on the viaduct, looked in their ceramic armor equipped with antennas like bizarre, upright crustaceans.

I was giddy with happiness. I had done it. Apparently my warning had reached the right place at the last second? But I had conducted that telephone conversation on that imaginary day that didn't even exist in this universe. Nonetheless, in the universe in which I was now, the attack had been thwarted and the lives of more than five hundred people saved.

But where was Father?

III

Exit Roads

The heavens will vanish like smoke, the earth will wear out like a garment, and its inhabitants die like flies.

ISAIAH

Shortly thereafter—and yet years later—I ran into my father again in Rome. I was sitting in the lobby of the Vatte hotel on Via Cavour, where I was staying, when he suddenly came in through the entrance. Hesitantly he stopped when he saw me, placing his hand on his forehead for a moment. He walked with a bit of a stoop and was no longer quite as elegantly dressed as I remembered him. Then he came up to my table, took off his sunglasses, tipped his straw hat, and asked me with a polite bow whether he might sit down with me.

"Of course," I said.

How strange he had become to me. He pulled up the creases of his somewhat threadbare dove gray gabardine pants, took a seat in the chair across from me, and laid his hat on the chair next to him.

"May I ask you something, signorina?" he asked with a soft voice.

"Go ahead."

"Have we met before?"

Oh God, please no!

"Not that I recall, Signore . . ."

"Ligrina. Jacopo Ligrina."

". . . Signore Ligrina."

"Remarkable," he said, scrutinizing me intently with his dark brown eyes. "The resemblance. It's been several years, but I remember quite clearly, because it was the day an attack was planned on the Naples–Rome express, which was foiled at the last second."

Growing curious, I said, "Go on."

"Signorina, I don't want to offend you. But the resemblance is really striking. I had been in Naples for a few days on business and had a reservation for that very train. Then I met an extremely charming young woman in the lobby of the Grand Hotel Terminus."

"Just like we're meeting now . . ."

This couldn't be happening!

He gave me a flustered look, then smiled wistfully and went on, "No, no. I'm sorry, the circumstances were completely different. We drank a bottle of champagne at the bar and got along fabulously right away. To make a long story short, she agreed to have another drink with me in my room."

"Do you really want to tell me this? Is this going to be a confession?" I asked emphatically.

"Oh, there were no intimacies. Probably she was married or engaged."

"But she went with you to your room anyway?" I prompted.

He shrugged. "As I said, we got along well."

"And you have the impression that I have a great resemblance to that . . . lady?"

He gave me a dismayed look. "No, no. Really only purely externally! Nothing could be further from my mind than . . ."

"So there were no intimacies," I said, to make sure.

"No. She left the room. Apparently, she was suddenly in quite a hurry. I don't know why. At first I was a bit annoyed, because I realized that I had missed the train to Rome and had to try to get a new seat reservation."

"You must have forgiven a charming woman for that and accepted the minor inconvenience."

"I was deeply *grateful* to her, signorina! For I had missed the train that was the target of the terror attack. She had, so to speak, saved my life."

"I don't entirely understand. The terror attack was thwarted. Why do you think that woman saved your life?"

Pensively, he wrinkled his forehead and stroked the lapel of his dark blue blazer with his thumbnail. The liver-spotted hand poking out of the worn sleeve shook.

"Well," he said with a helpless gesture, "how can I be absolutely certain that the attack would still have been thwarted even if I had been in the train?"

I nodded. His shoes caught my eye through the glass tabletop. They were meticulously polished, but cracked, and the heels desperately needed repair.

"So my doppelgänger played the role of your guardian angel and contributed to the fact that you were able to return home in one piece to your wife and daughter," I said.

"How did you know . . . ?"

"That was really just a guess."

"May I ask you your name?"

"Oh! Domenica."

"What a coincidence! That's my daughter's name. She's now—let me see—twenty-three. Unfortunately, I haven't had contact with her for years. Since the divorce from my wife . . ." He broke off and then, after a while, went on, "I work in the fashion industry and am very often traveling around the world. You know, Paris, New York, Budapest—where fashion is made."

He didn't look the part. I didn't believe a word he said.

"You don't know what became of her? Your daughter, I mean," I asked him.

"Back then she moved with her mother to Genoa. My wife was Genoese. It wouldn't surprise me if Domenica—my daughter, I mean—were now in Rome. She wanted to study botany here, if I remember correctly. Unfortunately, I don't know whether anything came of that. We completely lost touch. My wife forbade her to meet with me, and so . . . I don't even know what she looks like now."

He stood up. "May I treat you to a drink, Signorina Domenica?"

"To be completely clear, Signore Ligrina, I will not go with you to your room . . ."

"Please, what are you thinking!" he said, raising both hands defensively.

"I just wanted to have said it. If you absolutely want to buy me a drink, then I'd rather get a soda or coffee at a sidewalk café somewhere."

He smiled, grabbed his hat, took his sunglasses out of the breast pocket of his jacket and put them on. He stood up and bowed gallantly.

We walked down Via Cavour and were turning the corner onto Santa Maria Maggiore when the guests sitting at a table in Emanuele on the opposite side of the street caught my eye. Marcello and Birgit—and with them CarlAntonio. They looked over and whispered to each other. For a second I had involuntarily stopped, but Father had noticed nothing of my moment of shock.

"Shall we go to Emanuele?" he suggested.

"I'd rather not," I said. "Let's look for a different café."

"As you wish," he replied.

Later, when we had parted, I wondered uneasily what I should make of the daydreams that sometimes overcame me. I had already had them as a child, and they were sometimes of such clarity and coherence that in my memory I couldn't distinguish them from reality. Sometimes it seemed to me in retrospect as if I had truly experienced them. But how could he, Father, have known about that?

I remembered the woman who had come plunging out of the elevator and rushed past me, sobbing, when I, returning from the train station, had entered the lobby of the Grand Hotel Terminus. And then I gradually began to suspect that I would have to learn to live with such overlapping, only partially aligned realities.

A FEW DAYS later I walked across to Trastevere to visit Stavros. The front door was locked, but in the passage to the courtyard a short round man in a gray work coat was sweeping the pavement.

"Are you the super here?" I asked.

"Yes," he said tersely.

"Does a Signore Vulgaris live here? Signore Stavros Vulgaris?"

"No foreigners live here," he replied in an unfriendly tone.

"Are there vacant apartments in the house?"

I had seen that nameplates were missing on a few bells. The Bartocellis apparently didn't live here anymore either. "My" apartment seemed to be available.

"That you should ask the house management," he replied. "I can't give you any information."

Shouldn't Stavros already have been super here at this time? The Aegean conflict was already three years in the past. Had Stavros been killed in the battle of Icaria by the laser beam that in my memory had only seared his chest? Had he died in Turkish captivity when they had knocked out his eye and cut out his tongue?

Suddenly the thought occurred to me: Hadn't I already lived in this house myself at this point? I could no longer recall the exact date I had moved in, but nor did I remember ever having met here this surly dwarf in the gray work coat.

Confused, I looked up to the windows from which I had seen the victims of the massacre on the Gianicolo that morning. I turned away and walked across to the convent of the Sisters of Santa Maria dei Sette Dolori. The gate to the small front courtyard was open. A car was parked by the wall and covered with a dusty tarp.

The door to the entrance hall flew open with a click when I pushed against it. The second door wasn't locked either. I cast a glance at the ancient secretary made of dark wood between the entrance to the chapel and the glass case made of cherrywood in which the life-size Christ Child stood—a blond boy in a pale red robe and with a golden halo. Over the hand raised in blessing was a white sash, on which large golden letters spelled IO SONO L'AMORE. The figure had not yet been blown to pieces. Bright light fell in through the tall, narrow windows from the convent garden, in which a fountain burbled. Involuntarily my eyes wandered to the point on the wall where Stavros's outline had been spray-painted on the floor. No blood, no shards.

"Can anyone just mosey in here?" I asked the small pale sister sitting behind the desk in her black habit.

"I saw you a long time ago," she said, pointing to the monitor next to her. "You didn't make a particularly dangerous impression, so I let you in," she explained with a laugh.

"You never know," I remarked. "Times have become unsafe."

"The Mother of God will protect us," she asserted. "Besides, we don't have any artworks here; a robbery would hardly be worth it. We're a poor order."

"I know."

"May I help you? Would you like to see the chapel?"

"Very kind of you. But I've been here often. I live nearby."

"I can't remember ever having seen you here. And yet I do reception duty almost every day," she replied.

I shrugged. "Thank you anyway, Sister."

I ALSO TRIED to find CarlAntonio, but the Siamese twins seemed to have dropped off the face of the earth. No one I asked about them seemed to have heard of the bizarre pair—Antonio with his "backpack." Had the two of them never come to Rome? Had the Brothers of Mercy in Regensburg "selected" the newborns? Or had they fallen victim to their ambitious surgical experiments?

Bernd, on the other hand, I ran into unexpectedly. It was directly in front of Stazione Termini, on one of those hot summer days in those years.

The sun was burning down mercilessly. I stood in the shade under the large overhang of the train station, considering whether to take a taxi to the hotel or to walk the short stretch. Then I caught sight of him coming over from the metro. He saw me at the same moment and came hurrying toward me before I could turn away and disappear in the crowd of passersby.

"Domenica?" he asked uncertainly.

He looked at me in shock with his large blue eyes. He hadn't shaved for days; blond fuzz covered his chin and cheeks. How young he was! His T-shirt had large sweat stains under the arms, and I smelled his youthful body. How I had desired him! Memories welled up.

"Do we know each other?" I asked, and my throat constricted.

He shook his head. "You can't fool me," he replied. "My God, what have they done to you? What happened to you?"

I forced a smile. "I got a little bit lost," I replied offhand, "between times, worlds."

He eyed me from top to bottom.

"Yes, I've gotten old, Bernd. I've gone through a lot in the meantime."

He brushed his long blond hair from his forehead. How I had always loved touching that hair!

"Domenica, I will . . ."

"No, Bernd, you won't do anything. You won't even say anything. To anyone, you hear? Not even to me, to the Domenica who still doesn't know anything. Promise me that!"

"I can't . . ." he replied, almost sobbing.

"Yes, you can. I know you can. The Domenica you know and maybe love lives in another world. You would destroy her and your world."

He looked at me uncomprehendingly. "But . . ."

"Farewell, Bernd!" I cried, and left him standing there. I strode away quickly and didn't turn back.

THUS I'VE TAKEN leave little by little of all my roots. What living thing can exist without any roots? Single-celled organisms, perhaps.

"What are we actually?" I ask Don Fernando. He utters an excited squeak, as he always does when confronted with a difficult question.

"That's not at all so easy to answer," he says, scurrying a few paces, turning around, and scurrying back again. Finally he plumps down with a sigh on the black stone tabletop. "You're a biologist, Domenica. You must understand it better than I do."

"What is it I'm supposed to understand?"

"Well, every organism needs something like messenger substances that can travel freely and unhindered through the body and maintain the connection between its parts, which convey information, make resources available, detect and eliminate disturbances. We're something like that."

I think about that.

"You mean hormones that travel in the bloodstream? Serotonin, dopamine, L1?" I ask him.

Again Don Fernando squeaks. "Not exactly," he says. "We're among those who can also move freely outside the system. Outside the tunnels."

"You mean . . . antibodies? Suppressors? Cytokines? Lymphocytes?"

"Yes, something like that. I think that's not a bad comparison. But I was thinking more of enzymes, RNA genes, microRNA, riboswitches, the smart little helpers of life. Along those lines," he replies.

"And who is this organism we're helping?" I ask, even though I know the answer.

"The multiverse."

"And this organism, like any other, is in a process of evolution. It tries incessantly to improve itself, is in search of ways to optimize itself. New cells grow, others die off."

"That captures it really well. It's a being consisting of membranes of space-time continuums, of countless universes—real universes, which emerge, grow, and collapse, and virtual ones, which can unfold at any moment into the dimensions. They're linked to one another and together form a whole. Perhaps it's only a mechanism or even only a computer program, as some believe. That's a philosophical question or a question of faith. We don't know. We know only that we ourselves are part of it."

I look across to the smoking ash seams, the sediments of innumerable failed possibilities. There are cells that cannot find their balance and in their insatiability suffocate in their own excrement.

"Why should we work on behalf of this . . . monster?" I ask.

Don Fernando chuckles. "We live in it. Where else could we exist?"

"Are we directed by it? Do we receive orders?"

Again he scurries excitedly back and forth. His paws patter across the polished stone tabletop. Then he again plumps down.

"Perhaps we're programmed. How could we ever find that out?" he asks, licking his front paws and cleaning his face. "To speak of passing the time doesn't befit us, does it? The reduction of indeterminacy sounds terribly stilted. How about curiosity, the joy of discovery, the pleasure in play? Qualities that distinguish intelligent creatures. We're restless and curious. We come across problems and try to solve them. That's all."

I think about that. For a long time, we're silent. The sky above us is empty. There's no eye in sight.

"Where are we actually?" I ask him.

Don Fernando gets up and looks around as if he has to make sure himself.

"Highgate," he says.

"And what does that mean?"

With an elegant movement he winds his tail around his backside.

"The border," he explains. "It's the outermost world in which life is still found. Beyond it begin the universes that have borne no life. And it's the turning point of time. Here it has reached its maximum expansion. The time arrow faces indecisively now in this direction, now in the other. Many things thereby lose their validity."

And as if to underscore his words, the sun, which rose just a short while ago from the sandy sea, descends again toward the horizon. The rocks, which yesterday evening still stood on the beach, have disappeared. Perhaps, taking advantage of a temporal anomaly, they have moved on to seek a new berth on the coastline. Or, following the seductions of a capricious gravity, they have sunk into deeper regions of the continental shelf to be closer to the last warmth at the heart of this dying world.

"Here the solitons, which accompany and tend the temporal dimension like shepherd moons, turn around and begin their descent into the past. They roll like a swell over the pole: They change direction without changing course."

I AM NOW often on Highgate. I love the cool, salty smell of the morning and the bitter taste of midday, when the wind comes from the desert. Sometimes the sky breaks open and Sir Whitefang and his companion Kertschul come for a brief visit. I see them already from afar, because they come tramping up the glacier tongue of time—for every one step the man takes, the wolf takes four.

"Where do they live?" I ask the ancient young man, the widely traveled one some time-natives call the angel, when the sky has closed again and the icy breeze is gone.

"They live on the other side of the biophilic zone. They guard the border to the universes of cold and darkness, which are also without life," he replies. "The borders overlap here at the end of time."

"Why do people actually call you the angel?" I ask the widely traveled man.

"Perhaps because I can fly."

"Do you have no name?"

"Oh, I've had many names. Some call me Hermes."

"Hermes? The messenger of the gods?"

With a scarcely perceptible shrug, he answers, "The time-natives are very inventive in giving a name to the strange. They believe that they have a better grip on it that way—that they can grasp it."

"Are we who travel so freely through the times special?"

"Freely? Are we free?"

He looks at me mockingly with his odd honey-colored eyes.

"We're very mobile, yes. But are we therefore free?" he adds, leaning back in his rocking chair and folding his hands over his chest. "Special? A difficult question, Domenica. There are billions of lymphocytes in a body. They come into being and pass away. They have an important function. But is one of them therefore special? I don't think so."

OCCASIONALLY I RETURN to Amsterdam—to Venice, to Rome. I take a short walk with Grit, sit in the Waag while Leendert, preoccupied with intricate thoughts in his effort to track down contradictions in the sources, stares silently into his beer mug. I visit Grandfather at night after the last guests have gone, when he sits in his wheelchair on the terrace, and let him show me the stars.

"You should come sometime in winter," he says, "when the sky is full of stars."

I promise him. Sometimes I ride for a few hours by Renata's side through the stony bed of the Isarco or sleep with Frans in his small apartment in Castello. But I notice that they all increasingly have trouble perceiving me. Have I become for them a hazy apparition, so that I encounter them only in their daydreams—in the languor of midday or at night when their senses are enveloped in sleep?

At times I have trouble focusing on the present in which I happen to be at a given moment. I look around, marvel at the facts between which I find myself, for my consciousness is constantly straying, roaming my virtual future and my virtual past, which are in a state of constant flux. The multiverse must experience itself in a similar way.

Then again, when I direct my attention to the reality surrounding me, I run the risk of getting tangled in the thickets of the factual. It is of a terrifying, overwhelming density. An unbearable flood of data assails me, which exceeds my receptive power. Time seems to stand still, and I feel as if I'm looking at a photograph in which I keep discovering new details, though I would like to close my eyes to them.

Sometimes I penetrate deeper into the dark regions of this universe, areas full of horror, in which the smell of fear and torment is overpowering. There, at the fortresses of darkness, I encounter no more travelers I know, for they all rely on technology—on the arteries through time and the stations along the tunnels.

Wherever I go, I gather information, for I think that even those events the historians call "constitutive facts"—those ugly encapsulations of violence and death, the pernicious knots of chance, negligence, and indifference—can be unraveled and disentangled by prudent probing, gentle smoothing, subtle changes in the period leading up to them. You only have to try. I hope we still have enough time. Our universe still exists. But for how long?

MIDDAY ON HIGHGATE—the time when the blaze reaches its zenith. The sepia haze of the depths is gone, and from the salt of the dried-out ocean a light bursts forth that extinguishes all colors, consumes all shadows, and turns the contours of reality into trembling chimeras, which melt over the desert into pearly puddles and seep into the sand.

"What is it like when a universe disappears?" I ask the widely traveled man, who sits beside me in his rocking chair under the pergola. "Does it go fast?"

"Very fast," he says, without opening his eyes.

"The speed of light?"

Don Fernando stops licking his paws and squeaks. "Do you think the end comes creeping through the galaxy?" he teases. "No. It's like a hand going through cobwebs."

"And how does it happen?"

The widely traveled man shrugs. "An additional force decouples—or one of the curled-up dimensions unfolds. One of the physical constants changes or begins to oscillate. The elementary particles decay. Vacuum bubbles tear apart space-time, and matter evaporates into vacuum energy. A moment of motionlessness—then: *nada*. You wouldn't feel a thing, Domenica, wouldn't notice a thing."

I gaze into the distance. No shadow darkens the landscape. No eye stares indifferently down at us. The sky is empty. It's the hour of absolute stillness, no sound can be heard, only the soft creaking rhythm of the rocking chair. It's as if time itself were moving—forward . . . and back, forward . . . and back—a swell like the breath of someone peacefully sleeping.

But sometimes, when the heat becomes almost unbearably stifling, the fear creeps up on me that this soft rhythm, this soft breathing could stop— and with it the very last sound would go silent.

Acknowledgments

This novel makes forays into several fields in which I'm not—or not sufficiently—adept. I'm grateful to everyone who helped check the data I compiled and answer questions, among them Fariborz Abedinpour (immunology), Willi Geier (botany), and especially Alexander Seibold (religion and Church), who also gave me valuable insight into the work of the Cusan and taught me in the park of the Catholic Academy in Munich how the balls must be released onto the board of the Cusanus game. For numerous details about Rome I am indebted to Manfred Fischer, former director of the Bad Boll Protestant Academy, with whom I had the privilege of taking several interesting trips to Rome. With respect to Holland and the city of Amsterdam, Carla Remé, who resides there, was helpful to me. Her husband, the artist Jörg Remé, called my attention to many details in Venice. Should mistakes or inconsistencies have nonetheless crept into the text here and there, I am responsible for them.

My thanks are also due to the literary models from which I made borrowings—the connoisseurs will have identified them easily: *Time and Again,* by Jack Finney, must be mentioned, as well as *Hard to Be a God,* by Arkadi and Boris Strugatski. Dieter Kühn, with his subtle approaches to a world that is absolutely foreign to us in *Ich Wolkenstein* and *Neidhart aus dem Reuental,* emboldened me to enter the exotic terrain of the fifteenth century and take on the narrative challenge of depicting it. And, of course, Carl Amery's *Königsprojekt* (*The Royal Project*) was and remains the origin and wellspring of all speculations about dark machinations of the Vatican along the timeline. From the conversations he and I conducted over thirty years about the endangering of Creation through carelessness and rapacity, a great deal found its way into this book. How I would have loved to press this novel into his hands with a wink and hear his laughter when he read one passage or another. It wasn't meant to be, but I tried to weave in for him, who came up with a fitting verse for every occasion, a small tribute on page 400.

Finally, for their work on the original German version, I offer my thanks to Friedel Wahren, who took on the task of line-editing the voluminous manuscript; Sascha Mamczak, who provided helpful editorial input; and Erik Simon for his suggestions and improvements to the text of the most difficult chapter, "The Cusan Acceleratio," which he published in advance in 1999 in his anthology *Alexanders langes Leben, Stalins früher Tod* (*Alexander's Long Life, Stalin's Early Death*) and which was awarded the Kurd Lasswitz Prize for best story of the year. Thomas Schlück, my agent, managed to place the book with a German publishing house where I could be proud of it. Hans-Peter Übleis took it upon himself to read the manuscript, though he is a very busy man, and then made a flattering judgment and gave the green light. Thomas Tilcher put the finishing touches on the German text, went through it with a fine-toothed comb, and gave me wise counsel and practical advice on the final draft.

For the present edition I have above all to thank Ross Benjamin, who translated the novel into English. I have never before worked with such a knowledgeable and precise translator. He dissected every sentence, and the e-mails flew back and forth across the Atlantic for a year. In addition, I am grateful to David Hartwell, who oversaw the project and made sure that the novel would be translated by a first-class man. I'm enthusiastic about this edition, and I think readers will share that enthusiasm.

And of course, I thank my wife, Rosemarie, who was always my most merciless critic and over the eight years I spent working on this book gave me heart again and again, and was convinced of success from the beginning, as well as my son, Julian, because the thought of him repeatedly inspired me to contribute with my writing to a better future, which would, of course, be his.

WOLFGANG JESCHKE
Munich, Summer 2012